When the Little Wings Are Stronger

Published by AKA-Publishing
Columbia, MO 65203

Complete Unabridged Edition

     ISBN 978-1-951960-33-9 Trade paperback
     ISBN 978-1-951960-35-3 Ebook

Special acknowledgment and appreciation is due Sharon Warner, the author's daughter. Realizing her mother's dream to see this book in print, Sharon's caring diligence has ensured that Oleta's voice lives on for future generations.

When the Little Wings Are Stronger

Oleta May Nichols

What does little birdie say
In her nest at peep of day?
Let me fly, says little birdie,
Mother, let me fly away.
Birdie, rest a little longer,
Till the little wings are stronger,
So she rests a little longer,
Then she flies away.

—excerpt from *Sea Dreams*
Alfred Lord Tennyson

CHAPTER 1

1941

"Oh, m' gosh, oh, m' gosh," Shandol breathed the words, barely audibly to herself. "Nobody must see me like this—oh, m' gosh." She mopped the dusty perspiration from her forehead with the short sleeve of her faded cotton print dress; but that did not stop the feeling of the heat still radiating from around her neck and whole body.

The object of her concern was a black shiny sedan moving slowly along the unpaved street a short distance in front of her. The automobile was moving so slowly she thought it was going to cease moving at all. And it was between herself and home, a house almost directly in front of her. Oh, golly, had she been seen?

It was a warm August day. The sun blazed down in a glare from a cloudless azure sky. It was so warm each breath brought almost stifling warmth to her nostrils. The smell of the warmed, lush growth of deeply matted long grass and moist earth also welled up around her. She felt stifled. She was in a rather low-lying area, actually an abandoned street, which was no longer maintained, and the drainage had in places become virtually nil. It stayed damp, sometimes marshy following a rain;and was always green in season.

She stood still watching the car, keeping barely out of sight, barely breathing, peeking from behind an oak sprout, brushed by skunk brush, part of a variety of small brush growing in the almost unused area. The sprout was only slightly taller than herself. She wondered if the light color of her faded cotton dress would make her easier seen.

Earlier in the warm afternoon, she had been on her way to a wooded area, just east of the meadow now a block or so behind her.

She had to go a short distance across the corner of it to reach the secluded spot she liked to claim as her own. But she had no more than crawled under the barbed wire fence when voices shouting for her to play ball with them reached her. She had begged them not to ask her even, pointing out how hot it was, but to no avail. She had pleaded she didn't even want to because she was so terrible at it. But the pleadings that they needed more players, and for her to "come on over" finally made her realize she could not expect a quiet time in the woods. So she knew she would at least have to talk, and perhaps plead more, as one of the girls in the game came over to walk with her to where there were others grouped around to watch. Her two brothers were among those there to play, and she also knew the other young people there.

There seemed to her plenty of young people there to play, including more girls. But most preferred to just watch. Some had to because of health reasons, some vanity—they simply didn't want to get hot, sweaty and dusty; others doubted their ability because they had played so little; jokingly pointing out somebody had to watch.

It was an ideal place to play their loosely called version of baseball. There was plenty of room, the ground was level, the grass was kept short by grazing cattle, as it was a corner of a large pasture. However, the "ball diamond" was in evidence, so the owner had no objections to that corner being used for that purpose. There were markers at home base, and the catcher's position evident. There was a path to the bases; and the pitcher's mound was bare.

The players promised her she could have her choice as to where she'd play, which was already suspected would be pitcher or catcher, when her team was not at bat. After all, as had once been said of her, she'd been playing with some of them since she was "knee high to a grasshopper."

Bucky Sandler, who had done most of the talking, and who usually had the last word on their rules and regulations because he was a known baseball fan, had known she did not like the uncertainty of being at the bases and having to catch a ball coming at her, with perhaps a runner headed for the base also; or in the field where she would be sure to miss catching a high fly batted ball because she was afraid of the ball hurting her hands; or perhaps fumble trying to figure out where to throw the ball. She also had her own doubts that she would ever get the ball where she wanted to throw it, or where it belonged, as the excitement mounted.

"It's gonna be hot everwhar yer at," he had pointed out. "Well, maybe for awhile," she'd agreed, doubtfully, but seeing their predicament. There weren't really enough anyway for two full teams so they needed all the players they could get.

To her, pitching meant trying to hit the bat with the ball she threw. Of course she never told anyone that, and actually couldn't have really hit a bat the batter held up no matter how hard she tried. It was simply her way of getting the ball somewhere in the vicinity of where it should be for appearance's sake. If the batter didn't happen to hold the bat where she could aim, she had to guess where it should be; not that she could judge exactly, or even throw where she aimed. But apparently her ruse sufficed because she was often asked to play—or was it simply her lack of resistance when begged? But this was with friends and neighbors, choosing up sides and playing because it was something to do on a warm summer afternoon.

On the other hand, catching was, to her, keeping out of the batter's way, trying to keep out of the way of a pitched ball in such a way that she might be able to stop it also; then get it back to the pitcher as soon as possible, or somewhere else if a yell came for it. A few redeeming times she had caught a foul ball, and had helped get runners out who were trying to run to home base. Yet she realized they needed more players desperately to want her. She would much rather watch, because she couldn't compare to some of the older boys, who were practiced and some were pretty good. But she was probably as good as any other of the girls—except one.

She had actually done better than she had expected today.

With some unexpected luck, she had made some good plays. She had decided to pitch. She soon lost her usual self-consciousness at being watched, got caught up in the competitive excitement, and thoroughly enjoyed herself. But now the game was over, they had won a close game and she had had quite enough. She was tired, dirty and simply wanted to go home as soon as the after game chatter would allow it. The crowd would scatter. A few dating couples lingering along on their own paired-off separate paths. Some of the players might climb over the high embankment of the railroad tracks nearby, because on the other side was the Big Pond, where they could take to the water for a cooling swim, if there were no women about. There were times in the afternoons when women or girls went there to swim or just splash around; other times to fish. So if any players, who likely didn't own swim trunks anyway, wanted to cool off, they'd just have to go into it clothes and all—and sometimes did just that.

But now here she stood hot and dirty, barefooted, and wondering whether to go on and risk being seen, or—but the black sedan did not stop. It had moved slowly out of sight. She did then take time to slip on her black patent leather sandals, which she had taken off after leaving the pasture. The deep thick grass covering seemed soft as a cushion and soothing to her hot feet. She laid aside the steno-type tablet, pencil, book and white ankle socks to buckle the strap across her bare feet.

She crossed the street, diagonally, to the large, unpainted, weather beaten-looking house on the corner of the block, crossed the green grassy yard and entered the house from the back porch, the door going into the dining room. She had completely lost the mood to go to the woods now. She thought of the trees with patches of green lush moss around them, and scattered small wild flowers had beckoned because she had supposed it would seem cooler there.

3

She could fantasize and dream fine dreams of better days and a good life ahead. There were things she would like to do and see. Sometimes she wrote down these thoughts and dreams—the "what ifs" she called them in her own mind. And with four brothers, who sometimes saw her scribblings, she had to have an excuse to answer their teasing.

"They're only 'what ifs'," she'd defend them. "Don't you ever wonder what if something happened, or if things were different?" She hoped the shorthand book explained her wish to practice. She might need to explain she had to keep practicing shorthand, which in fact she sometimes did. But incentive came hard with no teacher or guide other than the book.

Right now all she could think of was the need to wash and feel refreshed in clean clothes. Preparations for that was uttermost in her mind. But first, she was interrupted by her mother, who was just coming from the front room with a book in her hand, one finger between the pages to mark her place. She apparently had been reading and was going to the kitchen for a drink of water, which was where Shandol was also heading.

"Shandol, you look—rather terrible," Audrey Sonnett exclaimed, as she had a chance to take in Shandol's appearance.

Had Shandol not been so accustomed to her mother's appearance in the everyday, nondescript dress, she might have returned the comment. However, her mother did not appear hot, dusty, and disheveled as she herself felt. In fact her mother made the most of her drab attire. Even at thirty-nine she was still youthful and a beautiful woman. She had sparkly brown eyes, dark hair, worn with a short natural wave. It was becoming to her fine features and wrinkle-free face. Her face was almost oval except for a softly squared chin and jawline. Many people thought Shandol favored her mother in looks. Yet Shandol knew her eyes weren't as dark, her hair much lighter and her nose more pointed, which favored the other side of the family, along with a broader forehead. This Shandol tried to disguise with her hair style.

"I know, Mama," she replied, looking down at herself. "But I've been over in the pasture with the boys and a gang of kids playing ball; and I'm in the mood for a wash-up and change of clothes when I put this stuff up," indicating the things she had in her hand.

"When are you going to quit runnin' and playin' like some kid? You're gettin' too old for it. You look sorta pale, do you feel all right? Nothin' wrong is there?"

"Mama, I'm hot and tired," she said, hoping her mother could see she wanted to go on. But Audrey waited, as though she sensed Shandol had more on her mind.

4

"Well, we chattered a bit after the game," she went on, "and Dolene had some gossip she did pass along, which wasn't good. I know—" she raised her free hand, "why do I bother with her and her know-it-all notions? Talk about someone who should quit runnin'—you know her condition. Anyway, I'm surprised someone hasn't made it a point to come and tell you with so much happenin'."

Shandol didn't want to go into that now, standing almost in the middle of the large room. She wanted time. She'd rather wait and discuss it with her mother in a more leisurely way.

What had it all to do with them anyway?

"I just want to go wash and clean up," she replied. "I'm so hot and sticky feeling, and dirty. I am really, can't you see?" She grinned at the picture she must make, but Audrey thought her smile was a bit sheepish.

"But what was Dolene's gossip?" Audrey persisted. "You can't always count on her to get things straight, remember."

But Shandol knew her mom wondered if it had been fit for her daughter to hear.

"I'm sure it's true, there were other girls with us whisperin' and goin' on." She paused thoughtfully. "Wanita Strawn is going to have a baby, they said," she blurted abruptly.

"Oh, no. Poor kid," Audrey replied, frowning. "Who—uh—who does she go with?"

"I didn't hear any name, just that he's some hillbilly singin', guitar playin', good-for-nothin'—uh—according to Dolene. He lives around Plainesville somewhere, and they met at parties and dances he played at, I suppose, and just began datin'."

"Oh, the things that happen now-a-days makes one wonder," Audrey said, shaking her head negatively. "But maybe they'll marry?" she brightened.

"Nah," Shandol said, "Dolene said he's already goin' with somebody else." She muttered under her breath, "Wonder what line he fed her."

"Musta been a good one," Audrey retorted, which startled Shandol as she hadn't realized she had spoken loud enough for her mother, with her impaired hearing, to have heard.

"That's something to watch for," Audrey went on. "And by the way, Shandol, why gossip with Dolene? There were other girls there, I gathered."

"Mama, you know how it is," Shandol defended, "she was just there. And she's a good ball player, if she is pregnant. We were all just talkin' after playin', and that—just came up."

Dolene was a Wittever. They were what some thought of as the town's disreputables anyway. At one time the four brothers had all lived in Greenway. Now, only two remained. One had moved his family to near Plainesville; one had died of cancer—or syphilis—depending upon who did the talking. The two that remained were not as rowdy as they once had been. In fact they had tried to turn decent. They had all served short prison terms except Dolene's father. He was the oldest and hadn't had much luck trying to keep them on the right track, though he had had to try after his father died when they were still young. His mother still lived in Plainesville with a granddaughter staying with her. But when the Sonnett family had first come to Greenway they had been told about, and warned about, associating with them. And they had seen the drunken brawls they had had, actually fighting and cutting one another with knives. They would have to go to the doctor in Plainesville to be patched up; yet, when they were sober they were the best of friends. It seemed only when drunk did the resentments, the enmity and antagonisms erupt into violence.

Even so, the gossip didn't stop. It was still rumored his wife, Edith "entertained" men while Ruben was away. They were not as poor as some of the people who talked about them. He worked regularly for the railroad, on the "section gang," so they lived in a neat white bungalow. It was said to be nicely furnished and clean as a pen. Very few people actually knew for sure; they simply did not go there. It was also whispered that Dolene, though married to Judd Fargon now, and was expecting a baby herself next year, had also been of questionable character. Certainly wise beyond her years.

Shandol had not had to be warned about her. She had had her own run-in with her. Years before Dolene had simply taken all the things from Shandol's "playhouse." It was a crude affair in a garage, which had formerly held the cow, but when pasture was rented it had been cleaned out and Shandol played there. She had makeshift furniture of wood crates, wooden boxes, rocks and boards, even broken dishes had to do. Why Dolene had resented it no one knew; but she had simply got up one morning early and carted the whole thing to a nearby ditch. She had been seen by a neighbor who promptly informed Shandol's parents. It had shocked the Sonnett family into action. Audrey had confronted her, learned where she put it, insisted she take it back where she got it and apologize to Shandol. She had complied, mocking the whole thing. As time had gone by, Dolene's talk had become coarse, and sometimes shockingly revealing to the sheltered Shandol, when they'd been in school together. Dolene hadn't finished, even the two years in high school in Greenway.

"That isn't all, is it?" Audrey prodded.

"Not exactly. Somebody's been arrested for statutory rape whatever that is. But I don't know much about that. Dolene didn't say that. I think it was Evelyn Kenders. Her brother heard it. If it's so, I remember the girl from school-"

"Go take your bath," Audrey interrupted, motioning with her hand. She smiled. "That's enough gossip or news or whatever it is. Don't worry about it. It seems there always has to be something people have to talk about." She changed the subject. "I'm readin' one of the books you brought home, and been restin', and I just wanted a drink of water." She went on into the kitchen, Shandol standing thoughtfully where she was, until she saw her mother go back to the front room and her book.

Shandol had thought no more of the black car, then the mental picture returned as she thought of how nearly she had been seen. Who was it anyway? Strangers in town?

CHAPTER 2

Shandol went directly to the kitchen for a drink of water, after her mother had done so and left. But the water she drank from the water bucket on the washstand in the corner of the small kitchen she found to be tepid and not very satisfactory.

"Warm as dishwater," she muttered.

She collected what she needed for a bath, however: A washpan of water from the reservoir of the large wood-burning cook stove. The water was still sufficiently warm. She took a towel from the double doors of the washstand, and a suitably sized portion of another, salvaged after much wear, to be used as a washcloth, from the washstand's one drawer, and placed them over her left arm. She also took the used bar of soap, went back through the dining room, through the front hallway, and climbed the steep stairway to her room. In her own room she'd be sure of privacy; and her clean clothing were there.

After washing, she smoothed a few shakes of talcum from a flower decorated can, over her skin, dressed and with the paraphernalia she had taken up with her went back downstairs, replacing everything, which included caring for her soiled clothing, the damp towel and wet washcloth. The soiled clothing was deposited into the "dirty clothes box" in the downstairs bedroom, the towel and washcloth she hung to dry on a small length of clothes line behind the stove in the kitchen. She felt fresh and fragrant, and as she tidied her hair at the medicine cabinet mirror at one side of the dining room, she saw it still looked clean and shiny, and despite her activity, easily made neat.

Now, if only she had a cool drink of water. The tepid water she'd had to drink had certainly not quenched her thirst. She decided it would be worth going to the well to get more water. She often did go for water, despite her mother's protests. Had she but known of the change it would make in her life, she might have reconsidered this time.

"Shandol, there are enough men with stronger backs than yours to carry water around here," she'd heard her mother's protest even now in her memory.

Shandol, however, poured the water into the teakettle on the stove and went out the kitchen door, across the same back porch, which also opened into the dining room, though the porch seemed to be in worse shape on this end. Some of the wide boards sounded loose, and it had a dilapidated look.

Outside, Shandol faced the glaring sunlight. The heat closed around her, which in turn caused the essence of fragrance of her bath radiate around her, even reaching her nose. It seemed a quiet Sunday afternoon now. The summer sum, beaming down, encouraged most people to remain out of it as much as possible. Bees were busy buzzing over the white clover, which was abundant in the yard. A tiny lavender butterfly flitted past. She was soon at the edge of the back yard, where the woodpile, as it was referred to, was located. There were chips of various sizes, even to mere sawdust, along with a small pile of split wood. Most of the wood was ricked in a long neat row, a post separating it into ranks. A rank of wood, they had had to learn, was stacked eight feet long, four feet high, and the sticks as long as ordered by whomever used them. These were suited to their own need. The path, however, skirted the edge of it and continued beside the street, seen even through tall grass and weeds, and on to the well.

As she was just passing the woodpile, however, she saw the black sedan was again going along the street in what seemed to be a crawl. It surprised her, and for a startling, breathtaking moment she thought it would surely stop. She could see two young male occupants. They stared at her, momentarily, and she at them, wondering who they were and, if they were looking for someone, who it might be. She hoped they wouldn't ask her. She hated trying to give directions. Yet that was the only thing she could think of which might explain the slowness of the driving. She didn't recognize either of them and she doubted they recognized her either. The car moved slowly on; so slowly in fact that it was only at the corner of the block by the time she reached the well—about halfway between corners. But it didn't go on, it stopped.

Shandol set the white enameled water bucket on the ground beside the well, which had a three feet high boarded wall around it. Her back was to the road. She faced a row of trees, which was along their fenceless garden, although directly in front of her was their corn patch.

The well was called The Town Well, and was so considered to be. Above the boarded sides and built into it was a frame of two-by-fours, which held a pulley for drawing the water from the well. She

9

took the bucket from its board hanger and was ready to swing it into the well, but then, as always, she looked down into the water. When she put her head over the opening, mirrored on the water below was that portion of the outside directly above it, which then included her face against a background of blue sky.

It's a pretty picture and so plain to see, she thought. It's far down there, yet clear as a mirror; perhaps better because it flattered her because there were no flaws. It's just a pretty me, she thought. She fantasized owning such a lovely color portrait of herself. She would want just the coloring shown. Her pink thin cotton dress had blue cameo-shaped print, with tiny dainty white flowers inside each "cameo." Her hair style was becoming and stylish.

But, as always, she must cut her fantasy short. Someone might be looking. And it made her self-conscious anyway about getting water, having been told so much she shouldn't. Also, there were houses along the street across from her, who also used the well for drinking water. This was either because they had no other source, or they preferred the spring-fed coolness of it. She completely forgot the car and its occupants in her fantasy. Besides they were no concern of hers. The pulley wheel creaked its usual protests as the bucket was lowered, and the picture shattered as the bucket reached the water. The bucket sank immediately, as a large steel nut had been wired to the bail, just at the top of the bucket, which weighted the one side down quickly.

She brought the water up hand over hand on the rope and poured the water into her pail. She was about to pick up the pail and start down the path, but she had hardly made the move to pick it up when a strange masculine voice nearly startled her out of her wits.

"Ain'tcha 'feared that'll gitcha down?" he asked.

"Hasn't yet," she replied quickly, and turned toward the voice. That shiny black car! She noticed it immediately. After all it was the third time today she had seen it. And it too would have to do with the turning point in her life—but not that day.

The shock lasted only a brief moment. It was just the unexpectedness of it, and she was surprised to say the least. Well, if they were hunting someone it seemed she'd been elected to help them; though giving directions even here in the small town would not be easy for her.

As the surprise and uncertainty ebbed away, her brown eyes came alive again, the veil gave way to sparkling awareness and expectancy, she was completely unaware of. The sun shone on her fair hair, which seemed a silken screen as the sun enkindled the dancing gold highlights in it. She smiled, hoping that would hide her natural reticence and nervousness with strangers—especially men strangers.

10

The car's occupants exchanged a few words, which she was unable to catch; but the one on the passenger's side opened the door and got out of the car. He was so tall he seemed to unwind. He's over six feet tall, Shandol decided. He was decidedly a blond. His hair was very light, his eyes baby blue, and a pinkish fair, though somewhat tanned complexion. He wore khaki pants and shirt set. He helped himself to the battered tin cup, which always hung on a nail on the pulley frame, on the opposite side of the drawing bucket.

"That there water shore looks invitin', " he said, adding, "cool 'n nice too. Kin I git a drink?" He smiled, and not really waiting for an answer, helped himself.

"Oh, sure," Shandol replied, unnecessarily, nervously, knowing she was blushing. "How'd you get here and me not hear yuh, anyway, I'd like to know," she babbled.

"Purty good," he nodded. He dipped another cupful and handed it through the car window to his friend.

What do they want, she wondered. Will they go now? Wonder if he's as old as I am; and then was appalled that it should enter her mind.

"We just rolled down slow, stayed outta the gravel as best we could," he said, answering her question. He grinned, which almost closed his eyes.

"Which house you live in?" he wanted to know.

She decided he wasn't really handsome. His eyes were too small, or perhaps too close together for his long full face.

"That ole big one," she replied, and pointed to the unpainted, weatherbeaten, two story house she'd just left. It was practically the center block of the town. On the next corner, north, was the town's post office. In between was the town warehouse, which resembled a rather large barn. It sheltered the street maintainer on one side. On their near side, the Sonnett family used as a barn and chicken house. There was a pen for chickens and enough room for the cow, when she was brought up to be milked from rented pasture. Sometimes they also acquired and fattened a pig to sell, carefully separated from the chickens. A pig was usually a gift, or perhaps payment for some work done. In exchange for the use of the barn, Joel Sonnett served as town clerk.

"It used to be a hotel is why it's rather big," she explained, more for something to say than supposing they would be interested.

"Yore Miss Sonnet," he stated. It was not a question. "I betcha don't 'member me, but I know who you are."

But he doesn't really remember my first name, she thought. She grinned with a hint of mischief in her eyes at the thought, then let it pass quickly.

"Maybe yuh just think yuh know me—but isn't it really only the family that lives in the house?" And turning she nodded toward the house. "I know I don't know who you are. Haven't seen yuh."

"Oh but yuh have," he contradicted, "several times in fack. I seen yuh look right at me."

"Where at?" She asked dubiously.

"Differ'nt places—mostly Oak Grove church. Yuh e'en talked to me onct. Hey, 'member ole 'Pluto'—He's uh friend uh mine." He looked at her, squinting, as Shandol had turned her face from the sun.

"Oh, sure I recall Pluto," she said, adding, "you're not kiddin' are you?"

At the name the image of a tall, dark, gangling hillbilly preacher, who lived in a large, new looking, rambling house somewhere in the woods, so far as she knew. The house, located on a hillside was made of roughhewn lumber (not logs); but the rough, unfinished, unpainted look was rustic, and just suited the hill, wooded surroundings. The lumber had been cut from the nearby woods. "Pluto" lived there with his mother, a retiring woman, petite, but plump, in sharp contrast to her tall, gangling son.

Her gray hair was pulled back from her mature, serene face into a knot on the back of her head. "Pluto" had practically built the house with his own hands, he had said; yet he was barely literate enough to read his Bible. Of course Shandol remembered him, and probably would for a long time. The nickname was used affectionately, yet Shandol could not recall having heard his real name. He was well liked by his fellow hill people and parishioners. The thought was fleeting as she fantasized briefly the events of the previous summer, which flashed through her mind.

There were the three preachers who had come from the west central part of the state. They consisted of a young divorcée, her fifteen year old sister, who was the star attraction, and child prodigy. She had preached since she was seven years old. She wore her blond hair parted in the middle, her pretty face was set off by sky blue eyes, and she had a vivacious personality for one so young. Her sister was also a blond. She wore her long hair waved at the sides and pulled back to a knot at the back of her head. She was plump, and her face showed it. She was quieter, her smile sometimes strained looking, as she seemed to shrink into the background as her young sister kept the limelight.

There was also a large middle-aged, obese man with them, who acted as protector and driver of the old model car they drove.

Shandol's oldest brother, who'd married his childhood sweetheart earlier this year, had that summer become quite infatuated with the

12

fifteen-year-old, who did not discourage him. It had been at this insistence and invitation that the three had spent some time as guests of the family. This in spite of the wide differences of the respective church affiliations. Lester had been disappointed and hurt more than he had let on that the innocent affair had turned out to be no more than a summer romance. But while it lasted it had been a fun summer. Not only Lester, but Shandol had been invited to go with them. She was supposed to be company for the older sister. This meant they visited various churches in the area; and also had been invited and gone along with them as they had held street meetings in Plainesville, the county seat. This was something they had not known about and a completely new experience for them. They were also carefully cautioned by their parents to stay strictly in the back ground, and take no part in it, such as singing, or even being identified with them. Shandol's mother pointed out to her she still had another year of high school there, and no telling who would happen along the street.

The object of the street meetings had been to collect money in the form of an offering. When the man of the group placed his hat, crown down on a Bible near where they stood, those persons who enjoyed the service or merely felt compelled to do so, dropped whatever coins they could spare into it. The girls sang, accompanied by the guitar played by the younger one. She also gave the "message." A few times her older sister substituted for her sister, but the offerings were better when the younger one did the speaking. Even she could see she hadn't the personality to hold an audience her younger sister had. The same held true of the large man, who usually just introduced them and was in charge of the service in that he explained who they were and why they were there, which was "to tell them of Jesus."

The offering collected was used mostly to buy gasoline for the old car and in general keep it going. The tires were bad, and it often seemed a miracle that they actually withstood the sometimes quite rocky country roads they'd traveled over from time to time, as they went from place to place. They depended on people to provide a place to stay and food to eat. Lester Sonnett had been crushed when they left. He had accused the older sister of interfering because she thought they were getting too serious. That was only to his family, but he was bitter toward her for some months. They all felt they had been used, because they had taken advantage of the situation for board and room there; even while he had to admit he had enjoyed the experience—and time took care of the rest.

"Of course I remember 'Pluto,'" she repeated, coming back to the present after the brief flashback, and added, "I've even been down where he lives—well, once with some people," she blushed. "But I still have to wonder if you're kidding me."

"Nope, I ain't. Ask Jim here. He'll back me up." He'd been leaning on the car and bent down to put his head at the window opening. "Right, Jim?"

"That's right if he says so." The one called Jim agreed, and nodded.

"Yeah, you gave him a wink or something." she accused. "Never needed to," he replied, amicably. "But, hey, let's git in the car; this sun's hot." He had no more than said it than he opened the door and got inside. "How's 'bout goin' for a ride," he added.

"Oh, I couldn't do that," she replied quickly. "I'm carryin' water, don't yuh see?" She giggled.

"Why not? We'll take care of the water," he replied.

"Oh, boy." She put her hand to her forehead. "I told you I don't know you," she replied firmly, but patiently." I don't even know your names. And so if you know me as you say you do you'd know very well I don't get in cars with strangers."

They both laughed good-naturedly at that. There was a pause as each one took a pack of cigarettes from his shirt pocket. Shandol was offered one, which she declined. The one called Jim found a light first and his friend's cigarette was lighted before his own. Each blew a stream of smoke.

"My name's Dean Leonard," the sandy-haired one told her. The oil on his hair gave his hair a light sandy look. Shandol noticed even his eyebrows were almost white, they were so blond. "And this here's James Brown," indicating his friend.

"Yeah," James Brown said, "excuse us not introducin' ourselves. What's your first name?"

"Shandol," she replied.

"Do you live around here?" she asked.

"Uh course, 'bout four mile out," Dean told her, "ceptn' Jim. He lives in Pollard. His dad has the store there. Jim here drives a truck same as me."

"So you drive a truck?" She repeated it as a question. "Not full time," Dean admitted. "I help Dad farm, too.

But I do sometimes and I like the job."

"What do you haul?" she asked, looking first to one then the other.

"Anythin'," Dean answered. "But me, livestock mostly. I work for a guy who buys, sells—even trades. But Jim here, he hauls milk on a regular route to Folks Consent."

A short silence followed. Shandol looked around the familiar landscape in front of her. This part of the town was between two hills. Facing west, as she now was, was the railroad tracks midway up the hill, with two houses on the hillside to the left in between. And across one grassy yard, where a house had burned, some oak saplings were already in evidence.

"Yuh're shore yuh won't go ridin' with us?" Dean asked again.

"I'm sure," she replied, drawing her lips in a straight line. "I've already said—"

"Yuh don't know us—yeah, we know," Dean interrupted, grinning.

"Exactly," she came back at him, as she felt he was needling her.

"Hey! I've just thought uh somethin', Jim spoke up, suddenly animated. "Know what's this week, Dean?"

"Can't say off-hand as I do," Dean replied.

"Why, it's reunion time at Titan Springs," he told them, eagerly, and as though the idea had occurred to him.

"It sure is," Shandol nodded agreement. "Wednesday's the first night, isn't it?"

"Do you ever go?" Dean was searching her face.

"Of course—almost every year," she answered.

And it was true. Her eyes dropped as if to hide her embarrassment, as her foot scraped a small pile of dust back and forth. She wondered what they would think of the transportation she had to use—the back of a milk truck, converted for hauling people by removing the cans, the low boards needed for that, and adding the higher stock racks. This, as a means of getting to go somewhere, was a regular thing here. Few people could afford automobiles, and the young people (dating or not), and the not so young often had to depend on the truck to go somewhere. There was usually a "load" to go to Plainesville on Sunday nights, especially in the summer. Some went to the show, some to a special church, and once a month there was a Singing in the courthouse. This was a gathering of singers: soloists, duets, on to groups who sang. There was usually a good-sized appreciative audience, as Shandol well knew. Of course there was the county fair to attend, the reunion and such varied events to which a group would be interested in going.

"Say, how 'bout Wednesday?" Dean cut into her thought. "Go with us."

"I—I don't know about that," she replied, doubtfully. "I really don't," She wondered what her father would say. She doubted he'd approve, on such short acquaintance. It would take away the joy and anticipation if he criticized, which he so often did. Sometimes it seemed to her there was some fault with everyone she considered going with, no matter who it was.

"Won't cher ma let yuh?" Dean asked.

"Oh it's not her," she could reply, truthfully. "Well, then I'll be by to git yuh," he said.

"But I didn't say I'd go yet," she replied, astonished at his self-confidence.

"Nope, but I did," he replied, as though it was, after all, up to him to make up both their minds.

"Wait!" She exclaimed, "I can't go with two guys anywhere and I won't; so there!"

"Git Jim a date then," Dean replied.

"I'm not sure—" she began, then said no more. She supposed it to be useless anyway. Why, the very nerve of him she thought.

No more was said about it, though there was more light chatter before they finally drove on. Shandol thoughtfully watched them go. After they rounded the corner at the block she picked up the bucket of water and went back to the house. It was clean water, she knew, but she was sure it could not be as cool after being in that hot sun as she would like it to be. So she finished filling the teakettle on the cook stove and the rest she poured into the reservoir of the stove, which was on the end farthest from the firebox where the wood burned. She immediately set out again for a fresh cool bucket of water to drink. She was feeling exuberant and expectant; feelings she seldom had, except in fantasy. She looked at herself in the well again, smiled a glad smile, which showed clean white teeth; she was quite unabashed at herself, and more reluctant than ever to break the pretty girl's picture.

* * * * *

Meanwhile, the wheels of the shiny black sedan had rolled smoothly down the dusty, rocky, grass-lined street, with a row of spindly weeds and grass defiantly growing between the car tracks, to the main street. They turned right, to across in front of the general store, which was across the street from the post office.

"Stop here at the store," Dean said, turning to his friend, explaining "I need some cigarettes."

Jim looked at him quizzically. "Yeah, sure," he replied. But he was remembering the satisfied "hot dog" exclamation of his friend, who had also said he could hardly believe it; his fervor showed. He was obviously anticipating his date with the elusive, assumably unattainable Sonnett girl, who was always with some family member, and who was so shy she could hardly look at a man, with some exceptions; and with a father who cared little about her being interested in anyone—even discouraged it, it seemed.

The store was a stone, one story building, with glassed front, and a concrete porch with a tin roof across the entire front. It was large

16

enough for two stores of its size, actually; one side, however, was used as a warehouse and storage area. An assortment of men loafed on the porch. These were mostly men who'd come to meet the mail train, because the post office was opened only a short time on Sundays. The men had just stayed to talk and pass the afternoon. And some would stay so long as there was anyone there—even to suppertime.

Dean purchased his pack of cigarettes at a glassed counter near the front door. He glanced around briefly, and yet unseeing. It was just the usual country store with its assortment of merchandise, from food and candy to medicine and clothing—even gasoline and kerosene. There were other odds and ends, which might be necessary to some type work or otherwise be necessary and handy to have around. The store was opened when the first passenger train came through, and hardly had a chance to be closed. It was opened by Clive Thomas, who met the train to carry the mail both to it, and the incoming mail to the post office. Clive, a short stocky man in his early fifties, had a small bunk room partitioned in the back of the storeroom, though be took his meals with a family across the block, up the street from Sonnetts. He was usually followed inside by someone needing something from the store, and others followed. Harry Bright, the owner, who would be at church when the store was opened, would frequently drop by. He was a checker player, and if an opportunity came he would stay to take on any challengers. At other times he would go to play checkers with Joel Sonnett. They had, in fact, played a few games earlier, when Joel had gone to the store, after stopping at the post office. However, Harry had expected company so they hadn't lingered as long as he sometimes might.

Dean did not tarry long. There was no one inside the store except Clive, who had waited on him, as he could see back to the pot-bellied stove, which heated the place in winter; and where the checker games were held summer or winter. Dean ventured leisurely back outside. There he could see three young men approaching the store porch. Dean went on to the car to Jim.

"I been talkin' to a guy," Jim told him, "he's—well, sittin' over there now," pointing unobtrusively, and nodding in the general direction of the men. "It seems he seen you talkin' to a certain young lady. He was just walkin' along the road at the corner. He asked about it."

Dean was leaning on the car, his hand on the top, his long lean frame slouched, one thumb hooked at the edge of his pocket.

"Didja tell 'em I had a date with the Sonnett girl?" he asked, slightly raising his voice for the benefit of the young men, now at the gas pump at the porch corner, as he eyed them.

The three boys were dressed in faded blue denim patched overalls. One wore no shirt. The others wore faded print shirts, one of which had had the sleeves cut away to the shoulder seam;the other had unhemmed short sleeves, with rips to the shoulder. They stopped at the edge of the porch and eyed the speaker.

A youth with handsome features, thick brown hair and nut brown skin, even where his shirtless shoulders showed the deep suntan.

"Sonnett girl, huh?" he asked, eyeing Dean.

"Yeah, I gotta date with 'er," Dean replied, grinning smugly; the grin almost closing his sleepy-looking eyes.

"Really, now," the young man returned.

"Know 'er?" Dean asked. "Anything yuh gotta say?"

"Not a thing," the young man replied, and added an aside, "see yuh fellas," to the other two in farewell. He crossed the graveled street, entered a well-worn path beside the post office building, and, as was plain to see, was headed for the back yard of the Sonnett place.

A silence followed.

"Her brother," one of the youths finally volunteered. "And he didn't believe yuh, I could see that, 'cause she don't go nowheres with no boys less'n her brother er somebody is along. Her dad's purty pa'tic'lar where she's concerned."

"Well, I'm takin' 'er to the reunion Wednesday night, I'll tell yuh," Dean insisted. "Say, was that Phil? Why I'd orta knowed him. I wasn' thinkin'. And he dit'n know me neither."

"She don't go with nobody she don't know," the taller of the two boys insisted, stubbornly. "I'd betcha on it."

"Yuh gotta bet," Dean challenged. "What's the stakes? 'Cause she knows me now."

"Uh—uh Coke?"

"Hell," Dean taunted, "ascared to make it worthwhile?"

"Okay, six of 'em."

"Shake," Dean grinned, triumphantly, assuredly. It was taken and he added, "thanks," walked around the car and got into it. "See yuh later," he called and threw up his hand. The car sped away, kicking up gravel and fogging the dust behind it.

18

CHAPTER 3

Wednesday dawned clear and beautiful. It held promise of another dazzlingly bright August day. The deep blue sky was flawless. The sun had already turned the dew-drops into gems, and stolen them. But Shandol did not care about the weather right then. Her brain was still befogged from lack of sleep; and she was entirely too bogged down in doubt and dread of even having to face the day. She hadn't slept well, and it hadn't all been because of the heat. In fact a slight breeze had made it pleasant, as she had moved her pillow to the foot of the iron bed so she would be able to feel the air.

But she couldn't seem to turn off her mind. Her thoughts kept churning with questions. She puzzled over regrets and disappointment; and wondered if the new plans she had made could be carried out. For by now she had made up her mind there would be no date tonight; and only hoped the truck would show up so she could be gone. She regretted the fact it might be considered breaking a date. But there was no way to let Dean know, and she didn't much care anyway. It had virtually turned into a nightmare for her.

And it all went back to Sunday when she had made that ridiculous date; and the absolutely inconceivably foolish way it had been done. How could she have done it? For being the strangers they were and only the first encounter? Now she knew that that was just the half of it. And she couldn't help puzzling over whether to take it seriously or not. She didn't know those young men no matter what they said. That meant she had no idea as to what kind of reputation they had. And for all she knew the whole thing had been done on impulse. Suppose that's all it is, she thought. Suppose they have steady girl friends, and Dean conveniently forgets about me? But Dean had seemed so sincere, she would mentally argue with herself. In fact he'd seemed insistent. But why? And the bets? She had learned of that only last night. Her thoughts churned on despite her decisions. And she wished she had listened to her mother about carrying water; she would never have been at the well, and she wouldn't be in all this dither.

Still, it put her thoughts right back where they were: Could she manage to make the truck in time? And since last night there was the added embarrassment of knowing it was no longer her own personal matter. She was sure that by now everyone in town knew about it.

19

Her brother, Phillip had told her about the bet, which he'd heard about from Buck Sandler, who'd made the bet with Dean. Shandol had no idea Phil knew about the date. She had had a chance to talk to her mother about it only yesterday. She had hoped her parents would object, a perfect excuse, but no such luck.

By Monday and Tuesday, she had begun the vague questioning and being unsure—but resigned. Her doubts had floated first about whether to believe in the sincerity of it, in the first place. Then she hoped she had made it plain she would not go out with two men alone. She had made up her mind if Jim had no date she would not set foot into that car. They had given her the idea it would be a double date, and that was that so far as she was concerned. She had no intention of trying to find him a date. Which brought up another doubt. What if Jim brought a date and she turned out to be a stranger and a snob? How could she, Shandol Sonnett, keep from being self-conscious and clumsy? She had thought it all just dubiousness; just a huge question mark. Now she was stunned. She was so shocked and bewildered, as she decided it one huge joke. And that hurt. Just an excuse to make a bet.

Had it all really been since Sunday? She listlessly sat on the edge of the bed, and wished she could just crawl back into it. Actually, what it seemed was weeks. She felt she was entangled in a web—no, strangled—and somehow she must extricate herself.

She hoped it worked out that way. And to think, she reminded herself, that Sunday she had felt good about herself, and somewhat incredible. She had been glad she had attracted someone. Of course, there had been skepticism, too, because she was not better acquainted with either of them; and it was an unusual thing for her to have done. But she had not allowed herself to be overly preoccupied with its rightness or wrongness. It was done.

She had aimed to confide in Phil later Sunday. She had in fact followed him into the front room, where he had already picked up the violin he had left on top of the pigeon hole desk.

Shandol had listened to him "fiddle," as he himself called it. And she silently wished she could pick up tunes by ear as easily as he did. At least he made it seem easy. When he had finished a tune and she had hoped to get his attention, her mother had called her to get tomatoes from the garden and peel and slice them for supper, so the chance had passed. She had hoped to have asked him if he knew, or knew of, a Dean Leonard. If he'd heard anything, good or bad; and what would he think of her going with him? Of course she would tell her mother, but she wanted to discuss it with him, also.

Shandol helped her mother with supper and the dishes afterward.

Following that it was time to get ready to go to Young People's meeting. They went despite the fact it was not held at the church they usually attended, where no Sunday evening services were held. This small church was called the Union Church, supposedly non-denominational, but due to a once-a-month preacher who came, it was more or less identified with his denomination. It would be somewhat like attending a church service, though informal; and to many it was merely somewhere to go. But there would be songs sung, prayers offered, and a leader, who had volunteered to prepare a Bible study lesson. And all age groups attended.

Shandol went with her parents and two younger brothers. The other two had gone to Plainesville on the truck. Shandol sat apart from her parents, who sat near the front because of Audrey's hearing problem. For awhile Shandol sat alone on the crude pew, a few rows back. The pews were little more than wooden benches with back support boards, and there were two rows of pews, with an isle down the middle.

Then she was joined by a former classmate, Arlane Gilmire.

She was a slender brunette, a little taller than Shandol, whose dark brown hair was worn in a shoulder-length pageboy style. She greeted Shandol pleasantly, with a broad smile, which reached from her wide mouth and high cheek bones to her dark shiny eyes. Her mother, a small sister and young brother sat elsewhere. The girls, who had been friendly rivals for good grades in grade school, really hadn't much in common now. Arlane had dropped out of high school after her second year. So their conversation consisted mostly of incidental exchanges. That is until Arlane made the startling (to Shandol)announcement she was getting married next year. The date depended upon when David, her fiancée could get leave from the navy. Shandol was surprised and showed it; but managed to smile and say she certainly hoped everything worked out happily for them.

"I just hadn't heard about it," she added, silently thinking such news got around faster, usually.

The meeting began when Mr. Follerson, who was at the front of the church, in front of the pulpit, in his wheel chair, announced the first song. Audrey Sonnett was asked to play the piano.

While the first song was being sung the leader for the evening passed out slips of paper, on which were scripture verses and their location in the Bible. They were consecutively numbered. As the numbers were called the person having that number stood and read the verse aloud, including the Bible location.

The leader tonight was Mr. Follerson's daughter, who was going with the high school teacher. There were only two grades in high school, and he taught them both. By making some courses for both grades, and alternating subjects year by year it could work out. She was of medium build, with dark snappy eyes, a dark creamy smooth skin, a firm assured voice and was late twenties in age.

Shandol looked around to see who was in attendance, It was about the same ones every Sunday, both inside and outside. Some who came for somewhere to go lingered, and gossiped outside all men and boys. There were young single men who were waiting for their girl friends, or a likely one to ask to walk home.

Shandol was proud to see her mother at the piano, even though they had to show her the song page number, rather than to assume she could hear it. She was sorry her conversation with Arlane was cut short, but she knew better than to be caught whispering in church. Unthinkable; her father would criticize. As old as she was!

Despite the fact, Shandol tried to keep her mind on the service, her mind wandered. She assumed the lesson would be well prepared and presented; the leader was mature and had had experience before the public. She thought of Arlane's approaching marriage. Would she, herself, ever—marry? Arlane certainly seemed happy. Shandol considered her lucky to find someone she was so in love with, and someone she thought was the only one for her. She was so self-assured. Shandol remembered them going together in school. Arlane s father, with only a third grade education had dared to open a grocery store, after quitting the highway department—or was he fired, as some claimed?

Who knew, really? Yet, the store had succeeded. It was located along an interstate highway—a crooked two-lane blacktop, but the highway bus route.

Shandol recalled when once she had tried to be the leader. Her shyness and self-consciousness had made the thing a flop, in her own estimation. She had forgotten most of what she had planned to say, and even her notes hadn't helped. They weren't complete enough. She had also hoped her father would help, but he had refused to participate, even. The subject, which was Love was chosen for the next two Sunday nights—"because it was such a broad subject." So Shandol was sure she had made a mess of the whole thing, and had been truly crushed at her poor effort. In fact when she got home she could barely keep a straight face until she reached her own room, and let the darkness envelope her before she wept bitterly at her failure. It was later she realized that feeling as her father did about what women should and shouldn't do, that he had refused to encourage her effort. And that was one thing his daughter, at least, should not do.

Shandol remembered hearing him tell her mother he would hate to think a daughter of his could make more money than he could, when Shandol had graduated from high school. His schooling had stopped at the eighth grade, but he had studied and never quit trying to make up for it. Sometimes Shandol thought he was better educated than herself, even with her high school diploma. And his knowledge of the Bible rivaled, if not exceeded, that of Mr. Follerson, who before his health failed had been a preacher. On the other hand he considered it foolish to educate girls—except for teachers. He reasoned most of them just married and settled down to raise a family, anyway. It was her mother who harped about Shandol needing to finish high school, even though times were hard and it had been a struggle. Shandol had had to work to help with buying her clothing and books. She had picked blackberries in summer; stayed with a lady who had had an operation, doing the housework. There she had had to wash, iron, help cook and clean, and was paid one dollar a week. It seemed there had always been someway—even at school she had been allowed to work a couple of hours a day and the government helped with that.

She became so absorbed in her thoughts and the news she had heard, and the happenings of the day, she almost missed hearing the number of the scripture she was to read. But she looked at Arlane with a resigned shrug, arose, and with no comment, read it aloud, timidly.

There were other songs, prayers, and a scripture text read by the leader, who in a short talk used the scriptures for a worthwhile lesson. There was then allowed a time for further comment on the subject. There had been none, as she had prepared well. Mr. Follerson, Benita's father had helped her, Shandol was sure, or he'd have added more comment. As it was he only complimented his daughter on the fine job; and announced it was time to choose the next Sunday's leader and a word, which must be the subject, and used in all the scripture text slips passed out. Tonight it had been *Heart*. Then there was a final song and Joel Sonnett gave the benediction, and it was all over.

Shandol had walked home with her parents and younger brothers. The younger boys tagged along, sometimes behind, tagging one another and running, or romping along a short distance ahead, shoving one another, scuffling or throwing street gravel at imaginary, unseen targets along the side of the graveled road. Audrey cautioned them about their clothes and falling down, because the gravel made walking uncertain and stepping sometimes meant sliding with variable steps, as it was a dark night.

"It's dark as a stack of black cats," K.C., the younger of the two boys had observed, repeating what he had heard.

They were accustomed to walking in the gravel, even in darkness, and they had long ago accepted it and were hardly aware of it.

It was a warm night, but seemed cooler now that the sun had gone out of sight. Only the glitter of the stars overhead, resembling twinkling gems tossed haphazardly into space pierced the overhead curtain.

Monday had been such a busy day, Shandol had not had a chance to talk privately with her mother. It was a day when it seemed someone, or everyone, was near one or the other—or both—all the time. They had canned tomatoes and Shandol and her mother welcomed any help offered; and even asked for it. After all it was a time consuming job. There was water to carry to wash jars and to boil to scald the tomatoes, so the peelings were removed easier. They also had to have the stem end removed, as well as any other imperfections. It was Shandol's job to help prepare them; she washed and filled the fruit jars, as her mother directed her. So it had been a time of family cooperation, complaints at such hard work (or women's work), opinions expressed, and the inevitable "horse play" among the boys. There was joking and laughter, as well as seriousness, as Joel sometimes called order if he supposed there was too much noise and confusion to get anything done. But during it all Shandol had not mentioned her encounter with Dean and Jim, though it had been on her mind a great deal. She had supposed she had a secret!

It had been much the same the next day, with everyone busy, except that it was wash day. It was certainly no secret that Audrey, whose health had suffered in the past, could use the help of the family. The men were around to carry water, though they used what rainwater they could catch, including in a rain barrel at the corner of the house, and from an old cistern, just off the back porch near the house. It was low this time of year, however, and some would be brought from the town well. The water was put to heat on the large cook stove in an oval wash-boiler, made to fit the stove top with the lids removed, so the bottom of the boiler could be next to the fire. The first water heated was put into a tub, with cool water added so it wasn't too hot for the hands, and more added to the boiler. Shandol scrubbed the clothes on the washboard first. She would soap them with a bar of home-made laundry soap, made with lye, she and her mother had made. Some of the soap, usually a small used bar from a past wash day, was cut into slivers or thin narrow slices, so they would melt quicker, and added to the boiler. The clothes were mostly all boiled in this soapy water. Shandol was conscious of her job this day. She hoped she could keep from scrubbing a blister, and consequently the skin from her finger joints, which she sometimes did. She tried to go slower so her hands would not be blemished and sore.

Her mother punched and poked at the boiling clothes with a

24

short round clothes punch. It was just larger than a broom handle, unpainted (but shorter) and only about four feet long. For all Shandol supposed it had been made for the purpose.

Audrey punched the clothes as they boiled; she also took them from the boiler by buckets full, using the punch; then rinsed them through two tubs of clean water, and hung up the clothes, at least until Shandol was through the scrubbing and could help finish whatever remained to do.

The clothes were clean. People remarked of the nice looking washes on their lines; when they were dry they were collected from the line and folded to be put away, except the ironing, which was dampened, if not gathered before completely dry, rolled as neatly as possible and put into the paper-lined bushel basket to be ironed the next day. There was usually a large ironing as the sheets were "pressed" and the pillowcases, as well as the tea towels were included with the family's clothing.

It was while they were washing Shandol and her mother had managed to have some private time together. After all, washing wasn't a popular chore, and as soon as they had brought water, the men had gone to the timber to cut wood. So it gave Shandol a chance to tell her mother of Sunday afternoon, and how she'd met the two men and the date she hadn't been able to object to or contradict, and assumed was made.

"Ive decided I'd really rather go on the truck," she finished, sincerely, "but that one who talked to me wouldn't have taken 'no' for an answer, I'm sure. He said he'd be after me. Do you suppose Dad will say anything?"

"Who are they?" Audrey asked, her heart going out to her shy, sheltered daughter, who so often showed misery in her timidity.

"Their names are Dean Leonard and James Brown—or did I already say that? That's about all I know, except Jim drives a milk truck on a route that takes milk to the cheese factory at Folks Consent. Dean, the one who talked to me, helps his dad farm, and sometimes helps a man who buys and sells livestock—also driving his truck. They'd gone out to get the Martin girls, they said before they left. The girls weren't at home so they were just drivin' around town, and came around this block here at least three times that I know of. And the last time I was gettin' water from the well, and they stopped and talked. Finally that Jim remembered that the reunion begins this week. Then the one named Dean asked me to go—no, he insisted he'd be by to get me."

"Your dad'll likely leave it up to you," Audrey replied, smiling. "You're over eighteen years old, and must learn to trust your own judgment. It wouldn't look right going with the two alone, but otherwise, why not?"

"But I don't trust my own judgment," she sighed, audibly. "I can't make up my mind if I'd have a good time, or even if I should take it seriously, or just be scared of it—which I am, I guess. They are strangers," she added, "even if Dean says he'd seen me before and knew who I was."

"For pity's sake where'd he see you?" Audrey asked, looking at her.

"At Oak Grove church, he says," she replied. "You know when we went—down somewhere in the sticks—with the preachers. But all that didn't mean a thing to me. I sure don't remember seeing him."

"Oh, me," Audrey sighed, resignedly, "time to get back to work. Don't worry, it'll work out. Just remember what your grandma would say: 'If the women behave themselves, the men have to'. " Audrey believed it to be true and it was also true there was plenty to do, though they had mopped up their water mess and emptied the water, while the clothes dried.

Now it was time to think of suppertime and Shandol was starved. The other thing she disliked about wash day, next to the hard work, was the scant noon meal. Usually all that was cooked was unpeeled boiled potatoes, which Shandol found unappetizing, but which Audrey found convenient. Sometimes bread and gravy were added, but usually they were lucky if there was milk to go with the bread, though there was usually butter, also used on the potatoes. Because even when the cow was "dry" or with calf, they bought, or sometimes were given, whole milk, and it was skimmed for the cream and churned into butter. The churning was usually done by putting the cream into a half gallon fruit jar and shook up and down until the butter foamed. She was glad when suppertime came.

Shandol thus realized she would have no help from her parents. She wished they would advise her. In fact she needed someone to talk to. She wondered if it would be as once before when "Drummy" Drawlson had gone to Joel to ask permission to escort his daughter home from a party to which they had all gone. Joel had agreed, and Shandol had supposed he approved; perhaps even impressed by "Drummy's" asking for his permission even before asking Shandol. But when they had reached home and were alone, he had let her know in no uncertain terms he was not pleased about it. In fact he had criticized "Drummy" as an undesirable character, especially where young ladies were concerned; and herself for not using better judgment. It seemed Mr. Drawlson was getting quite a reputation with young women and not very popular. He was a tall, handsome man. He had curly light brown hair, and was well-built—even mannerly when he chose to be. His parents were divorced and he had spent many summers with his grandparents, who lived on a small farm just outside Greenway. He had lived in the city with his mother to go to school, his father helping in his support. But he had quit school by now. But before, it seemed to make up to him, he had been indulged and spoiled, and had had things better than most of the local children had. Now, one never knew when or if he would come to Greenway, though he still came to visit in the summer, and supposedly to help his aging grandparents in the garden. But he was irresponsible and did as he pleased, including his fly-by-night comings and goings. He seemed never to have a steady job, but joked about it.

Shandol had resented her father's criticizing her, but she realized he had only been testing her judgment. She must learn to make decisions after weighing the facts carefully, which certainly left her in a quandary now, because she was so lacking in facts. She realized she didn't know enough to make an intelligent decision. She was sure she had been somewhat influenced by the chance it offered to go with someone who had a car. It was certainly something to think about. Boys who had cars—or more likely, had access to a family car—were indeed few in the town. Because of that, going somewhere for most young people and the not so young, meant either going to whatever was within walking distance, such as to church, play parties, school related activities and games (during the school year)or going on the truck. It was a milk truck, with a regular route, that is, which took cans of milk to Plainesville. For hauling the passengers, the milk cans were removed, of course, and high stock racks put on to replace the low sides used to haul milk, which made it easier to load and unload the cans. If enough people wanted to go the truck would go. That included going to such places as Plainesville Sunday nights.

Some people would go to the movies, some to church; and there was a singing there once a month. There was the county fair every year to attend; the reunion, which rated more than one trip, as did the fair. Sometimes there were other special events which came up from time to time. Because of this it was usual for Shandol to go only when her parents, her brothers or a friend went along. Because of this also, the idea of going in a car alone with a man she hardly knew disconcerted her.

What could she think of to talk about, for instance. She tried to remind herself a butterfly stomach was normal for her, but she was also in such a dither of indecision. She had heard other girls talk about their nervousness before a first date, but she thought it was just that—talk. But now that she experienced it she wondered if it was worth all the worry and bother. Thus her mood had see-sawed from wishing she could get out of it, to being certain it was impossible even to consider it. But what could she do?

That was until last night when Phil had come. He headed for the front and motioned for her to follow. Shandol followed, wondering what he had on his mind. He leaned against the old pigeon hole desk, waiting, so she knew music making was not on his mind. He searched her face momentarily, then spoke."Do you know they're bettin' on you and this so-called date?" His face was unreadable. The animation and twinkle was gone from his usually expressive dark eyes.

"What's to bet?" she asked, lightly, "and why on that? Hey, I thought we'd play some, but you've never time or patience to help me learn and practice the guitar chords so I can accompany you playin' the fiddle." He couldn't seem to understand why she couldn't pick it up as he had.

"They're bettin' yuh don't have a date with Dean Leonard," he persisted.

"Well I—I," she stammered, then more heatedly, "how'd you know so much about it?" He's teasing me surely, she thought. "Don't get het up now," Phil chided, gently, his expressive eyes lighting up a little. "Dean's told several. Even bet six Cokes hisself that he had a date with you. That was Sunday afternoon. Now several are bettin'. But just Cokes, root beer—stuff like that is all."

"Why do they think I can't date?" she asked, so deflated her face seemed to change to a mask. "I don't look or act so much different from others who do, do I?"

"It's not that, Sis," he replied. "They just don't believe yuh'll be allowed to go with 'em by yourself."

"Oh," It was almost a sigh. "Maybe some people know something we don't. Maybe he won't show up."

"Would he bet if he didn't aim to keep the date?" he reminded her. "They just don't think yuh'll be allowed to see him and have the chance."

She was near tears. She was sure if she could be alone she would cry, and she would liked to have had the chance. It was all so foolish. All her worry, indecision and uncertainty she had gone through, and she hadn't known the half of it.

Secret indeed! Why, to Dean it must be all just a huge joke to feed his ego.

"Are you bettin'?" she asked, woodenly, afraid he would guess her feelings. He was two years younger than she was and they had been close as children, as Shandol had no sister. It was important to her what he thought about it.

"Course not," he said, "seems silly to me." He looked at his downcast sister with sympathy. He could realize she was sensitive, and hurt.

"Yeah, silly, silly," she said, "and why? And what do I do now?"

"They don't mean nothin' personal, Sis," he told her, wondering if he should have told her after all. "They're just jostlin' opinions, that's all." He brightened, threw back his shoulders and reached for the violin. "Whew, I've got that off my chest. Wanna play some music?"

"No, I'm not in the mood, after all," she replied, dejectedly.

"Uh—watch 'em, Sis," Phil added, meaningfully. "He was braggin', I think."

Bragging? About going with me? She brightened up a little. What did that mean? But her mood fell just as fast. It was all just something to brag about and bet on, wasn't it?

She turned and stalked from the room, a determined look on her face, her mouth set in a straight line, her mind made up. She wanted no part of such a mixed-up, silly outfit, and when the truck left to go to the reunion tomorrow night, she intended to be on it as one of the passengers. She was thinking, the nerve of the whole impossible lot of them. Muckrakers all—men, too: Let 'em bet; and win, lose or draw, it wasn't her game and she wouldn't play it! Furthermore she didn't care of the consequences! She'd just ignore it and Dean Leonard, too.

In her wildest fancies she would never have guessed at such a thing, even knowing the town had its fair share of gossips. It's so incredible, she fumed to herself. I suppose I had a secret. What a laugh! It hadn't even occurred to her that Dean might talk about it; and, indeed, why had he?

But then it reminded her of what had happened earlier in the summer. She was at the Little Mission church, and though it wasn't the one she belonged to, there was nowhere else to go. Besides there was a young, tall, handsome, guitar-playing preacher, who also sang, holding a revival. He drew good crowds, which had cut into the attendance of Young People's meeting on Sunday nights. But on this night Shandol had sat about the middle, and four men came in and sat down on the same rough wooden bench, which, unlike the church in the hollow, had no back board rest. Shandol thought nothing of it, because she was sitting in the middle of that bench, and they on the end of it. Besides she was with a girl friend, Margery McNeely. But then the men scooted closer, though it wasn't necessary. The girls moved also until they were at the end of the bench, and the men were next to Shandol. Shandol became quite embarrassed because the man nearest her was a married man, and a known flirt. She supposed her blushing, and the forbidding glares she gave them only made them want to tease her all the more. As the bench actually filled with people, and the small church as well, she tried to ignore the one next to her.

However, the next morning as Shandol was just getting up, sure enough a blabbermouth across the street had already come to tell Audrey. Their voices trailed up the stairway as she came down, and she listened at the hallway door before going into the dining room where they were. Shandol realized it was not old Mrs. Kasper, as she might expect, but the younger Charlene Frist, who had three small children, one a cute chubby curly haired blond. Shandol waited until they had finished that part of their conversation before entering. She did note that Charlene admitted the girls had moved to the end of the bench, but Charlene said she thought Audrey should know. Why? Shandol wondered.

Audrey, of course, wanted to hear Shandol's side of it, but made no fuss, because there was nothing else to it. Actually she didn't mention and luckily Charlene couldn't have known, he had put his hand on the bench beside her thigh, but Shandol put her hand between, glaring at him again, and being careful that their hands didn't even touch. Otherwise it was chance seating so far as they were concerned. The girls hadn't wanted to sit on the front row, so stayed put.

Shandol already knew about girls who had crushes on married men, and how foolish it was considered. Her mother's only brother, and Shandol's favorite uncle, was a high school teacher, who besides mathematics, biology, or some other subject he was qualified to teach, one subject he always had included was the music department. There was a band, orchestra, or both, and individual music lessons. He was a tall handsome man, who had the problem of getting love notes and calf-eyes from young girls in a class from time to time. Shandol had heard her aunt tell Audrey they had usually invited them (one at a time of course)into their home, and usually learned they were really the shy ones with few dates. They would make a point of having them to meals, perhaps with others, and try to get them interested in music, sports, or whatever activity they seemed to prefer, which would be revealed sooner or later. Soon they'd be interested in persons their own age—perhaps even dates. Mostly it had worked, and no hard feelings or "broken hearts."

Shandol was often impatient and exasperated about so much town gossip and grape-vine news guessing. Usually the whole point of it escaped her. And it certainly did now. Except : Was this another example of what was and wasn't expected of the Sonnett kids. It seemed more was expected of them, and they had to be careful. Better behavior, more discipline—after all Joel Sonnett kept his children in line, didn't he?

Yet they were tempted to learn to play cards, begged to smoke cigarettes, to sneak off to their nickel and dime dice games, and then it was thrown up to them: "The Sonnett kid:; do it." "Why us?" Shandol had complained the first time she had been told this was the case. She even brought it up at the supper table.

"We're not preachers kids, are we supposed to be perfect or something?" she'd blurted out, her annoyance showing. "I get a little tired of hearing what my brothers do, even though they might be doing the same things other mortals around here are doing with no judgment."

"Christians are supposed to try to walk a different life," Joel had conceded, "but not perfect. We can only do the best we can, but failures and triumphs will be evident." He'd pause between sentences so he would not stammer. "It's the trying that counts, I suppose. Ignore what you can't help that others do.

"I know I should," Shandol replied, "but they act like it's some discovery to find feet of clay in this family."

They laughed it off, put like that, but Shandol would not soon forget it.

Now Wednesday had come at last, and she wished it were all over. But breakfast was being called, and face it she must.

The day passed slowly for Shandol because of her anxiety. She wanted the day to go quickly and be over with, because she wanted to be gone before those men showed up again. She had to stay at home while her parents went to Plainesville. It was time for Audrey's checkup. Her confinement was due in five months, and with her history of poor health, another child hadn't really been in their plans and Joel wanted every care to be taken regarding her health and the unborn child. Audrey had just yesterday complained of not feeling well.

Shandol was left to do what ironing she could get done, and to keep an eye on her younger brothers. And she also took time out to wash and roll up her hair.

By late afternoon her hair was dry and ready to be combed and styled. It was full of curly bounce and silken sheen. The soft water and homemade laundry soap she had used washed it clean and brought out golden highlights as well as its baby softness. But she took it all for granted; and only passively noticed. She was so preoccupied, and as nervous as the proverbial "tomcat in a roomful of rocking chairs" all day.

As the day slowly passed she supposed she had answered when spoken to, or had done what she was supposed to have done, but it had hardly registered. That included her bath as she got ready to go; she had had that one thought which had dogged her all day: That was just to be already gone when—or if—Dean and Jim came for her.

They had had an early supper because Shandol and her two brothers had asked for it.

Shandol had not softened her idea about Dean and Jim. She thought of the bets—and what else?—and she wanted no part of the affair. As a result she was actually ready to go long before it was actually necessary, as were her two brothers, who were also going. She stayed inside lest she be seen and asked questions before the truck left.

Then she heard a car honk outside.

CHAPTER 4

Hearing the car honk outside nearly made Shandol's heart stop. She thought she would surely faint if they had indeed beat the truck. With her feelings bordering despair, she had to know and managed to move to sneak a peek from the dining room window, which faced the street on the back porch side. It wasn't the car she had seen Sunday afternoon, but a more familiar one.

"Thank God," she sighed under her breath, in pure reverence.

Phil went outside to see what they wanted. It was two young men, Follerson and Nephew, from town in a car which be longed to the brother-in-law of one of them. They talked a while to Phil, and then he came back toward the house. Shandol, who was leaning over a birdcage, still looking out the window, straightened and turned to face him as he came back into the room.

"Steve wants to know if we'll go with them to the reunion," Phil said.

"Both of us?" she asked.

"Yeah."

"You'll just have to tell 'em no," she replied, "and you can't tell me he won't know why. As if I didn't have enough complications for one night. And all because of that—that braggart!"

He will know why, she thought, as she watched Phil go back to the car. Everyone in town surely knew about Dean—surely. And just why was Steve bothering to ask her now? Refusing to go with him stung, because she honestly wished she was going with him. *Why was he asking now—this late? Perhaps he didn't realize I could go before,* she decided mentally, *or else he is just making up for taking me for granted so much lately. I'm usually always here, and he can just pick me up when he's ready he thinks, I suppose—even to get married.* She dismissed the sarcastic thought quickly, wishing he would just leave.

But then she saw Steve Follerson get out of the car and walk with Phil toward the house, and coming on into the dining room where she was.

"Well whataya say we go?" he asked, and grinned in the charming self-assured way he had. He was about as dark as Dean was fair. He had dark brown eyes, slicked back black hair and a deep-tanned-look complexion. He was tall, though not as tall as Dean, but well built and handsome, which he seemed well aware of. But she had known him for a long time and had had a crush on him since she had been a sophomore in high school. He had been a classmate, except for the last two years of high school. But—the dates they had had, if they could be called that, had consisted of his walking her home from church, some school activity, or being together at parties; but to go in a car with him somewhere, he had never asked her until now.

"I just can't go," she said, with a silent plea for understanding. "I already have one date I'm not sure I want to keep, but I'd better not go with anybody else. We'll be goin' soon, I guess."

She hoped Phil had told him she planned to go on the truck, and how she hoped it got there first.

"May as well go on then," Steve smiled, "see yuh." As he left Phil walked to the porch with him, exchanging small talk.

Shandol and her brothers, Phil and Bobby, left the house soon after the car was out of sight. They headed directly toward the store, where they were to wait for the truck. It was about time for it to be going, and sure enough it soon showed up, coming down the hill leaving a dust trail billowing behind it from the dry graveled road. There were several people already on it.

There were adults. One family with young children; a small group of young people; boys and girls, though not together, as they were not yet dating age. There were a few dating couples, Shandol knew, and they had no other way to go.

The back part of the truck bed had the high stock rack, though without the end sections. They were joined in the back by a chain. A portion of the end gate was placed on the ground, leaned against the truck and was used as a ladder, of sorts, for climbing into the truck, which most adults and young ladies used. It was placed near one side, which helped them balance themselves by holding the racks, as they climbed it. The younger men were just as likely to climb from the back wheel over the side as not. The end gate was then tossed inside the truck bed to be used to disembark.

"Nice night," Shandol smiled in answer to a greeting from two older women, who frequently went places together. They were Mrs. Sandler and Mrs. Duniway. Their husbands just seemed not to care to go where they did so they went together. They were also close neighbors. They each had grown children and were older than Shandol's parents. Mrs. Sandler's two boys were on the truck. They were both older than Shandol, yet both were at home yet. One was on the truck with his girl friend. All Mrs. Duniway's five children were married except the youngest boy, who had quit school earlier this year to go into the navy. She was a short, plump woman, whereas her friend, Mrs. Sandler, was a more matronly, average size.

34

Shandol smiled a "hi" in response to others who spoke to her, which seemed to be everyone near enough to her, and some not so close, as she tied a three-cornered print cotton scarf over her hair to keep it from blowing wildly as the truck sped down the highway.

"Hang on," came the usual shout, as soon as the half-dozen or so got on the truck. The truck started to move as smoothly as possible, as the driver hoped everyone could remain standing. Everyone knew—or was told—to hold on to the truck racks, or to someone who was. Shandol did not know of a single case of anyone's having lost his balance and actually fallen.

The truck was headed east, climbed the long hill, and as they turned onto the highway, headed south. Only a short distance from the corner was a gasoline service station, where two more passengers were picked up. They were Shandol's best friend's brother and a girl, whom he lifted onto the truck. Shandol was quite disappointed when Margery was not with him. She was so disappointed in fact, that as the truck picked up speed going down the highway, she wished she had slipped off and gone home. She had so planned on being with Margery she had looked forward to going, even on the truck. She could have just hidden somewhere until Dean had come and gone. It left her wondering how she could possibly enjoy herself. She would either be alone or having to tag along with someone, or group, who wouldn't even want her company. She would be practically by herself. No, she could tell Phil and Bobby, her own brothers, of her predicament. Phil would understand, though he might not like the idea, but would allow her to go along with them. After all he had no date, and she would promise to be agreeable and go where they wanted to go, as well as expect them to allow her to do some things she came to enjoy.

Shandol joined in with the spontaneous singing, which interrupted her thoughts. It happened every time. Someone or some group would start it. It began this time by a group of young girls. Some of them had parents among the adults. Soon almost everyone joined in with the songs they knew; or started one they hoped the group would sing. This sudden bursting into song was such a usual thing it seemed an automatic part of it. The girls started with "You Are My Sunshine" followed by "Playmates," which Shandol could help sing. There were hymns sung, also she knew. There were also some she new were quite old, some so-called "songs of the hills," and some she supposed were so new she hadn't heard them yet. There was that advantage to those who had radios. The Sonnett family had none. They did not have electricity in their house either. Sometimes they went, or were invited to a friend's home to hear something of interest, such as the Grand Ole Opry on Saturday night. Other times there were special things such as a speech by the President of the United States, which always interested Joel. But not all visits were to hear the radio, of course.

They went their merry, singing way through the first small town, Folks Consent. But then somewhere along the way Shandol became quiet. She was first preoccupied with the wind in her face, as she stood at the front. She found if it hit her full in the face with her mouth open just so, it almost seemed to make the sides of her face flap. It was indeed a force to reckon with, and was rarely actually faced up to for very long. And to sing was impossible unless turned away from the front, as the words seemed to be blown back into the mouth and strangling anyone who tried.

Without realizing exactly when, Shandol became aware of the fact she was being stared at, as she glanced silently around at her fellow riders. Her returning gaze was, however, unflinching and not friendly, and she offered no explanation or rationalization. Actually, her first impulse had been a mind-your-own business disdainful shrug. But it soon came to her in sudden understanding that they were probably wondering why she was riding on the truck in the first place. So she began smiling back at them. They were her fellow riders, curious friends and neighbors. She was sure they were that, despite their nosy ways. She was also sure the reason for her change in plans would be learned: Explained by someone, somehow, who in someway would garner the information from their usual unimpeachable sources—or so they'd be considered.

The thought persisted about being on the truck. She tried to see herself and the situation as they might. But she knew all the details and her own mind's reaction to them; while they could only speculate. One thought made the whole thing brighter. That was that she hadn't *had* to come this way; there had been those other offers. But it was still little comfort, because here she was. She also thought about the guy who had made the bet. He was also a fellow passenger. Bucky Sandler was not only the local authority on the rules they played ball by—even making new or bending them if the situation called for it—but he was also the town wit. And Shandol was somewhat uneasy lest he make some snide remark about winning a bet. Of course he could handle it in teasing banter, too, because he could usually make things funny, or with a double meaning, which could make one forget who the joke was on. She hoped, because it would not be a popular subject, he would be quiet, as so far he had.

Her thoughts also went to Steve Follerson and the reason why he had chosen tonight of all nights to come by for a date with her. She thought of all the years she had adored him. He had been her party beau many times, and he had walked her home afterward—except on a few occasions when a new girl came to town and he had to assure himself he could be first to date her. Actually he was not breaking a date with her by doing that. They would not have made a date. It was just an understanding, or pairing off, as each expected the other to be there. Shandol was often hurt by the disregard he showed her at such times, but she was always sure there would be a next time. Shandol simply resented his asking new girls out to be first to date them, rather than because he cared to find out if he could care for them or not. This left Shandol to have to go home with her parents, or her brothers, sometimes another boy, so it was not that he left her to go home alone.

He is somewhat conceited, she thought. A regular dog in the manger. Why else had he come by tonight? She was considered his girl, or had been, and so when he was around she received little attention from anyone else; though she did not lack for partners when he was not around either. But he was her favorite. He was so handsome, and even gentlemanly when he cared to be; and she was proud of him. He was only a few months older than she was, so they had been classmates from the time the Sonnett family had moved there until the last two years of high school. Greenway had only a two-year high school. Shandol had gone to the county seat, Plainesville, Steve had gone to Folks Consent.

Once when they were both seventeen, they had promised, each to the other, that one day when they were older they would be married. He had been walking her home from church that night. They had been alone. Soon they had walked silently after awhile and then he had stopped. Shandol was nearly home. The church had been the Little Mission, which was on the same block, but on the corner diagonally across from where Shandol lived. But they had not gone the main street, and cut through by the post office as her family would; they had gone the opposite way. It was longer and they would be alone. He stopped under a tree in a grassy triangle where the road forked. He had taken hold of her shoulders so she faced him, and said rather abruptly and solemnly.

"Promise me something, Shandol, now."

"What?" She had turned her questioning gaze to look into his face, which she couldn't really make out even on the bright moonlit night.

"That someday you and I will get married," he had replied. "I love you."

"Wh—why, Steve. Oh, Steve," she could barely breath it. "Oh, yes. That would seem so wonderful." She had added, after the surprise ebbed somewhat, don't let's ever change our minds, will we?"

"That's what I mean," he had answered. "Someday—"

She now realized how young they had both been. She was sure she still loved him, though going to the separate schools had made a difference. He had tried Plainesville briefly, but then decided he preferred the smaller school, so left in only two weeks. Shandol felt compelled to finish where her brother had. If Lester could she decided she could, and, encouraged by her parents stayed the two terms. Anyway, their Someday seemed no closer now than then. Jobs were so hard to come by these days; but there was hope that someday things would be different. But would they still feel the same?

She could still fantasize now as then. She could see him with his jet-black hair, oily and slicked down, his casual clothes and tall well-built body. She, herself, would be in a pretty cotton dress of a pastel color, and the white low-heeled pumps she had had that summer. There would be the faint aroma of the flower-fresh talcum she used, scented as though sweet blossom petals rained over her. How bright that moon had seemed! And he had kissed her so romantically before they were on the creaky boards of the back porch, as he always did. But this time Shandol felt it sealed a pledge. Her heart ached longingly as she thought about it.

Perhaps that is why he came tonight, she mused—to protect what he considered his own. But she couldn't be sure. She hadn't really been with him much lately. He double-dated with his brother, whose girl friend had a sister old enough to date. His brother drove their brother-in-law's car. So she supposed he could have forgotten all about that long ago pledge. She wondered briefly where his brother and his girl were tonight. Steve had had the car, and it was not his brother who had come by with him.

"State line!" was called by someone, rousing Shandol from her thoughts.

Well, we're about there, she thought, and realized she did not recall going by the last town. By now she could see the spring lake, for there was a dam there and a power generating plant. The water looked deep and greenish blue. The lakeside across from where they were was lit up, yet was not completely in view until they were almost there because of the trees.

As soon as the truck came to a stop, the driver got out and placed the end gate against the back of the truck bed for the make-shift ladder, which allowed the older women, at least, to climb down, backward, as with any ladder. Shandol, as most of the young people, sat down on the edge at the end and then dropped off to the ground.

The group of young girls headed their own way, she noticed.

Shandol saw her brothers and followed them.

"I'm stayin' with you," she said, stepping up beside Phil. "I'm sorta by myself since Margery didn't come. I had so hoped she'd make it."

Phil was about to ask her if she wished she had waited for Dean, but he could see the pleading and misery in her eyes and softened toward her.

"Sure," he replied. "What's first?"

Shandol looked around fleetingly, and saw a couple making their way to the grounds hand in hand. The man wore a loud cowboy style shirt and dark pants. The slim, dark haired girl, pushing back her shoulder-length hair, wore a simple cotton print full skirt and white blouse. They had been on the truck so Shandol recognized them. They were now so engrossed in one another they seemed unaware of other people1 and didn't seem to care what others might think. Shandol sighed somewhat longingly, and turned toward her brothers, the bright lights, noise, mob and smells of the carnival.

"Let's look a bit first," she replied. "There's time to decide what to do."

"Look." Phil stopped. "Remember that stand there. We go by it to get back to the truck."

"Thanks for reminding us," Shandol said, as she took note of where they were.

Then her eyes seemed to come alive. The questioning brown eyes were now also wide and bright in anticipation. The crowd was thick, the carnival noisy with its merry-go-round music, barkers chanting their monologues about games and goods. Shandol secretly wished she dared play some of the games of chance, or skill really, but would certainly be chance for her. She would want to win. Even the lighting on the turning Ferris wheel was just starting the excitement. The smell of popcorn and hamburgers with onions was hanging in the air. The looks of happy faces searched all parts of the entertainment. There were surely no sagging moods here, and Shandol's rose also. She would be no exception.

CHAPTER 5

Shandol and her two brothers began walking, looking first to one side then the other. There were eating stands and game booths, and the rides could be seen or heard before getting to them. Shandol wondered how much money her brothers had been allowed. They had had to ask for money, she knew, even though they got an allowance, which they earned. She also knew their father would be as fair as their circumstances would allow. They earned money by being responsible for milking the cow night and morning, and they had to help Joel cut wood, both for the family's use and for sale. She supposed they were able to get a reasonable amount, but still she knew they also spent more of the money they were allowed than she did. Joel had sold the calf last week for sixteen dollars, so perhaps he had allowed extra. The calf had been sold as soon as feasible because it took the cow's milk, and the milk was needed for the family. Also there was Joel's job. He worked on the road. It was a rather uncertain job, but was certainly a help, as Joel himself was quick to assert.

Last month he had been sent a "four-o-three" (the title given the notice of job termination) and five days later was laid off. He had gone to Plainesville as soon as he could to begin interviews, and whatever else needed, including signing papers of citizenship, to get reinstated. He was working again, as he had received his work card ten days ago. There was so little else to do—except cut wood. One of the men he worked with had a small truck, an older model, rather nondescript in looks, which he had fixed up to haul the men for which he charged them a small fee. He had built a weatherproof, box-like cover on the bed of it. There was a small window on each side of the shelter. It had no heat, so was not so warm in winter. The work on the road, as Shandol understood it, was for the most part, pick and shovel work for most of the men. There was a boss to oversee the job. At least the job, with the best hourly wage obtainable around there, allowed a breathing spell. It allowed them to obtain what necessities they could surely use.

Shandol was given a weekly allowance of one or two dollars a week if there was any money available at all. After all, Joel reasoned, she was a high school graduate and should have had something better to do; but she was so badly needed at home. Some days her mother spent mostly in bed, and wasn't considered well even without the coming of another child. Shandol mostly saved her money to use for what she needed, which was not candy or soft drinks or other foolishness, except for a treat such as this once in awhile. And then she would be miserly.

Shandol eyed a doll stand longingly, hardly listened to her brother's comments and walked on. Then she saw the photo booth. Pictures while you waited. Oh, yes indeed, she must have pictures made of herself. They were three for a dime, and she stopped, her brothers soon beside her. She almost felt alone sometimes, the way they dragged behind or went ahead or ignored her, she felt. But now Phil eyed her. She looked around furtively and seeing no one else she knew, stepped to the end of the line.

"You guys wait on me," she said. "Hey, Phil, do you want to get some pictures of yourself? I'll pay for 'em."

"Nah, not now, maybe later," he hedged.

Soon there were only two ahead of her, then it was time for her to enter the curtained booth. She smiled broadly for a front face view, as the light flashed. Then she turned her body so her pose would be with her chin just over first one shoulder, turn, then the other; and with the flashes of light it was done. She was told to wait, as she paid the dime from a small zippered, cloth handbag. Her mother had made it out of a men's suiting material, a brown and beige tweedy design color of rayon. It was big enough for a handkerchief, in a corner of which she had tied the coins of money she had allowed herself. There was also in the bag a small comb, lipstick, the headscarf she had taken off and poked into it, and a small pencil. As she stood waiting she noted her brothers to one side patiently waiting for her. She wondered if they were tired of her. She realized it was time to tell them to do something they wished and it would be her turn to wait, as she and they were waiting now.

We must talk, she thought. I must know what to expect and just see what we can do together. She hoped one thing would be to ride the Ferris wheel with them. And they could each get a hamburger and soft drink. It was strange, she mused, she wasn't sure what her brothers would like; and if it would be different from last year, whatever that had been.

She turned back to watching the pictures being dispensed, and soon saw what she was sure were hers coming up next. When she saw they were hers her face lit up. She could see they had turned out to please her. She put out her hand to reach for them, but just as she was ready to take the pictures, which were snipped apart for her, a large tanned hand fell over hers and tightened ever so slightly.

"I'll take 'em; I wanna see 'em," a vaguely familiar masculine voice said, and took the pictures from her. Shandol was so surprised she mutely offered no resistance. Then she looked up and saw she was staring into the face of Dean Leonard.

"Why Dean," she cried, "what on earth—" Shandol then looked around for her brothers, even bending to look under his arm.

"I told 'em tuh git lost," Dean grinned, superiorly, seeing her looking around and suspecting for whom she searched. Her shoulders sagged in resignation as she realized there was nothing she could do.

"These're purty good," he remarked, looking at the pictures. "I'll jest take this un." And he showed her one and handed her the other two. He had kept the best one. He put it into his wallet and put the wallet back into the back pocket of his khaki-colored, neatly pressed, pants pocket. His shirt was the same color and material.

"Yeah, I guess I like 'em too," she said, smiling. "They flatter me. The other one's the best—" She seemed to come to herself. "Just you give me back my picture! I didn't say you could have it. In fact you didn't even ask me."

"Okay, I'll ask. Kin I keep it?" She was sure he was mocking her. "Now it's settled, and I woun't trade a purty fer it."

"Oh, you," she began, her exasperation finally showing. "It's not settled. Please," she begged. She had mental pictures of him flashing it about for others to see and saying, "My girl." And right now she wasn't sure whether she wanted to be his girl or not. But she wisely decided not to make a scene. It would do no good, she reasoned, with all that well built six feet of him, there was little she could gain by it anyway. In fact she was being steered quite firmly by the arm away from the photo stand.

"Don'tcha try to leave," he told her, holding her arm. We got a date, 'member? Why dit'n yuh wait?"

"Turn loose of my arm," Shandol hissed, between clinched teeth. "I don't want to be dragged along like some tow-sack you can't carry."

"Wanna bet I can carry you? Oh, sorry," he added quickly, seeing her frightened, yet angry look. Her face was turning red. "Ennyway coult'n yuh've waited fer me? I kin tell yuh why I'm late."

They were walking slowly on the trampled grass, which was beginning to look quite wilted because of the traffic over it. Soon, she knew, not only would it be gone but the ground would also be dusty.

"That was no date," she retorted sharply. Then smiling derisively, added, "just a big fat joke. Those bets—" She let the sentence hang without finishing it.

"Oh, that," he replied, sheepishly. "Yeah, that," she said scornfully.

"Guess yer brother told yuh, huh?" Yet it was more a statement of fact than a question.

"But not until last night," she nodded. "High time somebody did. At first I couldn't believe it. Then I decided if that was the way it was I wanted no part of—of such a date. Wonder where my brothers are."

"No brothers, and I'm sorry," he said, humbly, "really and truly sorry. It 'uz that guy—he dit'n believe me. I wanted to prove it but you let me down. I meant it—the date I mean."

"But how could I know that? I felt let down too, you know," she defended herself. "Besides I was so embarrassed because I'm sure everybody in town knew about it, except me."

"Oh, lets jest fergit it fer now," he remarked, off-handedly, and added, "Hey, it's time we started enjoying this reunion. We've not been, yuh know."

"Well, okay," she agreed, since she saw she was stuck with him anyway. "If only Margery could have come. I thought she would. But I guess she had no one to go home with. She lives a mile out of town. She sometimes goes with her brother, but he's with a date, so she couldn't tag along, I suppose."

Thus, Shandol found herself being taken among, through, and around the milling throng, hand in hand with Dean Leonard. She felt no embarrassment or self-consciousness. For once, she completely forgot herself. It simply did not matter whether or not she impressed Dean Leonard one way or the other. He was generous and agreeable, what more could she ask?

They rode the Ferris wheel—how many times? Three? They looked at the stands. They each had a hamburger and soft drink; he had a Coke, she chose an orange flavor. He threw baseballs for a doll and won one. It wasn't a large one, but a small darling one. He threw pennies and won a "birthstone" ring of his choice. He slipped it on the third finger of her right hand.

Her class ring was on the other. She couldn't read the look he gave her, but she smiled lightly. He seemed to look serious, she thought passively.

"Will you go to Jim's car with me?" he asked rather abruptly.

It was so unexpected Shandol stared at him, and swallowed; and simply couldn't help the thought: *Not on the first date, surely.*

"To get my comb," he explained, after eying her a moment.

He thought he saw something like fear in her eyes, and guessed he knew her unspoken thoughts.

"Oh, I suppose so if it's not far," she replied. And they set out from the crowd to the parking area over the much trampled wilting grass. It seemed they hadn't gone far when she could see the car that belonged to Jim, and it looked just the way she remembered it: Black and shiny. She looked back toward the crowded area. She always marveled that anyone could leave a crowd like that, especially at night, and find anything so quickly. She was sure she would have taken off in the wrong direction; and then she recalled Phil had wisely called hers and Bobby's attentions to the stand nearby which they would pass going back to the truck.

Shandol sprang ahead quickly and opened the door to the driver's side. She wanted to be sure they went nowhere. He want around the car and got in beside her. He opened the glove compartment and took a comb from it as he said he would, combed his short blond hair. Shandol took from her small cloth bag the lipstick and her compact with a mirror. The compact had been an unexpected, surprising and cherished graduation present from a girl, a former school friend, now gone, but who still sometimes wrote to her, though the letters were getting fewer and farther between now. Things in the family had not been the same after one of the girls had given birth to a child out of wedlock.

"Okay," Dean teased, "put it on so I can take it off."

Shandol looked at him warily out of the corner of her eye. She unlatched the door, pushed it open with her elbow and was outside in a wink.

"N-not this," she stammered, and thought that if he had some idea it would be a necking party, she had better put that matter straight.

"Aw come on back in here," he protested. "Let's just set a spell. Yuh afeared of me?"

"No," she replied. "That is I don't think so. Maybe a little suspicious. It's just that I hardly know you."

"Come on and set down," he ordered gently. "I won't bite—won't touch yuh if'n yuh don't woun't me to. Honest and truly."

"Well—" she began, and then silently got back into the car beside him, slammed the door and placed her hands at the top of the steering wheel. She was trembling a little.

"Only a minute though," she turned to him. "I got to find the truck so I won't miss it going home."

"But we'll take yuh home," he sounded surprised. "Jim will. He knows I found yuh."

"Oh, I can't do that. Dad wouldn't like it." she replied firmly. "He'll expect me to come in when the boys do on the truck."

"Here have some peanuts," and he held a sack he apparently also had taken from the glove compartment. They had had popcorn earlier.

"Thanks," she said automatically, and took a small handful. "Um-m they do taste good."

"We gotta git better acquainted," Dean said. "Maybe we kin come again. And next time fergit that truck, will yuh? We'll git a gurl for Jim and make it a double date. How's zat?"

"It might be fun," she admitted, still munching on the peanuts slowly and silently.

"Would yuh help find Jim a gurl?" Dean persisted.

"I can only try," Shandol replied, "I can hint or ask around. Maybe even Margery."

"Now see," Dean put up his hands as though they showed lily white, "I ain't touched yuh. Are you sure I can't just touch the lipstick?" He put his arm across the back of the seat.

Shandol smiled. "No," she said, "or shall I just take another fast dive out?" She was more at ease with him all the time, she found. "But you must help me find that truck so let's go."

"You're right agin," he sighed deeply.

They got out and walked along. "I wished yuh'd let us take yuh home though."

"You're stallin'," she exclaimed. "Dad'll be suspicious. It would look like I was meetin' yuh away from home. I'm not sure I should have been with you tonight except I didn't have much choice as it turned out. So unless you want him to object *next* time—"

"Yuh win," he cut in, "let's find that truck." He took hold of her hand. "Yuh know," he said after a moment, as they walked, "when I put the ring on," and he held up her hand as though to look at it, but it was on the other hand, "yuh have this ring on. Is it yourn?"

"Of course, It's my high school class ring." she replied, pride in her voice. She *was* proud of it. She had supposed they would never be able to afford one, but Grandpa had helped. He'd given them seven dollars a week from his pension when he was there, so her mother had saved some of it along for her to be able to get one. She had been so surprised and grateful.

"How'd yuh git out of high school at fourteen?" he asked, grinning. "Yuh sure it's yours?"

"Yes, it's mine. I am out of high school and I'm sure not fourteen," she stated flatly.

"Yuh coultn't tell by lookin'," he teased.

"So go ahead and be funny," she fumed. "I worked hard for this ring, I'll have you know."

"How old then? Sixteen?"

"Nope, If it makes any difference I'm eighteen," she replied, and added, "I missed a year of school years ago, so it did make me a year late." Then she wished she hadn't said so much. Why should he be concerned?

"'When'll yuh be nineteen?" he wanted to know.

"In December."

"I'm already nineteen," he told her. "Turned nineteen last February. We're close to the same age. They coultn't keep me in school that long though."

Shandol silently noted it showed. She wasn't sure she could ever get used to his grammar, though she realized her own was far from what it could be. But his was pure hillbilly, she decided.

"We haven't found the truck yet," she reminded him. "And I may have already missed it. If you take me home I won't be able to go Friday night, I'm sure of it. Or any other for that matter."

"Okay, okay," he said. "It's right over yonder under them trees."

"Did yuh watch?"

"Shore I wuz watchin' fer yuh," he admitted. "Just got here right behind you, so I wasn' so late really. I aimed to make it look like I seen yuh accidental like, though."

They had little time for more small talk. Shandol was worried. He said he wondered if he would try to find his friend or if he would go to the car and snooze until Jim came. Or he might already be at the car. Shandol wailed that it was probably later than they thought and that she had probably missed the truck. And when they came in sight of it, sure enough it was loaded and ready to go. They could see the driver as he got in and heard the engine start.

"Wait! Hold it !" Dean yelled, waving his arms.

The passengers took up the yell, and the truck did not move. Shandol squeezed his hand, which she took in both hers, said, "Thanks; see yuh Friday," and ran toward the truck. She had to climb the back wheel and up and over the high rack, but she made it, and, as modestly as possible she hoped. She noticed some shy meaningful glances her way, but she paid no heed. She knew what the looks meant: You with a guy alone? Incredible!

"Thanks," she breathed to no one in particular.

She searched for the faces of her brothers and when she saw them, was content. She was completely alone with her thoughts. She tied the cotton scarf over her hair again and they were ready to start. Most of the passengers were also quiet. Perhaps tired. After all it had been a big night and was now getting late. Shandol thought every detail of her evening, and realized she had enjoyed it. She could be so comfortable with Dean. Perhaps it was because she wasn't sure she really cared to go with him. He was such a "hillbilly" and particularly when he opened his mouth. She was so engrossed in the thoughts she spoke only to assure a few who asked that yes, she had had a nice time, and received the expected affirmative answer when she had returned the query. They were back in Greenway before she hardly realized it.

"How'd things go?" Phil asked, as they were walking up the path from the main street to the house. Bobby was quiet. He looked worn out.

"You deserted me," she accused. "But in the beginning," she said flippantly, evasively. But then she added as she suddenly felt he deserved a better answer than that. "No, really, I enjoyed myself. Did you?"

"Yeah," he said in answer to her question, then asked, "but whyn't he bring you home?"

"Oh, that again," she sighed. "He expected to, but I said no. It didn't seem right with two men I hardly know. And you know Dad. He'd been waitin' up if I hadn't been on that truck. I told Dean Dad might not allow me to go next time, which he might not. Or make me feel so bad I wouldn't want to go. It was hard to convince him I really wanted to come back as I'd went."

"Oh, goin' again, hmm?" Phil grinned at her.

"Yeah, Friday, if Jim gets a date," she replied. "I can't really make up my mind about them, but guess I'll go if someone else will go to make it a double date."

"Still mixed up?" he grinned good-naturedly.

"Nah," she grinned back.

The three did not linger long, but went straight to their respective rooms. Shandol carried the kerosene lamp, turned low, which was waiting on the dining room table for them to climb the stairs by. She took the lamp to her room, after she had washed her hands and face.

Before Shandol went to sleep she smiled to herself, pleased. She had enjoyed herself, and had another night to look forward to, if things worked out. She rather hoped they would. She thought of the bets. She was glad they had held little significance after all; and she was glad because she felt no one had really won, after all.

CHAPTER 6

In the days that followed, Shandol had expected some teasing or ridicule from her brothers; and some comments, probably negative, from her father, concerning her Wednesday date. If nothing else the way she had handled it by going on the truck. Even though she had had such a good time, she had felt some dubiousness about it. Still, as she had reflected upon it and considered the options, she didn't see how she could have done otherwise and still have gone. She would not have gone with the two of them. And because Dean had seemed forgiving, and even guilty, as he was later than he had expected to be, she had simply refused to dwell on it with regret or apprehension; and now she didn't worry and dread the next time as she supposed she would.

There had been comments and questions of course. And she had made no more attempts at secrecy. Perhaps, she reasoned, that is why she had been so miserable before. Her parents were aware of the fact she had been with Dean at the reunion. They were glad she had had presence of mind enough to have gone and come home on the truck. They knew she had dates for the weekend, if she could get someone to go with Jim. Joel had merely, and somewhat jokingly, asked about what kind of "scalawag" she was going with.

"So far he seems all right," she had answered. "He treats me good anyway."

"If he don't I'll sic my bulldog on 'em," he grinned at his own joke. But she had no doubt he would let his indignation be known if there were no good report. It was something that was to be indeed in the months to come, but which no one thought of considering now.

Phil had teased her only briefly. He had reminded her about the Bible story of Isaac and Rebekah. How his bride-to-be had drawn water for the servants of Isaac's father and their animals. This was to be the sign she was the one. And one of her favorite stories. And now she had met this man at the well, right?

"Oh, I know you're kiddin', but don't be so—so trite with the Good Book," she had replied, amicably.

"He may be a big guy, but he ain't as good lookin' as Steve," he'd answered.

"I know that too, for goodness' sake," she replied, "but Steve goes so much with Emilie Baker, and so I never know about him."

"Yeah," Phil agreed," with Alvin and his girl and her sister."

But what Phil couldn't know was that she held him, her own brother, up as contract with other boys and young men she knew, also. She hoped Phil never became as wishy-washy as Steve, if he ever cared for a girl—or gave her the impression he did. She was glad there had been no issue made of her going with Dean.

Shandol thought of the bulldog joke again. She had supposed her father would forget about that when she got older. Joel had always threatened to use his mythical bulldog to protect his daughter. At one time the dog was considered real and a threat, and the boys may have had doubts, because they couldn't be sure there was no bulldog who, like a caged lion, was living beneath that house. There was certainly open space beneath the house. It had been a fruit and wine cellar once, and there were still steps under a door on the wood floor of the long back porch. But the area was now a damp dark hole, certainly not fit for even animal habitation, and hadn't been for years before the Sonnett family lived there. But Joel was amazed at the fearful reactions or the stares of incredulity because he could seem so serious—so undaunted by their doubts. Also, he seemed so sure nothing really threatened his daughter due to her careful upbringing. Joel had had a lot of attention and amusement mileage out of the whole thing.

This was the one part of the lighter side of Joel Sonnett. Other bantering consisted of his straight-faced claim, "I'm th' purtiest in the family! Mom's purty but I'm th' purtiest." And at that at the most unexpected times. He affectionately called his wife "Dovey," except in public or in serious discussions. He could recite long poems and sing a variety of songs (though he did not consider himself much of a singer). The songs included some Indian love songs, which he loved. And he was a good hand to tell a story in his own way.

But he was also a serious man in a mild mannered, agreeable way. He was not one to air his worries, if he had them, and of course he did. He must often have wondered where the next meal would come from, and how they'd make it through the winter. How they would manage to obtain shoes for the family and clothing enough, especially as the children were in school. He taught a Bible class in the Sunday School, took an interest in the church and studied his Bible faithfully; and his good reputation meant a lot to him. The members of the church who could were considerate of his circumstances and realized his struggle. They often shared with the family when they could. They put work his way which they knew he could do, such as put a roof on a building; there were fruit crops to gather and he was usually one of the first of those chosen to help pick peaches or apples. One family on a large farm near town allowed him a plot of ground for a truck patch every year for a third of the crop -sometimes less. Thus, they could grow almost all the food they needed, except sugar, coffee, flour and the like. Also, there was the wood he cut. Actually it was not only families in the church who helped. He was well-liked and respected even for what he was by most people in the town. But it was usually the church people who furnished the boxes of hand-me-down clothing which was always a help.

On the other hand, he could be quite firm in what he expected from his family. His stance concerning moral virtues were right or wrong, true black or white. His beliefs seldom ran to shades of gray—or pastel—the in between. But he was a thoughtful, affectionate, if somewhat inflexible at times, husband and father. He obviously adored his frail, sickly wife and was solicitous of her welfare. If he had a weakness, she was probably it, or so the children thought. Yet she looked up to him and deferred to his judgment and opinions and considered him to be the head of the family.

Joel had been brought up by a stern father, who had owned and operated a restaurant. His mother had died in childbirth, and in time his father married again; although no more children were added to the family of five children. His stepmother was kind and had been a good influence on his life. Joel tried to temper his firm handling of his family in kindness and reasoning, rather than the domineering, virtual bullying of his own father. He had left home to go out on his own as soon as he was old enough with only an eighth grade education, though he continued to study and learn on his own. He had learned a lot about cooking from his stepmother in the restaurant. He could even now make light bread every bit as good as his wife's and that was good because she was frequently asked to sell a loaf of bread to a neighbor and could have sold more. At one time they had thought that between them they might make, and to sell bread, candy and cheese; the candy, peanut brittle, a Christmas time seasonal thing mostly. This was to begin with. It was soon after they had made the move to the south part of the state, as they had made extra cheese on the farm. However, the selling was a hassle as they were unknown, and, Joel feared, too much work for Audrey. They had lived in the county seat then, and after moving to Greenway had not pursued the idea any farther. Before his marriage, Joel had worked on the pipeline and farmed, following the harvests. He liked the farming best. He loved the animals and liked to plant seeds, and just watch the living things grow. He felt he was his own man when he farmed for himself.

He had met Audrey when he came to her father for a job on his farm. Although he was sixteen years older than she, he had adored her almost from the first time he had seen her. He then became a regular on the farm, at first in the summer, then almost the year around. Audrey's father was away a great deal. He served on jury duty, and had wood saws, thrashing machine and helped other farmers in various ways. He was also a blacksmith. Joel and Audrey had married after a few years and moved into the small, now somewhat crude original home on her father's farm; the four rooms adequate for their needs. The larger home had been built by Audrey's father before she was born. It was on the next hill, less than a quarter-mile away.

Eventually, as Joel's family had increased, he had farmed independently on rented farms. It was hard work, a living, but he never seemed to get very far ahead. And so it happened when Audrey's mother had died, they had moved back to the home place, as Audrey thought of it, and still did.

Joel, despite the uncertain times following the "crash of '29," had invested in dairy cattle there on borrowed money. It soon became evident there was no way he could come out ahead with the country in the grip of a depression, so he had lost it all. It had been a defeat which had shaken his soul and pride, but his faith had not wavered.

Joel was of a stocky build and average height. He was fifty-five years old now and had, since leaving the farm, developed a "thickness through the middle." He had a full face, "cat eyes" as he called them, because of their yellowish brown color; he had a slender though prominent nose, and dark hair with no visible gray as yet, which meant he looked younger and was guessed by those who did not know, to be only a few years older than his wife, whose age he'd likely furnish for comparison. He was flattered more because she did not look her age either. He seemed not to want to age too much ahead of her.

Audrey had been little more than a child when she first met the itinerant farmer, who would show up each summer earlier and earlier as time went on, to work on her father's farm. She was still a teenager when he had courted her properly, taking her places in his own buggy, with his own team, which he had told his children could find their own way home without his always driving them. Audrey fell in love with him and they were married before her eighteenth birthday. She had had to help on the farm since she was considered big enough and so had been a great help to Joel. She was the youngest of seven children. (Joel the oldest in his family.) But Audrey had grown up with a brother, a sister and an assortment of nieces, nephews and cousins, because her other sisters were so much older than herself.

51

She was still a pretty woman, a trim average size, with snappy brown eyes. Her dark hair, which was cut short and blowy, and had a narrow, fascinating streak of gray above the right temple, framed her oval face of classic features. Her pouty, sensuous mouth was still youthful, her features unlined, and her skin seemed perpetually tanned and creamy smooth. She was docile and yielding to her husband and almost childlike in her dependence on him. She was content for him to assume all responsibility possible for the family. And because her health had been impaired, it was easy for her to get attention and help with the work, even excuses for allowing Joel all the responsibility possible.

They had left the farm in the north part of the state, an area where the both of them had always called home, and moved to the southern part, because of doctor's orders. Audrey's health had been poor since a bout with pneumonia one mid-winter, in which her condition had been critical for a matter of weeks. It had made her a virtual invalid the rest of that summer. The doctor warned she should not go through another such illness, because, he admonished, she either would not make it through it or would be left consumptive. In the fall she had given birth to twins. The girl of the two had not survived, and the other one was Thomas Edmund. (They had called her Tina Sue) Joel could not bear the thought of going through another winter as that last one on the farm had been. He was convinced in his heart that only through answered prayer had Audrey lived.

The doctor had advised the southwestern states would be ideal, but the southeastern slopes of the Ozark mountains would be milder and that would help.

It had been late fall when they had moved. A trucking man had been hired to move what was necessary, such as furniture, dishes and cooking utensils, bedding, clothing, and the incidentals every household needs.

The children, the dog, who had since died, and Joel rode on a mattress on a large wooden box near the back. The driver, with Audrey and the young baby, rode in the cab. It had drizzled and was cold. Joel had seen the land in the early morning hours, as they had driven all night, and his heart sank. His farmer's sight showed him land looking terribly bleak. It was hilly and rough, rocky and barren, or with woods and brush. Joel and Audrey debated about whether or not to say; Audrey, as usual, more or less leaving it up to Joel. Joel wondered how people lived; how they made a living. But to go back was the only alternative. There had actually been nothing to go back to because all their farming equipment, tools, livestock and feed had all been sold. Joel had reasoned, then, that perhaps they could stay at least a winter or two, hoping that Audrey could regain her strength and enjoy better health, and then go back.

Eight years had passed since then. And of course there had never been enough money even to consider going back even if they had wanted to. And the money from the farm equipment sale, after it had been properly divided with Joel's father in-law and everything settled otherwise, had been used to live on that winter. The farm had also eventually been sold. There had been no way to get the furniture and other belongings which had been left behind with Audrey's sisters and cousins. But they had been content not to go back. They had only to remember the colder winters and "all that mud." It had taken awhile but soon they began to feel they belonged and had no real regrets that they couldn't go back. Audrey's health had improved, though she was still not considered strong, and was saved as much pressure and heavy work as possible.

There had been many changes. The children had grown up; though one had been added and now another expected in a few months. It had been a struggle, an uphill one it seemed, all the way. But Joel was sure God had had a hand in helping them have enough for sustenance through the years. It had been through people who could help, and, even the government, which had provided jobs and corn-hog bonuses. It had all made a difference in their lives, as well as countless others' as well.

CHAPTER 7

By the time Friday came, Shandol had seen two girls about double dating with herself and Dean that night. The first, who lived up the street from Shandol in the next block, she had doubted, but decided to sound out any possibilities. Because they lived so close together the two girls had spent many afternoons and early evenings together, perhaps two or even three times a week, almost all summer. Many times they went for an ice cream cone. The only place in Greenway it was available was the gasoline station alongside the highway. So they would walk up the main street, east. Sometimes they would choose a candy bar, gum or even a lollipop, usually depending on the amount of money they had or the whim at the time. Once coming back down the hill it had been later than usual. The sky in the west was red with sun glowing on the deeper grayish-red clouds and in between. *This is pretty,* Shandol had thought. *The view from this hill, the hill to the west dotted with homes, trees, yards with shrubbery—it seemed a picture-pretty scene. Sometime I may miss it,* she mused, *and wish I could see it; but right now I would just like to be far away where I could feel I was doing something—anything with my life but just waiting!*

Other times the girls had gone to the store for the candy or gum. There were also times when they had had no money at all of course. If Shandol had no small change, sometimes Carol bought ice cream, candy, gum or a lollipop, depending upon how much she had from her allowance. But if neither had money they would go to Carol's home for iced tea, perhaps just after a walk, or having gone to the home of a lady who had a library of books she had loaned them. Carol's mother or sister would make the tea and perhaps there'd be cake or a cookie. They had spent happy times talking, singing, while Carol chorded on the piano; or they might copy lyrics one or the other wished to add to her notebook. One Shandol had wanted was the song "Falling Leaves" she had finally heard sung and liked. Carol had had a copy.

Shandol had known Carol ever since her family lived in Greenway. The Middletons had also just come (from Oklahoma) a few years before the Sonnetts. Carol was now a young lady of slender build and taller than Shandol. She had thick, wavy dark blond hair—"dirty blond" she called it, laughing. Carol was younger than Shandol and a year behind her in school. They had been friends and friends of mutual chums so they had mixed in the same group in school. Shandol hadn't seen Carol since the week before, as Carol had been visiting her married sister in Plainesville.

It was late Thursday afternoon when Carol had finally come by for Shandol. She was carrying two books. The sky was deep blue and cloudless. The sun, though still hot, was well on its westward journey, as the girls set out. They both carried books, as Shandol had taken the cue, and had gone to the desk to get the books she had. Luckily, Shandol thought, I washed and changed clothes earlier so there's no worry about not being ready. Supper was also over.

"We'll go by the store," Carol said. "I have two pennies so I'll get us a stick of gum a piece."

Carol purchased the gum at the store, exchanging light comments to Clive Thomas, who had waited on her; then Carol ceremoniously, rather than privately, offered Shandol the stick of gum. Each tore in half her stick and chewed one piece. Shandol carried the rest of hers in a handkerchief in her hand; Carol had a blouse pocket. Carol was dressed in a ready-made button front skirt of blue and white striped cotton, and a plain white cotton blouse. Shandol knew she had shorts that matched the skirt, which she sometimes wore unbuttoned to the waist. Today she would not be dignified that way, Shandol supposed. Shandol wore a princess style dress of lavender flowered cotton she herself had helped to sew.

They walked up the dusty gravel road, lined with dust-covered weeds, west, crossing the railroad tracks. At an intersection just over the hill they turned right onto an almost identical road. The dark green bungalow was the third house on the left side of the street. It was an attractive place. The yard had bare spots, but what grass there was, was smoothly short. The barren spots were under tall pines, which served as shade on one side, a large oak on the other. Pines were also visible in the back of the house, and seemed a back drop curtain to the place. There was a wide, open concrete porch, which had a two-foot rock wall around three sides, except for an entryway. There were two chairs and ornamental pots of blooming plants in various places with mostly geraniums and petunias blooming with a few foliage plants mixed in. Some dead tree branches were about on the ground lending a rustic look, yet neat enough.

Mrs. Davis herself greeted them at the front door and with a smile invited them inside, nodding mute reply to the girls, who showed they had brought back the books they had borrowed, and hoped to make other choices. Mrs. Davis was a tiny elderly widow with gray hair and twinkling gray eyes.

Her sister, who also came to see who had come, was larger by comparison, with a more serious look, though they looked some what alike, lived there also. They were dressed in dark toned dresses.

The house inside was as lovely and as well kept in appearance as one would expect. There was an entry way and elaborate woodwork archway on into the front room, with French doors on into the well-furnished dining room. It all seemed so modern, so luxurious to the girls. There was a wool rug of a colorful design in the front room, shiny hardwood in the dining room. The furniture looked modern or shiny and hardly used.

The sisters seemed pleased to have company, even two teenage girls who came to borrow books. They chatted about the books, the weather and friends in common. The ladies were shy however, and hardly went anywhere, and supposedly visited very little.

There was quite a large selection of books and there were built-in shelves to accommodate them. There were novels of romance and adventure; biography and history; children's stories and even some of the classics. Shandol chose those she really wished to read. Audrey usually read them also, but rarely kept Shandol waiting to return them. Shandol suspected Carol chose those books she thought would impress Mrs. Davis; and Shandol knew she never quite finished reading some of them. In fact Carol admitted skipping some of them, which gave Shandol the idea in the first place. But Carol gushed on about a book she had borrowed from the library in Plainesville at her sister's which was talked about because it had been made into a movie. It was *Gone With the Wind*.

On the way back they had talked about the things Carol had done while at her sister's home. She had attended the movie matinée; they had gone shopping, including a lot of window shopping, as Carol did describe some clothes she had seen in a window, which she would probably never be able to buy, and she knew Shandol could not. They also went for car rides and Carol was learning to roller skate. She had joined the side-walk skaters of the neighborhood; made some friends, though mostly younger than herself.

Carol suggested they go by Shandol's home to drop off her books and go on to her house. The Middletons lived in a small house of only three large rooms. In the front room was a piano wicker sofa and chair, a small wood coffee table, a magazine rack and lamp table. It appeared lived in, comfortable, but certainly unpretentious. The kitchen, a large room, was large enough to include a large dining table and chairs. The beds in the bedroom were divided by heavy curtains for privacy, but only one dresser and closet. Also there was a large old fashioned trunk in the room.

56

Carol lived with her parents and an elder sister, who worked as a clerk in a hardware store in Plainesville. Evelyn rode back and forth with her father, who also worked there.

Occasionally Evelyn stayed with another of the girls, Janette, who was married and lived there. But they had returned now and had eaten. Carol said she'd eat later, though she did ask if there was enough cake for them. Shandol could smell fried chicken, which they would have had to buy. Mrs. Middleton brought the girls, who were in the front room, tall glasses of iced tea and a saucer of cake with a fork, and greeted both fondly.

Mrs. Middleton was a large, but handsome woman, who stood firmly behind her daughters' wishes to be well-dressed, stylish and to put up a front of importance to the public. Mr. Middleton was a mechanic. He was a hard-working, gentle man of medium height and heavy build. He was proud of his beautiful daughters and so it was said he had spoiled the ladies of his household, being hopelessly outnumbered. They demanded to eat well and dress stylishly. Everyone had heard they were extravagant and wasteful, which in turn gave Mr. Middleton the name of being slow to honor his debts and pay expenses. The people who hauled garbage around town to feed their hogs, for example, said one extravagance was the waste of food. There was apparently no attempt made to salvage anything from food which was not cooked perfectly. There were cakes which were burned, some beyond salvaging, but others which might have been usable, at least in part. And other foods as well. Whether it was a case of too many cooks or just carelessness, it was talked about as being selfish and wasteful in these hard times. They were church going people and respectable, though he was considered slow pay. He seemed to like Shandol. He called her Janette the second.

Shandol tried to keep these things out of her mind because they made her self conscious in their company. Yet she knew the lady-like atmosphere was good for her, as she was so often in the company of boys, with their slang and rougher ways. So she tried to take the cue from Carol and eat cake and drink tea in a dainty way, as Carol. But sometimes she was also criticized as being a tomboy and not grown into a lady as yet, as they hoped she would in time. Mr. Middleton soon left, they said to get gasoline. He would leave early and did not want to make any stops.

Mrs. Middleton and Evelyn had apparently been talking about their getting an apartment in Plainesville, because they soon came into the front room and talked more about it. Apparently they had considered it for sometime, but now that Carol would be going to school there the idea of moving there became a sure thing. They had in fact found one, Evelyn told her sister; and it was already available and they would be moving as soon as some cleaning and decorating could be done, possibly by the first of the month.

Later the subject of the reunion came up. It was something everyone talked about, and almost everyone went at least once. The Middletons would be no exception. They planned to go Friday night as a family with Janette and her husband, which answered Shandol's unspoken question as to whether Carol might like to go on a double date with her. When asked, Shandol replied she supposed she'd be going, and let them draw their own conclusions as to how she would get there. She doubted they had heard about Dean, as they kept somewhat apart, being what they considered themselves to be; but she wasn't sure. Not around this town—one could never be sure. But she even doubted they would be interested and she just let it go.

Shandol left soon after. Carol assured her they would see one another before she moved, to return the books at least; and Carol walked a little way with Shandol. The sun had gone down and it was dark. Shandol ran the rest of the way home. She was lighthearted about having that settled; and, she realized, relieved rather than feeling any disappointment. Shandol thought she might feel overwhelmed and self-conscious with Carol along. She could turn on the charm and wit and talkativeness. In fact Shandol was surprised at having been so chummy with Carol all summer. They had seemed to have drifted apart since elementary school days. But still there weren't many girls for Carol to choose from and Shandol was certainly the closest. Shandol realized Carol had learned how to converse and subtly show herself to advantage. Shandol knew her sisters were of great help to her in such things and Shandol envied her the advantage.

The only other girl Shandol had seen also had a date to go to the reunion.

Thus it was that by Friday Shandol decided to ask Margery McNeely to go. If she couldn't go she might not get to go either. It had to be some one Shandol knew, her mother had specified, and Shandol couldn't think of anyone else. There were other girls in town to be sure, but there were obstacles to overcome as Shandol thought of them. Two or three had sisters who would want to go; some had close girlfriends to be considered, others had boyfriends. There were those who had already established a wrong kind of reputation, which Shandol knew she dare not even consider being with.

Shandol had supposed she would see Margery's younger sisters when they came to the post office, so she'd started to watch even by nine o'clock, though it was nearly noon before the first passenger train, which brought the mail, was due. She was sure they would wait until then, perhaps even for the later train. So as Shandol went about her work, she tried to keep one eye on the road to the post office; and somehow keep the mounting tension inside her in check. It became as though a life or death proposition.

By early afternoon she had not seen them and she felt she could not stand the suspense any longer. The thing to do was go out there. She could cut through the fields. It would still be a mile or so, but she felt the suspense was worse than the mere walk.

She raced to get ready once she made up her mind. She ran up to her room and put on white cotton anklets, and the crepe-soled saddle oxfords of two-toned brown, the "saddle" being the lighter shade of brown. She had worn them to school, but they were still in good shape. She put on a lavender cotton dress she had also worn to school except in cold weather.

It was faded now, and she had cut the short sleeves off, leaving only enough for a small hem, to make it as cool as possible for every-day summer wear.

She told her mother, who was putting water into the bird cages in the dining room, where she was going. She added: "I want to ask her if she'll go with us Friday night—if she can. She's about the only one I can think of that I could get to go with us."

"Be careful in the fields," Audrey cautioned. "And don't be gone late."

Shandol stepped out into a bright warm day. Honey bees buzzed in the white clover blooms in the yard. Tiny purple butterflies darted about. The still air smelled warm and sweet from honeysuckle running rampant, across the street and on the corner from their yard. It had smothered the roadside, crowding out all other growing things.

She went around the block, which was by the well, to the corner, and down the block on the other side. This was to miss the loafers, which were usually sitting or standing around on the store porch. She crossed the main street and on to what was little more than a wagon trail. It consisted of a pair of ruts with tall, uncut grasses and sweet clover at all edges and through the middle. She had practically to blaze a trail along the now abandoned street, which led to the fire blackened ruins of the church where she had gone when they had first moved to Greenway. The church now rented the one room community hall, which was a low compact building. It had once been used as a dance hall, a voting place and public meeting hall until the church took it over. It had been rather a source of contention, expecting people to accept as a church a former dance hall. There was condemnation from outsiders. But there was nothing to do but ignore it; believing God would be anywhere people were gathered together in his name. Already it was being heard less and less. In one concession, the voting was moved to the schoolhouse, and no dancing allowed.

Shandol sat down on the steps of the church ruins in the shade of a tree which was fire scarred, and on one side, dead. What a secluded place, she thought. If only I could come here more often. But it would be impossible, she knew, not to be seen and a possibility of being followed. Anyway, to be seen carrying a notebook would be something to snoop on. She would be so embarrassed. The thoughts decided for her not to tarry long.

The road, such as it was, had ended there. She would have to go through a small patch of timber, which had a path through. It was so spooky being alone. There was a dip in the terrain and there were moist mossy places, with lizards scampering over and under dead leaves, also a part of the woods floor. She dodged blackberry briers and buck-brush undergrowth, and her anklets soon became virtually covered with pesky stick-tights and other weed residue by the time she had gone the short distance to the next road. There she had to stop to remove the uncomfortable stickers and burs from her anklets and skirt.

Once on the road it was only a short distance to the black top highway, which she crossed and climbed over a fence at the corner to enter a pasture, that she could cross diagonally. There were two more fences, a patch of young trees and brush, and a field with black cattle, including a bull. She hoped she would miss them. She had no intention of facing them and it would add distance if she had to walk the brushy fence row.

She watched the yellow of the ragweed blossoms fall around her ankles. How dusty and stifling they seemed. She saw the cattle under trees some distance looking peaceful and contented. They hardly noticed her, though she paused briefly to size them up and then admire them. She was soon climbing over the gate into the road again. It was at the corner, which went to town to her right, but straight on was her destination. There were no more field shortcuts. She rested momentarily under a large oak tree, which hung over the road side from the field. As she gazed north she realized down the hill into a bottom was where Joel had his truck patch. There was rolling woodland all around it, so the truck patch itself was out of sight. There was still popcorn, peanuts, white beans and butter beans that she could recall still to be harvested. Things they could never have if they did not grow them.

Shandol mopped her forehead with the underneath of her dress-tail, and walked on down the road. As she walked her mind was on

60

her errand. A crow winged its way toward the trees on another hill. Leaves rattled as a lizard moved along the roadside weeds and dry leaves. Goldenrods bloomed about her, but Shandol hardly noticed. She had to rationalize the reason for her coming. It *was* the only way to find out anything: Just go and ask. That raised doubts to her mind.

Perhaps Margery isn't home, she thought. She may be busy somewhere about the place. Her mother may think it's a wild idea dating a guy she has never heard of—even with Shandol along. And what a lot of trouble I'm going to, she thought. "For a date," she muttered aloud, which embarrassed her when she heard herself. She was in front of a neat white bungalow, empty now, as the owners had moved to Plainesville for their daughter to attend high school there. Shandol put her hands over her hot, damp face; running her hands on into her short curled hair. She looked around to be sure no one had heard her talking to herself. She did that sometimes and it was company to her. Sometimes, as now, it made her feel silly.

Before she hardly realized she had covered the distance, she was entering the yard in front of a white, trimmed in green, freshly painted house. It had two gables and three dormers, though the upstairs was largely unfinished.

She knew almost immediately someone was at home. There were three little girls and two boys playing under the trees. One girl had hold of a rope swing under a blackjack tree. The others were in a dirt pile nearby with cans, a small shovel, old spoons, etc. They were "playing house" Shandol surmised, smiling at them.

"Is Margie here?" she called to the oldest of the three girls, though she needn't have. Farther to the back she could see the wash hanging on a line, moving ever so slightly in the almost still air. Of course, Margery would have helped scrub clothes even as Shandol had to do on wash day. Margery had to do more field work than Shandol, however. Shandol had brothers and no sisters, whereas Margery's one brother was older and now in the army, and now home on leave; and the other girls and boys were too young to be of much help. Her brother's leave would soon be over Shandol was sure; perhaps Margery would mention it.

"Yeah, she's here," curly black haired Iris replied, shyly, coming toward Shandol. Her spindly bare legs under a short dress made her look less than her eight years. She was dark like Margery with surprising large deep violet eyes, large in her small thin face.

"Hello, Iris," Shandol greeted her. "Can I see her?"

They crossed the narrower width of the long porch, that had a porch swing on one end. They went into a rather dark, after the bright sun, front room. The room was familiar to Shandol and the furnishings, which consisted of a cot, the heating stove being left up all summer, a mirrored old-fashioned bookcase and desk, a bench and two rocking chairs, a small stand table with a few family pictures, and a box of assorted children's toys: some blocks, a small doll, and odd toys scattered on the floor. It was covered with a linoleum that was showing wear in the heavy trafficked areas.

Shandol hardly noticed, as she followed Iris on through to the kitchen. Shandol saw Margery was mopping the faded linoleum there; the chairs out of the way, with the seats on the table, the legs in the air. A wood-burning range, a dish cabinet, the oilcloth covered table. The latter had a cloth over the sugar bowl, salt and pepper shakers and a few biscuits. The chairs, a washstand completed its furnishings—except for the inevitable bench behind the table. It was in almost every family home around there, Shandol knew, even they had one. It seemed they were like a unique style of furniture, yet a convenient, inexpensive necessity.

"Hi, Margery," Shandol smiled, genuinely glad to see her. As the floor was still damp she had stopped at the kitchen door. "I sure caught you at a busy time, didn't I?"

"Yeah, I guess," Margery replied, smiling and mopping her forehead as she raked her dark wavy hair out of her face. "But I'm about to get done in here. Always the cleanup after washin' though. Hot day ain't it?" She was leaning on the mop handle.

"It's sure hot walkin', too," Shandol agreed. "The sun's hot; I didn't realize it'd be so hot. I watched for the girls, I thought they might be in town, but—no, finish your work and then maybe you'll have a minute." Margery had hesitated, but Shandol did not want her to stop she was so nearly finished.

When she finished she dragged the small tub of dirty mop water through the back screen door onto the porch, pulled it to the edge of the unpainted plank floor, dumped the water on to the ground three or four feet below, and turned the tub up side down in the corner of the small porch. Back inside the kitchen she emptied the washpan out the same door, returned it to the washstand to wash her hot face with cool water and soap. She tiptoed out, after drying her hands on a bath towel hanging on a nail nearby. She tiptoed out to keep the still-damp floor as untracked as possible.

The two girls went on outside to the front porch and sat down on the edge of it with their feet on the wide board step.

"I'm glad you've come," Margery said, grinning broadly, "and I'm curious too. You don't come out here very much except Sundays, so it must be something besides just a visit."

Her eyes were dark pools of blue. She was dark complexioned, with dark wavy hair. She smiled easily, her eyes sparkled and her teeth were even and white.

"Uh—have you been to the reunion yet?" Shandol blurted.

"Oh, is that it?" Margery's grin dimmed somewhat. "Yeah, I went last night. Have you?"

"Un-huh, I went Wednesday night," Shandol answered. "You uh—haven't talked to anyone—or—heard anything about me?"

"No," Margery replied, "not much anyway. The two girls went with me; they sure got tired and sleepy. Say, what are we getting at anyway?"

"Would you go again tonight?" Shandol asked, peering at her friend from the corner of her eye. "With a boy?" she added quickly. Then she turned to look at Margery directly. "I don't know him, I must say that. In fact I don't know the one I'm to be with very well either. I was with him awhile Wednesday—shall I go on?"

"Oh, sure," Margery grinned broadly. "Sounds interesting anyway." Shandol was encouraged by Margery's close attention, her expressive eyes getting mischievous, her smile wider.

"The truth is I can't go unless someone goes with me, that we know," Shandol went on, "you know how it is? Two guys? Mama says it don't look right. I've only talked to two girls. Carol is going with her family, her sister, really; one had a date already, so I didn't really mention my date. I don't know who else might be able to go that I'd care to go with us, if anyone."

"Who are the guys?" Margery wanted to know.

"Well, the one I'll be with is Dean Leonard," she replied. "The other one is Jim Brown. He lives over in Pollard—where ever that is."

"I know him!" she exclaimed, suddenly. "That is—a little. My aunt Alice lives out near Pollard, and I've been there. They run the store in Pollard—Browns, I mean. And—of course! I know Dean too!" Triumphantly. "He lives about three miles on down that road."

"Well, I do know!" Shandol ejaculated. "Well, I'm glad I asked you, I mean if you'll go. Think you can?"

"Yeah, fairly sure," she replied.

"I've really been worried about going with them when I don't know much about them. Surely Jim isn't too bad if they own a store. You know people would have to like them to trade there. So Mama agreed if someone would go."

"But how'd you come to know them?" Margery asked, "It puzzles me."

"They were driving around Sunday and tried to pick me up," Shandol replied, grinning. "I couldn't go of course. But I about half-way made a date for Wednesday. Then I heard there were bets being made around town there was no date, or that I'd not be allowed to go, so I got mad, and just went on the truck. He was there so we were together, but I wouldn't allow him to take me home; I came home on the truck. I was afraid Dad wouldn't like for me to be with the two of them. But I did say I'd go tonight if we could be with another couple."

"I'll be dogged," Margery said.

"I enjoyed myself," Shandol went on, "but if it turns out I don't like him or don't enjoy myself, I don't have to keep going with him."

"I'm sure I can go," Margery reiterated. "I'm glad you asked me. Oh, I hope we have fun!"

"I suppose I'd better go now," Shandol said, "I imagine you'll still have things to do. I was so afraid you'd be gone somewhere around the place and I'd not even get to see you."

"I've a notion to walk into town with you," Margery said, "if I can get someone to get the clothes in off the line. I'll go ask Mama."

"Oh, could you?" Shandol asked. "Goody."

"Listen," Margery added, "if I can go, and I'm pretty sure of it, I'll get ready. I'll have to wash myself a little. I can't go like this. Wait here so I can hurry."

The children were playing, so Shandol's attention turned to them. A small boy, in faded overalls cut off just above the knees, appeared at the corner of the house. His hands had dirt on them. There was dirt around his eyes also, as though he'd tried to get dirt out of them by rubbing them with his hands. Shandol wondered how he had kept from worsening the problem. She smiled at him. "Hello, Dickie," she said.

Iris came up and took hold of his hand and they moved closer. "Where is Margery?"

"She's cleaning up so she can go into town with me," Shandol answered evenly.

"Oh, I'm going too," she replied, and hurriedly went inside.

"The porch is nice since it's fixed," Shandol said, conversationally, to the oldest of the younger girls. She had almost auburn hair, and looked unlike the other girls. They all said she took after her dad's aunt, who lived in town. Though the youngest of the girls had lighter hair, she looked a lot like the others in the family. Lily didn't. It was pointed out she was aunt Harriet all over again, except for the illness. She had spasmodic coughing spells. The phlegm expelled was thick and yellowish. It was not, they protested, tuberculosis; but more like asthma, as it choked her at times usually at night. Their aunt Harriet lived with her brother, Dan Smith. Neither had ever married. They had raised their nephew, Margery's father, and was sometimes a great help to the family. The two were something of a mystery to the people of Greenway. They had come shortly after McNeelys had, which was only a short time after the Sonnett family had moved there. The Smiths and McNeelys had all lived in the county, however, for many years; having lived in many different rural localities. It was thought the Smiths had money, or a small income of some kind. Dan Smith never had a job, yet they were able to have what they needed, as well as help the McNeelys—though in quiet, unpretentious ways. Some doubted just who McNeely's parents really were. It was gossiped the child had been Harriet's illegitimate son! They, however, claimed his mother was their sister, who had died, and the father was unable to care for an infant, had been glad not to have to care for him. He had left and was never heard from again, and also assumed dead. But, was it, they wondered, the explanation for their seeming independence? The Sonnett family, took them at face value; assuming their claims to be true. They seemed to be good, God-fearing people, so why all the smear and mystery? If the family knew of the speculation, they had never let on, that Shandol knew.

But at least the McNeely's had the small farm and were proud of it. The couple worked hard, and managed to eke out a living out of it, with some outside help along. They raised hogs, cattle, poultry and crops for feed; as well as a garden for family use. Shandol knew the oldest boy, who had entered the army was a help to them now. He had, perhaps, helped buy the paint for the house, and materials to fix the porch; also some labor for the jobs.

Mr. McNeely was a small man. He was dark complexioned, dark eyed, with sharp features and a long face. The latter characteristic had been passed on to his children. His wife was a larger than average woman, so almost his size.

She, too, was dark, but with the blue-violet eyes, which made her a comely woman, despite heavy eyebrows.

Iris soon appeared almost in tears. She had, Shandol guessed, been informed she would not be allowed to go to town with her sister, because she would not be coming right back. Shandol gazed at her sympathetically and watched as the girls drifted back into the yard to play.

Margery soon followed looking refreshed, clean, and lipstick added a becoming bit of color. She wore a blue cotton print dress, which had been a school dress. Shandol smiled. Everything was indeed working out well. Another breeze blew around the house, causing the dust to fly momentarily. A cricket echoed her happiness from under the porch. The leaves in the grass rustled dimly. It was cooler in the country, Shandol decided.

"I'm so glad you're goin'," Shandol said immediately. "But aren't the girls goin' to get the mail or somethin'?"

"Sh—h—h, no; we want to talk, don't we?"

"But wouldn't they walk ahead or behind, you know—?" Shandol asked.

"They'd never do it," Margery replied, "I know 'em."

They'd want to hear all they could. "Little pitchers have big ears," you know."

"Yeah, it sounds about like a brother, too," Shandol laughed, "which I'd know more about."

Shandol and Margery started out for town across the bare path of the tree-rooted, sparsely green, stony yard. Just as they reached the road Margery called back a warning to the children: "Don't yuhns foller me now. Mama knows I'm goin', so stay there for she's gonna be checkin' on yuh any minute now."

The girls walked in silence a short distance. It was as though there was so much to say and no where to begin; and anyway they might be heard so they'd wait until they were well away from Margery's home. It was quiet, except for the crunch of their steps in the rocky road. A wren sang his brief song in the brush at the roadside and then repeated himself.

"I'm glad it's settled," Shandol finally broke the silence, and skipped once to be in step with Margery.

"Yeah, I wish yuh'd come out sooner," Margery replied.

"I could hardly bring myself to do it," Shandol admitted. "It made me feel silly to take it seriously and go to so much trouble."

"Do you like Dean?" Margery asked, looking at Shandol. "I'm not sure," she replied, "just being with him once, but he acted all right and we had a good time. He said he did too."

"Where were you when they tried to pick you up?" Margery asked. "Tell me all about it."

Shandol explained about being at the well drawing a bucket of water when they were just driving by. And how they had stopped to get a drink.

"Really?" Margery had interrupted at that.

Shandol had explained they had told her they aimed to get the Martin girls, who weren't at home, was the reason they were in town. Also that Dean claimed to know her brothers as well as herself.

"Let's rest under this tree," Shandol said, as they reached the corner. "The breezes seem to gang up here to play; while on a day like this they should be scattering themselves around. Isn't it nice?"

"This ridge is cooler," Margery agreed. "Yuh know it won't be long until cold weather's here. Summer's goin' so fast."

66

Shandol didn't care to be reminded. It seemed a long time out of her life. Her mother had tried to reassure her something would turn up, though Shandol knew her typing and short hand skills would get rusty. Audrey encouraged her to enjoy herself. "Just don't lose heart. It's a wide world out there before you. Maybe a beau even. You can date you know." Then later Joel had touched on the same subject. "No need to rush into the very tide of life," he had told her. "Wait and it comes to you. You'll get in less of a rush that way, and not in too deep before you can handle it, so maybe it's all just as well."

"Yes," Shandol agreed, aloud, thoughtfully, "summer is going. Soon kids'll be in school. Time to start hullin' beans after supper. We'll miss Grandpa for that. He's sometimes hulled nearly all day. I don't know if he will be back this fall in time or not—just if the notion strikes him," she grinned then. "We hope to have a basket full of peanuts again to use, and popcorn, too. And then old cold weather."

"Will you miss going to school?" Margery asked.

"I suppose," Shandol replied. "Actually, I can't yet imagine not going to school. I though I'd be glad to get out of school, but as I think of it, it seems sad—lonesome or something. We must hurry on."

"I guess I'll go this next year, anyway," Margery said, "I don't know if I'll finish or not. I know I'll be glad to get out; I don't know if I can make it two more years. It won't be long—what *are* you looking at?" She broke off laughing.

Shandol had ventured to the side of the road to some weeds and brush and was peering into them.

"Excuse me, but what luck," Shandol replied, "it's just what Tommy will want. He had a big green worm and now here's another kind. He just wants to see what they do. Let me see if I can make a leaf cage to carry him, in case he bites. And if I have a screamin' fit yuh'll know it's touched me?"

She broke off three leaves, and holding them by the stems, put them around the twig with the worm, and hoped it would 'ride' along and not fall off. She hoped they'd not meet anyone.

"How'd yuh see that thing from the road?" Margery wanted to know. "Yuh couldn't a known it was there."

"No, just luck. I just happened to see it. It was in plain sight, and I just looked at the right time."

"Boys must like awful old things," Margery observed. "I couldn't handle that thing."

"Me either, really," Shandol admitted. "But I can't admit I'm too much of a sissy. Boys are all I'm around it seems. Your brother is older so you probably don't recall his younger days. Your sisters are older than the younger boys—so just wait. Phil is the nearest I've had to a sister—or playmate in the bunch. I've worn Lester's old out-grown overalls, so I'd be dressed like Phil. I carried a little pocket knife, and I could keep track of mine, Phil never could. We'd even wrestle. I could get the best of him for awhile. Then, too, he'd play dolls with me. But that's all changed, natcherally. He teases me sometimes, gouges my ribs, or holds onto something of mine until I beg. But we had good times and are still fairly close anyway."

Shandol took a deep breath and paused. Margery said no thing, so Shandol went on talking. The sun beamed down on the two girls walking along the rocky, dusty, narrow road.

It was almost level on the ridge, the countryside rolling hills around them. Tree foliage almost hiding the few dwellings on this side of town, even as they got closer.

"Hey, more about this here worm," Shandol went on, "the truth is, we've been around Mama's brother, Uncle Lafey. He teaches biology in high school, among other things, always including music. He has this huge bug collection and adds to it all the time. Right now at home we have two tarantula spiders in some half-gallon jars, some scorpions the boys found under rocks, some creatures called preying mantis, he asked us to look out for—even some lizards. Then Tommy has some big green tomato worms, ugh! The last summer we spent on the farm Uncle Lafey and aunt Ruth were there. We spent time tramping around with him hunting bugs and butterflies to add to his collection. I suppose he's our favorite uncle."

"How'd those kids catch the spiders?" Margery asked, finally, "aren't they supposed to be dangerous?"

"Yeah, supposed to be," she said. "They usually find one behind a rock or something and put a jar over it and then rake it on in with a stick or whatever's handy. I couldn't do it. It worries me they're on the back porch. They're on the old cabinet that is the wall on the east of it. Makes about half the width, but is handy for things and keeps snow away from the door, too. If those jars got broke and the live things let loose, I don't think I'd ever sleep. But as long as they aren't loose it's okay. Uncle Lafey is on a trip through the west and will stop overnight with us. He knew it last year and told us to be on the look out for some of these things. Maybe his classes will look at them and think about the Ozarks. He's in Iowa. He will have his in-laws along, and a young man to help him drive. They will have to think of school starting also. Mama had a card from 'em."

The walking and talking had made the trip much shorter to Shandol than going out had seemed. They were soon at the post office. Margery walked to the porch of it and stopped.

68

"Shandol, I'd better get back after all," Margery said. "My brother doesn't have much longer to be here before he goes back to camp. He might feel bad if I'm not there for supper. He'll probably have places to go or things to do then, but I can be with him that much. I was so excited guess I forgot all about anything else. But I'll be waiting for you to come by anytime after six thirty. Don't forget me." She laughed, and turned to go home with a skip and a spring in her step. The post office was closed.

"It's settled," Shandol told her mother later, as they prepared supper and straightened up the house. "Margery even knows the guys. Her aunt lives out near there and Margery has been to see her. Oh, she don't know him really well, but she knows him when she sees him; and knows of him. That makes it some better, doesn't it?"

"It does," Audrey agreed, smiling, with a knowing wrinkle in her eye.

Phil took a moment from his guitar strumming to tease Shandol good-naturedly, with his tantalizing smile and mischievous eyes.

"The first guy that ask yuh, huh? I'm surprised. Wondered if anyone would. Yuh know, I always thought yuh'd rather go with your notebook with a dream man in it." He was also taking a dig. Shandol had once jokingly said she'd go with anyone who'd ask, if he had a car, or a way to go. Joel had heard. He had cautioned, "You don't catch wild horses by flinging yourself in front of a stampeding herd. I can't imagine anyone wanting the wild anyway, when the tame or civilized can be had just as well." She knew who he had in mind, and agreed he had a point. So she had orally and mentally qualified the statement. Parents were sometimes exasperatingly right! But then Shandol did not really want to go with the "wrong kind," did she?

"Oh, be still," she replied to Phil. "At least I don't intend to be stopped by mere teasing," leaving a dangling meaning that he *had* at one time. Just a few months ago he had been seeing a girl home about his own age. She lived a mile out of town, however, and as he walked back alone, older boys had tormented him with weird noises, dressing as ghosts, even with owl hoots. He had finally quit walking the girl home. An older guy began dating her.

Phil walked away. He could make nothing of her. He was still sensitive about Gloria Lankers, but she wasn't sure if he was hurt or just embarrassed by the whole thing. He went back to his music. This time Joel's violin, which he played by ear. But he carefully avoided playing Shandol's favorite of those he fiddled—"Ragtime Annie."

There was the usual busy time near this Friday evening mealtime. And to add to it Shandol herded Tommy and K.C. to the washstand to see that they were clean. She intended to see that there was no half-hearted washing done by them this night; that is instead of their usual method of barely getting wet and drying on the towel. She didn't notice her mother's knowing smiles and glances to her father. Shandol also insisted they change their dirty patched overalls to clean faded and patched ones. They didn't wear shirts, so Shandol had more skin to scrub. They fairly shone that night for the supper table, despite their loud protests.

Shandol ate hurriedly. She hadn't much appetite either.

One ear was tuned only to hear a car horn. After what she considered was plenty of time at the table, she left the table and busied herself getting ready. She was completely ready before six-thirty. The truck left shortly after that time and Phil and Bobby were on it. She watched the familiar sight of its going from the dining room window, almost wistfully, and almost wishing she were on it. It was such an uncomplicated, simple way to go.

By seven-fifteen Shandol began to wonder: Where on earth were Dean and Jim: Her hands were moist as she unmindfully clutched the zipper bag. What time had they come before? She had been told only that they had come awhile after the truck left before.

Seventy-twenty: Shandol felt she could not stand it! He was paying her back for the way she had done him. Of, course that was it. He was standing her up. Oh, what a fool I was to drag Margery into it, she scolded herself.

She was too stunned and furious to cry. With heavy steps she climbed the stairs to go to her room. She could hardly get it through her head; he had seemed so sincere and serious when the date had been made.

She looked in her round mirror. She could not see her self as pretty—only dejected. The color in her face was heightened, perhaps, by the sheer mortification and displeasure. Her sensitive mouth was pink with a natural looking lipstick. Her fair hair was clean, curled, and becoming. The lavender print dress, of material her father had chosen, because he thought the color becoming to her, and which she and her mother had made in a style showing her young figure to advantage, would be completely wasted.

Her mirror could not speak to assure her that her beauty *was* youth and innocence, which looked back at her, and was the most effective she would need. It could not hear or be mindful of her moans of distress and disgust at herself for being taken in, or see her utter desolation, as she lay her head down on her arm resting on her white painted dresser, as she sat on the one chair in the room. The mirror was not talking; it merely reflected the top of her head impersonally.

70

CHAPTER 8

Shandol sat on the edge of her bed, her spirits at a very low point. It seemed that everything wrong with her life came surging at her, and further overwhelming her! It was this not doing anything, not getting anywhere, not working at a job, and being so penned up, as she often felt. Even dates were hard to come by, she now conceded. It seemed high school didn't work all that much magic after all. There were a dozen after every job opening, and most of them managed to be the necessary minutes ahead of Shandol. Three times she had gone to get a job at Plainesville to use her shorthand and typing. She lived twelve miles away and had to depend on friends to get there. The last time she was only ten minutes later than a classmate, who had made no better grades, and was a country girl, but ten minutes earlier! Ten minutes! It seemed a tough break as it would have been quite a good job in a department-hardware store. The last girl, who had given up the job, had married and moved away.

Joel sometimes reminded Shandol of the little verse he used to say to them. He had seemed to sense her mood at these times of restlessness and impatience. But how did that verse go? "Let me fly, says little birdie / Mother, let me fly away. / Birdie rest a little longer, / till the little wings are stronger. /. . . then she flies away."

Well, perhaps that wasn't exactly it, she thought. Funny that I should forget that. But the meaning's the same. When the birds are ready, they fly. I should be ready sometime; I can't be a "bird in the nest" from now on, can I? She knew she was a help to her mother. But there was so much of the time that she wasn't needed. It just seemed life was going to pass her by.

"I feel more forgotten than a sparrow," she muttered in self-pity. "They have a simple, free, busy, cut-out life and are counted when they die. Life for people gets so complicated, elusive and threatening. So what about me? I'm never counted. I'll probably never go anywhere. Dad probably won't even let me. I just stay here and beat against a wall of disillusionment and uncertainty, while the 'world goes on its merry way!'" That wall alluded to a dream she sometimes had about being up against a wall. All her life was on the other side of it. It was always dark and shadowy where she was, and on the other side of Light. It seemed she could get just far away enough to see it, yet she could not puzzle out a way over, around or through it.

Curiosity as old as Eve, she supposed, to see what made the world turn and people tick. Just a sampling is all she hoped for, with perhaps a ringside seat to view the rest, so long as it didn't get too rough.

"Funny old conscience," she muttered aloud again, "Dad tells even you what to say to me. I don't want to get involved in the basest of things, just see something besides dirt and kids with sores and patched britches. Kids who've had enough to eat so they don't beg for bread, when they supposedly come to play."

Only this week Shandol had washed sores for a little boy. "Only mosquito bites I scratched too much," he had said. But they were red and ugly with dried scabs over yellow pus. Scratched with grimy hands, and never cleaned. A small opening had to be made to allow the pus to drain, and thus making the cleansing more complete.

Almost every summer, if not every one, Audrey washed and cleaned such sores on any child who had come to play, and she could see it was not being properly cared for at home. There was no offense meant and none taken; it seemed to be taken for granted she *liked* doing it. For the most part washing with warm water and the home-made laundry soap a few times was enough, especially for the "summer sores." They were discovered on visible areas of the skin. Some of them came already treated, routinely, with a sulfur and grease (lard) salve, which, Sonnetts had been told, was also used for scabies, or "the itch," as it was called. The odor hovered offensively strong and clung to the sores. Sonnett's had been lucky, Audrey commented many times, about such things. Her children had not been plagued by the sores, if they were contagious, which was something of which they were never sure.

The worst sores were those scratched and infected through the lack of cleanliness. Few were really full of pus, but open, possibly the result of scratching insect bites, and with bacterial infestation. In winter something more serious was suspected, but still the Sonnetts had never had them. Audrey did her best, so far as diet was concerned and insisted on a germicidal hand soap, along with a pleasanter smelling toilet soap, at the washstand. And no germs could survive a washing in lye soap and hot water surely.

Once good friends of Sonnetts did get "the itch." It was as humbling experience to them to have to come to Audrey for the name of a lotion Audrey had once been told would cure it with a few applications. Audrey was not only glad to give it but glad it could be purchased. She was thankful her family had never had to use it. It was ironic, however, these same friends had at times, bragged of their ties with large churches, the "right people, and patronizing and uppity to the family. They had tried to please an "upper class" at outside churches.

They had also been good friends. They hired Joel to pick fruit in season and farm his rented land on shares; and in fact had put other odd jobs Joel's way, as they knew the necessity. The girls had remarked to Shandol how much more they were able to contribute to the church than Sonnetts, and how much higher in "society" they ranked. So it had been a humbling and humiliating experience for them. But so far as Sonnetts knew only the two families in Greenway ever knew. No one would have guessed, as they were outside of town enough not to have so many in and out at odd times.

Besides few were good enough for them to associate with. Sonnetts vowed secrecy and kept the vow, though there had been times when Shandol had been tempted to remind *them*, at least.

But that was no comfort now. They too had moved from Greenway. Tears of self-pity were finally squeezed from Shandol's eyes. She didn't want to cry. She dared hope at times things would improve. But she fought that too, thinking it was little use to hope. It wasn't fair. She tried to be as little trouble as possible. She was sometimes even given credit for it.

"She's quiet and retiring," was said of her. And "she's quiet as a mouse, and a mama's and daddy's girl." Why, she wondered, didn't they just say a "mousey nothing?" Why couldn't something have been worked out so she would have gone on to business school? She wondered often. But Joel had determinedly put his foot down concerning her chances for that, or anything for that matter.

"Too much temptation for girls," he had said, "to be away from home alone even if we had the money. Too many girls go wrong that way."

"Sahndol! Shandol!" Someone was coming. Shandol blotted her eyes and tried on a smile. As she tried it it became easier, brighter. New hope! I can't quit, can I? I shouldn't they say, she thought. Life is a living, breathing, dreaming, hoping and waiting thing. Oh, yes, waiting.

Shandol went to the door. She could tell by the slow footsteps it was her mother. She met her at the stair landing in front of her own room's door. Audrey studied her daughter's face. Shandol's smile was still awkward and forced. But she smiled affectionately at Audrey, then her face changed to concern. Audrey shouldn't climb steps, should she? Suppose she fell?

"I've called and called," Audrey told her. "What are you doin'? And them men down there are tearin' up the neighborhood with that horn. Can't yuh hear, child?"

"I was so busy thinkin'—" Shandol began. "I'd given 'em up anyway. I was gettin' 'poppin' mad, thought he's standin' me up. So I fretted about it. So they're here, huh? I better git!"

Abruptly she pecked Audrey's cheek. "Sorry yuh had tuh climb up here," she apologized, and raced on down the steps. "Bye now," she called, excitedly.

Audrey shook her head a moment, then started down the long, steep narrow stairway of bare boarded steps, carefully descending, sliding one hand along the banister.

Shandol went into the dining room from the hall, looked at herself in the clear mirror of the handsomely made, unfinished walnut wood medicine cabinet Grandpa had made, which hung on the wall by the door. She smiled at herself, decided she looked all right and calmly stepped out onto the back porch. Dean was waiting. "Wasn' yuh ready?" he asked.

"Oh, sure," she replied, "and just about ready to get un-ready. I was upstairs, and about decided yuh wasn't comin'."

"I'm a bit late," he admitted. "But I'm here now. I worked late. I drove the truck today. Went after some hogs. Hey, let's go, come on."

"Oh," she said, and followed him off the rickety back porch, and they walked across the yard to the car.

"Hi," Shandol said to Jim, as Dean opened the door. Jim nodded a mute greeting with a slight wave of his hand.

"Say, Margery will be waitin', too," Shandol said, as she got into the car beside the driver. Dean followed and they were off. Shandol caught a glimpse of her father watching her. Of course he would see her off, she thought. And she had been given a time to be home— before midnight.

They drove out the country road to get Margery, who had only just begun to wonder, she said. Shandol and Dean then got into the back seat and Margery sat in front with Jim.

They returned to the highway over the same dusty road, the gravel occasionally hitting the car with a bang, in what seemed only minutes. Shandol had a good feeling. She felt like hugging herself. She was riding in a nice car, looking forward to a pleasant evening with friends. If only she could measure up. Or did it matter? Unhappiness again seemed far away.

There was light conversation and laughter. The top of Margery's head seemed to just barely show above the seat. Her dark brown hair had surprising bronze streaks, caused, Shandol supposed, by over-exposure to the hot summer sun, but it was shiny and clean looking. The top of Jim's head was about the same height. He was in fact only slightly taller than Margery's five feet, four inch height. They must, as Margery stretched up to say to Shandol, get acquainted all over again. Margery had met him before, while visiting her aunt, she reminded Shandol.

74

Shandol and Dean also had more getting acquainted to do, but Shandol couldn't resist a friendly jab.

"How's the bettin'?" she asked low and off-handedly. "Anymore takers? By the way, who won?"

"I'll say only onct," Dean replied, stonily, sharply. "Darn anyway. But wasn' nobody won, yuh know that."

"I'm only kiddin'," she said, surprised at the sharpness, the defensiveness. "So maybe I shouldn't tease, but it's over and done. Yuh've been patient with me, are yuh always?"

"No," he replied. "Depends on the gurl." He picked up her hand and moved closer to her. He examined the cheap ring he had put on her finger Wednesday night. She hadn't worn it all that time, so decided at the last minute to wear it, as she saw it on her dressing table, along with the small doll she had been given that night and which she had placed at one side. Their eyes met and Shandol wondered what he was thinking. She hoped he wasn't too serious, as he held her hand in both his own.

"Is it hard work, haulin' cattle, or was it cattle?" she asked.

"Not cattle, hogs," he replied. "Not such a bad job. Sorry hit made me late though."

"It's okay now," she smiled. "It's just me I guess. I thought yuh'd decided tuh pay me back. Stand me up, I mean."

"Why would I do that?" he wondered. "When wanna go with yuh."

It would have been in character for Shandol to settle back comfortably and daydream. To just gaze out the window at the even-changing landscape as it passed, and yet hardly seeing the rocky, hilly timberland, or the flatter, green farmland, nor see the occasional livestock along the way in the "open range" country, after crossing the county line. But she came to herself and realized she was not on the school bus or just "ridin' into town," but really on a date. Future company would depend on how good a companion she could be. It was practice if nothing else.

I'm part of this one, so normal a situation, she thought.

Young people out for an evening. They were to enjoy the entertainment and test each the other's company. It was all to lead eventually, in a hopeful way, to that someone with whom one wants to spend the rest of one's life. Perhaps not as they were now, but it was all part of the search. Was dating really a fair test? To be in company and be company each on his best behavior; and to be entertained and enjoy another's company a fair test of temperaments, of abilities, interests and strength of morals? Shandol wouldn't question yet, it would only be a vague wonder to her. Experience she had had could not teach her—only guidance now.

That is what Joel, as he watched his daughter leave, was thinking, concernedly, prayerfully. How young and untested she really was, even for one her age. These misgivings and doubts he would have each time she left the house in the company of a young man, he knew. Oh, that. I've been able to guide her right, and that she will heed what is right without malice toward me. I shall do my best to guide her right and hope to keep her safe and pure, he vowed prayerfully.

The car made the trip faster than the truck. To Shandol it seemed much faster.

"How fast're we goin'? she asked Dean conversationally. "'Bout fifty or sixty, I 'spect," he replied. "Worried?"

"That's pretty fast," she said.

"Are yuh really worried?" Dean asked, crossly. "Take it easy. Jim's uh good driver. Besides that ain't too fast."

"I was just testin' yuh," she replied, smiling. "I looked as I already knew. I just wondered if you could guess, that's all. I've a cousin who drives fast—as fast as he dares in fact. He considers if the road's safe, I guess."

They were soon on the incline that took them across the state line and past the edge of the lake into the park. The lake was the Mammoth Spring dammed for use as a power source. They drove along it and then across the bridge over it. The water was deep and dark blue in color, and rippled by the activity of a few boats and skiers, and swimmers. The water later would take on a darker, richer hue, and the light strung along it would reflect as special jewels.

"Well, we're here," Jim remarked. "Now to find a place to park the car as easy to get out as possible."

The park was already lit up. Lights were also winking along the lanes to the parking area, even among trees, though the carnival itself was in a more open area.

"Look out at that little porch—like a building over the water," Shandol cried. "There's dancin'. It's so pretty—and romantic lookin' out there." She blushed at her own words.

It was a smallish building over the lake, with a short walkway from the water's edge. The upper part of the sides were open all around, as a screened-in porch might look, if it were not attached to a house, and open all around. Shandol had noticed the building before of course. Now it made her curious and envious. How she wished she weren't so afraid of water and be a part of what seemed to be so much fun. But she was afraid of so much water. She supposed it must take some getting used to being around.

"I don't never wanna see *you* dance," Dean told her emphatically.

"Why? Oh, you're as bad as my dad," she replied, lightly smiling, eyes shining.

"I cain't dance and I wouldn't want yuh tuh be dancin' with nobody else," he explained. "So that's why."

"Well, don't worry. I can't dance anyway," she admitted. "Dad wouldn't ever allow me to learn. Looks like it might be fun though. We had to learn a little in school in phys ed, but I never try it otherwise. I had tuh pass it though. Probably be as stiff as a board." she giggled.

"I sorter figured it," he replied.

Since it was getting late they had to search awhile for a parking place. Cars lined the lanes on both sides and the parking area crowded. They finally found a place at the rather far end. It was a little farther to walk, but that was pleasant too. Shandol and Dean walked hand in hand, behind the other couple who walked side by side in front.

Dean was wearing matched khaki shirt and pants, neatly pressed and brown dress shoes. Jim wore dark trousers and a light blue shirt and black dress shoes.

Both Margery and Shandol wore white anklets and black shoes. Shandol wore sandals; Margery's were oxfords "because I'm hard on 'em walkin' so much and far," she had once explained. Margery's dress was of reds, blues, and orange print cotton. Shandol wore a fitted style of shades of lavender, flower printed cotton.

"We've decided to try tuh ride 'bout *ever'thing*," Margery said, turning to Shandol. "Ain't we Jim?"

"Shore, if yuh want," he agreed.

"Will you, Shandol?" Margery asked.

"I sorta doubt it," Shandol laughed. "I don't think I could take some of those rides."

"They do seem rugged," Margie agreed. "But I'm a gonna try 'em."

"Are you gonna ride everything with 'em?" Shandol asked Dean.

"Nope. Only what we kin ride together," he replied.

"We can be their audience, can't we?" she laughed.

He nodded agreement and added, "I don't think I'd try to ride ever'thing ennyway in one night."

They were walking among trees on the uneven ground, made as uneven by mounds of tree roots or clumps of grass, though the green of it trampled severely and many places ground into the dust. The carnival loomed ahead. The midway with its booths, games and rides began.

"No pictures," Shandol laughed pointing as they passed the booth.

The first thing they did was to humor Shandol's insistence they ride the Ferris wheel. They teased her about her childish fascination for it. She merely agreed with them but agreed they had to start somewhere.

"Besides it's just the first time. I hope we ride again. So there," she defended.

That was the first of the rides for Margery and Jim. The second was the merry-go-round, though they all sat in the booth-like seats. "I suppose ever'body likes the music," Shandol mused.

"Let's git sumpin' to eat next," Dean suggested, as they passed a large, roofed stand, the sides open with benches around the crude counter–serving area, which was on three sides of it. The aroma of cooking meat and onions beckoned. "We ain't et yet," he added.

Dean and Jim each ordered himself and date a sandwich and bottle of soda. The men chose Coke, the girls orange flavor. Margery following Shandol's lead. The men ordered a second sandwich. They sat on the hard bench at the crude plank counter in front of them and waited for the orders.

As they talked and laughed they noticed glares and frowns from other diners, who apparently hadn't anything funny to laugh about, or considered eating a more serious ordeal. So the two couples moved to a nearby bench to be more to themselves.

It was, surprisingly to Shandol, Jim who was the clown. He began a chant, which she wasn't sure if he figured out or if he had heard it somewhere. He repeated it at intervals, and perhaps it was their mood, or his clowning, but they laughed hilariously as he would chant, "Goody! Goody! Get 'em while they're hot! Pickle in the middle, onions on top." There were other variations that were suggested, but that was the easiest to remember, most apt, and was repeated again and again at intervals. Each time he would draw a deep breath as though he was going to bellow, only to chant in an ordinary voice the chant. Soon they were repeating it softly with him, and hesitantly.

"Well, that's that," Jim finally said, as he threw away a paper napkin.

"Oh, my, I've laughed so much I've not been eatin'," Margery said.

"Me neither." Shandol held up a half-eaten bun. "But I guess I wasn't as hungry as I thought I was, after all. But just please don't leave me."

The girls finished hurriedly, quietly, as Dean spotted the peanut and popcorn cart and got a sack of shelled peanuts, when Shandol declined popcorn. He gave the peanuts to Shandol to carry, who looked up at him wondering how to make him understand she didn't want anymore to eat.

"Carry 'em fer me," he grinned at her.

Jim who had volunteered to return the bottles, caught up with

78

them, chanting and prancing, "Goody ! Goody! Eat 'em while they're hot. Pickle in the middle, onions on top," as they moved on into the crowd again. At odd or silent times during their stay, the chant would be repeated, or parts of it, as they moved among the crowd. And they had decided to walk around awhile before any more "rides." The men seemed to be drawn to the shooting stands. Dean won a souvenir cup and glass; Jim a thimble and beaded necklace. They turned the prizes over to the two smiling girls.

When Margery and Jim decided to ride again, Shandol of course suggested the Ferris wheel, it shouldn't bother them even after eating. Then there was more walking around, looking, talking, even going to the water's edge to see them dance in the small pavilion, though their view from shore was limited.

"We're not gonna git to ride 'em all, after all tonight," Margery conceded. "It's gettin' late. But Jim says we're gonna do it tomorrow night."

So, thought Shandol, there were plans to come the next night, which was the last night. Were Dean and herself included?

"And I can't be out too late," Shandol said. "I've been given a time limit."

They were quieter on the way home. There was some discussion of the evening's events, sometimes with renewed laughter of "Jim's chant." As Dean talked she realized it was assured they too were going the next night. And they were looking forward to that, reiterating the fun they had had this night.

Shandol was taken home first because Margery lived on the way home for both men. Shandol allowed Dean to give her a brief goodnight kiss at the door on the back porch, breathed a brief goodnight and went inside. His "see yuh tomorrer" reached her as she closed the door.

The next night, Shandol supposed would be much the same as the one before. But there proved to be differences. Almost from the first the couples were more relaxed together, because the evening itself got off to a better start. The men came early. Then picking up Margery they drove out to where Jim lived, and to the gasoline station and general store there. They went inside and Dean handed soft drinks to them all, including Jim. The store was quite typically country, not quite as large as Greenway's, but with a surprising variety of merchandise, from food and home necessities to clothing and livestock feed.

Jim introduced his parents, who were a youngish looking middle-aged couple. Both were short, plump and smiled easily. Mrs. Brown had dark brown eyes, as had her son, and fat cheeks. Her husband only inches taller than herself, had brown curly hair, blue eyes and a dimpled chin. Jim was much like his father except for the cleft chin, curl in his brown hair and Jim's brown eyes. Mrs. Brown, whose greying dark hair was short and curled, asked Margery about her aunt. But they were soon ready to go, having exchanged other pleasantries. Jim put gasoline in his car and Dean insisted upon paying for it, after which they left.

"Nice place ain't it?" Margery asked, looking at her friend, "even for a country store."

"Yeah," Shandol agreed. "And to think it's that close and I didn't even know the place existed!"

It seemed to Shandol, as they continued on the strange country road, they drove a long way, with deep mysterious woodlands, some open grassy land, green despite the rocky ground. She saw only a few homes. Eventually they came again to the highway. She was surprised to see and recognize where they were, which was actually about six miles south of Greenway and a mile or so north of Folks Consent. She had seen what was to her completely strange territory and she had not recognized a single landmark, until they were on the highway. She was relieved. What a place to be lost, she thought, especially alone.

It was still early evening when they arrived at the reunion grounds, chatting and laughing among themselves in good humor and with anticipation. They were enveloped into the crowd and the din of it. There was again the music of the merry-go-round calliope, the game and side-show barkers, and at the water's edge the music from the dance pavilion which was on records. The smell of food and popcorn, both stale and fresh odors, hung over the air. An occasional southern breeze blew feather soft and whispery rippling over the lake.

"'We're gonna ride, ride, ride," Margery opened wide her arms and almost sang out.

Shandol and Dean decided they would join them in more rides than just the Ferris wheel and swings. Again they took time between rides to eat in a leisurely fashion as they again enjoyed hamburgers and soft drinks. Shandol, at that point stated she would not dare ride anything more than the Ferris wheel, if anyone happened to want to besides herself.

"You and that thing," Margery mocked. "We're gonna ride again!" She laughed good-naturedly.

"Okay," Shandol agreed. "Then what? You're so determined."

"The tubs again," Margery answered quickly.

But when time camebto ride the tubs, Shandol demurred. "I'll wait this time. I don't think I can stand it again."

"Come on," Jim urged. "Dean will if you will."

"He can go ahead with you two," she replied, but firmly. "I think it would just finish me." She put her hand at the pit of her stomach.

"Go ahead. I don't care to neither."

"Wait for us," Margery admonished them.

"Shore will," Dean waved.

Jim got tickets and they got in line, laughing and talking between the two of them. It seemed the huge, noisy, churning Octopus never lacked for passengers. Shandol and Dean stood at the edge of the passageway to wait and watch. Dean produced a sack of popcorn Shandol hadn't noticed him buy. They nibbled it, though neither was hungry enough to enjoy it.

"I wonder if they'll do the swings again before that Rolly Rocket thing," Shandol said as though musing aloud. "I know they are saving it until last. I've ridden those—whatta ride!"

"Will yuh tonight?" Dean asked in a coaxing voice.

"I didn't like it very well," she said hesitantly, shaking her head negatively. "It just scared me."

As the tilt-a-whirl had begun to speed up, Shandol and Dean watched for the couple. Soon a large blurring noisy ring was all they could make out. It was all churning, thundering noise and the tilting twisting tubs jerked first one way then another. Soon after reaching the maximum speed it began slowing down and finally stopped. Dean and Shandol moved nearer the exit lane to join Jim and Margery as they came in the line to join them.

They soon realized that neither Jim nor Margery was smiling and as they joined them Margery was almost stumbling.

"Margie!" Shandol cried, alarmed, though not loudly. "What's the matter with you?"

"I don't feel so good," Margery mumbled, sickly, holding her head to one side and allowing Jim to lead her.

"Let's go somewhere to set down," Jim said, calmly.

"You're sick!" Shandol cried nervously. "Your face is so *green*! What must we do for you?"

Off to the sides, away from the heavily trampled area, grass was still long, green, and thickly matted. They found just such a patch close by, screened by a nearby food stand. Shandol sat down on the grass.

"Here," she told Margery, patting her own lap gently, "come lay down and put your head here."

"I'll be all right in a minute, I think," Margery said weakly. "Good thing I could get off when I did or I'd really been sick. I mean upchucky sick. Whooey."

Shandol, at a loss as to what to do rubbed her hands over Margery's moist forehead, smoothing the dark wavy hair from her forehead and temples.

"Thanks, Shan." Margery looked at her. "Your hands feel so cool."

Dean watched Shandol. The girl fascinated him. No small detail did he overlook, and put his own interpretation to each. The cool hands, the sympathetic, sweet nature, he supposed. So easy to look at—indeed quite lovely. *How lucky can a follow like me be*, he wondered.

"Just rest awhile anyway," Shandol told Margery. "You've had quite a-churnin'."

"Yeah, guess my ridin's over." she laughed lamely.

"Yuh scared me half to death," Shandol scolded mildly. "I swear I never saw anyone that color before. I just thought any 'green' look was exaggerated or joke stuff. But, gee whiz, it's not. You're gettin' better color back now."

"I'm feelin' better too. Just too much too soon after eatin' I guess. I shouldn't a eat. I really wasn't hungry. But I so like eatin' out sometimes—tastes so good." She raised her head braced on her hand by her elbow on the ground. "Yeah, I'm gettin' okay. Whatta' way tuh act," she scolded herself.

"Too much excitement," Shandol soothed. "This bein' the last night, yuh wanted tuh crowd too much in it. Ridin' all those things. But yuh almost made it!"

"Maybe we better go," Jim said. "Wonder what time it is."

"Let's wait awhile," Shandol said. "She's still a little pale, but the color's comin' back."

There was nothing to do but sit and wait. They visited in a congenial way, as though they had known one another for years as they talked, laughed, and rehashed the events of the past two nights. They were oblivious of curious looks of passers-by, having no idea they might be stared at disgustedly as guilty of some folly such as drinking the wrong thing. They were simply apart and completely alone with themselves. Then a group from Greenway had stopped to see what was wrong. Was she hurt or what? It was explained to them the simple truth, which was the way Shandol hoped it would be repeated—if repeated it must be.

"It must be gettin' awfully late," Shandol finally remarked. "But hey, what are they doin' over there?"

"They're gettin' ready to tear down to move this thing pretty soon would be my guess," Jim answered.

"Let's not be the last ones out then," Margery said.

"What a short evenin' it has seemed. There's still a lotta people here. But we better go. I'm all right now, don't worry." She stood up to prove her point. They all followed suit and walked slowly from the park to the car.

"I'm so sorry I got sick and—and over-excited," Margery apologized. "I really am. I sure never thought I'd do somethin' like that, I just never did."

"No problem now," Shandol replied. Maybe yuh never will again."

"But the idea!" Margery groaned. "Wantin' to ride ever'thin', I'm embarrassed!"

"Could've happened to anyone," Jim consoled her. "But nobody nicer," he added, starting the car, shifting gears to reverse and then into a forward going vehicle.

"I wish't it uh happen't tuh me," Dean joked.

"Oh, my goodness," exclaimed Shandol, "And why, for Pete sakes?"

"So yuh'd been worried 'bout me." he answered.

"Were yuh so terribly left out in the cold?" she mocked.

"Nope," he grinned, "just no pretty hands to cool my brow."

"Oh now I see," she replied, joining the fun. "But it'd been Jim's lap you'd been restin' on and his hand to cool your brow."

"Now, that wouldn't be so good," he admitted. "Guess yuh can just put yer hand on m' brow ennyhow."

"Silly," Shandol laughed, but complied. She put her hand on his forehead and smoothed it back over his oily fair hair.

"'Cold hands, warm heart'," Dean quoted lightly. "Dirty feet and *no* sweetheart'" He took her nearest hand.

"I've heard," she answered.

They became quiet. It seemed Jim and Margery were finding conversation unnecessary. They each seemed to settle back becoming relaxed, resting, letting the rhythm of the moving vehicle soothe taunt nerves. They had not gone far in this silent fashion when Shandol, who was leaning close to Dean's shoulder, his head bent to near hers, began to sing softly. A song she had heard her brother sing was on her mind. She was hardly aware she was singing it aloud. The song, "Old Shep" was about a boy and his dog, and years passing, the dog old his life about over. Shandol sang part of it, then paused. Dean made no comment and she continued, finishing the song.

"Very purty," applauded Dean, low.

"My oldest brother used to sing that song. I like it. Of course I miss hearin' songs, not havin' a radio." Her voice trailed off. She hadn't meant to admit they had no radio at home. The house was no longer wired for electricity. There were wires visible in some of the rooms upstairs, mute evidence it might have been wired after the house was built. But there was now no hope of getting it done again. Occasionally Buck Sandler brought a battery set down. She wasn't sure where he had acquired it. Perhaps he had rigged it himself. She could recall her uncle had had one at her grandfather's farm years before. Bucky came, at these times, on Saturday night to see Shandol's brothers; sometimes a group gathered. But that was less often now, and then usually in the winter when little else was going on.

Dean apparently hadn't noticed. Lack of a radio was no rarity there. Radios were almost the exception, though that was changing as more and more people strove to acquire them.

"I'll allus remember yer singin' that song fer me," Dean told her, softly, pecking her cheek.

"I had a good time again tonight," Shandol replied, somewhat embarrassed. "I've really laughed a lot. Jim can be a clown, can't he?"

"When yuh kin git 'im started," Dean agreed. "I wish't there'uz more nights we could go back. But maybe we kin do sumpin' else."

Shandol was silent.

"Cain't we?" he persisted.

"I guess so," Shandol smiled to herself.

They sped on, stopping first at Shandol's. At the driveway Dean got out and helped her from the car, and walked her to the back porch. "Tell me sumpin'," he said, before they got to the porch.

Shandol had stipulated going to the back porch as that door would be left unlocked. She could let herself into the house and no one would have to unlock the door. She knew it would be almost impossible for anyone to enter that door and her dad not know.

"Is thar a basement door on this porch?" Dean asked.

"Yep," Shandol replied, curiosity made her try to see his face. "The hinges're right here." She showed him in the darkness by feeling with her foot, then tapping it gently, as she could feel the bump where one hinge was.

"Thar's a dog in thar," he stated.

"A wha—?" Shandol laughed aloud. "What kinda dog?"

"I've heard about that bulldog," he replied seriously. "Aw, not really—that mutt—" she stopped. Who had told him that? She found it hard to keep a straight face and was glad it was dark.

"Hey, I'll see yuh now next Sataday night," Dean said, and before she could reply or turn away, he had her in his arms kissing her soundly on the mouth. "Such a perfect night, Shandol," he whispered.

Stupefied and speechless as usual, Shandol watched his long strides take him to the car. She was feeling foolish because she felt so deeply what he had said and how he said it. She said nothing, still feeling the lingering motion of his kiss on her lips. She stepped inside, watched the car pull away, and closed the door.

What's happening to me? she wondered, silently, as she went through her face and hand-washing ritual before going to bed. Is it what I want? But it's all I have now. Perhaps some day—or is that my lot? Waiting for a someday which doesn't come? She hated the comedown after such high spirits.

CHAPTER 9

"We're goin' t' town t'day," Audrey announced at the breakfast table one morning. It's 'bout time tuh see 'bout the boy's shoes, clothes 'n' things for school."

"How'll yuh go?" Shandol asked, "and who's we?"

"Your dad and myself," she replied. "And I'm leavin' you in charge, Shandol. We're goin' with Mrs. Bright."

"Get me a new tablet, colors 'n' pencil," Tommy said, happily, but fidgety.

"Me too, me too," K.C. added, clapping his hands. "Alright, I'll see about it boys," she replied. "But be good boys while we're gone and don't pester your sister."

"Will you please tell 'em now if they can go anywhere or must stay here? Then I'll know and so will they." Shandol said, so she wouldn't get any arguments about who was boss. She eyed her mother, briefly. She supposed Audrey would also see the doctor. But somethings weren't to be discussed before the young boys.

"They better stay here until we get back," Joel answered. "And we're not sure when it will be. Mrs. Bright is going to get her car worked on today before school starts. That's not far off. But she don't know how long it'll take."

The family members were seated at the large dining room table. Breakfast consisted of fried potatoes, gravy and biscuits. There was plenty for all and they all ate heartily. Sometimes there was rice also cooked for breakfast, prepared with boiled plump raisins added. And this was one of those mornings. It was usually eaten as cereal in a small bowl with milk and sugar, if desired, and it usually was when prepared.

The early part of that week had all seemed normal. Back to normal except for Shandol. She had a date for Saturday night, which was unusual for her and hard for her to forget. It had been unusual for her to be up past midnight on Saturday night, and because of it allowed to sleep late rather than get up to go to Sunday School. Audrey had not gone, which may have helped account for it. Audrey had complained she did not feel up to the walk, though someone from the church usually gave her a ride home. However, they had all gone to Young People's Meeting at night. Shandol sat with her parents. She decided she was not ready to face talking about Dean to anyone as yet. The truth was she wasn't sure as to how she felt about the whole thing. She, as well as her parents, she gathered, did not know enough about him to draw conclusions. Thus, she felt her parents attitude was mostly tolerance so far. She, herself, actually dared to go with him only because she was double dating with Margery.

Earlier in the week also, Shandol and her mother had discussed the new baby in town. None other than Mrs. Bright's grandson. Audrey declared they must go see mother and baby because Mrs. Bright was a good friend of long-standing. Mrs. Bright's daughter was at her mother's home, as Mrs. Bright could take care of her. Mrs. Bright's mother also spent a lot of time helping anyway she could, Audrey had learned. Audrey had also been told the child's name, but couldn't recall it—but a "junior" she thought.

Marcia was the younger of Mrs. Bright's daughters. She had finished high school a year ahead of Lester, and in fact she and Lester had gone to the same school that year. It was a small school east of Plainesville. Della Bright, at that time, had taught a country school, which was on the way to the other. Mrs. Bright drove that far and Marcia took the car and the three others on to school. Only one day did they decide to try to spend the day other than in school. It was known in Greenway by noon. Shandol had learned it also. But Lester had finished his senior year at Plainesville and Shandol two years.

Della Bright was married to Harry Bright, who was owner of the store, but they did not live together. He lived with and cared for his elderly parents. Della had had her daughters to care for since their father had died when they were small. She preferred her own home. She had taught school and had remained independent by still doing so. No one knew if there was more to it than that or not. It was simply accepted as each one lived an exemplary life. Sonnetts were on good terms with both. Harry and Joel spent many Sunday afternoons playing checkers. Audrey admired Della because her life had not been easy. She had even had to finish her own education in order to teach. Both girls were married now, but only Marcie had a child. The older of the two had been deliberately "fixed" so she could never have children. It was considered a smart thing to do, if finances allowed it. Della had gone on teaching after her marriage, as did her older daughter. It was what she wanted. She could hardly imagine her life without it. Now, she taught in Greenway's elementary school.

"That baby is nearly a week old now," Audrey had told Shandol. "And I'm beginning to feel we're not being very neighborly."

"Should I go?" Shandol had asked, "Or would I just be in the way?"

"Of course go with us," Audrey replied. "Don't yuh want to?"

"I suppose so, but I thought Marcia was feelin' so bad."

"Yes, she had a rough time," Audrey replied. "But she's goin' to be fine in time. That's one reason we've put off goin', she's so nervous I've heard. But Mrs. Bright said it would be all right now. Dad asked when he saw her about when she'd be goin' to town."

It was still early evening when the family, as a whole, set out up the road. The two oldest boys expected to stop at Horns, the house just before Mrs. Bright's. They walked west on the main street, across the railroad tracks, over the hill to the T-corner, turned right. All but Phil and Bobby would go to the second house on the left. It was a brown, one and one-half story house, one of the nicer built ones of the town. It was next to the "book lady," as Shandol thought of the next house past it.

Phil and Bobby had hastened their gait. They were "seein' how fast they could walk without actually runnin'." It was hard for Bobby to keep up without running. They talked and joked. Who'd be at Horns? And would Horns be going to Plainesville on the weekend? The Horn family had their own transportation and often asked the two boys to ride along.

Tommy and K.C. skipped along the rocky road, flopping tousled hair this way and that. They pushed one another, played tag, threw rocks at fence posts to see if they could hit them. They would even scuffle, though Tommy was older and larger than K.C. Joel put a stop to it lest it lead to wrestling, which wouldn't do in the dusty road.

As they entered Mrs. Bright's rather bare, twig covered, rocky, but simply tree filled yard, they noticed an extra car in the driveway, but recognized it as Marcia's sister, Martha, and her husband. Of course they had expected other people would be there. It would seem impossible to expect to go there and not see other visitors.

Tommy and K.C. were cautioned they would have to sit still. No "rough-housin'" would be tolerated by Joel. They might go outside or stay on the porch in the porch-swing. But they would have to do that carefully so as not to disturb anyone. The porch was screened so almost seemed to be another room.

Martha's husband answered their knock on the door and invited them inside. There were several guests. Some were from the Little Mission church were Della was an avid church worker, though her husband chose The Church on the east hill, Harry Bright was also there. There was talk and light banter, even laughter, so far from the quietness Shandol and her parents had expected. No wonder the young mother was nervous, Shandol was sure they were thinking. Audrey's "no wonder" Audrey had breathed to Joel, had justified her thought. They wondered why so many were there and how they could all be seated.

"You ladies go on into the kitchen," the tall man said, and they were met at the dining room door by Mrs. Bright.

The faint fussing of the infant was audible. But Della welcomed them with a ready smile and warm greeting.

"Come in, it's nice to see you," she said. "I'm so sorry we're so busy canning tomatoes. But first come with me to see my grandson. I must see if there's anything his mother needs anyway."

They went back through the dining room, into the crowded front room. The bedroom was through a door leading from it on their left. Marcia lay on the bed, which was propped noticeably high at her head. The fussy infant, wrapped snugly, was beside her.

"How are yuh?" Audrey greeted her, while Shandol smiled shyly, and murmured "hello" almost inaudibly.

Marcia smiled weakly and said, "I'm doin' all right I suppose. The baby's so fussy and I don't get much sleep so I'm sleepy all the time." Yet she smiled at the infant fondly as she drew back the blanket so they would see him. Audrey wanted to see of him so she opened the blanket further to gaze wonderingly at his tiny perfect hands and feet. The baby put up an extra loud protest at that precise moment, making a fact with his loud "wahs!"

"It must be time to feed him," his grandmother said. "My, the time has passed swiftly. Seems only awhile ago we fed him." She left to prepare a bottle.

"I'm trying to nurse him," Marcia explained," but it doesn't satisfy him."

A straight-haired girl of about fifteen entered the bedroom. She wore a faded skirt and gray-white blouse. She began to shake the bed to rock the baby.

"Please don't shake the bed, Erma," Marcia moaned. Erma's brown hair flopped over her face, partially. The baby cried anyway.

"See, the beds propped up?" Shandol spoke up. "It might fall off the bricks or whatever's proppin' it up if yuh shake it anyway."

"It does make me feel so ill," Marcia said. "I'm sorry to be that way."

Marcia was a dark-haired girl, with dark brown eyes, and her face now almost colorless. She was covered with a white sheet, with all other bed linens also white.

"I hope I didn't shake the bed as I leaned over to see him better," Shandol said apologetically.

Marcia looked at her, smiled weakly, and closed her eyes. She's so tired, Shandol thought. I wonder if she wouldn't just like to be left alone.

"She's worn out," Audrey whispered. "Let's leave and not wake her if she can sleep." The baby still fussed but Marcia made no move toward seeing to him.

Audrey and Shandol went back into the living room. Erma also left and wasn't seen again that night. Audrey aimed to wait for Mrs. Bright to take the bottle to the young mother. They stood as there seemed nowhere to sit. It seemed awkward to Shandol. It was not long before they saw Mrs. Bright take the bottle into the bedroom. Surprisingly, she soon returned carrying the baby and bottle, explaining that Marcia was much too tired tonight to do any more. "The baby has cried a lot and she doesn't rest," she said, and added:

"I'm needed in the kitchen. Marcia really tried to breast-feed this baby, but the third day the doctor said he wasn't getting what he needed to eat. So we feed him extra. Marcia's been so weak and nervous it really keeps us all busy. Mother has helped too, but she's really not able to do much.

Could you help? I hate to ask but we're so busy and rushed at that."

"Shandol can give him the bottle," Audrey said, taking the baby. The tall man got up from the soft overstuffed sofa when he saw them coming with the baby. "Sit here, please, and feed him." Mrs. Bright smiled acknowledgment at her son-in-law and turned to Shandol.

"But Mama, I'm afraid he'll choke," Shandol protested. "I'm scared to feed him. I'd rather just hold him, but I'm scared to do that."

"No, here," Audrey said firmly. "Learn to help a little if yuh're needed. If he acts like he's strangled lift his arm or stroke the top of his head gently, back to front. You'll be all right."

"Mama " she cried. "Maybe Dad will," she whispered, hopefully, lowering her voice. "Or the baby's dad."

"Aw set down, Shandol," Audrey told her. "You'll be fine with all these people here."

So Shandol sat down on the soft cushion of the sofa at the end where a space had been provided for her. She was sitting beside a man, she couldn't see who, whose wife was no doubt helping in the kitchen. He was so interested in the conversation, and, as his back was to her, Shandol felt she had been shoved into a room all to herself and the door closed.

Shandol's heart went out to the tiny, helpless form she held. She held his head on her left arm, which she could practically prop on the sofa arm, and held the bottle in her right hand.

"His daddy is leaving now," Mrs. Bright explained. "He comes on the weekends when he can and won't take them home until Marcia is stronger and able. He's stayed awhile this week because Marcia's felt so bad."

"Uh-oh, she's heard me," Shandol thought.

"I see," she said. Mrs. Bright stood and watched a moment to see how Shandol would do, and soon, apparently satisfied, went toward the kitchen.

Shandol's hands became moist. She felt completely isolated. The men seemed so completely absorbed. But Shandol was so preoccupied with her own fears and apprehensions, she could not follow their discussion. She was so afraid the precious delicate child might strangle to death there in her very arms. She became almost frantic thinking about it. And after a few minutes he did choke and cough faintly.

Shandol, with her heart in her throat so that she couldn't even cry out, lifted his arm and turned his head to one side but to no avail. She was so frightened her heart pounded in her ears. She then remembered to smooth his head from the crown toward his forehead. He was all right in a very few strokes. He had such a pretty little head, and the short dark baby hair barely covered it. The worst, to her, having now happened Shandol sighed in relief. It had been over in seconds. She realized she, at least, would be aware of it when or if he strangled again.

"Why shame on me for being so afraid of you," she crooned low. "You're really a fine little fellow, you know that? Popular too it seems. So many people here to see you. Too many I think to suit your mommie. She's so tired and can't rest, so she can take care of you better."

He squirmed and Shandol was sure he was going to wail like a steam powered freight train locomotive. She felt like it too.

"Now, now," she soothed, and patted him with her left hand, as his head was near her elbow crook. "You'll worry ever'one, 'specially me." She straightened his light blanket and shirt, in case they were wrinkled and uncomfortable. He was soon quiet again.

"I'm a terrible scaredy cat, anyway," and Shandol went on talking to him softly and low so no one could hear. She realized it helped her relax.

Audrey finally came to see how Shandol was doing. She even changed him so if he fell asleep he would be dry.

"How's it goin'," she asked Shandol.

"All right I suppose," she answered, smiling. "He got choked once but we made it okay. He's fine—quiet as can it seems to me."

Mrs. Bright came in also to see about him.

"What are you doing for our baby?" she wanted to know. "That's the longest he's been quiet in his life!"

"He's takin' his bottle," Shandol answered. "He seems to be doing fine, I believe he's about finished though."

"I must tell Marcia what a good baby tender you are," she praised, smiling broadly. "She's wondering about the baby being so quiet all of a sudden."

Mrs. Bright left them and so did Audrey. The baby was doing fine. He never did get choked on his formula again, though Shandol had mental fantasies of making a desperate attempt to get to someone in the kitchen, and falling over something in the attempt. She fought the wild ideas. After all, she had made it all right before. She looked down at him fondly, wondering if she would ever become a mother. She noted his tiny features. How perfect they were! How tiny he seemed, yet he was a normal-sized baby. He was really rather pretty she thought. He was not red and wrinkled, but filled out rather nicely, and just pinkish. The tiny nose, cute ears, and she touched them, crooning, "he was a cute one."

"You're bein' nice," she told him, low, "And I appreciate it. Do they ever talk to you? Do you get scared and lonesome? People do that all the time you know. Wonder what they'd say if they heard me talkin' to yuh?" She pressed her face to his forehead in a caress. She was sure she shouldn't kiss him—even his tiny forehead.

Though there were still people talking and going to and fro through the rooms, Shandol paid no notice. She wondered where her parents were and when they would go home. It was impossible from where she was to see everything and everyone. However, when she found herself becoming tense she talked to him softly and it seemed to help drain away her own nervousness. Even as he slept peacefully, after having his hunger satisfied, she held his tiny hand, watched him, crooned to him and he too seemed at peace. "Why, he's worn out, too," she murmured to herself, and to him, once.

It was a good feeling to help a neighbor, she decided, as she walked home with her parents. She had been a success she knew. Her parents mentioned then that Mrs. Bright had told them she would be going to town the next day and they would be welcomed to go if they were in no hurry. They wouldn't be.

It was past mid-afternoon when they returned from the trip to Plainesville. Shandol heard them talking and when she looked through the hall and on outside she was surprised to see Mrs. Bright coming up the flat rocks "sidewalk" to the front door with Joel and Audrey. She was even more surprised when Mrs. Bright made it known it was Shandol she had come to see. She came to the point abruptly.

"Shandol, we need you to help us with the baby," she said. "We already know you can and do you know he was good all night last night. You can't imagine how relieved his mother was, though she doesn't understand it." She smiled.

"Oh, I'm sure Dad would think I'm needed here—" she began.

"I talked with them before asking. I know your mother isn't strong, but they seemed to think they can manage for a few weeks which is all it will be. Mother will be there all time, as well as myself some of the time. But she couldn't cope with it all when school starts and I won't be home as much during the day."

Thus Shandol found herself with a temporary job. She knew it was because they had been impressed because the baby had been quiet when she held him. It was agreed Shandol would have Saturdays and Sundays off. But next week Mrs. Bright would be teaching, as school opened on Monday. There was no excuse Shandol could think of not to help, since her parents had no objections. She was too surprised about the whole thing to think of a single reason, except her own qualms, which she did not know how to express right then.

Later, Shandol realized payment for the work was never mentioned, but Shandol was sure she would get something out of it. Perhaps whatever they could afford to give her. She would have supposed Joel would want her at home to help Audrey. She was rather bewildered he hadn't. But Harry Bright had been good to them as had Della herself. Perhaps they felt they owed them this favor. So Joel may have decided they would all pitch in for the few weeks and they could make out even if less important things weren't done.

"Just, please, no Saturday washing," Shandol muttered to herself. "I can't stand it if they throw that in. It won't be fair." But she wondered, fearfully. But it was not so. A Saturday had passed.

Shandol had begun her job that first morning by awakening with a feeling of dread. It was not really a weighty kind, something like facing a test, coupled with the vague fear that she always had when facing a new situation. It had grown fainter, but would never quite leave, as she spent the few days. On the first day she had been nervous and afraid she could not measure up; that she couldn't please them. After all how could she know she could keep the baby quiet again? It might have just been luck and they, as well as herself, would meet with disappointment.

It was the first of the week. Again changes and qualms for Shandol. In the first place Mrs. Bright had asked her to be there before eight o'clock because she would give Shandol more specific instructions before she left for school. After all, Mrs. Bright would not be there to do the cooking, for instance. Mrs. Bright told Shandol she had tried to anticipate things which could come up so she could give Shandol instructions accordingly. Shandol had on a clean cotton print dress. She had bathed the night before, anticipating the early hour. She wore the comfortable, crepe-soled, brown tones "saddle" style shoes, ate breakfast with the family, and was ready to walk to her job, wondering what the day would bring.

The three youngest of her brothers were getting ready to go to school. Shandol could scarcely believe school could be starting because she wasn't going. Phil wouldn't be going until next week, however, as Folks Consent school started a week later. He would be riding the school bus.

Shandol had by now realized things would go better at home if she could be there. But she could see they were determined to let her have this chance to do something for herself.

Mama always considers ways for me to have clothes and things, she thought, as she walked along.

Shandol arrived well before eight, as directed. Mrs. Bright's mother, Mrs. Bennett, wasn't there yet, but she could give Shandol instructions. One was she was to heat water and wash the diapers using the washboard and warmed water. There would also be other baby things. Under no circumstances was she to use soap. There was a small tub quite full of soiled diapers soaking, which she must get the "worst out of" before adding them to the wash. Later on, Mrs. Bright explained, when they did the main washing in the machine, the diapers would be washed and boiled in a tiny bit of soap. But first, Shandol was directed to clear away and wash the breakfast things, including a final hot rinse.

"Mother will bathe the baby, though I already have for today," Mrs. Bright told her, smiling warmly. "You can peel and boil some potatoes and have them ready for dinner. Also peel and slice some tomatoes. These she indicated to Shandol. They were on the window sill. "I'll see about something to finish the meal when I come in, so don't worry about it. I've Jello fixed too."

Shandol was relieved about the meal, but couldn't help questioning about the washing.

"Will just warm water and scrubbing take the stains from the diapers?" she asked.

"No." Mrs. Bright admitted. "But the sun and air will take care of it."

Mrs. Bright left soon after and came back shortly with her mother, then Mrs. Bright was gone again without coming inside. Mrs. Bennett was a gray-haired, tiny woman. She had gray-blue eyes and a face mapped in wrinkles. Her gray hair was neatly done and waved becomingly. She smiled at Shandol in her exaggerated way, as she toddled in her elderly way on into the house.

Shandol waited to tackle the diapers when the dishes were finished. Shandol had tried to prepare herself for doing soiled diapers. She would have made a face in distaste but felt it would be belittling the baby. Besides she had never seen her mother flinch at much more trying circumstances.

However, she was surprised at the number of diapers. She wondered how one tiny baby could use so many. She added a stick of wood occasionally to the cook stove so the fire wouldn't go out. She did not want even to try to build a fire when it was time to prepare the noon meal. By that time she had the diapers on the line. She hated to hang the yellowed stained ones, when she knew soap and boiling water would remove it, and extra rinses remove the soap, but, she reasoned, perhaps Mrs. Bright could not use the extra water. She had soft cistern water, which would have required little soap.

It was a joy to Shandol to go about the convenient kitchen. There was water in the house with the small hand pump by the sink. The sink had a real drain, not just a large pail beneath it, as Shandol had remembered the one on Grandpa's farm. Where they lived now, despite its history as the Old Hotel, there was no sink in the small kitchen—only the low chest for the water bucket and wash pan, a soap dish back center of it.

The floor in Mrs. Bright's kitchen had bright colorful linoleum, where Sonnett's was so faded the pattern was no longer discernible anymore, except perhaps behind the door and stove. Mrs. Bright's dining room had a shiny hardwood floor, and the wide door into the living room showed that room to be comfortable and neat. It had a blue rug, Shandol noticed, with a large floral design in the corners. The living-room suite was dark red-maroon, she later heard someone call the color. The two bedrooms downstairs were furnished with thick rugs and bedroom suites, seeming to Shandol modern and very nice, in contrast to their own sparsely-furnished bare-floored ones, except for crocheted rag rugs by the bed.

At noon Mrs. Bright came in. She opened a store-bought can of peas as another vegetable. There was butter and jelly to spread on bread. Shandol ate heartily following her morning's work, as she listened to Mrs. Bright and her mother exchange light conversation. A lot of what was said concerned Marcia and the baby.

"These potatoes are good," Mrs. Bright told Shandol, possibly to include her in the conversation. "I aimed to tell you to salt and season them, but I see you have, Marcia forgets sometimes."

"I did it when I first put 'em on," Shandol replied. "Mama says the seasoning cooks right in that way."

"Maybe that's it."

"Oh, you're just tired of your own cookin'," her mother suggested.

But Mrs. Bright wondered again how the baby had really been.

"Fine," Mrs. Bennett smiled, her wrinkles seeming to rearrange themselves. "Slept all morning—now that we've somebody to help with him." The last added significantly.

Later on in the afternoon, Shandol did not know if she was supposed to sit down or not. There wasn't anything else she had been told to do, unless the baby cried. He was quiet except to be fed and changed.

"When we had no one to help us care for him he squalled at the top of his lungs," Mrs. Bennett observed once again during the afternoon.

"I'm *so* glad he's quiet," Marcia said. "I feel he's all right so it's peaceful and restful for me."

The radio was on softly to the daytime serials. Shandol wasn't interested. She hardly realized what they were.

Shandol held the baby in the afternoon for his feeding. Then Mrs. Bennett suggested she had better lay him down soon after she realized he was asleep. Shandol would have liked to just hold him awhile: just to rock and cuddle him, but did as she was told.

"No use spoilin' him," Mrs. Bennett said, as though she had the last word in baby handling experience.

Shandol soon decided she could get the diapers and the other necessary baby things she had washed, from the clothes line outside and fold them. She was pleasantly surprised and delighted that Mrs. Bright had been right. The things were all snowy white, smelling sun-kissed. When she finished Mrs. Bennett told her she could go home. Shandol left reluctantly as she felt she should go only when Mrs. Bright told her. Before she left she turned the baby to his side from his stomach.

"Guess I'm gettin' old," Mrs. Bennett said. "I can't remember such things anymore. It's so thoughtful of you."

"Mama told me," she replied simply. And Shandol had learned the first night he liked a change of his position. Audrey *had* reminded her, explaining he could get as tired as anyone just being in one certain position.

Mrs. Bennett explained she would go when Della took her, but mentioned it wouldn't be very long now.

Shandol was glad to get home. She got home before her brothers were home from school, which was let out for the day at four o'clock. Audrey was resting. Shandol straightened her room, made her bed and took a sponge bath. She did not want to be teased about smelling "like a baby." It wasn't that she had held the baby all that much, but she had handled his clothing, his oil and powder, and it seemed she even smelled it on herself.

She then helped her mother with supper, helped with the dishes and sat with her brothers on the front porch awhile. There was no church or other activity so everyone seemed to be staying home or otherwise occupied. Later, after they had gone inside, Phil picked the

96

guitar and sang. For anyone passing they would scarcely realize there was no radio in the Old Hotel on the corner.

Shandol's days, therefore, more or less fell into a routine. The baby continued to be good.

One morning when she arrived Shandol found the baby had not been bathed, but there was a huge wash on the line. It was not baby clothes, but bed linens, gown's and women's apparel. It had been washed the night before and hung out then.

"They should be almost dry by now," Mrs. Bright told her. "If it rains get them in as soon as possible. It looks a bit threatening."

Mrs. Bennett bathed and dressed the baby and Shandol took time to watch. Then they scalded the baby's bottles, after a thorough washing. These were the ones he had used the day and night previously. These were prepared for him for today and tonight. They were kept in the refrigerator, and warmed in water as needed.

Shandol scraped and sliced carrots, as asked to do, for the noon meal. She also peeled and stewed potatoes. She sliced red, luscious-looking tomatoes. In between she had dusted the furniture.

"The baby cried again last evening after you left," Mrs. Bennett told Shandol. "How he knows when you're gone is beyond me," she added, smiling, the wrinkled face crinkled more around the gray-blue eyes.

At noon, Mrs. Bright came in again to lunch. She added a can of spinach, which she took time to heat, and season, to the meal she had had Shandol begin. There was also bread, butter, jelly and milk. Marcia was still eating in the bedroom.

"Get the clothes in after the dinner things are out of the way," Mrs. Bright told Shandol. "Fold it all, including the ironing—mother will help you sort it out. Tomorrow we'll do the baby's things again and boil them. And please, stay longer this afternoon. We've had a time the few times you've left early. I've almost gone back after you."

"That would've been all right mostly," Shandol replied. "Except I wouldn't have been home last night. I was with Carol Middleton."

Shandol recalled the afternoon in a flash of fantasy. In the first place she was always glad to be home a little earlier. She washed herself, as usual, hanging the dress she had worn that day over the foot of her iron bedstead to wear the next day. It was not dirty. She put on a clean dress and was just wondering how she would spend the rest of the afternoon, when Carol came by.

"It's been awhile," Shandol greeted her.

"Yeah, I know," Carol replied. "Wanna go for a walk or somethin'?"

"I suppose I could. Anywhere in particular?"

They had already returned the last of the borrowed books to Mrs.

Davis, and had decided not to borrow anymore. Carol had used the excuse that she would soon be moving and going to school. Then Shandol had demurred saying she would not enjoy coming by herself. Not yet anyway. But they had assured Mrs. Davis they had enjoyed being allowed to read the books and visiting her when they came. It had certainly added some purpose to their summer. Shandol added a special thank you from Audrey, who had said she had enjoyed reading the ones Shandol had brought home.

"Yuh know how my dad likes to play checkers whenever he can, and he also reads and studies for his Sunday School class. So the books have been company to both Mama and me," she finished.

So the girls had just started walking. They walked to the service station along the highway for an ice cream cone each which was Carol's treat.

"This may be the last time we'll have much time together for awhile," Carol told her. "We're goin' to be movin' this week and then I'll be in school."

"Yes, I know," Shandol smiled. "Thanks for the cone. I've really enjoyed these times we've had together, Carol, and the times you've treated me to candy or ice cream, chewing gum or just going to your house for iced tea or a piece of good cake. I hate to see this summer end. I don't mean that to sound greedy or anythin' like that. I've enjoyed it." Then her face became pensive. "It's sad really, not going back to school."

As the girls were walking back down the hill, having passed two short streets which were access roads to the highway to their right, when they became aware of a persistent, air-filled, loud droning sound. It began to produce a steady roar to the northeast, the direction of the highway.

"I've learned what that noise is," Carol cried, excitedly, grabbing for Shandol's hand. "Let's hurry and we can see."

They raced the short distance back to the road which turned toward the highway. They started running toward the sound. Someway they managed not to spill their ice cream!

"It's an army convoy of trucks—and men!" Carol exclaimed, meaningfully.

They reached the highway breathless, yet after a moment could continue eating ice cream, now nibbling the cone itself. They stood in lush matted green grass along a bank well away from the highway.

Shandol thought they must have reached the highway in time to see nearly all of it. She could hardly realize it would take so long for it to pass. Later, Shandol recalled the trucks with men, jeeps, more trucks, and waving shouting soldiers! Some of them flung pieces of paper toward the girls which contained their names and addresses. Some were home addressed, so perhaps they hadn't thought to put where they were going—or did they know? Would any of these have a wife at home?

"Shall we write to one or two?" Carol asked.

"I might if Dad and Mama say it's all right. Wonder what one should write about."

"About oneself and try to get them to write about themselves. You know what you do. Just write an ordinary, friendly letter. Some may be good letter writers, some hate to and may not answer—Mama says."

"You've already asked her?" Shandol asked, surprised. "Yeah. As I told you I learned about these convoys and what they mean, and that they throw addresses too, of course. So I wondered and asked. A letter from someone might help a homesick soldier. They do get homesick I bet."

"I suppose you're right."

The girls had smiled and waved, they had yelled "hi" and "'lo" and to Shandol it finally became automatic. She stared fascinated, mesmerized and in absolute awe.

They found several addresses, Carol, four and Shandol three. Shandol decided only two was all she could afford to write to—even if they wrote back. She realized there was a chance they wouldn't. It could be they wondered if anyone would care enough to write. Shandol already wrote to a school friend who was in the navy. Carol supposed the men might be lonely or curious about anyone's finding addresses. Carol decided to "write to all to see how many answers she would receive.

Carol walked Shandol home and as they were about to part Carol told Shandol she had something to ask of her. She asked if she could buy Shandol's last year's school books. After all, Carol remarked what Shandol already knew, she would be a senior this year.

"I hadn't thought much about sellin' 'em," Shandol admitted. "I didn't suppose I'd be able to go up there to find anyone who'd want 'em. Well, you know livin' here."

"I think I can use most of them," Carol told her.

"I'll really have to ask the folks about sellin' 'em and what they're worth. Some are Lester's and he may not want to sell his. He hasn't yet. I don't know what to say, except I'll ask and you can see me later, if you haven't found any first."

"I probably will then," Carol answered, "because I'll need books and the sooner I get 'em the better."

Shandol had asked her parents about the books that very evening. They helped her decide on prices and the ones they would let go. Some were Lester's. They were from his senior year also, which might or might not still be in use. She could accept them or not as she chose.

But another thing, a visual thing, Shandol would remember about that evening was a beautiful shades of red and gold western sky looming before her, just as they came back to the main road from the highway, Exploding before her in reds, oranges to gold was a sight blended into being by a master hand. The clouds, translucent, and colors above the ridge seemed to defy a painter's imagination. The red made a splatter of the sun, the orange seemed more distant, fading the red, yet blending into it. Spokes of gold framed it as a sunburst. The ridge skyline topped by trees of various sizes were waiting to swallow it all. Shandol could not miss seeing how gorgeous it was as she silently admired it.

Someday I may think of it and wish to see it again, to see it painted or an attempt, and I think I'll cherish it in my memory, Shandol thought, but right now I wish I could go far away. She knew she was made more sad because Carol was going away to school, and how she, Shandol, would miss her.

Shandol's fantasy did not get in the way of her doing what she was supposed to do, or being aware of where she was and the goings-on, including what was said. It had been merely flickers of thought.

By the time the meal was ready and eaten and Mrs. Bright had taken Marcia her meal, and talked to her a few times, it was time for her to go back to school.

It seemed a longer afternoon as Shandol stayed longer. The radio was going softly, she supposed, the serial stories were on. There was really very little to do.

It rained a shower which seemed to freshen the air and lighten it somewhat.

The baby aroused in the afternoon to be fed. In the dampness a light blanket was kept closer around him.

"He's right on schedule," his great-grandmother beamed.

He was, as always, put back into his basket bassinet to sleep, as soon as he was fed and asleep.

Marcia was waited on mostly by her mother and grandmother. Shandol, on occasions, carried her water to drink or a pan of water for washing her hands and face, but one of the others carried her her food, helped her take sponge baths, change into clean gowns, and change her bedding.

The baby cried after four o'clock. Shandol took him and held him in her arms, his head on her shoulder. She patted his back, hoping to make him belch, as she had heard sometimes helped, then hoped he would be all right.

Mrs. Bright found them so when she arrived, though the baby was quiet.

"Hello," she greeted with a smile on her wide mouth. She had blue, wide-set eyes and sharp features. "Uh-oh, a fussy baby again? Nice you're here, Shandol."

Shandol nodded and said "hello" in a low tone.

Mrs. Bright laid her stack of books and school papers on the shiny dining room table, which had only a lace centerpiece.

"Mother," she said, "I'll take you home now since Shandol's here. And then I have to stop at the store for some groceries and things."

Shandol was then alone with the young nervous mother and tiny baby. She was worried and feelings of inadequacy threatened to overwhelm her. She felt so responsible for both mother and baby. Shandol was sure she had been around more small babies than Marcia. Just having a baby didn't bring much experience for his care. But Shandol remembered her mother had said mothers were given insight or instinct, which helped. Her mother had gone to help families with newborn infants when Joel wondered whether or not she was up to it. She had bathed and dressed the babies, or help the mothers anyway she could, including washing diapers, or perhaps straighten up the house or prepare food.

She recalled in her mind and thoughts, of once when Tommy was small she had been left with the others. The older boys had started teasing her and one another. She had pleaded with them, threatened to "tell mama" on them, which had had no effect. Finally, in a sudden bursting forth of exasperation, she had laid Tommy on the bed. "I'll just get Dad's razor strap," she fumed. "You need it, I'll use it."

She hoped to scare them with her determined grown-upness and the intimidation.

But she had placed Tommy much too close to the edge and Phil had plopped down on the bed to get near Tommy, as he knew she would not risk striking him there. But as he landed on the bed the jar on the bedsprings had bounced Tommy off onto the floor with what seemed like a very harsh thump.

It frightened and quietened them all. Shandol picked Tommy up and he started to cry as loudly as he could. He yelled so hard and got so pink in the face she thought sure he must be dying. Tears had rolled down her thin pale face. She rocked Tommy in the creaky rocking chair, which had faded cretonne covered, cotton padded cushions on the back and seat, tied by strings of the same material to hold them in place. Shandol talked to Tommy, and declared him too much a little man to cry, even at four months. She berated herself and conceded wickedness at allowing such a thing. Oh, how she loved him and please not die.

"Mama, Mama," she cried, her face next to Tommy's.

He finally hushed and looked at Shandol. She felt on his head for a lump, but found none. She felt his arms and legs to see if they were broken, but she knew she didn't know. How long it seemed before her mother came. She was afraid if Tommy slept he'd never awaken.

Audrey came in a half-hour or so. The boys had hung back, though Shandol had ranted it was as much their fault as hers. She burst into tears. She would be blamed. The boys went into the bedroom to play cars and bandits.

Shandol put Tommy in the middle of the bed, then to run to meet her mother to tell her what had happened to get it over with. But Audrey had smiled, knowingly and in sympathy, but told her daughter it was said a baby hardly started to grow until he had accidentally fallen off the bed, it was so common an occurrence.

"As soon as they learn to roll over, watch out," she smiled. "But it happens no matter how careful you try to be." She soothed Shandol about his crying as being more scared than hurt. Shandol felt better and of course nothing happened. In fact he had other tumbles much worse than rolling off the bed on a rag rug.

Shandol determined nothing must happen to the much tinier infant she now held. It had taught her not to be careless. She looked at him and smiled to herself at the thought.

Shandol had little idea of the thoughts and feelings of Marcia. She doubted Marcia would ask her to get anything if she needed it. It annoyed her, because Shandol felt there was a distinct, yet unspoken, plot to keep her ignorant of somethings concerning the whole thing. She sensed and felt it. Yet she was doing a woman's work, yet she had the idea she was being treated—no, sheltered, as a child. She thought she might otherwise learn from the experience, but what?

She could talk and croon to the baby anyway. She saw his mother look at her through the door. She was sitting up now and taking a few unsteady steps. She saw Marcia look at her. Was it tolerance? Wonder? Envy? Ridicule? Or revelation in the look? Perhaps all of it. Shandol was natural and herself.

"I'm foolish I know," Shandol said, smiling and then looking at the sleeping little tyke. "But Mama says it's a secure feeling to hear a voice, low and soothing. Or maybe we're just sorta odd that way."

"Maybe I'd better do it," Marcia said. "Sometimes I feel like talking to him, when he's so quiet and peaceful. But I feel so silly too. I suppose it will come to me in time."

When Shandol finally arrived home she learned her sister in-law had come to spend a few days. Shandol would hate to leave while she was there, but Jane insisted it was perfectly all right because they

102

were depending on her. Jane and Shandol were good friends as well as sisters-in-law so they visited that night on into the night, when the others were not crowded around. Shandol had been jealous of Jane at first because she was their new "Sis." She had never had anyone to be called her pet name before and she couldn't bear to be replaced. But she was still "Sis" and Jane had once more become Jane.

The next day was Friday and fair. Shandol walked to her job aware of the cool clean morning air. She knew she would be doing the baby wash and felt ready to do it. She had left home as they were putting wash water on in the iron wash-boiler at home. The boys and their sister-in-law were going to do the wash there. Audrey would oversee it and perhaps help some if she felt like it. Their job would be much larger than hers, she mused, but there were more of them. Shandol hoped her mother made them do it and not try to take over herself, thinking she could do it faster or better. Sometimes the boys could act so foolish, too, and get so little done. Shandol or Joel should be there, but he was working on the road. Shandol had left reluctantly, but also pleased Saturday would not be a wash day for her.

The first thing Shandol had to do when she arrived, however, was to hang out what Mrs. Bright had washed the night before. It was hanging on the back porch, in the other bedroom, and seemingly everywhere. Shandol wondered how late Mrs. Bright had been doing it. There were baby things that had to be dried to be used. They would dry sooner now outside in the sunshine. The sheets and other straight articles, such as towels, were already outside. But the starched things and ironing were not, in case of rain.

The day went much the same as the others, though she was later with the remainder of the baby's wash. The day seemed to speed by as she was so busy with the wash, the baby, helping with the meal and housework.

She was surprised, but delighted, to arrive home to find her uncle Lafey, Audrey's only brother, his wife, Ruth, their daughter, Ruth's parents, and a young man who had gone along to help drive, were there at last. They had been on a vacation trip through the western states, and were expected, if even for a short stay. They were now on their way home.

It was near chaos there.

CHAPTER 10

Shandol was sure "near chaos" was the correct description. Everyone seemed to be trying to talk at the same time and it would be a marvel if anything were understood. Sonnetts were anxious to hear how they were and about the trip, and they to talk. But it seemed everyone wasn't talking or listening to the same one. So the greetings and introductions took time. That included the young man who was along.

Shandol looked about her at the house. In appearance it looked fairly clean and tidy, considering it had been wash day. Perhaps Jane had been responsible for much of that. But how Shandol wished they had a home like Mrs. Bright's to which to welcome guests! What a delight it must be.

The visitors were tired but in good humor. They mocked and apologized for their wrinkled clothing. They were verbal in anticipating their eventual arrival home. It was Ruth's mother, Mrs. Souther, who remarked she had heard one of the nicest things about a trip was getting back home again, now she could believe it. Of course, she had enjoyed the experience she was quick to add. She was a tall dignified appearing woman of unreadable age. Her hair was gray which belied a youngish look. She was not handsome. Her mouth was too wide. Her cheeks flared at the corners of her mouth giving her a false smile look. Her eyes were a redeeming factor. And she needed glasses only to read. Her husband was the opposite. He was heavy-set, bald and wore glasses. He had even features and had been handsome perhaps in his young days. His look was pleasant, but Shandol doubted much escaped his consideration. She considered him a businessman. Their daughter was dark-haired, worn short, with composites of their features. She was average in height and had taken the best features and was quite nice to look at, as one would expect her uncle Lafey to desire. Of course to the Sonnett children he was the embodiment of perfection. He was the maiden's answer to tall dark and handsome, though he was not all that tanned as his work was inside; except now it seemed he had acquired some sun tan. His was not a rugged good looks, but "movie star" handsome. His hearty, unexpectedly genuinely pleasant, completely spontaneous laugh broke into Shandol's thoughts, as she considered how really stylish and successful their guests looked.

"The first thing on the agenda," Uncle Lafey cut into everyone's conversation, "Is to make a big pot of vegetable soup! I've been looking forward to it."

He disappeared into the bedroom and emerged with his clothing changed from the dress slacks to more casual trousers of a white and blue stripe. It was obvious he was going to have a hand in it. In truth he had written his sister before the trip that he would be looking forward to that very thing. He had said he wanted every vegetable to be found in the garden at that time of year to be put into it. And he might want some canned, if not in season, such as corn. The concoction would then be cooked in the pressure cooker-canner.

"How long have you been here?" Shandol could finally ask her aunt.

"Not long," she replied. "We just got here you might say.

Audrey said you were at work helping a neighbor. What do you do?"

"Helping take care of a baby," she answered, carefully. "A baby at this grandmother's, a friend of ours. She teaches, so the great-grandmother is there to help look after his mother and him. But I help by doing the baby wash and help with the housework. I also help keep the baby quiet. He was so cranky and just one little 'wah' and they all melt to butter. He does just fine now. Much better."

Shandol dared glance at the young friend of Uncle Lafey's, who had been eyeing her as she spoke. Her aunt saw the exchange of glances and introduced them. Jake Lutiss was his name. He nodded politely as Shandol murmured, "How-do-you-do." Shandol wondered who he was, what year in school. Who were his parents? Perhaps his father was a teacher, doctor or merchant. Or was he someone needing help and Uncle Lafey took him "under his wing" because he considered him deserving of a chance? It would be like her uncle, Shandol knew. But he looked so trim and neat in dress slacks and pale blue shirt.

Shandol noticed Tommy finally had Uncle Lafey's attention, talking a mile a minute. He was not one to hang back waiting to be noticed. He could make the first move with persistence if necessary to get his say. She strongly suspected he was telling his uncle about the living things they had acquired for his uncle. Uncle Lafey had written even during the early spring to ask them to procure certain ones for him. He apparently appeased Tommy by promising to give them his full attention as soon as he helped with the soup. But he did want to help with that.

Audrey was already on the way to the garden as he followed, leading his small daughter, who had been at his heels, as far as the edge of the garden. There she was left to play with K.C. Ruth had admonished her husband to watch her. The other boys also were outside, feasting their eyes on their favorite uncle, but Audrey suggested they help and directed them as to how, mostly picking beans. Ruth and her parents visited. Shandol supposed they compared their home now with their former one, and perhaps their own most presentable one. Mr. Souther had been a merchant in a county seat not far from her grandfather's farm. But they had moved their business nearer their daughter a few years ago.

Audrey and her brother visited, though a lot of what they talked about the garden and what they could use. The boys and their uncle must have joked because his distinctive, spontaneous laugh rang out at intervals. There were tomatoes still ripening, beans, both green and "shell-outs" on the same vine. The ground was soft but not sticky muddy. The porous soil settled soon after a rain. The garden was near the house, across the path and perhaps twenty-feet from the porch.

Inside there was a lull, the guests resting as best they could, Shandol supposed. They moved from the dining room to the front room. She was sorry she hadn't suggested it. But she had been so preoccupied with her own thoughts. She did so want to change from her work clothes, but simply could not bring herself to comment as to why. She was sure she smelled of baby things. She actually became ill at ease. She thought she had detected a smirk on the face of Jake Lutiss. If he didn't look so bored, she was sure, he would feel like hiding his face to laugh. He was a tall slender youth and she saw younger than she had at first thought, at least two years her junior. He had a pale smooth face, high forehead, wide-set blue eyes, fine even features almost feminine. His fair hair had tiny waves and curl, and Shandol decided he was pretty in the way a girl is pretty. He was quiet with an air of superiority, she thought, and that was the reason for a smirk on his handsome face. He was probably wondering why Mr. Bregmanson and his in-laws could possibly want to stop here. And even if Audrey was really his sister. Shandol felt resentment, but left alone she realized it would be a chance to freshen up. She took it.

She went to the kitchen for the pan of water and other things she needed. She took them through the back screen and into the dining room from the porch. She was less likely to be seen from the front room. She went into her parents bedroom. She went upstairs only to get her other clothes. The bath was also important to her because Dean was coming.

As she went up the stairs, they did not seem to notice her. She could barely get a glimpse of them. She did hear groanings and arguing they had "been sitting all day," which proved tiring. That room was a presentable as it could be made, and tidy because the company had been expected *sometime*, and special care had been taken to keep it neat. The old-fashioned wainscoting had been repainted at one time and the wall papered. Shandol was not going to be ashamed of it she determined. It was where they lived. And people accepted people, not their houses, didn't they? And their home was as well furnished as the majority in Greenway, though she knew the exceptions. She even realized the old divan was probably old fashioned with "horsehair" stuffing and varnished wood arms, also across the back, the leather upholstery showing age somewhat. And there was the old desk and the rocking chair of unknown pedigree.

Shandol decided in her mind the Pretty Boy, as she thought of him, was a snob. Then she remembered something which made her heart hammer. She took a deep breath, her chest heaving above the bare torso she was washing. She had, modestly, draped her bath towel shawl fashion across her shoulders. *The Ozarks!* That was the vague thing she had been trying to bring to mind. The idea was illuminating. How simple. He had probably heard of The Ozarks. Did he see it as he had heard, perhaps, of its hills, its rocky land, its brush and woods, razorback hogs, even ignorant, shiftless people, poor and crude? Why shouldn't he want to learn of it so he could go back home and talk. She had completely forgotten he had been other places, seen other sights also. But perhaps he would poke fun at them and laugh. That is if be could laugh. Or could he? His face might crack. Shandol smiled at the thought. She judged him to be selfish and conceited and a bore. Perhaps he knew nothing else. Just comfortable and smug and completely unmindful of how others less fortunate had to manage any way they could and as best they could. Or had his present company gone to his head? She dared not guess. She just supposed people having hard times were about everywhere, some even worse than themselves. Was it funnier here? Shandol resented him. His neat clothes looking so right for him. Would he notice anything other than the "typical Ozarker" here? He should know they weren't "natives" of the area, if it made any difference, typical or not. But there was crudity and the lack of money was evident.

But they were the rather large family with crude or old and homemade furnishings. Not that the homemade things were rough and ugly. They were well made. Audrey's father had made them on visits he had made from time to time. He liked to be busy or perhaps Audrey would ask him to make something she wanted or needed. He made the things smooth and fine, some were walnut. But they had no finish. No varnish or paint. There was the dish cabinet in the dining room by the kitchen door, with a glass door at the top.

There was the "tea table" with no casters, near the door to the back porch, over which hung the medicine cabinet he had made, complete with a mirrored door and a drawer at the bottom. It was handy in the dining room. The washstand in the kitchen he had made. They were all nicely made and they all wished there was money to do them justice. But the dish cabinet only had a coat of cheap white paint.

The Sonnett children had, however, been reminded they had much to be thankful for, which should concern them. They had good health, good minds, were cared for, and God himself seemed to help care for Audrey. But the house, no matter what they did, was still old and usually seemed shabby, though they were proud of the front room. The bright blue linoleum with rose and green floral design, looked as good as new, except the few places marred by someone leaning back on two legs in a straight back, dining room chair. The faded cretonne curtains in the dining room, freshly washed now, had a large floral design. Curtains made of white feed sacks hung at the one window in the kitchen. It was a long window and they were two-tier pairs. In the front room there were clean, starched and stretched cotton ones, with window shades, because it was the company room. The rest of the curtains in the house showed wear, sometimes tear, but bravely managed to look better than none at all.

That bench behind the table! Joel had made it. That may brand them Ozarkers, Shandol thought. They were in just about every household, Shandol supposed, unless some obvious exceptions. The benches were functional and, in most cases, necessary.

Did any of them know or guess about Joel's job working on the road? Well, no matter she thought, powdering her body lightly, which did not smell of the baby things she had been aware of most of the day. She had had the bedroom closet door (under the staircase) open so she could dart inside and close if anyone came near. A handy table held her pan of water. But she was soon dressed, hurriedly, and realized how her thoughts had turned. All because of a surprising boy she hadn't considered before. But she resolved he would not ruin Uncle Lafey's visit.

A measure of self-confidence returned to Shandol after her refreshing interlude. She went into the kitchen to see if she could help. They had not returned from the garden as yet. They were visiting. She wondered how Jane liked her uncle. She set about peeling potatoes, which she procured from a tow-sack behind the cook stove. She peeled and washed several, sliced them and put them into the large open pressure cooker, which was already on the stove with water in it to heat. She could hear the others coming from the garden. There was hardly room for them all in the small kitchen, so some spilled over into the dining room. There was much to be done. The beans to string and break, as well as wash; carrots to scrape, cabbage to be shredded, and the other odds and ends prepared. Shandol shed tears over a large white onion, which had been hanging in a bunch, one of several, in an out of the way area to an overhead rafter on the back porch. Before freezing weather they would be moved upstairs.

Uncle Lafey shredded cabbage into the cooker, Audrey scraped carrots, washed tender okra pods and sliced them to add. A quart jar of canned corn was opened and a pint jar of peas were added. There were busy hands with the beans. And a handful of large lima beans was added. (It had always been a source of delight to the children when they were younger, to find a large butterbean in the soup.) A green pepper was added, red ripe tomatoes, salt, pepper and an adequate slab of fat-back bacon were added for seasonings.

"Looks like you've all cleaned up." Uncle Lafey noticed Shandol.

"Yes," she replied. "I usually do. It seems I smell like baby things and just generally untidy."

"Member, Unc Lafey," Tommy interrupted, "when the soup's on and Mama's watchin' it, I wanna show yuh the tarantulas and things."

"And I have some things to show, too," he said, smiling and winking at Tommy.

"We could go see a sinkhole, a cave or Grand Gulf," Bobby suggested, not to be ignored.

"Sounds fine," Uncle Lafey replied. "But we're so tired. And we aren't home yet. Traveling is tiresome if you're not used to it. We've seen a lot of scenery and other things to do this trip. Maybe another time, when we can just see things around here. We were in Arkansas and came out of the way to see the Shepherd of the Hills country west of here."

Ruth appeared in the doorway from the front room where she and her parents had stayed to relax.

"Where's Jean?" she asked, looking at Lafey. He looked at her startled, glanced around, obviously surprised and disconcerted. Forget Jean? He had been so busy, so enveloped in the crowd, he supposed.

"Well, we left her outside," he recalled quickly. "She and K.C. were going to see the chickens I think. She's all right."

"She'll get dirty, wait and see," Ruth fretted. "I'd better go see to her myself."

She found her daughter. Jean and K.C. were playing in the pile of wood ashes in an out of the way edge of the garden. They were contentedly playing they were driving on a "road," also used by Tommy and K.C. The toys were rather wretched looking affairs. There was

109

an old truck cab, and toy cars, barely recognizable. Tommy and K.C. had even made some of narrow pieces of boards. They fashioned the "car bodies" of wet clay mud and allowed it to dry, which, to them resembled the real thing, minus wheels, of course. And also their older brothers and sister had also done this on the farm some years before.

Ruth, who saw them before she came directly upon them, listened only a moment and turned back into the house to tell her husband to take over their daughter and the dirt. She could not cope with it just then. She was quite frankly amused nonetheless. Because as usual Jean was imitating her fat her as she did at home in everything from eating to giving music lessons.

"Go see Jean, Lafey," Ruth told him. "Hurry. They're—they're on a trip and she's explaining about the scenery, the mountains, the desert, the seashore—oh, everything I think."

Lafey left his place by the stove where he wanted to be in on the soup making to check on Jean. He watched briefly, and, with effort stifled his urge to laugh.

"You kids get out of that dirt and play somewhere else.

Just look at you Jean!" He had to be cross or laugh. "You need sand or something to play that, so go somewhere else to play."

Jean, her small round face serious, looked at K.C. There was a smudge on one cheek. Her blue eyes turned to her father and then to K.C. Her straight short dark hair was amazingly unruffled, the short bangs across her forehead seemed to keep it from her face. She waited expectantly for K.C.'s next move.

"We'll play on the front porch," he said. "We'll git Tommy to make us a road there. And they ran toward the front side of the house, after getting Tommy's word he'd help them.

Inside the house the soup was cooking. The aroma of the mixture of vegetables hung deliciously in the air. Audrey, alone in the kitchen, except for Jane, who hovered where she could help if asked, watched amazed as Audrey stirred raisin pie filling on the stove in a heavy iron skillet, while juggling with pie dough soon ready to "roll out" on the "bread board," which pulled from its own niche in the cabinet, under the metallic top. She made enough dough, she told Jane, for a blackberry cobbler, which Lafey might like for a change. Raisin pies were Lester's favorite, as he had told his mother many times, and Audrey often made one when he and Jane came for a Sunday dinner.

Lafey and Ruth, while outside, and without asking her parents and young friend, still resting, or waiting, in the front room, became absorbed in Audrey's collection of houseplants, outside now and at their best. He knew she had obtained them from different places, usually having started them, he knew, from small cuttings from a neighbor or friends of the neighbors. He even saw some he was sure he had given her and was only mildly surprised. He knew his sister loved flowers, and as they were a hobby with her, as well as himself, she took care of them. Too bad she couldn't have a small greenhouse, as he himself kept. There were shrubs and rose bushes in the yard. Audrey also had dahlias, gladiolus, cannas and other flowers, some of which had bulbs or roots which had to be dug every fall. There were annuals planted in rows, also, in a potato patch, which was north of the house, between the house and the shed. Audrey pulled weeds, but Joel cultivated the soil, or hoed, as he did the crop.

Finally, at Tommy's repeated insistence Lafey went with the boys to look at the small live creatures they had captured.

"I sure hope I can keep them alive, long after school starts, too," he told them, looking pleased at the variety and apparent good shape of the specimen. "Now, I've got to find somewhere for them to ride, even if Ruth has to hold them on her lap all the way," The last he added looking at her, as she hadn't yet returned to the inside. His look was affectionate and he was grinning broadly, expecting her grimace.

"I heard that," she replied, returning the grin tolerantly and retorted, "Yes, let Ruthie do it. We can just start on a two hundred fifty-odd mile trip with my lap full of spiders, lizards, and whatever else those things are." She was treat it all as the joke she supposed it to be.

But they did have several *other* things for the haul back home. He had other live things, including a horned toad from the desert, which Lafey fretted about, afraid it could not survive in such confinement. Also some plants. These included cacti and other unidentifiable, except to Uncle Lafey, plants, rocks, or anything he dared try to bring across state lines, and even some he actually wasn't sure about. But how he loved the living things! "Preying mantis are so intriguing," he mused aloud.

Joel came in from his job on the road. He was late because of car trouble. He was let off the small truck at the store and walked the path past the post office, the lot and through a fence opening, the potato patch on one side, the garden the other. He went inside the house by way of the kitchen screen door to place his black speckled (done by peeled paint) dinner pail. The cabinet was already cluttered by utensils and a few vegetables peelings, which hadn't been put in the garbage pail. Later, with table-scraps, the garbage would go to the chicken pen.

Joel went to greet his guests, apologizing briefly for his appearance. He was introduced to the young man and settled in the front room to visit with the older couple. He supposed correctly his family was around, possibly as close to their favorite uncle as they could handily stay.

Shandol began watching the clock. It was Friday night and she and Dean were to go with their friends on a double date. Audrey realized her preoccupation and hoped to have supper over by the time Dean and Jim arrived. Then began the mad rush to get things on the table.

"Do you suppose you could get Dean and them to go see Lester and tell him Uncle Lafey is here?" Audrey asked, as she placed bowls and spoons on the table at place settings instead of plates. "And do tell Tommy to run to the store for a box of crackers, and bring back the charge ticket. Yuh know Jane would like Lester here."

"Do you think I should ask?" Shandol asked, nervously. "He might say no."

"I wish yuh'd ask," Audrey replied. "He can no more than say no, even though they prob'ly have something in mind."

"I've run out of bowls," she answered. "Even those that come out of the oats boxes. But only one or two needed yet. I guess I can eat out of a plate, for I want my soup to cool quickly anyway."

Shandol hurried to find Tommy to dispatch him on the errand. "Hurry," she prodded. "Everyone will be washing and getting ready while you're gone."

"I dread asking to go get Lester," Shandol worried aloud. "Must we ask Jane, or what?" Jane had been a help all day, even to her share in helping to get the soup on.

Then Shandol went to tell everyone supper was ready. There was much stirring around while everyone in turn washed and milled around waiting to be shown where to sit.

Mrs. Souther noticed K.C.'s idea of cleaning up for supper.

"Well, I suppose you get a bath at bedtime." It was almost a question.

"If you can call his washing up a bath," Shandol replied, evenly, quickly, and somewhat defensively. I wonder if she thinks he's supposed to look like he's ready for church after playing all day sweaty, in and out, *and* in and out! Shandol thought. She's a snob. I know the word now. But Shandol hadn't forgotten the snide remarks she had made to Bobby when he was about that age. They were still on the farm then. She seemed a mean old woman to me then, Shandol thought, who didn't like little boys. Shandol had told her parents. She mimicked her occasionally for the delight of the rest of the family.

But K.C. seemed to take no offense. "You're Mrs. Souther, ain't yuh? You a nice lady?"

She squirmed sheepishly. Given time Shandol believed K.C. could win her over.

The meal was not exactly a quiet one. It was a warm night and actually quite hot weather for such hot soup. Uncle Lafey boisterously, but good-naturedly laughed at them. He was enjoying himself thoroughly. He even asked Audrey for some chili powder, which she managed to produce. No one else cared to add that, however. He asked.

Bobby left after he had eaten and excused himself, seeing Joel's look, to go deliver his newspapers. He must meet the highway bus at the bus station, which was located at the gasoline station, to deliver the twenty or so papers to the customers on his route, bringing one copy home. The others with Joel soon left the table to go into the front room again, leaving the women to clean up. Audrey asked the company, except Jane to go rest too as the kitchen was so small.

Shandol slipped off upstairs to get ready to go out with Dean. She took care in dressing as much for those in the house as for her date. When she was ready she simply sat in her room. She was nervous about asking to go for Lester. But so far as the company was concerned she doubted she would be missed. She also wondered if Dean would decide they could go somewhere another night.

Soon she heard a "beep" and she went to a window in a back upstairs room where she could see to check. It was Dean, but he was alone and in his parent's car. So tonight they would be alone, she thought. This she hadn't allowed for either, trying to sort it out as she started downstairs.

"—The country'll be run by a dictator. He'll make himself one yet, wait and see." Shandol heard Mr. Souther's remark as she was descending the stairs and knew he meant the President. She had heard rumors of such remarks before. But she had been reassured by her father it was all just loose talk. That the President had no such ambition, in the first place; and he, too, was proud of the country's freedom for another. No, that was really irresponsible talk or just plain political propaganda. But words her uncle spoke next startled her.

"We'll be at *war* in six month's time," he vowed.

Why they're talking politics, really, she thought, and wondered how Joel would take it all—possibly silently? Joel was not much to argue where he considered it a futile thing to do, though he did enjoy a good Bible discussion with one as knowledgeable as himself. Joel realized his brother-in-law's father could not possibly know they had somewhat changed their politics, as so many it seemed, to what Joel called "New Dealers."

"Not unless we're attacked and must defend ourselves," she heard her father assert. "So it won't be the country's fault. There's some that criticizes the President for wanting to be prepared to defend the country. In my opinion," he continued, "we aren't all that ready to jump into war yet."

It was hard for Shandol to realize her uncle would think they still thought the same about such things. It only brought back the changes in their lives, especially those they had undergone since coming to this area. The Sonnett family had been through some hard times that the relatives and their kind would find hard to imagine. The government helping had made a great deal of difference. Did they understand the help the government had given so many hard pressed citizens? The work to do for pay? Corn hog bonuses? But no doubt her uncle would not have been affected by these directly. It would not have made the difference between having a place to live, food to eat, and clothing to wear.

But the war talk was something else. It was certainly real enough in Europe. Fortunately there was a wide deep ocean in between, which gave some comfort, but would it be enough? Would Hitler really be satisfied to just take over Europe? There were many people beginning to doubt it very seriously.

"Not unless we are attacked and need to defend ourselves," her mind echoed. It agitated her. She wished they would forget politics until they realized a meeting ground. But she supposed it was taken for granted they would all agree fairly closely with Uncle Lafey. They had no way of knowing Joel's mind.

Shandol knew about the war talk. It was news in the papers and talked about everywhere. It seemed to be a real monster looming huge and close and threatening. And the question was could it rain its fire and destruction upon this country? Yet there had been opposition when the President had chosen to begin some defense measures. "He'd just be invitin' war," seemed to be the consensus, "when he promised we'd stay out of it."

Joel thought the national defenses should be built up—just in case. He did not think the United States would choose to go to war, but if it were thrust upon us, be prepared. If no war then thank God we were able to stay out of it.

"We'd look as defenseless as David must have to Goliath, though," Joel had once said, thoughtfully, "to those countries who've built up armies and military might, and who had made military training a national project. But God has prepared his 'David' in the form of our president, in the right time and in His own way. I'm sure he has. We must hope, and pray He has and will always do so."

Shandol knew she would have no say in such a discussion even if she had the time. She doubted her father would argue about it.

Their stay was too short so he could keep peace. Time often proved speculation futile anyway, so why have any battle of opinions, no one being the winner or changing one the other. She hoped they soon changed the subject to the trip or something else, perhaps reminiscing.

As she went out the dining room door there was no way for her to go to miss Jake seeing her. She supposed he would be smirking his snobbish boredom. She felt a little better about letting him see her. She had on makeup, her hair was more fluffed out at the ends and reversed becomingly at the sides.

"Mama, I guess I'll be going," she called. "We'll go by to get Lester if Dean will," she added.

Giving Jake a Mr. What's-Your-face glaring look, she deliberately left the house, the small purse in one hand.

"Got company?" Dean greeted her.

"Yeah, my uncle, his family, in-laws and a guy helping him drive." she had counted on her fingers. "Uh, Dean," she added, nervously, "Mama wanted me to ask if you'd mind going out to see if Lester would want to come see them. They are leavin' in the mornin' so they don't have time to go see him. Besides they are tired of goin'. They've been on a long trip. Would we have time, yuh suppose, to go tell Lester or didja have somethin' else in mind to do?"

"I'll take yuh," Dean said, opening the car door for her to get in. "And bring 'im in if'n he don't have no other way." "Well, he's been stayin' here. In fact Jane's here. But he has to go to town in the morning to work, so her dad will take 'im. She's only here for these few days. He'd aimed to get her this weekend anyway."

"Where's he work at?" Dean asked.

"The cheese factory, or whatever yuh call it, in Plainesville," she replied. "He's only worked there since yesterday."

"We're on our way, "Dean said. "Then I thought we'd go to that dime show at Folks Consent."

"Is there a theater there?" she asked, surprised. "Nah, it's to be in a big empty room over the feed store down there. Naw, hit's too little for no theater all its own. Whar's yer uncle live?"

"In Iowa, but he'll go see other relatives north of here before going home. He teaches in high school. And he's always been our favorite, I guess."

"Say, I do appreciate you a takin' me out to tell Lester. He may not can come in unless he can go back tonight, because uh work and that's the only way he can get there in the mornin'. Um, turn left here," she directed, "after a few miles of driving west, and on out of town. Then just keep on the main road. That's about all the directions I know. I think I know where it is. Part of this I went over as part of the school bus route. But we come in from up the highway, so I do get turned around. The roads still finally get tuh lookin' all about alike tuh me."

"This here's a whale of a lot outta the way, ain't hit, fer goin' tuh Plainesville?"

"It certainly is outta the way, but it *was* the school bus route. On cold days it was a long miserable ride, too. There were these hard benches around the sides of the bus and one down the middle to set on. No heat. Sometimes I sat on my feet, one or the other or both just tucked under my coat—almost all the way, on real cold days. They'd practically go to sleep. One winter the bus driver put a small coal oil heater in the bus, but only a few days. It was considered too dangerous. It could get turned over and be a bad fire."

"Yep, that'd be so," Dean agreed.

"I must be home on time," Shandol changed the subject. "I don't think I could stand Dad gettin' on tuh me in front of the company. Yuh know what I mean?" She appealed to him. "By the way, where's Jim at?"

"Jim couldn't make it. And yeah, I see about the company," he laughed. "You shore we're on the right road?"

"Fairly sure, yeah," she returned. "It always seems like such uh long ways to me too. We may miss the show."

"There s a chancew they won't have it," he replied. "They have better crowds in the winter when people'd druther go to things. More places to go in summer."

"Could be," she agreed.

They finally arrived at Chiltons and gave Lester the message. He was quite excited and Mr. Chilton, could see it would mean a lot to him to see his uncle, told him to go ahead and take his car. Shandol and Dean left when that was settled.

Dean's prediction that there might not be enough to have a show proved to be correct. So the couple ate a sandwich at the small cafe in Folks Consent, had a soft drink each, lingered awhile in the car outside talking and watching the young people dance in an adjoining part of the cafe where there was a jukebox. Some of the dancing "couples" were young girls, because there never seemed to be enough boys. Shandol and Dean also drove around to see if they could find another couple Dean knew well and Shandol had met. They saw no one, however, and soon after decided to go back to Sonnetts where they could sit on the front porch awhile.

Shandol had considered Dean's car. She was disappointed it was not shiny and new looking as the one Jim drove. It was a smallish car, and she had never seen one like it before. It was an older one. Shandol thought it must be an odd make, but was told it was a Chevrolet. However, it looked nothing like the one her uncle had, which was a sedan. She wished that for tonight they had been in the other one. It seemed more impressive.

"Tell me about that bulldog under the porch," Dean said lightly, and Shandol supposed he was teasing her.

"Sometime I will," she declared, "but not now. Later sometime if yuh still wanna hear about it. Of all the things—" she let the sentence fade away.

It's that silly, she thought. *I can never be sure if he's serious or not.* If he were merely mocking and pretending she couldn't be sure.

"I must go in, I guess, before Dad comes bellerin' at me," Shandol grumbled.

"Yeah, the company'd hear," Dean mocked.

"Yeah, and that goose of a guy—" she stopped.

"Guy? What guy?" Dean was suddenly very interested. "Oh, that boy that's helpin' Uncle Lafey drive on the trip," Shandol stage whispered. "Sh—h, not so loud. I told yuh. They been on a trip out through the western states. I think he's laughin' at us all time. He's probably a doctor's or lawyer's son. I think he's a dope. If he wasn't Uncle Lafey's friend I'd call 'im a snob. He fits in with her folks— they're snobs. But he's prob'ly enjoyin' the Ozarks and us 'hicks' first hand." She chuckled, mirthfully.

"Has he said nothin' to you?" Dean wondered. "I'll beat 'im to a pulp. Wonder would 'e fight?"

"No, he don't say much to nobody," she replied. "Him fight? Ha ha. I doubt he could ruffle up enough. He'd be afraid to touch anythin' strange, or muss up his pretty face and curly hair. He's really prettier than a girl should be. And I mean *pretty*."

"Purty!" Dean yelped.

"Sh—h, they'll hear," she scolded lightly. "So'll Dad.

Besides we'll never see *him* again. Bet he don't notice girls much. He's shy."

"Well, he'd best be too shy fer you." he said.

"SHANDOL!" Joel roared from the open front doorway. Both doors of the old-fashioned double doors were open.

"I'm right here," she answered. "Scare me half tuh death."

"Oh," he replied, "I thought yuh might be still in the car. Come on in purty soon."

"See? What'd I tell yuh?" Shandol reminded him.

"Well, he didn't hear me," Dean returned. "He thought we's still in the car."

"I just gotta be goin' in now," she said, and she got up and went to the door.

"Well, I'll see yuh tomorrow night," he replied, and took her in his arms and kissed her fully on the mouth, before Shandol had time to guess his intention. "G'night," he said, fondly.

"Goodnight," she replied, watched him go to the car, then went inside. She washed her face and hands, learned the visitors had decided to try to get some rest, and she went on to the living room, where she knew she would be trying to sleep on the sofa.

The next morning the first thing that seemed to keep coming up was that the visitors would be leaving. Uncle Lafey asked his sister to prepare him a country breakfast of bacon (even fat-back, as she called it, and asked about it), eggs, fried potatoes, gravy, biscuits and her rice. He had a big day ahead, another overnight stop to make before going home.

"I'm getting anxious to get home, now," he said. "I've a lot to do before school starts. Some class arranging, getting music lessons lined up and started. I hope I have a bit of time to rest after our trip. And we've Ruth's folks to get home."

They began getting ready immediately after breakfast. Uncle Lafey put things in the car, but Audrey refused to allow Ruth and her mother to do dishes. Audrey would see to them later. She had help. Jean looked washed and ready.

Shandol noticed Jane had gone home with Lester. Perhaps she should have stayed. Was she wrong in going with Dean? But then Lester wouldn't have made it otherwise, she reasoned.

"How was the show?" Audrey asked. Shandol was standing around not really knowing what she should be doing.

"They didn't have it," she replied, honestly. "There just wasn't enough people showed up. So we went to the cafe and ate, sat awhile watchin' people and drove around to see if we'd see anyone we knew. We didn't so came on home. They may try again in a few weeks to have a show. School'll be started and it will be better advertised, they think."

All too soon it was time for the visitors to go. Good-byes were being said and good wishes, as well as promises to write. It was already nearing eleven o'clock. There was just so much talking, but so little time.

"I'm glad we stopped here," the tall youth told Shandol in an aside manner.

"I'm afraid there wasn't much for yuh to enjoy," she replied. "It's nice of yuh to say so anyway. You were rather a surprise. Wish we coulda got Phil to clown around. But he's bashful till he knows people. Wish they'd made some countrified music, but no piano for Uncle Lafey, I guess."

She couldn't understand his sudden friendliness. Perhaps he was being polite, she supposed. She could even smile because she was really thinking about what his reaction would be if he could hear the almost (?) Ozark language her boyfriend used—even though the schooling children received what they heard from outsiders who moved there, much of the "original" language was being changed.

"Your brother Phil's a nice guy," Jake was saying. I wish I could know him and all of you better. In fact I wish I had Mr. Begmanson's— that is, your uncle's ability to enjoy every situation."

"We all think Uncle Lafey's pretty special," she told him still smiling.

"Well, guess we're going. Nice meeting you and all that. So long now."

Was it possible she had misjudged him? Perhaps they should have tried harder to show him a better time. But he was probably too tired anyway she reasoned. But I should know a friend of Uncle Lafey's would have to be an all right guy.

Everything and everyone was packed and crowded into the car, and no one would have to hold anything. As on all the journey, extra care had been taken with his quart jar of water from the pacific ocean. Lafey had allowed everyone to dip a finger into it and taste. It was hard to believe it could be so awfully salty.

But if anything had to be held it might well be the form of a tired little girl, who would no doubt, sleep some. She was also travel weary, but taking it very well, her parents had admitted proudly. But the crawly things found other places to ride.

For the Sonnetts it would then turn into a rather empty day, yet everyday busy-ness would help some. Of course Shandol had a date for the evening. She wondered if Jim would be along.

CHAPTER 11

The emptiness of the day continued oppressive. A pall seemed to have settled around everywhere. Shandol wondered if everyone were affected or just herself. It was the contrast, she supposed, of having company, the excitement and then have to see them leave. Even Jane's being gone added to the loss.

The task facing her then did nothing to dispel her gloom. Her elation that the wash was done by the family yesterday was short-lived. Today, as she was not required to go to Mrs. Brights, she could get what ironing done she could. The irons had been on the stove heating since breakfast and she was getting such a late start. And ironing was such a tiresome task to her. Her hands were busy, but she frequently found her mind wondering elsewhere. There were times, as today, she resented having to do the large ironings. There were times her mother did the more "difficult pieces" such as shirts, wash pants, which were creased and things Shandol thought a waste of time to iron such as tea towels, especially when company seldom saw them. Today, however, Audrey would rest. The company had been a physical and emotional drain upon her, though she had been very happy to see her brother. It did, to her, mean extra work.

Shandol caught herself watching her mother that day, and realized she had been doing that of late. At first she was hardly aware of it, and then she couldn't seem to help herself.

She kept trying to see signs her figure was filling out. She decided now it had. She mentally did some figuring and realized she was five months, more or less, along. Yet, Shandol realized Audrey might not look pregnant to anyone who did not know her. She merely looked matronly, partly because, instead of wearing actual maternity clothes as such, she wore a straight coverall apron. She was also careful that her dresses were not fitted or tight.

Shandol watched for clumsiness also, which Audrey was not as yet. She sometimes moved slower or with precise and deliberate movements, as though carefully planned, she was none-the-less not large enough to be clumsy yet.

As the ironing progressed it seemed to Shandol her mind was busier, more impatient than ever. She tried to picture a new baby as a member of the family. But she had little luck. She could just think of her mother as expecting, a fact she had now accepted. At first she had thought of it as a nuisance, because the situation meant she would be needed at home.

She also thought it ridiculous, and yes, disgraceful at the age her parents were. It was ridiculous because of the ages of their children. Lester was married and she was old enough to be. And disgraceful because she thought her parents should know better, though she suspected it was quite unexpected. Besides Shandol felt embarrassed now because of the young people who came—especially older boys. She resented its keeping her at home. She had so hoped she would get a job elsewhere or go on to school. These, she supposed, were so impossible it was not even worth day dreaming about. And the coming of another child meant added expense.

Just how impossible the dreaming of school was brought home to her more completely following her graduation from high school. Two or three times, at least, already a representative from a business college some one hundred miles away, as remote as a thousand miles to her, had been there to talk to Shandol about continuing her business education. Joel had been appalled that no such interest had been shown Lester the year before. Although Lester's business courses had been few, Joel wondered why no such offers, or interest, had been shown concerning college. It was Shandol he had come to see each time to encourage, and even persuade her. He had wasted no words in pointing out she had the looks, personality and credits to do justice to such a course. He could see it would benefit her need for self-assurance and poise, and he had persisted. The fact there simply was an appalling lack of funds to even consider it did not seem to faze him at all. Anyone, he had reasoned, could work their way through school if they would so set their minds to do it. But, Joel had reasoned, that was fine for young men, but he could not see it for a young girl. And Joel would not go into debt. He would hesitate to encourage his son, though Lester had shown no actual desire to go on to school. Shandol had. Joel not only did not encourage her to hope, he had been verbally negative about it. Girls didn't really need to be educated, he resolutely affirmed. They would get married and raise families, and that was the way it should be. The exception was unless they chose to teach school or some such vocation, and not marry—or before marriage anyway. But that didn't take much education with which to begin.

There was no doubt that Joel Sonnett loved his daughter; and that she was the apple of his eye. He wished he was sure it was known, as well as the fact he would like for her to remain the innocent girl she still was. She could not be other wise for he had guarded her well. But it was still his opinion that it was unthinkable a girl-child of his could make more money than he did. She already had more schooling than he did, but he was sure his overall education exceeded hers. He knew she depended strongly on his opinion and direction. But he saw her as a *female* person needing these from a strong personality. That he was cultivating, promoting, and condoning by feeding from his own fears of inadequacies, hesitancies, and reticence he had almost banged into his own head and implanting them into another generation he could *not* see. Or that he should be glad to see his family working for better things. Though he did not have the means to accomplish it, he could at least encourage them. But he had not received such either. He had wanted to be a preacher, but his speech impediment had been too much for him to hope to overcome. The fact that others who had stammered or stuttered had overcome the handicap he had heard. But he had been defeated before he started because he supposed his case too different and difficult.

The matter of Shandol's furthering her education just fizzled out, rather than any profound decision making on her part, or a dictatorial mandate on Joel's. Shandol began realizing how dependent she was upon her family. Not just their physical presence and her moral support met, but their approval, their help and encouragement. Yet she was fed upon feelings of unimportance and inadequacies.

Her father had nothing to prove—or was it everything? She knew Joel considered himself a poor but honest and decent citizen. He was liked, though that was not the total sum of it. He was respected by about everyone in town, Shandol supposed. He also placed himself into the position of being a devout Christian. And because of it, his actions were watched. Perhaps not in a conscious way, but judgmentally. Also his family. This Shandol learned by word of mouth and she had caught herself staring unbelieving, her mouth open, as some fault of her brothers was brought to her attention. It was not that she believed her brothers above reproach, but that the idea came to her they should be. She had learned when Lester smoked cigarettes, played hooky from school, gone to a party where the party games turned into square dancing and he hadn't left. Now it was Phil. Some of the same things including playing cards, though Joel had done the same himself years before. "The Sonnett kids can do it," it was quoted, as though that settled it. To them it was a nuisance and incredible!

Of course, Shandol replied to some of the charges. She could sometimes say they were punished, or scold the tattler for thinking them so different. She had gone to her mother also about it. Sometimes she felt she needed to share it with someone. But because Audrey frequently told Joel, Shandol was at times on the outs with her brothers for tattling, as they called it.

122

"Well, your so-called friends tattle to me first," she replied, heatedly. "How do you think I feel? I always hear about your faults and how perfect you're not!"

And Joel shrugged off the words religious or religion as applied to himself. They were very broad terms, he insisted, and meant non-Christian as well.

Joel was the dominant one of the family and he tried to be a guide and leader, not a driver. He took it upon himself, with Audrey when possible, to visit the "sick and afflicted" where feasible, and to be friendly and tolerant of the young people in an aloof sort of way. He did not try to join them, but hoped they would come to him if he could ever help them. However, they mostly stood in awe of him and had no wish to draw his disapproval.

Shandol's thoughts ambled along these lines. She was not proud of the fact he had a job the government had fashioned for the destitute and jobless. Joel *was* proud of it.

"It's a chance to give a fair day's work for a fair day's pay," he had defended. He admitted there were a few exceptions to the chagrin of those who tried. But some had to keep mouthing dirty stories, such escapades and gossip of who was or wasn't whoring around and with whom. Audrey had confidentially told Shandol a few, mostly silly jokes, hinted at others and Shandol had overheard a few Joel had told Audrey, though he admitted most he forgot. But Joel liked the pay. Nowhere else could a laborer work for eighty cents an hour. The problem was he was limited as to the hours he was allowed in a given time. But that left time to cut wood in winter, garden in summer and in general worry as to how to meet the bills when he was laid off. The lay-offs he dreaded and came too often. The work was manual labor and he tried to keep busy as he did the road work. He knew there were other jobs consisting of the construction of buildings, which he had never done. He even appreciated that because he knew very little about road building, it was someone's responsibility to tell him and the others what to do.

Once coming home on the school bus Shandol had seen them doing the road work, on a road which was part of the school bus route. The boss's daughter rode the bus. She had waved proudly, it seemed to Shandol, as she had pointed him out, joking about her daddy, the boss. Shandol had seen her own father and waved, but most of the students had waved, and yelled, in friendly, but knowing, way.

Joel guarded his pay and budgeted it wisely, he thought. He bought groceries on what he called a "pay-on-payday" basis, yet he never went over what pay he would have already coming. He kept account of it and never spent more than he had already earned. He also tried to have some money left over for any unforeseeable emergency. Or even to replace clothes, and shoes, especially when time for school to start. It was important to him to stay out of debt, though he could name some of the so-called respectables, or so self-appointed themselves so, as being hundreds of dollars in debt. To Joel it was a matter of decency to owe only what he could afford and he had no intention of having the worry of deep debt. He knew it would take him a long time to make so much money. As poor as he was it was respect he craved. And though the store owner was a very good friend and they played checkers, even far into the night, usually at least one night a week and many Sunday afternoons, he never took advantage of that friendship. If he ever did need groceries, or other necessities from the store, as during bad weather or a lay-off, he wouldn't go into debt deeper than the value of the milk cow, which was his one asset (along with a calf she produced every year). Also the store was heated by burning cord wood so he could also pay in that way—and had done so. He liked himself better this way and seemed to be satisfied in a resigned way to his lot in life. Shandol was not. To her, her life had scarcely begun.

Shandol had sometimes wondered why Joel had settled in Greenway in the first place, and seemed to like the town. It was a sprawling village, going nowhere unless downhill. Proof of that was visible even in the eight years since they had lived there. There had been three stores then and a small lunch and coffee shop in the post office building then. It was run by the widowed sister of the maiden lady postmistress, though she was still postmaster by title. Now Greenway had only the one store downtown, and no lunch could be obtained at the post office—not even a candy bar. The gasoline businesses along the highway were still there, as was one grocery store. These hadn't changed, except for fewer things handled for sale. Greenway, therefore, had little to recommend it, and living there was a struggle, even with living costs cheap. It seemed to satisfy Joel, however, and this was a wonder in itself because it had a history shrouded in wickedness and a tinge of mystery. None of this could possibly be connected to Joel Sonnett, so perhaps he could remind himself he was not guilty of some of the sins others had committed and felt a certain satisfaction from it, because in a small town such things are certainly well known. The wickedness had had to do, strangely enough, with the vineyards and winemaking of past years. It seemed there was too much sampling of the product after hours, and otherwise "respectable" people—one a minister—had taken to loose and unseemly behavior. There were women—*other* women—in those carryings-on. Shandol was shielded by as much such gossip as possible, but the deeds done did not die so long as the gossips lived.

The mystery was with the house on the land itself, which had burned in a brush fire only a few years ago. It had been known as the haunted house. A woman had disappeared during the building of it, conveniently setting a husband free. It was supposed she was encased in the concrete of the basement walls or the vineyard cellar. It was not quite clear if known. In truth it may have been only legend, as many suspected, to keep intruders away. The mysterious light in the house's windows when it was still standing, dilapidating, but stately, on its hill south, which was a ridge showing from where Sonnetts lived, could have been the daring curious or the light of the passenger train reflecting in the window. But a few of the old timers could not let go of the ghost story and it was still repeated, if less confidently.

Greenway had at one time been a growing, prospering, bustling town, with the vineyards and fruit orchards being the main reason. Besides the wine making, there were the peach orchards especially, and the fruit was picked and shipped out by railroad in season. The changes began in the early 1900s. For a few years the climate was such that crops weren't so good. There was a train strike which caused more growers to go bankrupt. The vineyards and distilling business slowed, and, with prohibition had stopped. There was a tornado in the late 1920s which wiped out a portion of the town which was never rebuilt.

Now, only a few peach orchards remained, but even they were coming nearer ending. Older trees weren't being replaced. There had been several good crops of peaches since Sonnetts had lived there. The fruit, picked before completely ripened, was usually trucked out now.

Also, added to the fruit growing and vineyards, there had been the iron works, which had to do with the old iron ore smelter, now lying in ruins—and even the ruins were almost stripped of what metal or other scrap which could be salvaged or used. Some said it had never really amounted to much.

The town, which had been named for the man who had donated the land on which it was located, had even boasted a hotel in those early days. This hotel still stood, now referred to as the Old Hotel, and was home to the Sonnett family. The town had once prospered, reached its peak, and then a sure and steady decline was begun. It was like a fanned flame. It had flared up, and was still in the process of dying down.

There were certainly discouraging aspects of living there.

It might not seem much of a place to bring up a family in a responsible way. However, Joel contended, there were drawbacks, undesirables and "unfortunates" everywhere. Yet he realized that for young people there was little future to it. Those choosing to remain there would either have to make their own employment, such as farm, or work for farmers. There was a large farm and dairy operation just across the tracks, lying to the south of main street in Greenway a few blocks. A small white caretaker's house was evident on the next rise, as were the large milking barns. Two large old houses, also haunted according to certain ones, which were not considered inhabitable. There was the dense timbers nearby, which might invite a sawmill. Or they could choose to go elsewhere for employment. Even now young people must supply their own entertainment, or go elsewhere, as on the truck, to nearby places for it.

At first Joel and Audrey Sonnett, straight from farm life, found some of the ways the leisure time was filled strange. There seemed to be a lot of spare time, too, when compared to farm living where there was almost always something to do. There were the boys and young men who roamed around in the woods a lot, hunting or just to target practice. For these seldom were guns used. The ammunition was the immense supply and easy availability of the stones on the ground. Some of these "hunters" were excellent shots with "throw'n'rocks," as they were called. They could soon learn exactly the type of rock which carried truest, farthest, and easiest when thrown. There was also the slingshot, a stone slinging devise, hand made from the fork of small limbs, perhaps seven to nine inches long. A one-half to three-quarter inch wide length of rubber from an old automobile inner tube, and nine or ten inches long was attached to it. This when pulled back provided the force to send the stone projectile. A rounded leather piece joined them together by string an inch or so from the stretchable rubber. The leather was rounded neatly and held the stone. They were also whittled out of small boards, to fit the hand. The fork was also made more a squared U, the prongs holding the rubber, and the U deep enough for a stone to pass through. Boys desired these from a young age and kept them all their teen years, so far as Shandol knew. Sometimes they were kept even though a gun, whether rifle, pistol or shotgun, was purchased. The bullets cost money. A slingshot could be carried in the hip pocket. In the winter there were rabbit traps, which Lester already had learned to use.

There were other times the boys were just around town loafing idly. A few even hid out occasionally in a secluded, reserved spot, which they had stripped of vegetation, where they were sometimes joined by older men and "shot craps." Once Lester had lost a dollar from his paper route money, which Bobby had now taken over, "shooting dice," as it was also termed. Joel Sonnett had then laid down a law of absolutely no dice playing while under his roof. It was obeyed. They occasionally watched a game and admitted it. They always pleaded they had no money *to spare*, and could jokingly point out they were unlikely winners as they hadn't even had beginner's luck.

The parents of Bucky Sandler and Dale Lankers had bragged about their boys' winnings, and even their losses, the satisfaction being the boys had the money to play. Joel maintained it was gambling even though on a nickel and dime scale. He considered it un-Christian and not to be sanctioned. He feared it would create a craving for easy money and cause problems. In a similar class was liquor he considered wrong: (though he taught the "temperance lesson" at least once a year in the Sunday school class). These were things which kept those of the town in wonder of him.

And just these very things had come up when efforts had once been made to make him a justice of the peace, a constable, or some such official. Because the town was incorporated it was a possibility. And though he had joked about being able to perform wedding ceremonies as a justice of the peace, he politely refused the "honor." He knew that only the letter of the law would be good enough for him. He was sure this would cause antagonism and alienation of his friends and neighbors. This he did not want. He considered his part best served by hoping and praying "boys would be boys" and let the games go as a form of amusement. Even they had reasoned they had to pay for some forms of amusement anyway. Joel did, himself, like to play checkers, though he never gambled at it. And Joel went his own unassuming way.

Joel noticed a change in his own family after living in Greenway awhile. On the farm children were close. They were dependent upon one another for companionship and help, and learned certain diplomacy. But it gradually became different here in town. There were other boys and girls close by, and around a lot of the times. Even Joel and Audrey marveled at so much company so much of the time. They wondered why other parents allowed their children such freedom. They soon learned that there were those children who could come and go at will, their parents did not worry. So they had come to play ball in the alley near where they had lived then. They also played marbles and other games. Joel would not even allow his children to "play keeps," a marble game in which all marbles won when the games were over, were kept. They played with a large circle marked on the ground with a stick, the marbles in the center. They shot from the circle line with a favorite marble. There were some excellent players which had a distinct advantage over the Sonnett children who had never even heard of the game. They had played with holes in the ground so many inches apart. The first to finish putting their marbles in the four or five shallow holes fourteen to eighteen inches apart won. But theirs was a favorite place to play, because it was a place to go where other children would be. Even inside games and activities were held there in winter. They played checkers, dominoes, certain card games were allowed, or if there were enough, party games. They could pop corn or perhaps there were cookies. Sometimes their friends came simply to study.

They had lived in the Old Hotel only just over three years now. The other house had always been small which had necessitated a bed in the front room. As the children got older this made it uncomfortable for company, and especially Shandol when a boy walked her home and might have come inside. A few occasions they had, into the kitchen. So it was soon recognized by all that a larger house was the answer. And when the large old house became vacant they rented it.

It was quite a mess at first. All the rooms downstairs were just bare plaster walls met with a three-foot wainscoting, painted gray, as was all the woodwork and trim, in every room. The gray-glazed plaster on the walls was scratched and marked with initials, graffiti, and cracks of various veins, showing still in all except the front room. They had successfully papered over the plaster, after Joel and Lester had scraped and sanded the gray glaze-like finish off. It had proved a choking, dusty job. The doors were kept closed so only the three windows offered ventilation. The dust fogged and they "came out for air" even with wet cloths over their faces. They had been warned paper would not stick on it. But with that extra work it had. Audrey and Shandol had helped with the papering. Shandol dabbed paste to the back of it, Audrey applied it to the walls, keeping it in line and matching seams exactly. She was good at it. The room had smelled so fresh and clean when it was aired and the woodwork, windows, floors and curtains washed and cleaned. The ceiling added new light to the room with its plainer, white-silver design paper. The other was striped. It was mostly used as a company and visiting room, and in winter unheated, except for company or special occasions. In summer it was used with care. Only the kitchen and dining rooms were heated in winter. The rest of the house had been cleaned as well as laundry soap and kerosene could make it, which meant the floors and woodwork.

The smaller, sparsely constructed houses had been at first topics of conversation and amazement to Joel and Audrey Sonnett when they had at first moved there. They were built with a box frame and weather boarding outside. But inside the unfinished two by fours were covered by a heavy, gray building paper tacked to them. Occasionally wall paper was put over it for looks, but it was so easy for a hole to be punched into it, it was hardly practical. Sometimes newspapers were added in bed—or back rooms to cover such holes or to freshen the paper. These houses were hard to heat in the winter, but few hardly noticed. Wood was used for fuel and plentiful, and they were inexpensive to rent. There were the better conventional homes of course. Some of the small shoddy ones had been finished inside and were quite respectable, if small. They were usually owned by the occupants. Sonnetts had yet to be able to purchase a place and were required to take what was available.

Lunch was late. Shandol's mind, at first call, had returned to the present as she was ready to eat with the family. Her "wool-gathering" had made her time go rapidly and she had accomplished more than she realized, as she could see. Shandol was preparing to get back to it, rubbing the back of her hand over her forehead, when Audrey offered to iron awhile.

"Nah, I think I'd as soon iron as do dishes," she grinned, unless you just want to," she amended.

"It don't matter to me. Go ahead," Audrey told her. "But I'm faster," she added with a smile.

Shandol nodded agreement. She was tired and her hand brushed at her forehead again, and went back to ironing. Audrey would make up for it tomorrow, Shandol feared. Shandol was ironing in the dining room, as handy to the kitchen stove as possible where the irons were kept hot. She was vaguely aware of Audrey as she cleared the table, scraping clattering dishes and flat wear, but there was little small talk, because of Audrey's hearing handicap.

"About done?" Audrey finally asked again.

"Only two more shirts then the easy part," she replied, which meant tea towels, pillowslips, a few more odds and ends of clothing. Her mother usually pressed out the sheets beginning after they were folded twice, "Because they look better in the drawer," she always said.

Later her mother went into the front room to do some mending and sewing. The boys were outside, she knew not where. Perhaps Tommy and K.C. were rolling their discarded automobile tires, their bare feet toughened to run after them in the stony ground. If anyone had come in Shandol would hardly have noticed.

Shandol knew her mother sewed baby clothes, if she finished mending. She had to do all the sewing for the expected baby as materials could be cheaper than the ready made. Shandol's mind went back to the time she had first tentatively learned about it and marveled, yet she was mystified as to how it could be, because she was sure she was not supposed to know anything about it just then?

Shandol had gone to Plainesville with her parents to apply for another office job she had heard was open. It was one of the first she had tried. It occurred to her again she hadn't heard of any job openings. Perhaps they weren't drawn to her attention anymore because it was considered she had a job here at home when needed. But at the aforementioned time Joel had hired "Little" Horn to take them. It had cost a dollar, which was still cheaper than the bus or train for all of them, and more convenient. Joel had ruled out the milk truck as unsuitable for Audrey now. It was a route almost as long as the school bus route, Shandol supposed. Actually Joe did not expect his women folk to ride the milk truck, though free, though Audrey had with him once. But Audrey had convinced Joel she must see the doctor. She had complained of a "fagged out" feeling, as she often did, and though she said she supposed it might be her blood pressure was low again, she decided she wanted it checked. Shandol supposed that a cover-up, but at the time seemed not unusual.

As it happened Freda Bell, "Little's" daughter, had gone also. And it also happened Shandol was nearly a half-day late to get the job. One of her former classmates had already been hired. Shandol was so disappointed she was near tears, but there was nothing she could do about it except feel sorry for herself. But there was Freda Bell, who talked too much. Shandol had to control herself.

The girls were then left with some time on their hands, because there would be a wait for Audrey to see the doctor. At first they window shopped. Then Shandol bought some writing paper and pencils. She bought very little else without her mother. Audrey had told her she felt she could help Shandol make her "money go farther" and get more value for what she did spend. The girls "finger shopped" around in some of the stores. Soon there was little to do except walk around the public square, which had the county court house in its center, and gaze at the displays in the store windows again. They crossed the four streets, leading in each of four directions, located in the center of each of the square's four sides. Each street had a sign in the middle of it advising "Keep To The Right" for the benefit of motorists entering or leaving the square.

"We may's well go to the waitin' room upstairs in Mayer's Hardware store and wait," Shandol finally suggested.

Mayer's Hardware was rather an inadequate name. There *was* a hardware store, but it was mostly in the basement. There were small tools and nails, bolts and odds and ends on the street level floor.

Back of that was the office. The remainder of the street level floor was much like a ten-cent store or even a department store. There were cosmetics and grooming aids, jewelry, candy, novelties, toys, school supplies, stationary, a large assortment of dress goods and patterns, kitchen utensils and notions, seeds in the spring and men's ready-to-wear. It was a large store.

On a balcony floor was a square waiting room, lined with seating of padded benches and a few chairs and one mirrored wall. A low divider separated it from women's ready-to-wear, including hats and undies, and children's wear. Up a stairway to the left—near the mirrored wall, to a much-used ladies' restroom. To the right a stairway to the furniture department. She had also been there seeking a job, but had been only a few minutes late then. A girl who was not only a classmate, but also rode the same school bus, was hired. She lived closer to Plainesville and her parents had their own means of transportation.

The waiting room was a popular place and practical. It was the first place to look if separated from a friend, or to see who could be seen. It's value to rest tired feet or backs was a thoughtful accommodation, exceptional and incomparable. Actually Shandol had eaten her school lunches she brought from home there on days fit to walk the few blocks from the high school. She was with friends. Otherwise they ate in the gym, on seats above the basketball court and physical education location.

"No, Shandol," Freda said, turning to her. "I gotta better idee. Let's git are fortunes told!"

Freda was taller than Shandol and of heavier build, almost plump. She had dark eyes set close together, fat rosy cheeks which diminished the size her eyes appeared, and a plain mouth of thick lips. Her curly brown hair, which she oiled, fell to her shoulders. She had on a calf-length straight-skirted dress of bold cotton print in reds, pinks, blues and greens, floral, with print on white ground.

"Is there a carnival here or somethin'?" Shandol asked quickly, surprised, her left eyebrow raised.

"Nah," Freda replied, grinning sheepishly. "Leastaways I don't guess so."

"Then how can we?" Shandol asked. "Besides, it's kinda wrong, ain't it?"

"What's it gonna hurt if'n it's done in fun?" Freda asked, her narrow brown eyes glinting questioningly. The curly hair framing her face made it seem babyish. "Come with me and I'll jest show yuh. There's this woman in the north of town. She ain't black, but just brunette and darker'n us."

"It ain't that," Shandol replied. "I hadn't thought of that. I can't decide if I should. If it's all right. And what Mom and Dad would say."

But Freda, pulling at Shandol's arm, had persuaded her.

The north part of town meant across the railroad tracks in every sense of the word. But this did not bother either Shandol or Freda. The fact is was considered the "colored" section did not bother either girl, and Shandol knew none of them. Freda had a speaking acquaintance with a family or so, she would admit. In truth the poorer white people lived there because of cheaper housing. Shandol knew this because when she was in high school she had had to go to a new school house in the area, built by government worker's project, to grade papers for the few NYA hours she could get. She had graded papers of pupils up to the third grade, the only grades there. She also checked workbooks and so on. The children were all white, but they had a decided underprivileged look about them and their clothing. Shandol had felt compassion, almost kinship with them. Shandol had also gone to the home of a girl, in the senior class, as she herself was then, to her home in this part of town. She was actually a friend of a girl Shandol rode the school bus with, though Shandol did recognize her as a girl in her business courses classes. Not only were they poor, but also the family was large, the father a drunkard and all too often spent too much of his meager income on liquor. He worked on a government project also. Shandol recalled how happy they all were when she had visited. It had been payday, and the younger children were excited about having chili soup and crackers for supper. Shandol's friend ate, and Shandol, not knowing how to get out of it, tried to also. Yet it worried her that she was taking food from the children, who apparently didn't always fare so well as to have enough to eat all the time. Shandol wondered then if they would have had to live in that part of town if they lived in Plainesville. She was glad they did not. The smaller town was better for them, she decided.

"Honestly hit's okay," Freda persisted. "And yuh know yuh wanna know what's ahead as well as I do. With Doug going off to school to study tuh be a preacher I wonder about things.

He told me he'd be gone so long he'd not ask me tuh wait for 'im. As if I'd cared, just so's he'd want me tuh wait. But since he ditn't, I won't, would you?"

"No," Shandol replied patiently, but thought: *How many times must she ask me that? She repeats it to everybody though, I believe she feels jilted and hurt.*

"Yuh're jest outta school," she reminded Shandol. "Don't yuh really wanna know? It only costs a quarter, have yuh got that much?"

132

"Yeah," Shandol answered. "I guess I can spare it from my graduation money. It don't seem much so guess I will, if you do." It just might be worth it, she thought. I just hope the folks don't think it the devil's work!

Freda had the name of being a quiet, decent girl, if perhaps somewhat boy crazy. She had been fond of Lester, and in fact had openly thought she was in love with him and he with her. But Audrey and Joel had not encouraged it. They considered her hardly comparable to Jane, whose father had always held a good job working for the state highway department. She was a relative of, and in company with, more educated people, and was firmly guided as to the company she could keep. It all seemed to Lester's credit that he was considered suitable. But Jane had loved Lester since grade school days. And to the correct manners and neatness of Jane, Freda, plump and rather slow learning just could not measure up. Freda wore long, calf-length cotton dresses, longer than anyone else's. The print of them was usually a bold floral print, the more colorful the better she considered the dress to be, until many washings relegated it to her everyday clothing. She wore low saddle oxfords and anklets everywhere, on every occasion, even to dress up for church.

Shandol had known Freda since her family had first moved to Greenway, because then Horns were fairly close neighbors. Even then, though a younger girl than Shandol, had done her share of the housework. She was now a good housekeeper and cook and did most of it for the family, even the many times her brother brought a small gang of boys home with him from the CCC camp for the weekend, as it was only some thirty miles away. So as housekeeping was her one accomplishment, she seemed to realize it. Because she actually realized her schooling was so limited, marriage was her main aim in life and she made no bones about that fact.

Shandol could even recall when Freda had decided not to go back to school anymore.

"I ain't goin' back to that school no more," she had told Shandol. "They cain't learn me nothin' at that school."

"I've managed," Shandol had replied vaguely, and changed the subject. But she was piqued and wondered if it were another gibe at her family again as Joel was on the school board. Freda made it seem the school was at fault or inadequate, and she was superior to Shandol for not needing it, while Shandol stayed in school. It had actually hurt Shandol's feelings and she had told Joel. Joel in turn had mentioned it to the school principal to see if there were something lacking for some of the town children. Yet it was not unusual for children to quit or attend school irregularly. Frequently they used lack of clothing as an excuse, especially shoes being inadequate. But this had not been the case with Freda.

The principal had paused briefly and replied in the hesitant way he had, the thick heavy lens of his glasses giving him a scholarly look.

"She's really right," he said. "Though it's not the school's fault. She has simply reached the end of her capacity to learn, and the fifth grade is probably as far as she could go. Perhaps it's just as well she blame the school, she couldn't really comprehend otherwise—or care, I dare say."

But Freda had a good reputation. She was a great help to her mother, who demanded it, as she preferred to spend a lot of her time in her favorite rocking chair embroidering, chewing her wad of tobacco, and spitting (actually more like squirting) in an old dishpan of ashes in front of the wood burning heating stove in the front room. In the summer wood ashes from the cook stove were put in it to "change" or freshen the pan of ashes.

Because of these things Shandol had wondered how Freda had rated a boyfriend such as Douglas Lindersilt in the first place. Shandol had even heard Freda, in her straight forward bluntness, criticize Shandol and the family because of that very "Campbellite church outfit." She was now part of it herself, because of Doug? They went to the small church in Plainesville, however, because of the people in That Church (as it was sometimes called) were so about who was welcome there, and people knew it! Shandol wondered if Joel, in his quiet, unassuming, but profound way, had not helped that family simply by example. One could never be sure, but Joel was sure he could leave a more lasting impression in such a way as to hope people could follow his life's trail to know by his faith he was sure where he was going, and was a lamp to those who needed a spark to get them to follow.

Shandol reasoned that Doug must have seen Freda's limitations, or, most likely, had had them pointed out to him by his parents or trusted friend. As of now he must have been shown her ultimate unsuitability as a minister's wife. Besides he would be years preparing himself, and would meet many young ladies along the way. It had been hopeless, except to Freda. Shandol had to admit Freda was particular about her boy friends. She rarely bothered with the boys from the CCC camp, because she did not expect to get to know them well enough. The town boys were just in and out, as at Sonnetts, and, as Shandol, could hardly get serious about them, except Lester Sonnett. Perhaps she had at first been too sure of him. But he had been married these three months now and, of course, had not been qualified to remain in the CCC camp.

134

Freda had been rambling on about Doug, Shandol suddenly realized, startled, and she hadn't been listening. Apparently Freda hadn't asked her anything so she was unaware Shandol's mind wandered. But Shandol was sure she had heard it all before. On the north side of the square they turned north on Penn Avenue, which was as usual, a busy, crowded street. They soon noticed that farther down the sidewalk of the long decline a smallish crowd had gathered. When they had reached it they had realized it was a "street meeting." A man and two women possibly, his wife and daughter, were singing, as the man and older woman strummed guitars and a mandolin, respectively. As they sang, a Bible lay at the edge of the sidewalk and a hat, crown down on the book, was nearby for the inevitable donations. As Shandol and Freda made their way through the crowd and walked on they heard the end of the song, "Jericho Road," and the man began delivering a "message." It was not an unfamiliar sight to Shandol and had they sung again she might have wanted to have stopped. But she and Freda made their way through the crowd to hurry on to their destination.

After several blocks they were out of this part of that business district, having crossed the railroad tracks and gone up a steep hill on an orangey-colored gravel road. They turned to the left for a short distance, then north again two blocks and then Freda pointed out the modest white bungalow at the right far corner of the next crossroads. The small house was situated in a small neat yard with rose bushes, a few other shrubs, evergreens and a small flower garden in the front. It had a front porch, well kept with grey paint. Dormer's hung into the roof. A neatly dressed, auburn-haired lady answered their timed knock, and invited them inside. Shandol immediately surmised the woman "did something" to her hair, as she could see she actually looked older than her mother. She wore make-up which was tastefully, subtly applied.

"We're here to git our fortunes told," Freda blurted nervously.

"Come right this way then." They went inside.

There were few preliminaries. Both girls were too nervous for light friendly chatter. Freda followed the lady first, after she had inquired which of the girls wanted to be first. Shandol had time to look about her as she sat in the comfortable living room. The carpet was colorful and floral, she noted, the furnishings usual and functional for a front room. It all looked well kept and clean. On one shiny occasional table she noticed photographs, one a young man in an army uniform. *He's likely her son,* Shandol thought. She also noticed through another door a clean, shiny kitchen, all white and red, though black and yellow colors were added to a colorfully blocked design inlaid linoleum on the floor.

Shandol could hardly keep from comparing it to her uncle's and their own. (She had seen her uncle's home six years before when he had paid a man with a small truck to take them.) Of course their own worn ones hardly compared, so she quickly turned her mind from it. It was depressing.

Then it was Shandol's turn. She was shown into a small room which resembled an oversized closet, though there was a window. Then it came to her it was perhaps actually a small bed room used as a sewing or store room, as she realized the small space they were in was actually due to its being a curtained area. They were seated near the window, with a drawn, opaque curtain, at a small square table, the chairs on opposite sides of it so the two were facing each the other. The lady did not introduce herself, nor did Shandol.

Shandol saw she was facing a rather large woman, dark despite all her auburn hair. She looked all of forty-ish, which bore out the supposition the young man in the photograph in uniform was her son. A gold band on her finger was the only jewelry Shandol noted. Her piercing dark eyes were missing little, Shandol was sure. The first thing she handed Shandol was a deck of cards to shuffle. Shandol was stupefied. She took them as she might a hot potato, undecided and carefully. Shuffling cards was something she did not do well, especially this type. She was abhorrent first, then shocked and ill at ease. It had not occurred to her to wonder what this entailed. She took the cards, trying to control her feelings. She was sure her awkwardness showed. There was a vast difference to her in cards with "aces and spades" and the ones Shandol played "Books" and "Snap" with her brothers and friends at home. They were the only cards allowed in the house.

Shandol knew that her brother, Lester, could play "pitch." How he had been criticized: In fact it had been Freda in her blunt, gloating way, who had informed Shandol. He had learned at her home, then had the nerve to taunt Shandol! "Sonnetts do it. Lester hisself right hyear in our house!"

"It won't be the way to get Lester," Shandol had fumed. "Dad don't like it!" There, that shut her up—until next time. But Shandol found herself in this defensive position more than she admitted; or was perhaps becoming more sensitive to such slurs. Are we like preacher's kids? she'd asked herself. You'd think it sometimes, instead of the poor laborer working on a government project job! The same had happened when Lester smoked cigarettes. Joel had punished him once, threatened his privileges, what few he could, but apparently the urge to be accepted, the wish to belong was greater, the coaxing such that he found himself unprepared to resist the temptations.

And Shandol resented the fact she was made to feel guilty about it. They seemed to want the stigma—if that is what was implied—to rub off on her, especially by Freda. And Shandol had long since vowed to herself that no matter what she would never take up that habit. No matter where she went or under what circumstances she found herself she would never be taunted behind her back for doing that. Freda herself did not smoke—though she knew as well as Shandol, some girls were sneaking around doing it. Even Freda recognized the busybodies, making things known, and tearing at one's reputation.

Shandol watched the "fortune-teller" lay the cards in groups on the table. She was too nervous to notice how many stacks or recall much about them at all later, much to her chagrin. But the woman had picked them up and placed them about as she spoke. No questions, just comments.

"You are just out of high school," she began. "No job yet. You received some graduation gifts, but none were elaborate. You're of a rather large family. Your mother is in poor health, but your father is worse off as you'll find out. Your mother is expecting a baby at this very time." Shandol squirmed in her chair, causing the wood chair to squeak. "Your family likes music, one has talent he should develop, but it isn't you. Do not go into a nursing career, you are too frail in build for the demands. You will marry a garage mechanic, or of some such trade, and have three children—two girls and a boy." Shandol was unaware of the sparkle that brought to her eyes. Mostly girls! She'd love them. She got so tired of boys. "You're a brown-eyed blond," the fortune-teller continued, "and you will go with several young men before you marry. But none will appeal to you as will a curly, dark haired, blue-eyed man about four years older than you are. You will be married within two years, however. Look into NYA work, yuh might get a start there." And on and on. She clicked off predictions as rapidly as she could pick up a card replace it and "read" the groupings and their positions, Shandol guessed. Some of the things frankly amazed Shandol, she had to admit to herself. How *did* she know or guess what she had said, which was right.

"What's the charge?" Shandol asked, when it was over and she rose to go.

"Oh, I'm not allowed to charge," she replied quickly. "But I'm usually left a quarter consideration for my time."

As the girls had retraced their way back to town, Freda was truly excited. She would hardly listen to a word Shandol could say, if she could have said anything. Freda had been told she had met the man she would marry (which was of most interest to her, but that she wasn't as yet going with him).

137

"Well," she reasoned, "I ain't hardly had time jest gettin' over Doug and all, have I? *She* told me he was tall and blond and well built. I cain't 'magine who it can be."

"Do yuh know anyone whose like that?" Shandol asked. "Maybe someone from camp Loren has brought home?"

"Well, I do have a date Saturday night with Orville Brock, but he's goin' to the army—how awful!" she replied. "Hey!" she perked up and continued, "he's tall and blond, blue-eyed and I ain't never gone with him before. But I'll wait fer 'im if he wants me to if he's the one. I shore will!"

Orville Brock, Shandol had heard, was the son of a gasoline service station owner, rather recently arrived. There were two such stations. This was across the street at the northeast corner of the crossroads, and was not the bus station, which was the one past the house on the corner on the Greenway side of the highway. Freda had tried to recall everything she had learned about him. At first she wasn't sure, she told Shandol, she even cared to date him, but then she became anxious about it. She was excited and nervous, because then she thought so much might depend on that first date. (By now Freda and Orville had indeed become a serious twosome, and most considered a wedding imminent, sooner or later.)

Freda had also been told her brother was secretly married. That had turned out to be true. It helped clinch the idea for Freda that Orville was her true intended indeed.

Freda, in time, asked Shandol what she had been told, as they dawdled, sometimes completely stopped, on the way back up town. Shandol told her about the dark-haired, blue-eyed mechanic and the three children, smiling, as she was sure Freda would be interested in that, adding what she could recall handily between Freda's exclamations: "She's a real great fortune-teller! How does she do it?"

Shandol mentioned her mother's supposed pregnancy. At Freda's interested look, Shandol regretted it. She should have asked her mother first. And Freda was so taken in by the whole thing. She was afraid Freda would repeat it, because she was taking it all so seriously. Shandol hurriedly tried to explain how very unlikely that was; tried to laugh it away, wondering how a mere woman claiming to be a fortune-teller could know! But Shandol continued to wonder aloud.

Her mother had gone to the doctor. Shandol saw a knowing look come into Freda's eyes and the grin on her face, making her cheeks look even fatter. Shandol had tried to dispel any suspicions until, at least, she knew for sure.

"It's not unusual for Mama to go to see a doctor," she reminded

Freda. "Her health and nerves bein' such that she has to have a check up on it every so often anyway. Her blood pressure's either up or down, I don't remember which, so she worries and first thing Dad takes her to see the doctor."

Shandol had later asked her mother, who had replied, defensively, as Shandol now thought, though she hadn't then. Audrey had merely seemed meek. "The doctor said he could find no reason for me to have such suspicions. So far as he'd say, I'm not." Audrey seemed insistent. Shandol was sure Audrey wanted to believe it herself. But Shandol realized the reason her parents had gone to Plainesville was to check into that very possibility. And when they had gone back in two month's time there was no doubt. Shandol had been told then, and the suspicions that her mother was covering-up by being evasive and vague left her. It had been hard to accept at first for the older children, but now they had accepted the fact and hoped there would be a baby sister. Shandol often wished for a sister, but nearer her own age. But she too decided there were enough in the family.

Shandol soon finished the ironing. She had been so engrossed in her thought the time and work had gone by smoothly. Audrey put it away, except Shandol's own. Then it came to her it seemed she had been working for hours and the afternoon was almost gone, but the remainder of it would be her own, for awhile anyway. She took a book to her room to read. These were in a room between her own and the front of the house. These were also her favorite magazines, which had mostly been given her, some clippings she saved, and the box of books, her favorites separate and on the floor. There was no furniture in the room. This was one of her favorite books her father had had for years, she supposed, and she had read it several times already, but she had nothing else. Shandol had scarcely noticed the bits of lint which gathered at the joining cracks of the four-inch planks which made up the wood floor. As Shandol relaxed on her bed she realized how nice it felt to rest her back and legs. And, being more tired than she realized, she soon drifted off into a peaceful sleep.

She awoke to the sound of music downstairs. She felt refreshed and in a brightened mood. Her mother had gone ahead with the evening meal, which was almost ready when Shandol went downstairs.

Phil and Bobby were making the music. Bobby, like herself, was slow in learning the chords and having confidence to use what he knew, which meant when to make the changes. It had been only recently Phil had ordered a chording manual, which included reading notes and so on, and until then could barely identify what he was playing by ear. Since then he had learned more, dared more difficult chords, and because he seemed so interested and loved doing it, it seemed to come so easy to him. Bobby never played anywhere except at home. He was unsure of himself, discouraged when he compared himself to his brother, because he knew he hadn't the ear for it as Phil did.

Phil had had only a few lessons on the violin from Joel, who played mostly old-time fiddle tunes, a few hymns he loved, also by ear, though he knew and could read notes also. Phil had added other tunes from Greenway's fiddler, Steve Werst, who played for dances and parties for miles around. By now Phil could learn the tunes fairly well by himself by ear, enjoyed playing, or practicing to perfect the ones he was learning. Shandol had a hard time recalling the titles of most of them, and wondered how Phil could, besides remembering which tune was what. She marveled at it.

Lester and Phil had enjoyed many sessions of making music and when he left Phil missed him, because that left only Shandol and Bobby. Either one of them wasn't much of a choice, but he did put up with them, which they admitted was about what it amounted to.

Sometimes there was criticism of this music. Why couldn't Phil learn it properly? It was, of course, out of reason. But some of their *church* friends were not so appreciative of it, Shandol had learned. It was referred to as hillbilly (or humorously as 'Ozark' mountain William) music. They would admit they liked it they would declare they wouldn't admit it to anyone else. Shandol and the whole family had practically been raised on it. Joel played, Audrey's father and even Uncle Lafey would join in when he was there, while they were on the farm, chording on the piano. Audrey had also done this, but they had no piano now. They could not move it so far. Uncle Lafey had learned to play many instruments through correspondence courses, preparing for the work he now did. Shandol frequently brought this favorite uncle to defend her brother and the music, to those few who would not accept it, then let the matter drop. It was her only argument and should be sufficient so far as she was concerned.

That was just one of the things she must defend concerning her beliefs. Once she had heard some girls defend their wearing red nail polish. Gloria Dahle had remarked her cousin thought clear nail polish should be used. It wasn't so evident one was wearing polish and was natural and pretty too.

"Why be a hypocrite?" Gloria had said, in defending her own red fingertips. Gloria's mother belonged to a church which frowned on the use of cosmetics in any form. Shandol wondered if Gloria were trying to get at her. The truth was Shandol preferred a faintly pink polish which she thought enhanced the natural color. It also kept

Joel from making negative comments, which encouraged her. Her brothers had similar opinions. Shandol supposed Gloria thought of her as meek and undaring and she did nothing to dispel the notion.

Was old-time fiddle music so old-timey? Was pale nail polish a sign of weakness? (To Shandol any at all was daring!) Couldn't one have one's own preference? So some of the fiddle tunes were played at square dances—not in their home. What did keeping up appearances prove, she wondered. Well, perhaps she'd learn. Meantime, any comeback she could think of was usually after it was too late to give it.

So if she felt like it, which she now did, she would tap, or even dance by herself, lively, gracefully, smoothly in time with the swift tune of the fiddle, in her own interpretation of it. (But that strictly and only within the confines of her home and family.) Or, with it, as now, sing aloud to one she did recognize: *"The possom's tail am bare / the rabbit has no tail at all / just a little bitty bunch of hair!"*

Joel looked up from his paper fondly. Shandol had hardly been aware of him.

"Yuh still hafta 'physical ed', don't you?" he asked. This he joked about and it stemmed from Shandol's dancing, tapping, practicing the exercises (some in song) she had had in high school. She had added some of her own. How self-conscious she had been in high school! It had been sheer torture. She could loosen up, lose her inhibitions and do them all much better at home, than before the class and the critical eye of the teacher. But dance with a young man? The thought terrified her. She was glad The Church forbade it, at least in teaching.

Then Shandol realized she shouldn't be fooling around so much. It was Saturday night. She had a date. She took a bath, a good tub-soaking one; at least the best one can get in a wash tub. She was ready when Dean came, but stayed in her room to be called. She had heard "nice girls" did not appear eager and ready to date anyone, and casual was what she wanted to be with Dean.

It was proved a difficult date for her, almost a frightening one to the sheltered Shandol.

CHAPTER 12

"Look hit's glowin' now in the window," six year-old Kenneth Casey Sonnett insisted. "That house's on fire!"

Fire? FIRE! Oh, no!

"Don't say hit," Audrey Lou Sonnett scolded her youngest son automatically.

"Danged if it ain't," Phillip Wade replied. "Hey, Dad!" He yelled at his father though Joel was nearby ready to open the screen door to go inside. "Rhodes's house's on fire!"

The Sonnett family had just returned from Sunday night Young People's Meeting, the nearest thing to church in Greenway on a regular Sunday night basis. The two oldest boys (still at home), Phillip Wade and Robert Blake, had arrived first and were lingering on the front porch, already sprawled in almost sitting positions, Phil leaning back on an elbow on the rough unpainted boards of the small front porch, while Bobby was leaning against the unpainted, rough weather-boarded side of the house, at the opposite sides of the door, yet well away from Audrey's various, large potted plants there. Per haps they dreaded going inside lest it still be hot from the summer day. A slight breeze had shoved the sun from view and it was yet barely dusk.

K.C. had pointed to the white frame house to the west, approximately halfway between their home and the railroad, and on the far end of a lane that turned off from the main street, approximately a block west of the Old Hotel. An alley at the corner of Sonnett's yard was also an extension of that street, east and west. The place cornered the lanes on the hillside.

"That there's smoke comin' from that house," K.C. had said. "Ain't in no chimney neither," he added excitedly.

First, Phil reminded them all, including his youngest brother it could be a trash fire. After all the family was planning to move. But K.C., then Thomas Edmund, his next older brother, had watched: And before their horrified, very eyes another "Greenway's Nightmare" became a reality.

Others walking along also saw and neighbors and townfolk soon began to gather, as though the "grapevine" were mental telepathy.

Shandol, who hadn't gone, pleading a headache, came down after hearing Phil's excited yell. Phil, Joel and Bobby were already leaving the front yard. Lester Lee kissed his wife, Jane Ann, and said he would join them. They had walked home with Joel and Audrey. They had said they hated to leave Shandol alone, but she assured them not to worry; she would not be good company because of her headache, and she simply hoped Dean didn't show up, her head hurt so.

"What's up?" Shandol asked, looking first at Jane, then her mother. They had just come inside the screen door, which opened to the now old-fashioned double doors into the front hallway. They had, of course, been commanded to "stay here" with the "little boys."

"Rhodes's house is apparently on fire," Jane answered. "They maybe can get to it in time and save it."

But it soon became apparent that was not to be. There were people milling around, they could see, carrying out furniture. Then a large blaze broke out in the roof, following what appeared to be a small explosion. Fire seemed to engulf all the rooms at once. Those there could then only back off and watch it burn.

What a waste, Shandol thought. It was one of the better built, better looking homes, though an older one to be sure. It was not modern, but how many were in Greenway? Shandol knew of none even in the finest of houses, except running water in the kitchen. The house was adequate for a family if not too large.

"Wonder what happened," Shandol mused aloud. "At this time uh night I mean."

"Can't imagine," Audrey said, obviously concentrating on the sight before her and "her men" there. They watched and waited until they saw the men drifting away, even toward their house. Walking along with the boys was Bucky Sandler. Shandol and her mother went to the porch to meet them. Jane had already gone outside. Joel was not one of them and it was learned he had stayed either to help or just talk to other men there.

"They ditn't woun't nobody to help." Bucky spoke matter of factly. He was a youth of average build, light brown hair, with shifty, mischievous blue eyes, tanned face, and a few years older than Phil. "I think they set that far," he added. "Theyze ready fer it! Rugs all rolled up—"

"They're gonna move," Shandol reminded him.

"But they woultn't let nobody in only to carry stuff out," Bucky insisted. "Finally they just threw a lit lamp on some rags 'n papers 'n stuff."

"Surely not!" Audrey replied, aghast.

"Uhnuther house burnt fer insurance, shore as shootin," Bucky declared, unabashed.

"But they can't—" Shandol began, but stopped. She had been about to say they couldn't hope to get by with that, but decided it would be futile. Besides, she knew the gossip would persist. Such rumors had followed other such fires, hadn't they? How'd they get by with it if it were true?

How was it the gossips weren't challenged if it weren't? Or did they even know of it? Was it all considered accidents due to carelessness or unavoidable accident. In most cases the owners lived elsewhere; did they care? It seemed not as they were all insured. How had the store owners, a few years ago, managed? Of course the store had burned during the night and virtually gutted before discovered. Arlane Gilmire's boyfriend's parents and when they moved she was sure her life was ruined. But they hadn't gone far so the romance had blossomed. But that did not stop the gossips declaring they "heared" it was not doing much business, relatively new as it was, and the owner managed it. Had they done something? Dared they? This fire, on the other hand seemed so blatant! But Rhodeses would be gone so they wouldn't care about gossip. Why had they decided to move? They never stayed anywhere long it seemed.

"Where'll they go tonight?" Audrey wondered aloud.

"Prob'ly tuh one of her sister's 'er mother's place, or here 'n there, Miz Sonnett." Bucky replied.

Perhaps. Her mother lived directly across the street, south. She would no doubt welcome her virtually blind daughter. But their three room rented home seemed hardly adequate for the family. The older boy was married. He was a good looking young man, dark wavy hair, falling over one side of his forehead no matter how hard he tried to slick it back. He had a handsome, though rugged face, with forceful brown eyes. That one summer Lester had paid him on occasions to drive his Model A Ford to take Lester to go see the "child preacher" after they left Greenway. Shandol had gone also, which had caused the gossips to circulate that fact, adding that Sonnetts had had to pay so that Shandol got to go somewhere! It was quite ridiculous. She went with her brother because Lester asked her and he paid for it. She would not have been allowed to go with Bill—with or without Lester. His background was too "shady" and how he made his money, which he seemed to have, bet wasn't gainfully employed that much. Anyway, they were all also surprised, especially Shandol herself. She knew he had a serious girl friend, whom he had since married, a very young bride. But they had to quit that means of transportation. Lester tried to explain it to Bill and others over and over. Bill seemed to enjoy the joke, and said nothing, so the gossip persisted until he married. Then the gossips passed the rumor that when he had gone job and house hunting and was gone a week and his young bride stayed with his parents, she had slept clutching a pair of his trousers. They had finally settled in Plainesville. Perhaps his parents would also.

The other Rhodes boy was younger, twelve or so. He was dark like his brother but chunkier built, He did not have the muscular look his brother had.

"Maybe they've got a truck comin 'and be gone yet tonight," Phil said. "Heck, they're all packed up ready tuh be loaded." Joel also believed this because they seemed not to fret or be concerned about their plans.

Well, another family was leaving Greenway. They would rarely see them. The gossip would die down, when something else came along.

"It could be me ag'in," Shandol muttered to herself, "after today."

Once the family went inside it took awhile for the excitement to abate. The members of the Sonnett family discussed it. After all it had caused, not only excitement, but also terror! It became a huge blaze and there was concern for awhile that, should the wind shift directions, sparks could land on their own high roof, which was of dry wood shingles that would likely ignite easily and perhaps burn rapidly. It caused ripples and shudders to discuss it—even with the many people to help. The Old Hotel was two stories, old and high and would be difficult to get to to extinguish a fire.

"If this keeps up, so many fires, no one will be able to get insurance here pretty soon." Joel observed.

Shandol thought of it apprehensively after going to bed. She worried that a spark might have landed on the roof and was smoldering, waiting until they were asleep to ignite into flames. She also feared fires could result when the flue burned out. That frightened them all. So much so that a ladder was kept handy to reach the back porch roof, and one had long since been attached to the roof near the kitchen chimney, which was also used from the dining room for heating. They were used to carrying water up to dampen the dry shingles around it. The flue to the front room had never burned out—yet. But it wasn't used so much. Shandol did not know if the place was insured, but what they had was not, and so much of it could not be replaced. No one would even consider Joel Sonnett to want a fire. His reputation would eliminate such a possibility.

Shandol sighed. Because she recalled something else which she had temporarily forgotten. That fire would not be all that she would remember as being significant about this day. Not for her. The Rhodeses would be gone only to be recalled upon occasions. They had not been close as neighbors. Nor would she recall the day as one in which a member of the prestigious county singing quartet, with his brother-in-law, Harry Bright, who was Joel's favorite checker playing partner, had come by for a few games. They had not stayed long and it still left a long afternoon. Shandol had had to entertain the quartet member's young daughter, which had proved to be no chore. They sat on a round, crocheted rag rug on the grass in the shade of the house, at the edge of the potato patch, with the border of annual flowers now in bloom nearest the house. The girl had talked about herself, her family, school, her likes and dislikes and so on to Shandol. She seemed too dressed up to play games and too hot to care to anyway. Shandol was vexed at herself as she drew a blank trying to think of riddles or some quiet game. But the time had passed rather quickly and the girl, so self-assured, and almost citified, was gone.

Shandol would remember the day in a very different way, and now with much speculation! It was the day after that night! She would recall how it all came about, and it took her mind from worrying about a blaze. The events seemed to form in her mind so vividly.

Sunday mornings were unhurried in the Sonnett household. Sunday school was later at The Church where they attended than the other town churches. This was because so many of the members were farmers who had chores to attend to before they could leave home, and then some distance to travel. They were sometimes accused of just dragging around by those from town, impatiently awaiting, grumbling because they were delayed, but nothing seemed to change.

Shandol headed almost straight for the kitchen that morning to bathe her red eyes, while deciding an aspirin might relieve the tightness that gripped her aching head. She dreaded to face herself in a mirror, feeling sure she would find herself as aged and faded as a mauled, mishandled blossom, yet she could not contain the overwhelming compulsion to do so. She went to the medicine cabinet to get the aspirin and furtively, defiantly glanced into the mirror, expecting that it too might crack, but found her face relatively unchanged. Perhaps the barely visible redness, much diminished now, would be taken for being mere sleepiness after being out on a date last night. It wasn't unusual and she felt better after it had been washed, except for the tightness of her head.

"What did you do last night?" This was Audrey's inevitable question after every date, and as now, came after the family had all been seated, at the table, the blessing said, and Audrey was pouring coffee for the older members of the family. The question, by now, Shandol expected and could usually answer honestly, off-handed and with glib tongue. But this morning she was quaking in her shoes, and "scared fitless" lest she say or do something that would bring about a third degree questioning. It was sheer torture.

"We went to Waiton to see a show," she replied, nervously, glancing about to see if anyone could see she felt differently and make some remark, which would cause her to burst into tears. But it seemed breakfast as usual and the question so usual it hardly warranted attention, except from Joel. He would appear to be busy eating, but his ears would be on her words, luckily, rather than on her pale face. "If it seemed long it's a double feature—I think I've said. And then we ate and—and visited and then home." She deliberately neglected to make it clear the "eating" was a box of popcorn they each had eaten during the show, instead of having stopped for a hamburger or other snack, as she had had to explain so explicitly before; or that the visiting was a brief encounter with some friends of Dean's before they left Folks Consent.

"He'll be here today, I suppose," Phil asked, automatically.

"Strange you wondered," she replied, more offhandedly than she would have thought possible. "The fact is he may not. His mother may want the car to go see her sister or somebody. That is if she don't change her mind."

The truth was Shandol didn't know if Dean planned to come or not. It was true his mother had said she might want to go visiting a sister. Shandol wasn't sure if that meant Dean's aunt, or a sister in the country church, where the women were sisters and men, including the preacher, Pluto, brothers.

And if they ask me why he doesn't come anymore—if he doesn't— I'll just excuse it all by explaining it may have just been an excuse. Perhaps he has a new girl friend. He is young, after all, and wouldn't mean all that much. Perhaps he liked less timid and rowdier girls, how was she to know?

"You're rather pale," Audrey looked concerned. "Yuh feelin' all right?"

"I'm all right, Mama," she said, "just sleepy, I guess." *Oh, I wish I could be let alone,* she moaned inwardly. *If it isn't one hovering over me it's the other.* No use letting them know what a dismal failure she had been last night on her date, she thought.

"She jest loses uh pound ever' date," Phil chided, amusingly, the twinkle in his eyes, the slight wave of his brown hair falling over one eye. He was merely teasing her, he thought, and that all was normal. "She's so afraid she don't say the right thing at the right time and makes her a nervous wreck!" He would never have guessed how true, especially the "nervous wreck."

"Oh, bug dust," she replied, low. "You and yer eagle eyed mind-readin'." *If only you knew,* her mind said, *how terrible I feel, even though I didn't do anything—I didn't! Could you understand why I do feel such a failure.*

"Well, I gotta be gittin'," Phil got up to leave the table as he spoke, "if I'm gonna make it to Horn's to go to Plainesville to church with 'em."

The Horns went to Plainesville, though to attend the same denomination as The Church. They simply had never had the encouragement to go to Greenway's. There Freda had met Doug. Calvin, her brother, and Phil each had a girl friend in the small church, near, though not across, the railroad tracks in Plainesville. Calvin was older than Phil, in fact older than Shandol. Sundays were about the only times the boys saw the girls, unless they met at Plainesville on Friday or Saturday nights, when the truck, usually other than Horn's small one went. At such times they attended movies or whatever other there might be to attend. Sometimes Horns spent the day on Sunday visiting relatives or friends and the girl friends could stay. The girls were sisters, but hardly looked it. The one Clavin went with was nearer Phil's age, and not as pretty as her sister. Phil's girl was a petite blond, with large blue eyes, perfectly shaped face, with strikingly even features, a smiling mouth showing perfect even white teeth. Her complexion seemed baby fresh. She was six years older than Phil but looked about his age. Shandol had seen only her picture, and Phil's biased, she was sure, opinion. Phil added that Cal's "girl" was dark-haired, darker complexioned and dark violet eyes. But her mouth was large, he thought, and her nose turned up. Not ugly, he had quickly clarified, just not the beauty her sister was. So the young men could team up some social life with the spiritual and the family rarely missed a Sunday, including evening services. The oldest Horn boy had joined the army soon after marriage; and Freda left her heart at a certain gasoline service station, if her boyfriend did not go. He and Freda sometimes attended the evening services. The youngest Horn child was a boy of three, "Little" Horn worked on the same job as Joel Sonnett.

Shandol went with the other members of her family to Sunday school. Audrey said she felt fine and knew she would be offered a ride home, which she'd be glad to accept. There was nothing else for Shandol to do but go, she had no excuse. She had a distracted frame of mind, a lack of feeling she wanted kept secret. She felt apart even from herself. And because of the Saturday night baths helping to see her two younger brothers were ready, in light colored cotton shirts Audrey had made and hand-me-down pants kept for church.

It was a gloriously bright early fall day. It seemed a day to reach out to the warm sun and late but abundant flowers, grasses, even rag weeds, which lined the road up which they had to walk. A day to greet people who came to the post office when the train was due, as they were going home from church. Then was always a time of activity. The dust hardly settled from one car until another went by, or stopped, which ever the case. Shandol was so preoccupied she failed to realize she could remember little of the service, who was there and her part in it. She supposed she acted normal enough, or she would have heard.

To Shandol there was only this churning distraction with in herself; and before mid-afternoon proclaimed she had a severe headache, which she hadn't been able to shake off, and if anything, was worse. She swallowed another aspirin, went to her room and laid down upon her bed with the book she had started before. She tried to read awhile, headache or not, but soon realized she was reading the same paragraph several times and still not getting anything from it. The words she read did not register. So she put the book aside and lay miserably prostrate. She tried not to think, but just shut out everything, but she soon discovered that impossible.

She wondered if Dean would really ever dare come again. She actually hoped he wouldn't. And what a change in her life if he didn't, she realized. She knew how much she would miss going places with him. She could, for friendship's sake, over look his obvious lack of schooling, rationalizing it was just the hillbilly upbringing, which he had had no control over. But he also amazed her sometimes at the things he had picked up, useful to him and his way of life. He was worldly wise beyond most young people she knew, yet that too served him making him self-assured and independent.

Her mind went back to their first meeting. Then she remembered he wanted to do it all over again! How quaint she thought that, because she doubted it could be done that way ever again. Never. There would not be the same surprise element, spontaneity, the reticence, and the absolutely completely unexpectedness of it. She remembered the beauty of that glorious day and how perfect it now seemed. She herself felt lovely, lighthearted and exuberant. No, it couldn't be reproduced just exactly like that ever again. She could never recapture her feelings of expectancy and the novelty of it again. How pretty she had looked peering down into the well water! How marvelously she had felt! But just as surely as that bucket had hit the water and shattered the image, so now had her heart and well-being been shattered as though a bucket of rude experience had hit her full in the face as cold and shocking as the water might have been.

All about the house was quiet and the warmth gnawed at Shandol. She knew there was a checker game downstairs, but she wasn't interested. Her mother was likely reading the Sunday paper in the bedroom downstairs. Tommy and K.C. were playing outside, coming occasionally to ask their mother to settle a disagreement or register a protest as to how one or the other was playing. She finally told them if they couldn't play together without so much quarreling and fussing they would both have to stay on the back porch where she could see for herself. They didn't dare disturb Joel as he concentrated deeply on his games. The boys seemed to make up as usual. Later their little friend came to play and they seemed to do better.

As the afternoon wore on Shandol became more tense. She wished she had something else to occupy her mind. She realized she had forgotten herself while the young girl had been there the hour or so. What a lot she had to learn! But still Shandol wished for something to occupy her mind now. She wished that Dean might come, reassure her that last night had never happened. As that was impossible all she had was a load of misgivings, both that he might come and then that he wouldn't or couldn't dare possibly show up. If he didn't what more could she say to the family? If he did what could she say to him? How had it all come about, so premeditated and deliberate on his part? And then all became so out of control. The date had started as any other date they had had, so far as she could see.

Dean had come early. The date was to go to a movie; and because it had been Saturday night they had gone to Waiton, which was south of Folks Consent on the same interstate highway, to the movies. Every Saturday night there was a double feature there. One was inevitably Gene Autry or Roy Rogers, usually, and a love or adventure story, some in color and very pretty, such as *Aloma of the South Seas*, she thought was the name of it, which she had particularly enjoyed. In fact Shandol enjoyed the dates, watching the shows, munching popcorn, since she had met and gone out with Dean. She could be so comfortable and at ease with him because she had no worry as to trying to impress him. She was simply herself, as he so plainly seemed to be himself.

As the movies came to an end Shandol supposed the evening would end much as the others had. Usually they would stop at Folks Consent and park in the center of main street, as it was so marked. They watched the dancers through the large glass windows. The young girls in shorter skirts danced the jitterbug. Some girls danced with dates or other fellows, but some still younger ones danced together. Usually Shandol and Dean watched during the time it took to eat a sack of potato chips each and drink a bottle of soda pop each. Sometimes there were couples who knew Dean and likely wanted to see the girl he was dating, who would come to the car to

150

be introduced and exchange light conversation. At other times fist fights had broken out in the tavern and the fighters were promptly evicted to settle their differences outside. Dean was usually amused as he usually knew those involved and realized they were drunk. It did not amuse Shandol. She hated to see them in that state.

Neither Shandol nor Dean had a desire to go inside the dance hall, though next to it was the cafe and tavern. Shandol's dancing experiences were very limited; she was much too unsure of herself. In fact her dancing lessons had been restricted to those she had had in her high school physical education class in Plainesville and Joel had complained about them being taught his daughter when he did not believe in dancing. It had been a difficult course for her because she knew how her father felt about that part of it at least. It made her so self-conscious she was miserable. She learned to take the tests with some of the good dancers and had made the grade, but it hadn't seemed so enjoyable when being graded on it, and that usually was before she had had time to catch on sufficiently and be good at it. So many already knew how. Some had been fun, but they had been little more than singing party games. Simple square dancing she hadn't learned very well because they didn't dwell on it long enough. But she had learned the waltz fairly well. But it was still almost impossible for her to relax and enjoy it. In school she had preferred games, volleyball, girl's basketball, but only for the exercises were these gone into. So she and Dean would laugh at how im possible their dancing would be. Shandol with her "board back" and Dean with his proverbial "two left feet."

Last night they had not stopped at Folks Consent, but a mile or so past they had turned into a dark, lonely lane which was not unusual either. Spoon Hill Pond was there. It was a square formed by the highway connecting country lanes and back parallel to the highway the lanes joined. It was near a cemetery. She supposed this would be their destination and wondered who else might be there. There were trees, brush, rocks of various sizes and even bare places due to travel of couples frequenting the spot. There was a small frog pond in the middle, usually in some chorus or a lonesome baritone. There was some semblance of privacy here. Though there was love-making, it was not "heavy-petting" leading to a girl's undoing. There really wasn't *that* much privacy. It was actually a place for couples to go to talk, to plan and just be together. Sometimes the cars were close enough to each other to hear a car radio (Dean's car had none), or even to talk back and forth. Sometimes a couple would leave their car and go sit with another couple. Other times couples brought their snacks there to enjoy.

Of course the parents considered it a promiscuous place for a boy to take advantage of and to weaken a good girl's morals, and strongly warned them not to go there if they knew. Shandol had not tried to explain it to her parents. They would not be able to see it as it really was. Parents seemed to suffer agonies of lack of confidence in the young at such times, lamented their lack of judgment as to what could happen, hoping and praying for the best. Shandol had no hope of making them see there was little more privacy there than in the front room at home with family members strolling about. At Spoon Hill Pond some fellow might go to a car and ask for cigarettes, or a light. Perhaps he would need a push. ("Sorry to bother, but I can't get my car started. Wouldya help?") This happened especially if the radio had played too long perhaps. Again, someone might ask to have headlights beamed on his car to change a flat tire, or try to ascertain some engine problem. Sometimes also a small amount of gasoline was needed to prime a carburetor, jokingly admitting he must be low on "push water." Only to be answered by, "well yuh can't wean it!?" All these had not happened to them but she had heard of them and Shandol decided the main difference here and at home was that here there were no little brothers to be going in and out with pestering comments or embarrassing questions, or just traipse in and out for attention and curiosity. Even Phil might want to entertain them! So in her mind, unstated, unofficially but steadfast as a rule, Shandol considered it essentially a decent place to go. There could have been exceptions, she supposed, not everyone went by the rules.

But Dean had not stopped there! He had driven past it, down the brush and tree-lined narrow road and pulled to a stop at a gate entrance to a woodland pasture.

"It's so spooky here," Shandol said, wonderingly, trying to see out but there was only darkness. "And so lonely, Dean."

Dean leaned back as though stretching (in anticipation?), and after a puff or two more on the cigarette he was smoking, threw it out the window onto the bare ground, impatiently. "Two things I'm gonna find out tuh night," Dean said, without preliminaries. "What about that bulldog in yourenzes' all basement?"

"Well, what about him?" she asked, cautiously. *What's he driving at*, she wondered. *Why are we way out here? To go into that?*

"I heared he's purty bad," Dean went on; "as bad in fack as the one the peach orchard man had. That ugly yeller'n thet got shot. They say this'n looks like 'em. But he ain't to be let out 'cause he ain't to get shot."

"I get the idea," she replied. "Who told you about him? And I do wish yuh could see 'em." She wanted to giggle and glad it was dark to

152

hide the grin. It was neither the time nor the place to enlighten him. She wasn't sure how he would take it.

"Well, never you mind. I've heared," he stated, mysteriously, nervously lighting another cigarette.

Shandol was by now accustomed to this bulldog of her father's invention, and how he had given it substance in an off-hand implied manner. Her father had merely said a good mean bulldog was a perfect way to protect his only daughter. He had been joking, but the implied warning was there.

"Some dads might threaten with a shotgun and buckshot or salt—"he had added good-humoredly, "yet most could figure that wouldn't be my style, even to scare someone. Accidents happen with guns, especially to those who know little about 'em. So for me that means a good mean bulldog. One who'd obey me to the letter and trust me, even to any command." Perhaps he was actually voicing a private dream he had to own just such a dog, but perhaps any good dog, not necessarily an old ugly "bulldog." But people had a terror of them because of the "peach orchard man's" dog.

Yet, how the word had been spread around so convincingly Shandol could only guess. But he had taken on more reality as he was discussed, apparently. It even seemed in character that Joel should let it be known jokingly, rather than belligerently proclaiming his intention to have anyone mangled to within an inch of his life, if they should trifle with his daughter. No, he'd kid them along and let them take the hint or learn the hard way.

The younger boys were no help to the curious. They could honestly say they didn't "know nuthin' uhbout it—they weren't allowed to go down there." The older boys merely went along with the joke it was, wondering about the curiosity. "Yuh might find out someday," they'd say, or some such remark.

The bulldog story was passed around as fact. It had been intended as a family joke. But as so often happens in the case of gossip, it was propelled all out of proportion. Shandol secretly thought that if she were really all that popular someone might just be trying to scare Dean away. Was it possible? But who? Steven? Cal? The dog was by now a myth the family actually enjoyed, privately, even though Joel didn't seem to need him. Grandpa Bregmanson had even whittled out a delightful and apt likeness, complete with a tiny dog-house and a ten cent pocket knife chain for his neck. He had brought it from a visit with another daughter where he spent time also. He had a name—Tugo. He was painted an orange color with a white T marking on his face and forehead. T for Tugo—or Terrible? He also had white on his feet and underside. That then was the rumored bulldog Dean

153

and Shandol were discussing. He was a joke, and the tiny wood image the only one they had. Shandol could hardly suppress a chuckle, but seemed to sense Dean's seriousness. She was sure he was seeing a fiery-eyed animal seeking the lifeblood of anyone foolish enough to harm the girl who sat beside him.

"Yuh know why we're here," Dean said matter-of-factly, moving closer to her. "I want tuh tell yuh that I'd aim tuh do right by yuh and no reason for that d--m dog. Don't yuh know? Git m' meanin'?"

"Meanin' what?" She nearly shrieked. Then truth slowly dawned. "Yeah, I git it." She scarcely breathed.

Dean moved to get closer to her. But she shied to a corner. Shandol got his meaning all right and she was astonished, speechless, and afraid. She seemed to become dizzy and her head spun and seemed to be emptying of all reason. The silence then became so intense a numbness enveloped her. The silence deafened her. Then she was near panic.

What's the matter with me? I can't even think straight she thought wildly. Dean, who perhaps had half-way expected her to flail him open handedly, took her silence and stillness to mean she did not object and he moved closer to take her in his arms.

"Just stay where yuh're at," she snapped, coldly, finally becoming animated again. "And just take me on home!" She swallowed nervously and with difficulty.

Oh, dear, what was she supposed to say? Terribly disappointed in him? Well, she was! That she was. She had read it was old fashioned, and now incorrect, to slap a fellow's face, though why she had resisted that first impulse, she didn't stop to analyze. That was one thing, she thought, about going with a guy. You can't just say to them something like: "Now look here, I have brothers and I know a few facts of life from my mama, which includes especially that such guys gossip and brag! I don't approve of certain things, including guys who go with girls for no other reason than to take advantage of just such unsuspecting or weak girls as I'm supposed to be." No, she couldn't say it, but she could think it, and thinking it made her furious!

Dean moved closer and tried to kiss her, but Shandol, unresponsive, pushed him away.

"I'm tryin' tuh give you the idea. I mean no, N–O; no!" she cried, jerkily. "Now just take me home!"

"We're really alone," he persisted. "No one'll bother us here. I said I'd do right by yuh— " He caressed her nearer to him.

In a sudden burst of strength and determination, she took his arm from around her with one hand, and immediately opened the car door with the other and stood outside the car in jig time.

154

"Whar yuh think yer're goin'?" he asked, surprisedly.

"Right here to enjoy the fresh air," she replied, sarcastically. "I hope that foul mind of yours gives yuh a sick headache. If yuh think I'm *that* kind—O-oh, if I had a six-penny nail I'd bite it's head off," she hissed...

"Huh?"

"Mind yer own business," she retorted.

"Yuh wanna walk home?" he asked, cooly.

"Of course not," she replied honestly, then daringly added: "You maybe a dumb hard-head, but yuh're not that bigga dope! I've no idea where I am, and if I'm not home at a certain time Dad will have the sheriff and half the town huntin' me? Yuh know where they'll look first? He won't wait until mornin' neither. He says there's no decent place to be after midnight, so I'd better be home or along the road in case of car trouble. Do *you* get my meanin'?"

"Git in hyar," he ordered. "I see I'm to get no where's with you."

She sheepishly got back into the car.

"Yuh're exactly right," she agreed, "so yuh don't need to bother tuh come around me anymore."

"Yuh're mad," he said, accusingly. "Yuh shoultn't be, yuh know. I uz jest testin' yuh—yuh know that?"

"*Testin'* me!" she mocked. And thought that if she had failed it how he would have gloated! She added aloud, "Well, I hate tests, and in this case the one doin' the testin'. Take me home or I'll tell *Dad* on you!"

"Don't do that, fer cryin' out loud," he exclaimed, startled. "Shandol," he went on, "let me jest say I'm sorry and let's us start over ag'in. Why, I want tuh go with yuh more'n any gurl I know. I jest had tuh know what kinda gurl yuh are."

"Yuh've heard so much about a certain bulldog," she said, as quietly as she could because she wanted to scream at him, "but yuh've not heard nothin' about me? That may make sense but it ain't worth much."

"But yuh've allus had a brother er two with yuh," he tried to explain. "Sometimes yer mother er dad, girlfriends—yuh know what I mean," he added lamely.

"So yuh draw the conclusion I need a chaperone?" she replied, heatedly. "Yuh figger I can't think things out for myself, and without bodyguards I've the spine of a woolly worm! Or did yuh think I'd give in just so I could see yuh again? You're much too immaterial to me for that. Right now I don't care if I never lay eyes on yuh agin!"

"Don't get so het up," he admonished, spiritedly. "Hit's done all time, don't yuh know?"

"I'm not finished," she raved on, so hurt she hardly realized the torrent of words she had spoken and those in her mind. "Yuh see all time I've gone out with yuh, I've tried to act decent. Talk without rough language. I said I tried. My dad gets onto me a lot about the slang I pick up, but they're not dirty words. I tried to be a lady because I wanted tuh be treated like one. I thought yuh'd see that, and with what yuh could hear about me, *know* what I am. So testin' I don't appreciate. You learned the lesson the hard way as far as I'm concerned."

She wanted to cry. Tears stung her eyes. Later she probably would but not now. Her cheeks felt hot and her hands cold, as she twisted her white handkerchief almost into a knot, loosened it only to twist it tightly again, over and over. Her mouth trembled. She caught her teeth over her lower lip.

"Now," she said low, to herself and into the quiet darkness, "I know what the second thing yuh wanted tuh find out is."

Dean, with rough, jerky motions and rough jerking at the gear shift got the car going as he prepared to take Shandol home. He was stoney-faced, impatient, and, Shandol decided, a bit surly. But he was deep in his own thoughts. He seemed not to care to reply to her stormy reaction. It had rung all too true. But how he had misjudged this girl! A timid little soul indeed! Mostly, yes, like a calm sea if the wind don't whip it up. Jumpy as an unbroken filly. Not the type he had seen around the dance hall. He had supposed she might try to play hard to get, use some vague idea maybe later—or—but what had he expected? That he might wear her down surely. But jumpin' jiminy, fiery smoke and national defense, she had just hurled point blank blasts of facts, fast. No minced words, either.

"Shandol," he broke the silence after they had driven on to the highway, a few minutes having passed. "I'll be in town tomorrow. Let's start all over. I'd e'en meet yuh at the well. That was so purty that day. Yer so purty, Shandol. Wouldja do it fer me?"

"If a bulldog practically took yer leg off would yuh still want tuh follow 'im around so's he could lick yer hand?" she asked, her voice dripped sarcasm. She gave him a hard look, then turned away.

"Yuh're bein' stubborn. Yuh wouldn't believe me when I say I'm sorry. I apologize with all my heart and yuh don't accept."

"Well, I just don't care to go through it again," she replied firmly. "I may forgive and forget the whole thing, you included."

"That ain't fair," Dean exploded, impatiently. "Look, Shandol, yuh look like uh kid. How'd I know how growed up yuh are?" And added, off-handedly, "now yuh can explode."

"Twas just the chance yuh took," she returned, "and yuh make it sound like yuh'd take candy from uh tot!"

Shandol was thinking of the tom boys. Boys young men now, too—who would sit on their porch, or come to the house to play games, or just to see her brothers, they would not even tell a smutty joke in her presence. Not even when they shut up when she appeared, laughing, at whatever she must not hear. They've *spoiled* me and I'm just shocked, she told herself. I must think. Is this part of dating? I've hated it! I can't imagine Lester doing Jane that way before marriage!

"Shandol," Dean broke into her thoughts, but then apparently changed his mind, said, "oh, nut'in'." And Shandol thought he added something under his breath which sounded like "H--l." He drove the remaining few minutes in silence.

"I can find my own way," she said stonily when they were in the back yard. She got out of the car quickly and left him, running the few feet from the car to the porch. The nightmare was over. She was home. Only tangled, uncertain thoughts remained. And anger. What a conceited jerk he must be not to see a thing or two.

She groped her way into the dark kitchen. She wanted to take no chance of anyone's seeing her face. She washed from habit, but then did it again, seeming not to be clean. Tonight removing makeup was secondary. Because they all washed after being out anywhere. It had to do with germs, yet they were hardly conscious of it. But if the Jasper Bright family could get the itch from going to the churches they thought grand and bragged about, anyone might. There were also the preachers, who had stayed there. They were particular about washing after shaking so many hands. They worried about getting something such as that and passing it on. They'd joked about "preacher's itch" but did not treat it so. So they washed in a "germicidal" soap, usually. Sometimes Shandol had had to smell her hands later to be sure she had, it was so automatic.

Tonight was different. In her agitated state she had dumped the water in the washpan into the garbage bucket, which sat beside the large cook stove, making sure first it was there and would hold the water. (Otherwise she'd have had to toss it out the door and off the porch.) She took water from the stove reservoir with the dipper and had warm water and soap. She would have liked to have taken a bath, but was sure someone, perhaps Joel, would be aroused and ask questions she didn't want to answer. She wondered why she felt dirty. Or did she just need to wash her wounded pride? Water had little effect on that. Though unbruised, she had felt trapped and had come out clawing!

Shame. She felt shame. Of course she had had fellows hint around "and sound her out" she supposed now, as they teased her. There had been parties when she had been alone with boys. In fact there was a party game they called "Pleased or Displeased." Someone was "IT" so-called because he or she would go to each of the others in the party, in turn, as the players would be sitting in a line or circle, with the question: "You pleased or displeased?" If the answer was "pleased" IT would go to the next player. If he should say "displeased," as was inevitably the case, IT would ask, "What'll it take to please yuh?" Usually it was for some couple to take a walk, holding hands, around the house, down a lane a certain distance, or some such thing, depending upon where they were. Other times it was a kiss, which was an embarrassed peck on the cheek, or they'd have a brother sit between a girl and boyfriend, some were ridiculous as someone should say the ABC's, or perhaps not so ridiculous as to sing. Some of them, Shandol thought, were quite inventive sometimes. Even sending someone for a cookie or the like if that were possible. Shandol had no fear of these boys. She had no reason to be. They treated her as she supposed they should, whether they feared a bulldog, or what ever the cause. But Dean had trapped her by taking her far away. He had not teased, no plan of seduction, just practically demand she please him, she thought, and "he'd take care of her," meaning if she got caught. She was sure it was an often used line and perhaps a good one in some cases. But Shandol had to admit to herself she was completely unprepared, as it turned out, surprised, enraged that he thought her so cheap, and it also hurt her feelings.

Shandol got matches from the painted tin dispenser on the kitchen door facing, but went upstairs in the dark. She was glad she could. Her father had not called to ask the time, nor was he up to take some bicarbonate of soda, as he so very often had to do he thought for his "sour stomach." She undressed in the darkness of her room. She lay on the bed clutching her head with her hands, while her jumbled thoughts rippled through her brain, turbulently, as a swollen stream. One thought plagued her: How should she have handled the whole thing really? It was normal for her to place herself in the wrong, or to be unsure of herself if she were right.

I believe I did right, she thought. *But was it the right way? It would have been simple to just have slapped his face, as I do Phil or otherwise try to get back at him when he pokes my ribs, pinches my arms, or flips me on the hips with his fingers, which stings, not to mention the surprise and disgust.*

It might have saved a quarrel. Just bop and said, "just you take me home, pipsqueak. I don't go in for heavy pettin', take it or leave it." That would have been that! But was it lady-like? She knew it was important to Joel she be lady-like. It was a delicate, lady-take-care situation to her. She supposed she had failed the lady test, she had been so angry. But according to her psychology course, in high school, one semester, such slapping was frowned upon. A slap wounds the male ego! (*How about my wounded pride by insult?* She inwardly fumed.) So is one really supposed to be such a brilliant talker one can talk her way out of such a situation? Be calm? But how can one keep one's head when suddenly all reason flies out the window? And a fuzzy, unreal, shocked feeling takes its place. She had supposed she'd be ready for "a pass." She had expected a subtle approach at seduction, not that bold "I wanna know how far yuh'll go for me" approach. Shocked is what she was. She had gone on the defensive, she realized, because his attitude had been so offensive to her.

Shandol's thoughts drifted more to the psychology course she had had. Lester wanted her to take it. She remembered they had laughed about the rats, the four legged ones, which had been used for some types of experimenting. But also in that course, she reminded herself, she had learned the sex (or mating drive) hadn't been considered the strongest force in this animal called man. Self-preservation, necessities of food, clothing and shelter; even ambition and a good reputation, or feeling good about oneself, were stronger than the sex drive. Shandol hardly knew what is meant but learned by association and implication, rather than a direct discussion of it. But she thought Dean was a stupid jerk who probably thinks it's the sun, moon and stars (of course, he's a man!) Or a ring in the nose one is to be led by!

Girls do get "caught" she knew that, even knowing better, just simply by taking chances. She was reminded how Lester had walked the floor one night, talking to Joel, and she was kept in the dark about it until sometime later. He had learned Penny Rose Winsh was expecting a baby and unmarried. He supposed she would blame him, and he didn't love her enough to want to marry her. But he had been with her. He couldn't think what to do. And for a few days he was irritable and verbally explosive, with misgivings. Then he learned a few other fellows had had the same harrowing experience, and the crisis passed. Penny had finally left town and went to a "home" for such purposes, to wait for her baby. When the baby was about a year old the family had left Greenway and gone to a western state. Shandol had felt sorry for Penny. She thought Penny was trying to catch a husband the wrong way, and too many around to take advantage of her ignorance.

A man might forgive and be sincere, she knew that, but one never knew, not really. Anyway would the right one promise or not? Shandol just knew she could never face her family in such disgrace. Her father would be so disappointed in her. She was sure she was right, but not sure it was done in the right way. But suppose, her mind churned on, she loved a guy? Would she react the same? Would she be easier worn down? In short she would then care about his feelings and could she handle the whole thing better?

She moved to the foot of the bed, so that her head was in front of the open window. Was it the window which looked so dark or her thoughts that failed to take in anything else?

The far away screaming, yet lonesome, wail of the midnight passenger train cut through the night and into Shandol's soul. It was called the midnight train because it was due to pass through town at ten minutes before midnight. The mail sack was snatched from a special hanger installed on a painted iron pole, especially for that and near the tracks. Clive would meet it and pick up a sack which was tossed out. The lonesome steam whistle shrieked its warning again at the bend, and as a soul mate, Shandol wanted to cry out with it as the sound tore at her heart's core. Tears finally came. The train charged noisily and jarringly on through town and Shandol wept. The whistle was soon dim and farther away, not piercing, meant the train was carried courageously, deliberately on, and the lonesome sound failed to soothe her. She wept quietly into her pillow for all the frustration, shame, and uncertainty of her unprotected self. The pillow muffled heartbreaking sobs, and the muffled, "Mama, Mama." The darkness hid her tears, until she had cried herself out. Then as a child who cries itself to sleep, she gave one last sigh, caught on a sob and slept.

Shandol decided to go for a walk, not unusual for her on a Sunday afternoon. She had gone down the deserted, grass matted former street, and saplings, buckbrush and some weeds. She crawled under the barbed wire fence at the edge of the pasture, where they had played ball the day she saw Dean for the first time. She had to crawl under another fence of three strands of barbed wire, after crossing a triangle of the meadow, to a tree at the edge of a wooded area. She saw cattle grazing toward the southwest in the pasture from where she now was. The warm air was filled with the earthy smell and some elusive floral smell. She carried a tablet and pencil. She wanted to finish some verses. She wanted to make a poetic picture, the setting by a pool for a pool portrait. Not one just as a glimpse into a well, but big enough for a fluffy cloud in the sky, a tree perhaps, in bloom, of course, flowers, and a pretty girl. She knew how she would end it. "The vanity of the girl to hold the picture" would mean she would put in her hand and each ripple would distort her picture, breaking the pretty pool portrait, just as her own had been broken at the well by the bucket. Soon Shandol, still dissatisfied with her poem, decided

160

to leave it for another time. She could not bring her mood up enough to give the poem the light touch she desired. She strolled back slowly and thoughtfully the way she had come, leaving her favorite spot of moss, dry leaves, spindly small flowers beneath a large oak, complete with a fallen log to hold her pad of paper.

Shandol learned they had company upon returning home. It seemed she had missed a couple of women of the town, who had dropped by to see how Audrey was. Also Jane's parents had brought their daughter and son-in-law to visit, stayed a short while themselves and had already gone, leaving Lester and Jane.

Shandol was always glad to see her brother and sister-in law. Her head still hurt and she was preoccupied, but if they noticed or wondered they did not ask outright for which she was glad. Shandol had firmly decided to confide in no one about her experience, not yet anyway. Perhaps in time she'd understand Dean—or men. She realized it had been such a letdown she couldn't be sure if Dean were the type who went with a girl to try to wear away her defenses; or if, as he implied, he had to "test" a girl before he would get seriously interested in her. She had had no experience to guide her, and no one close enough to confide in as yet, not even Jane. She would merely be as shocked as Shandol herself. Her doubts plagued her as to the way she had handled it. She had become so angry and hurt. She was miserable and felt she was a failure, not only on dates, but as a person because she needed someone. She was so lonely, a miserable shell of her former self, she felt.

"I'm surprised Dean ain't here," Lester finally remarked off-handedly. To Shandol he couldn't have made a worse comment, but she was sure he hadn't intended to be tactless. He considered it brotherly. Her face became pale.

"I don't know if he's comin'," she said, hoping to sound as near her normal self as possible. "He warned me earlier he might not could get the car. Said his mother might want to go see her sister or something. Yuh know the first time we dated we went with another guy. So maybe his mother didn't change her mind and he couldn't see Jim—I don't know," she ended throwing apart her hands.

That was true enough so far as it went. Of course he might just let her sweat (with curiosity as to what he thought of her now). He could also be out with some other girl.

"Well, maybe he goes with other girls, too." Jane added, as though reading her thoughts. "They've not been goin' together very long and maybe not steady yet." *Bless her*, Shandol thought.

"Thinks you're too young for 'em," Lester teased. She knew he didn't realize how close he came to her own wondering about that.

"How'm I suppose tuh know," she teased back. "Ask him if he's ever around again. She shrugged her shoulders, smiled secretively, and in mock shyness. But the usually innocent, doe eyes were veiled; directness averted.

"Don't protest too much, didn't some sage say?" Lester persisted.

"Quit teasing her," Jane interrupted. "Shandol feels bad as it is, not havin' a word if he's comin' or not—or just late. Yuh don't look good, Shandol, feelin' bad?"

"Yeah, one of my headaches," Shandol answered, glad to change the subject. "Mama said she usta have headaches too. She used to worry that I was comin' down with somethin', but I think she's decided I inherited the tendency, along with the palest skin in the family, the lightest hair and palest brown eyes." She was ticking the features off on her fingers.

"Danged if yuh didn't at that," Lester conceded. "Hadn't thought of it before, little sister."

"I'm gonna take more aspirin and take it easy," she said. "Don't expect I'll go to church."

"Oh, people would stare because you're not with the tall, fair country one?" He chided.

"Yeah," she agreed, "and with this headache I might just yell at someone, 'What's it to yuh?' and they'd think I was jilted or somethin'." *Is this really me talking like this*? she marveled. "Well, he *could* find someone else, or maybe there was some girl who was rather mad at 'im and he just went with me tuh make 'er jealous. So let's change the subject again, huh?—Oh, say," she continued, "speakin' uh teasin' do you know Dean teased me about Dad's bulldog?" *Is this me?* She thought. *I must pinch myself. How can I?*

"Really?" Lester asked, a broad grin. His mouth was large, his chin strong, dark eyes, well set, a heavy crop of dark hair and broad forehead and wide nose, gave him a rugged handsomeness.

"Yeah, I was flabbergasted. "Yuh know K.C. once asked why he never heard him bark! He was told merely that being as he was and where he was, and K.C. not always at home, well, so it went. We're gettin' too old for him. But maybe he's the ghost of Burgland's dog—yuh know, the 'peach orchard man' out for revenge. It's so silly. I just told Dean I might tell 'im about it someday."

"What?" Jane wondered.

"I'll tell yuh sometime," Lester promised, squeezing her arm affectionately, still smiling.

Dean did not come and Shandol felt better once the tension, questions (or just looks), and uncertainty let up. She wanted to think about tomorrow and going back to help the new mother and baby. It promised to be work and she needed something to think about.

On Monday Shandol learned that that week, perhaps next week for sure, would be as long as she'd be needed. Marcia was up now, less nervous and was doing more and more to care for the baby herself.

On Tuesday Freda stayed while Shandol went to Plainesville to see about a job at the telephone company exchange, which Mrs. Bright herself had mentioned. But there she was told of the irregularity of the working hours, which would require either she stay there in town or have transportation to go back and forth. Joel had gone with her and had told her to reply they would have to see what they could work out. Later Joel was vague about it all and Shandol supposed the matter would drop there. She knew there would be no way he would make it possible for her to stay up there, and there was simply no way such transportation could be arranged.

Shandol was disappointed, but had no idea how she could go against his wishes. He said he'd worry about her living away from home, going to work at no telling what hour, perhaps alone. He had a point, she supposed. But is that all it is? She wondered. Other girls made breaks from home. In fact are encouraged to do so if they can better themselves. "But not me," she pitied herself.

It's his silly pride, she thought, every nerve balking in side her. *He's so afraid that I, a mere slip of a girl, as he often refers to girls in general, and me in particular, could and would make more money than he could—perhaps ever did bothered him. Why couldn't he see it would help them all?* If only she could do it anyway. But how? It would be nice and she could maybe hire someone to help Mama.

Joel himself offered little sympathy at her disappointment. "Somethin' will turn up later, surely," was as near consolation as he offered her. "There're simply too many things that could happen to girls who live alone in towns the size of Plainesville," he added.

On Wednesday night Dean came to see her.

CHAPTER 13

When Shandol saw Dean standing nonchalantly at the door that Wednesday evening, she had been so surprised she had to give herself time to get over the shock, and think as to best handle the situation. She did not want a scene because there was a gathering of several friends and neighbors. Was it a streak of luck or had he bided his time?

It had seemed a long time since she had seen him, so he seemed a stranger. She was reticent and kept distance between them, It was easy to do with so many people there; and their being there was not all that unusual. But it was turning into something like an impromptu party. Bobby was in the kitchen popping popcorn in a skillet, and it smelled delicious. It was conceded by family members it was one thing he did best. In fact he was good to help Audrey in the kitchen. Audrey and Jane were making taffy candy (for a "pull"). Dorothy Landers, the only other matron there, had brought a batch of homemade cookies, as though she had known others would drop by when hearing the music, and the children had perhaps said to a few they would go there, and having her own family, it seemed only fair to bring something, as Audrey might not be prepared to furnish refreshments for so many on such short notice.

Phil, Bert Lankers, Sam Wolken and the Landers children, who took turns actually playing some musical instrument, were already making music in the front room.

Sam Wolken, the fiddler, something of a character and individualist, was a small, stoop-shouldered man, with graying hair, steel gray eyes and looked fifty to sixty years old, though no one seemed to know or care how old he actually was. He lived alone now in his two-room shanty just up the hill, a very short distance from the church in the valley, as it was frequently identified, the supposedly non-denominational church. Sam had two grown sons, who had lived with him as boys growing up, doing about as they pleased. The older one a woodsman, his brother took to music as their father, but got their education out of the classroom for the most part, after learning some 'readin', writin' 'n 'rithmetic' they considered adequate. Sam and his wife were separated and had been for years, though never actually divorced. Sam was also the town handyman. He did carpenter and repair work, besides being in demand as a fiddler. Actually he played for parties and dances for miles around. In truth sometimes the actual date of a local birthday party or get-together, as tonight, depended upon on whether he would be available or not. If he promised to attend a local party he did not let them down to go play for a dance. Fridays and Saturdays were his busiest nights for dances and parties. For the dances, many times, he was paid, especially if he had to go out of town.

Albert Landers, better known as Bert, and few people actually recalled his real name at times, was the father of a musical family. His oldest daughter, Rayda, could play a mandolin and guitar. Two younger girls, eight and ten years old, also played these instruments passably well. Dale, the only boy, except for an infant now two, who was twelve, three years younger than Rayda, played the banjo and guitar. Bert, who could also play these instruments, "sawed a little," as he himself put it, on the violin. He had taught his children what they knew, and they had had enough natural talent to be quick and apt to do it. They all played by "ear." They owned their own instruments, and the children helped make music, usually taking turns, because while they liked the idea of joining the music-makers, the older ones also wanted to enjoy the party. They had moved to Greenway from a county west of there, and he, too, "worked on the road" as did Joel.

Rayda was not at the time joining in the music making. She was sitting apart with Rod Sandler, now considered her steady boyfriend. She was a taller than average girl, slender, with dark wavy hair, large blue eyes and prominent jaw line. She was attractive, however, and neat in appearance, wearing a flowered print gathered skirt and white blouse.

The custom was at these parties, when they were, though this one hadn't been planned, if there were to be refreshments, every family helped furnish them. Usually the hostess made a cake and furnished coffee, and cocoa for non-coffee drinkers who were mostly children. Tonight only Mrs. Landers had brought anything, except Steven Follerson, who had brought the sugar. That is what prompted the taffy making, and later "pulling." Audrey had neither cookies nor cake, but she did have graham crackers. She quickly stirred up a frosting of powdered sugar, a bit of cream, vanilla, salt and butter and made "sandwich" cookies, breaking them into squares. It had to do. After all the party hadn't been planned, but she did wish to contribute something. It was not a large party, compared to others, so it seemed adequate. Audrey made a pot of coffee, and also cocoa for the younger ones.

Dean had finally been offered a chair and sat in an out of the way place near the door. Shandol noticed, but had been keeping herself much too busy, flitting around from person to person in welcome

165

and friendliness, as she usually did. But then soon she noticed he had gone and wondered if he had decided he would never see her alone in this mob and just left, having spoken only when spoken to. She had not been aware when he had actually gone.

Freda Horn followed Shandol into the front room, where Shandol hoped to get the young people interested in games of some sort. But outside of the checker game she couldn't seem to make much headway. Those who could took turns playing checkers, the loser giving his place to a next challenger.

So far Joel, who hadn't joined the music makers, was keeping his seat, playing the young players, some even fairly good, but hardly a challenge to Joel. Harry Bright was not there. Freda had come to remind Shandol the taffy was ready to be pulled, though pretty warm. Shandol saw it was a light color and appeared to be a good batch.

"Youns maze-wells give a party," she said, "here we are ennyway."

"Maybe somebody'll give a party soon," Shandol answered. "Oh, ain't yuh heared?" Freda asked. "Next Saturday is Bert Landers birthday. The very reason they're here tonight is to invite youns. He don't know it yet so don't say nuthin' he kin hear."

Shandol saw Dean standing at the door again, and for an unguarded moment a questioning light leaped into her surprised eyes.

"Ain't that yer boyfrien'?" Freda asked, as she had followed Shandol's gaze.

"I've gone with 'im, why?" she replied.

"I jest ain't seen yuh with 'em tuh night," Freda explained, with a look that Shandol knew was all question, and the unspoken question was—"why?"

"I'll get to 'im if he'll stay still long enough," Shandol laughed. "I'm tryin' tuh talk tuh ever'body a little bit. If he'd stayed put, I'd been to him by now." I think, she added to herself.

"Oh, he left tuh smoke," Freda informed her. "I heared somebody tell 'em he'd not needed to a-done that."

"He needn't 've," Shandol agreed. "But I'd best be goin; on tuh see if people seem tuh be enjoyin' themselves."

Then Shandol felt color flood her face, as she had a sudden thought. Dean would likely rather leave, he's probably bored to death, but he's determined to see me first. I'm sure of it. But standing between them was Bucky Sandler, dressed cowboy style, even to gun and holster. Shandol stealthily slipped the gun, which was near her, out and as quick as a wink was holding it against his ribs.

"Put 'em up," she ordered, in a mocking deep voice. "I gotta gun—yours, so you're out-maneuvered!"

He felt his empty gun holster and turned on her in a fury. Shandol

166

grinned back bravely. Even when he saw who it was he scolded her soundly.

"Yuh wanna shoot somebody? That ain't no toy!"

"Of course not," she mocked. "I didn't pull the trigger did I? In fact I wouldn't touch it. I hate guns. I only did it to see if I could."

"It shore ain't no toy," he reiterated, patiently. "Yuh shoultn't ever do such uh thing."

Shandol then examined the gun in her hand. She turned pale, and her mouth became dry. In her hand she saw a real, fully loaded .32 caliber revolver. She knew what it was because Lester had one just like it he had bought from money he earned carrying papers, and other odd jobs including picking fruit in season, catching rabbits to sell, helping Joel cut wood and so on. Lester's was mostly left on a top closet shelf in her parent's bedroom. Sometimes he would get it down, flip it around in mock movie cowboy style, but without sufficient funds to keep shells it wasn't very interesting to him now. He hadn't purchased enough shells to practice and become a good shot. So his mostly nestled among quilts, extra bedding and other paraphernalia, which accumulated there also, unmolested—most of the time forgotten.

A loaded gun! In this house! Shandol was horrified, terrified, terribly embarrassed and pale as a ghost.

"Yuh're gonna get in turrible trouble, for cryin' out loud," Shandol scolded back. "How'd I know it was for real. I supposed it was that look-alike cap pistol yuh used tuh carry so much. I mighta shot yuh! Oh' m'gosh. My-ee gosh."

Shandol was still sure he carried that cap pistol sometimes. Perhaps it was why that when, or if, he had the real one no one wondered about it. He could shoot it accurately, Shandol knew. She had heard he could strike a match but she had never seen that. She had also seen him come in from hunting with squirrels or rabbits, some he had shared with them, without a gun, because he was just as good a shot with a slingshot, or just a "throwin' rock." And gun or no gun he probably also had his slingshot, as most of the time boys did.

"Yuh're not really supposed tuh carry that thing are yuh?" she asked. "Somebody'll tell on yuh or somethin'."

"Naw, yuh woultn't do that," he teased. "Anyway how'd I go huntin'? It ain't concealed or nuttin'."

"It's still a gun," Shandol said. "But I don't know about 'em only what I've heard and decided sorta myself. I hope you know—" Her voice trailed off. They were creating a scene. Others had gathered around closer, now realizing the gun *was* real, and some wanted to hold it. But Bucky demurred, reminding them they were in a house full of people and someone could get hurt. He also could guess how Joel might feel about it.

Shandol moved away from the milling persons. She stopped to exchange a few words with Rayda Lankers and Rod Sandler, who was Bucky's older brother, though the boys were quite different in temperament and personality.

"I hope yuh'll sing sometin' tonight," Shandol told her. "Sing 'You Are My Sunshine'" or just whatever yuh like, and maybe your sisters'll help."

"I'll see about it," she promised.

"I hope yuh'll spare Rayda a few minutes," Shandol told Rod. "And, hey, does that brother ever bother you with that gun? Even in fun I mean. Did ya see me point it at 'im? What if it'd gone off? I'm still quakin' in my boots," She smiled rather grimly, shuddered and moved on.

But it was with Cal Shandol flirted a little, or tried to make it appear she was. She knew Cal had the girlfriend near Plainesville, she was only showing Dean, meaning nothing by it, yet felt compelled to do it. She could hardly take Bucky serious, even without the gun incident. He was in and out so much he almost seemed a member of the family. Calvin was a neat enough fellow, with a small face. He was shorter than average, so quite short compared to Dean. He had a protruding stomach from a congenital defect, which had been corrected, but the characteristic remained. It was hardly noticed as everyone was so accustomed to his looks.

"Pretty soon I can bring yuh somethin' tuh eat," she said. "Should it be cookies, crackers, candy and coffee or tea with it?"

"Coffee and cookies, but I'll get it," he said, looking away.

"Don't yuh wanna talk tuh me?" she asked.

His look at Dean standing nearby watching them gave her the answer. He shrugged and said, low, "yuh see how 'tis?"

"Yeah," she agreed, aloud. But cowardly, she thought as she moved on. She stopped at the checker game, but couldn't have told a thing about it, because her mind was on other things. She had talked to everyone, she supposed, but Dean. She walked toward him, determination written on her face. If he came to see her, see her he would.

"Lo," she said, looking up at him, " I guess it's about time I said 'hello' to you. I do try to go around and say a few words to everyone. I do want them to have a good time. I've done that since I got a compliment for it once. It was a bigger party and I was inside and outside.

Dean was silent so she rattled on, "there were some inside talking, listening to music, playing checkers or dominoes or cards. Outside were the party games such as 'Johnny Was a Miller Boy'; 'Pleased or Displeased'; 'Where You're At, Who You're With, and What You're Doin', which really gets silly sometimes. Yuh see, three people are *IT*. One to tell where yer at, one, for who you're with and the other what yer doin'.

Each *IT* has no way of knowing what the other *ITs* are going to say. Once I wound up in a teacup, with Cal, picking' blackberries! Wasn't even blackberry time. Anyway it was a nice party. We heard about that party for weeks. This isn't really a party. I mean no one planned it. Just these people come in."

He was still looking at her and said nothing. In fact his woe begone expression hadn't changed. Shandol had tried to be exuberant, but it was difficult. It wasn't easy, trying to be animated while talking to a stone face.

I'm really just babbling, nervously, she thought, and she was incensed at herself. If it made no difference, why was she so nervous? At what people would think?

"So why the silent treatment?" she finally asked in a whisper. "Why are *you* here? And tonight of all times?"

"I come tuh talk tuh yuh," he replied evenly. "How'd I know there'd be a party. Just whar kin we talk at? Let's go to my car, er take a walk er sompin'."

"Now, really, Dean," she scolded, "yuh surely know better'n that, don't yuh?"

"Come on, don't be silly," he replied firmly. "I uh come tuh talk and I ain't aimin' tuh leave till I do it." He took hold of her elbow and steered her through the dark hallway, through the open double doors to the front porch. There was a standard sized screen door built in to fit the double door opening on the outside of the door.

"We can't talk here," Shandol reasoned. "We'll be heard. Let's make it some other time. I gotta go inside now."

"Wait un listen tuh me," he coaxed. "With the music no one kin hear all that good out heer. I'm comin' Saturday fer yuh as usual."

"Just like that?" she replied shortly. "I'm not sure I care tuh go anywhere with yuh. I just can't, expectin' I might be threatened."

"Look. Slap my face and git it over with," he replied, suppressing a grin, which she didn't see. "Maybe I got it comin' scarin' yuh so. But yuh cain't hold that agin me forever, kin yuh?"

"Oh, boy, I will." She pursed her lips and indeed gave him a resounding slap, which, she thought, surprised him after all. She even hoped she had been seen. "Now, leave me alone," she said. "I'm goin' inside. Shall we say 'good-bye' or is it worth it?"

"Good-bye, h--l," he ejaculated, not as softly as Shandol would have wished. "I sed I'd be here Saturday."

"Stop it! Why bother?"

"I'll have somethin' tuh tell yuh then," he replied softly.

Shandol gasped and he guessed at her thoughts, which he knew were full of doubt concerning him.

"No, not what yer thinkin', but somethin' as important as that army—tuh me ennyway."

"But what?" she begged. "Tell me now, please. I can't stand to wait and wonder till Saturday."

"Nope," he replied firmly. "It's a gotta be Sattiday."

"You're a meanie, I knew it," she taunted. But when he took her hand she did not pull away.

"After that slap I get a forgivin' kiss," he said and kissed her before she had time to consider if she agreed or not. "Uh kiss tuh make up," he said low, still holding her.

"Sorry about the slap," she conceded. "It wasn't so satisfyin' as I supposed it'd be."

"Don't worry. Might remind me tuh be uh gentleman," he replied, laughter in his voice.

"This is the first time we've kissed on the front porch," she reminded him, conversationally. "Always the back. Does that sound bad? But we almost always use that entry, as I've allus said. Dad can hear if anyone comes in better there. The front is mostly locked."

Dean must have regrets, Shandol decided. Perhaps he feels he has been punished enough and we can start again even if not at the well. Was the banishment too much for him?

Anyway the quarrel tonight, which had been mostly in undertones, was over. If all quarrels could be held so it would be better, Shandol thought, because less can be said, and in a low cutting voice and hurting way. And the making up is so sweet and maybe quicker.

"See yuh Sattiday," Dean said.

"If you're sure yuh know how tuh behave," she couldn't help sparring.

"I'll see yuh then," he promised.

"Let's go see what's goin' on inside now," Shandol invited. "Wonder if I've been missed."

They were still in time for refreshments, though most had already helped themselves and were eating and milling about. Just as Shandol was getting cookies she was joined by Dean, who said he would take hot cocoa as she did. She was then horrified to see K.C. eating popcorn off the floor, also embarrassed because so many were around.

"K.C. what *are* you doing?" she demanded.

"Eatin' like a pig," he replied, laughing brown eyes meeting hers. "Pigs eat like this." And he giggled delightedly at two other youngsters who had joined him.

"Dad! Dad!" Shandol fairly shouted. "Come 'n make K.C. behave." Then added threateningly to K.C. in a lowered voice. "I'll have him put yuh in the pig pen and see how yuh like bein' a pig!"

Joel appeared at the door, saw what Shandol meant and immediately told him to get popcorn from the dishpan or eat a cookie right, as pigs weren't allowed to come to parties at this house.

"That kid!" Shandol felt she should say something. "Or the lot of 'em. What one don't think up another will." "You should see one of our parties," she continued to Dean. "I don't mean just here, just about every family has them if there's a birthday or some other excuse. It gets people together and we have fun. This really's not a party. This one family, Lankers, came to invite us to a party at their house Saturday night, and somehow others heard, or just followed Steve or—"

"And you won't be goin' to no party," Dean interrupted softly.

"We could go," she amended, "and stay only a short time. Yuh don't really need to be invited. People invite all they see and send word to those they don't; as Mama sometimes says. Well, you can't just go see everyone, so they have the word passed around. And that is something that really gets around here anything worth tellin', that is, that's for sure."

"We'll see," he agreed. "But choo gotta 'member yer goin' out 'ith me."

Rayda sang, as Shandol has asked her again, shortly after she and Dean had gone to the living room. A few still munched cookies, or the sandwiched graham crackers, or popcorn, which was passed around in a stew pot in the room. Rayda, in turn, asked Phil to sing and Rod joined the suggestion, lest anyone think him jealous, Shandol supposed. Phil said he would sing if Shandol would help. She tried to demur, but was reminded "turn about, fair play," so they sang "I Guess I'm Just a Little Old Fashioned" in harmony. Steve Follerson, not to be outdone, sang his version of Rancho Grande, to Shandol's delight, and Joel was prevailed upon by his daughter to sing an Indian love song. She loved the ballads of the romantic, but usually said fate, of the Indian maidens. Joel had also fiddled a tune earlier, Shandol learned. Then everyone joined to sing "Precious Memories" and by then the slow but steady leave-taking began. Soon all were gone except Dean and Steven Follerson, who was playing checkers. He also left after the game. But how he would love to have won over Joel Sonnett! Dean stayed until Steve left. He had seen the way Shandol listened to his song, her heart in her eyes. But Shandol went to the back porch with Dean when he left.

"I'll be here Sattiday night," were his parting words, as he cupped her small, lovely face in his large hands, bent down and kissed her tenderly.

"Bye now," she replied.

When she was alone at last, Shandol wondered why the mystery about what Dean had to tell her. And why so secretive: She wondered if that were just his excuse to come again, or if he really had something to tell her. What a jolt she was to receive over it.

I wish I'd made him tell me, she thought, *or I'd not go with him Saturday night. Why, oh why, didn't I,* she berated herself. *I am so curious I don't see how I can stand such a long wait. It must have something to do with us—maybe me, directly or indirectly.*

And in a dream that night she seemed to be running, running from wild horses. On one road a corpse. Fear made her feel she was barely moving and couldn't seem to get closer to home, to close the door, *wash her hands* yes, her hands must be washed, and she'd feel safe. Then the corpse disappeared and only the driving need to get home plagued her. Yet all her running seemed to be getting her nowhere. She became so frightened she awoke with a start, sat upright in bed, feeling her heart pounding. She looked out the window and realized where she was, safe in her own bed. A dream? Yes, of course. But why such a nightmarish one? Probably that loaded gun, she shuddered. Then, trying to think of Saturday night to get her mind off her dream, she pulled the light, colorfully handmade quilt up and over her head, she soon slept again.

CHAPTER 14

Saturday it rained in intermittent showers. Between showers there was a denseness of low clouds and mist which seemed to cloak everything in gloomy oppression.

Joel could not go to his job working on the road as they were rained out. The boys listlessly sat about, looking at the papers, making music, and finally became so bored left the house as Bobby followed Phil's decision to go to Horn's house where they could listen to the radio, talk or perhaps just decide to go wandering around despite the wet weather. Tommy and K.C. had settled down awhile on the long back porch to play with toy cars, using the rocking chairs made by Grandpa Bregmanson of hickory switches, and the porch's other paraphernalia, as mountains to go around, towns, their "homes," or whatever their fancies dictated to "play like" at the time. They were not allowed outside to roll their old tires, or running with hoop and paddle. The "hoop" was an iron rim of perhaps ten inches in diameter and one and one-half inches wide. The paddle was a board two feet, more or less, long with an eight inch by two-inch wide cross piece nailed at the bottom to push and guide the hollow rim. Joel had denied them permission to go to a friend's home, who had an unused upstairs room where they could pay with strange things in the attic to see and use for pretend games.

Sometimes they played cowboy games, hide and seek, besides making up their own from stories they had heard. But Joel has vetoed the idea lest they carry mud and muss on the neighbor's floors.

Shandol ironed for two hours, then Jane insisted she must iron. That would include her husband's clothes and the few things of her own. Shandol was glad to oblige so she could wash her hair, pincurl it, and then she tied a triangle head-scarf of cotton print over it, because she had other work to do.

It was also up to Shandol to clean the house on Saturdays. It was a large house and there was quite a bit to do when done thoroughly. However, a Saturday cleaning was hardly that, but made a considerable difference. It was also a depressing task to Shandol, but she knew she must go through the motions. Audrey seldom helped with it, as the dust gave her hay-fever sniffles. She had tried tying a damp cloth over her mouth and nose, which helped, but usually got the sniffles anyway, perhaps taking it off too soon. So Audrey and Shandol had bargained. If Shandol would do the sweeping and dusting, she, Audrey, would cook and wash dishes. Of course, the downstairs rooms were swept more than just on Saturday. Though Shandol knew she should learn to cook. Audrey excused her by saying she would like for Shandol to learn at a time when Audrey could teach her more when they had more to do with than now. There were exceptions to the rule. If Audrey felt bad, then usually her father cooked, with some exceptions, and she did have to wash dishes.

Shandol began by sweeping the bare floor in her parent's bedroom. There were things to put away, mostly in boxes either on or under a large grand piano, which had long since deteriorated to a despairing impossibility. It stayed intact because it belonged to the owners of the place, who, for sentimental reasons did not want to part with it, and could not possibly realize its deplorable condition. Sonnetts did the best they could by it. But it did make a catch-all, which was almost impossible to keep neat. It was the only piece of furniture in the room except the bed, a cot, and a small bedside table. The closet took care of most of the clothing and some other things. A shelf in the closet also helped. But there were things which had to be boxed. Between it all there were quilts, comforts, other bedding, odd clothing, mending and so on.

As soon as she had done the best she could there she went upstairs, leaving the room with a fresh damp smell, as she always sprinkled with water the bare floor of wide planks of wood to help settle some of the dust.

Next she went upstairs to do the bedrooms. She made her own bed first. She stripped it from the pillows, quilts, even the sheet itself. She shook the feather tick, each corner and middle front, turned it over, shook and plumped it some more, then smoothed it evenly. When the sheet, quilt and pillows were replaced and it all covered with a white counterpane, her bed was smooth and neat. The counterpane had belonged to her grandmother Bregmanson. It was old but still in good condition. It was the only bedspread in the house used regularly. Occasionally one was used on the bed downstairs. It was embroidered on white cotton muslin, which had to be starched and ironed, as did its matching bolster.

In Shandol's room was a smallish wood dresser her grandfather had made of some discarded cabinet. It contained a door with one shelf, and two drawers. There was a small mirror hanging on the wall above it. Shandol straightened her few trinkets and cosmetics on top of it and flipped the dust from the embroidered scarf and top of it. There was also a "stand table" by her bed, which had been made with broomstick legs. Shandol used the top of it for her lamp, and a small shelf-brace was beneath the top for a book, usually, as it was not very large. The only place she had to hang her dresses (coats were kept in the downstairs closet or in the hall on a long, gray-painted plank with clothes hooks screwed into it)was a plank, a shorter replica of the hall coat rack, except it was nailed to the wall near her bed. Somethings she put in the dresser drawers or inside the door. There was a what-not shelf with glass door in her room. Audrey had given it to her. It was painted white, had a glass door which hooked, two shelves and a deep bottom. She had been told her grandfather had made it from an old clock. It rested on the floor near the foot of her bed. She kept her few pictures and souvenir treasures in it. Some of these her grandfather had whittled out of wood with only soft wood and a sharp knife. There were small pliers of wood, so perfect in design and so precisely cut they opened and closed as the metal variety did. There was no glue used in their making. There were also puzzles he had made of various sizes, that actually came to pieces and could be put back together again, if one dared remove the one key piece. They were not easy to put together the first few times. Also he had made links of chain with the whittled in links, again no glue. One he had made round which had made Shandol happy when he let her have it. These were more precious as years went on, as he sometimes complained his hands were stiff. Who knew how much longer he could manage this unique pastime. Shandol had accumulated picture postcards, letters, handkerchiefs, and other souvenirs, including a white handled pocket knife given to her during her tom-boy, early puppy-love stage. She had talked a school friend out of it. Its pretty white handle had so caught her eye she knew she had to have it. Luckily the boy had cared enough for her to part with it. Now he had moved away. They had been such children, and he had been "sweet" on her for two years in grade school. He was younger than she was, small for his age, and vowed his everlasting love for her—then. She was not particularly fond of him but she did take advantage of his feeling for her to get the knife. His sisters were her friends. One was a classmate, one older, nearer Lester's age and always tried to make a hit with him, which she never could.

Shandol sprinkled the bedroom floors with handfuls of water, that is the ones used, to sweep them. She had to pick up a few pieces of soiled clothing and toss them over the banister to the hallway below. She shook the crocheted round rug she had in the middle of the floor in her room, out on the upstairs balcony, which was over the front porch. She swept the dampened floors, and made the other beds. Only a mirrorless dresser served the boy's two bedrooms. The rooms then smelled fresh, but damp. Of the four front bedrooms only three were used. The one next to Shandol's room, was mostly empty though it faced the street. Shandol had an old, large, hatbox of dolls and doll clothes, and boxes of other playthings such as dishes, that the hatbox could not hold. She had kept a large doll. There were also her schoolwork papers, books, notebooks and so on. There were also things she wanted to keep but were not in sight in her room. There were three other bedrooms which opened off a narrower hall, which had a closet, and was more over the rear of the house. These rooms were only occasionally cleaned and straightened. The first and smallest one held the jars of canned fruit, vegetables, and meats. Audrey added to their own crops raised to "put by," by canning for other people. She helped with the preparation and processed the jars for one third the total-trading equal numbers of empty jars for those she took filled. It gave the family variety and besides many people realized they preferred the pressure cooker method of canning.

Another room was directly over the dining room and had a floor vent, which meant it could be, and was, heated in winter. It had two windows facing south, and this is where Audrey kept her rather large collection of houseplants in winter. It was a family spring and fall project getting them out for the summer and back inside for winter. There was also a crude table-like desk, a reminder of Lester's study days in high school. He could not tolerate any noise when he studied so the desk area had been prepared for him. Though he had been out of school for sometime now, the desk had not been moved.

The other room and small closet held books and magazines, which were usually in an untidy way, strewn about. It seemed no sooner had someone sorted and stacked them neatly, usually at Joel's request, until someone wanted something to do on a rainy or cold day; hunted a book for information, or perhaps a magazine for picture cut-outs, and never bothered to replace them as they should be. The books were old, as were the magazines, some even belonged to the owners, mostly books, who resided in Oregon and hadn't seen the place for years. The magazines were discards of their own few, or given them by others. But there was never a decision made to destroy them.

Shandol soon finished her tasks, leaving the rooms smelling refreshed, but herself feeling warm and dirty. Next she must tackle the remainder of the downstairs, beginning in the front hall. She picked up what she had thrown down from upstairs, swept the stairs, and the bare hall floor, as upstairs. Then she would need to mop all the linoleum covered floors, after having first swept them. Then dusting. The dining room always gave her the most trouble because of the tiny bird feathers. They were breezed about even by the movement of the broom and it was hard to keep them in front of

176

it. They wanted to whirlwind every which way. The floor had been last mopped after doing the washing, so showed only a few tracks from the wet to outside would remain. She could wet mop the floor this time.

Though Jane had not finished her ironing, and there was visiting and just going about, but they moved out of Shandol's way as she came to some particular area.

After mail time Phil came in waving some letters.

"Looks like Shandol rated the mail today," he said. Then waving them over his head, teased, "how much for these?"

"Give 'em here," she snapped, her energy too sapped to play games. Besides she wanted to read them.

The family was gathering for a late mid-day meal, so Phil handed them over. Not much chance to really taunt her as Joel already sat at the table, and his rule concerning respect of the property of each member of the family was known. He didn't forget the golden rule and found cause at times to remind them.

Shandol looked over the letters. There was one with an army, and one with a navy address. She opened the one with the navy address first because it was from Hugh, a personal friend. His father lived in Maple Hill, though Shandol had met him when he visited, actually had stayed, with his aunt in Greenway. His name was Hugh Burdett and he had gone with Shandol. He had walked her home from school functions, parties, or church, many times. However, he had not asked Shandol to wait for him. She was such a sweet kid and everything was all so uncertain he had said. But he had so insisted she write to him that she answered each letter he wrote to her. She had admired him. He had been the star basketball player because he was tall and could jump so high; this during his two years of high school. His letter now informed Shandol he would be home in October. He asked her to please write soon so he would be sure to receive it by the time he would be getting leave. He wanted to see her, he wrote, so hoped she wouldn't be busy with other things.

The letter with an army address came from a fellow who had thrown his name and address alongside the highway as the army convoy had passed. It was a nice chatty letter about life in the army, some complaints, some humor. And he hoped she would write again and let him know how things were going with her. Shandol wondered if she could measure up to his letter writing ability, although he had complimented her on her lovely handwriting.

Audrey made light bread that day, as she hated doing it on Sunday. She usually made nine loaves every other day. However, today she had made only seven, using the remainder of the dough to make a large pan of hot light-bread buns. The aroma was so tempting it was hard to resist until mealtime. Tommy and K.C. sampled one as soon as they could handle it. Audrey buttered the top of the loaves and buns while they were hot so they would be golden brown, but soft crusted and fresh tasting.

The day sped by. Shandol at times was so preoccupied by her date she was hardly aware of exactly what went on around her. The family knew she had a date. No one, by now, considered it of but little consequence. She had gone about her tasks trying to be her usual casual self. It had not always been easy. She still had nagging thoughts and misgivings. Was she doing right going out with him again? Would it seem like a compromise and she be undoing all she had tried to do? In short, would he suppose she was backing down? Still she had emphasized that he had to learn how to act, hadn't she?

What a lot I'm going through, she thought, *to keep from being asked questions I don't want to answer. Wouldn't Dad be furious if he knew! What kind of guy is Dean anyway, really?* She was going through all the agonies of her very first date with him. The fact he seemed so genuinely sorry for the whole thing gave her heat, at least enough to keep her mood bolstered.

But what's he got to tell me?

Dean came somewhat early. And he was being a dream of consideration from the very first. His gaze and every action dripped with tenderness. Shandol even worried that her parents or Jane would later wonder if he over did it! He commented on her good looks; he caught her arm to assist her off the rickety boards and steps of the back porch. His concern that she be helped into the car was just short of a caress.

Well, he does know some manners, she thought. *I just hope he doesn't think he's buttering me up.*

It was a movie date. On the way to Waiton, Dean said he had to stop at Folks Consent for gasoline.

"Some guys try to impress their girls by telling the service station man to 'fill 'er up'," he laughed, mockingly, "then hold up fingers, one, two, three or however many gallons they want outta sight of the gurls, to show they kin only pay fer that many. Tryin' to impress 'em," she said again, and added, "but I mean fill 'er up!"

They parked in front of the tavern-dance hall. The parking area was in the center of the wide street, rather than at the curbing. Already a few had gathered to dance to the jukebox music, so it was blaring. A few men were openly drinking.

They were there only a short while. Dean went by the filling station for the gasoline. He said "fill 'er up" and took out his wallet obviously to keep his fingers in sight. As the tank was being filled, a short, small man, obviously already nearing inebriation, came to the car on Dean's side.

"I'm needin' money," Shandol heard him say to Dean. "How's 'bout lettin' me sell yuh a ole sow? She's a goodern and'll have pigs in 'bout two, t'ree weeks. Take twelve dollars fer her," he nodded expectantly.

Shandol had seen him around the tavern before. He was called "Grandpa" because his shoulders were so stooped. He had an old-looking steely glint in his rather bleary eyes. Shandol, however, had learned he was actually only twenty five years old. He was often taunted and made fun of, because he was small and caused no trouble about it. Shandol thought it cruel, though he seemed to accept it, as he was accepted, in this taunting, humorous way.

"Yuh gotta deal," Dean replied, "'n we'll jest take keer of it right cheer." He leaned toward the glove compartment, as Shandol sat on her side of the front seat because they were there and Dean was busy, gave it a wop with his fist to make it open, and to Shandol's surprise took out a checkbook. He then wrote out a check for the amount agreed upon. She noticed, because he was writing on his knee next to her, he signed his father's name, then his own under it.

"Thanks, Grandpa," muttered Dean as he moved away.

Grandpa went in front of the car, said "Haddy" to Shandol, bashfully, without meeting her eyes, as he passed the car window, somewhat unsteadily at times, to the corner and toward the tavern.

"He's gotta git drunk Sattiday nights," Dean explained to Shandol, grinning sheepishly.

"Is that why he needed money right then?" she asked, deciding the whole thing incredible.

"Shore is," Dean replied, replacing the checkbook and fountain pen.

"But weren't yuh takin' advantage of 'im a little?" she asked. "Was he capable of realizing what he was doin'? I mean, maybe he's past being able to decide or care, or—or realize."

"He named the price, yuh heared 'em," Dean reminded her. "So 'twas fair 'n square, right, Sam?"

Sam was the station's owner and attendant, who working near the car putting in gasoline, checking oil, wiping the windshield, and eyeing "Dean's girl," had seen and heard the whole thing. He was a large, ruddy faced, snouted looking faced man of perhaps forty, wearing a set of khaki colored pants and shirt. A strand of dark curly hair fell just short of one of his blue-gray eyes.

"Sure was," Sam agreed. "Even the check's good," he kidded Dean, winking at Shandol.

"He'll mess up the bookkeepin'," Shandol, who had taken such a course in high school, replied offhandedly, "if ever' one writes checks."

"Pops'll be glad," Dean replied defensively. "That tuz some bargain. I'd uv jest as easy give 'im five dollars more. The sow's worth at least twenty-five dollars and if'n she has good luck with 'er pigs so much more's the better."

Dean paid for the gasoline in cash, replaced his wallet and they headed on south to Waiton.

"He must've been in bad shape," Shandol marveled at such poor judgment, "tuh need tuh drink that *bad*. Half-price for that hog! He's some dope, 'n he's too young tuh be senile."

"I ain't never seed a Sattiday night that he ditn't get drunk," Dean said again. "Sober all week, works hard helpin' 'is dad, but come Sattiday 'Grandpa's' gotta get drunk. He don't keer about no women'er nuthin', jest a big drunk. If'm he cain't then yuh see how 'tiz."

"I think it's terrible," Shandol said. "And what's his dad gonna say?"

"He cain't say nuthin'," Dean replied. "Uh deal's uh deal. Anyways he knows how y 'Grandpa' is. Besides he'll spend the money and the sow'll jest be gone. She's a fat un too. I've seed 'er. Oh, boy!"

"Too bad for 'im. He'll prob'ly wisht he hadn't done it tomorrow." she decided thoughtfully, rather impatiently.

"Hey, whoz side yuh on? Don't pity 'im," he coaxed her. "It's a break fer me cain't yuh see? His bad luck is my good luck. If'n it hatn't uh been me, it'd uh been somebody eltz."

"Yeah, I suppose," she conceded. "But it's too bad he's in such shape he needs tuh do it, I meant."

"Show's 're gonna be good, I think," Dean remarked to change the subject.

"Whatta yuh got tuh tell me?" She suddenly felt less gloomy herself after the disconcerting brush with the shiftless drunk, as she was inclined to consider him. "Please tell me. I've sure wondered and can't think why yuh think I'd be interested knowin'."

"After the show," he replied firmly.

"Well, there's tuh be no sparkin'," she pouted, "so yuh maze well tell me."

"Oh, we'll go tuh Spoon Hill," Dean replied. "Yuh gotta start trustin' me agin', beginnin' now."

"We'll see, she replied. "Anyway I'm here ain't I?"

It may take some effort, Shandol vowed silently, *but I'm not going to mention that other night, and my disappointment and sassy reaction even try not think of it anymore, beginning tonight.*

And with the decision, a wave of tenderness swept over her, which she let linger because of the sweetness of it. It was the first time the thought had occurred to her, and she wondered if this was how one fell in love. Could she possibly fall in love with the big lug? It was too great a realization to toss about lightly, as she wondered if that were really what she wanted.

The movies were a cowboy show and a love story. Shandol enjoyed them both. After the love story, ending happily, Shandol was riding her own gossamer cloud of dreams, and she wouldn't have been surprised if the man beside her, given her own magical kiss, turned into Prince Charming himself.

When they arrived at Spoon Hill there were two cars already there, so they turned into a lane apart in the wooded area, The car lights lit trees, green underbrush, red-leafed sumac, and privacy. Yet Shandol did not feel apprehensive and isolated. It was better than being in the front room at home, even though someone might could, and might just walk up and rap on the window for attention anytime.

"Now," Shandol breathed expectantly. "I hope it's good.Do get on and tell me!"

"Don't be so happy now," Dean replied, almost sharply.

"Why?" she asked, somewhat deflated.

"I'm goin' away," he replied flatly.

"You're leavin'? Just like that, huh?" Shandol cried, stunned. "But why? How can yuh? Uh—uh uniform?" Her voice shook. She couldn't bare to say the army—or any other branch of the armed services.

"No," he laughed, nervously, "nuthin' uz *permanent* uz that. I been thinkin' 'bout this uh week or two though."

"A week—'er two?" Shandol repeated, haltingly. She was so stunned with surprise her head reeled. It made her dizzy trying to let it all soak in. She had been floating on her cloud of dreams, of romantic endings to hearts entwined and living happily ever after. But the gossamer was weak material to hold so much fancy. Ah, the fall of innocence! The drop bounced from earth to reality, abruptly and joltingly. As a whiplash it hurt and she was thoroughly shaken.

She burst into tears. She was mortified at herself for doing it, and that was the last thing she wanted to do. But she couldn't have helped if her life had depended upon it, she was sure. It was so frustrating. Was Dean moody and undependable after all? How could he deal her such a blow, now of all times? Why had he given this lovely night such a horrible ending?

"D-don't th-think I-I'm c-cryin' 'cause y-you're leavin'," she sobbed, as coherently as possible. "I-I thought th-things were tuh be different. But just you go: Leave! A-and I-I d-don't c-care if yuh don't come back—ever!"

So he's been thinking about it for a week or two had he, she thought, trying now to control herself. *Before that night! What if I had really been so-so stupid? So that's one way those things happen? Supposing I had already been head-over-heels in love with him?* A blanket of self-pity settled over her and she sobbed silently.

"Take me home," she cried, forcefully, so she wouldn't stutter so much. "I think I hate you. Take me now! I tell yuh, now!" She began weeping all over again bitterly. She blew her nose on her small handkerchief, which was becoming damp with tears. Tears of remorse, disappointment, tension.

"Shandol, please," Dean pleaded, finally breaking an equally stunned silence. He was taken by surprise at her outburst, and was puzzled why she was so heartbroken, disappointed, or just like a woman? "I ain't tole yuh all yet."

"Yuh needn't neither," she sniffed jerkily. "Don't I already know? That night—and yuh'ud left me flat! I can't believe it! I can't stand it! I can't—I just can't! After all your pretty speech? I can't stand you right now neither, and I wanna go home! So take me. Just please take me," It was a child's plea. She was begging. She moaned as though she had been dealt a blow, she rubbed the side of her head.

"Shandol, no, pleez," Dean began again. "Wait, at least hear me out."

"No! No!" she cried.

There was silence again and Shandol tried to get hold of herself.

"I can't take yuh home like this," he said, abruptly. "Cryin' and carryin' on over—I'm tryin' to unnerstand what."

How true. He wouldn't want to take a near hysterical girl home. As her weeping subsided somewhat, Dean moved closer to her and she allowed him to hold her to him to comfort her.

"My darlin'," he whispered, "I ditn't realize it'd upset yuh so, and 'cause of that other. But don't yuh know I wouldn't hurt yuh for the worl'?"

"But yuh said—" she began, realizing it was the first time he had really used an endearment when talking to her. She looked at him, still wiping at her nose and eyes.

"My dear, I see now how it must've seemed, I do." The endearments seemed wrung from his soul. "I know what yuh think it coulda been, but it ain't. Don't cry now, just don't. I don't like tuh see yuh cry."

"It tuz like a slap er somethin'," she explained. "And, boy, yuh don't know my family. Mom allus said she druther have boys, because things happens to girls that disgraced families. My dad's heart would've broke. How'd I ever-a told 'em? Whatever woulda become uh me? I'm scared." And had she known the term, could not have felt more vulnerable. She was sure if the world's weight were on her shoulders she couldn't have felt heavier.

She turned her head to look out the open window, thoughtfully. She looked into the darkness. Crickets chirped. A lonesome bird seemed to be calling home. The grotesque figures of large trees, saplings, the trampled down places, dead stumps, huge rock formations and fallen limbs all made an uneven "skyline." All seemed still.

"I bet it'd been like yuh to of tol' yer dad," Dean mocked.

"For your pin-head information," she retorted sarcastically, "the man I marry must love me as much—though different too, I guess. So there!"

"Hit beats h--l outta me," Dean slapped his leg, "but I got more 'pachens' with yuh than enny gurl I've ever went with. I've took more too. Why, I don't rightly know. But any other gurl I b'lieve I'd jest took 'er home and let 'er bawl!"

"Well, why didn't yuh?" Her lips trembled. She thought she might cry again. All the pent-up emotions of the past several days were perhaps not all spent. "I asked yuh to anyway, didn't I?"

"I cain't say," he replied in a softer voice. "Yuh're diff'rent somehow tuh me. I coultn't hardly stand it when I thought I'd not git tuh see yuh no more. Shandol, I hadta come back. An' when I got there that night and seed all those people then I thought, lord, yuh don't e'n keer. Wuz e'en havin' uh good time at the party. I knowed I had tuh talk tuh yuh ag'in. Now, I wanna tell yuh how sweet yuh were then. Yuh were, yuh know."

He leaned down and kissed her beside her nose. She was sitting with her legs under her, feet toward the door, her hands on her lap, she turned slightly to face him and he was close to her.

"Shandol, write me when I'm gone," he went on. "Write 'n most uh all think uh me often."

"But where're yuh goin'?" she asked, "if not to the army or navy, where else—?"

"There's uh new army camp gettin' put up over near the state border—west uh here. They need workers, and I'm gonna see if'n I kin git on. Will yuh write tuh me? Say yuh will, Shandol."

"Well, I suppose so," she replied," But yuh'll hafta write tuh me first or how'll I know where tuh write to?"

"I will don't worry," he hastened to reply. "Just yuh answer. I want yuh tuh write yer name 'n address down so's I'll be sure 'm git it spelt right and have it with me. Will yuh?"

"Uh—Uh, sure," she replied. "when'll yuh go?"

"I'm goin' with Brad 'n his brother. Soon's they git ready, I reckon."

"Who's Brad?"

"Oh, he's uh friend uh mine, neighbor too. Knowed 'im all my life. His brother's married and got two kids."

"Oh," she said. He handed her paper from the glove compartment, obviously ready for it. She wrote her name and address, including their post office box number.

"Feelin' better?" he asked, after a moment. "Yuh know yer actions are somethin'. But yuh jest act before the facks are all give."

"I suppose so," she agreed. "It's just it was so unexpected, and I put two and two together, and it hurt, I guess. Besides with boys around I have tuh take my part, don't I?"

Can it hurt even before falling in love, she wondered later, after she had gone to bed and was thinking about it all over again. *What's next? I must learn to be more prepared and less "tear-trigger happy."*

CHAPTER 15

Shandol went to work the next week for three days only after all. Marcia had grown stronger and was not so nervous about being left alone with her small son. Freda, who lived nearby, also liked to go see the baby and hold and coddle him, which she often did. They realized they could call on Freda in a pinch. Thus it was agreed that because of these developments Shandol would not be needed after Wednesday.

On Monday she cleaned and straightened the house; Tuesday she did a large washing, and Wednesday she ironed. With these chores out of the way, they reasoned, they were sure they could manage afterward because Marcia's health was so improved.

Wednesday afternoon, just before Shandol left to go home she was paid for her work. The pay consisted of two dresses. One was a nice green print summer voile, and one a flimsy one of blue crepe. She was also given a maroon-colored wool skirt, plus one dollar and fifty cents in cash. Shandol had supposed she would be given one dollar for each week she worked, but she realized the clothing was worth much more than she could have purchased with the cash.

The skirt was a slim style and would go nicely with a white satin blouse, which she, Shandol, her mother and a neighbor had made of a remnant. Shandol had worn it to school. The blouse had wide long sleeves. She supposed she might even wear the skirt with a pale blue one almost like the white, for a contrasting effect. But mostly she preferred the blue with a dark gray jumper she had and liked, which had cost fifty cents on sale. The satin had worn well, washed and ironed beautifully, and both were still good. The money she was given therefore, she would save for now for something she would need. Now that she was going out she wished for some type of short jacket for early fall. She did have a good winter coat. In fact two. Audrey had purchased for fifteen dollars a new one only last year. Her mother had managed the money from the sale of young canaries she had raised and shipped to the pet shop in St. Louis. Also some of the money had gone back into supplies that feeding and caring for the birds necessitated. There was bird seed, cuttlebone, and Shandol scarcely knew what all, but these were usually special objects or medicines to be replaced. The coat Audrey had bought, made a modified fitted style, had a removable fur collar, which had never been removed. Shandol's friends thought it becoming, and prevailed upon her to leave it. Audrey had agreed it just suited her.

And last year during the school year the study hall teacher, who had rather taken up with Shandol, partly because she had attended school where her nephew was teacher, and partly because she knew she was timid, shy, quiet and sometimes frightened, coming from a small school as she had, to attend a much larger one, with different ways, had given her a darling winter coat. It had a narrow fur trim and had a textured, almost nubby, and more expensive look. Though it had been a hand me-down, from whom Shandol never knew or worried about it. It was so pretty. It was kept back for more dressy times and she had worn the other to school. Also, Audrey, at times wore the one she had bought Shandol, as Audrey's own did not look as well, though Audrey felt it good enough for Greenway. The used one was made fitted, therefore smaller, and did not fit Audrey.

Shandol also had a dream of owning a dress of spun rayon, she had heard so much about, and thought the material quite pretty. Also gabardine. If they could not find one or the other at a low sale price, Audrey had agreed they might have to make one. She hoped she could remember to price the yard goods at Plainesville the next time she went. She would need to know first how much would be required and then calculate about how long she would have to save. Joel also gave her money along, as he could spare it, for her helping at home; usually a dollar each week if possible. If not at each pay check for sure. This money she hoarded for the things she wanted, or needed, and could get no other way.

Audrey was delighted at Shandol's "pay." The clothing was well made and nicer than they could ever have been able to afford. And the new mother, as Shandol explained, was looking forward to a new wardrobe. She was sure anyway she could never use the other things again, hinting there might be more. She was taller than Shandol, but had now filled out. So the alterations would be at the waist length, skirt length and little bother.

With mixed feelings Shandol began her routine at home again. There was little to do except to accept her share of the housework. She had a lot of time to think. She was inclined to think that right now her life now amounted to just marking time. Just so much time had to pass before she could really consider calling her time her own. She wished she could be sure that after the passing of that time that somehow things would be different. Sometimes it seemed just a dream of a far away time and so very dim she could not see how it would be possible for her to get there. She wondered if she were foolish to think of it and hope. If only she could somehow *see*, could somehow *know* if she would ever realize her heart's desires and do the things she most wanted.

She knew she did not want to stay in this place, which sometimes seemed to close in upon her as a prison. She wanted to see something of the world and learn about the people and their different ways, of those fellow beings who populated this planet earth. It seemed a large order for one person such as she knew herself to be. Yet, she reasoned, if she could get to work somewhere else, where people were doing all different things, and seeing these things getting done, and being where such things were just everyday life, one was sure to see, hear, and learn quite a lot. And a lot of that she was sure her father would rather she was shielded from knowing. But, after all, she could read a few things in the newspapers.

That was, she supposed, what she wanted most was to be a part of a city newspaper. It was necessary for reporters to know first hand to report accurately what went on; or so her idea of it was. She would occasionally try to visualize in her mind mangled bodies in wrecks, or someone horribly burned in a fire, waiting for an ambulances. It might be something she would have to become accustomed to seeing and she realized it would most likely shock her. Could she bear to see a brawl in which guns or knives were used? The thought made her shudder. Or perhaps she would need to give newspaper accounts of murders, which would be expected to be reported from police files— or wherever and whatever source she would have to use to find the facts. Could she? She knew only vaguely of "houses of ill repute" but scarcely considered them enough to put a name to those involved, and except for women being used by men for selfish purposes, cared little about such degraded women. She had no patience for their otherwise lack of what to was moral character. Could she see, learn, and write of such things, yet never be a part of them, or "tainted" by those involved? Could she learn to see, or hear about, to report these things objectively? And, as it would possibly be horrible for her at first, how long would it take her not to be shocked or horrified? Could she live, work and walk on the borderline of everything, sometimes perhaps precariously, and keep her strength of character, her mind unsullied, and purity of soul? Then she could go safely to her own home when her work was done. She envisioned that home a compact, comfortable place, stylishly furnished, feminine, and all her very own. There she could go to wash and feel clean, or perhaps bask in a real bathtub. Would it be as simple as washing off the "itch germ"? She wished she could hear or read about someone who really did these things. Were women limited in what they were allowed to do? But there was always her father pointing out to her that the more she saw and learned of "worldly ways" the less she would like it. Was that so for her? Was she so much the better for being ignorant? She wished for a middle ground, perhaps objective view. And she knew that for now there were only the vaguest of daydreams.

The urgency she felt for these things was due in part to the fact school was going on and she was no longer a part of that anymore. The realization of this jabbed at her, though she was trying to adjust to the fact, and to hide how she felt at not belonging anywhere anymore. It was a lonely feeling, not going to school, not belonging to a group or her class. She was realizing also there was a certain security about not having the pressures or uncertainties about what she should be doing. Any ambitions now were still in a *hoping* stage; trying to plan was hopeless and self-defeating. Her father's consent for what she might want to do would be a problem. She was already getting suspicious of certain postponements now. Were there hurdles being deliberately put in her way? That was a wall-building thought in itself. She wondered if she would be able to go *anywhere* if her father did not agree? How could she? How far could she go, perhaps by bus, and have money to live while searching for a job? Which seemed to point to some semblance of parental support and consent, and of these things she had never been assured. Not really.

At night she saw the old desk busy in the front room, someone with books. Or perhaps it would be the dining table. Sometimes, even now, Phil studied there, though the desk was usually used by the older ones. This was when he had some subject he had to work on. He would do only what was required of him, seldom making any extra effort, as Tommy and K.C. would do. Bobby would check his work, but it seemed to some easy for him, as Shandol thought it had for Lester also.

At times Shandol could not help berating Phil for his exasperating lack of concern for his schoolwork. He reminded her he had time to do some at school. She hoped he did. But it seemed to Shandol he was always too ready to finish and he and Bobby go somewhere. Where? To listen to the radio, or just loaf around and visit, she supposed.

"You should appreciate school more," she once told him. "Yuh'll sure miss it when yer out of it."

"What's it gettin' you?" he had asked, pointedly. "Not one thing. Yuh should set the example." he had taunted.

"Don't rub it in," she replied. "I didn't plan things as they are. I'm just doin' what I can under the circumstances. Surely yuh know that? I hope it's only a delay. Besides yer a boy. For boys it's easier."

"Ain't fer Lester," he replied. "Besides yuh've already done yer great deed," he teased then, not taking her as seriously as she would have preferred.

"Oh, be serious."

"Yup," he went on, undaunted. "By the age uh three yuh'd shown up the wickedness in this family for what it was, and broke it down completely, once and for all, I guess."

"Must yuh always make jokes?" she retorted. "Besides yuh coulda done the same thing. Prob'ly would've if I hadn't. I just got here first. Har! Har!"

"Oh, no," he replied good-humoredly, as usual. "Just yer luck."

"Whadda yuh talkin' about?" Tommy interrupted.

"Haven't yuh heard?" Phil asked. "Shandol here, she stopped Dad's cussin' habit when she was less'n three years old. She'd cuss right along with 'em, so he had to quit tuh make 'er quit. Seems he didn't want his baby girl cussin' aroun' ever'body and havin' 'em guess where she learnt it."

"Well, I'll be jiggered," Tommy said. "Whew, I guess not."

Joel was out for the evening to the school board meeting.

There was no sign Audrey had heard this conversation. She could hardly have objected. She and Joel had both, in a joking manner, informed them of the fact in the first place.

Hence there was no way for Shandol to forget about school. Phil rode the bus to Plainesville, Bobby, Tommy and K.C. could go to Greenway. They usually spent more time studying than Phil. Bobby studied until he was satisfied. The other two kept going over and over theirs, especially Tommy. He helped K.C. and they copied words and numbers, cutting and pasting even—with paste made of flour and water—just to amuse themselves. K.C. thought he must learn the alphabet in order, and had had enough help he could about do it. He had been so proud he had learned to write the numbers to ten before anyone else in his first grade class.

Shandol considered visiting Mrs. Davis, the book lady, and get books to read again, now that Dean would be leaving. He hadn't been sure when that would be. He merely laughed and told her if he failed to show up some night when they had a date, she would know he had gone. But he assured her he would write as quickly as he could whether they had an address or not.

Shandol and Dean did get to go to the Plaines County Fair together, shortly before mid-September. It was to be their last real date for awhile. They enjoyed taking it all in, much of the time walking hand in hand as they went from place to place to view the exhibits. They possibly spent more time around the carnival area. They rode the Ferris wheel, swings, and "tubs," then the Ferris wheel again. Shandol could not help contrasting it with the good times they had had at the reunion and this simply didn't measure up. Of course she enjoyed herself at the fair, but they seemed to be trying harder. The reunion had had such spontaneity, such naturalness they had enjoyed in spite of the fact they were almost strangers. The fact Dean was leaving was, here at the fair, mutely between them. And try as they might it seemed to put a veil of gloom about them. The reunion had also had a more romantic setting. The nights had seemed beautiful, with warm breezes, soft darkness cloaking the bright midway and then being able to see it all reflected on the glittering ripply lake. The couple was quieter and they were concerned over their immediate interests. Dean had said earlier he did not want them to dwell on his leaving. Yet it was so close to the front of their minds they had to remember to stifle the obvious. They had both been glad they went, when it was time to take Shandol home. Dean had even commented on the time he had had not to refer to his leaving. But if inadvertently a sentence had to remotely recall it they had given each the other meaningful glances. Dean's treatment of her had been tender and sweet, she thought. Even his good night kiss, though tender, had been deeply searching and she sensed hunger.

Dean came for Shandol the following evening. He had come early. "I want to spend as much time as I kin with my sweetheart," he had explained to her.

There had been nothing planned, so far as Shandol knew. So she was not surprised they were just riding around; then decided to stop to eat and talk. But the surprising highlight so far as Shandol was concerned, was that it was the night Dean and his father had decided to get the sow he had bought from "Grandpa." Dean wanted her to go along. Dean and Shandol had gone in the car while Dean's father had hired a small truck to haul the large hog. Dean went to "oversee" this actual obtaining of the prize. Because, as Dean had predicted, his father was pleased.

"He's tried tuh git me tuh sell 'er back to 'em," Dean told Shandol as they watched the large awkward hog being loaded. "But I woultn't," he went on. "I jest tole 'em she warn't fer sale. A deal's a deal and we made the deal fair and square."

"I figured he'd be sorry later," Shandol murmured.

"He coultn't git o'er it. Guess 'cause we waited so long to git 'er. But she'll soon have this litter uh pigs and then be bred ag'in in a few months, for more profit—with any luck a-tall," he amended.

"Dean," Shandol pleaded shyly, "let's not talk about it."

"About what?" he asked surprised.

"Uh—gettin' animals to—uh—be born and things."

"But I like raisin' animals," he objected. "In fack it's necessary to uh farmer. Farmers discuss sech things with their wives."

He looked at her, but she dropped her eyes. He looked away, thinking *what a baby* and the subject was dropped. *Another day,* he thought.

But to Shandol it was a confusing contract! Her father had never allowed her "tender ears" to listen to the subject of getting their cow bred, for instance. Yet Shandol knew from Audrey's telling her on the aside, that the cow was led by a rope halter to the large dairy farm across the railroad tracks for the use of the bull (for a night). There was a small fee, Shandol gathered, but she was not present to hear discussions concerning it. Now, at even her age, and in this stage in time she was embarrassed. She had not been prepared for Dean's openness with her on the subject.

In truth Joel had been shocked and showed it when Shandol had told them she heard someone say that if the cow were bred in the morning, instead of evening, the calf would be a heifer. Joel had had dreams of adding a calf to mature to another cow to the one cow he had. He often wished for a heifer, hoping to keep her. And, although Joel chided Shandol passively for talking of things she wasn't supposed to understand, he did try it. It had worked! Whether by coincidence, a trick of fate, or fact of life they did not question, they could not know. They were just amazed that it had worked.

Shandol had felt the same shame, or sheer embarrassment, she had been made to feel as she wondered about these things. *He sees me as such a little girl,* Shandol rationalized to herself. Yet now it had caused a strain between herself and Dean she felt, because he took it all so for granted. It was his way of life—this breeding and raising of farm animals.

Shandol and Dean followed the truck to where Dean lived. She decided, privately, it must be the farthest from civilization possible in the whole area. It was also at the end of a lane, off the main road at least a quarter of a mile of trees, brush and grass lined fence rows. The farmstead consisted of a large barn, farrowing sheds (these he had pointed out to her as the sow would possibly occupy one), poultry houses, a privy and sheds in various stages of disrepair. The home itself was not a large one though a story and one-half high. The elderly-looking couple had "raised" seven children, as Shandol was told again. Dean was the youngest, and was born late in his parent's lives. Inside the white house, itself showing signs a paint job would soon be in order, was about as Shandol had grown to expect from having visited other places. A quilt covered the sofa, with toss pillows in the front room; crocheted rugs in front of the chairs and at the doorways. A picture of Christ was prominently hung on one wall. A faded rug covered the floor, but linoleum covered the floor in the room beyond, which Shandol guessed was the kitchen-dining room.

She met Dean's parents and was surprised. She hadn't expected them to look as old as they did. Dean was, after all, her own age. Mrs. Leonard was plump, short, with gray hair and gray eyes, whose very countenance showed disenchantment. Hers had likely been a hard life, yet she squared her shoulders as though determined to go on. Her husband, and Dean's father, was larger, also fair with a ruddy complexion and pale gray eyes. He complained of his back, apparently a rather constant thing and more important than his wife's complaints, because Mrs. Leonard did much of the work. He had managed to help unload the "sow-hog." Shandol had watched also, noting the barnyard animal waste, and jimson weed which hadn't been cut. Shandol noted the strong resemblance Dean shared with his mother. She wondered if she saw it in her son. And wondered if Dean were like her in personality, or his complaining dad.

Shandol had looked beyond the immediate area. It was nature at its prettiest, and, yes, wildest; she had not seen the likes of it in a long time. To the east was a low bluff, at the base of which a creek ran. There was woods and saplings, weeds and brush between she could see, which apparently spread to the creek also.

"It would be so perfect for deer and other wild things. If I lived here I'd try to get deer brought here." She was almost musing aloud. Just any type of animal might love it, she thought. It was so enchanting, almost breathtaking, because of the surprise of it, she fell to daydreaming that one day she might live here with Dean. His parents were old now and he'd be a lot of help. She had no desire to live with them. They would just have to build nearer the creek and bluff like hill to the north, so she could see the animals she envisioned there. She even hoped she could make friends with them, with pet fawns, squirrels and rabbits and they would trust her and be close to her.

When the unloading was finished and Dean decided it was time to go, nothing would do Dean's mother but that they must go inside and have some blackberry pie. Shandol was given a small glass of milk; the others preferred coffee. She realized they considered her quite young, as so many did. Shandol did enjoy the pie and milk and said so.

After small talk and pleasantries at having been "made acquainted," Shandol and Dean were on their way. There was much Shandol understood about Dean then. Particularly in the way he talked. Dean had actually improved on his grammar some! But Shandol was sure they talked the old-time hillbilly-in its purer form, if there were such a thing. One remark stuck in Shandol's mind, which Dean's mother had made. "I seed Nancy at town Tuesday," she said. Nancy was Dean's cousin, Shandol learned, but Shandol thought about that "seed." Had Dean used the word in that sense and she had ceased to notice? She wasn't sure.

Dean and Shandol still had time on their hands, as it was still early. They drove to Spoon Hill. Shandol had no qualms concerning Dean's treatment of her now. She was sure he was serious about her (if only she would grow up, he implied). There was little to do but talk. He was still excited about acquiring that hog, and they talked of his leaving. And once, as he kissed her, he remarked he wished they could be married before he left.

Soon, Dean spied Brad, one of the young men going away with him to work. He had his girl friend in the car. Dean moved his car closer, as they had not seen Dean's car and its occupants.

Shandol was introduced to Brad's girl friend, Frances. She was quick to point out everyone called her Fran, and she hoped Shandol would. She also remarked of the unusual name Shandol had, asked if she had a nickname, and Shandol, used to it by now explained how she got her name.

Fran was a tiny blond, with a plump baby face, a quick dimpled smile and a few pimples marred her otherwise fair skin. Shandol learned she considered the pimples a curse and she over-emphasized them. However, they gave her the school-girlish look, which indeed she still was. She was a junior in high school, and Shandol wondered if she would ever finish. She was quite obviously in love with Brad, and even vowed she would not consider going with anyone while he was gone. In fact she confided to Shandol she wished that Brad would consider their being married before he left.

Brad was average height and handsome. His hair was dark and wavy, a strand falling over his brow, and he combed it frequently. He combed it straight back. It was a marked contrast to Dean's short blond hair, which he combed to one side. Brad had dark eyes, which Shandol finally realized were a deep blue. They were twinkly, mischievous eyes. Shandol decided privately he was proud of his looks, his trim manly figure—and was rather spoiled. He was certainly less concerned about settling down than Dean. However, Fran saw no fault in him, such as his dependence upon his parents. He made few attempts to get a job outside his father's farm. His older, married brother had finally persuaded him to go with him to help with the army camp. He pointed out he had a girl friend now, and the pay would be excellent, so he could hardly refuse manfully.

Later the two couples decided it was not only past time, but they could do with some food. It was decided Dean and Shandol would go into Folks Consent and get lunch meat, cheese, potato chips and soda pop, and make their own meal in the car, in the form of sandwiches, as the list also included bread.

After returning with the meal "makin's," Shandol and Dean got into the back seat of Brad's car, a two-door, which necessitated Fran's seat back being pushed forward, but she was small and it did not squeeze her completely from her seat. They decided upon Brad's car because it had a radio. They chose a portion of the school grounds behind the schoolhouse itself to eat. They could park on a hill in case the radio sapped the battery so badly the car wouldn't start. At least it could be pushed down the long grade to start it.

With a musical background, they visited, joked, and Fran and Brad even sparred good-naturedly. There was also a comedy program which they giggled about. They talked of the job to which the men were going, even though the men had to admit they were not sure what they would be doing, or where they would stay.

They discussed the "inevitable" draft. Also the lengthening of the stay from one year to eighteen months. An even longer time was a possibility, and was being discussed they knew. The war was unanimously termed a grim proposition. The United States had hoped to stand behind the free countries, but there was France on the Nazi side now, as was Italy. The Soviet planes had carried out their first bombing raid against Berlin last month. But the Germans were sweeping up the Ukraine, and the Russians had blown up their Dnieper Dam.

Japan was more and more being considered wishy-washy, it seemed, with an unsettled government, yet apparently out to sow seeds of war themselves somewhere. Last year they had bombed Chungking, China. But the United States, the young people supposed, seemed fairly safe. After all there was, they had been told, an American navy in Hawaii and Manila. Names and exactly what these meant it would never occur to them to question. They were satisfied, as gathered from older people, they would more likely turn their forces upon China, who had no navy, or upon Russia, if the new cabinet felt ambitious. They were a cautious people, weren't they? The young people did not always agree, but one cloud did hover, however flimsy it might seem or they hoped it to be: What if the United States became involved? Only perhaps, the United States was too far away.

They also discussed Plainesville's county fair some. Brad and Fran had not gone as neither lived in Plaines county. The next county east was only two or three miles down the highway from Greenway, which meant Folks Consent was in the next county.

"It was not nearly the fun the reunion was, but we had a good time," Shandol told Fran. "But we could never duplicate that reunion in a million years," she laughed. "And that's so strange. Dean and I were practically strangers."

Of course Margie McNeeley had not been along that time Dean and Shandol had gone with Jim and his new girl friend, Ellen Garfield. She was plumpish, with light brown hair, a pretty face and good complexion. Her large blue eyes were expressive, her features were molded for her pixie nose and even hairline. She was a good conversationalist. She had a quiet self-possessed, yet self-confident way one immediately grasped. She frequently, as she talked, batted her large blue eyes, glancing sideways, and elsewhere, to see that she had all the attention as she talked. She was from a large family, also obvious as she told interesting anecdotes and doings at home. And she could make them all seem so worth the telling. Jim seemed never to miss a word. Jim was proud of her, Shandol saw. They were about the same height, he perhaps some taller, so they made an interesting couple. Later Dean told Shandol Ellen's father was a successful dairy farmer, with a splendid heard of dairy cattle. And with cheese factories in both Folks Consent and Plainesville, there was plenty demand for the milk. There were also some store and delivery demands, so no doubt he made a profit. Though there was a large family most of the food for both the animals and family was home grown. Now two of the older boys were in uniform.

Shandol was mostly quiet and observant, however. In fact she was shy and self-conscious comparing herself to Ellen's quick wit and easy conversation topics. Ellen seemed not to notice. She could talk non-stop. Yet she seemed so friendly and down to earth, Shandol really hoped to get better acquainted with her. Ellen was also still in school which made Shandol feel still not only more inadequate, but rather old and stupid.

However, the real highlight of the county fair, for Shandol, had been, she recalled, was having met Phil's girl friend. She had beautifully luxurious hair, to which her picture could not do justice. Shandol could only prejudicially recall she was twenty-two years old to Phil's sixteen. She looked no older than Phil and acted no older. She was short and childishly vivacious. But Shandol could not understand why such a lovely girl did not go with someone her own age. Her wide-set eyes were strikingly innocent and childlike. They were almost the color of mahogany, as though reflecting somewhat from her dark auburn hair. "As fire behind a grate," Phil had teased Shandol. She recalled one speech Phil had made about her rich brown eyes with sparks—and those lashes? They had length, were thick, dark, curly and beautiful. Even Shandol, who had been proud of her own, considering them a redeeming feature, she thought did not match them.

Shandol supposed Phil was practicing a pretty speech as he had spoken at the time. And under ordinary circumstances Shandol supposed she might have liked her. But with Phil so wrapped up in her and at her age, Shandol could see no future in it for either of them. I don't think I like her, Shandol thought, a mite jealous of her beauty, and decided she would not be flattered, merely friendly, by her exclamation to Phil so Shandol heard, "Oh, you didn't say your sister was so beautiful." It was a mutual feeling perhaps, each thinking the other beautiful.

It had, however, been a pleasant, satisfying evening. Shandol and Dean had been together and it seemed with better understanding between them. It was a quiet enjoyment as there had been no controversial bickering, no subjects to hassle over. His leaving was certain, or at least tentatively settled, and his coming back to see her whenever he could was also certain, he assured her. Their good-bye at Shandol's door was sweet and promising in mutual kisses. Shandol later wondered how it would be to send a sweetheart off to war—if it came to that. Or what about a husband. She again thought of what her mother had said: "It was easier to send a sweetheart than a husband," and she wondered why.

Now, all she need do was wait for him to write and she wondered if he really would—or could. And she wondered how she could write to him not knowing how well he read and what would interest him in a letter. *That* she was to learn!

CHAPTER 16

It was Friday before Shandol heard from Dean. She received a postcard with no return address.

During that week Shandol tried not to mope and be glum about his being gone. She did admit, to herself at least, she did miss anticipating their dates. Because by now these had begun to include a mid-week one, usually not made in advance. He would just drop by and have her hurry and get ready and they'd go somewhere. Now she wouldn't expect him and she realized she did miss him more than she supposed she would.

Her mood apparently showed because she was reminded by her father she could not spend time moping, thinking of Dean, and reading romantic stories. There was work to be done and she was expected to help out with it. So she helped pick-up and can apples. They were free for the picking up off the ground. They were referred to as "fallen apples." The whole family had also helped Joel dig sweet potatoes, which he sold. There was still some left for their own use, which could be dug when convenient. Joel also "worked on the road."

There was fall house-cleaning, which was almost a repeat of spring cleaning. Curtains were washed, and the lacy ones starched and stretched in a wood frame on a stand, the curtain edges placed over small scant headed nails driven quite close together. There were the winter comforts to air; and the washing of the lighter quilts, used during the summer, which would be stored away until next year. It meant giving the house a good going over inside, cleaning and scouring as necessary, including downstairs windows. This work was done and projects accomplished as time and routine permitted.

* * * * *

On Tuesday Shandol saw Margery at the store and hailed her, waved, and as she saw Margery was coming toward the path to the house, went to meet Margery part way.

"I volunteered to come to the store so's I could see yuh," Margery said. "I heard Dean's gone, so wondered if yer lonesome."

"I do sort of miss thinkin' he might show up at almost anytime," Shandol admitted.

They exchanged light conversation and then Margery told Shandol why she had made the effort to see her. Margery wished Shandol to go visit school with her one day.

"Oh, I couldn't, could I?" Shandol asked.

"Sure, " Margery answered, quickly, the grin broad on her pleasant face. "Let's go ask your mom if she can spare you tomorrow. Yuh can go home with me tonight and we'll just ride the bus down tomorrow. No use waitin', is there?"

Shandol had doubts but she supposed Margery knew if it would be all right or not.

"It will take your mind off things for a day," Margery had told her, "and yuh can see my school."

It was decided they would ask Audrey, Margery was so enthused about her idea. Audrey could see no reason why Shandol shouldn't take the day off if it was all right with the school. So it had been settled. The girls had spent many nights with one another over the years, so it was assumed it was all right with Margery's mother also. And with both being from rather large families, it hardly made much difference at mealtime.

Margery went to Folks Consent to school. She rode the bus so it would mean an all day visit. Both girls carried a sack lunch. Margery introduced Shandol to her teachers in turn as her classes changed. They were friendly and cordial usually commenting on her unusual (to them)name. At the noon hour and morning and afternoon recesses (which even the high school had, another novelty to Shandol). Shandol saw both Fran and Ellen and talked and visited with them. Ellen seemed glad to report she had a date with Jim Brown again Saturday. Ellen knew Dean was gone and that Shandol had no idea as to whether to expect him or not.

"Can't tell about these guys, can yuh?" she sympathized. During Margery's classes Shandol tried to be as inconspicuous as possible. She tried to read a book she had suggested to Margery to choose for her, but it was hard to concentrate. She felt curious eyes upon her; she felt she was a distraction to those in the classes, and invariably ill at ease. She hoped she was keeping no one from his or her lessons. She made every effort to appear interested in the book and ignore them. But she did "soak up atmosphere." The class noises, the smell of books, seeing a teacher in front of the room, it was all so classroomy, that had been so familiar to her in past years.

She indeed enjoyed it. She had so wanted to be in a classroom again, she hoped with no bother to anyone, or a nuisance to the teacher. And it was all so easy with no lessons! But that only brought the nostalgic realization she was visiting. Once she felt she might have been a bother when a boy was asked to get her a chair—from she knew not where, possibly the auditorium, she supposed. But she had to remain objective about it all, because she wasn't really a part of it. She enjoyed being with Margery, but it made a difference. She had not felt she was in school, only visiting with her friend.

There was one thing Shandol could marvel at, which was the short ride there and back. Shandol had gone to Plainesville, and their bus route had included rough country roads off the highway. Shandol had heard it was at least a twenty-five mile route, but seemed nearer forty to her sometimes. For awhile it had been a touch-and-go situation as to whether she could stand the trips. Her parents had worried when she lost weight, and was sometimes dizzy headed, woozy, and nearly car sick. But Audrey so had her heart set on Lester and Shandol graduating from there, they decided to give it a few weeks. Shandol had adjusted. Not only to the long ride but the tension and nervousness of the abrupt change from the small friendly school, to the large, strange, sometimes cold receptive newness of the school. It had been a cold ride in winter in the unheated bus. Many times she had sat with her cold feet on the seat, her coat covering them, which helped slightly. Sometimes snow or ice made the traveling slower and more precarious. But they had been lucky having had no flat tires or other trouble and being stranded far from school or help. Only once could Shandol recall having trouble and then they had slipped into a small roadside ditch. There had been enough boys on the bus to push and so it was a minor happening.

Margery, on the other hand, went from home down the highway to Folks Consent, which was only about one-half the distance to Plainesville by highway.

Shandol got off the bus as Margery did, along the highway. Margery would walk the short distance home. Shandol noticed how much less tiring the bus ride had been. The girls parted, each to go to her respective home, after a brief discussion and Shandol expressing appreciation for getting to go, and thanking Margery profusely for taking her and also thinking of doing it for her.

But now it was Friday. There was to be a marshmallow roast at the schoolhouse at night. It had had little planning, but word did get around. It was to be in honor of Hugh Burdette, a sailor home on leave from the Navy. Shandol corresponded with him, when he was able to write and get a letter mailed. He was Mrs. Bright's nephew and would stay there.

The way it had come about was that on Wednesday night, the day Shandol had visited school, Hugh had showed up at Sonnetts to see them. He had gone to school only as far as he could in Greenway.

He had played on the basketball team, before going into the Navy. He was a tall, brown-haired young man, with large gray eyes and a wide mouth when he smiled, which he frequently did, showing clean white even teeth. He was in a white naval uniform, but would don the blues soon, he informed them, smiling broadly.

He had stayed for supper, much to Shandol's embarrassment—and consternation at her father for asking him. Not that he wasn't welcome to a meal with them, in fact she would like that, but they weren't expecting company and Shandol did not consider what they were having a company meal. They had tomato soup with cheese and white crackers. The soup was already steaming in individual bowls on the large dining room table, couldn't he see? But—

"Stay for supper," Joel had invited off-handedly yet warmly and sincerely.

"Don't mind if I do," he had replied, with his easy broad smile, and without being coaxed, offering excuses or hesitation. Audrey ladled a bowl for him, assuring him there was plenty.

Surely, Shandol thought, *he can see this is no "company" meal.* But apparently he couldn't see, or thought no such thing. He sat next to Phil and across the table from Shandol, who dropped her eyes each time their eyes met. She was frankly embarrassed. She thought he rated a chicken dinner. But then she realized he actually seemed to be enjoying himself. He smiled warmly, and contributed to the light conversation, some of which concerned his life in the Navy. Shandol relaxed as the meal progressed, and smiled back when their eyes met and his broad smile lit his face. After all it *had* been his choice. He could have made some excuse had he so wanted.

Every head had bowed as Joel had prayed: "Our Heavenly Father, we thank thee for this expression of thy bounty. Bless it to its intended use. Forgive us our sins and save us we ask in Christ's name. Amen."

"We're sorta a soup eatin' family, I guess," Audrey had said at first. "And we weren't expecting anyone. Well just make out everyone. There's plenty of what there is."

"Dad made the cheese," Phil said, conversationally. "Yuh'd never realize that," Hugh replied, already having eaten some with the white crackers.

"We had dead fish for supper last night," K.C. recalled, seriously.

Phil laughed heartily, though embarrassed, the others joined him. Shandol also blushed scarlet.

"Here now," Joel scolded, quickly. "we'll have no more of that." And K.C. hung his head, his pert smile vanished. He had smiled when Phil laughed his merry eyes danced.

"He means the canned kind," Shandol hurriedly explained.

"Dad likes 'em occasionally and last night just happened to be one of the nights he had brought some home."

"Besides," Phil noted sarcastically, "who eats live ones?"

Well, I hope we got over that one, Shandol thought. *Whew! What kids'll say who can predict?*

Shandol looked at Hugh to see how he took it. It seemed not to have bothered him. How nice he looks, she thought. A decent, clean cut, handsome man. He has nice manners, and she was sure he would treat all girls nicely not just herself. He had always been a gentleman around her. He had walked her home from school ball games or programs, and had even been her escort at parties.

As he talked about going back to his ship on the west coast, possibly to go "across the waters," she wondered what it would be like to be going with him instead of Dean. Hugh acted older, and was, though only a few years. Yet Dean had an outdoorsmanly quality about him, which was appealing, and belied the adverse experience she had had with him. But, anyway, Dean was nearer and handy and they did like one the other well enough to be led on by each the other, if that is all it would turn out to be. But who knew? Who could say?

After a make-do dessert, which Audrey felt she should come up with, and which was home canned peaches and graham crackers, the peaches served in small individual dishes, Hugh suggested he and Shandol do the dishes. Shandol agreed, as there wouldn't be many, comparatively speaking, and they could visit alone.

Hugh carried dishes from the dining room, where the others still sat, to the small kitchen where Shandol was preparing the dishpan in which to do them. There was warm water in the teakettle. There was a large dishpan to wash them in, in which she made a slight suds of her mother's home made soap, and she put out another pan in which to drain them.

"Sometimes we pour hot water over them to rinse them, but not always. Let's do it the quick way," Shandol suggested.

He agreed.

Shandol kidded him about how well he did the dishes, as he dried them on a grayish white tea towel, stained from canning fruit or vegetables, but clean nonetheless, and wondered about if he had to do KP in the Navy—or was it called that? Would he mind it? She also joked about the small kitchen.

"Mama says sometimes you almost have to back out to turn around," she laughed. "It's a bit of an exaggeration, but you see how she might think it."

The dishpans were near the end of the stove, which was near the washstand and the back door. So they touched almost each time he dried dishes to carry to the cabinet top on the other side of the stove, near the window, where Shandol had wiped off an area on the cabinet for a place he could put them until she could put them away.

Once he purposely put his hand over hers in the dishpan.

"When helping with the dishes a guy always gets to steal a kiss," he said, his wide smile reaching up even into his eyes. He promptly gave her a brotherly kiss on her flushed cheek.

"I'm gonna see yuh agin," he said. "Wonder if we could get up a party or something for Saturday night."

"Be better to make it Friday," Shandol suggested. "The truck goes to town on Saturday almost every time so a lot of the kids will likely go. It's sort of short notice—" her voice trailed off.

"Well, I couldn't really have a party. My aunt would be too worried about Granny," he told her regretfully. "I'd as soon have a marshmallow roast or something like that, and it wouldn't be a bother to anyone."

Hugh's mother was dead and had been for several years. He was staying in Greenway with his aunt, a widow, whose divorcée daughter and young son (Jack, a friend of Tommy's) shared her home. Also living in the home was his aunt's mother, and his grandmother, who was quite old, nearly blind and bedfast. His father, who had recently remarried, lived in Maple Hill, and he would also spend some time there before his leave was over.

"Yuh know, we might could do that," Shandol replied, wringing out the dishcloth to go over the oilcloth-covered table again. She brightened with bubbling enthusiasm, and stepped lightly to the dining table to swish her dishcloth over the table.

Shandol and Hugh talked it over with her family. They agreed it was a fine idea and it was agreed to start passing the word. Of course the idea had caught on as soon as word got around. And get around it did. Everyone who possibly could was to bring a package of marshmallows and meet at the schoolhouse. There would be firewood there and plenty of room for games and youngsters to race around.

Shandol went with her brothers, Phil and Bobby. She told herself she really had no date with Hugh, but she would go to help make up the crowd. She did so want the party to be a success for Hugh's sake.

The men in the group, including Hugh, Phil and Bucky Sandler, helped get the fire going. They also went to the edge of the timber-lined school yard for tree limbs or sprouts for those unable to get their own, or as a courtesy to the ladies, on which to place marshmallows for roasting. As it happened (quite on purpose) Hugh found one for Shandol. It had a forked end and he remarked, rather smugly, she thought, that she could roast for both of them.

"One for you," he said, with an affectation of daintiness, his little finger poised above the rest, placed a marshmallow on a prong, "and one for me," repeating the process.

"All right," Shandol agreed in a sweet tone. "And I hope I haven't lost the hang of it and burn 'em."

It proved difficult trying to get a game of any kind going. The responsibility seemed to have fallen upon Shandol, and she did so want the party to be a success. The younger boys dashed around in circles tagging one another, pushing contests, or hiding and "booing" at the finder. They tried to play Hide-and-Seek until dark, off and on. Among the older ones, however "Pleased or Displeased?" seemed to receive the most suggestions. It was decided to start with that. "I'll be pleaser," Shandol volunteered.

"Oh, no you don't!" A chorus almost sang out, including Hugh.

"Let one of the younger girls, Rayda's little sister, or someone like that," Rod Sandler suggested.

Della, Rayda's sister, agreed to start it.

Everyone sat on the grassy ground, mostly facing the blazing fire. They hardly realized when darkness came and there was no moon.

"Pleased or Displeased?" Della was a small twelve-year old, with straight brown hair, instead of the black wavy hair of her sister, asked the first in line—Phil.

"Pleased right now," he answered.

"Pleased or Displeased?" Della asked the next one, tossing her straight brown hair nervously.

"Pleased," Steve Follerson said.

"Aw, come on," Bucky Sandler exclaimed. "Somebody get this here thing goin'."

The next one was Rayda's brother who was displeased.

"What'll it take tuh please yuh?" Della asked, dutifully. "For Rayda and Rod to take a little stroll around the schoolhouse, hand in hand," It was, of course, assumed that only this would please him and they must do it to play the game. But they were quite a safe bet as they were considered going steady anyway.

The game then began moving along. Sometimes the dozen or so couples were gone, leaving only the younger ones, who carried on, quite pleased. They refused to send any friend lest they be done the same way and then teased.

In the meantime, Shandol would roast marshmallows for anyone who cared to share with her. She was beginning to feel left out, yet, she rationalized it was all a game. They knew she went with Dean and she supposed that explained why she was not coupled with anyone. She thought, rather morosely by now, she truly only helped make up the crowd and wished she had insisted on being "pleaser." She had gone out a time or so with guys who had no girls, and didn't care. She knew they were being good sports.

Then Steven Follerson came back and helped himself to a marshmallow from her forked stick. Then, shortly, as a joke, Rod, who was back from a walk with Rayda (again), sent them around the schoolhouse. Shandol wondered if Steve put him up to it, which was sometimes supposedly done. They went. Steven wanted to sit on the north side steps of the schoolhouse, but Shandol declined. They were not only the highest steps, but it was also the darkest place. The school building was a large brick, looked square, or a cube, building of two stories with a basement. The basement windows were tall and about three feet wide, which made them seem long and narrow. Because of the basement there were steps required to reach the ground floor, where the classrooms were. Upstairs was the auditorium, with the stage, a wide hall at the top of the steps led to a small library, which also served as "dressing room" for the stage. Across the hall from the auditorium were two classrooms. These were used for the high school, as was one of the four large class rooms downstairs, connected by a T hall. Downstairs in the basement was the gymnasium, with "bleachers" just the concrete-like step-ups. They were wide enough to hold folding chairs. To be really close the school children often sat at the bottom step. The gymnasium floor itself was a smooth, hardwood one and just right to play basketball on, though cramped and smallish by some standards.

Shandol explained to Steven she was more or less taking it upon herself to help to see that things went smoothly. She supposed he wanted to "smooch " a little, but Emily Martin was also present so she saw no reason to show interest. It was indeed so like him to want all the girls at his beck and call. If only he could be content to be a steady boyfriend because he was so handsome a date. But he was not really trustworthy. He might leave a girl stranded to make up to a new girl in town, even a visitor. Shandol had learned? She had had a crush on him long enough and still had, hadn't she? Yet, by now she had made up her mind not to be treated like that. She had learned a girl had to be attracted to someone else before he cared. It seemed he needed to prove girl's attraction for him, which was not always the case at any rate. He was easy for Shandol to talk to however. He was her age, out of school, having gone to Folks Consent, rather than Plainesville (except for a few weeks so he and Shandol could be together)to finish. But he gave that up because they weren't together that much. And he did not let Shandol know or she might have paid him more attention. But she had no idea and it was all so new to her, such an adjustment to make they could have helped one another. If only— she had often berated herself. Now he too found himself at loose ends, with only temporary, occasional jobs. He considered going away to work, considered the service of his country, even a defense plant when work became more plentiful, and every prediction was work would become more plentiful. Meantime, indecisions.

When Shandol and Steven returned, Hugh took the stick from where Shandol had temporarily placed it on the huge woodpile, placed a marshmallow on each of its forks and handed it back to her. She smiled at him understandingly, roasted them nicely, evenly browned, and held the forked stick out to him to help himself. (Actually Shandol liked the inside of the ones nearly blackened, but it was unpleasant eating them sometimes if some of the black became embedded in it.) She and Hugh ate them standing close.

"Good," he praised her, his broad smile evident. "Thank you," she replied briefly.

"Well, let's try another."

Phil got the game going again saying he was displeased. He promptly suggested that to please him they must go to the corner of the schoolhouse. The game was rather an on-or-off-again affair. So when the marshmallows were done they started off, minus the stick, walking slowly, eating the sticky sweets.

"He didn't say which corner," Hugh remarked, "we'll make it the one on the opposite corner, and go the long way and come back to the same corner."

"As you like," she agreed.

"Maybe we should change the game now," Hugh suggested. "Do yuh suppose ever'one is gettin' tired of it? But I've been waitin' for this chance. The other girls can't hold uh candle to you. I guess I should thank Phil."

"Hugh," she groped, taken aback. "Are you flatterin' me? Oh, never mind. Should we think of a game to suggest?"

"Not much use," he replied. "Let's leave it up to the crowd."

"Well, yes, they'd all have to agree or be agreeable I suppose. I just thought we might just have suggestions, others too, and then decide."

They were beside the schoolhouse. The fire was behind them and some distance away for safety's sake, though there was little about the outside of the building which would burn except recessed windows sashes, set well back in the high concrete there. The brick was above the basement, high because of the basketball court.

"I sure have set on these windows ledges out here many times," Shandol recalled, pointing to a special recessed window, which appeared only a wire-meshed dark aperture, and which looked down to the lower floor.

"Yeah, and the good ole games on down on the floor," Hugh reminisced, meaning the basketball games, she knew.

How bright his uniform seems, she thought. *How are they kept so white?*

"Oh, yes," she said. "And you the best player here! Easy, Hugh, honest."

"Thank yuh, dear one," he said, obviously pleased. "Lester was good," he added, "and Phil is too."

"But not as tall as you are," she reminded him. "But my brothers aren't too bad I suppose. Being tall *was* an advantage to you. Yuh carried yourself well. Some tall guys seem awkward. Um-m, *you* know. You were so nimble and light-footed to jump so well too."

"Do yuh miss school, Shandol?" he asked, looking seriously at her.

"Terribly," she admitted. "I feel rather *old*, like life is just now passin' me by. And I miss bein' with the kids, studyin'—and just all of it I think. And I used to get so tired of it? I never ever thought or dreamed I'd see the day I'd miss it all. All that worryin' over grades and teacher's looks." There was a hint of mirth as she said 'grades and teacher's looks,' "Do you miss it, Hugh, or did yuh?"

"Yeah," he replied. "I did. And I realize now I shoulda finished like you and Lester. But I quit after the two years because Dad was so unsettled. But I like navy life pretty good. It takes me away from some things I like, but it's not a bad life either."

They had started back around the building. After passing the high steps at that, the north, side, where Shandol and Steven had been only a short time before, there was a large oak tree a short distance from the sidewalk. (Sidewalks joined all the school's doors and steps on the three sides. It faced west and there was another door on the south. It was near the water pump.) Hugh stepped off the sidewalk gently leading Shandol beside him, and took the few steps to the trunk of the tree, and stopped. Shandol stopped in front of him. There was a pause as they reached the large tree. The night sounds were muted. It was a quiet night except for distant crickets and answers from some neighboring, more persistent katydid. The breeze was pleasant, sometimes bringing the faint scent of books, the cleaning oil for the schoolroom floors—familiar scents of school. But it was just there and only recognized it in a passive way, as it was not what Hugh had in mind. The soft elusive flowery scent of Shandol's talcum mingled with the equally faint scent of a clean manliness emanating from Hugh's person. These too were not spoken of if realized, which likely were not except that each could think the other nice to be near. And

206

it made up Hugh's mind to say what he wanted. He could only sense her sweetness.

"Let's just rest a minute," he said. "Just stop and talk. We'll go back to the others in a minute but I have more to say. That is uh—yuh must know that I think yer so sweet, Shandol. I think of yuh often when I'm away. That darling sweetness of yuh. How dear yuh'd be tuh me if yuh were just mine. What I'm gettin' at is I'm askin' for a memory to take back with me. I think when I go back I'll be shipped out somewhere. Yuh, understand, don't you, dear? Something real and definite I can take back with me to think about, and remember all the dearness of yuh. You do see, don't yuh?"

"But, Hugh, what about me?" Shandol hedged. "You know I'm chaperone, don't cha? Oh, it's not official really, but I do know there are those here who wouldn't be if I wasn't. I don't know why but it's true. I don't even like it. I don't know how it got to be so, but yuh see, don't yuh? Maybe it's because I'm older, and bein' outta school—" Words failed her, as she let the sentence hang unfinished. *At least he's honest*, she thought, yet with a twisted knot where her stomach should be. *A memory indeed? "A sweet girl and a 'precious' memory to take back," she thought, to talk about—or brag about? Not you, Hugh, surely. I thought you too fine, so manly and well-behaved to make such a request. I can't believe it! It's awful. A bad dream. But, oh, what a perfect excuse! I must wake up from this nightmare! Are all men the same after all? Oh, Hugh!*

"I expect that's true," Hugh conceded, but pleased. "Who'll know? Oh, I know to lotsa girls a kiss don't mean so much. But to you, Shandol, I know it will. Just please, a real one for a memory. And just for me."

A kiss, she thought. *Oh, I don't deserve that either. My mind must be getting dirty, thanks to Dean. A kiss. A memory? What a treasure you are, Hugh.*

"A kiss, Hugh?" she asked aloud. "Oh, Hugh." A glad lilt in her voice could not be denied. She moved toward him trance-like.

"A real one," he repeated, "not cheek peckin'."

"Yes, I know," she replied, breathlessly. "Hugh, I think it is sweet of you."

She did have uncomfortable qualms about so deliberate an action, which made her nervous, afraid it would all be clumsy and awkward. But she hadn't reckoned with Hugh's taking over. In fact it was so natural, so completely, pleasantly marvelous and dearly charming that he kissed her a second time. Shandol's heart sang in happiness. The kisses were pure, natural and sweet rather than emotionally draining. It was a compliment, too, she decided, one of the nicest she could think of. She had always heard guys didn't collect the "easy" type for fond memories. Emotion was behind it, and involved, but was not all of it. The source but not the whole of it that it should become the blind passion she had feared he meant. How long, she wondered, had he dreamed of it, and dreaded working up nerve, to ask her? She could only wonder. How could she ever live without singing it out from every housetop!

"I'm gonna walk yuh home, remember," he said low.

Perhaps the rest of the evening went normally, Shandol couldn't have said. There was wonder in her heart. A secret trembled on her sensitive mouth.

There were a series of other party games played, having finally been started. There was a song fest around the fire. The roasting of marshmallows and eating went on until the marshmallows were gone, thanks in part to the younger set, who sparred, tried to out-talk, sometimes loudly, or out-eat one another in their special attention seeking way.

In due time the couples began to bid good-byes—sometimes to no one in particular—and drift away, presumably toward home. Some with younger brothers and sisters following a short distance behind.

Hugh considered Shandol his girl for the balance of the evening, and after what Shandol considered the flattering compliment, she felt drawn to him. She was glad Dean was absent! How jealous he would have been! But the consideration Hugh rendered was a tribute, she felt, and she was glad she could share the time with him, without interference from a jealous boyfriend who would like to think he owned her. The selfishness of his ways and the fact he couldn't see or understand her hurt at his sometimes lack of thoughtfulness or consideration was, tonight at least, emphasized. Dean compared so unfavorably with Hugh, she wondered why she bothered with him. Of course he was near, while Hugh would soon be—no telling where.

Hugh teased her fondly about the chaperone title she had given herself, as they walked toward her home together, his arm entwined with hers, their fingers woven together.

"The sweetest, most innocent one chaperones," he chided. "I hadn't thought of it but it just might be so. It seems funny though—you're so *little*. What couldja do? 'Whup' the whole bunch? Or just tell Papa?"

"Don't overdo the sweet innocent stuff," she laughed, though she wanted to stomp her feet sorely. "I feel dumb enough anyway. But then don't think all chaperones are old ladies, gray-haired and someone's misfit kin, acquaintance or somethin', who'd glare at a girl who looked at a fellow. Some are I suppose," she went on, "But no one expects me to *drive* them down some virtuous path, using a switch or ruler to keep 'em in line. I'm just tuh see what goes on, sorta, so the gossips get their stories straight!" She added with a smug smile, "And lest some wound my sense of modesty, they figure's over sensitive anyway, really behave quite well, don't yuh think?"

"Um—yuh may be right."

"I'm not sure when I began to suspect the idea," she added conversationally. "But I feel I'm terribly lacking in whatever it is I need. I don't have the knowledge of the opinions—or pitfalls—it's not fair. I don't feel I can measure up."

"But aren't yuh glad yuh're looked on like that?" he asked. "I mean if some mother feels her daughter will behave better simply because you're along?"

"That's it," she countered. "Do they behave better? I don't *see* anything wrong of course. But what do I know? I'll tell you once I walked all over the countryside, or so it seemed to me, before I realized what my being along meant. I went on this picnic hike with some kids. There were some couples, of course. We took sack lunches, water, and went to Helsum's sink. I was told I'd have to go for the other to get to go. I also knew I was one of the oldest, though not the oldest. But I didn't get the real significance until days later. Wasn't I dumb? I thought they wanted me just for *me*. I did enjoy it. I'd never seen such a big sinkhole before. Just that huge, *huge* round bowl-shaped dent, and some *dent* believe me, in the ground. It was grassy ground, with trees, broken limbs, weeds and underbrush, rather over grown, but I sure hadn't seen it before. Yuh know the place?"

"Shore do," he said. "Go on."

"Sinkholes are odd," she mused. "Deep round holes yet no water stays in 'em. I sure was tired when I got home. Everybody was swell. We climbed down the sides of it, nearly straight down I thought. And coming out was like climbing a mountain. We strolled around at the bottom of it, which happens to cover a lot of territory, I declare. We ate picnic style in the shade, then the hike back home. We ran out of water by the way. Most of the time I was lost. If Rod Sandler hadn't known about it we'd have been hopeless. But then if someone hadn't known, we'd not uh gone. It sure was a tiring day to me, and so later when I was called the chaperone it was something of a letdown."

"Some hike," Hugh observed. "Wicht I coulda gone."

"Tonight was a nice night, wasn't it?" she asked, to change the subject. "A nice gang and a good time had by all—I hope."

"Yeah," Hugh agreed, smiling his broad smile. "I hope so too. And Shandol I hope we can go to Plainesville while I'm here for a real date. I suppose we can go on the truck. In fact we'd have to. Shandol, I want to very much. Would yuh—uh—like to?"

209

"I think I would really," she answered, being fairly certain it would work out so far as Dean was concerned. And anyway he had no say, and all he could do would be to create a scene.

"I gotta go to Maple Hill to see Dad," Hugh told her. "He expects me. But I'll try very had to get back tuh see yuh." He put one arm around her shoulders and looked around to see if he could see anyone. There was no one in sight.

"We can see," she said. "And yuh can let me know."

"I'm sure I'll see yuh," he said. "Gee, I hate yuh go back this time."

"Hugh—uh—" Shandol faltered. "No, I won't say it," she finished.

"Say what?" he asked. "Yuh can ask me anything."

"I'd best not," she demurred.

"Come on now," he begged. "My curiosity is aroused. Yuh shouldn't start to say something and not finish it. Remember how Mary always used to say so?"

Mary was a high school freshman friend of Shandol's, an attractive girl only slightly larger than Shandol. She was blond, blue-eyed with a few freckles on her otherwise perfectly fair complexion. The freckles on her nose were bane of her life. Once Hugh had walked Mary home from church, but then caught up with Shandol, explaining Mary had no one else. But they hadn't asked Shandol to go along either! But only once. He doubted he liked the situation Mary was a part of. There was a large family, a non-working stepfather and a small house to crowd the whole family into. Mary was a responsible girl, pretty, but overworked. The baby was only nine months old. The house smelled of baby things, mostly spoiled it seemed. There was such a demand upon Mary's time to care for younger children or doing mounds of family laundry, she missed a lot of school.

"Yes, she could get me to tell things I decided not to," Shandol admitted, fondly, smiling. "I don't hear from her much anymore. She got married, did yuh know that? Mama thinks she did it just to get away from home, I never wanna do that."

"No, I didn't know she married," he replied.

"Yeah, she lives between Maple Hill and Plainesville on a farm—somewhere."

"And now," Hugh turned to get her attention, "Back to the subject. What were yuh gonna say?"

"It's nothin' believe me," she replied. "Don't be so serious. It's not important. I'm sorry I said what I did. So there."

"I won't forget it. I'll wonder and be sad," he told her. "So, please, get it off both our minds."

"Oh, it's just that a friend of Mama's has a coral rock and shell's 'n things from those islands out there somewhere," she finally replied, grudgingly. "They're so pretty. One sparkles like a jewel, though we have those here, don't we? Mama would like something like that. She wonders if they have to be bought like souvenirs, or are they just there for the takin'."

"I don't know," he sighed with relief. One never knows about girls and women. "But I can find out. I'd love to for you," he added.

"Well, Mama would pay for any cost, if not too much. So don't go too high."

"Oh, no," he objected quickly.

"Now, yuh see," Shandol said. "I knew I shouldna mentioned it. Mama didn't. I thought she just forgot, but I bet she knew how it'd be. Please *don't* mention it no more."

"Well, now I can see about it," he pouted. "I'm glad yuh said it. Now I'll know what to look for for souvenirs. Rocks! Since we have so few here, just none like those, huh?"

"Now yer mockin' me."

"No, just tryin' tuh getcha outta that mood."

"What mood?" she asked quickly.

"Oh, bein' sorry yuh told me what yuh did," he replied firmly. "It's okay, believe me."

"Well, here we are," she said. "Are yuh comin' in?"

She felt perfectly comfortable asking him inside. He would go with hot cocoa and cheese sandwiches—or cookies and milk. She mentally decided she should fill the cookie jar vacancy in case he did come again. She recalled his helping with the dishes that time, and it might be the thing to do, and something he'd enjoy.

"I better not tonight, Shandol," he declined softly. "But I've loved every minute of tonight. But I just doubt your dad appreciatin' us awakin' 'em up."

"That's thoughtful," she remarked. "He does wake up easy."

"Remember, I'll see yuh agin," he reiterated. "I'll be gone awhile to see Dad. But I won't forget. I couldn't."

"All right," she whispered.

He bent and kissed her gently, goodnight, and Shandol responded. He kissed her again. She could sense the sweetness, the beauty, the cleanliness of his mind, she was so sure of it, and it was a relief, and a contrast from Dean's kisses. He seemed determined to arouse passion. Not Hugh. In complete trust she could surrender completely to it. This was still searching for love, not ready to jump into some quagmire of passion which only seemed to would get one dirty or disgraced! She was sure he felt the same as he kissed her, holding her firmly, fondly again. How wonderful she felt! Oh, the mystery of passion!

"Tuh take back with me," he murmured. "So I can think of you and the kisses. Lovely memories from such a lovely girl—Shandol, you."

Shandol later wondered of other girls with whom he was bound to come in contact. Perhaps there were different responses! But *she* was the girl he asked for kisses for memories to take back with him. As though to wear? Kisses for him to take back to the ship; perhaps to a war. No one knew for sure. And things were looking bleak. Even preparations were being made. There was still the see-saw argument that either the country might be caught unawares and unprepared, and hence would require time. On the other hand did it invite war if they did prepare for it? But the people, mostly, just hoped the country could keep out of it.

But Hugh would be safe either way. Someway he would be safe. For herself or someone else, because she would pray for him. She did: "Dear God, let fate be kind to Hugh. He's a good man even without having a mother for so long to guide him. Keep him safe wherever he goes. Guard over our country too, even bless all who must defend our freedom. Grant wisdom to our leaders—in Jesus name—."

It was how she felt about Hugh. For out of it she would have memories also. After all, women and girls need memories too while the men are gone. This would be one of her sweetest, she was sure, ranking with Steven's and she would guard it fondly. It was precious to her, and the last kisses seemed to seal a secret sweet memory packet, hidden treasure from Hugh, to keep forever.

* * * * *

But this had been the day she had heard from Dean. It had been a silly postcard. Shandol thought of Dean as she recalled her good time with Hugh. She had taken the card to her room to read it. He had dated it simply Tuesday. He wrote they had got there "yesterday." They had camped out, but "we have not got a job yit." He hoped they did, but if not considered going to Oklahoma. He wasn't sure when he would be home. She noticed the non-capitalized I's he used and slips in grammar—as he talked so he wrote. Shandol knew she was sometimes guilty of that. Her talk was worse. Dean hoped when he worked he got weekends off so he could see her. He promised to write soon and tell her more. He had included no return address, so she need not write to him—yet.

CHAPTER 17

Shandol was called the next morning earlier than usual to help her father prepare breakfast.

"Your's mother's sick," Joel told her briefly when he called up to her from downstairs. "And she's still in bed. I need yuh to help me."

Joel had a fire roaring in the cook stove and was sitting at the table peeling a pan of potatoes, which he held in his lap, in his slow deliberate way. He had no doubt but that Shandol would respond to his first call for her to get up. And Shandol had by now learned it was futile to ignore his order, for that is what she considered it and had learned the consequences long ago.

Shandol began helping by preparing water and washing the potatoes he had peeled, then slicing them. He had what he considered enough peeled by then, and she could put them into a greased iron skillet, already warming on the back of the stove, to fry. As she did this her father painstakingly mixed up a batch of biscuits. These he let Shandol roll out on the cabinet's pull-out flour board, which she pulled out only enough to accommodate the dough. There was a biscuit cutter, which she used to cut them to size, put them into a greased rectangular pan and place into the hot oven hoping she would remember to watch them. She was not accustomed to doing much cooking, both parents being good cooks, which gave her an insecure feeling when she was called upon to do so. They seemed to feel because she was grown up she could automatically cook. Perhaps it was so, but it made her nervous, shaky and very full of qualms. She fried a few pieces of "fat back" bacon as she'd seen her mother do many times, for grease to make gravy. The coffee was perking merrily and fragrantly in the aging aluminum coffee pot and she moved it aside. As soon as Joel was assured Shandol would take over without supervision, he went out to the barn to milk the cow.

By the time Joel returned everything was ready, as they had tried to plan it so. He strained and took care of the milk himself, all before the rest of the family was called. Shandol and her father had talked— mostly light conversation.

"Didja have a good time last night?" he asked. "Or do yuh need tuh be out gallivanting in some *automobile*, maybe parked somewhere, tuh enjoy yourself? (He emphasized the "automobile" instead of saying car as would have been more like him.)

Usually, Shandol was intimidated by her father for when he was crossed he could be outwardly mildly, but firmly, furious. His jaws rippled, as though he was gnashing his teeth to hold his temper, which he could keep very well under control in most instances, but his stance was firmness and he seemed the need to feel in control of his family, as he always had. It was important to him to be looked up to and be assured his words carried weight. Shandol, though she admired him, occasionally spoke her mind, perhaps because she was somewhat like him, perhaps also she was tired of being treated like a child. She was also sometimes taken down a peg. As for instance the time she impertinently told him he was just going to the store on wash days to hear the radio news, sure, but then "loaf around" until the washing of clothes was finished.

He had replied she was young and selfish as well as mouthy. And it wouldn't hurt, he had continued, if she and the boys did do the wash. But didn't he always help do the overalls? So they could wait on him for that (which they usually didn't and he knew it). Shandol would not want Audrey to do it, which she might try if it weren't done. It *had* been unfair to accuse him at the time, Shandol learned. He had made it back for part of the heavy overalls, which Shandol could barely handle. She could soap them at the dirty spots, the pocket openings, the knees and front in general, and use a scrub brush over them, and did this at times, but to wring them was a problem as she had to go the length to make her small hands reach to wring the water from them. Also by then she was usually getting tired, because the dark "colored clothes" were the last to be done, and there was still lots to be done, even though their individual clothes weren't actually all that plentiful. But for a family that size there needn't be to make a lot.

But it was at that particular time Joel had wanted to see if an appropriation for more money for his "road work" job would go over. Yet, because it wouldn't have affected him anyway for a few days at least he could have read it in the newspaper, she had thought. Joel scolded his daughter for doubting his judgment and urged her to allow him to take care of his affairs in his own way.

But there had been times she had been correct to speak up, disagreeing. One such time was when Tommy had had whooping cough. He was just a baby, but luckily he hadn't had a hard case of the disease. But as the family sat eating one day at noon, he, being in the adjoining room, had become strangled with phlegm in his throat. Shandol told her mother who couldn't have heard him.

"He's all right now," Joel had said, to save Audrey a trip to see about him.

"Oh, no!" Shandol had cried, and arose herself.

"I said he is better," Joel said firmly.

Shandol could only shake her head in defeat.

But Audrey had already decided she should check on him. She depended on Shandol, so that was all she really needed to hear: That Tommy needed her. And he had needed her! He was helpless on his back, unable to expel or swallow the obstructing phlegm. He was soon all right again as Audrey first turned him to his side, but then she had to get him up and lift his arm over his head. She fondled him lovingly and concernedly before leaving him. And as young and helpless as he was, no one dared even speculate if he would have ever been able to get his breath or not. Joel had looked at Shandol sheepishly, and she had looked back at him shyly, but nothing more was said.

"I had a very nice time," she answered the question Joel had just asked. "Hugh is swell, you know that. As for that "auto" Hugh does want to take me somewhere, such as Plainesville to go to a show or something. We'll prob'ly have to go on the truck though since he don't have a car. Not much choice for anything around here to do, unless we figure something out such as the marshmallow roast."

Then she could not help adding an impish smile and mischievous twinkle in her brown eyes, so like his own, as she had forgiven his grouchy way of asking about her good time. She reasoned to herself why shouldn't she ask about his. He was young once.

"Is it all so different from years ago when young people went out with horses and buggies?" she asked. "The horses, I've heard you say could almost go by themselves and certainly find their way home. Surely you wouldn't try to tell me those couples sat stiff, formal, and silent, talking of nothing but the weather or the moon if there was one. Or that parties, love and kisses were taboo, because the girl's 'old man' would see to it that his daughter got married—why should she have a good time while she is young? That don't work. Dad, really! I shouldn't read my mind out loud," she added quickly, sheepishly seeing his shocked expression.

Shandol supposed her father would remind her the expression 'old man', meaning a girl's father was slang, but he was silent.

"Such perfect people," these parents, she mumbled. Joel glanced at her, too surprised for words. Surprised because Shandol was usually docile and considerate. He wondered if she had aimed to be sarcastic, and if it resulted from his putting his question as he did. At any rate he was learning that when she did bare her mind unreservedly, it either surprised, embarrassed, amazed, shocked, and sometimes provoked him. Now he was a little of each.

"Get to the breakfast," he told her as he left the room. "We've babbled enough. Don't burn the 'fatback' with your mind elsewhere. Sometimes the clay feet show," he added ruefully.

"I'm being a sorry outfit, myself," she said. "It's not that I accuse *you*, and perhaps cars don't seem decent dating to you, but what about buggies. It still depends on the people! If they want to be something else, there'd be a way—car or no car, buggy or no buggy. And the other way around."

"Just be careful," he replied. "The two men may not be of the same mind," he amended, moving his palms to and fro.

"That's true, she thought, but kept silent.

There was little doubt in Shandol's mind that her dad had treated her mother with the utmost consideration. He still did the best he could. Perhaps he was much like Hugh, she decided. But why must Joel worry so about her, his daughter?

Perhaps he perceived the intent of the "human animal," she mused.

Audrey got up for breakfast. She was pale, hollow-eyed and, pleading an upset stomach, ate very little. She promised to try to eat a little off and on during the morning if she could for nourishment she supposed she needed the baby.

She did manage a slice of bread and butter.

Shandol knew what was to be done today was her job. Joel, with Phil and Bobby, went to the timber to cut wood. This was to go on their own winter's supply.

It was a busy day and went quickly. Audrey laid around. Shandol prepared meals and straightened up the house. She talked Tommy into helping feed and water the canaries. Even though Audrey didn't feel like cleaning the cages today, and wasn't sure Shandol would have time, someone had to see they had food and water available in the cages. Shandol boiled eggs so each cage could have a portion of one. Sometimes Shandol did help clean the cages, but today Audrey decided they could go one day. Shandol still hated the flying tiny feathers when she swept.

At noon the men came from the woods. Goody, Sis's got beans cooked," Phil exclaimed, and patted her hair.

"Yeah, good." Joel agreed. "You know they argued on the way home if it was bean day or tater day."

"Yep, bean day," she replied, "and taters. I know I should be more economical but I can't figure out things like Mama so here we are— beans *and* taters. I put onions in the taters like I like' em."

They ate heartily as working men do. Phil bemoaned the job and idea of going back. Audrey picked at the food and said little.

"It used to be I'd get too sore to move," Phil sighed. "But guess I'm getting used to it now."

He and Bobby took turns working with Joel on the crosscut saw; sometimes they worked together as Joel trimmed and prepared another tree. There was brush for the boys to stack also.

In the afternoon, after the dishes were done and the house "spruced up" as well as could be expected, Shandol and her mother read awhile. By then Shandol must prepare another meal and take a bath.

Hugh came soon after supper. They sat and talked and played games with Tommy and K.C. They helped them study and played dominoes, checkers and simple card games. This meant when they played partners, Shandol and Hugh were rivals, as they each took one of the boys to equalize the competition. He stayed until he had to leave to catch the bus to Maple Hill to see his father. He was natural and friendly but hardly dared hold her hand because of boys and Audrey and Joel. Occasionally accidentally—he hoped it appeared. But he promised to try to see her again.

x x x x

Dean came unexpectedly Sunday afternoon. He had not said for sure in the card if he could make it home, so Shandol hadn't been expecting him. She supposed when he didn't come Saturday he wouldn't make it. Shandol dressed hurriedly, and they left rather early.

"Nobody's beatin' my time?" Dean questioned in jest, but Shandol was sure he was serious.

"No, but the 'fleet' came in," she replied, eyeing him, wondering if he would know what she meant.

"Meanin' zactly what?" he asked.

"Uh, the 'fleet'—you know?" she teased.

"H--l," he exploded, "some sailor been here, or what?"

"Don't roar. I won't be roared at," she answered calmly, her hands in her lap. "I won't even answer that tone of voice."

"Okay, sorry," he said meekly. "But what about this sailor?"

"I shouldn't have said a thing," she retorted. "He hardly counts. He's almost like my kin. I've known him a long time. I write to him is mainly why he came, I suppose. He went to Greenway school, has relatives here and used to be our basketball star."

"And you like him?" Dean asked.

"Of course I like him" she replied. "He's a nice guy." *And oh, my head and heart are entirely too full of the 'memories' for it not to spill out, even though I know I should have kept still.* "But let's not talk about him," she said, smiling and moving closer to him in the moving car. "No use being in a bad mood just because of him. Anyway what are you doing here?"

"You got my letter?" he asked. "I said we'd be home if'n we ditn't git a job and we ain't chet."

"I got a card," she replied, "but not letter. It only said you didn't know when you'd be here. But you didn't have a job then either. So when you didn't come Saturday, I just didn't look for you."

Gosh, what if he had come when Hugh was here, she thought. *Wouldn't I have been in hot water? Or we?* "Is there work up there?" she asked.

"Lotsa work," he replied. "We joined the union so's maybe that'll hep. If we git a job thr', we work on Sattidays and Sundays and git paid fer it. I won't git to come home very often though. That I don't like a-tall. Ole Brad made fun uh me fer writin' to yuh."

"Is it—uh—hard work?" she wondered aloud.

"All kinds—truck drivin, jobs helpin' carpenters, just a lot uh things. Good pay, too."

"If Brad made fun of you writin' to me," she couldn't help asking, "I'm wondering if he wrote to Fran."

"Nope," Dean answered, "that's why he came on in, though we was late gettin' started. Bet she'll git on to 'em too. Of course his brother's got a family. He kept wonderin' how they was makin' it and him gone."

"I expect they missed 'im," Shandol answered.

"Yuh know they *did*," he snorted. "If'n we git jobs up there the whole Walt Lawson family may go up there with us. Guess we'll go to the show tonight—that okay?"

"Why I suppose so," she replied, and wondered briefly why he asked, then thought no more about it until after the show.

"The show was good," she said, "but there're usually two. What about the cowboy one?"

"They're only on Saturdays," he replied.

Then she knew why he had asked her. He wasn't sure she would want to go on Sunday night! She usually didn't. She was usually expected to go to church. His parents also liked to go to church, which sometimes left Dean with no car. Once she and Dean went with his parents. But she had actually forgotten it was Sunday, because he usually came on Saturday—first anyway. That was why she asked about the cowboy show.

She knew they were only on Saturdays. Of course, Shandol hadn't always gone to church on Sundays with Dean when he came. But then there were get-togethers with other couples; just spending time together, perhaps riding to places she had never seen; eating out somewhere was quite common—and the church a time or so. But it was the first time they had gone to a show.

They drove by Spoon Hill, after a soda at Folks Consent, which they obtained at the filling station. They spied Brad's green shiny car, which Shandol conceded looked much prettier than the older one Dean drove. Dean's was a colorless, grayish—she wasn't sure what color it had been. Brad's was not so new as Jim Brown's but was as nice in appearance.

Brad and Fran were having words because he hadn't written to her. Fran was pouting. Dean and Shandol went to the car to spend time and talk.

"Didja get a letter?" Fran asked Shandol, after they had settled in the back seat of Brad's car, Fran turning toward her.

"Only a card," Shandol replied, "but he said he'd wrote a letter, so I suppose I'll get it tomorrow."

"I didn't get a word," Fran said accusingly, "not a line and I looked for a letter everyday. I think I expected to get one every day for sure. I'm mad at 'im."

"I said we didn't have a good place to write," Brad reasoned, defending himself.

"How did Dean manage then?" she wanted to know.

"I wrote by uh flashlight and he made fun uh me," Dean told her. "Told 'em yuh'd expect a letter or some kinda note."

"I'm proud yuh wrote me, it bein' so inconvenient and all," Shandol said low, so that the couple in front weren't likely to hear as they were so concerned with their own squabble. Fran was really hurt; more so perhaps when she learned Dean had written to Shandol.

Brad was apologetic. Fran looked so dejected and crushed she was almost childlike in the hurt. She hardly realized she presented her cutest, vulnerable, most desirable self.

"If he don't write next time, I'll never speak to 'im agin," she vowed.

"Shandol here kept comp'ny with the navy," Dean said, joining Fran in feeling affronted.

"Oh, Dean, don't be like that," Shandol replied. "It wasn't nuthin', he just came down. We've known 'im a long time."

"I don't like it," Dean said.

"You don't know much about it," she pointed out.

"Well, there was a party I suppose, and you flirted as yuh did before."

"And if yuh recall yuh said I was sweet to mingle and make people feel so welcome," she nudged him. "Only it wasn't a party—only a quickly got-up marshmallow roast. And he only walked me home."

"Did he k–kiss yuh?" Dean asked.

"Last night he dropped by and we played games with Tommy and K.C.," she evaded. "We had to play against one another so the sides wouldn't be so uneven."

"Yuh ditn't answer me," Dean reminded her.

"Hadn't we better go home?" she interrupted. "It's Sunday. My folks will wonder where I am."

"But I been gone," Dean pleaded. "But we will go back to my car so Brad and Fran can patch things up."

"Yeah, we better let you get the score settled," Shandol told Fran lightly. "We'll be going soon. Hate to be a bother."

"No bother," Fran denied, as they crawled out beside the front door, as the car was a two-door.

"I ain't kissed yuh," Dean finally spoke, "and after all this time too," and he proceeded to take care of that detail.

Shandol kept talking and gabbing and asking questions so Dean wouldn't begin harping about Hugh. She wished she had kept still. What had she expected to prove anyway? She mentioned everyone in the family. She tried not to be obvious about it. She did go into more detail about the marshmallow road and Hugh's kidding her about being the chaperone. It made her feel like an old maiden lady.

"I straightened him out on that," she said. "But there were some there who couldn't otherwise have gone. Chaperone sounds old maidish or something. And I'm out of school, not married—nor about to be."

She mentioned Tommy and K.C. and reiterated her embarrassment when they stuck their hands in his pocket, as they had done the other guy who came around. He had encouraged them, saying they'd find gum or a penny (whichever he had). He was amused they took only one thing they were told. If there were more coins they put all but a penny back, etc. He had given her a lot of attention, Shandol admitted, but secretly suspected Joel asked him not to come. He had left town now. He made a great thing of asking Joel to take her home, bragged about Shandol's finishing school, her good looks—even flattered Joel and Audrey, but they still considered him phony. And he didn't care what effect taking things from his pockets would have on the small boys. Dean had been surprised, to say the least, when they had tried the same thing on him. Shandol had explained it as best she could.

She had asked Dean not to blame them—but herself. She should have stopped "Drummy" from letting them do it. Then she had scolded the boys. She had explained Dean hadn't asked them as "Drummy" had. But Dean, not to be outdone, gave them each a nickel. Shandol declared that the end of it. Dean said he shouldn't have made anything of it, but was so surprised.

"The Sonnetts, you know."

"And oh, how perfect they must be," she mocked. "But we don't want them to be pickpockets," she said seriously. "So it's best nipped in the bud. Dad didn't like it. Maybe he figured they'd embarrass us sometime."

Dean tried to make a point of noticing them, and asked about them when he didn't see them.

They talked about other dates and wondered about Jim and Ellen. Shandol was sure he would forget Hugh.

But when they reached the back porch at Shandol's, on the step, he asked her again.

"Sh-h-h, the folks'll hear you," she cautioned, whispering.

"This time yuh gotta tell me," he insisted. "Did that sailor-man kiss my gurl or not?" Dean had his arm around her.

"What if I lied—one way or the other?" she hedged, glancing at him sideways.

"Yuh won't lie, that's why yuh been so gabby all evenin'," he said. "But what do yuh think I'll think if yuh can't answer me? In fack I'll know!"

"He did, Dean," she admitted lightly, "but it wasn't like *you'd* think. He only wanted a kiss to remember me by—a memory to take back, he said. Besides we haven't been going together long enough for me to be your girl—just like that—all yours!"

Dean bristled. "To me yore my gurl. He'll go back and talk about it—and my gurl. I don't like it one bit."

"Talk maybe, but not bad," she flared. "It was just a very light kiss. Surely it's okay when he'll soon be going so far away. He wanted a nice memory. I really felt good about it."

"Are yuh seein' 'em agin?" he asked.

"I'm supposed to," she admitted, "and just don't try to stop me because yuh can't."

"The uniform," he spat out, "Gurls go nuts about a uniform! I'll be working just as hard and be away from yuh too."

"I said I'd write," she reasoned. "And I do kiss you too. He's in the service for the country and soon be gone. If he comes I'll see him."

"I'm jealous," Dean pouted. "I can't help it. Just thinkin' of 'im. A gurl in every port and here too. Ain't yuh heared sailors have gurls in every port?"

"I'll be careful," she told him sarcastically. "Anyway he's not like that, he's a nice guy. Comes to see us all too."

"I'll bet," Dean replied, but the tone denied the words.

"Get mad then! I'm goin' in," Shandol shot back.

"No, wait," he said, "let's not quarrel. I won't be mad. Write, will yuh? Don't be mad. Promise. No, say it. Say 'I'm not mad'."

"I'm not mad," she conceded, "you are!"

"It's jest I hate tuh share yuh," Dean said. "That's natural when yuh like somebody a lot."

"I guess so."

"Good night Shandol," he said, "I'll write and see yuh ag'in as soon's I can."

Shandol had the bad dream again that night. She dreamed of a great explosion of an enormous building of several stories. Soon there was a crowd with people poking around in the smoky ashes. How it had burned and become ashes so quickly she didn't know. It was just so in her dream. Soon the debris was being hauled away. And then a fat, well-dressed man, except his coat and tie were missing, handed her the dainty index finger of a woman's hand. It was smooth and beautifully manicured, she saw in color, and completely unscathed by the fire.

"Get rid of it," the fat man ordered her. "I can't see to and it may cause trouble."

Then there it was in her hand. Soon she became aware of uniformed policemen and she became alarmed. Perhaps she shouldn't have it either. Perhaps they'd guess there was a corpse somewhere. *A Corpse!*

She felt she must hide it so she placed it in some ashes. Then she heard a policeman say the whole "gigantic thing" had been done to hide the murder of a woman, they suspected. But who was she?

The finger in the ashes began to glow, Shandol noticed, and the mound grew. She was compelled to get it from there. So she got it, and, watching to be sure no one saw, she threw it.

No body remains were found yet. How strange. Was there no one missing? But there was the finger. She had it again. What was it—a boomerang? She must get rid of it! Burn it? But it wouldn't. Just wrap it and leave it alone and leave. But it glowed. She wrapped it, it wasn't hidden; more wrappings, a larger package.

Finally, she was drawing attention, suspicioned and being stared at. She wondered if she'd become the hunted. She decided to take the seeming tenacious, unyielding, immortal bit to the river. Instead of a bridge there she discovered only a huge culvert of concrete crossed it. The sides reminded her vaguely of the side of a huge stone wall, damp from a mist that seemed to hang over the river.

She tossed the package into the stream current. But it *floated*. *Floated!* Yet now she couldn't retrieve it, and it seemed to be floating straight toward a policeman, who was waiting beside a tree trunk. Dejectedly, forlorn, frightened, but hopeless, she waited in the mist by the damp wall, which was outside the waterline, for the policeman to come for her. The evidence couldn't be destroyed, whatever it meant. The finger always pointed at her. Why? Was she guilty of something she didn't know about? She hoped the finger would slip on past, but knew it wouldn't. Perhaps she should try to get it. No, she was afraid. The water was deep, the mist unnerved her. Yet she could see the finger. There was no escape. She was so frightened.

She awoke. She sat upright. She was so scared she wanted to cry out but couldn't. Then as she became awake enough to realize she had been dreaming, she looked out the window into a moonlight night, and she realized she was in her own bed, instead of on a strange riverbed ready to step into the deep water.

She tried to solve the mystery after she awoke. It was not to be dismissed easily from her mind. It had seemed so real, even the unworldly. The wall wouldn't give, the package wouldn't sink, there was no shallow water. No escape. Why? She thought about it. The finger—was it a finger? Or perhaps a soul, or no, perhaps a spoken—or unspoken—word? Could it be a deed done or undone. A conscience? At any rate it seemed to *be*. As an aggrieved conscience it might return to haunt her. As a lost soul could not die. It couldn't be hidden because it *was*, and would always *be* somehow.

Her heart cried out *why*? She was fully awake, still frightened and dwelling on the dream, as though someone or something tried to tell her something. It hurt her feelings.

She was not only afraid but enraged and very, very lonely.

Perfect and secret? These things didn't exist at all.

Am I innocent, she wondered. *I didn't do anything—or is that the problem? A very sick woman died as I prayed she would. I didn't kill her did I? I couldn't have. But these frightful corpses! I shouldn't have run that night. I should have gone to phone. They depended on me. Maybe I should have touched her. They say you never dream of people who have died if you touch them. But I don't dream of her, do I? Besides I didn't see her. Except she had looked dead a long time—almost anyway. It's like a curse—though I don't believe in such things.*

She decided to pray: "Dear Father, I didn't aim to hurt her, but did I? I've tried to keep it out of my mind, and I have—a little—but it sometimes comes back. Daytimes, I'm all right; I can turn my mind, but not my dreams. Please, forgive me for whatever I did wrong—for your Son's sake—amen."

She pondered still, when did the dreams start? *I can't stand it. Oh, what can I do?*

She put her face forlornly into the pillow, allowing herself to breathe. She clasped her hands behind her head and her elbows rested beside her. Her body shook. Shandol wept.

CHAPTER 18

Hugh kept his word and came back that same week on Wednesday evening. And weatherwise it couldn't have been a worse time. It literally poured down rain. Shandol hadn't expected him to show up. And they were certainly stuck there at home. There was no way for them to go anywhere.

You wouldn't put your enemy's cat out on a night like this," Phil had remarked, as light conversation included the weather conditions. Games and visiting soon got underway.

"I guess Hugh better stay all night," Tommy stated, matter of factly.

Audrey and Bobby popped a dishpan nearly full of popcorn, the aroma filling the air. Bobby was quite able to have done it himself, but Audrey wanted to be sure Shandol gave her time to Hugh. They took turns with checkers, played dominoes and the few card games allowed. Most popular they called simply "books." Whoever had the most of sets of four of the cards won. The "sets" were gained by each player calling for a card in his turn. Sometimes he got it, sometimes not. If no one had a card called for the player drew one from the stack, which was left after each player was dealt seven. If lucky they might even draw the one they had called for. Tommy could play; K.C. couldn't, but he "helped" Tommy.

Sometimes Phil took time out to play the guitar. He both picked out tunes and sang some.

Joel and Audrey busied themselves working the crossword puzzle in the newspaper. Audrey kept a notebook of scraps of paper for strange terms—goddesses or gods, Latin and other word pairs hard to recall, but which appeared time and again in the puzzles. They too took for granted Hugh must stay all night. Joel had also insisted and Hugh had agreed with little extra coaxing.

After the evening had ended and they had all gone to bed and Shandol was alone in her room, she recalled her grandfather telling about the nights Joel had had to stay with them when he was courting Audrey. A few times it had been bad snow storms. Other times it had been rumored that a former friend of Audrey's was "laying" for Joel with a knife "to cut him to ribbons." It was perhaps exaggerated somewhat to catch the imaginations of the children, but no one doubted the threat. And there was such a man who boasted he would not allow someone to beat his time without fighting back. Grandfather hadn't considered it safe because such a fight would be unfair in the dark and Joel unaware of where he might be hiding. Finally, when Joel worked there he practically lived there. There was a small house on another hill where they moved after Joel and Audrey had married. Now it seemed to Shandol men must have these urges to fight or protect what they chose to consider their own. She wondered if such "cave-man" urges would ever leave the human race, or must each one have to deal with them all over for himself.

Shandol did not sleep well. She thought of Hugh. What kind of person was he really? Then as the night wore on and she became tired and sleepy she fought sleep. She was afraid of the dreams. Sometimes she would linger briefly at the edge of sleep and soon be seeing weird creatures or walking to higher places. Then instead of falling into restful slumber, awake, startled, with a bodily jerk, when trying to escape other falling sensation. Soon she gave way to the pull of unrest and finally slept fitfully, but not restfully.

"I had a very special good time," Hugh said, as he was leaving the next day. "There wasn't really the time alone with you I'd hoped for. We could have had such a nice time. I did have a good time, though it was you who provided it and I had wanted it to be me. See?"

Shandol understood. And they had hardly been alone. They were left alone for awhile in the front room. There had been a lull in activity. But Joel had had his ideas about when bedtime should be and expected all to comply by it.

"Let me kiss you good-bye," Hugh said. "Now, I may not get a chance tomorrow when I have to leave. I do have to go back to see Dad. This weekend I leave to go back to my ship."

"Oh, I hate to hear it," Shandol replied. She held up her face to be kissed. Would he peck her cheek tomorrow?

"Let's go get something to drink," she had suggested then, nervously. "Like hot chocolate."

So she had only sweet friendliness to remember. No really bad moments to dispel. Just her feelings and questions about them.

He had insisted over and over she be sure and write to him. She promised she would do so, faithfully.

"Just keep me posted as to where you are," she said. "*And* answer my letters."

He kissed her on the cheek as the family looked on. Audrey asked him to come again anytime. The good-byes over, she watched him walk up the street through the mist and drizzle, which was in the air instead of rain, as yesterday. He would go to his aunt's for more good-byes and their best wishes.

The good-byes tugged at Shandol's heart. She wondered if love for Hugh would flower or, no, not break her heart.

* * * * *

"What's wrong with Shandol?" Phil asked one morning. "Is it so tough on her all her boyfriends are gone? She's such an old gripe lately."

As the month of September faded and soon slipped away, time moved along and fall was in the air, and a change showed in Shandol. She had grown thin in body, sharp of tongue, pale and listless. Of course, there was less diversion and she seemed to stay to herself more. They had so far said very little about it to her. They never knew how she would answer. She had overheard Phil, however, and retorted.

"I'm fine as frog hair, as Grandpa says, and you can't get much finer than that!"

Once Audrey asked if she felt ill or needed to talk, but she denied anything. If they were suspicious of some outlandish condition she did not try to set their minds at ease. It was to her so far-fetched that she was actually passive about it and they were left to wonder and worry, and grope in the dark for an answer.

Joel decided it must be making her bitter to stay at home. He had broached the subject to Audrey and added: "Young people can be so impatient at that age." Then Audrey worried also that it was resentment toward her at being at home now. Yet they could not bring themselves to giving their consent to allowing her to go away from home. Even if she were to get a job, which could pay for help at home, she was yet too immature, too trusting and inexperienced. They needed her and she still needed them. Of that they were fairly certain. But they were still concerned.

Audrey suggested she go to Plainesville to visit Jane and Lester a few days. She didn't know it was an excuse to get her away a few days. The visit had not really been much of a success.

"She's still so withdrawn," Audrey observed. "Maybe she's just sad because Hugh's gone. Or she's quarreled with Dean over him, and now both are gone."

"We'll have to wait and see," Joel said. "Maybe *time* will tell us something."

"Oh, no!" Audrey, thinking of her own condition, did not like the implication the word time could mean.

"We must be brave," Joel said, "But I'd never forget such a thing— ever." Audrey realized he was horrified at the same possibility.

"She is punishing us for keeping her here," Audrey said. "Joel, I mean it. She's different somehow; I'm sure of it. Maybe she should have gone to business school. She may be one of those who has to just feel her own way along. There's so little here."

Audrey understood, she thought. She too had been stymied by lack of parental help. She had wanted to take business courses, but her mother had declared a woman's place was in the home not in some man's place of business, running it or helping him to do it. So she had just quit school and soon married. The only consolation was her family to care for and a husband who loved her and whom she loved. But she had always had the what-if regret. The lack of forcefulness of being kept away from—but what? That was it. You could never realize what you did or did not miss.

Audrey believed her mother had been a prude. Some subjects of life she had ignored. She was a dutiful wife and *duty* had given her seven children. But how her oldest sister ever learned the facts of life Audrey was never sure. When Audrey had asked her mother questions of certain things she had heard, her mother had stuck out her tongue at her and then shamed her. But Audrey was the youngest of the five sisters, so they had given her certain basic facts. Audrey told Shandol, and she had added if she ever needed answers to ask Audrey and if she didn't know, perhaps they could find out together. Had Audrey done any better, she wondered, than her mother after all?

Joel Sonnett saw Shandol only as a white-haired, dark-eyed doll of three years, running trustfully and lovingly to meet him. He would pick her up and carry her. Sometimes, however, she would be almost under the horse's hooves when he stopped to pick her up, she was so anxious to see him when he was returning with the team from the field. Once she had fallen and bumped her nose. That was as she came down the hard clay hill and stumbled as he was going up. How she had howled! Mostly in fury, her mouth wide open, screaming until he could soothe her. A baby girl. His baby girl. Why must she grow up and learn about life? Why couldn't he keep her sweet and innocent and unhurt? But then, why do rose blossoms fade? Why does time pass on so quickly?

Shandol had actually enjoyed the night she had spent with her brother and sister-in-law. She had visited normally, and was interested in their home. They had pointed out how well they liked having their own apartment; they showed the things they had acquired and she learned some of their routine. Shandol had had to sleep on the front room sofa, because they had three rooms and only one bedroom. They discussed plans for their own home someday; about their lives together; and wished they had even a small garden plot. It was a duplex situated at the edge of town, but was only a small lot. There

228

were a couple and baby living in the other part of the house.

She had slept soundly that night the first time in a long time. Yet she was afraid to stay another night lest she awake in some horror dream. She and Jane had gone shopping; she had bought the four yards of dark blue dress-weight gabardine. She had also priced light-weight jackets. But she was ready to go home the next day. If Lester and Jane wondered why she didn't stay another night they hadn't questioned. The truth was they had noticed a nervousness about her. Audrey had prepared them by telling them she hadn't seemed herself lately. They wondered if she was so broken up over Dean's or Hugh's leaving.

Shandol reassured them she had enjoyed her stay, and had. She said she hoped they would invite her again soon. Jane had walked her to the filling station only two blocks to the highway where she would have the bus flagged down so she could ride to Greenway.

She was glad to be home. It had been a strain, she realized. She had tried to be herself, to be enthusiastic in replying that she thought they had a cute place and she had enjoyed her visit. But then at home she felt very tired. She went to her room. She would change and think and ponder what to do. The steep bare steps had never seemed longer, as she felt certain she couldn't go on this way much longer. She was so unhappy inside and going or coming made no difference, except for a short while. She dreaded going to sleep, so she read until all hours. Sleep was going into a horror world that she dreaded to enter. The loss of sleep kept her edgy and pale. She had little appetite for food so she lost weight, and had little energy.

Her parents decided if there were no change soon they would have a doctor see if he could find anything wrong.

Shandol began to realize she had no secret, actually. Her family knew something was wrong. She would have to tell someone about it. She didn't trust herself to try to explain anything verbally, but she could write it down. Perhaps her father could guide her. Late that night she tried writing it all down. It hadn't been easy. She wrote, tore up sheets of paper, and, doggedly, wrote over and over again, until she was satisfied she had some semblance of what she wished to impart. She was afraid she had sinned and she would have to confess that sin before the church, as she had seen done. But first to ask her father; something had to be done. She could not live with this torment any longer. She slept.

* * * * *

229

"Dad, could I talk to you?" she asked, as they finished supper that night. He was not surprised. He had felt she had had her eye on him all during supper. He had not let on in anyway, in fact he tried to pretend he had not noticed, he was sure she had something concerning him on her mind.

After supper, Joel went to the front room to the desk, opened his Bible and Sunday school teacher's book. Of course he could hardly concentrate, he only pretended as he waited for Shandol to come to him when she could—alone. At any other time he might have studied, but now found he had his mind upon the upcoming interview. He told himself he was ready for the worst. Nothing was going to surprise him, and he determined he'd try to be as level headed as the situation warranted.

Yet, he was taken completely by surprise that she only handed him a page of lined, rough tablet paper filled with her neat handwriting. His eyes quickly followed the lines only briefly.

"It's as though you are confessing a sin," he remarked, thoughtfully. "Are you considering reading it at church?"

"I'm askin' you!" she replied. "I don't know. I'm so tired of it all, I must do something. Oh, I wish I were dead."

Tears fell as she wept briefly, silently. "Please, just read it all," she added, as she rubbed her nose with the palm of her hand. Her eyes she wiped on the sleeve of her faded cotton print house dress. "Did I *do* wrong?"

She remembered only three such confessions in the church since she had gone there. Two were young men who had gone to a tavern and became drunk. There was also dancing. One was a Sunday school teacher, and he had been reprimanded and told he wasn't fit to teach a class of young people. He had been told to make amends, but for the life of her Shandol could not recall what either had said as they stood before the small congregation and admitted doing wrong.

Shandol remembered local gossip: "Don't he realize he's sinned— that's worst of all." "Will he get by with it because his folks have more money than the rest of us?" Or, "so he's saved by grace so he thinks it don't matter, but it does." And so on.

Joel had said: "The world watches the church and things like that hurt it. People call 'em hypocrites and feel they're no better than themselves, though they don't know all that goes on. Such things are beginnin' to be *so accepted*, though," he had added.

But the world laughs: What crust!

It's better to have a millstone around the neck and drown in a river than mislead young people, doesn't the Bible say?

The things Shandol could recall seemed to convict her. Was she

230

to be one the church couldn't change? *Oh, no!* She knew some quotes from the Bible. She recalled the one the girl had used. She had stolen and felt she was a backslider, she had said. Shandol had felt genuine compassion for her. She was so sorry for what she did—not just for being caught. But she reminded them of "James 5:6:"Confess your faults one with another, and pray for one another, that ye may be healed."

Will I have to go so far? Shandol wondered.

Joel looked over the paper several minutes, before turning to look at her. He raised kind eyes, with obvious relief in them, had Shandol noticed.

"Well," Shandol swallowed hard, "If I do hafta stand before 'em, will you help me with somethin' I can say?"

"I must say, Shandol," he began carefully, "I've been stumped. I dared wonder if I should consider the worst. But I'm mystified. This death, Shandol, I simply don't understand."

"Just tell me if I had anything to do with 'er dyin'!" she burst out.

"First tell me," he replied kindly, "who was this person? And why do you question your part in it? Yuh better begin and tell me all of it."

"Well—," she began hesitantly, swallowing, dropping her eyes to her hands in her lap, which she clenched and unclenched. "It was Mrs. Wells—she died in August—buried the day I saw Dean the first time. I think I hated her!" It burst from her, and she was about to cry again, but controlled herself.

"But she died of cancer," Joel objected. "She was sick for so long and was so bad off everyone knows what she died of. No one would even consider your having anything to do in regards to her dyin'— even remotely."

"Yuh must think me pretty silly," she replied low. "No one would guess and I'm glad, but that hurts too—feelin' I may've done wrong."

"Get to the point Shandol," Joel admonished. "It surely can't be as bad as yuh think."

"Oh, sure," she replied, not knowing how to explain it. "Well, you recall how sick she was at the last? She was kept so doped up to kill the pain she didn't know anything or anyone. Remember how the town people pitched in to help, especially the Little Mission church. Since Mom wasn't able to go, I went to help out. For of course, they expected us of all people to pitch right in. It was only fittin', as they'd say. Actually they made it as easy for me as possible, I suppose. I just did housework and looked after the two little girls. I even had to put them to bed; so I hardly saw Mrs. Wells. But ever' night that I went a church group was there prayin'—prayin' for a miracle that somehow she could just get up and be well. It seemed unrealistic to me; having nothing to do with faith. It was her time to go. Yet they bragged, or it seemed like braggin' to me, that that is what kept her alive as long as she was. One even remarked a doctor had thought she should have been dead a month ago. But kept alive, mind you, to be kept full of dope and linger and breathe, yet know nuthin' or nobody—only pain.'"

Shandol paused, as though remembering. Joel was watching and waiting, so she continued.

"I'm not sure if I pitied her or myself most." She smiled wanly. "But I was so vexed at those women, though I wasn't there all that much. But they prayed so loud the little girls couldn't sleep, while I was trying to catch up on some dishes. I don't see how they had so many dishes. Maybe I just helped out when they all got dirty. I felt sorry for myself. I wasn't gettin' a thing for doin' it. I got so tired of it and bein' in that old run-down kitchen. I hated every board on that bare floor, having to scrub it sometimes. And it all smelled so bad. I—I—" words failed her and she thought she would cry again. Her mouth trembled, tears came to her eyes, but she poked at them with her hand, and gained control. Joel sat silently, lest he discourage her telling it all.

"I—I prayed that she'd die—*die dead!*" She said it hurriedly, as the one word she must say while she could. "Then and there—and, sh— she did, almost that very minute, I think."

"I see," Joel said. "Can yuh recall what yuh said to make it bother yuh now?"

"I just prayed that she'd die," she replied. "I think I asked God to have mercy on her dyin' condition. To clip the tiny frazzled thread of life and set her soul free. The ladies prayed it to be mended. I thought her life in God's hands—or something to this effect. I'm not sure I said it out loud; but the ladies couldn't hear me. I *felt* it more. Just all of me. And—I've been haunted by it ever since."

"Strange—uh—interestin'," Joel mused almost to himself. "And is this all that's botherin' you?"

"Yeah, I think," she said. "But *all*? I feel terrible!"

"Believe me," Joel commented hopefully, "you have blown this up all out of proportion. First, don't feel so terrible. But how are you bothered? Your conscience—or what?"

"The dreams," she cried. "Terrible, frightening dreams." She told him of the finger she couldn't get rid of. "I see skeletons or corpses. Not always, but sometimes, and they seem so real. I think about them when I wake up. That makes them worse. Sometimes I dream of being in a real nice crowd, then realize someone is really walking around dead. Sometimes it is a skeleton, dark holes for eyes." She covered her

232

face with her hands.

"Did you see her dead?" Joel talked more as though they were having a conversation.

"No. Well, I just saw her lyin' there. She'd looked dead a long time to me. But when they saw she was goin', they wanted me to go to the store to call the doctor. But I said I wouldn't. I was going home. I ran as fast as I could and I was so scared because it was so dark. I looked back and saw the small square-top brown house, all lit up, but it wasn't reassuring. Lights, when I could see from home were better. I guess I shouldn't have run. I don't know. But I don't know much about usin' a phone. So it bothers me—or somethin' does. Why?"

"Death," he said simply, shaking his head affirmatively. "People usually remember first experiences like that. And it probably bothers them more or less one way or another."

"But not so bad!" she exclaimed quickly.

"You're a sensitive, young person, so yuh should'uv talked about it sooner. You've lost sleep, your appetite and lost weight. Yuh shoulda let me know before it bothered yuh. Yuh bottle up yer feelin's so. Now, I hope yuh feel better. And I doubt your prayer ended Mrs. Wells' life. It was prob'ly an unusual coincidence. God's ways aren't your worry." There was a moment's silence.

"You talked to no one about this?" He finally asked incredulously.

"I couldn't think how to say such a thing," she replied. "That I helped somebody die? I figured I'd get laughed at and most likely teased. Can't you imagine? It just wasn't an easy thing to talk about. I don't have anyone I'm that close to. The girls take me too seriously. Once I was talking too much to Freda, I guess, and yuh know how she answered? Like she hadn't heard a word! She sort of put on a dreamy expression and said, 'I think yuh're real purty.' The only time she ever complimented me and then to change the subject!"

She's a lonely child, Joel thought. *Has always been a loner. Quiet but deep. What will become of her? She's so sensitive and her feelings easily hurt.*

"What about the church people?" she asked. "Was I disrespectful? They were tryin' to help a lady on her deathbed."

"Oh, maybe thoughtless and a bit selfish," he told her. "But they don't know to be hurt, how could it? Sometimes I think going to all the churches maybe confusin', yet the friendliness and help of some of the people cannot be ignored. So one must keep up one's own Bible study and let the Holy Spirit teach."

"Well, I meant no real harm," Shandol said. "Mrs. Bright was so good to me. I—I don't guess I need the paper anymore?"

"No," he replied. "I believe you'll feel better about it now—even if you need time. If necessary talk to me again. I mean that, Shandol. I had forgotten all about Mrs. Wells. She was a county case, wasn't she? Her husband in prison and all. The county had to help. Paid for someone to stay after she got so bad. I do recall your going. I recall how pale I thought you turned once when you were asked to go. I stayed out of it since you did agree to go. Do you remember feelin' bad?

"Must've been after the first time," she told him. I got so sick I had to run for the back porch; I thought I'd throw up. The terrible smell—even with all the disinfectant, it was horrible. Like rotted flesh. And it seemed to hang on. I couldn't feel clean with the smell in my nose. But soon I felt I was stepping into a different, unreal nightmare—like place. I wonder how people get used to it."

"Maybe they don't try," he replied. "Just accept what can't be changed, even if they don't like it."

There was already a change in the way Shandol looked. Her expression had changed, more relaxed. There was even a hint of sparkle coming back into her eyes.

"I feel like I can go to bed now," she said, sighing. "I think I can sleep better—I hope. Thanks Dad, for hearin' me out." She bent over and kissed his bewhiskered face, and she was about to go out of the room.

"Wait, Shandol," Joel said. "How're you and that young scalawag gettin' along?"

"Well, he's not around, as yuh know," she replied. "But I look for him back as soon's he's home again."

"Yuh know what I mean!" Joel gazed at her steadily. "How does he conduct himself? Does he treat you like a lady or is he selfish and wayward?"

Shandol's face fell and she felt uncertain. A pink blush spread over her face. Joel realized it was a touchy subject, especially between a father and daughter. He was glad to see she blushed. He supposed the blush was a sign of modesty and thought it becoming. She was embarrassed.

"We have an understanding," she finally replied, weakly.

"He's been brash and uncivil?" Joel asked, the ripple in his jawline meant he felt worry, fear, protective—strongly.

"Just a round about way—talkin' and hintin'. I can't say it very well, but I hinted I boxed bad guy's jaws and not see 'em anymore."

"So he's comin' back anyway?" Joel interrupted.

"Yeah, but before that one party I wasn't sure," she grinned. "He knew he had gone out of bounds—I'm not that dumb. But he was so apologetic I felt sorry for him—we made a date, but only if he'd mind his Ps & Qs."

"And yuh think that wise?"

"Well, he sounded so quaint," she reasoned. "I just had to reconsider. Wish I could recall how he put it—something about not hating someone asking for food even if yuh can't feed him—or some such thing. Rather far fetched but made his point too."

"Humph," Joel cleared his throat. "A brash young whipper snapper. No manners. I oughta send 'em on his way."

"Daddy!"

"I didn't say I would," he soothed. "I just said I oughta. But not much way for you to go places otherwise. Just be careful, that's all."

"Don't worry, Dad," she replied, as though sharing a secret. "Yuh know how Mama says Grandma always said if the women behave themselves, men have to! It's mostly true, I guess."

"Yuh're a caution," Joel said, brightening, "and maybe a credit to us. Go on to bed. And I'm glad we had this talk," he added, his jaw rippling again.

"Oh, but I'm the one's glad," she replied. "I'm glad I could talk to yuh. And you'll hear if I have anymore bad dreams. I do feel a little silly—childish is a better word. When will I grow up? I mean really? Sometimes I feel so ignorant and inadequate."

"Yuh'll never know it all," he reminded her. "As long as yuh accept that yuh'll be better off. It's the ones who think they know it all who get the biggest let-downs.

Shandol dressed for bed, and breathed delicious fresh air from the open window. But once in bed, and in a completely unaccountable way, she wept. She cried as though her heart were broken; uncontrollably for awhile. Then she realized she felt better—cleaner. All the horror, the worry, and unworthy feelings faded and she soon smiled, even as tears ran down the sides of her face into her hair.

I'm that much older, she thought, but did not stop to analyze what she really meant by it. For she soon slept the untroubled sleep of the comfortable and innocent.

If she considered it later at all, she would have supposed her parents discussed it, perhaps to some length. But she certainly wouldn't have guessed the sighs of relief of the both of them.

CHAPTER 19

September waned and gave way to October. As the month progressed and the balmy October weather began the fall painting of the timber and roadsides, Shandol appreciated the beauty of the trees and various colorful fall dressing as each variety had it's own color. There were shades of reds, yellows, purple and orange—some green remained longer to add that color. It was a brightening time it seemed to her. The spring had it's green-up time, but fall had it's paint-up, the mystery of the dying plants signaled nature's way of perpetuating itself, and the seeds would sleep until time to grow again.

Just as the month of October carried on day by day, with work to be done everyday, it could be seen the color was also coming back to Shandol's cheeks, the sparkle to her expressive brown eyes, and a smile ready on the sensitive mouth, which seemed to light up her face once more.

In the weeks at the ending of summer, there was always much to be done. It was a time of gathering in the harvest for one thing. There had been more apples picked up and canned. There was relish to make and Shandol had to help grind the peppers and onions in the old food chopper they had had since she could remember. Tears had run down her face, while the greenish juice dripped hurriedly to a pan beneath the table where the food chopper was attached. Her resentment arose with the rush.

There were more sweet potatoes dug; winter wood was hauled. Sometimes the boys had to cut wood on Saturdays while Joel worked, but most of the time he helped with it. Sometimes they all had to help on wash day, seeming a job which came entirely too regularly and frequently. Audrey just would not put it all on Shandol to "break her down to pay in poor health later." Even Audrey still helped. Occasionally she, Shandol and Joel did it.

"Here we have to help wash, but Sis never has to help cut wood," Phil would occasionally protest.

"Dad won't even *let* me saw wood, so ha, ha," she would reply.

"Well, I know women who saw wood," he'd retorted.

"Oh, so do I," she replied flippantly, "but they don't have a raft of brothers to contend with either. It's such a pitiful way to ruin the hands." She displayed in dismay her hands which were ruined anyway. They were brown, and ugly with apple stains and sweet potatoes. "Bug dust," she exclaimed, more to herself.

"Oh, your dusty bug again," Phil teased, having overheard. "Long cat claw fingernails all pink and pretty—or should be—but, oh, your hands—what will *him* say?"

"Honest toil, boy, honest toil," she returned. "Besides I hope it will leave when we wash, or I'll peel tomatoes and in the juice I can get it off—I hope."

"Well, dust the bug, I should hope so," he grinned.

"Don't be so teasy," Shandol snapped. "Dad said not to say 'shoot a monkey' or 'for cripes sakes.' He says it's slang, which it is. And he says 'cracky-dovey.' But it seems I just have to say something."

"What's he said about the new by word?" he asked.

"Don't know," she mocked. "He ain't heared it yet."

Fall cleaning was still under way, gradually being done.

There was so much. The cabinets would be cleaned out. Audrey lined the shelves with newspapers, but she'd fold and snip small holes and cut the edge in scallops to give the edge a lacy effect. Curtains would be washed, the rooms aired and everything cleaned—and every nook and corner. However, it had to be finished this month. It was handy actually, because this was Audrey's time to have the extension club meeting at her house. At least the house would be clean and fresh, though it might not last long.

It wasn't always that there was just cleaning either. It was also a time to check the beds and go over them with hot soapy water and wash the iron bedsteads, and dab the ends with turpentine as a guard against bedbugs! Always in the old houses there was that worry. There seemed to be *some* in everyone. Sonnetts had moved into one small house and just one back room seem infested. It had taken work, most daubing the bedding with a feather dipped in turpentine and kerosene. The turpentine seemed to serve as a repellent and the kerosene destroy the pest's eggs. It was a worry almost everyone in Greenway faced, or so it seemed. No one knew whether the pests would be found in any certain house. Because of the crude construction of so many of the houses, and the bugs' ability to survive, they could stay in them. Anyone who moved in would acquire a "bait." Here at the Old Hotel the Sonnetts hadn't been bothered much by them, though on occasion one had been in evidence, supposedly coming from behind the plaster through one of the many holes. This problem weighed heavily on any family's pride and even one usually resulted in a thorough bed cleaning—no matter what the season. It seemed an impossible task at times. Some people swore they believed they came from the wood from the timber; and everyone burned wood. It was something that had to be faced. Whether they came from whatever mystery place; carried on clothing, no one could say. Just try to battle them.

The new mattresses had helped. They had been made by the families themselves, with directors, of course, of government surplus, and made some less worry. At least the pests couldn't get inside them, hatch a new batch to march forth to bother.

But this chore was all a very real part of both fall and spring cleaning. It had not had to be a hurried job, because it was worked into the routine, but it was finished by "club day."

Club day was on the third Friday of the month. The boys were in school so there was no bother there. It was a dreary day and rain poured down at intervals. Audrey had gone all out to make a fine meal. She had made apple pies, a cake, baked beans, some salad and had other vegetables she had canned or had grown themselves. The club members all supplemented the meal with each one bringing a covered dish. Eating the large meal was the first thing they did.

The talk was light woman talk and chatter. They berated the weather; complimented one another on the food and especially Audrey for her part and the speed with which she had managed to get it organized. Shandol expected that however, as almost everyone commented upon the deftness of Audrey's hands in the kitchen.

It was a delicious meal. They all loved the tenderness of the boiled hens, for no one else in the club could have prepared them in a pressure canner. The chickens had been watched for non-layers and so retained for the occasion. There was also the "meatloaf" which hadn't been meat at all, but tomatoes cooked with okra. Several exclaimed about the delicious concoction, but Audrey admitted it was simple to "whip up." She could recall the "Not To Be Sold" can, which was out of sight, for the beef given in a "relief order" of groceries of some time back. Once Audrey had worked in such a cannery at Plainesville with many other women. It was employment for the needy, and had been one of the early winters of a tight squeeze and hard times for the family. The short lived job had furnished some welcome cash, little though it had been. There were so few hours to work to allow as many as could work.

After the luncheon, Shandol helped with the clean-up.

After that there was little for Shandol to do except sit through the club meeting or make herself scarce, which she had hoped to do. But it was hardly possible unless she went somewhere, which she decided not to do.

The business meeting came first. There were new officers to be elected, minutes to be read, visitors to be acknowledged (and Shandol noticed there seemed to be several visitors). There was new business and the suggestion was made that the club would, again this year, sponsor a pie supper to raise money for Christmas stockings of candy and fruit to be given out Christmas Eve. It would be held at the schoolhouse auditorium, as it was every year, and any proceeds left over would be given to the school for any small incidentals which could be met this way: New games or playground equipment—such as basketball or bats and softballs, etc. The suggestion, in parliamentary fashion came to a vote and carried favorably. The entertainment would be worked out by a committee in cooperation with the teachers. Old business and tiresome details, it seemed to Shandol to take a long time and they would never end. Yet it had only seemed boring to her. Actually the meeting had moved along smoothly and was soon over. Then the meeting was adjourned with a statement there was to be more to the social hour.

If there had been suspicions caused by so many visitors to the club meeting, as soon as it broke up several members began bringing in mysterious packages, wrapped in blue and pink and very pretty, should have added to the mystery. Shandol merely wondered, instead of trying to guess and she was taken completely by surprise when Audrey was directed to open them. The first one solved the mystery. Baby things! Of course, it was a perfect set-up for a baby shower. And what a shower it was! Nearly anything and everything Audrey would need for the baby. There were receiving blankets, and a large, heavier blanket; gowns, little undershirts, "belly bands," diapers, dresses, washcloths and towels—even safety pins. And one lady remarked there would be other things because The Church representation wasn't complete. Some things had been handmade. In fact many had, but it had certainly been a surprise to Audrey. But it made her very happy. It was thoughtful of them and met such a need on her part.

Once during the opening of the shower gifts Joel had come to the door to survey the goings—on. He had not appeared except at the dinner. Now when he saw what was going on, left in sheepish self-consciousness and decided it best to leave the women to their own affairs and he remained out of sight. Shandol was completely enchanted by the stacks of things and wondered if she would have a new sister or brother to use them. It had been a heartening day the weather could not dampen. It was a great boost to Audrey's morale.

* * * * *

Shandol, meantime, heard from Dean regularly, and she answered his letters. He had also sent a more colorful card than the first. It was a picture postcard, "Wishin' you a pleasant journey wherever you go," it read. There were two young children, a dog beside the boy, who was holding a wishbone, and a pigtailed little girl in front of him. It had given his address and admonished her to write. They hadn't a job yet and rumors floated that it might be a month before they were hired, as they hadn't added any men since they had been up there. The pretty card carried a gloomy outlook.

There had been letters also, lamenting the fact they didn't have jobs. All during September he had written of their plight; nothing to do. He dreamed of things he'd do if he got a job. One was to get his own car so he could see her every chance he could. In the first letter he commented he hoped they got the house cleaned in time, "but we don't have much to do, but eat and sleep, ho ho."

In the next letter he wrote it was raining and they were in their tent. Brad was tormenting him about writing, while he tried to sleep. Dean always asked her not to let anyone beat his time.

Her letters to him were friendly. She did write that she missed him, and news about the family and of the town she knew was inconsequential. But what else? She had also gone to visit her brother again, helped her mother tack a comforter, made of discarded coats, suits, etc., and pieced as the top. The backing was feedsacks dyed purple. That the men were busy cutting wood. And so time had passed that she hadn't seen him except once.

She had not been expecting him the night after the club meeting. In his letter he had hinted he might be home that week, but she just couldn't expect him. She was afraid she would only be disappointed. She reasoned that even if he came it would be so late he would not try to see her until the next day, as happened before.

But she cleaned up as usual. It made her feel better, whether he came or not, which she doubted. And when he hadn't come by for her by the time the supper dishes were over, she decided to go for a walk. She could take the books back to Mrs. Davis and get others and read. After all she was cleaned up and it was something to do.

She wore the smooth crepe dress of a rust color given her by Mrs. Bright when she had helped with the baby. It fit her so nicely in all the right places, the look pleased her and she half-way hoped Dean would show up. She told her mother where she was going, in fact, in case he did come by.

Mrs. Davis was at home, but it was obvious she was expecting company and going out, which she affirmed. Her son and his wife were taking her out for awhile—also her sister. But she cordially invited Shandol inside to choose her books and place the ones she had returned on the table, for Mrs. Davis to put away. Shandol had given up trying to recall where they went, after having taken so many, which she admitted.

Mrs. Davis was friendly and talkative, but Shandol rushed, so mostly they discussed the books she liked, comparing them to the list of those she had read to save time. She also had to admit, she had trouble recalling the titles of the books she had read, there were so many now. Mrs. Davis did inform Shandol she was going to Plainesville to church. She seemed so pleased at the prospect.

Shandol soon left with her books, promising to return them as soon as she and her mother had read them. She had finally asked Mrs. Davis about getting two at a time, as Audrey also read them. It was hard for them to be reading the same book. Audrey did not aim to read when Shandol would have, but Shandol would never interrupt to say she wanted the book. She never let on and busied herself at something else.

As Shandol passed Horns she saw Phil was there, so she stopped to visit with Freda. This was another place young people were apt to gather, but so far only Phil and herself were there. Young people gathered there to play cards, which was allowed, but not the kind Sonnetts were allowed. They could listen to their radio or just gab.

Shandol had not planned to stay long, just be friendly, as they were on the front porch of what had once been a two room house. Now three rooms had been added to the back and the porch to the front. It was all unpainted outside. They visited on the porch, soon watching the moon climbing in the trees, as twilight became overshadowed. It was a lovely night, with a hint of chill in the air.

When Shandol decided to leave Phil got up also.

"Guess I'll walk Sis home," he said, "if she'll let me."

"You'd better," she retorted, "it's gettin' so late."

Freda and Cal followed them to the gate at the near roadside. They still talked awhile and when Phil opened the gate for himself and Shandol to go through, they followed. They were all walking down the road. Cal had a large flashlight, a long shiny one. Why was it so long? Most were hardly half that long. As she looked at it he in turn took the books she had been holding all the time. He used it for a hunting light he explained.

Shandol had a light wrap which she had put on, as Freda remarked of the chilly air, and hugged her arms and rubbed her upper arms. The moon had now reached a point bright enough to cast shadows beside them, until they turned east toward town, and for Phil and Shandol, home.

Shandol had wanted to talk to Cal but hadn't had much of a chance. She wanted to ask about Phil and his girl friend. She wondered if something had happened between them. But Cal would not discuss it. "I don't know nuthin' about how they git along," and refused to add any more.

"You're impossible," she told him. "I just wonder about her. After all, Phil is pretty close to me. He won't talk either."

They were walking leisurely along, and then were at the corner where Phil and Shandol should turn to go home.

"It's not late and a pretty night," Freda said, let's go to the store and get some gum. Anybody got enough pennies?"

They did have. If only they hadn't! Why did they? Just to spend the time and not have to go home and little to do th re but prepare for bed. And the night was so majestic for the season. Soon it would be cold and being inside would suit better.

Exactly when they realized they were being met by horsemen, would be hard to say. They saw them in silhouette, perhaps as soon as the sounds had registered. It was unusual and the four were quite curious. So very few had horses to ride and they knew fever of them. So they wondered how far the horses had carried their riders almost as much as who the riders were, as they doubted they would know them.

There were three, and they seemed to race when they too must have spotted the onlookers. But before Shandol heard the "whoa" from one of them she knew it was Dean. He rode a large bay with white feet and face, it's coat shiny. One horse was dark, one a lighter brown with brown markings and not so large as the large handsomely built workhorse Dean rode.

"Dean!" Shandol exclaimed, "What're you doing here? And on that beautiful beast?"

"I come to see yuh," he replied, and led the horse to a tall telephone pole and tied him loosely.

Cal grabbed his flashlight in a hurry, handed Shandol her books and disappeared behind the stone wall of the store.

"Phil," Shandol called to her brother, "carry my books on home, will yuh?"

"I've got to take Freda back," he replied. Cal's gone another way. You're only a little way from home. You can make it easier'n she can." He looked at Dean.

"Yeah, shore," Dean agreed, and turning to Shandol said: "Wonder where yer coward boyfriend went? I'll find 'em and tear him limb from limb."

"You might," she replied, "and then you might not. Why, that flashlight he's got would make uh weapon. It's a long shiny one-and new. But he'd see you first, if he's hidin' and wham yuh over the head with it. I bet it's eighteen inches long if it's a hair's breadth."

"I'll git 'im," Dean vowed. "I kin wait. Come on, I wanna talk to you."

He untied the horse. *He is a magnificent animal*, Shandol couldn't help thinking. But she wondered why, after all it was only a path to the house, especially through the back yard. "Come on," Dean repeated, holding the horse's reins. "We're goin' round the long way. Yuh guys kin go or stay," he told his friends.

"But I have these books," she protested. "I must take good care of them because they aren't mine."

"Yuh better come on," he threatened, "before I decide to go huntin'—man huntin', I mean."

"Bug dust," Shandol spat, but joined him. He took her right arm, as she had the books in her left, but she jerked free.

"I know the way," she said, haughtily. "We go east to the corner and then a block south and then west almost another block. I live there."

"Why did yuh do it, Shandol?" Dean asked. "Why are yuh out with 'em when I said I was comin'?"

"I'd given yuh up," she replied. "I supposed it'd be Sunday before yuh got here. So I went to Mrs. Davis' house to get the books to read. See them?" And she held them out for him to see—not sure he could. "On the way I went by Freda's & Cal's, Phil was there talkin' to Cal on the porch. I stopped and talked to Freda. And when Phil and I got ready to leave they just walked along with us. We just aimed to stop at the store for gum and then Cal and Freda were going on back. I swear it. But you rode up, and well, that changed and so we didn't even get our gum."

"Th' coward had th' books carryin' 'em," Dean accused.

"And I had the flashlight," she replied. "It was so long I was just fascinated by it. I've seen 'em before, but I can't see why they are so long. Hey, that horse is breathin' down my neck. I don't want him to step on me."

"Yuh won't get stepped on," Dean said. "Besides, yuh rather like this Calvin, don't yuh? So does Phil. But I seen 'em eye yuh at that party."

"Which wasn't a real party," she replied, emphatically. "Will you listen to me? Cal has a girl in Plainesville! Phil goes with—or likes her sister, who's so much older than Phil. I don't understand it. I really wanted to ask Cal about it, but he just won't talk either. It's not like 'em not to talk, so don't guess he knows nuthin'. She's nice, just a bit old for Phil is all."

"Now, I wanna talk about us," Dean replied.

"I remember. Yuh saw 'em at the fair," Shandol rattled on. "Yuh should remember. I thought 'er rather cute: And besides they asked me about my blind date," she plunged on. *I may as well give him something to rave about,* she thought.

"A blind date, Shandol?" Dean said, a hopeless note in his voice. "Now what else?"

"Well, I didn't enjoy it, if that's any comfort." she replied. "This girl wants tuh go roller skatin' with this guy she met. But he has a buddy along. So she comes down and says she can't go unless I go to make it a double date. What a night! First, the driver, a soldier, lost his cap—then control of the car. So we landed in the ditch. I was so scared. I can't roller skate anyway, but agreed to watch. The driver had to go to a station and have the car light fixed. The girl was nice about it all, though. Apparently more experienced than I, even if younger. I felt so inadequate and just a hysterical female when it was over. Bet she'll never ask me to go ag'in. Hope she wasn't ashamed uh me."

"Yeah," Dean replied, "and every time I come in here yuh've been out with someone. I don't like it, Shandol."

"But I wasn't," she contradicted hotly. "Not tonight anyway. Just walkin' down th' road with my brother and friends. Let's miss this mud hole here," she added, and they walked to a higher part of the wide street to miss a low muddy spot, which stayed muddy almost all year, except in the dry hot weather of summer.

They then came to the crossroads, and a turn to the right was Shandol's home. The road made a Y as it came to the road, one road turned east, one west. On this small triangle, bounded by roads, grew a tree and there was a grassy triangle. Dean and Shandol stopped there before going on.

"Let's go on," she said.

"We're not gettin' much talkin' done," Dean reminded her, and he grabbed her and tried to kiss her.

"Don't say that," she pushed at him. "After all you've said and hinted to me. You think kissin' fixes everything."

"Well, yuh owe me one," Dean taunted. "Or did Cal beat me to 'em tonight?"

"I should beat you," she cried. "Such a thing never entered our heads."

"I bet not," he mocked. "Don't be like this. I'd do anythin' for you yuh know that."

"Then let me go on home, I'm cold." She shivered to prove it. "I'm goin' anyway."

"Wait," and he caught her to hold her back.

At that moment the horse stomped his feet impatiently. "Ha, ha," she laughed, "the horse is on my side. What's his name? Would he paw me?"

"Nellie is *her* name," Dean replied, slapping and rubbing its smooth, shiny-coated neck affectionately. "She wouldn't hardly hurt a fly, she's so tame and gentle."

"And seems so big," Shandol added. "But tame and gentle, huh? Why did you come on horseback—and where's yer friends?"

"I reckon they'll wait," Dean replied. "If not I still know my way home."

"I don't think yuh really come to see me," Shandol accused him. "Just to spy on me."

"Nah, I come to see my gurl all right. I coultn't get the car—Dad and Mom had already gone—tuh church I reckon, or somewheres. I aimed tuh tell yuh I'd see yuh tomorrow, anyway."

"Lets mosey along toward home now," she suggested.

They started down the road then, the horse stepping patiently, rhythmically.

"I reckon," Dean mused aloud. "I'm gonna beat th' tar outta a guy fer messin' up my evenin'."

"And I'll never speak to you again," she said, turning toward him, as though daring him to deny what she had said. "Just don't think I won't know it either. Freda will tell me or Phil. And gossip just gets around here."

"Well, he better keep outta my way," he fumed.

"I mean what I said," she went on, "but don't worry about him. His mother don't like me very well anyway, I've heard. I heard she once said if she had a girl like me she'd whup the britches off'n 'er. I don't know what I ever did to her—except not go with her oldest boy."

"So she's jealous," Dean laughed, "of your pretty face and I bet yer smarter too, goin' on to school and all."

"In schoolin', maybe," Shandol conceded. "But there's lots I don't know. At least Freda's boyfriend seems like a gentleman. Sometimes I wonder about mine. I may be the dumb one."

"If'n yuh mean I don't deserve yuh, nobody knows that better'n me," he replied tenderly.

They stopped at the end of the raw of trees, which was between the yard and well. They stood beside the stacks of neatly rinked wood. Nearby, the horse began to crop at the long juicy grass, his halter rattled, the saddle squeaked. Dean held the reins. The smell was faint and merely outdoorsy.

"I'm sorry," she apologized. "I shouldn't say things like that."

"It's prob'ly true," Dean admitted. "But I'm beginnin' tuh love yuh, can't yuh realize I want us tuh be steadies? I'd hoped I woultn't have to say it. Fran and Brad have just such a understandin'."

Yuh mean we'd go with only one another?" she asked, then added regretfully, "There aren't many to go with here so why bother to make such an agreement?"

"So I kin be sure," Dean replied. "Some guys wouldn't even bother tuh come back when their steady ain't waitin'. That's what I consider you."

"I don't know," she hedged.

"I'm in love with yuh," he replied. "Shandol, I ain't never said that to a gurl before. I ditn't need to. I could git any gurl to go with I wanted. I never found one I wanted as I do you. Whatta yuh say?"

"I suppose I'd be lost without you too," she finally said, thoughtfully. *At least that's true*, she thought. *At least I do get to go. Besides, it's no permanent commitment. This place is hopeless.*

"I feel I kin depend on yuh," he said gaily. "And yuh just practically give yer word."

"All right," she agreed, "we'll try it for awhile."

"No more uniforms," he teased. "Especially no uniforms."

"I didn't care for that blind date, I can tell yuh." she reiterated. "Next time someone comes and says they can't go without me, I'll jest tell 'em they'll have to stay home and go to bed then!"

"I'm glad uh that," Dean beamed. She couldn't see the smile crinkles around his eyes she knew were there.

"I still shudder," she said. "We mighta been hurt or killed when he lost control uh that car. All because he lost his G.I. cap. Oh, my."

They were silent only a moment when "Doll, baby," came thundering from the porch. It was the pet name her father sometimes called her.

"Doll, baby," Shandol retorted, embarrassed, "will he never quit callin' me 'baby'? Listen Dean, Phil has got in," then raised her voice and replied, "I'm right here, Dad."

"Come on inside soon," he said, and they heard the screen door close.

"I must go in," she said. "Uyh comin'?"

"Nah, I better see if Jack 'n Dick is waitin'," he said.

"One thing about the goin' steady," she said, "I do have letters I've promised to write. Not love letters, just letters to get from the old stompin' ground, and so on."

"Well, all right," he agreed, "jest so they're to faraway places. I'll see yuh tomorrer."

"Goodnight," she said, and they parted with a brief good night kiss. She went on across the yard to the back porch, leaving him with the beautiful horse. She watched secretly from the shadow of the porch as he mounted gracefully and rode back the way they had come.

CHAPTER 20

The last Sunday in October was a cloudy, dreary one, though it did not actually rain until about four-thirty in the afternoon. Lester and Jane were visiting, but Lester returned to Plainesville because he had to go to work the next day. Jane stayed at her in-law's. Lester promised he would be back the next Friday night even if he had to catch a bus.

The weather cleared Monday and turned suddenly cool. "It frosted last night," Joel remarked. Tuesday morning they were up early. "Froze ice."

"Oh, my flowers!" Audrey exclaimed, "I bet they are frozen or at least nipped. I must bring them in today for sure." She gave Joel and the boys a knowing look. Some were heavy and they had to be carried upstairs.

She found a few looking wilted, but few with permanent damage. Some might have to be broken back but would come out again from the root. The porches had given enough protection to make the difference she was sure.

With that issue settled, Shandol turned her thoughts to the day ahead. How she dreaded it! She wondered if Jane did.

Bobby milked and then he and the smaller boys got ready and went to school. Joel went to work early, as usual. Phil too had caught the school bus.

But Shandol and Jane had a very different day planned than any they had ever faced before. They got ready to go to the Church in the Vale, because today they would *tack comforters*! Of course, there would be supervision but Shandol dreaded it all the same. They were to be made of "government surplus." This meant cotton for the inside and print cotton material already stitched to size—a seam down the middle; all was ready to be put together. All that was required was that they tack them there and then take them home to be bound around the edges. The family had signed up for four. The number a family was eligible for was decided by the number in the family. Lester and Jane had been counted as they had been living there when applications were taken. So was Grandpa, though by now he had gone to visit another daughter awhile. That was all right, they had been assured. These had been entitled to one, Lester and Jane, even Grandpa, and it hardly mattered where it was finished. All the families in town were entitled to theirs also, no matter who they were. Shandol was glad Jane was to get one and she could help her.

Jane had had no experience with such. Audrey decided not to go as it would be awkward for her.

"Just tack 'em enough to be able to handle 'em" Audrey told them, while Jane and Shandol put on their coats. "Then bring 'em home and we'll finish 'em here. It will be easier for us and you won't have to hurry so much."

But they had had to hurry to get them all done. They arrived at the church and were given instructions. In fact they were told to watch a few moments and then try. It didn't seem so hard to Shandol, as it wasn't new to her.

"We're going to try to get all ours done today," Shandol shyly told the short lady who seemed to be in charge. "Mama said we could just tack 'em close enough to hold 'em, together and get them home and finish 'em there."

Mrs. Larway, a plump short woman with a prominent chin, but pleasant faced, laughed at them tolerantly at hoping to get finished. She insisted they must pass inspection and meet certain standards. But she put them to work.

The long hall-like room of the church was chilly. So Jane and Shandol realized they would have to leave their coats on. The wooden pews, which were actually crude benches with straight hard board backs were not being put to their usual use. The large wood-burning stove, almost in the center of the room, was without a fire.

The pews had boards placed across them to make work areas. The material was placed on them right side down. The cotton batting was placed evenly over that. The cotton was first beaten to fluff it and interlock it to hold it together as much as possible. Then the second matching length of material was laid over that, right side up. The tacking was done with a heavy thread (or light string) stitched through all the thickness at every two-inch intervals. It had to be tied—each stitch cut and tied.

The cotton material was white with small lavender flowers. There were two different designs of print but they were the same color. Jane and Shandol decided to choose two of each pattern. Both were the tiny flowers.

"Mom and Dad made mattresses last February." Shandol told Jane, as they talked while pounding the cotton with stubby switches. "It was a bad time then, too. There was three inches of snow."

"Just frosty's not quite that bad," Jane commented.

"They were about the same as the comforters—materials from the government," Shandol told her. "But there was real mattress ticking and when they were finished you couldn't tell 'em from a factory made one!"

Jane and Shandol had two finished by noon; tacking them only every other row and every other space in the rows, which was not the every two inches they were supposed to be.

Jane and Shandol worked steadily and rhythmically together, as they talked and laughed away their nervousness and the chill in the air.

"It's not so bad," Jane said. "I was really worried this morning—wondering what I was getting into." And, as they moved the boards, to get closer to the center it became like teamwork and they worked well together. A faint raw-cottony elusive smell was in the air.

Mrs. Larway hadn't much wanted them to leave with the unfinished ones, but relented as she knew Audrey, her condition and she was sure Audrey would have no trouble knowing how to finish them. The two girls went home to eat at noon, taking the two they had actually done as planned—enough to handle them and get them done.

After they had eaten they hurried back to the church to work on the other two comforters. Jane and Shandol were through early and were home by a little past four o'clock.

At home meantime, Audrey and Joel tacked more on the comforters. Audrey showed Joel he could tie the knots, as he had not worked all day after all. Audrey did not work hard at it, but busied herself as she could.

Shandol and Jane were glad to get home early, and Shandol decided later it was lucky they did.

Dean came. In the last letter Shandol had received from him, he had written he would be there in two or three weeks. Yet here he was. Shandol was tired, and looked forward to being at home to rest and relax. She had been under tension and they'd had to work hard, as well as rush. But at his insistence she got ready to go somewhere. He told her they could go to a movie and reminded her they had never had a Tuesday night date before.

The next day, as planned, they worked on the comforters some more. Shandol dusted the front room floor to lay one out, as Audrey had, as there was no better place to work. They hoped to get one finished for Jane to take home. Perhaps they could get them all tacked, but they wanted Jane's tacked and bound and ready to use.

"What happened last night, Shandol?" Audrey asked, "on your date, I mean."

Shandol winked at Jane. It was the usual "third degree" as Shandol called it by now, as Audrey invariably asked her about her dates.

"Poor me," she moaned low to Jane. "I have to be so careful what I do on a date, I can tell yuh. I'd be such a poor liar."

Jane looked at her and smiled. "Yuh always have to be careful—

250

anyyone would—or should," she giggled.

"Yeah," Shandol agreed, "but what a way to ask. What happened? What would? We didn't linger long after the movie."

"Just the usual, Mama," she answered Audrey, who didn't hear well anyway, so she talked louder. "We saw the movie, but we had hamburger and soda pop. I had orange, he always gets Cokes."

Shandol didn't like for her mother to pretend innocence, but perhaps it was just as well since Jane was there. She was sure (later) her parents had discussed the talk she'd had with Joel; and how he had even discussed Dean and their understanding. She wished she knew how their discussion had gone. Perhaps she would never know and anyway parents worried she could tell that.

"Golly, I'm in an awkward position," Audrey changed the subject, "Guess I'll just have to draw up a rug and sit beside my work. I can't crawl and move around on all fours as easy as you two can."

"I think I did an awful thing last night," Shandol said, aside to Jane, and went on, hoping Jane would be mystified. "It sure embarrasses me to think of it. And Dean was fit to be tied!"

"For goodness sakes, what was it?" Jane asked quickly. "Can yuh tell it?"

"She'd better can," Audrey replied, "for we're sure gonna try to find out." Shandol had supposed her mother wouldn't hear, but as sometimes happens with the hard-of-hearing, they hear what isn't intended for their ears.

"Well," she began, "we saw a different kind of show than's our usual Saturday night shows. And, in fact, it was funny. But once I was the only one who laughed, and I just haw-hawed right out. Ever'one else was quiet. Dean was embarrassed and then he told me some people might think he had his hand up my dress or something which didn't help. I was so mortified and if he teases me I don't know what I'll do. I explained to him why I thought it was a time to laugh."

Jane and Audrey tried to show sympathy but there were sparkles in their eyes.

"Oh, well, I'll tell it then," she went on. "The reason I thought it funny is that there was a sort of show within a show. And this one girl got up to sing and dance, and she just had on what looked like little more than under things, only on her backside there was ruffles and some kinds of gew-gaw that looked like a bustle and a flimsy curtain hangin' on it. She had on long black hose and long gloves with the fingers with the fingers cut out, all black—at least it looked so on the black and white screen."

"What's funny about that?" Jane asked. "Seems just immodest to me."

"Wait until I finish and you'll see," Shandol replied. "Anyway she did her dance kickin' and wigglin'—I bet I could do it. But with nothing on but my undies—I couldn't do that in front of the family here! I was embarrassed to see it with Dean. After all, women look pretty much the same way. And I wondered if he had his mind on me. I wonder what Dad would've thought of it." She looked at Jane, at the sudden thought, her eyes opening wider and she grinned. "Anyway when she got the dancing number done she went behind the scenes and then it showed her in a dressing room covered up head to toe, with a long robe, ruffles on the neck and sleeve. Seemed the other way around woulda been better."

Shandol was stretched out on her stomach on the comforter tying threads as Audrey talked, as they had done before making them of whatever Audrey could find. Once she had used old coats to piece a top, she put an old blanket and sheet inside, but the bottom was patches of denim stitched together from Joel's and the boy's overalls. "Anyway it should wear like iron, and be washable," Audrey commented, as they had worked on it. She had washed everything before making it.

"Are my feet in yer way?" she asked Jane. Jane cut and tied her own tacking, as she went along, so her pace was slower. "Guess I could stretch another way."

"Back to the show," Jane laughed.

"Oh, that's it," Shandol replied. "I thought it was supposed to be funny. Be in front of everyone so scantily clad and off to herself all wrapped up."

"Maybe she had to cover up like a basketball player," Jane reasoned. "Remember they put on a sweatshirt or jacket to keep from cooling off too fast."

"Oh, she surely didn't work *that* hard," Shandol said. "Maybe so. Anyway I was the only one who laughed. Dean made me feel so bad by having such a fit because I laughed out loud. He was as embarrassed as I was, so I felt awful. I wonder why he bothers with me. We do have our differences sometimes. And last night was among the worst. But I got mad last night, I said if I didn't suit him why not try to find someone who did, instead of giving me a rough time."

"No such luck," Audrey muttered. "Don't worry about it. It might be embarrassing, but I bet no one could point you out right now (except Dean) as the one who laughed at the wrong time."

"That's my one consolation," Shandol admitted and sighed. "It was dark, but I blushed. My face burned. It's a wonder I'm not an ash."

"You'll get over it," Jane assured her.

"Yeah, but Dean's mind ran to the lowest," Shandol replied in disgust. "I have such trouble. Wonder if ever'body has the trouble I do. Not possibly."

"Les and I had a time," Jane said.

"Did it seem so?" Shandol asked quickly, smiling again. "It seemed smooth enough to me."

"But I had so much competition," Jane remarked. "Yuh know, Freda and Betsy. Where is Betsy now? I heard she got married."

"Yeah, she's married. They went west—Colorado or Idaho, I forget which. She just ran after Lester. He didn't care a snap for her. I thought she was *my* friend. She come here often to visit and I went there. We had dinners or suppers together. They had a hard way to go, yuh know."

"Didn't they though," Audrey agreed.

Shandol's mind was carried back: Betsy's dad was a drunk—when he could get it. Yet he was on a special diet for a stomach ulcer. He had bread bought at the store while the rest of the family ate cornbread three times a day. Betsy's mother's sister lived with them. Her illegitimate son was rumored to be Betsy's father's. She had never married. It was a large family and the two women worked hard to keep body and soul together; and there seemed no enmity between them. They had to cut wood, as men would, or whatever they could find to do. The house was large and bare, though not dirty. The girls were responsible for it. But Betsy's father did little. He couldn't even get on the "road work." And the aunt living there had kept them from drawing "child's aid." However, it was rumored the latter might change. Betsy quit high school when she could no longer attend Greenway. She married "Goat" Wench—at least she's out of this dump. Shandol couldn't help thinking. Now maybe she will get lucky, though she had had a hard time. Shandol had to admit they had never had it quite so bad. *Can it be my time just hasn't come yet*? she wondered.

Soon Jane's comforter was finished and it was Shandol's job to sew around to bind the edges by sewing machine, turning down an edge as neatly as she could.

Jane went home that evening after all because hers was finished and she felt she must. Shandol and Audrey quit for the day when hers was finished.

Joel had been there at the noon meal. He had chored a round as usual and dug the rest of the sweet potatoes in the afternoon.

Audrey and Shandol worked on the other comforter the next day and kept on it until they were finished, skipping a day to wash. It rained the balance of October and Shandol hated wash day when it was rainy. They hung most of it upstairs, since they only washed what was necessary. In the winter it was worse. They had to do it all eventually and it was put over chairs, and short wires strung behind the stoves.

It was so rainy the Halloween party at the school gym had been canceled.

Early November was changeable. One day rain some, even tried to snow a day or so in the early part of the month. But life sped on as usual. Margery and Shandol went to Plainesville one Sunday night on the truck. She had stayed all day with Shandol that day.

Just past the middle of the month it became warmer. So when it was wash day that week the things could be hung outside to dry. Audrey was out hanging up clothes as usual.

Then, as Shandol carried another basketful outside to her mother, a neighbor lady was talking with her. When Audrey moved on down the line she remained talking to Shandol. She bawled Shandol out for allowing her mother to hang up clothes in Audrey's condition!

It hurt Shandol's feelings. She had always tried to do her best. She felt she was helping out however she could; and realized there was a lot she didn't know. But why, she wondered hadn't Audrey told her, as Shandol felt it was her place to do, instead of that old busybody.

Mind your own business, she thought, tears stinging her eyes after the tongue lashing. *I'm not a servant around here after all. I do help do what I can, but Mama tells me what to do.*

"Why do you allow your mother to do it?" Mabel repeated.

"Allow?" Shandol repeated, as calmly as she could. "I don't know. I just supposed Mama would tell me what I'm supposed to know—or Dad one."

Audrey came up about then, seeing Mrs. Colmay had stopped to chat with Shandol, which seemed unusual.

"Audra," she said, and always said Audra—never Audrey, "what do you ever mean bein' out here hangin' up clothes? Don't cha know it's dangerous?"

"I've heard it's so and not so too," Audrey replied. "I'm just helpin'. It's such a big chore for Shandol. She seems so little to tackle such a big job alone. I don't want her health all broke down."

"But—but hangin' up clothes," she sputtered, "you're riskin' that baby's life! How are yuh feelin'?"

"I feel all right,'t Audrey replied, "as well as can be expected—in fact sometimes better'n I have in sometime."

"Yuh look real good," Mrs. Colmay said, truthfully. "But no need in your working so hard."

Shandol left them to go on with her tasks. It seemed to her the two talked and talked. Shandol felt so hurt she was near tears and was certainly apprehensive as well as feeling sorry for herself. No one seemed to mind how she was made to feel.

She went on with the work. They were almost finished anyway. She thrust out her chin with determination and laid a dirty pair of overalls, which with others had been soaking, on the washboard, the soiled water running from them back into the tub. She took the bar of lye soap her mother had, rubbed the most likely dirty places and took the scrub brush and went to work. She was angry and worked with renewed energy. She soaped and brushed the fronts, especially around the pockets, legs, with emphasis on the knees, as well as the backs of them. She put them in the hot water bath on the stove to boil. That was easier than just scrubbing them on the washboard for her. Her hands were small and the bulkiness of them made it awkward.

She wondered what her mother and Mabel Colmay were talking about. At least Mabel wasn't a gossip, and Audrey disapproved of it also, though they might discuss some illness, church doings or children.

Audrey finally came inside as Shandol was rinsing the overalls. She had taken them from "the boiler" using a dish pan and "clothes punch" to handle the scalding clothes. The clothes punch was a round length of wood, of about one and one half inches in diameter—larger than a broom handle and perhaps a yard long. It was natural colored, smooth and had been made by Audrey's father. The overalls were put into a hot suds and into a final rinse. Audrey had two more shirts to starch.

"About your hangin' out clothes, Mama," Shandol questioned, "what'd she mean?"

"It's supposed it will loop the umbilical cord around a baby's neck and cause it to be 'hanged'," Audrey replied.

"Lordy, how awful," Shandol exclaimed. "Is it true?"

"Don't say 'Lordy,' Shandol," Audrey replied. "I don't know about your question though. I've heard it but I mostly suppose it superstition. I honestly can't say that I know."

"I suppose we shouldn't take chances," Shandol said, thoughtfully. "I never ever heard it and I told her so. I—I also said I had supposed you'd have told me—or us."

"I just never considered it seriously—at least this early," Audrey replied. "But we'll be careful. She's to help out when the time comes so we'll have to let her have some say—or think she does. Just goin' along with that won't hurt, I suppose."

Shandol supposed that is what they had been discussing—no gossiping as she had figured.

Mrs. Colmay was a self-appointed preacher and often gave talks when she could get an audience. However her weak, creaky voice and

her sometimes almost illiterate delivery made her sermons rather
few and far between. Besides she had a large family. She was a tall
thin woman, with large deep-set eyes, prominent cheek bones and
a long face. Shandol suspected that many times she hadn't all she
needed to eat, but rather let the children have their fill first. And she
was always ready to help a neighbor if possible.

And soon came the end of the long wash day.

CHAPTER 21

"Tommy, Tommy," K.C. rushed into the house almost breathless because he was yelling excitedly.

"What's goin' on here?" Audrey asked, drying her hands on her apron, as she had been doing dishes.

"Ripper's got a fit on!" he exclaimed, pointing and panting excitedly. "Ripper's havin' a fit!"

"Oh, my," sighed Audrey.

"Tommy, Tommy, come 'ere," K.C. cried on the verge of tears.

"Well, Tommy's right there," Audrey pointed out mildly because he was so obviously upset. She was pointing to the doorway between the dining and front rooms, where Tommy appeared having heard his name. K.C. again wailed his sad news.

"C'mon, let's go see," Tommy said, as though taking command. "Mama, come on," he added.

The screen door was opened and the three stepped onto the back porch.

"Is he runnin' or down somewhere?" Audrey asked.

"He's runnin'," K.C. answered. "Here 'e comes now."

And just then a rather ugly brownish dog came running wildly around the house west to east. The three on the porch called his name, each in turn, but he yapped rapidly and ran on. He hit the well curbing, which made Audrey wince. He nosed along it unseeingly, unconsciously, apparently, until he was at the corner and then ran on to circle the house again. Tommy had tried to catch him but the dog raced on. The next time around he had better luck.

"I thought sure after 'dog days,' since he only had the barking fits the last month or so, he'd be better by now," Audrey said. "Poor little old dog."

Shandol, who was upstairs doing the cleaning, came down to see if anyone else knew the dog was "having a fit." She had heard the furious barking and could tell he was running by the sound of it, and knew what it meant. Then she saw him running around the house. She got to the kitchen door in time to see Tommy catch him. A shudder ran down her spine and seemed to crimp the nape of her neck. She went out onto the back porch.

"Make Tommy leave that dog be," she exclaimed to Audrey. "He'll get bit." Shandol herself was ready to go back inside should the dog come towards her.

"Now," Audrey replied, "he won't bite now. Dogs in runnin' fits don't bite."

"They're liable to sometime," she pleaded. "He could go mad. Doggone old dogs anyway; always have to have fits noway. Scares me to death."

"Tommy run get the penny we saved for his next dose,"

Audrey said. "It's under the chiffonier cover on the corner by the window. We'll give it to 'im," she said, and went on talking nervously to Shandol. "If it's worms, that's supposed to help. I believe the others have helped him. He's not too bad yet anyway. Maybe we can keep the fits down a bit and he'll outgrow them."

"Yeah," Shandol sighed resignedly, "maybe we can keep this ugly little old mongrel dog. Surely since he's not very big and not fit for anything. Still pennies are as cheap or maybe cheaper than the pills you've ordered from the Pet Shop."

"Well, we got this dog early." Audrey mused. "We'll see."

"I'm gettin' to almost hate dogs anymore," Shandol told her mother, and seeing the dog's glazed eyes and tousled hair added, "Don't they look awful after a fit."

"Now, Shandol," her mother protested, "Tommy and K.C. love him. I really hope we can raise him."

The dog was standing, but just barking now, with Audrey holding a strap around his neck. Tommy came running out, banging the screen door, with the penny. Audrey forced it down the animal's neck.

"Funny way to buy a treatment," Shandol commented. "Well, that's that," Audrey said, getting up, somewhat awkwardly. Shandol noted Audrey's hands on her hips to straighten up. "Summer's worst. Maybe we can keep the worthless mutt."

"I never heard of such a place as this," Shandol shrugged. "Can't even raise a dog!"

And a strange part of it was no one seemed to know why, unless a veterinarian could have puzzled it out. He was miles away. But at a time when a doctor bill was always a hardship, a veterinarian for a dog was completely unheard of to most of Greenway's residents. Most people who had healthy grown dogs had bought them elsewhere, already grown. Trying to raise a dog from a puppy was where the trouble seemed to be.

Ripper wasn't doing too bad in some ways, so far. Some dogs did actually outgrow the running fits. But if, with the running fit, it eventually fell down on its side kicking and frothing at the mouth, the dogs might as well be killed on the spot, but seldom were. There was always a spark of hope, and they usually weren't destroyed until they gradually got worse, finally, and literally, going into one fit right after the other—convulsion-like, and finally resembling a "mad dog," snapping and snarling, sometimes even getting up (that is before they were too far advanced) falling and seeming quite senseless. Most of the time when they got up from such a seizure they would wander off and be gone for several hours.

What are these fits? the Sonnetts often wondered. *What makes them happen here? Why can't something more be done to prevent or help them?*

Actually the questions were bandied about by many people. Why would one out of just so many live? So the questions were wondered about, voiced, and puzzled over.

There were theories, of course. Many held it was simply a matter of a poor diet. People were thankful for enough food to eat and feel satisfied and had little concern about nutrition—depending a lot on milk. And most people needed what they had for growing children. The pets were allowed a share of table scraps, which might also, need to be shared with a few chickens or perhaps a pig.

Another theory claimed it was a parasite—a worm and their inability to cope with them due to their poor physical condition. It was also claimed when the fits began the parasite had entered the spinal column at the rear and the ultimate seizures when it reached the brain. How they went for several days, or even weeks, getting worse. Shandol pondered and it wasn't explained to her to her satisfaction. Worm medicines had little effect. Audrey, who had canary birds to ship regularly, and supplies to order at a pet shop in St. Louis had, on occasion, ordered worm medicine. But it hadn't helped. They supposed it the wrong diagnosis, too late or just hopeless from the start.

Ripper had been born in Greenway. It gave him a slightly better chance—perhaps a sort of natural resistance. But a dog brought from somewhere else had no chance whatever. It was like a disease. They got bad early and died or were killed quickly. It was sickening to Shandol, as well as the rest of the family to think of the dogs, good dogs, even pedigreed dogs that had died or had to be destroyed. One such dog had been a German Shepherd, a healthy looking gangling pup, who had been brought by a trucker who had come to get peaches. Learning the fate of most dogs, he knew he could never sell it so had given it to Lester; that was because he was the nearest to ask what he could do with it. But he became the worst case they had seen. He went completely berserk, and had finally tried to attack Joel. He happened to have a hammer in his hand, and though Joel only meant to defend himself, knocked the dog senseless. Another lick finished him and got him out of the misery, as well as the family. He had "advanced" to a fighting mad stage of one spasm after the other. Joel had made a pen for him of fence wire, crude but adequate. But then there was no hope.

Another dog, a yellow, long-haired dog had done the same. It was part collie, with markings of a collie and they would so loved to have kept him, but the same fate awaited him. Others had similar luck. Raising a dog could become a major project, which outsiders would not appreciate, as they had not at first. But always there was a dog needing a home, and little boys drew them as flies to honey. The boys in turn loved the idea of having a dog. Ripper was a good natured dog. He'd run and romp with Tommy and K.C. and they had all longed for a dog since losing the old dog.

Audrey and Shandol went back to their work, but the two boys stayed by the dog until he was himself again. They finally coaxed him under the front porch to rest.

It would be something to write to Dean about! He would be sympathetic about the dog and the boys' worry about him. He seldom failed to ask about the boys.

Shandol also wrote to tell him she and Margery had gone on the truck to Plainesville to see a movie. She made it plain they were alone. Shandol had even confided to Margery her understanding with Dean, though she wouldn't write to tell Dean so. It was the understanding she would date no others. Shandol found it hard to write to him. She could not write a love letter with flowery plans and words she did not feel. They were just newsy letters of things that happened in the family and town. She could honestly mention she missed him. After all she had given her word and there was little she could do.

* * * * *

It was near the middle of the month that Shandol learned a riddle and had a decision to make. Actually she had thought little of it until she had heard the discussion between her brothers before they had all gone downstairs one morning. Their talking had not awakened her, she had been awake. Then she realized that she should have been aware of the strange coincidences. It concerned Phil missing the school bus on otherwise mysterious occasions. The driver apparently did not stop for Phil as though he forgot a stop should be made. He lived with Mrs. Bennett only four houses, perhaps two blocks from where Phil did.

Shandol had not meant to eavesdrop, she simply couldn't help hearing them, the doors ajar. There, across the hall, Phil, who slept inside now rather than on the balcony above the front porch as on hot nights, was with Bobby and simply asked his brother to be outside when time for the bus to come by, and wave him on so that he'd not stop. She guessed that anytime Phil didn't want to go to school that had been the solution.

Shandol confronted Phil with the fact she had overheard the conversation. They were alone in the front room, Phil on the davenport, Shandol standing by the desk.

"So be a poor sport and tell on me," he said defensively.

"I'll see," she teased. "But yuh should be ashamed though gettin' Bobby in trouble. And what do yuh put on yer excuses at the principle's office?"

"Missed the bus," he replied.

"Well, yuh better watch it," Shandol told him. "Too much uh that and Prof'll be askin' the bus driver why he misses you all the time. And then the driver will explain that yuh don't live very far from where the route is and that he waved on. It'll get the whole outfit in a muddle. I know. I seen it happen. It's just like Prof to do just that—nosin' around 'n all."

"He might at that," agreed Phil, grinning a little sheepishly. "The whole set up scares me anyway. Don't like school up there. Too many kids runnin' around. I'd rather go to Folks Consent. I aim to next year or I won't go."

"I'm glad I finished at Plainesville," Shandol mused. "But don't ask me why. Pride I suppose, because Les did."

"Well, I'm scared and worried all the time," Phil objected.

"Yuh do have to work," she affirmed. "I worried too, though. But now I'm out, so it seems so different. I sometimes forget the work and worry—not having to go back."

Shandol decided quickly she wouldn't tell after all. She wanted Phil to like her and to have confidence in her. She had usually told on Lester with the result he didn't care to have her around. It was so exasperating of him, Shandol thought. She just wanted him to be just perfect; and it seemed others thought he should act above reproach. Shandol hoped to save him the adverse comments and criticisms, which he either didn't hear about or didn't care about—one way or the other. And Lester began to ignore her for being a tattletale and Shandol couldn't understand it. He hadn't just come right out and called her a tattler, but just that little sisters were a nuisance or got in the way. Yet she was sure what she did was for his own good. The same could be true of Phil, but she decided to give him a chance. She would warn him. She supposed she should mention it to her mother, but she could wait awhile. Phil had his books bought and it would be such a waste if he did lose out or flunk out in school. But would Phil care? She wondered.

It was a mild day and one in which Joel could go to work on the road. Phil would make sure of that, Otherwise they would be apt to go to the timber to cut wood. She was sure he would rather go to school than cut wood any day,

Shandol was glad she had kept still, because it paid off a few days later.

"At the pie supper that's comin' up," Phil confided, half heartedly strumming the guitar, "they're gonna keep runnin' up your pie and really make Dean pay for it. They are even offerin' me cash to let 'em in on which is your box. It's temptin'."

"Phil, no," she exclaimed. "Who are they? Oh, Dean would really blow his top," she predicted. "What can we do? He won't even go if he knows. he's prob'ly helped do some other poor guy the same way so knows it's a dirty trick!"

"Yuh have written to 'em about the pie supper?" Phil asked.

"Oh, sure," she replied. "But he says he can talk better about it when I see him. I suppose he's sure he'll know which is my pie. Oh, dear, I don't know. I'm in a notion not to go myself. Or at least not take a pie—or just send a bachelor one. They sell pretty good. Then a guy can get someone to help eat it, if he can find a girl; take it home to the family or just hog it all himself."

"I'll see what I can figure out," Phil said.

"Well, don't tell' em much," she cautioned him. "We have to keep 'em guessin'. Dean won't pay much more than is ordinary I'm sure, and he'd have a fit if I eat with someone else if they'd get it."

Shandol wondered if there were a rule about this type a thing; but mostly what would Dean's rule be!

The evening of the pie supper was a rainy one. This was a disappointment because it might keep some people away, especially those who would have to walk, which was practically everyone. Of course there would be those from the country and around who would have rides. It would mean extra cash too, because it was for a fairly good cause. It would furnish the candy, fruit and a Christmas stockings (of netting) to be distributed to Greenway children Christmas-eve.

Shandol walked to the schoolhouse with her parents and brothers. There were newspapers over her pie box and a scarf over her hair. She had been fretting about what a mess she would be by the time she got there and was still in a good notion to stay at home. In addition to Shandol's pie they were taking a bachelor pie. It was also protected, as was Audrey's hair.

Dean hadn't come. Perhaps he didn't care to after all, Shandol thought, as she tromped through the mist avoiding muddy spots and puddles the best she could, as did the entire family. Such a night!

262

Nothing but a disappointment was all she could foresee. Men! Were they always so unpredictable?

The program and pie selling was to be held in the auditorium of the school house, which was on the second floor. It consisted of one—half the second floor. There were two classrooms across a wide hall, and a small room usually referred to as the reference library at the end of the hall. Sometimes it doubled as a dressing room for the stage, which was at that end of the auditorium; and it also had become a storage space for odds and ends other than books.

The program itself consisted of music, singing and a skit. There were two quartets that sang some old time songs, one from Plainesville, one from Greenway. There was the popular fiddle music with guitar, banjo and mandolin accompaniment. Phil sang two solos, with his guitar, accompanying himself. The second was an encore by audience demand. The Lankers girls also sang and played their instruments. Shandol thought it a good program and seemed well received.

Then came the selling of the pies. Shandol wanted to just crawl under the seats and hide, except they were chairs and she couldn't. She felt dreadful and sick at heart. She was so sure Dean would be in a nasty mood if she shared her pie with anyone except himself. But she was *supposed* to take a pie! It was expected of her as well as any of the others. Audrey had made the pies and they looked marvelous. Shandol sat with Freda and Margery. She was even worried that no one would even bid on her pie, because fear of Dean might mean no one would want it badly enough. She wished again and again she had stayed at home—by herself, or not brought a pie, no matter what anyone thought. One would have helped—or two bachelor pies, just so it was not hers. But here she was trying to bluff it out. Her pie would probably be the last to sell so she would be miserable that much longer. She had to smile though she felt more inclined to snap back when anyone spoke to her. But the other two girls were giggling and pointing out pies, unworried, taking it all in, enjoying themselves. Shandol berated herself for her serious mood. But her feelings were dangling low indeed, and she couldn't bring herself above her fear and disappointment.

The auctioneer was an amateur but a good one. He was a local man who had picked up enough to bluff his way, improvising and with a jovial air. He did a good job, actually. And when Shandol's pie came up he had the audacity to say: "Now, here's the one you've been waiting for." And Shandol wished she had listened to hear what he had been saying. Had he said it every time—or even before? She wasn't sure, she was so mixed up in her mental misery. But it sounded more significant than was comfortable at that moment.

263

"Fifty cents," came a bid from the back.

Oh, it's got to bring more than that, she thought.

"Fifty-five," came back another bid.

I can't stand it, Shandol almost groaned.

"Sixty," another bid.

"Who's bidding?" Shandol asked Freda, who was craning her neck to look anyway.

It was a box covered with pink crepe paper and trimmed in blue. The blue bands covered the string which tied it, and there was a blue artificial flower bouquet in the middle of graduated heights and sizes. It was caught with green ribbon. It was simple but pretty.

"I don't know," Freda answered. "Wonder whose it is?"

"It's Shandol's, but sh-h-h," Margery said, "didn't you know?"

"Well, it's somebody biddin' who don't know Dean or that it's yuhrs," Freda concluded.

"Oh, he's not such a battle wagon," Shandol defended. "I'm not afraid of him and I'm not very big."

"Seventy-five," the auctioneer resounded, "Who'll make it eighty?"

"Eighty," a voice said.

"Are you sure Dean ain't here?" Margery asked.

"I don't know. But if I see him and he says one cross word—oh, I'll wring his neck," but hurt was in her voice.

"One dollar," a different voice said in answer to the auctioneer's fast talk, making swift decisions necessary.

"Somebody's goin' to be let down, is what I'm thinkin'," Shandol groaned. "They think Dean is here and has someone biddin' for 'em. Someone's gonna be stuck with me and I don't even know who."

"Let 'em bid," Margery laughed. "It may bring more than any pie here, even without Dean."

"Sounds like so many biddin'," Shandol mused. "I wonder who really wants the pie."

"One fifty-five." *It was still going!*

"Oh, my," Shandol cried, "there'll be uh hair pullin'. They think Dean is here. I'm gonna get up and tell 'em!"

"No, yuh don't," Margery said calmly. "The idea is to make money. Let 'em go. It's their hard luck if they're biddin' again' someone who ain't even here."

"One sixty—will yuh gimme sixty-five—got sixty, sixty-five. Goin' at one sixty."

"One sixty-five."

"One seventy."

"One seventy-five."

"One seventy-five, gimme eighty. Goin' at one-seventy five—once,

264

twice, three times—sold! For one dollar and seventy-five cents."

Shandol stared at the buyer. The boy, she was sure, who had ridden the pinto pony into town with Dean. What did that mean? With Dean's permission or what?

After the pies there were the usual fun-type things given or selections made by penny vote. First was the most love-sick couple there. There was keen competition. There was an elderly couple who had been married many years. There was a widow with a widower who were known to be keeping steady company, as well as the young couples. Rod and Rayda received that prize, the usual jar of sweet pickles, which they had to go to the front of the auditorium to accept.

Then came a broom for the dirtiest housekeeper. It went to a tall gangly bachelor, who was somewhat lazy and shabby, but he was a show off and seemed to enjoy the attention by sweeping a small section of the stage with the broom which was the prize.

Robert West, the fiddler, also a bachelor received a bar of laundry soap for having the stinkingest feet! He accepted it as the gag it was and he was cheered by everyone as he went forward to claim his prize.

Of course, there was always the prize for the prettiest girl present—or at least who could get the most votes. There were several candidates, some of whom did not live in Greenway.

Shandol, Rayda, and Louise Martin were the ones from Greenway. Carol's sister Laura and the oldest Allsup girl were other girls there. In the shuffle some began to lag behind until it was Shandol and the two out of town girls. Shandol third. Shandol was sure the Allsup girl would get it as her boyfriend was with her. But he reckoned without the pride and stubbornness of the boys in Greenway for their own, and she was kept in the race. She was sure Bucky had entered her name as a joke—or was he the one who had actually bought her pie? It would be like him—headstrong and being sure he was noticed.

Shandol won by three points. Her face in a flame, put her hands to her face and with wobbly knees, went to the front to claim the prize, a box of candy and murmur, "Thank yuh." There was applause, with whistles, as she returned to her seat.

The cakewalk kept the activities moving, and was a new attraction this year. The couples lined up, paying a nickel to get in line, getting ready to start the march. The fiddler played a tune and the couple with the broom in front of them, as it was lowered when the tune ended, won a cake. There were several cakes though only a few actually started it. But a chance to win a lovely cake, and with coaxing, the idea soon caught on, and more and more came forward. Freda's boyfriend had finally arrived and they joined the line. He was in uniform, so looked handsome. Shandol and Margery joined them, Shandol having some change in her zipper bag. When there was a good-sized line which was to circle a designated area, they were told to march along. A schoolboy was blindfolded and had the new broom, the "dirtiest" person had allowed them to use, and would, hopefully, lower it directly in front of the winning couple. A couple won from out of town, Shandol knew from church.

Soon it was over but the pie-eating or leaving. Shandol stood, staring, her hand on her forehead wondering if she could think of some excuse to leave, when Dean came and stood at her side. Then she sat down and looked up at his tall figure towering above her. She stared incredulously.

"Dean!" she exclaimed, "Oh, Dean, you're too late."

"Ain't I now?" he beamed. "I been here awhile." He went on to explain, "but nobody seen me, I don't think. I got your pie."

"Yuh did?" she replied. "But I thought someone else did!"

"I got' em tuh do it," Dean informed her, a little cockily she thought. "I knowed they'd run it up on me, so I stayed out of it. But here I yam! Glad tuh see me?"

"Why, yes," she managed, surprise still written all over her face. "If it wasn't for all these people—uh—"

"Yuh'd feel like kissin' me, huh?" Dean finished for her. "Well, we'll take care of that later and I'm gonna enjoy kissin' the purtiest girl. But right now it's pie time."

"So the prettiest girl, huh!" a smile dawned. Of course he'd helped. How much she'd never know.

"Oh, yes, the candy!" she exclaimed. "I think I'm supposed tuh open it and offer it around. But I do aim to save some for myself. I only got one box of candy before in my life; and it was for my birthday last year."

"Who got it?" Dean immediately wanted to know.

"A friend of Dad's," she answered, mischievously. "He thought I was just sixteen."

Then they went to the front where the pies were laid out, selected Shandol's by number, went back and sat down. Shandol produced two forks from a sack and wrapped in a clean cloth, already inside the box.

"I'll say I'm proud to be eatin' with the purtiest gurl," Dean teased, yet said it proudly. Perhaps he was trying to put her at ease. She was so nervous. "Purty box too," he added.

"I just have a sneaking feeling yuh helped me be that prettiest girl," she replied, eyeing him. "I wondered who backed me so determinedly. I supposed it was Jack—the guy who got the pie—and

266

Buck, who would want someone in town to get it. Don't know why he didn't back his brother's girl though. Or were you and Phil in on that?"

"Oh, don't worry about it," he said. "Let's just enjoy this good pie—my favorite, lemon meringue."

"I'm still glad no one gave away the fact yuh were here. I was worried. I wondered how I could keep from eatin' with someone else. Could yuh have blamed me if I had?"

"Sorry I couldn't face it," he admitted. "I just *had* to have it done fer me."

Before it was time to leave the amount taken in was announced—proudly—for it was a surprising figure.

Dean squeezed Shandol's hand. Then soon it was all over.

The family rode home in Dean's car.

The next day Shandol and Dean were together. It was a time when they had enjoyed one another's company, and of course rehashed the pie supper events in their conversation quite often.

It seemed there was nothing to quibble about except that Dean was becoming dissatisfied with Shandol's letters to him.

"Good lord, Shandol," he complained, "you write like Mom writes to me. Just friendly and nice really, but we're sweethearts. I wish yuh'd write like yuh think somethin' uh me."

"I'm sorry," she replied shyly. "I just don't know how to write love letters. Give me time. They must be natural and true as well as flowery, lovin' words."

"Make 'em true then." Dean replied, impatiently.

"I just can't decide how I feel yet," she said. "I like you. If I didn't I wouldn't go with yuh, though yuh have to admit we have our difficulties. I do miss you when you're gone, but if it was me that was gone would it be the same? I don't suppose you understand what I mean?"

"I'll try to, as long as yuh're my gurl and no one else can horn in," he said.

Shandol decided to leave it at that and the rest of the time went quickly.

Audrey had learned in the early part of the month the Winsch family was leaving Greenway. Two of the girls had already gone and were with their brother, "Goat," who was married and lived in a western state. The Winsch family lived at the end of an alley with a turn off the main road between the railroad tracks and the store. This meant they were about halfway up the hill, across a grassy lot from Sonnetts and next to the house which burned. There would be no farewell party for the family, Audrey knew, yet she felt it was unkind to see them leave without a friendly gesture of some kind. They had a hard time now that two of the girls were gone. So she decided to invite them to Thanksgiving dinner. For awhile they had milked for a dairyman and gone to school. But there were circumstances that had forced them to quit. Two of the girls had decided to quit when they could no longer go to Greenway to school. They also quit school. But the other one, Velda, who had a twin, Velma, wanted to go on to school. Velma had not. They were not identical twins so were not alike in looks or personalities.

Velda was still at home with her eleven month-old son; and was also invited for Thanksgiving Day. The child's father had been the school bus driver, so the gossip went. She discussed her "husband" openly, that day, and how much the child looked like him. And he must have because his round face, plump cheeks and body, dark hair, merry eyes and ready smile did not, in even his way, resemble the Winsches. He was a pretty little boy. His father had married his long-time sweetheart soon after the baby's birth. But Velda completely ignored that fact. There had been no divorce—no marriage in fact. Shandol would always remember her surprise and disbelief when she heard Velda had "gone away" to have a baby! Shandol still found it hard to believe he had deserted Velda and the child. Velda still believed he loved her and they would be together one day. But she had decided to go west with her family. Very few in Greenway had anything to do with them.

Shandol had hoped she would learn how it had all came about. Why Velda had "given in" before actual marriage. But there was no chance for personal girl talk. Shandol hoped to gain knowledge that way, but so far as Velda was concerned she still had a husband. And it was left so.

The meal went along well as did the day. There was neighborly talk of the Winsch's hopes and plans, which they were more hopeful of than actually knowing. They just wanted to be where the other children were. (And away from Greenway, thought Shandol.) They all enjoyed the baby. He was just beginning to take steps and was certainly made over, so cute in a blue romper suit. When it was over Audrey and Joel were glad they had asked them to share the day, and took the opportunity to wish them well on the journey to their new home.

There were a few who had asked about the day and activities, but little was said. Audrey's condition had not been alluded to. The Winschs stuck together. There was no gossip.

Shandol was more puzzled than ever. She and Velda were about the same age; and Velda had not finished the last year of school. She was so smart, Shandol mused. How had it happened? They only rode the bus a little way alone. How had any romance came about? Was it her fault or his? Surely his, because Velda thought they were in love. When they had gone Shandol felt as though she'd lost a friend. Or had she felt that when she learned Velda had "gone wrong"? Shandol wondered if Velda would ever marry. She hoped Velda could so she could forget the unfaithful man who had let his son be born without his name.

At the end of the month Joel was told he was transferred to another job. He went to Plainesville for further details. It was a wood-cutting job for the armory, a temporary job. He was to report there on Monday. It would be difficult to manage he knew, yet he would have to manage it somehow.

However by Monday he got word he could go on to work on the usual job. It had been a welcome relief, and so like the government to have a change of mind; it wasn't enough that it was an unreliable source of having to make a living. He had considered quitting and looking into the government farm loan set-up. But since his last failure he simply lacked the confidence it took for such a venture on soil he didn't even trust. He had heard of some failures.

Anyway in his trips to Plainesville he had finally been able to buy Audrey some turnips. She craved them and they hadn't any. She enjoyed them and expected everyone else to do the same. So far many meals they had to expect to eat turnips. Joel consoled their murmurings by saying there were stranger things women craved at such times, and in his easy-going loving way, took it all in stride.

CHAPTER 22

"Pearl Harbor's been bombed?" Shandol asked. "What's that supposed to mean?" Shandol spoke to Joel who stood by the large dining table solemnly facing the family. He had gone to the post office and stopped by the store for any late news or gossip. He was told the announcement had been made. He spent no more time there, but turned straight toward home.

"It means," he replied firmly, "if we are not at war with Japan, we surely, undoubtedly will be before long. They did it."

"War!" Audrey echoed. "War." She looked as though she might cry. She felt life so inadequate as she thought of the new life in store. Yet it seemed unreal to them all.

"Anyway Pearl Harbor don't mean nuthin' to me," Shandol said, and decided it must be some remote and faraway place, why make a fuss? "I mean," she amended, "it don't tell us anything. Where's Pearl Harbor at?"

"In the Hawaiian Islands, I think they said," Joel replied.

"The Islands!" Shandol cried. "But Hugh's there near Honolulu—what if it's around there? Is it? Is it? Is Hugh all right?"

"Wait a minute," Joel replied, "let's hope and pray he's all right. Maybe we can look up the location. I just didn't stay for any further particulars—if any's known. Just learned they'd been bombed and it's pretty terrible, I guess."

"I gotta find out somethin'," Shandol said firmly, and leaving the room went to the desk in the front room and pulled out an oversized book neatly stacked under some pigeon holes—an oversized book on geography. Turning to the index she hunted Pearl Harbor. Her hands shook, but she couldn't find it. She had decided to look under Hawaiian Islands when Phil came in about then, and as solemn eyed as Joel had been, guessed what she was searching for.

"It's not far from Honolulu," Phil said, evenly, "so look no further."

"It's no time to be silly," she snapped. "How'd you know?"

"I listened a minute longer," he replied.

Shandol put her hand to her throat, eyes frightened and large making her face seem small. Her chin unsteady.

"War?" she whispered. "War." Then she became angry. "They would have to bring it to us!" she stormed. "It's really comin' I bet—just like Uncle Lafey said. It may mean the end of everything—the end of the world! Oh, it scares me!"

That first Sunday in December had started out calm and pretty. In fact the whole month so far had been relatively mild and pretty. The air was crisp and frosty, almost every morning. This morning was no exception, just seasonal. The family had gone to Sunday school, looked over the papers as Audrey prepared a later than usual meal.

Joel had gone to the store to hear the news, play checkers or just visit around until it was time for the later train. Phil, having nothing better to do, had gone also.

The boys were out playing with the Parkley kids along the alleys. They would come in to warm, but would soon be outside again.

When the announcement came over the small radio in the store, the significant impact had hit every listener; and even those who hadn't been listening. There had been music, but the announcer had interrupted the program with the news. It came over the air even as they were being bombed, they thought.

Joel had come straight home. It wasn't two p.m. yet. Phil had stayed a few minutes longer and found out about the islands somehow and came soon after.

Shandol was expecting Dean that afternoon. She only half-heartedly dressed for his coming. She knew they would probably leave the house when he came, and there were so many questions in her mind. And worry. *What about Hugh*, she wondered.

Joel and Audrey decided to go across the street to the neighbors to hear their radio for more news and details.

How bad was it really? What led up to such a thing? Was war automatically declared? Were the Japanese really Hitler's friends? The Kaspers had a small radio and Joel and Audrey guessed they would surely listen, if not already.

Phil said he was going to Cal's to listen to their radio, and also to see if they still aimed to go to church in Plainesville. The younger boys would be playing and in and out, but they would know where their parents were, and they in turn could still keep an eye on the youngsters. Bobby went to see Dale Lankers.

It was nearly four o'clock when Dean came. Shandol had finished reading the Sunday funny papers and was scanning the news sections wondering if he would come for her. The bombing news would be in the paper soon and she certainly aimed to read about it then. What was it like when wars came, she wondered. Was she going to find out? But she hoped it wouldn't last very long.

Shandol arose from the table to answer Dean's knock. She had heard him honk his horn but she never ran out. It made Audrey frown at her, and Joel all but forbade it.

"Hello," Dean said, seeming glad to see her.

"Come on in," she invited, trying weakly to return his smile.

"How's my gurl?" Dean asked, shaking her lightly by her shoulders.

"Fine, fine," she replied, nervously, and moved to show him a chair lest he try to kiss her. "Do sit down. Folks ain't home now, but are across the street listenin' to a radio for news. H-have yuh heard the news yet?"

"Yeah," Dean replied. "At Folks Consent at the gas station. It's what I call stirrin' things up."

"Dean," Shandol explained nearly in tears, "don't be so flippy about it. It'll prob'ly mean war. I bet lotsa boys will join the army, navy, marines or somethin', to fight." She peered at him questioningly.

"Git yer coat then," he said briefly.

Shandol got her coat, head scarf and the small zippered bag and they left. They drove on to Folks Consent. It didn't seem like a time to be by themselves, and they hoped there would be others there. There were, parked in the middle of main street where a parking lane was marked. Brad and Franny were there, with another couple, who were already getting out. They had come in a bright red pickup truck parked next to Brad's car.

"We're just fixin' to leave," Brad greeted them, with a smile. "We're goin' tuh the schoolhouse. Come along. We'll try to hear my radio there. May need yuh to help me get started agin."

"We will if yuh mean it," Dean replied.

"Sure do," Brad said. "We're interested in the news."

"Who's that other couple?" Shandol asked Dean, as the couples left one vehicle behind the other; Brad first, Dean following last in line.

"Hal and Betty," Dean said. "Hal Fulbuy and Betty Ranemore— she's uh friend uh Fran's. They're in high school. They all live out in th' country and ride the same school bus, except Brad uh course."

Betty had long sandy-colored hair and fair skin. Her eyes in a rather slim face had frankly looked Shandol over, as Shandol also returned her gaze. Shandol smiled first and she smiled back showing dimples. Hal was a tall boy, slim with brown hair combed straight back. His face was broad with a high forehead, his smile ready showing even white teeth. The couple seemed to have a oneness about them one could almost sense. Shandol asked if they were married.

"Nope," Dean replied. "I *told* you their names."

"Of course," she said ruefully. "Engaged then?"

"Not that I know about," he answered.

As soon as they arrived at the schoolhouse the three couples crowded into Brad's car. Betty sat on Hal's lap in the back seat. The topic of war soon came up. They seemed to think it wouldn't amount to much.

"Ain't we been tryin' tuh make peace with them Japs?" Hal asked. "For sometime now I thought."

Yeah, the sneaky little yellow-bellies," Brad agreed. "Maybe it's jest their way—talk peace, act war."

"I bet it steps up volunteers," Shandol declared. "Do you suppose so?"

"Prob'ly," Brad agreed. "Think I'll wait. Maybe they won't need me."

"We gotta make a army camp," Dean put in. They had been working about a month by now.

"They're doin' that single-handed." Fran teased. "Then they will have time to go win the war."

"Well, do yuh want us to win the war first?" Brad mocked. "It's sure a mess to work over there."

"Oh, no." Fran replied quickly. "Just give a few guys a chance to see how it is."

Shandol stared at them because of their banter but said nothing.

Fran saw Shandol's stare and said, "Here we are jokin', but worried and scared to death. Maybe our men will have tuh go tuh war while we wait here. It's terrible is what it is!"

"I know," Betty agreed. "I could just cry for those who are already in this. There were a lot hurt and killed for all that sneak attack."

"If'n the war lasts we'll prob'ly have to go," Dean said, "and I'll worry about my gurl."

"I know of two guys who may've been 'round that area. It really bothers me. One is just a guy I went to school with, but the other is my sister-in-law's brother," Shandol responded.

"The navy, huh?" Dean drawled, knowing who she meant.

They talked more than they listened to the radio. There was too much confusion to hear the radio. It was also quite crowded in the car. Dean and Shandol soon after chose to go back to Dean's car. He turned it facing opposite the other car, yet beside it, hoping they could hear if something did come through.

"The music," Shandol mused, "makes one feel real good. But then they break in with that awful war news and it takes the wind from your sails. The war always seemed so far away before."

"We'll get used to it if war comes," Dean replied.

"Here I thought we'd have to fight Germany!" Shandol exclaimed incredulously. "We're helping England. Now then I wonder if we'll have to get both of 'em. That don't seem fair."

"All's fair in love and war," Dean quoted, smiling at her, as he reached for a cigarette and lit it.

"Oh, it ain't neither," Shandol replied. "If someone asked me fair and square for a date you'd say *ixnay erpay*, now wouldn't you?"

"What tuh beck's that mean?" he asked.

"That's Phil's version of 'pig latin' for nix per—meanin' no."

"Well, it shore wouldn't suit me," he admitted.

The couples went to a small restaurant to eat supper. It always made Shandol nervous but she went as she was expected to do. They each had a bowl of soup and crackers, then a sandwich and soda pop. The men bought cookies and potato chips for snacking later.

Then Shandol and Dean went to a movie as did the others.

Shandol worried about it because it was Sunday night. There was church everywhere it seemed. She kept silent. She was somewhat numb and preoccupied anyway from the day's events. What are we supposed to think? To feel? To know? And do? Where are we so far as this war is concerned? She thought. It was a puzzle to her.

When they returned from the show they sat awhile in the car. The heater kept it warm enough for comfort. Dean kissed Shandol then held her hand to his face. Into the quietness he spoke.

"Shandol, let's us marry," he said softly. "That way war woultn't be so likely to separate us. Will yuh, Shandol?"

"Gosh, Dean," she said, hesitantly, "I—I don't know what tuh say. I—I except I'm not—I'm just not ready to get married yet, I don't think. Yuh just wantin' to get out uh war?"

"H--l, no!" he exploded emphatically. "I love yuh, Verra much, Shandol."

"But I've done none of the things I want to do," she cried. "Absolutely none."

"And what's that?" he wanted to know.

"Be on my own," she said firmly. "Just have a job. I want to see how it'd go and be my own boss—" she eyed him speculatively.

"Oh, that," he said, almost taunting her. "You! Such a baby and want to go out and fight the world single-handed. Yuh'd be lost with no one tuh guide yuh. And get trampled on with no one to see after yuh."

"How do you know so much?" she asked piqued. "Yuh sound about like Dad. Not givin' me credit for havin' a brain in my head."

"Oh, yuh wish tuh sow wild oats?" Dean mocked, then sobered. "I woultn't like that, Shandol. Yuh want tuh marry some day, I betcha. Don't be so final. Think about it nohow."

"Yeah, I'd have to do that," she replied relieved.

"Shandol," Joel called from the porch. "Don't set out there! Come on in here!"

"Dad's so scared for us to set out here with the car heater on," Shandol explained. "He's so afraid we'll get smothered—or die of poison gas, I guess it'd be really."

"Come on in, now," Joel repeated.

"All right, Dad," Shandol called out, after lowering the window and turned to Dean. "I gotta go. Yuh comin' in too?"

"No, I better not," he replied. "'Member to think about what I asked yuh to."

"Are yuh gonna be thinkin' of enlistin'?" she asked. "It may help me think harder."

"Enlist!" he whacked the steering wheel with his gloved hand. "Me? Naw. They'll git me tied up quick enough now. No dependents, no nuthin 'tuh keep me out. I may can stay out awhile helpin' Dad farm. He cain't do much no more."

"What about bein' tied up in matrimony?" Shandol asked. "Or farmin'. Are yuh sure Dean? We must be so sure, yuh know."

"I'm sure," he said. "How could I make yuh understand that any man would be sure they'd want untouched, innocent, lovely you?"

"That's no reason to marry," she parried, "that's just— uh—desire or passion or somethin'."

"See? Yuh don't know what I mean," Dean replied. "I love yuh. I want yuh tuh be with me always. I want us in a home, with uh family. Yuh are my dream girl who belongs there. I'm lucky to uh found yuh so soon."

"I just don't know what tuh say, more than I already have," she told him, honestly. "I just won't say yet. It's so sudden—and now this war prospect and all I dunno."

I never thought I'd say that "so sudden," she thought. It sounds so silly, like I'm quoting somebody in a book. But it's a real truth. And besides he's hurrying me. I don't like that.

"I must go in before Dad comes out here in shirt tail and red longies," Shandol laughed. "A shirt is likely all he'd bother to put on. See yuh later? Bye."

"'Bye," he said, after kissing her lightly. "See yuh ag'in sure. Be sure and write."

After hearing the car motor running and fading out with the distance, Shandol went thoughtfully about preparing for bed. She was so preoccupied that she had to smell her hands for the scent of the soap to recall if she had washed them or not. Her face she washed also now felt hot.

War and a marriage proposal all on the same day, she thought. The world's a mess and I don't know what I want. They say we are practically fighting Germany, yet war's not been declared. Ships get sunk and the goods cost. Those sneaky U-boats how will we ever be rid of them?

But Shandol, having been taught to have complete faith in God and country, did not lie awake in worry over it. Everyone expected victory for our side over there, grueling though it might prove to be. The newspapers hinted of more taxes, rationed food, as before in the war, and there'd be a shortage of gasoline for people, but it would all be managed somehow. It was part of the American heritage to fight if necessary to keep this Republic free.

But she recognized there was a question for everyone: Somewhere, sometime, somehow, in all this, everyone would have to ask himself and wonder, where does it leave me? How or in what way do I fit into it?

The next day Shandol went to Plainesville to shop. She had saved the money given her as an allowance by her father for staying at home. She also made it a trip to look around at the Christmas displays, which most likely would be evident. Also, with some of her money she hoped to get material for a dress and some other articles she needed, especially hose and underthings. These things she bought at the stores on the square. She had gone on the school bus and was finished much too early to return to the school to wait to go home. In fact it wasn't even noontime. So she walked the several blocks east to where Lester and Jane lived. Jane was home and Shandol was glad to get inside. She explained to Jane if she hadn't walked to see her it would have made a long day indeed, and she enjoyed her visit.

Jane had to prepare lunch for Lester as he came in at noon to eat. But he told them he must hurry on back to be at the cheese factory where he worked before the whistle blew.

Then Jane and Shandol talked over old times, looked at photograph books and listened to the small radio Jane had. They also talked about the war, and the sewing Shandol would have to help do. Christmas season came up and they deplored the lack of money. Shandol told Jane Phil had had a spat with his girl friend. Jane's mother had had news by now Jane's brother was missing and presumed dead. Jane didn't explain further and Shandol hadn't the heart to question her how it was all done and if they still hoped.

Shandol told Jane it was nice to spend the day and talk girl talk and she had enjoyed it. But she had to leave in plenty of time to walk back to the high school to catch the school bus back home. It was a long tiring trip over the bus route home, and Shandol was so tired she was glad she wasn't making it everyday.

* * * * *

December was the month war was declared. Finally the nation was

276

at war with Germany too. Aiding the nations was not enough. The merciless Nazi beasts hoped to dominate the world, it seemed. The nation must rise up in wrath, protest and every or any effective help with allies to retaliate.

* * * * *

It snowed the day Shandol and her mother decided to make her dress. She wanted it fitted to her good figure and with long sleeves. It was a Friday morning. Bobby had come in delighted to find a rabbit in his trap back at the edge of the pasture. Near, in fact, to where Shandol liked to go. She hadn't gone for a walk there for some time now. The last time it had been chilly, so she had eaten a couple of persimmons that had fallen from a nearby tree to the ground, and gone on home. The snow today finally turned to rain and the snow left. It was still a gloomy day to sew, but Shandol wanted the dress finished as soon as possible.

Joel lost time on his job due to the rain, snow—bad weather—and break downs. But he had spent what time he could cutting wood.

One day Audrey had to go to the doctor again, and Shandol was sure it was partly an excuse as Christmas was drawing close and it was time to think of shopping if not actually getting it done.

But when they returned she could see no sign of any parcels, so she assumed it hadn't been a shopping trip after all. She wondered about it. She also worried. She didn't care so far as she herself was concerned, but she certainly didn't want Tommy and K.C. disappointed, as they surely would be. Tommy was at the age when he doubted Santa Claus, but went along with it because he could get more, he thought. Also for K.C.'s benefit. K.C. had no doubts concerning Santa Claus.

Friday night before Christmas there was a Christmas program put on by the school. Songs, plays and spoken verses, both of a serious nature by older children and Santa pieces by younger children. It was always worth the effort of braving the cold for the program. Almost the whole town's people turned out for it because they either had children, grandchildren or friend's or relative's children to see participate. Besides it was somewhere to go.

Dean came on Saturday night. He came early but Shandol was ready except for her wraps.

"Get cher coat," Dean said anxiously, almost brusquely, "let's go."

"What's the matter?" Shandol asked. "It's really quite early and I've not ate yet."

"I ain't et neither," Dean said. "But if we're gonna go to the show we don't wanna hafta hurry, so come on."

"All right," Shandol snapped, and went into her parents bedroom for her coat, scarf and small bag, which she had laid out ready.

"I guess we'll go then," she told her mother.

"But you've not eat yet," Audrey objected.

"I ain't neither," Dean interrupted, "we'll git a bite at Folks Consent."

"You're bein' so odd, Shandol told him. "Is something the matter?"

"Yeah," he replied briefly.

Shandol shrugged her shoulders and went on ahead of him, out the dining room door he held open for her; he also held the car door for her. The car's motor purred into life and he guided it from the yard.

"Maybe I shouldn't go," Shandol mused almost as if to herself. "Maybe I'd better not. I think something's wrong. Are yuh mad at me?"

"Naw, I'm sorry," Dean said looking at her nervously—or was it mysteriously? "But I got things on my mind. Got somethin' t'tell yuh. And besides that I notice that pretty new dress. I like that color blue."

"Thanks," she smiled. "Glad yuh noticed. B—but are yuh goin' to the army or somethin'?"

"Nope, not yit," he laughed. "Do yuh want me in uniform so bad?"

"Oh, no," she replied quickly. "It's just the first thing I think about I guess."

But the conversation broke the ice and brought back their more natural company. They talked more easily.

"The school program last night was real good," she told him conversationally. "Wish you coulda seen it."

"I'd uh liked tuh be with yuh," he replied. "Yuh know that. But I gotta work awhile yit at least."

"I suppose so," she replied. "Soon be Christmas," she added.

"Yeah, any plans?" he asked. "Like visitin' 'er lotsa presents?"

"Prob'ly not," Shandol said. "This dress may be my Christmas," she said, and thought, *even if I did buy the material and make most of it.* She had done most of the sewing machine work because Audrey wasn't supposed to pedal the sewing machine.

"Oh, there'll be Christmas for the small boys," she dared say. "They get so excited and expect it."

I may even have to help with it, she thought, *but I just can't let it take my allowance. The little money I have left.*

"There's a stocking given with candy and fruit at the 'Community Christmas Tree' Christmas Eve," she added. "Remember the pie supper—it pays for that. There's gum too and I don't know what all. What about you?"

"My married brothers and sisters always sends us things," Dean replied. "Mom sends things to them too o' course fer all o'us."

"Oh, that's right, we've a box from our Uncle Lafey." Shandol brightened. "It's all put away. The boys all know he sends somethin' so they're wonderin'. He puts a sticker on it 'Don't Open Until Christmas' every time, so Mama won't open it."

"How can yuh wait?" he wondered.

"Yuh don't know Mama," she replied. "She says he'd never send another box if we did. Anyway Mama says it takes the fun away from Christmas morning. So we just puzzle over it."

"Nice night," Dean reflected, after a slight pause. "Yeah, for winter," she replied, "but I just ain't crazy for the winter season."

"Not cold are yuh?" he asked, concern on his face.

"Oh, no," she said returning his look. As he turned back to the driving there was a short silence.

"I'm hungry," Dean remarked finally.

"Well, it could be about that time," she agreed. "Well, we got somethin' else first though," he said, "and I can wait that much longer." And with that he turned the car toward Spoon Hill.

"Why are we stopping here?" she asked pointedly. "I thought yuh were in such a hurry tuh get to th' show."

"M-m-m," was his reply, if that was what it was.

He parked in what seemed to have become their reserved space near a low clump of saplings, with dead brown leaves still clinging and rattling in the faint wind. The early winter night was settling around them, though it was not yet dark.

"Dean, I wanna go home," Shandol wailed. She was closer to tears than she cared to admit.

"Why can't yuh trust me?" he asked kindly. "It tuz so lousy o' me tuh make yuh suspratitious."

"Suspicious?" she amended.

"I regret it often, Shandol," he went on, "but now," brightening, "I only wanna tell yuh I gotta present fer yuh."

"P-present f-for m-me?" she stammered, stunned. "What? Yuh shouldna done it and you know that!"

"This here," and from the brown leather jacket he wore, took a small package. He laid it on her hand which was in her lap.

"But I—I," she stopped. She didn't know what to say. She stared at him, nervous and unsure of herself.

"Well, open it," he finally suggested.

"Oh yeah, I guess I should," she answered. "It's wrapped so pretty. I hate to tear it all away. She tore the Christmas paper and string from it with shaking hands. She saw revealed there a maroon silk lined box with a clear plastic covering, which opened, match-box style. Inside lay a wristwatch, silvery colored, with a black ribbon cord band attached to a small leather band which had a buckle on one side, holes on the other.

"A watch!" she exclaimed. "I said before yuh shouldn't uh given me a present. But this—why, it's out of the question. I can't keep it. It's real pretty though, but—" Her voice trailed off wistfully.

"Why not?" he demanded, undaunted. "It was my money, my idea. I can do as I like about it. I wanted to do it so there yuh are. It's yours."

"But I told yuh I wasn't ready to give an answer yet," she protested, "and if I take it anyway, it's just not right. Takin' presents from a man! I heard Mama say that."

"Shandol, I jest don't understand," he said obviously vexed. "I give it tuh yuh fer a Christmas present. What's wrong with that?"

"But it's a—a—uh engagement present, ain't it?" she asked. "I told yuh I'm not sure."

"Engagement?" Dean sputtered. "It's only for Christmas. "How'd yuh git that idea?"

"I know uh two men here abouts who are gettin' their girls watches instead uh rings this Christmas," she said, matter of factly. "The girls prefer the idea. And we have talked if you'll recall."

"It ain't that," he said. "I jest want yuh tuh have it."

"It's not right either, I'm sure of it," she persisted. "It's nice and you're nice to think of it, but— in fact, I don't think my folks will let me keep it."

"But cha do want it, doncha?" he asked. "No strings attached?"

"Yes, of course I do," she admitted. "Well, why wouldn't I, if that's the way it is?"

"Try it on," he told her. And he slipped off the transparent top of the case, and took the watch from it's cushioned base, put it on Shandol's left wrist and buckled the tiny fastener. Shandol's eyes were alive, her face radiant in the now glowing dusk.

"I don't know," she repeated. "Why didn't yuh give it tuh me at home and I could've asked them?"

"Yuh got tuh make up yer own mine sometimes," he replied. "And yuh want it so that settles it."

"But what if—" she began.

"If yuh wear it yuh'll have tuh keep it," he interrupted. "I couldn't take it back. See?"

"Wait. Turn about's fair play and I can't get you a present to match this. I can't possibly. I'd feet bad about it."

"Don't think about that," he laughed. "If that ain't like yuh. Just enjoy it. Keep it fer me will yuh? It might remind yuh uh me sometimes."

"Yes, it will," she replied, "and thanks so much. I guess I was afraid tuh take it and afraid it'd get away, so I really was in a quandary." And in a burst of gratitude she pulled his face toward her own and kissed him.

As they went into the small cafe for their supper, Shandol was almost too excited to eat. The proprietor's wife, who knew Dean well, noticed her radiance and excited look, when she want to the table to take their order.

"You kids gettin' married?" she asked.

"Oh, no," Shandol smiled. "It's Christmas and I just got a present," and she held up her wrist to show. "What time is it anyway? Oh, there's a clock." And she set the watch by it. And it shone bright and new like her eyes under the electric lights of the brightly lit café.

Shandol chose a sandwich and a hot chocolate drink, while Dean had soup and drank coffee. They each then had a piece of lemon pie and after the transaction at the cash register, they left to go on to the movie.

The next morning Shandol showed her gift. As she had expected was told it was not respectable to accept such gifts from men.

"But he gave it to me, he insisted I keep it and I want it so much as why can't I just keep it?" she reasoned. "Besides I've worn it and he swears he can't take it back."

"Are yuh engaged?" Phil asked the unspoken question. "Nope," she answered, a little embarrassed. "No strings attached to this, I have his word on it."

"Creepers," Phil sighed. "I can see what I'm out of since my girl got mad at me."

"It's nice, I agree," Audrey remarked, rather primly for her Shandol thought. "I still don't think it's good taste to take presents like that. I was taught that. Still, I suppose yuh can wear it as long as yuh go together, now that yuh are anyway."

"It's really not the most expensive," Joel rationalized, "but still seems a lot for just a Christmas gift. Shandol are yuh sure of the motive behind this."

"Yes. Love!" she giggled. "He's already proposed. Pearl Harbor was bombed that day! I said 'no' but he still likes me."

"Then what about him a gift?" Joel asked, soberly.

"Oh, he said not to worry about it. I mentioned it," she told him, more serious now. "He said anything would be okay."

"But is that what he means?" he persisted.

"I suppose so," she replied, "if it's not it'll teach 'im not to say things he don't mean. That's it. I'll get him something. Surely I can do that with my own money—what's left of it. I realize it can't be expensive, and if he doesn't, he's dumber than I think."

"Suit yourself," he said. "But don't get so involved you become his puppet, is to be considered too. That includes answering his proposals as yuh feel, not because you're obligated."

Later Audrey asked her if she had given a "hopeful" answer to the proposal—or any answer at all, for that matter. Would he buy such a gift if she hadn't?

"I don't know," she answered. "I just said I wasn't ready to answer, or be married or anything yet. We just left the matter there. He told me to think about it."

Shandol was surely the happiest girl in town about her gift. She supposed she was happier than the other girls who would—or had—received watches, even those which were finer than hers. Hers was truly a gift, while theirs carried a commitment. They hadn't received theirs until they were deeply involved. Hers was a gift, a true symbol of friendship and adoration. Just a gift. She could hardly believe it after all. So she looked at her now decorated wrist often. And she was so careful of it, because she was proud of it, and so learned to be careful because of it.

It was the day before Christmas Eve before she had a chance to go to town. Dean had said when he left he would see her the next weekend. She wanted to have his gift wrapped and ready by Christmas anyway. Her parents were going to town in the afternoon. She supposed it was undoubtedly to shop, but again she found no evidence.

Her own shopping consisted of only one thing: A gift for Dean. She had to look, ponder and figure. She put her whole mind to it as she scanned display after display counters. She was alone. She had agreed to meet her parents at Mayer's. So it would be her own decision as to what she should choose. She realized she didn't know what he liked or what he already had. She ruled out one by one items of clothing such as gloves, socks, even a muffler or even a necktie. She would have no idea of sizes, colors or what type anyway.

CHAPTER 23

That night at an early supper Audrey announced that she felt well enough to go help fill the "Christmas stockings," which Shandol knew were of a red or green netting. They had to be filled with the candy and fruit to be distributed Christmas Eve. Joel would go along as it would be after dark even as they set out. Audrey thought the walk in the crisp air might do her good; and she would wrap up so as not to get cold. Thus it would be up to Shandol to stay at home with the younger boys as they might not only get bored and sleepy, but would at sometime sure to become pests. At most they would be in the way. Besides it would take from the surprise and unexpected of what the "stockings" would contain, which might ruin it for them.

At first the two boys amused themselves on the floor. They had their own box of junk, as Shandol secretly thought of it. Most of it could hardly be called toys. There were toys of course, much the worse for wear. Cars with wheels missing, guns which perhaps had a flaw or just didn't work. There were bolts and nails, broken tools and an assortment of unidentified pieces of wood and metals; one could hardly guess where they got them. There was even paper, mostly numbers cut from discarded calendar pages, and school papers. Tommy made a clock first, using bobby pins through a hole for the hands. For one "kind" the wavy showed, the other plain. He put small calender numbers in the appropriate places, moistening them with his tongue. In the short time it took them to dry they were loose again. Wanting to learn about clocks and telling time soon bored K.C., so he brought the dominoes. Though he couldn't actually play the game, he liked to place them on end in a neat row and knock them down. This also interested Tommy and they were patient even if they fell before the line was very long. Tommy insisted Shandol help them and even play a game, so she did though making them promise they would go to bed when time—and, yes, she would read a story. She put aside her book with a frown but knew she couldn't read if they were going to keep interrupting her.

At bedtime they reminded her to read to them. She knew it would delay bedtime for them, but she had promised. She chose a Bible story supposing it might make them sleep quicker. Then she saw the floor.

"You hafta pick up your mess," she said, "so get to it right now and I do mean it!" She put all the authority she could muster into her voice. But they did pick up most of it leaving only a few bits of paper.

"There's more," she reminded them.

"We don't want that," Tommy objected.

"Well, pick it up and throw it in the stove," she ordered. But promptly changed her mind. "No, leave it alone. We won't bother the fire in the stove at all."

No wonder they can be so messy and get by with it, she thought, but better safe than sorry. She didn't want them playing in the fire and she didn't want any more fire in the stove than there was. It might cause the flue to burn out, which always scared her nearly witless.

They gathered at the table. Shandol arose, opened the door behind her to the front room, facing a blast of cool air, and brought a somewhat faded and worn book from the desk.

"I found a surprise," she told them. "This book, it looks sorta old but the readin's plain. But no matter how it looks outside, inside is the story of baby Jesus and with pictures. Now that it's Christmas time it's time to think about this part of Christmas—not just gettin' presents and stuff for ourselves. Christmas is really Jesus' birthday, a gift God gave to man to save souls. And God wanted to give this gift because of love, like Santa likes to give toys and gifts to boys and girls. Santa is nice but he isn't God's son and he can't save us from sins or wrongs we do." (Well, so she was saying Joel's ideas in her own way, they wouldn't care.)

Shandol was glad they were listening. That they weren't squabbling about one having his elbows where the other wanted his. And neither seemed to have his feet or head in the way. They seemed to want to listen, even if to delay going upstairs to a cold bedroom.

So Shandol read the story of Jesus' babyhood. How the Angel had first appeared to a good woman named Mary and told her she would have God's son and name him Jesus. And about how they had had to go to another town about that time to be taxed. Because so many others had to go also there was no place to stay. So they were offered a stable, which is where animals are kept, and there the baby was born. How there was a star to guide shepherds and wise men, who brought gifts and worshiped him. And that later they had to leave the country to go to Egypt because of the wicked king.

There were pictures so Shandol held the book so they could see them. When she finished and closed the book she said, "Now, wasn't that a nice story? It's a Bible one too."

"Let's read the pictures some more," K.C. suggested, coming shyly to stand by his sister.

"Well, yuh don't really read pictures," she told him kindly, "but we can look at them ag'in. And yuh can almost tell the story by talkin' about the pictures."

284

"Aw, he just don't wanna go to bed," Tommy declared, which was true, Shandol thought, but she decided to humor him by going over them once at least.

One of the first pictures was of Joseph and Mary on the way to Bethlehem.

"See how her dress looks and Joseph's clothes," she pointed out. "And see the little donkey. It helps to see the pictures, doesn't it? Now this picture—" Shandol was pointing to another picture, but K.C. put his two chubby childish, rather chapped hand's on her's and interrupted her.

"Shandol," he asked seriously, gazing at his sister, "if God is Jesus' Father then who is Joseph?"

"Who's Joseph?" Shandol repeated, "uh—he's, well, for heaven's sake yuh caught me off guard."

But K.C. waited for an answer.

"Let me see what the story says," she muttered. "Let's see. I seem to have forgot too." She turned to the book and read silently and rapidly and then said: "Oh, here. Joseph became Mary's husband of course and took care of them. Great guns, I couldn't remember for a minute, could I?"

"Why isn't God her husband?" Tommy asked off-handedly.

"You boys are really giving me a test aren't yuh?" She smiled at them. "Too bad Dad's not here. But let's us see how anyone can explain this. Well, you see, God's in Heaven and looking after the whole world and that's a big job. So he chose a nice man to take care of his Son and the mother, but with God's help too. But someone had to work so they'd have food, clothes and a place to live. Joseph was a carpenter we are told, and he did take care of them. Tell yuh what, we can see what the Bible says."

So forgetting she should be putting them to bed, went back to the desk for the Bible which was always there. She was sure what she was looking for would be in the first four books, so she turned to the first one in the New Testament, Matthew, and glancing through the genealogy she came to the story of the birth of Christ. Then reading only a short time, found what she wanted.

"Why, it's right here in this first New Testament book. I think I like it as well as the one we read. It tells about the angel that came to Mary, like the other story, but it also says one appeared to Joseph in a dream telling him about these things too. Look, it's time you two got to bed."

Shandol became silent for she was reading and thinking: Mary was a virgin and Joseph knew she should be or have to be to become his wife. So he was suspicious just as any man might be in such a case.

Expecting a baby. Shandol felt embarrassed and unworthy, but she felt compelled to know these things. And then because the answers were given, felt it was forgivable human curiosity after all. Of course people would wonder about such things, and God in his wisdom gave the answers in His inspirational account of the details. It was clear-cut and so far as she was concerned rang true. How thoroughly God anticipates the needs of people, she thought. How could anyone doubt if they had faith? Perhaps they hadn't taken time to wonder about it. She hadn't until now. Why?

She wondered.

"Why?" she repeated aloud.

"Nuthin' now," Tommy replied, supposing she was speaking to one of them. And he and K.C. hung close to her chair.

"You boys can go to bed now," she told them. "I'll take you."

"Where's Mama?" K.C. wailed.

"Yeah, it's so lonesome around here," Tommy added.

"Well, maybe Mama and Daddy are startin' home now or soon will be," she tried to comfort them. "They will be here—maybe any minute now. So get ready while I light a lamp. I'll leave it in the hall until I go on to bed when Mama comes."

The boys went into their parent's bedroom to get their nightshirts, made from white flour sacks, and put them on, as Shandol got the other lamp.

She noticed K.C. was puckered up about ready to cry. His chin was quavering.

"I'll read some more," she promised. "There's a 'let not your heart be troubled chapter.'" They went along the cold hallways. "Woo-o, but it's cold out here. I'd better get a coat if I'm going to read from the stair top." She got a coat hanging on hooks in the hall.

She carried the coat over her arm and the Bible on her arm, and insisted it was bedtime whether Mama was there or not. It was quiet and eerie climbing upward in the darkness with only the lamp to light the area around them. Of course there was nothing to be scared of except the boys' "spooks" and Shandol was not concerned with them. The silence was so absolute, even their footfalls, it was scary and made her jumpy which she hoped didn't show. If the boys supposed her frightened she wondered how she could manage them.

She took them to their bedroom across the hall from her own. Phil was sleeping inside now with Bobby, so the younger boys slept together. K.C. was getting that big a boy now they told him. He had slept on a cot in his parent's room while Phil slept on a balcony over the front porch. He had an old bed spring and pieces of carpet and quilts to make it comfortable. He felt he inherited it from Lester.

However, not many times did the house seem so empty especially to the small boys. It was strange that there was no noise or movement downstairs to give them reassurance.

Shandol set the lamp down at the top of the stairs, just out of the way of others who might come in anytime. She went into the bedroom and saw her shadow leap huge and quick before her, then Tommy's and K.C.'s, as she stepped aside for them to come in. She told them to crawl into the bed under the heavy comforts and she'd cover them.

"Now, I'll sit on the stairway and read." Shandol told them. "That way the light won't bother yuh. First let's say a prayer. Now repeat after me:" (Anything to put them at ease though they were supposed to repeat a prayer:)

"Heavenly Father, thank you for the day,
(They repeated the line after her and each succeeding one.) "Guard me through the night I pray.(Pause)
Bless this family, our work and our play.
And thank you for Jesus, in his name we pray. Amen.

"There now. I'll read and you guys try to sleep."
She shivered even with her coat on, but sat down to read.
If they weren't asleep soon she'd just have to lay down with them. There was faint heat from the lamp, but so little.
They shouldn't be afraid and neither would she.
She began reading the fourteenth chapter of St. John's gospel in a clear voice, but then letting it drift to a softer tone, hoping they might be lulled by it. But before the chapter was even one-half complete Shandol's teeth were almost chattering and her hands felt frozen. The boys were quiet. Anyway it was too cold to sit out in the hall. She closed the book, laid it aside, slipped off her shoes at the side of their bed and crawled between the covers beside K.C. She left the lamp in the hallway, because she aimed to stay only until she was sure the boys were fast asleep. They were warm and soon she too was warm and cozy and they were a comfort, each to the other.

The next thing she knew she sat upright in bed in total darkness now, wondering where she was. Also a sense of urgency. There was something she was supposed to remember. But she had dozed and was trying to become awake and she couldn't remember. Soon she realized she was in bed with her brothers, and fallen asleep as they had. She felt very foolish and got up.

What woke me, she wondered. She was sure there was something she must remember.

It all slowly came back to her. She remembered that she had stayed with the boys. But it was dark—where was the lamp? She got up, carrying her shoes, felt her way to the stairway and down it. Had her parents come home she wondered?

But there's *something* I *must* remember; something she was supposed to do, she just knew it.

She went to the kitchen for a drink of water which was cool. She took a few matches from the dispenser in case she didn't have any upstairs and then remembered what it was she had tried to recall. The lamp in the hall on the stairway landing!

"Sis, that you?" Joel's voice sounded muffled from the bedroom.

"Yeah," she replied, "who took the lamp? I woke up in the strange bed wondering where I was and trying to recall something—which was the lamp. Was it in a safe enough place?"

"It was all right," Joel replied. "We decided not to wake you up. Thought yuh'd sleep all night."

"I really didn't aim to sleep," she called back. "But K.C. wanted me to go up. I thought he was going to cry. I aimed to read but got cold so I just crawled under the covers too. Guess when I was warm I fell asleep."

"Well, go on back to bed now," he replied.

It would be cold in Shandol's bed and it would take her awhile to get warm enough to sleep. She tried to think other thoughts—such as tomorrow was Christmas Eve and Dean was coming.

* * * * *

"Kenneth Casey Sonnett, will you keep that door shut?" Audrey exclaimed impatiently. "And stay in this room! It's cold in there, and besides the warm air will dry out the Christmas tree faster. Please." she added, wiping her brow with the side of her thumb.

K.C. unhurriedly closed the door, which when opened let in a blast of cedar-odored cool air each time. The smell hung over the entire house faintly but surely.

"It's such a pretty tree," K.C. remarked. "Santa comes tonight and we get candy over't the store. Hain't Christmas nice?" he beamed.

"Don't say hain't or I'll tell Santy," snapped Shandol, who had just come in in time to hear the last part. She had been upstairs straightening up the beds. It almost had to be done or the covers would be in such a mess they would do little good.

"Say ain't," Tommy told him, hardly bothering to take his eyes from an old newspaper from which he was clipping words he recognized.

"Hain't our tree nice? Hain't hit?" K.C. chanted, adding the "hit" mischievously.

"Mama, make him shut up," Shandol burst out, "or I'll slap him."

"And I'll tell Santy," Audrey scolded mildly, "on the both of you."

"Ain't it now? Ain't it then?" he sang on.

"Ain't's not right either," she said. "Say isn't or aren't. Anything but that hain't. Where'd yuh hear that? And Tommy, that mess! Don't yuh know bits of paper are about the messiest mess to clean there is?"

Tommy just gave her a cool, questioning stare.

"It's Christmas Eve, Sissy," Audrey reasoned, warmly. "Where's your Christmas spirit?"

"Where's Dad?" Shandol asked.

"He's trying to find a way to go to Plainesville," Audrey replied.

"Oh," she replied. But what if he doesn't find a way what then, she wondered. *No Christmas? Why do we pretend I wonder. Exist and pretend to live. Surely there could have been something for the small boys. Christmas spirit indeed! With no Christmas?*

"Bug dust," she muttered.

"Your Christmas has been nice already," Audrey reminded her. "What's the matter?"

"Aw, she's sassy as a sore-footed cat," Tommy replied.

But Shandol knew she could not reveal why she was so miserable. It was bottled and corked too tightly inside her.

"I guess I'm not used to having the boys being underfoot," she replied lamely, "making noise and messes. Sorry I'm so cross. But gosh, I'm forgettin' to roll up my hair."

She rolled up her hair but the dread and gloom hung like a cloud over her. She worried that her present to Dean wasn't right. How could it be when everything else was so wrong? Well, she would just be glad and relieved when it was all over. It promised to be little different from any other day except the inevitable references to Christmas. That is, until the mail came. Shandol received a letter from Dean. He wrote:

Dec.22, 1941
Folks Consent, Ks.

Dearest Shandol

Well I will try and write you a line. I was thanking today that I told you iwould not see you anymore until next Saturday night. When I was talking to you I had forgot about Christmas being this week. Why didn't you tell me. We will have to go somewhere Christmas Eve night—that will be Wednesday so

I will be over in the eve and we will go somewhere. There will be something doing somewhere we can go. If not we can go to a show at Plainesville. We will have to be together Christmas night, if we was not it might bring bad luck, ho, ho. I can hardly write. Mother has got the radio on as loud as she can but i will scribble this letter to you. What did you do today. I just laid around the house. It has rained all day. I was up to Brad's today. Well I ges you will be surprised to get a letter from me but I was thinking today about where I was going Christmas Eve. I thought I told you I would not be over anymore until Saturday night so i want to go somewhere Christmas Eve night so I will be over after you so be ready when i get there. Well, honey I will close for this time. I have got to git up early in the morning to go to Waiton and also meet the mailman. We may get a package from my sister in Mich. She said she was sending it. I got another present from a boyfriend It was a necktie so he wants me to keep my feet warm, ho, ho. My cold is better. Hope yours is too. Well, I will see you Wed nite and hope it all rite with you. sorry I forget about Christmass eve when I was talking to you but its all the same ain't it. So good night and sweet dreams. Love and kisses.

Dean Leonard

Joel came in at noon announcing he had found no way to go to town. Shandol wondered if that would make any difference. Joel built a fire in the stove in the front room in the early afternoon. The cedar smell permeated the house more than ever. Shandol had already cleaned the room, wearing a coat as she did so because of the chill. This would give her a chance to straighten up the dining room somewhat. It seemed everyone had been there all morning, and Dean would be sure to come in that way.

Added to the scent of the cedar was the baking of a spice and "mock fruitcake," as Audrey called it. It was an addition and a part of Christmas to her. Joel had reminded them from time to time to try to keep her in a happy mood. But at Christmas they didn't have to worry. But Shandol realized she could see Christmas in a sack of flour they might need or the Christmas cactus blooming profusely upstairs; in the glow of pinkness in the cheeks of her healthy children, and in the good health of all of them. Shandol wondered if the evil of happiness would be stripped away into despondency when the hurt disappointment showed on Tommy's and K.C.'s faces? Or Bobby's— even Phil's. The latter wanted a Jew's harp to learn to play. Shandol knew they all expected something. Except herself. She didn't. She couldn't help feeling wretched and miserable and the whole thing just made her irritable. She tried to set her doubts aside, but they were just there. Everyone she seemed expectant about Christmas. Why couldn't she be so trusting? But she was sure, wasn't she, there could be very little Christmas around the place this time.

Bobby popped corn after supper, somewhat in Audrey's way as she cleaned up the dishes. Shandol was getting ready for her date.

Dean came after supper. As he came up on the back porch as usual, Tommy opened the door before he knocked. He spoke to everyone in turn as he went nearer the stove and held out his hands toward the warmth of it.

"Come see our tree," Tommy invited.

"Yeah, I smelt it," Dean replied.

And Tommy led him into the other room to the tree. Dean exclaimed properly over it, but Shandol, in her morbid state of mind wondered if he would think it shabby. It had been done over a period of time. Joel and Phil had brought in the seven-foot cedar. K.C. And Tommy had pasted with flour and water paste paper chains they had colored themselves. There was some twisted crepe paper; they had learned how to do it at school. There were no lights or candles, but a few bulbs that reflected light. It was rather pretty, she decided, in its home-made way.

"Yuh got a present here," K.C. finally remarked. "Have I?" Dean laughed, pleased.

"K.C., yuh shouldn't tell secrets at Christmas," Shandol scolded.

Bobby put his dishpan full of almost perfectly popped corn on the table. Soon everyone had drifted back to the dining room and took a handful. It tasted as good as it looked and smelled.

"Guess we'd better go," Dean said finally. "We'll be goin' to the show, I reckon."

"I'm ready," she replied, "soon's I get my coat."

She also slipped into the front room to get a square, rather flat box, which contained Dean's present. The suspense would be over sooner than she thought. She knew she wouldn't see him anymore until Saturday after tonight; Christmas Day he would be at home because some of his six brothers and sisters were expected to be there. She carried the gift—wrapped box to the car and gave it to him before he got the motor going.

"Here," she said shortly, nervously. "Merry Christmas."

She smiled but the smile did not reach her usually bright warm brown eyes. They were cool, veiled.

Dean glanced at her often as he took off the gay paper. "That's nice," he said warmly, sincerely. "Thanks," as he opened the box and gazed inside.

She wanted to admit it was so little, rather unimportant, but she didn't dare. There was a lump in her throat and her eyes were moist. The words he spoke had meant a lot to her. They seemed wrung from his heart. Her own heart had been so crucified the past days she wondered why she hadn't died.

"Somethin' I cin use," he said and winked. "I do like it."

"I'm glad," she murmured. "It was about the best I could do."

"Good too," he repeated.

Then they were both silent. They hadn't reached the highway yet when Dean realized she was not being herself. She was distant and preoccupied.

"What's the matter?" he asked, "somethin' botherin' yuh?"

"Nuthin'," she replied. How could she tell him or anyone there would be no Christmas for two small boys from "Santy"? Boys you loved even if they could be pests sometimes.

"Would yuh druther stayed home Christmas Eve?" he asked.

"I don't know," she mumbled, "it's the first time I've ever been away."

"Yuh act like it too," he replied grimly, "so droopy and quiet."

"Whatta yuh want me tuh do, giggle over nothin'?" she asked sarcastically.

"Jest smile like yuh mean it," he retorted.

"I suppose the sun never goes down for you," she replied, "or has a cloud over it?"

"Here's some gum, bright un," he teased, tossing an unbroken yellow package into her lap. She opened it, pulling the red paper tape and picked one part way out and offered it back to him, it's fruity fragrance hanging between them, with the faint odor of his cigarette smoke still in the car.

"Yeah, I'll chew," he grinned, and added, gesturing with his hand, as always, "keep the rest."

Shandol also took a stick of gum and put the rest in her purse, throwing the bits of paper out the car window.

"We either have a fuss or good time," Dean teased, "which'll it be? Shall we toss a coin?"

"All right," she smiled, "but let me while you drive."

"Okay, here's a dime," he replied, handing it to her.

"Okay, I'll shake it up like this," and she held the edges of her hands and fingers together bent to make a hollow, "let it flop around there, and then let it rest on my palm. Heads, good time—tails, huh-uh."

"All done, now," Dean said. "Look and see."

"Heads!" she exclaimed, brightening visibly, for the sheer silliness of it.

"Oh, maybe the show'll be a good un, at least we hope," he said, and reached for her hand and squeezed it.

"Let's do have fun," she agreed and smiled. The smile reached her eyes and seemed to erase the gloom on her then pretty face.

* * * * *

At Sonnetts it was gay. There could be no gloom where two exuberant boys waited impatiently for time to pass. There was no doubt it was Christmas time. There was the box of Uncle Lafey's brought out and placed under the tree. It would be opened in the morning, but the two boys looked at it, discussed it, guessed at what it contained for them, especially. Tommy continued to cut and color paper chains to put on the tree, though by now it hardly needed anymore.

And then soon K.C. came running into the room and announced the tree by the post office had lit up. Soon they began hunting their coats to get ready to go over for their stocking of Christmas candy and fruit—usually an orange.

Joel, on impulse, and in the spirit of Christmas burst into the song he had sung since the children were small. The song began: "It's Christmas Eve and Santa Claus is comin' here tonight"—He couldn't recall where or when he had first heard it, but possibly from a school book. But whose? He would never have guessed or known how much good it would have done Shandol had she heard it before she had gone. Joel also tried to read but K.C. and Tommy were so excited he finally gave it up, and asked them to remind him to finish it when they returned.

"Remember to say thank you," Audrey told them.

Christmas candy and an orange, no child should be expected to resist such Christmas tangibles. They were certainly coveted by the two young Sonnett boys. Every child in town was entitled to a "sock" of the goodies. To many it would be all such things they would get.

Tommy and K.C. were ready to return home when they had received their "prize." K.C. exclaimed the minute he was inside. "Open these socks, open these socks!"

"I got one for me," Bobby said, "though I wasn't really in line— just out with some boys. But they called us over and gave me one for Phil and Shandol too." And he held the three forward for all to see. "All because Tommy and K.C. said 'thank you', the lady said, but maybe she just said that. Guess she thought we all deserved one. I just thought it was for *younger* kids is all."

"Well, there's prob'ly plenty for them." Joel explained.

"Just open them and get one or two pieces," Audrey told them. "and save the rest for Christmas. It'll soon be bedtime anyway, and yuh can't be hungry after eatin' all that popcorn. There's even some left."

"Do as yer Mama says," Joel added.

"I see some nuts too," Tommy exclaimed in excitement, but a look from Joel told him he'd have to wait until tomorrow as he'd been told.

They played awhile. They played giving out candy. One was the giver and came by four times pretending there were four people the number of "socks" there was. Then the other was the giver. Audrey quickly put a stop to that, in case they would get it dirty handling it so much. They played Santa Claus then with their old things, They wrapped them in newspapers and took turns being Santa. While one "slept" he was given a surprise to wake up and find, All the time they discussed what "Santy" might bring and the old toys they would still want to keep. They were made to clean up the mess and go to bed at their usual time.

"We're not sleepy." Tommy dared protest.

"Naw," K.C. agreed.

"It's bedtime," Joel repeated firmly. "Now go on and get to bed. He and Audrey went to bed early, even before Bobby, who said he'd go somewhere in case Phil was there, came home. They came in together, and before Shandol did. Everything seemed Christmas-y.

When Shandol came inside after a "warm goodnight kiss" to Dean, as they parted at the porch door, because she really had enjoyed herself after all. But the odor of the Christmas tree brought back doubt and dread.

Her lamp was left on the dining room table turned down low, she noticed, and the flat irons were on the heating stove.

Audrey realized that because Shandol slept alone it must take her longer to get warm. But Shandol first turned up the light a little bit, went to the kitchen to wash her hands and the makeup from her face, using water from the teakettle, which was still warm. Then she got a section of an old newspaper and an old thin towel and carried one of the irons to take to bed to put at her feet to help her warm the bed faster.

Then, carrying the lamp and the iron, which she could fit in her arm at the elbow, she decided to go on upstairs and just forget it was Christmas Eve. But at the foot of the stairs she could not control the curiosity, as she was beside the hall door to the front room near the front door (which was closed because a fire had been built in the front room stove.) She just *had to peep and see if Santa had been there yet!* She supposed her parents would take care of it before going to bed.

There was nothing showing in the pale lamplight. She even looked again closer. Nothing there except Uncle Lafey's box and the few things the children got one another. They drew names, as at school, as there wasn't money enough to buy something *for* everyone *by* everyone. She wondered how the boys would accept it. Would they realize that Christmas is just the spirit of the thing and not just gifts and pomp and show? And that the right spirit is accepting what you have and are. It would be like her father to try to explain it that way. She would never forget once when they had drawn names at school she had had to give a high school age girl a rubber ball! Joel had picked it out for her to give and explained it shouldn't be taken all that seriously. Shandol was never so mortified. She was sure her life was ruined. The idea of giving *that* girl, whose family more or less considered themselves one of the better citizens of the town. And the girl had embarrassed Shandol further by showing her contempt at such a gift at the time. However, in truth she had enjoyed it. She had brought it to school and the whole school had played with it. She even finally grudgingly admitted to Shandol it hadn't been so bad after all. It was certainly a fair-weather favorite. But Shandol never quite forgot that embarrassment she had known, and before her classmates too—how ashamed, hurt and humble she had felt.

It had been hard to accept that and it would be hard to accept this. She and Dean, she recalled, had discussed Christmas in wartimes and especially on a battlefield—perhaps fighting that heathenish dictator. Certainly a soldier might expect a dim Christmas. Perhaps hoping for a letter or box from home, or think of something they might have already received. So many wouldn't even see Christmas as it was, because of Pearl Harbor's bombing.

"They must be brave," she muttered to herself. "And I'm acting a silly child, while their lives are on the line in war! I wish I wasn't so childish but there you are."

In her room she put the warm iron under the heavy cover where she thought her feet might be if she "doubled them up" a bit. She put the clothing she had worn on the foot of the iron bedstead, and put on her cotton outing flannel pajamas; which she and her mother had made. She also put on a pair of heavy men's socks, which helped to keep her feet warm.

She shoved Christmas aside, what else was there? She decided to keep her mind only on sleep and slept as soon as she became cozy and warm in her bed.

Christmas day dawned rainy, damp and gloomy. The Sonnett household became astir when two nightshirt-clad boys slipped noiselessly, they thought, downstairs much earlier than usual, to get a look at what was under the Christmas tree, and in the socks they hung behind the stove.

They exclaimed heartily over what they saw. Joel heard them almost immediately and got up to start the fires in the chilled house. Though he did get up during the night to add a stick or two of wood so the fire would not go out, it had died down and it was too chilly to be comfortable. He scooted the boys back upstairs to stay under bedcovers until the house was warm. They protested and grumbled with an "aw heck," but Joel was adamant.

They made reappearances every few minutes asking if it was warm enough yet. Joel decided it was hopeless and the "fanning doors around" was no worse then letting them stay up, provided they got dressed. There were roaring fires going in the stoves by then anyway and would soon have the rooms warm. Audrey also got up to check on the boys.

"Don't touch things that aren't yours," she admonished. "Get dressed and try to wait until after breakfast to eat candy and nuts." But she was smiling warmly, tolerantly, for she strongly suspected the candy would be a big temptation.

Joel awoke the others when breakfast was ready. It was an unusual task for Christmas and Joel also lighted Shandol's lamp for her.

Shandol aroused, saw it was a rainy day. *What a gray, ugly Christmas*, she thought. Her first impulse was to cover up and go back to sleep or try to at least. But the remembrance of the sting of a strap, when other such impulses had overwhelmed her, she got up. She had learned her father expected to be obeyed. She dressed, except for her shoes, in what was considered everyday clothes, and was in the hall just as Phil came from the opposite doorway. He too was barefoot, and fastening his belt to his lead-colored work pants. Shandol carried the lamp and the iron.

"A merry, west Christmas, Sis," he greeted, sleepily.

"Yeah, same to yuh," she replied, half-heartedly. "Has Bobby gone down yet?"

"Nope," Phil said, "but he's comin' I reckon."

"Here I am," he joined them. "Guess we'll git somethin' fer Christmas in Uncle Lafey's box."

"Yeah," agreed Shandol, "wonder if it's opened yet. And why we must get up so early. I suppose it's those two boys," she answered herself. "I heard them early in a sleepy sort of way. Seemed the middle of the night."

"They must be satisfied," Phil observed wonderingly just before opening the door to the front room, "or they'd be complaining."

The room and warm and smelled of the cedar. The boys sat on the round crochet rag rug with candy, bright red trucks, a harp and toy pistol each. Joel sat on the divan and Audrey sat beside him. The three at the doorway took in the scene not quite comprehending with stupefied looks on their faces. "We're goin' t' read a passage," Joel, who held an open Bible, explained briefly. "The world needs prayer and God now more than ever. We will open Christmas presents after breakfast."

For the first time Shandol really looked around. Everyone seemed in such a good mood. She noticed the "socks" still behind the stove, almost empty now. There were things under the tree which had not been there last night. She met her father's gaze meekly.

Joel read Luke's account of the birth of Christ. He then led in a prayer for peace, world-wide love, and thanksgiving.

"Now breakfast," he proposed, "before it's ruined." Later they returned to the front room and the gifts under the tree. Everyone had eaten because to be sure the boys ate they were told to stay at the table until everyone had finished.

There were presents for everyone. They became interested in one another's things from Santa and Uncle Lafey. There were toys for the small boys and socks from Santa. A jew's harp for Phil and guitar picks, which was what he wanted. A BB gun for Bobby and ammunition. Shandol received a lavender-colored glass powder box. On top of it sat a "colonial girl" whose full billowing skirt formed its lid. There was fragrant powder inside and large puff.

"Why, Mama, it's plum' purty," she exclaimed happily. "And a surprise too I guess."

Uncle Lafey's box held dress material for Audrey and Shandol and new shirts for the men and boys.

For their parents the children together (and with Joel's help) had given Audrey stockings and serving bowls for the table, which she often mentioned she needed. For Joel they had managed a pair of denim overalls. Joel got his wife a diary book every year, as she kept one faithfully.

The exchange gifts among the children were a puzzle, pencil, and gum for Shandol. Phil received two more guitar picks, because, they laughed, he was about to tear up all the combs using the teeth as picks. A comb tooth wasn't so bad and did fairly well in fact, but he couldn't keep up with one. So back to a comb to get another. Lester, Jane and the older boys gave Shandol a sweater.

The two youngest boys' things were similar in value and type. There were new crayons, tablets, card games and Bobby also got a jew's harp.

Shandol could hardly believe it. It was one of the best Christmases they had had in years. How everyone must have worked and saved— except the youngsters, who, no doubt had pestered Audrey and Joel. Shandol looked at Phil and Bobby and realized they too were puzzled. She realized they had had the same doubts she herself had had and tried to add their bit so it all wouldn't seem so bleak.

Joel went to church in the afternoon. He was the only one who had complete proper protection from the wet winter weather. The rest spent the day in wonder and pleasure with one another and their gifts.

But at the supper table Joel deviated from the usual grace at the table to say a prayer of thanksgiving and appeal, "God, our Heavenly Father, we thank thee for these blessings we've shared. Grant that we always accept our blessings with gratitude. Fill our lives with warmth as well as light to shine that thy goodness may be felt as well as thy way lit for others to see. Grant that peace may soon be the order of the world. And as you gaze upon us, thy humble servants, forgive our trespasses into sin. Guide and guard us always, in Jesus' name we pray—amen."

CHAPTER 24

"Christmas 1941"

The peak of wonder and excitement of Christmas was still dwindling when Shandol's ascending anticipation of New Year's eve began. And, even though New Year's day itself would most likely just be another day, time seemed to drag. Still that old monotony of marking time. She did try to help Audrey more, though Audrey often protested that she needed the exercise and maintained she felt fine, and worked around the house in her slow, and for sometime now, rather awkward way. She rested every afternoon, usually taking a nap, and sometimes took walks if the weather permitted.

Shandol looked forward to New Year's eve this year because her plans included something she had never done before. New Year's eve was also her birthday, which was certainly a secondary matter this year. Last year it hadn't been. She had been given a surprise party. There had been one of the largest crowds that ever attended any such party. And almost everyone commented it was the best party the town had ever had, though the activities and refreshments were about the same. One exception to the general rule was some of the girls who didn't always attend the parties (they were so "tame") had slipped away into the dark bedroom to themselves and danced. No one knew *that* until later. Even so, others who had attended still talked about it. But a party was impossible this year. Because of Audrey's condition it was never considered.

This year she and Dean had made plans to be somewhere together to wait the old year out and the new one in. They had talked of it on weekend dates and it was sure since the past weekend. Their plans, though not specific, included another couple—perhaps two. She hoped and looked forward to having as much fun this year as last, but in such a different way.

New Year's eve, as Christmas Eve, was in the middle of the week. New Year's day itself would be wash day, because everyone would be at home to help and would also allow their better clothes to be washed. Shandol did so wish wash days and holidays could be separate. She had even complained she would rather do it alone than have such a dread of holidays and Saturdays. Sundays were not considered proper days, nor was Christmas or July Fourth.

But that was tomorrow, now. Today was New Year's eve, a usual workday, to be sure and Shandol would have a birthday cake to be eaten at suppertime. It would be simple and Audrey insisted on it. It was while Audrey was making the cake that Shandol told her mother she might be late, and she related her plan, including the late movie. "Don't worry now," she said. "It will make us late. Be sure and tell Dad too will yuh?"

Dean came about dusk of the early winter evening. Shandol and the family were still at the supper table.

"Had supper?" Joel asked.

"Yep," Dean replied, "et jest afore I tuck off from home." He took off brown leather gloves, shivering exaggeratedly in a leather jacket. "Chilly out," he commented.

"Have some cake," Tommy invited, unexpectedly. He had been told Dean asked about him and forgave him, and he looked up to him. Audrey got up quickly, without comment to comply.

"Yeah, it's Sis's birthday," Phil remarked grinning.

"Oh, boy," Dean grinned mischievously, and slapped his hands together in a meaningful way.

"I shall retire to my room," Shandol remarked grandly, trying to imitate something she had read from a book. "I will not be—uh—be—*Well!*"

"Intimidated might do if you want a multi-syllable word. It means to threaten or con—a verb, and if I may hazard a guess, transitive."

"Oh, all right," Shandol laughed, knowing what a show off her father could sometimes be. "I don't know nuthin' about it. Yuh're just smarter than your high school graduated daughter, yuh know. Still I may check it out sometime."

"Thank you," he feigned grandness, and showed pleasure at the flattery.

"Here's yer cake Dean," Audrey said, handing him a saucer with a generous piece and a fork.

"I just won't be spanked by him like a—a kid just because it's my birthday," Shandol amended flatly.

"Oh, her poor dignity," Phil consoled.

"Mama, give this child of yours a large can of bread, milk and blackberries to fill his mouth with! Too much corn and mush!" she blazed.

"Hey, remember brotherly love," Dean said. "Don't fight! I don't see no corn and mush. This is good cake," he asked aside to Audrey. "Yuh make it?"

"Oh, yes," she replied, "if rather hurriedly. I want her to make mine in June." And her eyes met Shandol's stunned glare.

If I'm here, she thought. It had just interrupted her thought of how her brothers used large food cans to eat cornbread, blackberries, milk and sugar. The cans held a lot, and more plentiful than bowls. And Shandol hated to wash them, the edges rough after they sat awhile and the remaining food dried.

"This I gotta see," Dean declared.

"We've a name for her cakes." Phil said. "Deader'n a hammer cakes."

"Pipe down, fodder Mike," she hissed. "One bad job and I'm marked for life. If yuh don't like 'em, lump 'em, so there. I've made some good ones too, don't forget."

Shandol arose from the table then, went to the kitchen to wash and without another word went into the bedroom to get her things. She slipped on into the front room to repair her makeup at the chiffonier mirror.

"Ready?" Dean asked, when she reappeared. "We're to meet some kids at Folks Consent."

"Okay, yes, I'm ready," she said. "Be back late now, she called to her parents, waved good-bye and went out the door Dean held for her.

They drove to Folks Consent. Dean had told her the two couples they would meet there. The first part of their discussion they had was to decide upon how to spend the time until time for the "midnight show," as it was called. This was already agreed as to be the thing to do. It would be at Plainesville. It would actually start about eleven thirty, so the theatre should by then be cleared of the earlier movie goers. But before that there was time.

It was spent in just driving around, with a stop at Spoon Hill, though brief. They went to the school yard to talk and listen to Brad's radio. Then they went to Plainesville to eat, because they knew the hour would be too late when the show was over to even think of that, even if there should be a café open. They took time over the food talking and joking. They ordered more to drink—the men coffee, the girls soda pop. Though they sat at tables for four they were close enough for all to take part.

The time finally passed and they were inside the theatre. Shandol was surprised to realize they would not show the main feature until after midnight, because there were the usual, including previews and cartoons first. Then the fun of the midnight party, with "favors": noise makers, confetti, silly hats, and the noise and confusion became chaos, as they tried to sit talking, eating popcorn, and staying in their seats. When it was over, and it lasted, Shandol supposed, at least fifteen minutes, the main feature began. It was a song and dance show Shandol rather liked, though she was sure Joel would disapprove. She wondered if the others were enjoying it. Shandol could recall fragments of the song and decided she probably would for a long time. She wasn't sure she understood what it meant. At least the line "Daddy, let me stay out late', she could, but why should she want to if "tomorrow was my wedding date," yet it was apparently to "kiss the boys good-bye." She decided it was just a song, with catchy words and pretty tune. But the plot, if indeed there had been one, eluded her quickly afterward. Perhaps because the hour was getting late and she was getting sleepy. Even the others were beginning to yawn sleepily.

When it was over she was the first to get home. As they would first pass Greenway, Dean had asked Brad to take Shandol home first. Dean's car was at Folks Consent. They had all piled into Brad's car, Betty Ranemore sitting on Hal Fulbuy's lap. The girls lived near Folks Consent.

"I told Mama I'd be out late," Shandol said once, "but I didn't know how late. They'll prob'ly be worried. I've not been out so late before."

Dean had squeezed her hand. "Yuh're such a kid," he said.

When Shandol got home there was a light.

"They must be up waiting for me," She sighed, deflated.

Dean took her to the door but did not tarry because it was so late, and not wanting to detain the others. A good night kiss and, "see yuh soon" and he bounded off the porch and back to the car.

Shandol opened the door and saw the lamp burning on the large square dining room table, with it's four large round legs, which a tablecloth only partly hid.

How nice of them, she thought, to leave a light for her, but then she noticed Joel fully clothed, though barefoot, standing at the bedroom door.

"I was about to send somebody lookin' for *you* young lady," he said, almost angrily. "It's awful late. Where yuh been?"

"I told Mama I'd be late," Shandol defended reasonably, "didn't she tell yuh?"

"Yeah, and it's the only reason I haven't already done somethin'," he replied. "I been worried, wrecks 'n drunks and things like bein' asphyxiated in a parked car with the motor runnin' goin' through my mind. Go on to bed." And he turned back into the bedroom.

"I was the oldest girl along," Shandol told him, exasperated, before he closed the door. "And the first one home!"

"Well, I'm glad yuh're here," he said kindly. "Let's get some sleep now, Sissy-baby, huh?"

Tears stung her eyes, and she swallowed hard to keep a retort of protest and objection inside. Didn't he trust her? What about those much younger girls? And—

"Sissy-baby!" Is that all I am to him, she thought furiously. Can't he call me by my name to show he realizes I'm no child? And waiting up for me too! Those other girls are still in high school. Sophomores yet! And I bet they're not treated as I am.

She went to the kitchen for her usual washing ritual, got a drink of the cool water, then back to the dining table to get the lamp, which she noticed was her own. She had been bringing it down for sometime now because mostly it was still dark when she got up. She left it in her parent's bedroom and it was handy so she would not have to go upstairs by herself in total darkness, fumbling for it.

She was tired and went to sleep as soon as she was warm. But before she fell asleep she vowed that sometime soon she was going to find out why it was her father who was always worried about her. She wondered why her mother was not concerned. She was somewhat awed by Joel—perhaps still fearful of him. How long would they try to keep her so?

New Year's Day was a cold damp bleak day. A fine rain misted down. It was a terrible wash day, but wash day it was, and a family affair. All had a hand in it except two small boys who could help most by trying to keep from getting underfoot. A fire was made in the front room stove so there would be more room to hang wet laundry to dry.

The men carried the water, Shandol scrubbed on the washboard and Joel and Audrey rinsed. At the latter part Joel and Shandol changed jobs. Joel could still joke about it as he usually did. The truth was Audrey starched about everything except sheets, underwear, some finer fabrics and "dishrags," as they were referred to. It was extra work and the large pieces Joel had to wring out. Joel seemed amused, but tolerant, that Audrey thought it made things last longer and easier to wash, besides looking better. He often went over these reasons for doing it for her.

Phil carried baskets of clean laundry upstairs so they could be hung on lines put up there to use during the winter. There were two rooms available but still the things had to be hung close and thick—sometimes one clothespin held only a corner of a garment. The ironing was dried in the "flower room" upstairs because it was quicker. The room was directly over the dining room and heated from there by a stovepipe hole, which wasn't used. Also some of the ironing was hung on a short line behind the kitchen stove. The rest was put in the other room upstairs and on chairs beside the stove (sometimes the steam visible from them) around the table—all over the place. It was a problem lest something be knocked against the stove accidentally, or soiled from being knocked to the floor or touched with something such as small dirty hands or the fire poker. That they stayed clean was not so much deliberate as a miracle!

The next day was a cold one and by Saturday winter had come in a fury. It snowed all day, piling up to two or three inches. Temperatures dipped low over the weekend, still trying to snow. The boys went skating Sunday afternoon. Shandol bundled up to go with them as it was at the Big Pond, across the railroad from where they had played ball. However, Shandol could only slide around on the ice, sometimes taking a run, which was the way others did who had no skates. She soon realized she was spending more and more time by the fire because her feet got so cold and she soon went home.

And then school finally started again after the holidays.

Even Phil, who had had two weeks. And it was after this before Shandol had a chance to ask her mother why it was her father who worried about her when she was on a date, and not her mother. She asked Audrey in a self-conscious, timid way.

"Oh, but I do," Audrey said, "but mostly I don't have time to do much of it. She smiled, looking away as though remembering. "I'm having to try to calm your father's fears.

He can think up more things that could happen. Sometimes he's sure he's heard a strange car and he's sure it will mean bad news. He's a sight," she added.

"I'm still a child to him I think," Shandol said.

"Could be," Audrey agreed.

Shandol smiled, secretly pleased anyway.

It continued cold into the next week, and another inch of snow fell Wednesday. School was then dismissed for the rest of the week. The temperature dived to a chilly eight below zero, which was an uncommon thing.

But it moderated by the weekend. Phil and Bobby went hunting. It was a trek for nothing, but they reported they saw a lot of rabbit tracks. Lester and Jane came for supper "just to get out," they said.

Shandol had a date. She told them she hated going out every time they came, but they smiled and assured her they understood.

"Maybe we can all go out together sometime." Dean, who came for Shandol, volunteered.

"Really?" Shandol asked.

"I really meant it," he replied.

Shandol went all out to dress against the cold. She wore the maroon wool skirt, a white satin blouse, which she and her mother had made from the remnant, and the inexpensive white sweater her brothers had given her for Christmas. She wore hose, white anklets over them and the low-heeled brown saddle shoes. Her coat, a scarf for her head and ears, gloves and the zipper bag and she was ready.

They went to Plainesville to see a movie, after which they drove to a cafe down Penn Avenue for a sandwich and soft drink. They ate unhurriedly, talked and doddled until it was time to be going home.

They got into Dean's car and he inserted the ignition key as always to turn on the motor. But as he did the end of the key broke off and he held the other portion in his hand to show Shandol, a puzzled frown on his face.

"H--L," he fumed, angrily. "I cain't git the thing started now I've busted the key. Son of a b---h."

"Here," Shandol scolded. "Such language. Can't yuh get it fixed somewhere?"

"I was goin' to say bean climber," he mocked, but became serious again. "At this hour git it fixed?" he asked incredibly, "no chance—maybe in the mornin' around eight o'clock, and a Sunday at that—whatta pickle we're in."

"But that's nearly nine hours," Shandol exclaimed aghast. "And we'll freeze here. No motor going. No heater either," she reminded him.

"And we can't sit in that cafe all night," Dean said, and added, if it wasn't so cold we'd just stay right here and just sleep right here all night."

"Well, I wouldn't," Shandol denied firmly. "I hafta get home, before Dad comes out huntin' for me. Would yuh—um walk to the bus station with me? I can go home by bus."

Dean hesitated looking at her. She wasn't sure what his reaction would be.

"What a baby," he finally said, stonily. "Here we face something we should work out together, but all you can figger is how to git home. Home to papa," he taunted. "Only worried about your old man."

"And my reputation," she replied heatedly. "You wait for it to be fixed tomorrow, but I can't wait here with yuh. Dad would be wild with worry. That's settled as far as I'm concerned."

"I wish yuh'd say yuh'd stay with me," Dean almost pleaded.

"But I can't, I told yuh," she replied. "Guess I'll just hafta go to th' bus station by myself. Maybe," she added, knowingly, "yuh don't believe I have bus fare home—well I have! Good-bye."

And she was about ready to get out of the car when he stopped her.

"Wait," he said. "That's not what's botherin' me; it's stayin' here alone until mornin'."

"Go to sleep," she replied sweetly.

"Where?" he asked, throwing out his hands, "in the bus station?"

"It's an idea," she returned. "Or if yuh weren't so mean and don't

305

mind comin' back up here in the morning, yuh could go home with me—if I should ask yuh. If I carried K.C. from his bed to mine yuh could sleep with Tommy."

"Why don't yuh mean it?" he asked, catching her shoulders.

"All right, I do," she said.

At the bus station Dean asked about the buses south.

There was one that had left only a few minutes before. The next one was early morning. It would be about two-thirty a.m. before they could get to Sonnetts.

"If only we hadn't talked and debated so long," she said.

"It seems silly uh me to go at all," Dean said, "but I don't want to stay here. Oh, I could but it ain't much to go down and back. Besides I gotta see yuh home."

I believe he really wants to go she thought to herself. "Dad's gonna be in a bad mood," Shandol reflected, aloud, "until he understands. I wish I could get there sooner. I'm sorta scared, 'cause he won't sleep a wink. It might help if yuh did come too and show him that broken key."

Dean purchased the two tickets to Greenway. Shandol offered to give him her part but he wouldn't hear of it. They settled down to wait.

"We could go for a walk around the square," Dean said conversationally. "Care to?"

"Huh-uh," she replied. "I'm not even warm yet, let's just look at the books and magazines."

"Oh, well," he agreed.

The time seemed to drag. Shandol looked at her new watch often, and wondered almost as often if it had stopped. Dean remarked about it so she found a magazine she hoped might interest her and began to read. Dean didn't read, just thumbed through them. He would interrupt her reading to say something, show her a picture or ask her the time himself. She would be interested in what she was reading and was sometimes provoked, but felt it wasn't fair to say anything—even had she known how to do it tactfully. When the bus finally came, it did not tarry long. They boarded it without a word and rode silently, except once Shandol said, almost apologetically, "I'm sure sleepy." Then, hid a yawn and added, "I'm almost afraid I'll go to sleep."

She nodded and napped in spite of herself as she became warm, drowsy then numb in the moving bus.

The station at Greenway was dark. They had to walk down the long hill from the highway, which seemed twice as long this strange, cold night. They walked apart, each in a rut left by cars and trucks, in the snow and slush, now frozen, walking as fast as they dared to reach home. At first Dean's long strides almost left her behind. She fell behind. He noticed and slowed his pace.

"I can't run," she said briefly.

When they came in sight of the house Shandol noticed a light. But when they reached the door to the dining room, they discovered it was locked.

"Daddy, open the door," Shandol called, knocking briefly on it. "Daddy!" she called again.

"I ain't asleep," she heard him say.

"But won't yuh open th' door please, it's cold out here."

"It's chilly in there too," she muttered to Dean. "Not only does the fire die down a little, but he must be thinkin' the worst without even hearin' why. It's so unfair! Oh, my poor aching feet."

She went to him for comfort. He put his arms around her.

They kissed briefly, waited silently.

"What's yer excuse?" Joel called, finally.

Shandol could not answer. She refused to yell through a closed door, half frozen. Her whole being seemed frozen inside her. She was almost in tears from the cold, the lateness of the hour, she was tired, her father treating her worse than an animal, were taking a toll.

When only silence greeted Joel's question he wondered if they had gone. At first he supposed stubbornness, but then vague pictures of tragedy rose to his mind. He could just see them in the car motor running until their gas gave out, but they would be—. Or walking until they were exhausted and just fell asleep on the ground wherever they fell. Or would she go home with Dean? It seemed as bad as "Death by Exposure." He went to the door, opened it and the dim light fell on the two standing close together. Shandol sniffed, tearfully.

"Well?" Joel questioned his own action. "Come on in here."

"We had ta come down on th' bus," Dean explained quickly, once they were inside. "We just missed by a few minutes the earlier bus. But we went to a cafe to eat and when we got back to the car and tried to start it, the key broke off when I tried to turn it on. So I coultn't start it," He held part of the broken key in his palm after taking it from his pocket. "We took the first bus out we could. Waited at the bus station it's so cold. Sorry as I can be it's so late."

"M–m—m," Joel seemed relieved. He looked at Shandol.

She took the look to mean, "What do we do with him, now?"

"I asked Dean to come on too. I hated coming by myself. He can't get the car fixed until tomorrow, maybe not till Monday. I'll just put K.C. in bed with me and Dean can sleep with Tommy."

"Well, get it ready then," Joel replied. "It's late and I haven't slept neither."

Shandol washed her hands and got matches, getting her own lamp lit in the kitchen and went upstairs carrying it. She left it on the table beside her bed and then went to the boy's room to get K.C.

"Whatsa matter?" he muttered, sleepily, but she soothed him by saying he could sleep with her the rest of the night. He was too sleepy to protest or ask any further questions.

She went back downstairs, carrying the lamp. Dean was waiting. He had taken off his coat and it was hanging on the back of a chair. He was alone.

"Come on, let me show yuh," she said.

She led the way back upstairs after blowing out the lamp left on the dining table, still turn down rather low. She carried her own small lamp, the base of which was a pint fruit jar. It was strictly her own (bedroom) lamp.

She showed Dean to the door at the top of the stairs.

"First bed in there," she said, pointing. She turned to go into her own room.

It seemed rather strange, she reflected, as she prepared for bed, that she and Dean hadn't parted at the door as usual. She wondered if he thought of it. He's prob'ly too sleepy to think of it, she thought. I'm just foolish, and smiling to herself she blew out the light.

But Dean was staring disquietly at her closed door, until her light went out, then, still in the thoughtful mood he too got into bed.

It was rather late when they got up the next day. They weren't called when breakfast was ready and didn't awaken before. Dean left almost immediately to see about the bus back to Plainesville. He promised Shandol he would be back some time in the late afternoon if he could get the car fixed. If not he'd just have to go home the best way he could—any way, in fact—and wait until Monday, when perhaps Brad would take him back to see to it.

It was milder and thawing that day. The sun shone on the glistening snow, just making it a washed and painted fairyland and then watery slush and mud.

Phil and Bobby went hunting in the afternoon with Buck and came back with four rabbits.

Later, after cleaning the rabbits, or rather watching Buck do it in his quick unusual way, Bobby popped corn. Joel was playing checkers with Harry Bright. Audrey read and Shandol tried to read, but mostly napped.

As Dean came in the late afternoon she was glad she had slept some as she was rested and not so sleepy anymore. Nothing much was said of the night before except that it had taken awhile to find someone who would repair his car, and once it was done he had gone home, slept also, ate an early supper and come on over.

Otherwise the boys proudly mentioned their successful hunting trip, even giving Buck his due, as it had largely been his doing. They noticed the checker game, but the players were so absorbed in it they were hardly aware of what went on about them.

Phil put aside the guitar he had been playing in the front room. Of late a fire was being built in the front room on weekends, because of having people coming in and out.

Phil mentioned his disappointment at the cancellation of the basketball and volleyball games, which were rescheduled for next Wednesday. There were smaller high school teams who competed with schools of similar size. Phil played on a town team because he couldn't play at Plainesville. As he rode the bus he couldn't stay for after school practice unless he stayed with Lester and Jane. Joel thought that was too much for the young couple just starting out. At any rate, he and Bobby looked forward to the basketball games Wednesday night and were quite verbal about it.

But it would be very insignificant in comparison to another event due that night!

CHAPTER 25

Wednesday morning dawned calm, cold, but promising more seasonal weather. Shandol awoke earlier than usual, startled and then a note of urgency welled up inside her. But while she was still struggling to wakefulness, she heard voices downstairs. At first she only thought it strange she could hear them so clearly. Perhaps it was because of the quietness. After all when it was quiet at night she could hear the old fashioned clock downstairs in the dining room strike the hour. The clock that had belonged to Grandpa and Grandma Bregmanson, and sat in on its small shelf, with crocheted and tasseled "curtain" made to drape from the shelf instead. It was almost as old as Audrey herself. The muffled voices rose up to Shandol, and she heard distinctly.

"—just not workin' today," Joel was saying. "I don't see how I can leave yuh like this."

"But we need yuh to put in th' time for the money." Audrey reasoned, "now of all times. Besides it may not be today at all, and it could be the same tomorrow."

"Should I go tell someone then?" he asked. "Mrs. Kasper or someone just to be here."

Shandol waited for the answer, groaned and then held her breath. Mrs. Kasper! That snoopy, gossipy old thing! Oh, no! Someone else. She tried to will by pure mental force her mother to object to it. They had discussed it. Shandol wanted to scramble out of bed and dart downstairs to remind her. But she hesitated. She wasn't even supposed to be listening. Perhaps she shouldn't make it her concern. This was surely be tween her parents and her interference might be resented by Joel. He seemed worried enough. But Mrs. Kasper! She readily admitted she couldn't do a thing, was no help at all in a case like that. Yet every birth she could, she attended. Sometimes she was called, because it was supposed she could help, she went to so many. But in her reporting of a birth, she never gave the positive side—a fine baby, proud mother, or how the birth had gone. These were taken for granted or told by someone else. She hunted the negative and reported that. Such things as ashes under the stove, perhaps other untidiness of the home (which she didn't offer to help remedy)or in one case Shandol recalled, "a dirty mattress cover," and another "the baby had a few long hairs on his body."

Audrey had commented later, "She could have talked all day and not said that—surely."

310

What would she want to say about us, Shandol thought and shuddered. Most people, she was sure, hoped to be ready for the event, even uncomfortable as they surely were, and rest awhile and then busy again. All she would do today, Shandol, thinking continued, would be to go all over town telling what she knew, and still be of no help if something came up. Shandol's heart pounded furiously as she waited for her mother to reply. "No," she heard her mother reply, "not yet. Shandol is here and can go if I need anyone. I know it's no use to tell you not to worry, but I will be all right. I can even keep Bobby here in the afternoon if it's necessary. The neighbors are close. I'm just sure we'll all do fine."

Upstairs Shandol sighed audibly. Mrs. Kasper wasn't even on the list to be called, Shandol knew. Audrey already had her "team" picked out. Didn't Joel know she was one busybody who had no time to be busy *for* anyone, just *about* them. But of course, he was too worried to think.

"It'll be a long day," Joel commented forlornly.

"I know," Audrey replied. "But I wish I could make you see I'll be all right. I"ll be as careful as I can."

"I'll git Shandol up so she can start helping right now, Joel said. "She should know what's going on."

Shandol, nonetheless, gave a startled jerk at her father's call from the bottom of the stairs. Even though she expected it, he could make that "Sis" sound like a roar.

"Yes," she answered promptly, and sat up. She dared not delay a moment.

By the time she dressed, her father, carrying his lunch pail was almost to the store where he caught the ride to work.

Shandol saw her mother sitting in the rocking chair beside the stove. Shandol was surprised to see her looking so well. She had halfway expected to see deep worry lines and a frown on her face, ready to voice self-pity. But she saw no such thing. In fact she looked serene and expectant; Shandol felt less tense also. She hadn't known what to expect, but the otherwise utter naturalness was reassuring,

Shandol's attitude was hesitant and questioning, however, and she could not find words to voice her questions. Audrey sensed her plight.

"I think the time is soon," she said smiling, "goin' by certain signs and feelings."

"Yuh mean today?" Shandol asked, wonderingly. She didn't dare ask what signs or feelings. "Now? Shouldn't Daddy've stayed here?"

"Oh, not right away," Audrey amended, "just soon. Maybe tonight, tomorrow morning or even tomorrow night. Prob'ly sooner than that, though."

"Yuh just tell me what yuh want me tuh do," Shandol replied. "First I guess I'll finish with breakfast."

"It's all done." Audrey said. "It's keeping warm in the warmin' oven. First get Phil up so he can be ready in time tuh catch the school bus. We'll clean house today. There may not be time if we wait till tomorrow."

Shandol met her mother's smile shyly and weakly. It was all new. She couldn't decide whether to be excited or worry. It came to both. Her old familiar fear of the new and unknown was not to be replaced.

Shandol awakened Phil and hurried him to get up and around to catch the bus. The other three also got up and they too ate breakfast. They were told nothing, so unless they had overheard as Shandol had, they would suspect nothing. And the way they acted she was sure they did not.

Phil caught the school bus, combing his hair with a pocket comb. At the door he put the comb in his pocket and went on out putting on a cap as he crossed the porch.

Shandol washed the dishes. She also checked her younger brothers to be sure they were washed and ready for school, before they were on their way.

It was the beginning of a busy day for Shandol because Audrey wanted the house gone over and straightened. She began upstairs, as was her usual procedure. She sprinkled the wide plank floors with water from a small pan she carried up with her. She swept the dust and lint, which it was, mostly, with some crumbles of old plaster, all downstairs. The steps needed sweeping also. She straightened the beds and picked up until it looked as neat as the shabbiness of it allowed. She swept the steps and the hall out the front door, and even swept the small front porch and through wooden steps up to it.

But downstairs the rooms must be dusted, the floors mopped and everything straightened and put away as much as possible.

On Monday of that week the bed from the downstairs bedroom had been moved into the front room. This was necessary because of the stove and being able to heat it. Though there was a chimney in the bedroom it had not been used for years and was considered unsafe. And a warm room would certainly be essential to the birth and care of a newborn infant. The fire had as yet, not been built so Shandol opened the dining room door for warmth long enough to mop the linoleum covered floor, dust and straighten the book and paper on the old desk or poke them in one of the drawers. She did that task grimly as she wasn't sure what was important and what not. Audrey asked Shandol to take off the feather tick and put it in the bedroom in the corner where the bed had been.

"It's just for the time bein'," Audrey assured her.

Room by room Shandol went over the lived-in part of the large house. Upstairs she had swept and straightened up; but downstairs was scrubbed, dusted, tidied and even rearranged if she thought it helped any. She had even swept the walls and corners for cobwebs. She worked hard at it and knew it had to be. Not only would she have less time for such chores later, but the people in the town would come in bunches and one by one to see the new baby. Shandol knew this both from experience, as Mrs. Bright's daughter, and the remindings of Audrey from time to time, who at times offered suggestions, but did little herself.

It was getting on into the afternoon before she had finished. Bobby came home at noon for his lunch, ate bread and milk and a "bean sandwich" and rushed on back to school. Audrey felt there was no need to keep him nearby. The youngest boys took sack lunches. Shandol and her mother also snacked to their satisfaction. There was plenty of milk and bread, and there was butter—even peanut butter—and jam to go with it.

About three o'clock, which was about the earliest she could leave, Shandol went to Mrs. Bennett's to ask her to tell her daughter (Mrs. Bright) Audrey would possibly be sending for her sometime later in the evening or night. She was just to let her daughter know, who would in turn pick up her sister-in-law, who would be the only ones there. Shandol asked her to please let them know if for some reason she couldn't come.

Her daughter stopped by after school so she was sure to get the message. But Shandol was reassured there was hardly a chance of them not being able to make it. There was always Mrs. Colmay.

"How is she?" Mrs. Bennett asked.

"Well, she says she's fine, considerin'," Shandol answered carefully.

"What about the boys?" she wondered.

"They will most likely be in bed," Shandol answered, "or so we suppose and hope."

"If it don't work out just send 'em up here," she smiled. "Jack would enjoy having them. "Jack was her grandson, and he and his mother lived with Mrs. Bennett, and a good friend of Tommy's and K.C.'s.

Shandol hurried back home to be with Audrey. She did not ask Mrs. Bennett not to tell anyone. There was no need. She knew the uselessness of persons who only wanted to satisfy their curiosity.

Mrs. Kasper had stopped by briefly in the evening just before dusk to see how Audrey was feeling. Audrey sat down again in the chair near the stove.

"I feel like I'm doin' just fine," Audrey replied.

I wonder if Mrs. Kasper doesn't have a special sense about such things, Shandol thought.

Still she hadn't learned anything. Fortunately she was in a hurry as she wanted to be home before dark and she had been gone all afternoon and it was nearing time for her to prepare supper. She had also unwittingly given Audrey a loophole.

Mr. Kasper was so poorly," she said, though she'd left him alone all day. "And I ain't too well."

Audrey decided if she needed an excuse that would be as good a one as any not to call her that night, as Audrey by then had told Shandol she was sure it would be.

It had been a busy day to Shandol, but a strange one as well. Though Shandol worried Audrey showed no tension, so she seemed not particularly fearful. But there was the uncertainty, the "ignorance, she realized, and the expectancy was electric.

Joel came in at his usual time, vowing he hoped he never had to put in another such day.

"It was terrible," he confided to Shandol. "Why, I'd even think she might be callin' for me or wishin' she could get in touch with me. Then I wondered if it'd all be over when I got here." He shook his head negatively, "I can't go through another day like it. I'll just have to wait till it's over."

After talking to Audrey privately, he went soon after to the store to tell "uncle" Clive he might have to wake him up to use the phone, so for him not to be frightened or think him a robber. He'd know he meant they would be needing the doctor.

By seven o'clock Joel put a fire in the stove in the front room as Audrey directed. K.C. And Tommy were gleeful. They were sure that meant a party, which was about the only excuse for a fire there during the week.

"I remember now," K.C. observed, "the house is so cleaned up and we're fussed at not to mess up anythin', I bet it's a party tonight." He danced around happily, humming and making a song about a party tonight.

"Who's it for then?" Tommy wanted to know.

"Must be us 'cause we wasn't told not to tell nuthin'," K.C. guessed.

"No, it's not a party," Joel told them. "The room's just bein' warmed up in case it's necessary."

"But why?" K.C. persisted, not wanting to miss anything.

"It's cold," Joel replied briefly.

At eight o'clock, which was their usual bedtime, Shandol was told to take them to bed and go herself to make sure they stayed there. If Dean came Joel was to say Shandol couldn't go and he'd understand.

She had already discussed it with him so he would not think her angry or ill.

Tommy and K.C. protested, feeling sure there was going to be a party and they would miss it. Shandol dressed for bed and got into bed with them until they fell asleep. This was because that if she went to bed it would help convince them there was no party. They at first had not seemed sleepy. Shandol heard their prayers and they told stories. They finally fell asleep.

Phil and Bobby went to the schoolhouse to a basketball game. Before Tommy and K.C. fell asleep they made Shandol promise if there was a party she would awaken them.

"Yuh promised now, 'member," Tommy said.

"Of course I would," she replied. "We'd not have a party for everyone to have a good time and not include you. Yuh can be sure of it."

"Yuh're sure?" K.C. persisted.

"Absolutely," she assured him.

It was their last words before going to sleep, but Shandol did not go to sleep. She did go to her own bedroom as she was sure the boys would sleep all night.

Shandol had heard her father leave shortly after eight o'clock to get Mrs. Bennett. She was expected and her daughter-in-law were waiting. He still had to go call the doctor, he told them. It was shortly past nine o'clock when they got there, however. By then Joel had gone on to the store and "uncle" Clive had called the doctor from Plainesville. He was still surprised. He supposed it would be much later before the doctor would be needed.

Upstairs, Shandol kept quiet and tried to sleep. There were few sounds except muffled, low voices downstairs and the moving about. She knew when the ladies came. There was more waiting, talking, walking from room to room. Shandol wondered what was going on, but really wished she could just go to sleep.

At a muffled groan from downstairs, Shandol covered up her head. Then another and another. She felt her mother must be dying. She had no desire to see her mother die in childbirth as her grandmother Sonnett had years before Shandol's time. She had visions of herself having to take over the care of the family. "Oh, not that," she prayed. Yet she wanted to go to her mother. Tears came to her eyes. She heard Joel say something but she couldn't be sure what. She knew then she couldn't go downstairs. He would just be shocked at her daring and ask her to go on to bed; everything would be taken care of.

Then she heard the baby's cry. She had been told that was a sure thing, a baby cried at birth if alive. And it sounded strong enough for such a new baby and it's first cry.

"What is it?" she heard someone say, she thought. Audrey, it was such a breathless voice and so low she barely heard it. "A girl," a man's voice replied, louder and distinctly which she supposed was the doctor's.

"Thank goodness for that," Shandol muttered to the darkness.

"Nine and one-half pounds," one of the women called.

They were no longer talking in monotones.

"Name," the masculine voice again. "Birth certificate," she heard him say.

That was something else. It seemed to take awhile to get all the details ironed out.

But soon after that things quietened. The doctor left and the ladies soon after. Shandol heard first car then another pull away. Shandol wondered if Mrs. Kasper heard them, or even heard them come for that matter. The baby was quiet; soon the house was quiet. Shandol supposed her parents slept. She heard her brothers come in. She wondered if they had been asked to come in later if there were cars there—or if it just worked out so.

A glad feeling rushed over her. She tried to picture how Mrs. Kasper's face was going to look when she found out. I'm going to be the one to tell her, she vowed to herself.

She too, soon slept.

Shandol awoke the next morning without having to be called. She wanted to see her new sister. Yet, she dreaded the thought of being responsible for so much to get done.

Once downstairs the first thing she did was go to her mother's bed, and beside her near the middle of the bed was a blanket wrapped bundle. Joel had already been up. The fire was going and it was warm—if not all night.

Audrey pulled apart the blanket folds so Shandol could see her new sister.

"No danger in us fighting over our clothes," Shandol laughed."By the time she's eleven years old I'll be nearly thirty. Gee whiz!"

Audrey smiled. Shandol met her mother's eyes. She looks so pretty, Shandol thought. Her eyes are merrily twinkling, and she seems so alive. I thought she would be pale, wan and nearly sick. But she looks so sparkly and her color healthy. Maybe I should say so, she thought.

"Yuh look real good, Mama," Shandol smiled, shyly. "I mean—well—just pretty."

"Why, Shandol, thanks." Audrey replied. "I feel fine and proud as can be."

Shandol told her father how well she thought her mother looked. He agreed, and added to her surprise and discomfort.

316

"She had a fairly easy birth."

But I *heard*, Shandol thought, but said nothing.

Shandol was excited. She left Joel to finish peeling and slicing potatoes for breakfast to go get K.C. and Tommy. They weren't awake and she decided it was too early to get them up. She had to be told what to do—even the things she usually helped do and should have known to do them. And she spent more time than she should, mutely, at the side of her mother's bed.

She was called however to help Joel pack his lunch and also Phil's. Audrey had reminded her, besides helping with breakfast. But she did so want to see K.C.'s and Tommy's faces when they got their first look at the baby.

As soon as breakfast was ready she called Phil and Bobby.

Perhaps because of the early bedtime hour Tommy and K.C. woke up.

"Come see what we have downstairs," she greeted them, "a real surprise!"

"What is it?" Tommy wanted to know.

"No fair tellin'," Shandol replied and hurried on downstairs, knowing they would soon follow. She went to her mother's bedside and waited for them. When they came in and saw Audrey was still in bed they approached shyly.

"Look here," Shandol practically caroled, pulling away the blanket.

"Oh, ho," Tommy said.

"Ain't he nice?" K.C. chirped.

"This is a she," Shandol corrected.

"Karen Ann," Audrey said.

They got dressed and took their nightshirts to the bedroom, as Shandol reminded them. They had to be reminded about these everyday.

Phil and Bobby soon came in also, already dressed. They took a peek at their baby sister and went closer.

"Wake up, pint-size," Phil greeted, touching her cheek. "Not point-size," Audrey remarked happily, "nine and one-half point size."

"Only kiddin', Mama," Phil smiled.

"Don't wake her up yet," Shandol said.

Joel was ready to go to work by then and he came to Audrey for reassurance that it would be all right for him to be gone.

"Of course," Audrey replied, smiling. "Mrs. Bennett said she'd look in again today and I'm sure others will also as word gets around."

"We got another hillbilly," K.C. piped up.

"We sure have," Audrey agreed, her dark eyes sparkly.

K.C. had once heard the remark he was the only true native Ozarker in the family, as he was the only one born since the family had moved there. He had never forgotten apparently. It was a distinction and his only—until now. If only he doesn't get jealous Shandol mused.

"And yuh can be proud not tuh be the only one," Joel told him, "because you are still the only boy hillbilly, and she's a girl. That makes it just fine."

"Yeah, she's a gurl." he repeated.

"Boy's can take care of girls too," Shandol told him, "because they get big and strong. And you too can sometimes help. She'll be glad about you."

"She's purty," Tommy declared. Joel left for work.

"Before I catch that bus," Phil said, "I've got to see Mrs. Kasper's face when she learns what took place last night without her!"

Audrey smiled, knowingly.

Why Phil thought the same as I did, Shandol thought.

"It's so early," Shandol said, "but I'll go tell 'er to come as soon as she can. Be right back."

Shandol went to the hallway to grab a coat and put it on. A scarf in the sleeve fell out. She put it on and started for the door.

"I'm goin' too," came a chorus in unison from Tommy and K.C.

"Not without me either," Phil said. Bobby silently got ready to go outside also.

"Shucks," Shandol sighed. And they all left the house.

At the small house across the street, which was painted a dark yellow, they went to the back door. Mrs. Kasper was visible through the door glass building a fire in the cook stove. She was still in her night clothes, with a brown robe over them, so she had probably aimed to go back to bed, after building up the one in the front room if she hadn't done so, while the rooms warmed. There were three rooms in the house and their bedroom was in the front room where the heating stove was, they knew. Mr. Kasper was old-looking, feeble and crippled by age, and his rheumatism his wife claimed, and probably couldn't get up until the rooms warmed. They didn't go far enough inside to see the bed.

Mrs. Kasper opened the door at Shandol's knock, and her wrinkled face broke into a grin. She was a tall and thin, though stooped somewhat with age. Wisps of gray hair straggled from her white nightcap, which framed her aging face with a high forehead and expressive mouth which always looked over stuffed.

She thinks I've come because Mama needs her, Shandol thought. *I hadn't thought of that.*

"Oh, excuse us for comin' so early," Shandol said, "but you must come over as soon as yuh care to to see what's at our house. A new baby girl!"

The other children filed in one by one. If Mrs. Kasper was embarrassed Shandol couldn't tell, but she went into the other room and put on a coat.

"Now, tell me more," she said, veiling her shrewd gray eyes.

"Well, just come see, after awhile," Shandol told her. "She's nine and one-half pounds and came last night close to eleven o'clock. I'd gone to bed and the boys too. There were some women came and the doctor, I guess you heard *them*? Only Phil and Bobby came in later."

"No, I ditn't," she admitted.

"Well, it was late," Shandol went on, "but you're the first we've told. We'll go now and let yuh get yuhr fires finished and the house warmed up. We'll see yuh, I guess. Come on, boys." And they scrambled hurriedly back home.

"What'd she say?" Audrey asked.

"Not much really," Shandol admitted. " She was just getting up and I think she first thought I'd come for her, the way her face lit up. But the smile left when I told her about our baby girl. I told her to come see her, when she could. But she's disappointed, I betcha."

"Well, she may feel cheated," Phil added, "because she thinks its her job to report such things."

"I reminded her she was the first to be told," Shandol reminded him.

"We mustn't say too much more about it," Audrey told them. "After all it wouldn't be nice of us. She admitted she's no help, so we just didn't get her up, Remember K.C. hears such things and he might embarrass us by mentioning something or asking her about it." But Audrey smiled as she said it.

Phil had to eat and run to catch the school bus. The rest ate more leisurely, including Shandol. She had taken her mother's breakfast in to her on the doughboard, sliding it out of its groove just under the cabinet top. There was nothing else she could think of to use for a tray. She took warm oatmeal, scrambled egg, coffee, butter, bread and blackberry jam Audrey had made herself.

"Do yuh suppose we could find somethin' for a tray?" Shandol asked Audrey. "This breadboard is just too big and heavy so it's bundlesome."

"We might borrow one from Mrs. Bright or someone," Audrey said, "but I thought we might just use a lard can lid. Would it be big enough do yuh suppose?"

"It might be at that," Shandol admitted. "Where's one at?"

"Behind the breadbox behind the kitchen door, Shandol," Audrey replied.

Bobby went on to milk; Tommy put corn out for the few chickens. Later they would get what few table scraps there were. When the boys left for school Shandol began to tidy the house. There wasn't much to do, just straighten the beds upstairs. There wasn't the usual mess since the boys had gone to bed early and it had been taken care of.

Mrs. Kasper came over before Shandol had the dishes done, as she had done the other work first. But she went with Mrs. Kasper to see the baby, drying her hands on the tea towel she had in her hand.

"Right purty baby," Mrs. Kasper said, "not red a-tall."

Shandol was so surprised at this bit of praise she went sheepishly and deflated back to the dishes. She hadn't reasoned out what she had expected. What had she expected? A "why wasn't I called" rebuke? She just seemed pleased it was all over.

Mrs. Bennett came by to see if everything was still going all right. She washed the baby. They weren't sure it was necessary, but decided to do it so the habit would be formed right away. Shandol watched, but decided it would be awhile before she cared to try it. Audrey would likely be doing it first, she thought. The naval was such a delicate spot to cope with even to them.

There were people in and out all day, as they had expected. Word traveled quickly. Even one of Shandol's former schoolmates, who was herself married and expecting a baby any time. She had almost become the town's bad girl—yet not she, but her mother. The girl had married young, divorced and married again; everyone hoped she would settle down. Mrs. Kasper was her maternal grandmother so it was easy to know such things.

Shandol stayed close to Audrey when she was not busy. She knew that way she could better be told what to do. She kept wood in the stoves and got her mother, Bobby, and herself dinner at noon. She'd liked to have held her sister, and did for a few minutes sitting on the side of the bed. But she was so uncomfortable she decided she'd only hold her a little at a time until she got used to it. Besides they didn't want her spoiled, being held all the time.

Audrey told Shandol about the new conveniences of home births. Shandol didn't understand it all, she knew so little about it all in the first place.

"Were yuh asleep?" Audrey asked her.

"No," Shandol replied. "I couldn't go to sleep. I heard her cry."

"Yuh could've come on down," Audrey told her. "Yuh're old enough and there was nothing yuh shouldn't uh seen."

"I thought of it once," she smiled weakly. "But yuh know how Dad is. I didn't know what he'd say. He's funny about me and things like that. I was afraid he'd just say I was in the way."

I was also afraid and didn't want to face it, she admitted to herself. *I wished I wasn't such a goose.*

"He wouldn't a-cared," Audrey said. "I'm fairly sure of it. The doctor brought the things to do with, and the new ways make everything so clean and handy. There were disposable things and moisture-proof pads. Makes it much nicer. Used to have to use thicknesses of papers and old sheets and things. No use in a big bill at a hospital. I even got a little chloroform."

"Dad said everythin' just went fine," Shandol said. "He was sure relieved—at least about going to work. If only she's good. How long do yuh stay in bed Mama?"

"In fourteen days I can set up," she said. "By twenty one days I can be up and around good. It's usually only ten or twelve days, but he's keeping me off my feet longer."

The day went smoothly. Shandol helped her mother and learned to change the diaper to keep the baby comfortable, even helping Audrey get her to her breast at feeding time.

Saturday became the first wash day after Karen came.

Shandol had it all to do, except the boys helped with the water. Joel was on the job. It took her a long time as she knew it would, so she started early. She gave all the baby things an extra rinse, scrubbing, boiling first; and rinsing the rest as usual and hanging it all outside. And with checking on Audrey and the baby, she was quite busy. Bobby and Tommy washed dishes, but were sometimes considerably in her way.

She admitted it all once the wash was all hung out. The new diapers made it a pretty white wash, a delight to see blowing on the clear sunny day against the blue of the sky. Phil had had to add other clotheslines of wire from the corner of the house to two of the poles. It had taken a lot more clothesline to hang the added baby things, when the ones they used were barely adequate for the family wash. It had been a cold job hanging up the wet wash, but it did get done and most of it got completely dry.

While Shandol's hands were busy, her mind had time to wander. Why chloroform, she'd wondered once. Everything about Karen's birth had gone just fine.

After the washing was done there was always a mess to clean up. The floors had to be mopped from tracking around in the spilled water, which seemed unavoidable. And she still had to check Audrey and the baby from time to time. Once when no one was in hearing distance she asked about the chloroform.

"It makes the final stages easier," Audrey explained simply. Shandol imagined the rest and asked nothing more.

321

Dean came that evening just as they were finishing supper. The clean laundry had been brought in by the armload by Shandol. The clothes pin bag was tied around her small waist and the clothes carried inside and just placed on a table in the bedroom, near which still lay the wadded featherbed. The clothes even spilled over onto it. They had not been folded or taken care of in any way. The diapers she'd placed separately in case they were needed. She looked at the large stack and decided if she weren't careful the room would become quite a mess. Still no one needed to see it because the door was kept closed. But she would do more about the clean wash Monday.

It finally occurred to Shandol that Dean hadn't been to see her all week. It seemed so strange, and just as strange that she hadn't missed him! But then she had been quite busy. Yet what about him? What had he done Wednesday night? Surely if Phil had seen him and asked him not to come, at Joel's direction, she would have been told. He would suppose it was important to Shandol. But was it? She had been so preoccupied with what she had to do she had almost forgotten about him. Was that significant? Where was the feeling that had stirred inside her when she had thought of love before? At the thrill of a kiss? Wanting another kiss and his arms around her. *My throat doesn't tighten, or my heart go wild at imagined surrender,* she thought, *at real complete love sometime with him.*

I'm just tired, she decided. *So tired and emotionally exhausted. And I'm vexed at myself. I could have learned something. I could have had a new experience, seeing a baby born. But I chose to stay out. I could have just let Dad think or say what he liked. But I'm still where I started. No wiser, no nuthin'—just tired. So tired. I've done a good-sized day's work today with not much help. There was worry and taking so many steps. Now, what?*

When Shandol went to get her mother's supper tray she was told to go ahead and get ready and go. "But the dishes," she began.

"Don't fret about dishes," Audrey said. "The boys can do them. They haven't worked today like you have. I'll have your dad see to it. Phil can help, since Bobby milked."

"That I'd like to see," she smiled. But if Phil had to, why couldn't he do it? At any rate Shandol was free to go.

She and Dean went to a movie. After the movie they drove back through Folks Consent and saw Brad and Fran, seeing the car first, parked in the parking space beside the street. They stopped for greetings.

"Aren't yuh just awful mad at him?" Fran called to Shandol.

"I guess not," Shandol replied. "Should I be?"

"Oh, just that him and Brad went sparkin' Wednesday night," she replied, her usual smile rather subdued. She's so cute, Shandol thought, her blond hair and pink complexion, thick lashes and blue eyes.

"Fran, be quiet," Dean said in mock dismay.

"I hadn't heard," Shandol admitted, turning to Dean. "I did wonder where he was though."

"Did yuh look for 'em?" Fran asked.

"I expected him to show up, "Shandol admitted, "but I went to bed early. That night I got a new baby sister."

"Did you really?" Fran asked.

"Yes, really," Shandol replied. Was it possible Fran hadn't been aware Audrey was expecting?

Fran got out and came to the car door. "How really marvelous," she said.

Shandol explained why she had had to go to bed early, but not to sleep.

"And I practically had to drag Dean in to see her," she grinned at him.

"Yuh ditn't," he interrupted emphatically.

"Yuh acted strange, I thought," she said. "I thought yuh were just bashful; now I think yuh just had a guilty conscience."

"Can I come see her?" Fran asked shyly.

"But of course," Shandol told her. "I'd love for yuh tuh see 'er. We think she's pretty special. She's big for her age," she laughed, "and K.C. my youngest brother, thinks she was made to order for him."

"Oh, gee, I'd sure like yuhr job," Fran said dreamily.

"It's pretty hard work," Shandol told her. "A lot to do to get all the work, worry, and chasing around done."

"Let's go some place we can talk," Fran said, looking first at Brad and then Dean. They went to the cafe for candy bars, as they asked the guys if they would care for one. Each declined.

"Were yuh there?" Fran asked.

"No, I was upstairs," she replied. "As I said, I took th' boys tuh bed. I once started tuh go down but Dad is so funny about me and such things. So I figured I'd embarrass him or him me if he sent me away, as in the way. Now I'm sorry I didn't. Mama said it'd been all right."

Shandol could only tell her what Audrey had told her about new ways for babies born at home; at the groans she had heard and the chloroform for the last part to go easier. But Shandol knew it wasn't what Fran wanted to hear. She had hoped for an eye witness account of the birth itself.

"Well, I'd just thought yuh'ud been there," Fran was visibly deflated.

They went back to the car, still eating candy. Soon the subject of where the men had been Wednesday night came up.

"They had these girls," Fran said, "and just went to park somewhere. Prob'ly in an out of the way place. Ugh. I'm so mad at Brad!"

So Dean broke our steady agreement, Shandol mused, and aloud said, "I think I can get Dean real sorry."

"How?" Fran asked.

"I can't say yet," Shandol replied evasively, "but I just might can make him sorry. Tell yuh later, huh?"

But it was the next evening before Shandol had a chance to see if she could make Dean regretful. Fran was such a little dope over Brad that she practically wore her heart on her sleeve. She adored him and he knew it. But Shandol had no intention of letting Dean know how she felt. In fact she couldn't. She didn't know herself yet.

He came early. They parked at Spoon Hill. The car was comfortable. Brad and Fran were parked where they could see them. It was nearing time to go eat, before the couples decided what they'd like to do that evening.

"Yuh ain't jealous a-tall," Dean accused her.

"About what?" she asked innocently.

"That other gurl," Dean replied.

"I don't know much about it," she replied carefully. "Yuh haven't told me nuthin'."

"I wuz with 'er ain't that enough?"

"Is that all?" she goaded, "just with 'er? Parkin'? That don't sound so good."

"Mad," he asked superiorily, lighting a cigarette. And the aroma of the cigarette smoke and her chewing gum seemed to mix—a sensation she was sure she would never forget. It was not really unpleasant and seemed a part of themselves and as such she'd always associate it.

"Whatta yuh care now how I feel?" she asked, taunting him. "Yuh see, Dean, we had a goin' steady agreement. Yuh wanted tuh make it first—yuh also broke it first. So I think that'd give me a turn now too, don't you?"

"Oh, no," he said, jealously, "don't give me that now."

It was her turn to be nonchalant. "Well, it's true," she replied.

"Yuh should be jealous," Dean pouted. "Fran is. She's real hurt and heart broken."

"She's just actin' young, showin' it," Shandol said. "Yuh don't really know how I feel, but I'll say one thing, 'what's sauce for the goose is sauce for the gander' or how ever yuh say it."

"Then I might just git tired uh waitin' on yuh to make up yer mind," Dean taunted.

"Is that a threat?"

"Nope, a fack," he replied. "I"m tired waitin'. Why cain't we just go ahead and make plans; some sorta plans anyways?"

"I told yuh I don't think I'm ready yet," she said. "And after this I'm less ready to make up my mind."

"Well, I can," Dean looked at her his heart in his eyes. "You're my sweetheart."

"Yuh didn't act like it the other night," Shandol reminded him. "Out with another girl! Not even comin' t' see about me. That don't sound like gettin' married now does it?"

"Look, I was with Brad," Dean explained. "He picked up a girl and her friend with 'er got in back with me. It was nuthin'. I couldn't even help it. The whole thing's Brad's fault."

"Is that what he'll tell Fran? It was yer fault? I bet yuh'd thought it something if it'd been me in the back seat with someone. So if yuh must go—go. She might even marry yuh."

"I don't even want 'er," Dean said explosively. "Let's go on to town."

Shandol wondered if she had won or lost that round.

Perhaps, as before, they came out about even. She was hurt about it, especially her pride. But it still wouldn't help her make up her mind, so she could only wait. Of course, she was needed at home right now. There was no getting around that. But still she felt she should plan.

Here I am, she'd muse, as she often did, *a young person. My life is ahead of me, I expect. And I don't know if I should rush to meet it or wait until I'm sure. Positively sure. Life seems pushy—time is pushy. It makes me want to resist, is that it? Even Dean? He seems to want to push me too, into something, I'm not sure it's what I want. I want to blame someone—my folks or anyone expecting or needing something of me. Why must I feel so? I want to be something. But I just don't know enough about myself and what goes on in the whole thing. But nobody, nobody understands. Life must be a lonesome job just by itself.*

She took the disappointment in Dean, for it was that more than jealously, to bed with her, and mulled over it until she fell asleep.

Day by day the parade of visitors continued. There seemed hardly time to keep the house tidy and Shandol worked hard at it. There were some repeat visitors, of course, who came with friends, neighbors or relatives, to show off Greenway's newest citizen. They seemed as proud to show her off as the family was to have it done. She was a pretty baby. She had dark hair, a round baby face, clear and fair, with a perfect rosebud mouth. Her family were all so proud of her.

And it made a busy time for Shandol. Some things she hoped to get done just didn't get done. There wasn't time. Audrey repeatedly told her not to fret about it. She was to do what she could in a day of the necessary things, and that was all anyone could expect. Audrey reminded her sometimes the two of them sometimes fell behind, as when sewing or cleaning, so she couldn't expect to do more by herself.

Lester and Jane came on Friday. Jane, at first, because she hadn't been around babies much, was rather awed by her size and looks. She expected her to be red, wrinkled and smaller (as everyone). But she soon took up with the tiny one as everyone else had, and held her a few minutes.

Uncle Lafey sent a package and card. The package contained a new warm blanket, a dress, a gown and two pair of stockings.

Joel was kept busy on his job. He felt gratified he could get to work his allotted time. When that was done, he could help Shandol wash or whatever he needed to do. The two oldest boys went to the timber to cut wood. The "cold snap" and heating the extra room took more fuel, and more wood was hauled. Once the boys took a gunny sack and picked up bits of coal along the railroad tracks; but they decided it was as hard work as cutting wood. Besides, they still had to split wood.

Fran took Shandol's invitation to visit the baby as sincere, and sure enough came to see Shandol's sister, even before Audrey had even started to sit up in bed. Karen was ten days old by then. Shandol was proud of her work that day.

The clean white diapers seemed to fill the side yard, blowing in the wind, fresh and crisp; the sun making them a bright contrast against the blue of the sky. The floors were cleaned as always after the washing was finished. The things were tidy on the tables. Bobby and Tommy were mostly responsible for the birds, though usually were asked or reminded of them. The dining table was pushed against the wall. It was as though company was expected, as Shandol did expect Dean. Shandol was thankful she had gone ahead and done what she could.

Fran exclaimed over the baby. "Oh, she'll be pretty, like her sister," she smiled. She held her a bit but she couldn't get Karen to awaken so she didn't hold her long. By now Karen was so used to being held she could sleep or be awake when held. Shandol told Fran that now Karen's eyes were a big dark blue, but would most likely change, as had the rest of them.

"If only she could keep them that color it'd be so pretty. But we're all brown-eyed, so she prob'ly will be too."

"I'd sure love to take care of a little baby," Fran said, looking at Karen wistfully.

Shandol said nothing. She was sure Fran meant Brad's and her own baby. But Shandol knew he used the excuse she was too young to get married, though Fran insisted she knew what she wanted. Brad just didn't seem ready to take the responsibility of a family, Dean told her once, when she had remarked once they seemed so fond of each other she wondered why they didn't get married. But now the war. Would that make any difference, she wondered.

Shandol told Fran that the neighbors, especially Mrs. Bennett and Mrs. Bright had been good to come in and give the baby a daily bath. She also proudly told how she and her mother had done it when she was only five days old. Shandol said she was only worried about the "band" around the baby's stomach, but Audrey had just changed it, washed and powdered her back and put a clean band back on.

K.C. helped and Shandol was amused at his earnestness. He could hand her items of clothing, powder and so on. Once, as he handed her the large safety pins for the diaper, he told Shandol in a serious voice: "I think I know 'bout as much 'bout this as you do."

"Yuh might at that," she smiled. Then aside winked at her mother. Perhaps she hadn't heard but she would tell her later.

* * * * *

After Karen came, Shandol and Dean were with Fran and Brad more. It seemed the baby had given them something in common to talk about. Fran was in school and Shandol wasn't, so they hadn't that to discuss. The baby gave Fran an excuse to come more often. Sometimes Brad came with Dean before going after Fran. She was usually disappointed at those times, for Fran always made over the baby and held her if she could; that meant if they weren't in too big a hurry, the baby was sleeping or someone else had her, which was not unusual.

By the end of the month Karen had become quite cross and it was a puzzle to them.

"I believe it's a hungry cry," Audrey finally told Joel. "If I could hazard a guess, she may not be getting enough to eat, or the right kind from me. She'll have to be seen about."

Joel made a trip to see the doctor, repeating Audrey's remarks that her hunger wasn't satisfied. Joel was given a formula for bottle feeding, with further instructions to use either canned milk or *from a herd of cows!* (he emphasied). They chose the canned milk. Fran would hold Karen to give her the bottle when possible. Audrey was up and about by this time.

It was Dean who asked Shandol if she had heard the latest joke on Brad. Dean smiled broadly, his eyes nearly closed.

"I can't say that I have," she replied, "but it must be a good one. You're getting a kick out of it."

"They're sayin' at th' store I bring Brad along when I come see yuh so's he can take keer of the baby while we park."

Shandol was so dumbfounded she couldn't speak. But then the ridiculousness of it finally dawned on her.

"Yuh're jokin', o'course?" she replied.

"They're th' ones jokin' at th' store. Somebody jealous prob'ly started it. But I'm just talkin'—not teasin' yuh."

"How does Brad feel about that teasin'?" she asked.

"Well, he don't keer much fer it, o' course, but ain't nuthin' he kin do, so he jest laughs it off."

Shandol worried about what Fran would think. If it makes her angry and hurt, she too would be. But it seemed she didn't care and she just laughed with him.

"Maybe he could use some practice," she goaded.

Shandol hoped Brad liked children for Fran's sake. It just seemed so right that someday they'd get married. Perhaps even when school was out, if she had her say. But with the war and everyone saying times were so uncertain, it might be better to wait.

"It'd be easier to send a boyfriend to war than a husband," Audrey would reiterate. "It's just not the same," she'd add, "no matter how it seems."

It would be hard to convince Fran of any such saying.

CHAPTER 26

March came in as the proverbial lion, if it could be measured by the snowstorm. By the time it had stopped snowing there was snow everywhere, frosting a fantasy land of the whiteness, looking tempting enough to eat. Trees, fences, the bushes and brush all were covered with weighty mounds of the wet whiteness. Shandol was fascinated by the very beauty of it, as it lay unscarred. She thought of postcard pictures and wished she could paint it so she could keep the way things looked so "prettied-up." Yet she realized in reality it would be an inconvenience and a real mess-maker inside, as some would invariably be tracked into the house.

"But no groundhog didn't see no shadow last month," Bobby, who had to get out in it, complained. "I hoped that meant it'd mean fairly nice weather from then on."

"It's still winter," Joel reasoned. "And the groundhog sign may mean less severe weather, but not just sudden spring. That may not be this month, really."

"Yeah, I guess." Bobby agreed.

In fact it had snowed that February day also. The ground became white, but then the snow disappeared by evening. But it had stayed a gloomy day.

But groundhog day had not been the only event which had marked February's passing. It was the first Sunday of February that Audrey had prepared Sunday dinner since the baby's birth. She had seemed to welcome the task. So many days of virtual inactivity were beginning to become boring. Though she did have the main responsibility of the baby after the first two weeks. Until then the neighbors had come to bath the baby most days. On a few days Audrey helped Shandol do it, and everyday she had a bath and clean clothing. But now Audrey was feeling stronger and restless; and could think of so many other things she'd like to be doing.

So it was with an air of triumph she made a good meal, to the satisfaction of everyone. She was visibly pleased and adored the praise she received from her grateful family. Everyone was pleased and happy she was feeling stronger, and was not only up and about but would be doing most of the cooking once again. This, perhaps, Shandol appreciated most of all. Audrey would add subtle touches of variety with so little to do with, as Shandol had not learned to do. In fact, Shandol did not want her to become overly tired her first day, so she volunteered to clean up afterward. She supposed, in the back of her mind, Joel would have suggested it if she hadn't.

But February had not passed so uneventfully. The baby was good and the routine settled, though sometimes broken. Occasionally the baby cried at night, which was usually diagnosed as colic. Shandol held her when necessary now, as it seemed Audrey preferred to be doing other things. And Shandol loved to hold her when she was awake though she would hand her over to Audrey if she could do nothing to appease her when she cried.

All in all she was held a lot, awake or asleep, as there always seemed to be someone to want to hold and rock her awhile. So perhaps she slept good at night from so much attention.

In early February a siege of colds gripped the family. It seemed everyone in turn had it. Even Karen's nose stopped up and made her cry in frustration because she could not breathe through her nose as she nursed. So a small amount of petroleum jelly was rubbed around her nostrils, which seemed to help, at least temporarily. Shandol had it but still had to do the family wash; she seemed none the worse for having done it. She actually had it the easiest of all, though they all could keep going—except Phil.

It seemed at first he was going to escape even a mild cold, but ended up having it the worst of all. When it began he felt bad enough he decided not to go to school, perhaps rest *would* help Audrey reasoned with him. But the next morning he felt no better and went back to bed. After a couple of days Joel decided Phil had the flu and a fever and it was much too cold for him to stay upstairs. Joel and Audrey still had the bed in the front room because the baby must be kept warm. There was no alternative but to crowd a bed into the dining room. And with a heating stove, the large dining table and chairs, the bench behind the heating stove, the rocker beside it and the bird cages at the porch window, the tea table, which was under the medicine cabinet (both of which Grandpa Bregmanson had made and still lacked paint or varnish), a small cabinet, safe in the corner by the kitchen door, there was only the wall where the three doors were. One door went into the bedroom, one the entrance to the front room and the middle one to the hall. It was obvious the front could not be closed handily, so it was the other two. Of course the hall could be entered from the front room near the front door, as could the cold bedroom. The room was large and it was crowded but it could not be helped. Phil was a very sick boy. But Shandol, who had to clean and keep things as orderly as possible, wondered how she would be able to stand it. But by then neighbors and friends were coming in to help, because someone sat up with him at night—all night.

His illness caused turmoil. Audrey was cautioned to be careful for herself and the baby. Shandol decided it was the smell of the fever which reminded her of when they had the measles.

Clyde Horn was one who came to see if there was anything he could do. He was Clavin's and Freda's father, a short man, plump, with a full face, small nose and wore glasses. He could see in only one eye. He considered himself the unofficial town nurse and had even given vaccinations. He had used the pus from small-pox vaccination sores to "inoculate" other children in town. It had worked in most cases. The children developed identical sores and so were considered immunized.

Shandol's had not "taken," but ones she had later did not either, as it turned out.

Joel decided it was time the doctor was contacted so he asked Clyde to take him to Plainesville.

"He ain't got pneumony yet," Clyde declared. "He ain't got no red spots in his cheeks." He was talking to anyone listening but turned to Shandol.

Shandol looked concerned at her brother, looking so ill and helpless; his vitality sapped and he was pale and sometimes restless. She saw no red spots either, but doubted if she would have recognized them even if they had been there. She was very worried about him. It seemed he had been sick a long time.

Surely Dad won't let Clyde tell him how to handle it, she thought. Why, Clyde can barely read and write.

Joel went to Plainesville. Apparently the doctor assured Joel he had been doing all right by Phil. However, he did add some pills. Someone continued to sit up with him, put the mustard plasters on his chest and then one day the crisis was over. It left Phil weak and he had to take care, but his progress was steady and soon he sat up. He progressed more as he regained his appetite. Then in due time he was ready to be back in school.

Karen was kept separated as much as possible, though the family was in and out of the dining room as it was actually the dining room also. Phil then was the only one who had the flu, the rest having only colds. As soon as Phil was ready to go back to school, the bed was moved back upstairs. Shandol was glad, though she would miss K.C. sleeping with her, as Bobby had slept with Tommy.

Actually it seemed amazing to them later. There had been the wash to do, ironing, the baby to care for and Joel lost only two days of work, for which he was grateful because of the extra doctor expense.

Shandol and Dean missed no dates. They went to the movies or church as weather permitted on the day suggested. Lester and Jane had come two weekends; then one weekend they and Phil had gone to the show with Shandol and Dean. Phil liked to go with them especially Saturday nights as he, and Dean, liked the cowboy movies and Gene Autry.

The first outing for the baby came when she was a day less than a month old. Audrey and Shandol took her to the club meeting at Lavenson's. They lived in a sprawling, spacious, well kept home, off of any main road and surrounded on two sides by a large peach orchard. In summer the lawn was a work of art, but winter had now taken its toll.

There were none of Shandol's friends there. She wished there were; she was mostly tending the baby. Margery had been to see Karen and she too had talked to Shandol. After all, her mother was expecting in early spring. However, with her family she rarely took time for club, nor did Freda's mother. The rest weren't interested even if their mothers were.

After the middle of the month Joel lost more time on the job because of cold, wet weather. Some days they went but were rained out after a couple of hours. Some days they simply could not go. But other chores continued. Joel prepared boxes of soil and got them ready to sow garden seeds, which would be plants ready to plant when gardening time came. They had saved most of their own seed. Shandol had seen Audrey let large red tomatoes ripen to nearly mushy ripeness and then get the seeds by cutting open the tomato and taking the seedy centers, tie them securely in a cloth, squeeze out excess juice and any pulp which would go through. When dry it would hardly seem more than a stained rag, the dots of the seeds visible. They were then put away in a metal box with corn, varieties of beans, peas, cucumbers and others. Very seldom were the seeds destroyed by insects for it had a peppery smell. The hot peppers were put in whole, as well as sweet peppers for seed (lest they be confused).

There was a basketball tournament in Plainesville for the smaller schools of the county. Bobby played on Greenway's team, and when Greenway won first place he was declared the hero. Quiet Robert Joseph Sonnett was amazed himself. He was not a tall boy—about average for the freshmen and sophomore teams which played. But he said he just seemed to be in the right place at the right time, so it was luck, quickness and having a knack to play well.

This was hardly over and the excitement dying down when one evening as Bobby met the highway bus for the newspapers he carried, much to his surprise Grandpa Bergmanson got off it.

"Howdy, howdy," Grandpa said to him, at first wondering why

anyone was there to meet him as he had told no one he was coming. "How is ever'body?" he asked, smoothing his mustache.

He was a small man, bent with age, with gray hair, barely visible under the "bill-cap" he wore, rather than the hat he usually wore in warm weather. His gray eyes squinted at Bobby from a face of surprisingly few wrinkles, though not youthful. He was wearing a dark wool suit, with a blue cotton shirt.

"Hi, Grandpa," Bobby replied, "far as I know we're all doin' alright. I'm surprised t' see yuh. I come to get my papers. I got a paper route. Want me tuh help yuh get to our house before I go on my route?"

"Oh, no, never mind," he replied. "I know th' way—went over it enough times. Yuh, go ahead with your work, boy."

He picked up his suitcase and what was obviously a violin case and began the walk to the home of his daughter, Audrey. She was always glad to see him and now he had been gone awhile. So was the whole family glad to see him. They all made over him, taking his things upstairs, asking questions of how he had been and the people back in the county where they had once lived.

Grandpa fitted into the family life easily. However, K.C. was again to sleep with Shandol. She did not like the idea. She wished he were a girl. It would only be while the bed was in the front room. When the weather became warm it would be moved back to the bedroom and K.C. could sleep on the cot in their room, as Tommy had when Lester was at home. Shandol preferred her room to herself, though she missed him. She hated to admit she slept with him.

To Shandol the coming of March meant the time to take the teacher's examinations came closer. They were during the first week in March, in fact. Mrs. Bright had planted the seed of such an idea into her parents' minds. In fact she had voluntarily brought a thick paperback "course of study" which would help her, she was told, if Shandol would study it.

Shandol had struggled through places Mrs. Bright thought might be helpful for her. But it was hard to settle down to study just to cram, she wasn't sure for what. She had no idea what to expect and was as usual, miserable and a nervous wreck. She found it hard to find what she wanted to study, so she studied history and government and decided to take chances on the rest. They tried to encourage her by saying if she could get a school to teach, she could borrow money to go to college for the few hours credits—in case she found the examination too hard for her the first time. Grammar and mathematics didn't bother her unless she was nervous and got careless. She hated even trying it, she was so miserably unsure of herself. Joel and Audrey persuaded her.

Then Karen took sick with a high fever and all attention was given her. The encouragement and help Shandol so needed and sought almost ceased. She was on her own. She went to the county school superintendent's office; Mrs. Bright took her. There were three other women there. The examination started soon after Shandol got there. The other women were experienced teachers, who needed to renew their certificates to teach. Shandol was the only novice. It soon became evident that it was not any harder for her than for them. She was surprised, as she had supposed they would be able to breeze right through it, even with the questions on psychology, Shandol was sure would be a problem for herself. She had no idea of her grade but was worried. Some small relief she wasn't the only one worried. One of the women was from Greenway, much older than Shandol, but did not teach there in Greenway. There were two days of the examinations. The days went much the same, except different courses. The second day she felt more alone. There was no one waiting for her to finish. Her parents had decided to take Karen to the doctor.

When they arrived home Karen seemed no better, even after taking her to the doctor. Mrs. Colmay came over to see how she was and what the doctor said. She said she had come to pray for her if she was no better. Audrey quickly vetoed that idea, Audrey had been gone from home all day, the baby was cranky and she still had lots to do, including getting supper if Shandol could keep Karen quiet. Audrey was quite overwrought and really needed a few minutes away from Karen, though the baby was obviously in pain. She explained to Mrs. Colmay as kindly as she could the doctor had just seen her and he had assured them it was no more serious than an upset stomach.

But Mabel was not to be satisfied until she could see Karen for herself, to see how she acted. She considered children her specialty as she had six of her own, all quite young. She always seemed to care for someone else's more than her own. They had so little to do with for their children anyway. And Mr. Colmay was in poor health he always claimed.

She also insisted she had been called to preach, and to do good elsewhere. She seemed always trying to make a better go of things. She would try to find a congregation who could have her preach a night or two. She went to auction sales, though no one understood why, as she never seemed to buy anything. Her cow and pig she had purchased privately.

So it was that she wanted to see Karen and seemed she would not budge from her determination to see if she could help. She had been gone the night Karen came after all. Audrey finally brought Karen to her. She examined the baby as though she knew what she was doing. After the examination and quite by accident she noticed Karen's naval had broken and running as a boil might.

"Here's the trouble," she exclaimed, in her weak creaky voice, her anemic sallow face beaming triumphantly. She was a tall thin woman. Her brown graying hair was pulled back severely from a high wide forehead and twisted into a bun at the nape of her neck. The unbecoming hairdo made her face seem long, with undistinguished features except huge dark eyes. She looked old to have such a young family.

There was no chance now of getting a way of going back to the doctor at that time of day. Mrs. Colmay insisted there was no need now. She knew the perfect remedy.

"The only thing to do now," she told Audrey, "is scorch small folded pieces of cloths and apply as warm as possible without burning the child's skin. Find me a piece of any kind of old cloth and I'll show yuh."

Audrey brought her a portion of an old sheet. Mrs. Colmay tore from it a square perhaps a foot or so square and folded it twice to a three inch or so square. She put the cloth against the hot stove— moving her fingers often because they became too hot.

"A hot iron is better," she said, "at least easier to use."

She applied the scorched cloth, cooled somewhat, but still quite warm to Karen's naval.

"Nothing else is needed," she reiterated, "just scorch the cloths brown as I've showed yuh and put 'em in place under the band as I've showed yuh."

Karen seemed more comfortable almost immediately. Audrey of course wondered how it had happened, but Mrs. Colmay would not hazard a guess as to that. Soon after she considered her mission completed, she left.

Audrey puzzled over the cause each time she applied the cloths. She had put an iron on the stove soon because it was so much handier and easier, and she thought, perhaps cleaner, since there could be dust of ashes about the stove. Audrey had been so sure Karen had been kept clean. They had tried so hard to be careful when she was held. And there was a band over it. But there were so many who came and handled her, or perhaps it had no outside cause at all. Audrey marveled that she hadn't noticed. But she was sure she had noticed nothing irregular in the area. At any rate once the boil had drained healing was quick and Karen became a better baby.

* * * * *

Grandpa sometimes decided to be of help, so he and Bobby raked the vegetation on the garden and corn patch into piles and burned them. Though he got tired easily and Audrey had told Bobby not to let him feel he must overdo. But he watched the fires and gave orders and he seemed quite satisfied with his part in it. It had gone smoothly and well.

"What could be keeping your father?" Audrey asked no one in particular when Joel hadn't come in past the usual time. "We'll wait supper awhile," she said, to the children who were all ready to eat. "It could be a flat tire or some car trouble, surely it won't be much longer." She liked the family meals together.

By seven o'clock she was becoming worried, and still had had no word. She didn't voice her fears and dread, for there was no need to upset the whole family. She would let the car trouble be the excuse, but she worried if there could have been an accident. It gave her pause and concern. She finally decided there was no use waiting supper any longer. And in due time they all went to bed. There seemed no point in keeping everyone up and waiting any longer. Surely there would be word as quickly as possible. They might have to wait until tomorrow for repairs, but they would surely send word somehow, she hoped. And soon.

Audrey herself went on to bed as well, but did not sleep. She would doze but jerk awake at least little sound, even the wood settling in the stove, which she usually couldn't hear.

She expected his return at any time or someone to come to tell them why they were so late. Perhaps there would be a phone call made to the store.

Shandol, in semi-wakefulness, as she had slept rather fitfully also, heard Audrey let Joel in and exclaim : "Oh, Joel, it's two-thirty in the morning, where've yuh been? What happened?"

"We been fightin' a fire," he told her wearily. "The woods got on fire and they called all us workers nearby to help fight it. It was all out of control and pretty bad. But we finally got it under control and it's out now. Made quite a long day, but no work tomorrow. We all get to rest."

"Well, I'd hope so," Audrey agreed, "and, yes, now I can smell the wood smoke in your clothes. Whew. But I'm so glad you're here." And she embraced him fondly. "I couldn't imagine what was keepin' yuh, and no word so imagined all sorts of things. I was so worried about an accident of some kind."

"Wonder if I could get somethin' to eat?" he asked, "to do until breakfast. Only had a sandwich. All the money I had. We all put money together and got "dog" and bread at a store. Some didn't have any money. I could help a dime's worth. Ever'body got a sandwich though."

"If I'd only known. I'd had somethin' hot," Audrey said, regretfully. "Shall I heat somethin' anyway?"

"No, just a bit of anythin' now," Joel replied. "I'm tired now. I'll eat tomorrow—I mean later today!"

How strange that he should have to fight a woods fire, Shandol thought, sleepily. The woods were burned off almost regularly. Perhaps something else was threatened, she reasoned but with her father home, all was well; she soon slept peacefully.

* * * * *

CHAPTER 27

Shandol made personal calls on directors of two local country schools, where she had sent applications. The country schools would be the only type she could qualify to teach in one summer's study in college. The teacher-training class at Plainesville high school would make it hard to get a school anywhere around there. Each school usually got several applications, she learned. The two schools to which Shandol had sent applications hadn't received so many.

Mrs. Bright had volunteered to take her to see the directors or as many as they could see. She had also taken her to Plainesville earlier to see about her grades. At that time the county superintendent had had praise and encouragement for Shandol, although he did kindly inform her she would have to take a subject or two over. But, it seemed, that wasn't so unusual. At Mrs. Bright's question he had even offered to vouch for her if she needed to use his name. Would she, she wondered.

It was a frenzied, apprehensive day. It was a cool day, but still signs of spring were beginning to show. It was also a very trying day for Shandol. It was hard for her to talk to the strange men, who were responsible for the education of the children of their districts. It terrified her sometimes. She felt inadequate. Her own father was on the Greenway school board, yet she was in awe of these others. Perhaps that was why. Her father did not take his job lightly.

Later that same Saturday night she had a date with Dean. She told him about her experiences of what she had been doing. She mentioned she had one more school board member to see for the one school, which would be only a little out of their way to Plainesville to the show, to see him.

"I know I don't stand much chance," she told him. "I get so nervous and frightened I can't say much. And then there's all those teacher-training kids outta high school to make more competition."

"Sometimes yuh kin say too much," he replied. "Only thing yuh look so much like a kid yourself," he chuckled, teasingly.

But he volunteered to stop at the school director's place. In fact he knew of the man and where he lived, which saved time.

"I don't know about that," she replied in answer to his remark. "But be serious. The first impressions are important. I don't think I care much, because I know it wouldn't do me much good if I did. I don't even know if I've got sense enough to teach."

"That's the one thin' in your favor," Dean returned. "Don't worry about a thing."

They had to leave the highway and go a short distance on a gravel road. Then they turned down a lane. At the end of it was a small, new, but rather rustic looking house. Shandol realized as she was shown inside they had just returned from somewhere, and must have been gone for sometime, as the fire in the front room was out and the house cold. She had to wait while he shook down the ashes and got the fire going. Over the din she had tried to explain to his wife her reason for being there, but she had to speak so loudly, she felt it was rude, and she just stood patiently without a word. She smiled at each in turn and was so embarrassed she wanted to run away before she even talked to the man.

The fire in the stove was soon roaring warm and soon could be felt. He started a fire in the kitchen in the cook stove before he got back to her.

Shandol told Dean about it when she got back to the car and they were on their way again.

"The man said, for one thing, he didn't care to hire a young woman who might get married before the school term was out. He must have noticed I was with you," she began. "Yet actually he was really most encouraging. I met and I talked to his wife, who was nice and seemed to like me. I saw his four kids and they seemed nice and of course I can be quite myself with children—I've been around 'em all my life. They showed me their grades and they were all good. Must be smart. But he thought I looked awfully young for my age, too, and said some of the upper grade boys were as big or bigger!"

"Director's kids," Dean snickered. "Woultn't yuh know?"

"So was I, yuh know," she flared. "Don't talk silly."

Later she sent two other applications, but never even heard from them. She assumed they had hired—or rehired their teachers. In fact she learned as time went on she had not been hired as a teacher anywhere. At best her qualms were quieted. It meant she couldn't go to school either. But she wouldn't have been taking the subjects she would have preferred anyway. She'd prefer business college. It also quieted her fears of inadequacy, which she knew she was going to have to deal with and try to overcome. She was ashamed of the relief she felt.

* * * * *

Gardening was started. The garden was plowed and potatoes planted. A chilly wind blew that day. In fact it had been a cold March and those concerned wondered if the peaches would make it. They had to hire a man to plow the garden and he took his customers according to their turn, which was as he had them jotted down. It was potato planting time then.

A few days later a few onion sets were put out. Phil had been told to do that. How he did hate gardening! He quit as early as he dared. His excuse was he wanted to go to Plainesville that night and the school bus was going to take a load. This was not so unusual, so long as there were enough people going to pay for the trip.

By the end of the month Karen was cooing and laughing, and had begun to notice the people and things around her. Audrey made her cute print dresses of remnants. She also bought muslin and stamped blocks for an embroidered crib quilt. It was a Sun-bonnet Sue design. A girl with bonnet and long flowing skirt doing things such as work, play and going to town and church. There were twelve to do and it was to be Shandol's job—the embroidering. It would be the second one she had made. Sometime ago she made one for Uncle Lafey's daughter. Audrey told Shandol she should easily make a block a day. Shandol thought that a lot. It would be done in two weeks. More than that, actually, because of wash days and other allowances for the unexpected. Audrey wanted it done as quickly as possible.

"I want the quilt made," she said firmly.

Audrey had purchased a used baby bed for a dollar and a half from a lady in town. It was an old one, wicker in design, but quite sturdy and large enough to do Karen for a few years. It wasn't as yet in use. It was in the bedroom, but Karen slept with Joel and Audrey. There were some things needed for it before it was used.

Shandol began the embroidery of the blocks the next day—April Fool's day, to be exact, and finished the block. One a day as her mother predicted might not be too much to expect. Once Shandol asked Audrey why she didn't help with them.

"Yuh know yuh do prettier work than I do," Audrey answered. "I always liked to crochet, so never got as good as you are. You do real neat work, Shandol. Wished we'd had it already done, but wasn't sure there'd be a girl. Wouldn't be suitable for a boy as yuh can see."

And so it was April and spring was supposed to have already arrived. March bowed out, not so much lamb-like or lion-like as froze out. It froze ice even early in April. But still the signs of spring seemed to know their own schedules, and April took up where March left off in bringing in the newness, beauty and wonder of nature in the spring. Jonquils were early and pretty even when sometimes there was snow around them, which happened but not this year. The redbud, the dogwoods and the swelling leaf buds on the trees bursting forth with bits of green and tiny leaves. So no matter the weather the first of April, except for the fruit trees, which bloomed earlier usually, were not destroyed, nature took care of its own. While Shandol enjoyed this wonder, often marveled at it, actually it was too chilly to be outside and enjoy it.

Dean came April Fool's day, as he had called it, and Shandol had always heard the first of April called that also. Just before Dean had arrived in town she had been working on the embroidery as she lacked only some green stems and lazy-daisy stitch leaves of the small flowers which helped add color to the crib quilt block. She was surprised how quickly the work went as she had other things to do. She helped in the yard as well as with the baby and housework. Yet she now laced these few stitches.

She was sitting on the bench behind the heating stove, with a shoe box of tangled embroidery floss placed next to her. (No matter how hard she tried, there just would be some tangled thread in her box.) It was quiet in the room. Grandpa held Karen, as he sat in the rocking chair nearby. The birds hopped around in their cages, from post to post and to the floor of the paper-lined cage bottoms. The splat of their tiny feet on the paper was the loudest noise they made. Birdseed hulls and a few tiny feathers were always being fanned outside the cages; and no doubt there were a few under the low tables holding the larger cages, homemade of wood frame and hardware cloth. These with the occasional creak of the chair as Grandpa played with Karen were the only noise, except when Grandpa talked to Karen.

"Just a swell'un," he chucked, "yeah, yeah," and he'd click his yellowed teeth together. Then he would repeat, "Yessir, I'd bet stacks uh dimes on 'er, yessir, yessir," at intervals. Karen gazed at him wide-eyed, then he would rock her again. So long as she was quiet he didn't mind holding her, and talking sweet baby nothings to her.

Shandol was just putting away her embroidery, biting off the thread. When she had finished and taking off the hoop for the next block, she put the needle in a cloth, which had others of different colored thread, and dropped her thimble into the box and slid it under the bench.

It was the night Dean usually came so she decided she would get ready in case he did come, which she had already done. She wasn't sure but what he'd "April Fool" her and not come; she thought of it, but no second thought.

Suddenly, in the relative quietness, burst forth a loud report as though a gun had been discharged. Phil came from the front room, quietly, where he must have been studying, or perhaps he had just come in the front door. But he was grinning as he came into the room.

"Serenade again," he said.

Shandol was still on the bench behind the stove and looked out the window. The loud report came again.

"He's swingin' the block," Phil told her. "He'll be back in a minute again."

"Oh, him again?" she asked in mock surprise.

"Yeah, yer boyfriend," Phil replied, shaking his head. "Crazy young buck," Grandpa grumbled, "feelin' his oats. Sap runs high in spring."

"Grandpa!" Shandol exclaimed. "Don't say that. But, oh, I wish he'd stop that backfirin' that car. First last week, then Monday, and now again. The other two times he had stopped, but gone on. On Monday he told her he would see her on Wednesday to talk to her.

"Th' neighbors are a-gonna get tired of that," Phil said. "Can't yuh git 'em to stop it?"

The next time around, however, he drove closer and on in the yard and stopped. He got out of the car and came to the door. Shandol begun to wonder if he would ever stop.

Shandol opened the door. Phil sat in a chair near the table.

"If yuh don't quit makin' all that noise around here, yuh're gonna get arrested," Shandol accosted him, flatly.

"Who by?" he wanted to know. She supposed he wondered if they would do it.

"Just wait and see," she replied. "The neighbors don't like it and they're gonna start complainin'. I'm just warnin' yuh."

"Are yuh ready tuh go?" he asked, choosing to ignore the "warning" completely, wanting only the attention.

"Go where?" she asked.

"Oh, anyplace," he replied.

Shandol got her coat and was ready to leave. Audrey came in then with Karen's bottle so he didn't need to hunt to tell her.

"We're leaving," she said. "See yuh."

Dean would give no satisfactory explanation for his conduct, and refused to dwell upon it. But Shandol knew, she thought, he was getting back at her. Of course. She remembered that night very well. How long ago had it been? Only a week. Or longer? She should remember. Anyway she could recall it was the week before the extension club met at Mrs. Bennett's and Margery's mother had been given a baby shower. Margery hadn't gone and Shandol was so disappointed because she had wanted to talk to her about Dean, and what had happened, though Margery had probably heard one version of it by now anyway.

Dean had come for her on that Wednesday night as usual, and there had certainly been no reason to believe it would be different from any other date they had had.

As they rode down the highway Shandol spoke first.

"I suppose yuh are still comin' to dinner Sunday?" she asked.

"Figgar on it," he replied, lighting the familiar smelling cigarette, and looking at her with a twinkle in his eye.

The truth was she was supposed to prepare it. She felt she had been backed into a corner and had no choice but to ask him. It came about as Fran made the announcement, the Sunday before, that she was inviting Brad over for Sunday dinner which she would prepare for him herself at her house. "Have yuh figured out what yuh're havin'?" Shandol asked, expecting her to say fried chicken and something fancy.

"Sure," Fran replied lightly. "Macaroni and cheese."

"Oh," Shandol replied.

"She's never asked me," Dean reminded them. "So I don't even know if she can cook."

"I don't care to very well," Shandol admitted. "But you can just come anytime yuh like—just let me know first."

"How about Sunday then?" he asked.

"Why not?" she replied, and wished she hadn't almost immediately. "I'm sure Mama won't care, someone'll have to fix the meal anyway."

Dean seemed pleased. He clapped his hands together, rubbed them together briefly and said, "Oh, boy." But it was not to be. Shandol had worried about it, and asked her mother to promise if she hit any snags in what she would prepare to please help her out. She supposed she could have chicken and noodles and perhaps Lester and Jane could be there also, and she would not be so nervous. At least she could get Jane to talk to her in the kitchen. But even as she planned, she worried. What if it all came out a flop? What if she had to have blackberry pie instead of cake with icing? Could she even make icing? Perhaps she and her mother could see to that before hand. Shandol hadn't asked Fran what else she would have. Shandol didn't have to worry about vegetables. They had those canned.

But Dean came later that Wednesday night. His dad and mother had used the car to go to town that day and had made a stop somewhere else and talked too long, he explained.

She and Dean stopped at Folks Consent.

"Let's not go to any show," Dean turned to her. "It's late anyway. Let's just get somethin' tuh eat, and go somewhere and talk. Let's get somethin' tuh eat here. Yuh wanna go in with me or wait out cheer? We'll take the sandwiches we git and eat 'em out on the hill.

"Okay," she said, "but I'll just wait out here."

"Aw, come on in with me," he coaxed, and stood waiting.

She got out lest he make a scene and went inside the cafe with him. Dean ordered while she stood by.

There were a few people on high stools at a long counter eating. There was a couple with a young child of eight or ten at a table beyond. Across from the tables were toys, notions, souvenirs and other trinkets. Dean gave Shandol a nickel for the jukebox at the front of the cafe, she picked a song she liked and it blared out instantly.

With the sack of sandwiches, a small sack of potato chips each and bottled soft drinks, as was usual Coke for Dean, and orange flavor for Shandol, they left.

At Spoon Hill they parked in a wooded, more secluded area. It was dark and the peeper frogs were vocalizing from the pond nearer the roadside.

At first they talked of inconsequential things and enjoyed the food. Shandol decided it might be pretty here in the spring when wild flowers could be seen; wondered if other couples were there yet. They talked of the war and how he would feel about going.

As they finished the sandwiches but were still munching potato chips, and drank from their respective bottles, Dean became more serious.

"Let's get married next month," he exclaimed, as though the idea had only suddenly occurred to him, and pleased him. "I been thinkin'," he went on, "it's crop time almost and I could make my own. We'd live in the other house, across the creek from Mom and Dad."

Shandol's hand went to her throat as she swallowed what seemed to be a lump there. "But Dean—" she began.

"Lissen," he interrupted, "I'm tard of excuses. Either we marry or quit goin' together. I'm tard waitin' for yuh tuh make up yuhr min'. Wait? I wanna quit waitin!"

"But why next month?" she asked, suspiciously. "Are yuh scared uh bein' drafted?"

"Not yet," he replied. "It ain't thet. The house— we'd have tuh fix it up. We got hay and feed in it now. But it ain't bad, even has a upstairs. I got a box uh dishes. Mom's made all her seven kids quilts—each good uns."

"Why, Dean!" Shandol exclaimed, more animated, aroused from her thoughtful mood. "I didn't realize men kept hope chests too? A good idea, though, I'm sure."

"Course 'tis," he agreed. "I got th' dishes at a sale. They're good uns—whole set, only one cup has the handle broken off. Not too

344

many gurls got money for sech things. They're lucky tuh have a few sheets, pillowcases or even tea towels. And just don't have money tuh buy ever'thin' at onct."

"Well," she smiled. "Live and learn—'as yuh go down a pathway that has no return,' that's words to an old song Mama sings sometimes."

"Whatta yuh say?" He took her hand. "I won't wait 'til I'm ready tuh go tuh war and then marry, without no time for a honeymoon— at home o'course. It'd be silly."

"But what's the hurry then? I'd like to talk to Mama," she evaded.

"I said I won't wait," he replied firmly. "I want yer promise tuh night."

"Well, so be it," she sighed, "because I won't be rushed into somethin' so important."

"I haven't rushed," he denied.

"Well, I never really talked tuh Mama seriously about it, which she'd also discuss with Dad."

"And why?" he mocked. Then answered for himself. "Because yuh jest wanna keep puttin' me off—stringin' me along. Now, yuh gotta make up yer own mind without Mama."

"Th' answer is no then," she said stonily, "because I'm just not sure enough yet."

"That's th' answer?" he asked, a hint of surprise in his voice. "It's final?"

"Yes. Now, can we just go?"

"Glad to," he replied, starting the car and in jerky movements got it going. "I kin take yuh home and have some fun."

"Oh, yuh'd be the kind tuh marry and 'have yer fun' too, for all I'd know," she came back at him.

And they didn't talk on the way back to Shandol's home. "Yuh kin alloys change yuhr min'," he told her, as she was about to get out of the car.

"So can you," she replied evenly.

"Let me know if yuh do," he told her.

"Have yer fun," she flared.

"Walk yuh tuh th' door?" he asked.

"Nope," she replied. "No need. I can find the way. If this is the end just like that, let's just let it go at that."

As she prepared for bed she thought of how she would miss him though. And then how to explain his not coming anymore. She supposed the truth was as good as any. She had just refused his ultimatum to marry or quit going together.

The next day Shandol tried to go on as though nothing had happened, though she was somewhat preoccupied. It was a busy time so no one noticed, at first anyway. Joel had to work on the road five hours to get in his allowable time. Phil was out of school because of a track meet the last two days of the week. So there had been some corn and beans planted; also strawberry plants set out.

Margery's new brother came on Thursday, it was learned before the day was over. There were now four boys and four girls in the family. Shandol hoped soon she could see Margery and compare notes on baby care and doings. Margery would be busy for awhile certainly, as she had other younger children to care for also.

Shandol tried not to brood over the fact she would not have a date Saturday night. She told her mother Dean's ultimatum and that she had decided to stop going with him when she wasn't sure yet what she really wanted to do.

"If yuhr in doubt, it's best to wait," Audrey assured her.

"Maybe I shoulda made up my mind sooner," she conceded, "but it was a way tuh go and I enjoyed myself most times. But I believe I'm better off this way."

"Yuhr really not sure though either way, are yuh?" Audrey asked.

"No, I don't really know what I want," she replied. "And I just don't feel I know him that well. I know some people don't like him, for whatever reasons, I don't know."

"Don't be in a hurry," Audrey cautioned her. "This war will likely make a lot of marriages that never shoulda been. Not tuh mention broken hearts when a husband doesn't come home. And some won't."

"But wars also take a lotta men," Shandol pointed out, "taking husband material and some, as you said, may hafta be replaced."

Audrey gazed at her daughter thoughtfully for having such calculating thoughts.

"I don't mean to sound so—uh—deliberate," she answered, "but gosh, Mama, you know? Anyway maybe I won't want to be around here always. And there's not much choice here. Besides these guys seem so like kin I can hardly think of falling in love with one of 'um."

"I hope yuh don't marry until after the war," Audrey told her. "It's easier to say good-bye to a sweetheart than a husband."

"That again," she cried. "How can it be? It would be so different. Married people would have shared deeper feelings and have more memories, maybe a child. But a dead sweetheart—there's nothing except blasted and lost hopes."

Audrey smiled warmly, knowingly. Shandol, not understanding the look, looked away. She thought Audrey was just amused at her for worrying about getting married. Yet, her mother had said she expected Shandol to get married sometime. She didn't understand.

"Shandol," Audrey began, seeing her disappointment and

questioning look. "I wish I could tell yuh how things are. Things that I can see and know by experience from this side of marriage. But I can't. And even if I could you wouldn't really understand. And so I feel I just leave yuh gropin', I suppose, because I can't transplant what I know into yer mind. It just won't fit! And everybody's experiences may be different. Yet it seems such a waste that ever'one has to start from nothin' every time. Sometimes not even given the insight to profit by mistakes others have made. It's unfair. It's so—so—" she faltered, helplessly, gesturing outwardly with her hands.

"Mother, please," she pleaded. Rarely did Shandol call Audrey "Mother." Only at some deep feeling as now, or with some special request she hoped the pleasant sound would influence her decision. She wished she called her that all the time, but Mama she had heard all her life and had said since she could speak, so now it seemed an affection and only embarrassed herself. The outburst from her mother had been expected, yet Shandol and her mother had had what Shandol thought were serious talks.

"Just don't worry 'bout Dean," Audrey said. "Let 'im stew. Your Dad and I get tired of some of his highhanded ways and sometimes he seems so thoughtless, he's—he's uncouth. Besides he's plenty young for 'husband material' as yuh call it."

"I'll still miss him comin' and us goin' places, Shandol replied. "I reckon he was just gettin' tuh be a habit."

But she didn't stay at home her first Saturday night without a date with Dean.

She had just settled down in the front room—on the old fashioned sofa, with wood arms and black leather—like upholstery, to read when she heard footsteps on the front porch. Her first impulse had been to escape, but then she heard Phil's voice. Then she heard Cal, and realized Freda was with him also. She felt rooted to the spot, though she sat up. An unwelcoming hostility arose inside her. But it showed only in the temporary evil in her bright eyes, and gone at a few bats of her eyelids.

"Oh, hello," she said, hospitably.

"Not like yuh tuh be here on a Saturday night," Cal said significantly, yet good-humoredly.

"He knows," Phil said. "I told 'em." Shandol did not mind. After all it wouldn't be a secret long anyway.

"We thought we could all go up to our place," Freda said, "and hear the radio, play games. Wanna come too?"

Shandol was sure they had come for her deliberately, and she gazed at first one then the other. There was nothing she could think of she wanted to do less.

347

"Come on," Phil coaxed, "I can bring yuh home anytime yuh say." He winked at Cal. "Betcha old Dean ain't stayin' home."

"I'll see what Mama says," Shandol said. She put the book back on the desk and went in search of her mother. She was just goin' out the back screen door.

"Mama, wait," she called. "Phil is with Cal and Freda here and want to go to Horn's," she told her, "so I reckon I'll go. It's a good thing Freda's along or I wouldn't."

"As you like," Audrey replied, "though yuh don't seem very enthused. Don't be late, though."

"Oh, no, I don't expect tuh be," she replied. "Phil said he'd bring me home anytime I want. He's goin' too, by th' way."

Shandol called to Phil she'd be a minute. She went upstairs to comb her hair, change her dress and applied lipstick to her set distraught mouth. She didn't want them to know she had half-way expected a repentant Dean to be driving by—at least. Yet she supposed it was unlikely. He would expect her to give in first. Marriage or nothing. He was supposed to be punishing *her!* It was too much like marriage just to any man—just to be married. She wasn't sure what she was, but she was sure he was being childish. We must be too young to decide, she thought.

Shandol put on the blue satin, long-sleeved blouse and a dark navy grayish jumper. They were old, for she had worn them to high school, and she had been out nearly a year now. They had been inexpensive also. They had made the blouse and a white one—with help of a neighbor, from remnants, and her mother had purchased the jumper for a very low price at a bargain basement sale. But then Dean liked the outfit.

She got her coat because the nights were still cool.

Will Dean wonder what I'm doing tonight, she thought. *And he certainly won't be here for Sunday dinner.* She hurried back downstairs where the others were waiting.

"All set? Let's go then," Phil said.

As they walked along the dirt road, Shandol walked with Freda, the two boys, hurrying on ahead, decided to stop by the store.

"Yuh were smart not to marry him," Freda said flatly. "He's no good for yuh."

"Uh—well, he wanted me tuh make a quick decision, and I didn't want to," Shandol explained, and added, to change the subject, "How's the soldier?"

"Well, he's got a rating," Freda replied proudly. "He's a P.F.C. now."

"What's P.F.C.?" Shandol wanted to know. "I've seen the initials before and wondered."

"Private First Class," Freda replied.

"Oh, well, I sure don't know about the army, do I?"

"Yuh know it seems funny fer you to go out with the boys anyway," Freda told her.

"But why?" Shandol frowned. "I've as much right to go on dates as anyone else."

"I don't know," Freda admitted. "It just seems yuh're more the type tuh teach or somethin' like that and not marry."

Do I seem such a prude, Shandol wondered. *Why does it make any difference to her whether I'm an old maid or not? While she with her rather pudgy face and oiled hair—she oiled her hair to make it wave, but it would have looked much nicer if she would set it when washed and wet without all that hair oil! She hopes she's found her man and expects to settle down. No, thank yuh,* she thought. *I don't accept the invitation to be the town's other old maid—yet.* Shandol' s face turned red with embarrassment—or was it fury for even so she could be right. It seemed hopeless now.

Last year her shorthand teacher had said anyone can get married if they want to bad enough; she knew what she meant now. It might be just choosing anyone or the first one who came along. But when the someone, in your own book, was someone you didn't care for, or was at least uncertain about, it seemed an easy way to make a mistake. But what about Freda! Could she love anyone who would ask her?

"I'll just go along mindin' my own p's and q's," she retorted lightly. "I may never get married, that's true, but I've certainly had chances. I've never been actually jilted either I don't think."

And you have Freda, she thought. *You get serious fast. First it was Lester, but you were really too young for him then; then Doug Lindersilt. I could marry your brother Cal; and even your older brother said he loved me. He's love-ick! Sick-eyed and stupid! He repulsed me and Dean. But I still prefer Steven Connelly, but he don't know it. He never will. He's too conceited to appreciate it—and so young. But even he proposed. Kid stuff. He actually didn't jilt me, we just grew up, I suppose.*

"Um—m," Freda mumbled.

"Have yuh ever had a marriage proposal?" Shandol asked.

"Well, no, not yet, but I'm only sixteen," she answered, "unless yuh count Lester. And then he married someone else."

"I had my first proposal at second grade," Shandol laughed as she hadn't thought of that for sometime. "Know what I said? Well, the boy who asked me was a third-grader and I in second grade, said we'd meet in town on Saturday and get married. But I told him I wasn't sure I would be in town then. I wasn't. I don't know if he went or not. But we were still school friends until we moved to my grandpa's farm after Grandma died. I wish I could remember if I asked Mama about it. If I did, how they must have laughed ! Secretly of course."

"It was silly," Freda snorted.

"Of course," Shandol admitted. "Same thing with Bill Hollan in sixth grade. Only he didn't really propose, just said when we grew up he would. He'd write love letters. What a time I had. I liked his sister, but he was so much littler than I was. Then there was the one in high school who proposed, but said we'd have to wait until we were older. But it's all in findin' the right one. I wish yuh luck, Freda."

Phil and Cal soon caught up with them. Cal had bought chewing gum, as well as cigarettes for himself and passed the gum around. Shandol murmured, "Thank you." Cal lit a cigarette.

"There's a train comin'," Phil observed.

"What were you gals breezin' about?" Cal asked.

"Just mere men," Shandol retorted lightly.

"Yuh's smart not to git hitched with that 'un," Cal told her.

"So I've heard before," Shandol replied. "But he's not all that bad— at least with me. Some people talk like he's some kind of rogue or somethin'."

"He's a alecky outfit," Cal replied. "We gotta wait fur that train."

The huge steam locomotive was bearing down full speed toward the crossing, the "cow-catcher" pointing straight ahead. The signal dinged like a one-tone bell. The wheels with their own rhythmic beat rumbled on, and it seemed to jar the very ground they stood on. The engineer, looking so poised and alert, his cap just so, waved as he passed and they waved him on. A uniformed man stood on the caboose platform, which was lit faintly from within, and he too waved.

They walked on up the road. They had not gone far when it became plain Cal was trying to single her out. She could talk easily with him. He had heard she had taken the teacher examinations. And he had hardly exhausted his opinion of Dean in the one sentence. He offered no encouragement about teaching, but he said nothing against it. But Shandol was sure he had schemed with Phil to get her out that night.

It turned out to be a pleasant evening. There were a few other young people there. The Horns were tolerant of their children and company; yet none was known to get out of line. He and his wife sat in their respective rocking chairs, visiting with different ones. Birdie could sit in her chair and spit in the ash pan in front of the stove for she chewed her tobacco unabashedly. He smoked a pipe.

There was homemade candy and cookies if anyone cared to help himself. They were on the kitchen table where the games were played—pushed back out of the way. They visited, listened to the

says he won't go away until he talks to yuh."

Shandol crept from the dimly lit room and on downstairs reluctantly, leaving the lamp in her room. Joel was waiting for her in the dining room.

"It's after nine o'clock, Shandol," Joel reminded her as he looked at the large, old wall clock, "so don't get in that car with 'em. Make him come inside; we'll all leave this room, it's bedtime anyway, the doors will be closed and yuh kin talk in here. He might just drive off if he gets yuh in that car, and it's too late to go anywhere."

Shandol went out, somewhat shaken, but determined. She went to the car window.

"Yuh wanted tuh see me?" she asked. "Here I am."

"Yeah," he answered. "Git in so's we kin talk."

"If yuh're gonna talk tuh me, yuh'll have to come inside," she told him.

"I won't go in there and have a audience," he sulked.

"But we'll be alone, Dad gave me his word," she replied.

"We'll be alone here too," he coaxed.

"I have to go back in," she replied. "If yuh want tuh talk yuh'll come on in; if not then I done my part. Just don't try to badger me into what I can't do. It's prob'ly only because of me and Dad that the neighbors don't call the law. They could yet, yuh know. If they knew yuh were drunk—" she faltered, and quickly put her hands over her mouth.

"So yuh think I'm drunk, huh?" he flared. "They tell yuh that?"

"I don't know what to think," she answered, "but they said yuh'd been drinkin'."

"Do yuh believe 'em?" he wanted to know.

"Sure," she replied, "'cause I smell somethin' strange. I don't know what it is, but naturally that's my guess. I think it's terrible."

"But let me tell yuh—" he began.

"I'm goin' inside now," she interrupted to say firmly. "I'm too cold to stand out here. If yuh won't come in yuh'd better leave." And she turned to go toward the house.

At the porch steps he was at her side. They went into the quiet vacant room silently.

She sat down on the bench behind the stove and motioned him to sit in the rocking chair nearby. The birds were disrupted and fluttered about briefly in the cages.

"Why did yuh come here?" Shandol whispered.

"Shandol," he replied. "I changed my min'. I had tuh. I been through hell. I love yuh, Shandol, I tole yuh. I wanted us tuh git married. But if not yit, I still gotta see yuh. I jest gotta see and be with yuh when I can."

"But yuh hadta get a shot uh some kinda' nerve to do it," she reminded him doubtfully.

"Nope, this was part uh a weddin' celebration," he said smiling.

"Whose?" her eyes brightened.

"Truth is I ditn't know 'em verra well," Dean admitted sheepishly. "Jest a nephew or somethin' of the man I drive the truck for sometimes, invited me. Then I had tuh jest take a swig to satisfy 'em."

"Well, it don't much satisfy me," she replied. "I don't like it one bit. Are yuh sure yuh're tellin' me the truth?"

"It's true," he answered briefly, "but how 'bout me comin' up Sattiday?" he added.

"I have made a date," she hedged.

"Who?" he asked, immediately irritated. "I"ll brain 'em."

"Well, my stars, I'd better not say," she replied. "Look," she reasoned, "yuh caused the breakup, remember? Did yuh just expect me to sit around and wither away? Now really! I had the right tuh do it. How'd I know if yuh'd be back 'er not? And I can't back down. I gave my word. It wouldn't be right."

"Maybe next day then," he stated more than asked. "Don't make any date for Sunday, then."

"All right," she agreed, "though maybe I shouldn't. Dad don't like that drinkin' and may not want me to go anywhere with you. Yuh just may have some provin' tuh do for yourself. How could yuh do it?"

"Fergit it," he said, waving his hand to the side as though pushing the issue away. "I don't do it much and yuh know it."

"Just don't start," she retorted.

"I'll be here sorta early Sunday," he teased. "Yuh owe me a Sunday dinner, 'member?"

"Oh, yeah," she said, hesitantly, though he didn't seem to notice.

They talked only awhile longer, until he said he had better go. He again tried to get her to break her date, but she staunchly refused.

"If we don't have a way to go to town," she told him, "well, we'll just be here or at his house. It's nothing, don't worry about it! He won't even kiss me."

"He won't?"

"That is if I say," she amended.

"I don't like it," he said, "but what can I do? I'll try not to think of it. I see now I wuz so wrong tuh back yuh in a corner like that. I been sorry ever since."

He got up from the chair and went to the door. Shandol followed him. There he took her in his arms and his large frame seemed to enfold her. She looked up at him and saw his look was quite gentle and tender. She smiled, fondly. He bent to kiss her but she turned away so he touched her throbbing throat instead.

"Don't," she breathed.

He tried to kiss her again, but she could not bring herself to touch the source of the strange smell. "No," she smiled weakly.

What's happening? she wondered. *This is different somehow.* Always she had seemed to be standing aside, seeing herself, watching herself. And she always wanted to be proud of what she would see, because it might return to haunt or prick at her conscience. Yet now at his touch, clasped tightly to him with a strange repugnant smell in her nostrils, she was not *watching* herself, she seemed to be *involving* herself. She became aware of him as a man, as she hadn't before. She would not have liked seeing herself this way, but she did not *see*, she could only *feel* him near her and liking him there. He was not just a guy on a date and she must be on guard. Emotions arose in her that seemed to sense her mood and desire.

"I know what it means, now," she muttered to herself. If he heard he gave no sign. Or perhaps he sensed the time wasn't right and his position too delicate.

He looked covetously down at her mouth, and she forced a smile again. The clean, white, even teeth, her eyes aglow, shining and pure. His lips touched her temple and he let her go.

"'Lips that touch liquor shall not touch mine,' my aunt used to quote." She smiled the taunt as he left.

The words were spoken lightly, however. Words spoken so lightly, were they not to be, after all, in time forgotten?

But any ideas Shandol had wondered about for Saturday were solved and vanished, as she seemed to drop back down to earth. What kind of haze had she been in anyway, she wondered, to have forgotten. Actually she hadn't forgotten. The talk of the other members of the family hadn't allowed that, but the time was this week and she had vaguely considered it something coming up in the near future, with time in between.

But this was the Saturday night for the pie supper, the second of the school term. The first one had been for Christmas and the school; this one was organized by a few town women to raise money to have a "singing school" during the summer. This singing school was to teach singing by the "shaped notes." In this method, although they were placed on the musical scale the same, each had a distinct shape to identify its tone from any other. Why this method was necessary Shandol wasn't sure. Of course the church they chose to attend used no musical instruments in the services. Yet the church with no instrumental music had little to do with it, except as any individual might choose to participate. Perhaps it was meant for something the young people could look forward to doing.

Audrey made a pie, but it was sent as a bachelor pie. Phil participated by playing the guitar, as part of the program was music. In fact it was mostly musical.

Shandol had gone to the singing school, which usually lasted two five-day weeks. There was one held almost every year now. They hired a qualified teacher, one who sometimes helped in the song service at church revivals. There were usually grumbles that he charged a lot, but they had to meet his price. He was usually a young man just out of school or perhaps still studying for something else, such as the ministry. There were then singings held, quartets formed, but Shandol still thought the music was necessary, or was evident even with the shaped notes. The "schools" were usually held in the "church in the holler." It was a fun thing to do as well as a learning thing and, to some, something to do. There were still the same fundamentals of music to learn, but it wasn't always taken seriously enough, even Shandol realized that.

There were others genuinely interested, though, and profited by it.

Shandol didn't even go to the pie supper. She stayed at home worrying about the next day. Dean was coming to dinner! How could she manage it all? Audrey had made extra pies—should she make a cake? Had Fran and Betty worried as she was?

Shandol recalled having heard Fran and Betty talk of preparing meals for their boyfriends. She recalled they had talked and planned for such a big day—which she supposed was an occasion for them also. It all came back, the conversations. She had wondered what they would prepare to warrant such high hopes and large plans.

"Brad has said he's comin'," Fran had boasted.

"Oh, Hal's comin' too," Betty had replied.

"Well, Dean is comin' to our house, but I can't say I'll cook all by myself." Shandol remarked, bravely.

"Yuh've prob'ly done a lot of it lately though," Fran had replied.

"Why've yuh not ast him before?" Betty wondered.

"I just didn't think," she replied. " We were so busy and rather excited. Now I *do* wonder why."

"Yeah, so much tuh do'n all," Fran supplied.

"What're yuh servin' mainly?" she had asked curiously. After all there would be just ordinary food at her house, with only special dessert.

"Cheese'n macaroni," Fran replied, proudly, or defensively, Shandol wasn't sure.

"Sounds fine," Shandol had replied and hoped her surprise didn't show. Cheese and macaroni? She thought about it and then admitted to herself she had no idea what it was. She made a mental note to ask Audrey.

Yes, they had had their days and the day came that Shandol would see how such a day would go for her. She couldn't seem to get so excited as they had seemed. She worried that everything wouldn't be just so. She hardly knew what Dean would like to eat.

Shandol and Jane helped Audrey in the kitchen, helping get things ready and carrying it to the dining room. The men were in the front room. Lester and Phil made music as they liked to do whenever they got together. There was visiting between times and Jane and Shandol occasionally went to the door to peek in at them. Once Jane went to stand beside Les, fingered his hair, and patted his shoulder affectionately. Shandol looked at Dean. Their eyes met but she turned away and went back to the kitchen. She felt she could almost read Dean's eyes. She knew what he was thinking she was sure. "*See, they're married,*" *his look said, "and that not being afraid of showing love and closeness could be ours. Don't they seem satisfied and happy? Couldn't we be?*" *But could we, she pondered. Could I be satisfied as Jane is, when I think I want something else first? For awhile at least, just to get away from here. To see places I have read about and do things I'd like to do for a change.* There was no answer yet, so there was no decision as to whether to settle down and marry Dean.

Dean had never spent a day with them before and she wondered how he would fit in. She had to admit he seemed to take an interest in the music, could talk to her father about a mutual farm interest. Perhaps they were all on their best behavior but it was working out fine. Apparently they chose to allow Dean's and Shandol's stormy times remain their own for this day.

After dinner Jane wanted to take a few pictures. She had her mother's camera, but only a partial roll of film. Dean had not been interested. He plunked the guitar. He did pose alone at his car for Shandol's sake, though she didn't know it then. He wanted Jane to surprise her later. As the conversation centered around pictures, Dean wanted a picture of Shandol besides the small one he carried. The only one she had was copies of a snapshot of herself in her graduation dress. Her mother had borrowed a camera and she had also posed in her cap and gown. They had all turned out quite well and Shandol was rather proud of the black and white prints of herself and what it meant—that she had at least finished high school.

A lady from the country, Rose Hendallson, came in the middle of the afternoon to see Audrey. She bought a pair of canary birds, for which she paid five dollars, as reasonable a price as she'd find anywhere. In fact, the usual price for them.

Dean stayed until Lester and Jane left, which was almost nine o'clock. He and Shandol had not gone anywhere else. But later it seemed to Shandol that she could hardly remember anything had ever been wrong between them.

But the day was also a day of secret planning and conspiracy for the women. While the men were in the front room visiting, discussing jobs, politics, the war as was usual these days, Jane had brought up the fact Les' birthday was a week from the next day. She hoped they could have a party for him then, but here of course, where his friends really were. However, she wanted it to be different. Instead of the usual cake and coffee and hot chocolate, she wanted it to be a hamburger fry as well. She determined she should be responsible for the ground meat and also the buns. Audrey would bake a cake and someone else would likely bring one, and there were always cookies, some purchased, especially by bachelors who chose not to come empty handed. Jane thought she might make some also; they especially went over big with the children. So actually their plans were, if tentatively, fairly well complete. It was to be a surprise, so they would not speak of it openly until they had gone lest the youngsters give it away.

There was the following week to put the plan into action. Of course getting the word around town was no problem. The main thing was that Lester wasn't told, which wasn't likely as he worked in Plainesville.

It turned out to be a rainy week. Some days it poured down, but there were inside things to be done as well. Audrey cleaned up a mess upstairs in one of the back rooms where the sweet potato crop had been all winter. She also had patching to do and the care of the baby. On Friday she had a full day. There was the washing to do. Also club day. She reported she had seen a demonstration on cleaning and pressing clothing. One of the ladies also invited her to go to Mrs. McNeeley's to see the new baby. Shandol went also, but had little time to talk to Margery. But they agreed they should compare experiences sometime. However, Margery did confide to Shandol she had been at her mother's side, because she had had a difficult birth and she was considering the fact she might not survive. She wanted Margery to keep the children together. Of course Aunt Harriet and Uncle Dolphus would help. But Mrs. McNeeley also had the bright happy countenance of the new mother.

Lester and Jane came Thursday about noon on the bus. Lester would have no work until Monday.

Shandol and Bobby went to Plainesville on Saturday with Mrs. Bright. It was really the day she put in the last of her school applications at a country school. But Bobby needed new shoes. Les and Jane were at home and Shandol had hated to leave, but someone had to go with Bobby and she could hand in the applications.

The children were otherwise in school, with time for studying or competitive games of knowledge or other play.

By the weekend it was time to begin some cleaning up tasks for the party, so there wouldn't be so much to do Monday when everyone was expected at the party.

Shandol had had the date with Dean. He decided he must help buy some hamburger meat. Shandol could not convince him it was not necessary. They had gone to the movies, both Saturday and Sunday nights. They spent time with other couples, driving around and eating on their Wednesday outing.

Monday was a busy day. There was the house to get its final going over; never staying tidy all that long. Sometimes it seemed to Shandol the two younger boys could just go through the house to wreck it. It wasn't quite that bad but a whole family with an ounce of carelessness could mean work to be done.

Audrey baked bread so she could make buns. There was to be some purchased, but there was no way to judge the number of people who would show up. It turned out to be a good thing she made the extra effort, because there had been a large crowd. After all it was something new and different and promised good food.

It was also a good thing Dean had brought extra meat because it went quickly. Audrey had a fresh loaf of bread sliced and slices of cheese also, either to put with the hamburger or eat alone. There were home-canned sweet pickles and onion slices, which somehow seemed appropriate. And there were, as supposed, plenty of cakes and cookies brought by others.

Lester was taken completely by surprise. Though no one ever brought gifts, except food, to the parties, he soon caught on. He was very pleased. Additionally pleased at his wife for thinking of it and helping Audrey with it; also the larger crowd. The music makers were in evidence in the front room as the fiddles, guitars, mandolin, and this time, a banjo, kept music going almost constantly. Most of those playing could play more than one instrument, so that they could all take time to eat.

There were games outside. Joel's and Harry's checker games were inside allowing the winner to challenge anyone who would care to play. There were a few who considered themselves good enough and usually lost, except a time or two when carelessness or overconfidence would let one or the other underestimate a player, thereby letting his mind stray from his game.

The young children played games of tag or just pushing, wrestling and running. Sometimes they joined the older ones to make more and were sometimes in the way They also ate. Oh, how they could eat!

Shandol tried to mix in with the crowd as she always did. But she soon realized Dean may as well be her husband, as she was almost in the same boat as her sister-in-law. She shouldn't have been so surprised. There were girls there with steady boyfriends who wanted it no other way. They joined in some of the games, except for Freda, whose soldier was not there, but she talked of him in depth to anyone and everyone who gave her the chance.

Once Shandol went outside to check to see if the games were going smoothly, as she always had. She was not asked to join as in the past, however. She was sure Dean made the difference.

Dean met her on the porch on one such outing. She thought she had slipped out, but apparently he had been waiting for such a chance. He met her on the back porch. The games were in the poorly-lit yard. He caught her shoulders and would have kissed her, but in embarrassment she had turned her face aside and allowed only a peck.

"Not now," she whispered.

"Be a nice time to announce an engagement," he told her, giving her no doubt as to whose. He smiled broadly.

"Yeah, I suppose," she replied, meeting his look squarely and added quickly, "but there don't seem to be any to announce."

"Afraid uh me now?" he asked.

"Not necessarily," she replied and hoped she knew what she meant. That is that he would not act as he had in the past.

"Scared of yerself then?" he persisted.

"No! " she replied louder. "You're tryin' to rush me again. I'm in no hurry."

He suddenly grabbed her and kissed her full on the mouth anyway. She was caught by surprise but returned his kiss.

"We better go inside," she said, "or I'll get talked about."

Shandol left Dean as he went on into the front room after getting a piece of chocolate cake. As she watched him she was sure she heard something. It seemed to be coming from upstairs. She knew, after a moment of surprise what it was, but decided she had better go look anyway to see just who she'd find. She might have guessed and been correct. For sure enough in the dark hallway up there four girls were trying to dance. Joel would frown on it if there were any boys involved, but there weren't and Shandol decided they were not doing anyone any harm. They explained to her they were trying to learn the waltz, the two-step and square-dance steps. Shandol had no intention of interfering, because after all, she had had to do the same thing in school in gym class.

"We're just practicin'," Gloria Dahle defended, and added, "yuh don't know how awful it is to go tuh a dance and know so little how."

"But there's a boy-girl way," Shandol said, wonderingly. "The guy leads."

"Yeah, but we just take turns," Gloria's sister replied. "I didn't suppose your mom would allow yuh to go tuh dances," Shandol told them. "I knew yuh played around tryin' tuh learn, but do yuh really go?"

"Not much—yet," Gloria admitted, "but if I get a chance I will." Her mother was as strict on her girls as Shandol's father was. They were not supposed to wear lipstick or curl their hair when they attended church. But they had it done anyway. Their father did not go, however. In fact he drank a little, and so their mother did not have the backing and they could get by with more than Shandol. They simply did not have the example. Theirs was a divided discipline, and as they grew older chose more and more for themselves.

Dean was among the last to leave. And in an aside to Shandol, he confided that he was merely waiting for his good-night kiss.

"Or being sure no one else had one too," she teased. And the unanimous decision by everyone seemed to be it was a good party, a great idea being so different and all.

CHAPTER 29

"We'd all hoped it was just a rumor," Joel remarked one night at the supper table, when the family had finished eating, "But apparently it's not. The road jobs and building jobs will be closed down."

"Oh, dear!" Audrey exclaimed. "Without jobs what will people do?"

"Defense work," Joel replied briefly.

The rumor at first had been vague, as though just hearsay. Yet it persisted, and was now a known and accepted fact. It was certainly true that preparing for the defense of the country was surely more important than building roads and buildings, even necessary though they were, and providing jobs. But such jobs could come later. Defense work would provide many more jobs than were taken away.

Joel went on to explain the particular group of men he worked with could join the work forces building army camps. Some were young enough to be drafted if things got really bad; a few might prefer defense plants, now becoming more numerous. However, Joel's group were told they would be given transfers to a new camp being built about one hundred twenty miles, more or less, north. And the date of the required physical would be April twenty-first. That they must pass to get the work.

This would mean a change in the lives of most of the men. They would not be able to move their families, even if there would be enough housing, which there would unlikely be. As much as he hated being away from the family, Joel made plans to go. It would not be just government "contrived" to help the jobless.

The week before he was to leave was the last week of school in Greenway. Tommy and K.C. had their picnic near the school. It had been a lovely day for a picnic. So lovely, in fact, Audrey had the flowers brought down from upstairs. Everyone helped that could. That was a spring chore as sure to come as would taking them back up there be in the fall.

On Thursday Bobby's school room, which was called the "upper grades" went to a more distant spot. It was in an adjacent county, in a secluded, wooded and chilly country known as Greenland Cave Spring.

For the trip, the teacher, Mrs. Bright, had hired a truck to take the group. Family and even friends of the students were invited to

364

go along. Each family or individual, as the case would be, was to bring a lunch for themselves. They could spread it out with the rest or eat separately, whichever they chose. They hoped to eat beside the stream which tumbled from the spring somewhere inside a cave, and formed a pool of clear sky-reflected water, which kept would-be explorers out of the cave.

The pupils, the teacher, and any parents or friends who had decided to go met at the schoolhouse. They loaded the boxes of lunches onto the back of the truck, which would take them. Soon all were loaded and ready to start. There were several young children who had tagged along with a brother or sister and family, but Tommy and K.C. had stayed at home with Joel. Audrey took Karen as she was sure she and Shandol could manage her with perhaps some outside help.

Shandol wore pink slacks and blouse to match of a spun rayon material, and black sandals with white anklets. The blouse of the slack suit, which she had purchased with cash she had received as graduation gifts, hung loose and outside the matching slacks. Joel had expressed displeasure at her buying them. He felt they were not feminine and unbecoming clothing for girls and ladies to wear. Bobby wore his usual school clothing, denim overalls and cotton shirt. Audrey wore a colorful print dress she had made herself. Karen also wore a cotton print baby dress Audrey had made. Audrey, with the baby and the baby's things rode up front with the driver of the truck in a cab. The teacher felt it was her responsibility to ride with the children and others in the back.

Light-hearted expectancy, visiting and giggling had started before the truck left the school yard. They headed north to the main street, east to the main highway and then south.

Shandol worried that because she was older than the school children, yet younger than the parents, she might have a lonely time, except to be with Audrey. But even though she was among the oldest of the young ones, she was not much bigger and could fit in as she chose with the songs, giggles and small talk. Of course the children discussed some phases of the school year, such as their grades and how well they had done, but they were concerned only briefly as this was to be a fun day and they hoped to make it one to remember.

Shandol tied a scarf on her hair, but her arms were bare except for the brief sleeve of her blouse.

As they went along the highway there were brief comments of a familiar or interesting place to someone. All eyes were on Folks Consent as they drove through on the highway. But before they reached Waiton where Dean and Shandol saw the Saturday night double features, with one being a cowboy show, they turned off the main highway onto a gravel road. It would take them through the small county seat and they would still have several miles to go.

The county seat would hardly have been recognized, if it hadn't been pointed out. Even the courthouse resembled an oversized house. Perhaps it was adequate or a new one might have been built by the government workers.

They were well past the town when the truck suddenly jerked and died.

"Oh, we're outa gas," someone wailed. "I betcha."

It wasn't yet noon. The driver got out, raised the hood in a confident manner to see if he could find the trouble and repair whatever the fault so they could be on their way.

"Wonder if he knows anythin' about motors?" Dale Lankers snickered. He was one of the students and his sister had come along, though Rayda had quit school when she finished the eighth grade. It was a question perhaps everyone pondered and hoped he did now.

The teacher's sister and young son had come along. She had a camera and took pictures of the troubled truck and the group, before they were scattered. Audrey also persuaded her to take a picture of "my girls," which she did, Shandol holding Karen, who looked nice in a knit baby bonnet and seemed contented indeed. It was the first picture taken of her.

After being parked by the roadside for about an hour the driver had to admit the trouble was beyond his knowledge, and he'd have to go for help. He and Mrs. Bright began a discussion, on the best way to handle the situation. It all seemed to point to one solution. The driver would have to hitchhike back to the county seat for help. They also discussed a way to get transportation back home in case the truck would need to be taken to a garage for mechanical repair. Otherwise, they knew, they would just be stranded there, despite the fact he was hopeful the trouble would be simple enough to take care of there.

Meantime, a group of boys had set out to the nearest farmhouse to see if there might be a telephone, which was unlikely they knew. Also they wondered how far they were from the spring. They also took a container to get water. Though the driver had let the truck roll to a stop at the side of the road, there was a tree nearby, but the truck itself was in the sun.

They spread the lunch and ate. There was nothing for Mrs. Bright to do but depend upon the driver for the responsibility of the truck. He and two older boys left as soon as they had eaten. By that time the three, who had walked to the farmhouse, reported no phone, but that they were about "two to two and a half miles" to the spring turn off. They brought back water. They had made imitation fruit flavored drink in what they had had.

Everyone in the group enjoyed the food it seemed and ate ravenously. There was plenty. Sandwiches, pickles, salad, baked beans, canned fruit made into pies and more bread and sandwich spreads in case there wasn't enough. It was spread on a faded tablecloth brought along for the purpose. As in the case where any contribute the variety and amount was more than sufficient, which proved to be a good thing.

In the afternoon the older children decided to walk on to the spring. At first Shandol had hesitated leaving her mother with Karen. But Audrey assured her Karen could be laid down on the oldish quilt she had remembered to bring so she could have her nap and there were plenty children to help amuse her and other help if needed.

Because the school children represented the upper grades (seventh and eight) most of them who cared to do so were allowed to make the hike. A few chose not to go. Shandol chose to go. They seemed to form groups as they went along, depending on the pace taken, and Shandol was with a group of girls and one boy. He was not her brother. Bobby had been one of those to go with the driver.

"Under no circumstances is anyone to get into that water," Mrs. Bright directed, firmly. "It's said to be tricky. It may be clear and shallow looking, but here are deep holes which look no differently. So, please, no wading or swimming—though I'm told it is too cold where it's deep to swim in." She looked at Shandol. "Remind them if you see them try" Shandol nodded.

Their pace down the dusty gravel was steady but not pokey. They were all used to walking. Some trotted or ran on ahead, because they were excited about getting there. But for the most part, were in no hurry, but made good time.

The land around seemed relatively flat, as it seemed the road was on a ridge. As they neared the spring the more hilly scenery became evident. The road wound around so that Shandol wondered a time or two if they might be lost, and having missed the turn off. But she also knew all they had to do was turn around and go the other way.

A barn-like shed was to be the marker to turn off. There were also small signs marking the way to the spring and the rough paths on down, which were supposed to be only a half-mile off the road to the spring. It seemed as long as the walk from the truck.

The area was fenced so they had to climb over the woven wire fence topped with two strands of barbwire. There was little more than a trail to the spring, mostly downhill.

"Even a goat would have trouble in this place," Shandol observed, to no one in particular. "How'll we ever get out?" Some of the enormous hills seemed to go straight down. However the path was at an angle from the straight line down, then there had to be caution used. It reminded Shandol of the old Ozark saying she had heard, "it ain't that the mountain is so high, it's just that the hollers is so deep." Down one hill was a valley in the form of a v, which they had to climb out of in order to go down another hill, which they went down almost in a sitting position—at least one hand on something solid, whether the ground or holding to small brush which dotted the way; though sometimes eroded ground left tree roots which could accommodate them. Then they reached a plateau along a high hill, below which was the river. The shelf descend, tapering to low ground and a beach. Hidden only a little way further on among the trees and rocks and willows in a culvert-like formation the greenish water boiled and foamed and then ran more leisurely. The formation was the source of the spring. No one knew how far back the cave went or even if it were a cave, or simply a large overhanging rock formation. It was beautiful, rugged and wild. It was mystery because it seemed so untouched and untouchable. No one apparently wanted to be churned in the cold mass of lovely fury. But how gently it flowed along the small secluded beach. The water was clear, the pebbles showed clearly before the water surface.

Shandol looked around her. The huge trees, the mass of undergrowth and fallen dead limbs and trees, wild flowers were already in bloom and even bushes which she could not identify. How small she felt. But how much tinier the small fishes in the lazy stream. However, the spring churning to the surface fascinated her most.

She looked at the hills all around her, which rose up as though to hide and protect this wildness and beauty, and now looked unsurmountable. She supposed they could climb out, people always had. It gave her almost the same feeling she had had looking into the universe at night. The stars so far away. How small they seemed, yet she only a speck on a planet. And of all creation only people and the heavens to appreciate it.

They spent the early afternoon climbing around, looking at the quiet stream, the older ones keeping eye on the younger ones. Conversation mostly concerned points of interest, beauty or unusual rocks or flowers. Talking seemed so inconsequential. It was a quiet awesome place. Only flutter of an occasional bird was heard.

All too soon it was time to start the difficult climb back to the road. Shandol was glad her mother had not tried it, though she would have enjoyed it if she had reached it. It was a difficult climb because they still had to hang onto branches or brush to boost themselves upward.

At the top they peeped inside the shed. Someone had called it a mill house, rather than barn. But why way up here away from the stream? Others decided it was a barn or feed shed. There were no animals or feed evident. Perhaps it was used for a hunter's shack, or had someone hoped to make a business charging people to go to see the spring? They just would guess and speculate.

As they started back the pace was more leisurely. Going the other way they had more or less scattered along the country road, but they remained closer now. And there wasn't so much running, romping and horseplay. Shandol could see their walk had been tiring. It had been like work climbing the hills. It seemed her leg muscles shook —every one quaking, some she didn't realize she had.

By the time they reached the truck the warm sun was declaring a fading day. They learned there had been no further word from the driver. They were all wondering why. Could he have been unable to stand the trip? Or if something else could have happened. Perhaps they had had to walk every step of the way there and back.

The group at the truck had played party or school games as they could, running, tagging, romping in the grassy area and playing with the baby The adults tried to hide their concern over their plight, and, as the afternoon wore on and no word, concern for them deepened. How long would they be stranded here?

The boxes of food, which had been carefully kept in the shade, were brought out again. The children were getting restless and obviously getting hungry.

The sun was quite low by the time Mr. Cook and the two boys came back. They were walking, dusty and hot because they had tried to hurry. They informed everyone they had ridden most of the way to Ralton, but had walked most of the way back.

At the small town they found no one to come to see about the truck motor. The town had only one mechanic, who was just too busy with local service to leave. They had then had to make a call to Plainesville for a tow truck. Mr. Cook also had to seek alternate transportation for the people to get home. After numerous tries, waiting and much impatience, he had finally made connection with a school bus driver. But he would have to make his regular school route before coming.

The driver apologized to Mrs. Bright and hoped this would be satisfactory. She in turn thanked him for his concern for them and efficiency in making other plans. There was little else he could do.

* * * * *

At home, Joel Sonnett also watched the fading April day with misgivings. He realized now what it meant to worry about flat tires, motor trouble and accidents. He tried to console himself it was a long trip and perhaps they had stayed longer than they realized, or had a child got lost? He worried. He knew it was not like Audrey to be late and not have mentioned it. Still perhaps she hadn't known how late they would be. He was sure there was a reason. Anyway he was due at the schoolhouse for a school board meeting. Phil could stay with the boys. He had supposed Audrey would have been home by then. He decided if he hadn't heard anything by the time he returned he would see if he could learn why.

Meantime he had to get them a bite of supper.

It was dark when the bus arrived. The warm April sun had gone and left a chill in the air. It might have been a cold ride home in the back of a truck.

A tow truck had arrived before the bus, but the driver had refused to leave, though he decided to go with the truck when the bus arrived. He still felt responsible for their being there and he wanted to be sure they had a ride home. It was sparsely populated and the road had little travel.

Soon an eager crowd was scrambling aboard the bus and on the way home. The children were tired and quiet, some even slept. Karen had been good, Audrey praised her, but she was not out of milk. Audrey hadn't realized or planned on being gone so long, and the water Karen was getting from the bottle hardly pacified, though she slept fitfully. She too was tired.

They were met by Phil.

"Yuh musta had a good time or somethin'," he said, "yuh're so late."

The younger boys crowded around, glad to see their mother home again.

"The truck quit on us," Audrey explained. "and we sat along the side of the road most of the day. We had a good time though really. It was shady. Most of the kids went on to the spring anyway—the older ones anyhow. But too far for the rest of us, with small children and a baby to carry."

"And getting down through the woods and steep hills is some hike too," Shandol added.

And each in turn told of their activities of the day.

Audrey and Shandol listened to Tommy and K.C. as well as having them hear their own experiences on the picnic.

CHAPTER 30

Joel Sonnett was ready to go. His battered borrowed suitcase was packed with his freshly laundered work clothes, shaving mug and razor, a few of the better towels and washcloths, because Audrey wasn't sure just what he might need. He was dressed in his older suit (he had recently been given a better looking one) and a white shirt. He was not yet going to work but for the physical examination for the new job of helping build the army camp at Fort Lewis Woodward. He would go with the men he worked with in the truck in which they had ridden. But Audrey wasn't sure if they would return before the end of the week.

He was glad to be going. He felt fit as the proverbial fiddle and would be glad to begin work as soon as possible.

The whole family welcomed it, though it meant he would be away from home, with whatever visits he would be allowed to be home. They saw it as an opening into a new way of life at last. There would be more money and therefore security, more freedom from doubt, anxiety and want, then they had known for a long time.

They had already done some planning. They would try to save all they could. Perhaps they could buy an acreage of land. There would be some to till for food; farm animals; chickens. Perhaps they could manage to get enough milk for their own use and some to sell to the cheese factory in Plainesville, when the war was over. There would be other war work after the army camp was built.

"We'll get along someway till then," Audrey said. "Then we'd raise food, and have income from milk and eggs, and they could live as well, or better than they did now. Also cut and sell wood. It would always be in demand they supposed.

Audrey settled about the day trying to reconcile her mind to whatever came up. She hoped he would pass the physical of course and she saw no reason why not. Yet, she dreaded the responsibility of being left to her own devices. She knew she depended upon Joel for so many things and especially major decisions, and help in the discipline of the children. It meant a lot to the family, she knew, and this handling things alone could be her part for what they hoped to be building up of a better life for them all. If the long evenings became lonely, she could always crochet, which she loved to do.

The other members were happy at the prospects also. They felt they would have more and perhaps in time, they could buy some type of car; they would not be particular—just so it would run.

Shandol knew it would bring changes, but perhaps too late for her. She was still excited about Joel's chance of changing jobs. She felt it more dignified and worthy of him.

"This will be a long day," she predicted, "wondering how they came out and all."

"I just wonder how many of the men will go," Audrey replied.

"They don't *have* to go, do they?" Shandol asked.

"I don't suppose so, but they will probably want to," Audrey commented. "Work's still scarce and without the road work and all, it will be worse than ever."

Audrey had a busy day, however. School was out for the two younger boys the day before, and there were children in and out. Also Tommy and K.C. played between their friends' homes, yet Audrey always felt she knew where they would likely be.

In the morning hours, Mabel Colmay came by to see if Audrey cared to go green hunting with her, which of course Audrey did. She was fond of the cooked wild greens, as was the whole family, actually. Also it would take her mind off the trip and tests Joel faced today. Audrey would never realize Mabel came for that reason, as well as the free-for the taking food for her large family. After all, she could have gone alone. At any rate Audrey was glad of her company and that she thought of it. It really was more enjoyable to go with someone to hunt "greens." Audrey wondered if she would be able to can any as she had in past summers. Always there was plenty of poke. Eating the tender leaves of poke or poke weed, as she had heard of it, was something else she had learned since moving to this part of the state. She had always heard they were poisonous. But the natives had assured them only the roots and berries were poisonous, and they were left strictly alone. Audrey was taught how to cook them. They need parboiling before being put with the other greens.

The boys were excited about school being out but hardly knew what to do with themselves. But they were outside much of the time. As if it were still the last day they would discuss their passing grades and beginning school next year. It seemed far away—a whole summer!

"If yuhr dad was working on his job he'd be home by now," Audrey said to Shandol, as she prepared supper as usual.

Approximately an hour past his usual time to return, however, Joel returned from the trip. He sat aside the battered suitcase and faced his family gravely. He had bad news. He had not met the physical standard. He had not passed the physical examination.

"But why?" Audrey asked incredibly.

"Heart trouble, high blood pressure," he replied, disappointment and rejection written all over his drawn face. In that moment for the first time Shandol thought he had begun to look old.

"Heart trouble?" Audrey put her hand to her mouth awe stricken. "Why—why, it just can't be," she added, looking at Joel with genuine concern.

"That means that—there'll be no work there?" Shandol asked, almost faltering in her disappointment.

"No work," he repeated, and wrung his hands briefly, as though washing the deal away. It was a defeat he had not in the remotest way anticipated.

"But heart trouble can be a bad thing," she murmured. "But what did it mean?" she asked. If it was tactless she couldn't seem to help it, even as she knew her father was as disappointed as any one of them— perhaps more. He knew it had meant so much for them to look forward to his having a good paying job. Concern and disappointment and trying to understand brought her brows together in a youthful frown.

"It means," Joel said simply," they believe the work would be too heavy for me."

"Myocarditis, chronic, with irregular heart action and high blood pressure," Audrey noted in her diary before she forgot it, as if she ever could! Later she would think about it and what it meant. Right now she could only be shocked by it. She would not soon forget their dashed hopes.

"No more job," Joel told his older boys. "Guess we can always cut more wood. Have to grow a truck patch and keep busy at whatever we can."

"But I thought yuh couldn't," Audrey pointed out.

"Got to," he said. "We have to have some income some way."

"And prob'ly work just as hard," Shandol said, thoughtfully. "Walk three or four miles, do a day's work and walk home again. And handlin' the timber—" her voice trailed.

What sort of reasoning was that, she thought. Why hadn't they asked a few questions about how he had made a living? Or how hard he had had to work? But perhaps there were more people hunting jobs than there were jobs available. If he had some kind of visible handicap one could see, such as a bad leg or arm, there was ways one could get help for dependent children. But he looks so healthy, what a stir it would cause if he tried that! It didn't seem fair. What a mess we're in, she thought. She wrung her hands. Maybe we just weren't grateful enough for what we did have.

Just feeling humiliated, and, yes, humbled; and from the looks of things the end is not yet.

Later that night she remembered the fortune-teller's words when she had been told her father was in as poor health, and possibly worse, than Audrey. She had remembered then and certainly thought of it now, of how often he took baking soda with a glass of water, before going to bed, for his "sour stomach." He was always taking it, it seemed. But she didn't understand that because they hadn't found anything wrong with his stomach. Perhaps it could be helped. But his heart? A chronic condition, so it wouldn't stay helped, if there was help for it, which they couldn't know. And doctors cost so much. Chronic: Ever present or recurring were the words she remembered after checking it out.

The next day Audrey and Joel went to Plainesville. As it was "relief" day they had no trouble getting a way to go. Joel went to see his own doctor. They also wished to see if there were other arrangements they could make, even temporary ones.

While waiting for Joel, Audrey on impulse said she would just get in line where the government commodities were handed out. It was almost defiance. She received garden seed and grapefruit, because she had not "signed" up or been going.

She did learn the day before had been the day to see the lady about drawing money on children under sixteen. They just had to try some things to help tide them over until something else came up.

The doctor at Plainesville, Dr. Bushong, whose brother had a pharmacy, said much the same as the doctor at the army camp. He also added he should engage in *no* hard physical labor.

Joel went home, nothing more settled, having learned what he already knew. The next day he would see Joe David about cutting wood to sell.

A week later he went back to Plainesville, but could not see the lady about money on the younger children. He wasn't sure what to do except cut wood. It kept him busy.

The bees swarmed the last day of April and Audrey was determined to keep them. She had already done a wash with Shandol's help, and the cleaning up after. She brought a spare hive to the northwest edge of the yard, called the small boys to stay a distance, but beat on the bottom of the tubs or clang pot lids together to make noise. Such noise would hold them awhile she had always heard.

Using an old curtain for a net over her head to fall over her face, an old hat to hold it, coat and gloves, she took the smoker, and with a little help from Grandpa got the bees into the hive. She was sure Joel would want her to save them. There were three hives now. She got

374

stung once, on the lip, by a bee which had somehow maneuvered its way under her curtain net. She put a vinegar and soda poultice on it, but she was still quite annoyed by it. Usually she escaped unscathed.

Life went on. Little by little the disappointment and shock grew dimmer. The evidence of the setback soon faded. Occasionally they discussed the plans and dreams and the yearnings for the might-have-beens descended with heavy longing. But they were shrugged off with smiles of how fragile dreams can be. Besides there was the work, or other activities.

There was still music to make. The canaries still sang. There were friends who came to call and they went to see, who knew little of their fantasies. And while they conceded they would miss the income, Joel Sonnett would not lose faith.

There was a way and they would have to keep up the struggle to find it.

Because tragedy hadn't really struck yet.

CHAPTER 31

Early May was still cool, and it was a disappointment that it should rain the first Sunday. The whole family went to Sunday school and church anyway. A visiting preacher had done the preaching. He was, in fact, Douglas Lindersilt, the young man Freda had been so heartsick about when he had left to go to school. Theirs had been a summer romance and they still went to Plainesville to church so she was not present to see or hear him.

Joel remarked he had made a fine talk and should make a good preacher. He was still in school and could even improve.

It was nearly noon when they got home. Dean had already arrived and was waiting patiently for Shandol's return, as he wasn't sure where she was. It was true sometimes she went to the church-in-the-holler as a favor to a friend, which was frowned upon by the other congregation's members and she knew it. But it was Bible stories and Sunday school much as their own, except the music in the church—when there was someone there who could play the piano. There was also a piano where Sonnetts usually went, but Audrey was never asked to play it. It was never part of their worship.

Dean did not want Shandol to wait to eat at home. They ate at Folks Consent, then went driving aimlessly, it seemed to Shandol; back through the hilly, rocky countryside. They left the highway soon after Folks Consent and were on gravel roads awhile, sometimes on tree-lined lanes and then gravel roads again. One of the rougher most tree-lined lanes led by a place where Dean stopped and honked. It was Ellen Carfield's home and they visited her while sitting in the car. Ellen was a compulsive talker and they soon learned her brother was home on leave from the army. Shandol could see she was very proud of her brother and had missed him.

It didn't seem to matter if Shandol was so surprised to see where Ellen lived, which made her speechless, Ellen could make up for any silence. Shandol later decided she must have made out all right, because she received a letter from Ellen about her family and goings-on and her thoughts, which were just as she talked.

But then Shandol was surprised to see she lived in a large sprawling house, which was not very old. It was so much larger and newer than usual in this rugged area. It was painted a brownish red and had two stories, yet was so spread out that the height was hardly noticed.

Shandol knew theirs was a large family.

They must be rich, she decided to herself and decided to ask Dean how he made a living. She learned that he had a sawmill, cattle and trucks. And, as Dean put it, "He had did all right fer hisself." Shandol wondered why Dean didn't try to go with her, though she was younger than Shandol and still in school.

They went by the small Oak Ridge church, a small rough building set back in the woods. Dean reminded her the first time he had seen her was there in that "verra place."

"I fell in love then and there," he told her. "The first time I seen yuh I knowed yuh was the gurl fer me."

"My grandpa said he thought the same about Grandma," she answered. "So it may really work out that way sometimes. He said, 'When I saw 'er I says to myself, that's the girl I'm gonna marry someday.' His brother married her sister first, though."

"It should work out for us too," he exclaimed. "Shandol, yuh were meant fer me—why fight it?"

"I wish I was as sure," she replied. "It's so final, how can yuh be? Besides I just have this feelin' I need tuh do somethin' tuh pay back my folks for sendin' me tuh school. So I can't be sure just yet."

"It's easy fer me," he said. "But I suppose that means no more talkin' about it, huh?"

"Yeah," she replied, "if yuh don't mind. Maybe it makes a difference that yuh've 'been around' as yuh say, more than I have. As yuh know. All I know is home and school."

Am I over Steve? she wanted to say, but he would only be jealous. And just as important, did he remember his proposal and had he outgrown the idea now? Was it all puppy love? It hadn't seemed so at the time. But Shandol had been taught marriage was for life and she wanted hers to last.

It was a gloomy Sunday but Shandol still thought the scenery beautiful. The trees dripped from the recent rain and the leaves were shiny and clean. And still they drove farther back into the hilly, wooded country. Dean pointed out places of persons he knew and of interest to himself. They passed where "Grandpa" lived, the boy who had sold the hog to buy the booze; another place Dean had gone to a dance; another the farm of a pretty girl who spent a lot of time in Folks Consent. Of course he could go with her if he wanted to, he answered Shandol's questioning gaze.

"She's the one I was with the night yer sister was born and Brad had that other girl," he added.

Shandol remembered her. Fran had pointed her out. She had long dark hair and wore it with bangs. It was shoulder length and worn pageboy. She was attractive. Shandol grudgingly conceded. Her reputation wasn't "so good."

Shandol was beginning to wonder where they were when Dean pointed out the farm on which Brad had lived. Then she knew; the next place was where Dean lived. The road here was narrow, hardly more than a lane, with grass growing at the edge and middle and yet brush lined the road's edge, with weeds but little grass.

They pulled up past the barnyard into near the wood and chips yard. Across the driveway from the barn was the house. There were milk cans at the gate that entered the yard.

"We sure took a round about way of gettin' here," Shandol observed.

Dean got out of the car and invited Shandol to get out, going around the car quickly to open the door, as she was still looking around. She hoped they weren't here alone.

She was also taking in the weatherbeaten house with peeling paint, but homey looking. It was not a large house but there appeared to be at least two rooms upstairs. The roof sloped down over the rest of it.

The inside had large rooms, the floors covered by colorful linoleum. There were three rooms downstairs: The kitchen, a front room and bedroom. However, there was a bed in the front room also, nicely made up, and a heating stove. The kitchen was a step higher than the living-bedroom they had just entered, suggesting its addition later.

Shandol was first introduced to Dean's parents who were in the room. He was a heavy-set man, no doubt from lack of exercise, courser features and heavy eyebrowed. But hi's mother was the one her son's looks favored. Shandol could see many of Dean's features in her face: the deepset eyes, the pink complexion and the long; but fine, facial features. Her hair was gray, as was her husband's, which had darker strands in it.

Shandol sat in a rocking chair near the north window. She could look past the yard, which was bordered by a vegetable garden, though she could see only a corner of it. There was the woodland beyond— almost breathtaking. She would never later be able to remember exactly what they talked about. Dean had volunteered to tell about the way they had come because Shandol had never seen much of it before. His mother reminded him it would soon be chore time and he reminded her he could do with something to eat first. His father turned on a small battery-powered radio for news, music and a lot of static.

Dean brought Shandol a piece of raisin pie, and a fork on a saucer and she could see he had one himself. It was the first time she had eaten raisin pie that could compare to her mother's. And she complimented Mrs. Leonard accordingly.

She soon left to do chores and directed Dean to get prepared to milk. His father was "down in his back," a chronic condition, it was explained.

Shandol and Dean went to the barn together. He carried two milk pails, which he had fetched from the kitchen where his mother had left them. He went on into the barn where the cows were, their heads in stanchions. Shandol stayed near the door. The walk space between the cow and wall was too narrow, in case the cow kicked. The cows couldn't very well see so might be nervous and defensive at a strange noise or voice.

Dean milked two cows, leaving his mother one to milk, and strolled on past the barn into a pasture. It was still cool, though not now raining. Shandol was awed by what she saw—rolling green hills, very, very green. But then in the other direction, only a little to her left was a green valley and the creek. Across the creek rose a rocky bluff, high, but yet tree-covered. A perfect place for wild birds and animals, she thought. Wouldn't it be a perfect haven for deer? Why doesn't someone, or even the government, put some there she wondered. Couldn't the law protect them as were the pheasants protected up north? Shandol could still remember having seen the colorful, long-tailed roosters rise with a whistling noise from the fields; and the timid brownish hens staying almost out of sight. Sometime, she dreamed, she would ask Dean about the wildlife on the place and the possibility of some being added. Right now, however, she was put-out with him because he wasn't going to take her to church at Greenway. Perhaps, she decided she had said too much about the young preacher. She even taunted him for such jealousy but they went to a movie.

The next day Shandol learned the family where the preacher had stayed for dinner had brought him, and come to see them in the afternoon. She was disappointed that she hadn't been there. Yet she might have known. Phil and Shandol had visited the small church in Plainesville when he had been there.

And her parents were furious at her because she hadn't been there. She tried to explain she had tried to get Dean to bring her back, but he had refused, declaring he wanted to see the movie they went to see. And after all she hadn't been doing the driving. But Joel had shushed her excuses with the positive statement she should manage where she went better than that. There was a time for such perhaps but serious things, too.

"I feel bad about it," she defended herself, "and I was aggravated about it, but he was just sure I wanted to see the preacher and so I couldn't convince him." There was pleading in her eyes.

Joel realized there was nothing to do now but let it go.

Following the wet cool Sunday the men went to the timber but late because of the dampness. Tommy was allowed to go, but K.C. was too small to help and he could get lost if he roamed around. He might be of help at home. He could amuse the baby, hold her bottle or shake the crib, which by now was in the dining room near the window where the birds had been. The birds had been moved across the room near the dining table. It seemed more crowded, but was much handier. K.C. wanted to hold the baby also, but that he was not allowed to do by himself.

Shandol and her mother talked of going to see the new neighbors who had moved into town not long ago. They lived in the house Middletons had vacated, and it was considered their place to make the first move toward getting acquainted.

"They've surely had time to straighten up and clean up the place or whatever was needed by now," she reasoned.

It was not far to walk and carry Karen so in the early afternoon they set out.

Though Glenna Ruleton and her daughter Ardena Leigh were newcomers to Greenway, they were not really strangers. They had relatives here and had visited from time to time in the summer. Their home had been in Lampton, a small town about a hundred miles northwest. They had lived there since moving from their native Oklahoma, five or six years before.

Mrs. Ruleton was a widow. She was crippled in one foot from a disease she had had as a child. Her husband had been a World War I veteran, and had died when Ardena was a baby. He had been wounded and also contacted tuberculosis from which he had never recovered. But his daughter received a pension and this appeared to be their only income, and adequate. It seemed Ardena got about whatever she wanted within reason.

Ardena was now fourteen years old, having had a birthday, she said, last month. It had been her idea to move to Greenway. It had not mattered to Glenna, and perhaps as cheap to live as anywhere. But it was later learned Ardena had seen Philip Sonnett last summer, and, as she was beginning to notice boys, had not forgotten. They would simply have to move so she could make friends with the family.

Audrey introduced herself and those with her, and said they hadn't long to stay, and remarked they had been slow in coming to see them.

"The K.C. really stands for Kenneth Casey," K.C. piped up. "Ain't my sister cute?" It drew smiles and the ice was broken.

Ardena was tall for her age and taller than Shandol. She was a slender girl with thick dark brown hair, surprisingly green eyes and dark complexion. Her forehead was high, but her well-shaped cheekbones and well proportioned facial features made her an attractive girl who could have passed for older than she was.

Ardena and her mother made quite a fuss over Karen. The baby was in a good mood, playful and smiling. Audrey enjoyed watching. But it was soon time to leave. There was supper to prepare. Audrey invited them to visit and they took leave.

"They seem nice," Shandol said, "but she's young, though looks older than she is. She thinks I don't look mine, so we could almost pass for the same age—she thinks."

"How old?" Audrey asked.

"Fourteen last month."

"Well, I do know," Audrey exclaimed, "she did seem older."

"She aims to go and pick strawberries when we do," Shandol marveled. "Perhaps I'll have a friend close by again this summer."

I hope she works out better than Carol Middleton, Shandol thought. She had never received payment for the books Carol had used. She wondered if Carol hoped to sell them at the end of school, as she would finish then—or would she bring them back?

When the men came in Phil asked Tommy to go to the store to buy a bar of Lifebouy soap as he wanted to take a good bath. He handed him some coins and asked him to hurry. K.C. jumped up and down and informed Tommy he was going along. "Nah, I kin run faster'n you," Tommy told him.

But K.C. started out as he saw Tommy race down the path to the store. Audrey watched them through the window a moment, smiling. But then the smile changed to a frown. They obviously weren't going to watch for the traffic at the street, which they had to cross. Audrey remembered the traffic through town could be quite unpredictable sometimes unreasonably swift.

Audrey had hardly had time for the thought to go through her mind and she realized she must warn them, and she ran outside to do so. But there hadn't been time. The distance was not that far from the house to the street and the post office was there to block their view. As she stood at the corner of the house, by the well curbing and frame over it, she saw the cloud of dust west of the post office, and then Tommy's scream had rung out. K.C. was lying in the dusty track of that speeding car and Audrey knew it before she saw.

"Joel! Shandol!" she screamed, as she started to run toward the small figure she could see now. Shandol and Joel ran out and saw Audrey running toward the street. A small crowd had gathered from the store, before the dust had cleared. The car stopped, backed up and a young man in faded overalls and tousled hair stood apart. An older man went to him, perhaps to ask who he was and to assure him he couldn't possibly have missed hitting the boy.

Shandol was beside her mother almost by the time she got to K.C. Joel was not hurrying, but rather considering the newly acquired news concerning his heart, and running would be a strain.

Audrey sobbed, after looking at him briefly. There was blood on his head and from his nose. One side of his head looked crushed and broken.

"K.C., K.C.," Shandol said. "Listen. Don't die. K.C. yuh can say hain't. Ole Ripper won't make it without yuh. K.C. wake up! Please." She was sobbing.

"Stop it, Shandol!" Joel said. "Yer gettin' hysterical. It's no use uh that. Now git hold uh yerself."

"Oh, somebody help 'im," she sobbed.

Audrey turned her face away in shock. She put her hands over her face, her eyes full of tears. She turned to the inert small form and touched him tenderly, not knowing if she should move him.

The "postmistress," as she chose to be called, came out of the post office and was among the crowd. She came forward, knelt beside him and tried to find a pulse.

"He couldn't uh helped hittin' 'im," Steve Werst told Joel, spitting tobacco juice as soon as he had spoken. "The boy run right smack in front uh 'im."

"I shore am sorry, but that don't do no good," The pale youth spoke for the first time, shakily. "But I'll take yuns intuh town if'n yuh wanna see uh doc. He's gotta see uh doc. Kin we move 'im?"

"K.C.'s very hurt," Shandol said, hurt and bewilderment written on her face. "He must hurt all over terribly." And grimly, tears running down her cheeks, she touched him lightly and spoke his name very low. "K.C., oh, K.C."

"No, I'm all right," she added significantly.

"He's already gone," Grandpa said, almost as much to himself as to anyone.

The decision was made by Joel to take him to the doctor in Plainesville. There were men who volunteered to help pick up, as carefully as possible, the small inert body and carry him to the car which had hit him. Shandol wondered that her mother did not seem to want to go at first. She hastened to assure her mother she, Grandpa, and Phil could look after Karen. But Audrey dazedly and shakily got into the back seat with Joel and the child was placed across their laps. They immediately set out for the ride to Plainesville, Steve Werst in front with the white-faced, grim-looking lad driving the car.

"Drive careful," someone cautioned. The youth, who had been running his fingers through his tousled dark hair, nervously, bringing out the sharp features of his face, his large blue eyes veiled in remorse.

With an impulsive desire to comfort him Shandol touched K.C. through the open window of the car and quoted softly: "Let not your heart be troubled—" but they were ready to hurry on. It was actually Audrey who needed the comfort, she was in shock. Because she was sure now Kenneth Casy's heart was forever still, which triggered the soul's right to the eternal mansions, which K.C. already knew about, his heart could neither be troubled nor afraid.

A solemn Joel and pale Audrey came home later, empty handed, their faces mirroring their grief and loss. The small body would be brought back sometime tomorrow until funeral time.

A quiet ghost-like stillness descended upon the house; and a numbness that took away part of the pain.

Joel, next day, after a restless, grief-stricken night, went to make arrangements for the funeral. He took a family burial insurance policy, which was on the whole family and would cover the cost of the funeral and burial, though the cemetery plot was donated. They hadn't had the insurance very long and managed to pay for it a small fee each month. This was a convenience for many people, because it was not always financially possible to pay for life insurance. But now Joel realized how timely he had been in considering it as it would take the draining expense of such an unexpected death and funeral.

Friends came by for information, to offer condolences, and to help in anyway they could.

And then K.C.'s body was in the front room, laid out as though in a fine crib. The bruised side of his face was toward the wall and hardly showed. He looked so spick and span and ready to go, and ready to open his eyes at any moment. If only he could! But the sad hearts of the family knew he was merely ready to be taken from them forever. How final would be his going! And how they would miss him.

Volunteers came to be with the family on the all-night vigil. No one slept until late. Nearly everyone who came brought their own coffee. It seemed there had been a specific time worked out for different ones to come in. A member of the family stayed to keep them company, though they came in twos. Phil stayed up all night. He knew there would be no sleep for him, though he did doze a short while on the couch. The extra coffee, they had explained, they hoped would help keep them awake and give them something to do.

The atmosphere was hushed, yet low conversations took place. The tragedy of it all. How bright he had seemed! But how quickly snuffed, and unpredictable life can be.

Most knew of some cute or good thing he had done, even at his tender age. And they wondered how Audrey would be when it was all over and herself again. Of course she would never get over it, as a scar would remain. In fact none of them would and it was sad. They hardly deserved it, was the consensus. It was so sad, even they were stunned—the fellow townspeople and friends.

It was the next afternoon K.C. was buried. His funeral was sad. And well-attended. But what was said or why and how Shandol, later, could not remember. She wondered if the others did. She wished she could, but realized she was so numb she could only think of K.C. and the gap his going would leave. And she wondered *why*. She did recall the singing, the hope of meeting in another life. She knew who sang, but she would have known that if she had stayed home. There was only one quartet in Greenway. And there were people who came to the church who usually wouldn't have, in fact, were critical of it. But for the occasion all differences were forgotten.

Always there was the question *"Why?"* pulling at them. Why?

Whose fault was it? How could things have been different? The questions persisted as they were led away after the benediction, and Audrey had tossed a single blossom from one of her own houseplants into the grave.

At home, the grave apathy lingered on into the days ahead. They were all so near tears they could hardly bear to hear his name.

"I'm so sorry now I lost patience with him sometimes," Shandol sobbed. "He was just a small lively little boy, curious and noisy. Now he's gone and I can't tell 'im, can't show 'im it's all r-right—"

"Don't," Audrey said. "I wasn't perfect either. He sometimes got on my nerves so bad. Now I just wish he could."

Lester had been with his family, as had Jane. He would frequently hug his mother and say. "We must wait for time to pass. It may help some." It seemed to help her, as she loved this oldest son of hers.

Work was at a minimum. Even food was just picked over. Neighbors had been good to bring dishes of something for the first few harrowing days.

But there had been great hopes died with him. They hoped, by them all helping, he could be the one educated and perhaps become a preacher, or any other useful calling. So why was he taken—their little "Hillbilly" as he himself accepted the term as some title, because he had been the only boy—now with Karen's coming—who could claim it?

Audrey sat thoughtfully often as she rocked Karen, for care of the infant must go on. She was the only light in their lives now. She was always her sweet smiling self and almost demanded response. These thoughts went through Audrey's head now as she sat in the rocking chair applying baby oil, thanks to her shower, to Karen's scalp to soften the pale scales that seemed to form on her head no matter what they did. Audrey called it "cradle cap" and after the oil was on a few minutes Audrey would take a very fine tooth comb and gently scrape it loose and comb it away.

"Some babies are bothered by it," Audrey said, "and some don't seem to be. I don't know why."

Then bitterness seemed to begin to seep into their talk as they became more articulate about it.

"A car going fast hits a little boy and almost kills a whole family," Shandol remarked, resentfully. "Why? And what about that driver? Can't the law do somethin'?"

"He couldn't of helped it," Phil replied. "Th' men all settin' in front of the store would say that. As far as he's concerned it's uh unavoidable accident." And added as an after thought, "apparently he wasn't even goin' as fast as we thought. Just happened K.C. was hit just so."

"He oughta be sued if he's got anythin'," Shandol retorted.

"He don't have," Phil replied. "I'm sure uh that."

"He oughta get kilt hisself," Tommy calmly added.

"Vengeance is mine I will reap saith the Lord," Joel quoted, but little heart in it. "Still he's got his own private self to make it right with."

"Yuh mean his conscience," Shandol replied, thoughtfully. "How can he stand it? K-killin'a little boy. God help 'im," she breathed almost inaudibly.

Joel looked at his daughter, thoughtfully. How sensitive she was. He went outside. He had some thinking to do.

Dean came Saturday after the funeral. He had been gone he said. "Hauled a load uh hogs from south tuh here and took 'em north and ditn't know nuthin' about it. Sorry to hear too." Shandol begged to stay at home. She didn't feel like going out and knew she wouldn't be very good company.

But he argued, as was his way, that she needed to get out, to get something else on her mind.

"Yuh cain't spend yer life grievin'," he reasoned. "It just ain't gonna bring 'im back. Yuh gotta go on from here."

"But I just can't forget it just like that," she replied. "We all have so many regrets and are so miserable, because he was really a pretty good boy and I can't understand it."

"Yuh cain't 'spect to fergit so soon," he replied. "In fack yuh'll never fergit, but it won't be so bad after awhile."

And Shandol recalled what Bert Lankers had said as he set up with them while the body was in the house: "The Lord just retched down His hand and tuk 'em. Guess He wanted 'im. And yuh cain't change the Lord's way."

"Come on," Dean pleaded, "yuh look like some sad sack. Git ready and we'll jest ride if nothin' else. Yuh kin talk or cry or whatever yuh like. But jest leave th' house awhile. Yer not the only one tuh lose a brother, yuh know."

"Is it all right, Mama?" she asked.

"I don't see no harm," Audrey replied. "We gotta start tuh live again sometime."

They went to the Saturday night movie at Waiton, however, and Shandol's mind had been temporarily freed of the gloomy thoughts and she had enjoyed herself. At least more than she had expected.

Joel had done some soul searching following the half prayer, half sympathetic words of Shandol's: "God help him." But Joel realized his family was still inclined to consider him the villain who had struck at them and taken a precious possession. They spoke bitterly of the accident, blaming anyone, everyone, including themselves and God. Joel could understand it, but he must find a way to bring a different attitude to his family.

They must not remember it all with bitter hearts, it would cloud their love for K.C. What was done was done, and though he found it hard to believe himself, apparently it had been in the Lord's will, or it would have been avoided or K.C. only hurt but able to recover and be himself again.

He could not justify, as a Christian example, this way. And after prayers and Bible study he talked it over with his family.

"I'm gonna have tuh see that boy," he said firmly, the muscle in his jaw rippling as it did when he was thinking or feeling something strongly. "I hear he's been drinkin' pretty heavy, and even has wishes he'd just die. So I'm gonna let it be known I wanna see 'im; maybe word'll get to 'im somehow."

"Yeah, Dean told me he'd been drinkin' like he's tryin' to drink hisself to death," Shandol replied.

"But we gotta try to forgive as we'd want to be forgiven," Joel went on. "This is the Christian way. It's just that it's hard because we don't understand God's ways and we wanna fight back—At God and everybody—even ourselves. We're hurtin' ourselves and that won't bring K.C. back. We'll just have to see him in the hereafter, the Lord willin'."

"I'm gonna try to help the boy, to comfort him the best I can. Maybe even ease his conscience. I believe we need to assure him, and ourselves, he couldn't help it. I'm old enough to know I'm sure I'd appreciate such a gesture. You see, maybe we shoulda told him and Tommy more often to stop before crossing the street as we have the railroad tracks. There're people who care for him too. But it's us he's hurt. So I've decided tuh make a try at it. I had to wait until now. First, I had to realize it myself. Then I had tuh make sure I could be sincere. I hope and think now I can be." He had paused in his speech, fidgeted with his hands and sometimes stopped speaking lest he stammer, but all marked by determination.

Joel had not long to wait to see the boy. He made no personal attempts to corner him, just let it be known he would like to talk with him. He gave no indication as to his intentions, outside the family, when he saw him. Whether he wanted to berate him, beat him or just see what kind of guy he was, he left to those who would get the word to him. Whether there was speculation or not, he never knew, but the boy did stop by one afternoon.

"Mom sent me," he said first thing. "Name's Rolly Doorn—I hit yer boy. Mom heard yuh'd lack to see me tuh talk to—or shoot me whichever yuh'd like."

Joel almost smiled, as though at a joke, because the idea he might consider violence he supposed would enter no one's imagination. But the situation at hand was not funny, they both knew, and the light moment flickered and faded leaving Joel's face impassive. Yet it gave Joel the impression he had thought about what had happened, regretted the whole thing and wished with all his heart he could undo it.

Joel intended to say something that might ease his defensive attitude. He could understand it, but how should he handle it? How could he lead up to it reasonably? Was he reassured enough in his mind, heart and faith to show a forgiving spirit? He supposed it was right, but his feelings at his loss tugged at him. They must not show. But he remembered it was not just for himself, but others concerned. He still had to ask why.

"Why do these strange quirks of fate happen?"

He was surprised and rather startled that he had spoken the words audibly.

"What's that yuh said?" the boy asked, leaning closer. Joel had invited the youth inside but he shook his head.

So he stood on the top step with one foot propped on the porch floor. There was only one chair there, one Grandpa had made of hickory switches; two large plants, "elephant ears," Audrey called them, stood on the south edge. It was not a large porch.

Joel came outside and stood leaning against the porch support post, where a volunteer tomato vine tied with a honeysuckle vine for support defied the odds.

"I was just thinkin' the turns fate sometimes takes, the way things happen," Joel told him. "I believe yuh are sorry and hurt and hate what happened. I am sad and hurt too, for he was my son. And at first I was angry. I admit, I suppose because K.C. was so small and the car hit him. Yet, now I want to let yuh know that I reasoned, prayed and don't want my other children to hate and be bitter, so I must do what I can to go on. We realize now it weren't yer fault, too."

"Oh, it musta been my fault," he said, shaking his head. "I just wish't yuh'd jest take a plank and beat me up, maybe I'd feel better."

"But what would that help? Wouldn't change nothin'. And it's what I'm tryin' tuh say—I don't feel that angry anymore."

"But at first yuh did." It was a statement.

"I don't know." Joel answered truthfully. "I was numb at first. Then angry wanting to blame somebody, to hit back. I'm still tryin' to understand. Of course he shoulda stopped at the street before crossin'. It's gonna take time for us all to get over it; to realize he's gone. But the why just ain't for us tuh know yet."

"I shore hate my part in it, Mr. Sonnett," Rolly said. "At first I was glad I didn't know youns, but now I feel I almost do. It really haunts me and I've a time livin' with it."

"There yuh see?" Joel told him. "We feel yuh are bein' punished. But yuh didn't aim tuh do it. Yuh weren't out of the road and no way could yuh've stopped, everyone says that. We blame ourselves for not bein' more strict about the street crossin'. So we're at fault for not helpin' 'im take care of himself."

At that moment Phil came to the porch door with the guitar. Joel wasn't sure the conversation should end. Rolly went to Phil. Phil had that quality, to draw people to him and it turned out the boy'd had "a old beat up gee-tar" of his own.

I know you his manner seemed to say, but he turned to Joel and said: "Thanks heaps, sir, fer talkin' tuh me. I'll try tuh go on and fergit the best I kin, and not let it git me down, which it nearly wuz. Mama was right. Yer a fair man."

Joel felt he meant it and he left the boys alone. Soon they were in the front room having a session. Joel listened awhile and went on to the woodpile to split wood for the cook stove. Later he told Audrey that he thought Phil played better than Rolly, but maybe such would help the lad. And help he needed. Perhaps there was healing in music. Joel realized a weight had lifted. He hoped the boy would mourn and regret with themselves, but nothing more. Nothing would bring K.C. back, no matter how sorrowful they were, regretted their own shortcomings or wished it had never happened.

A few months later they learned, in a round about way, that a few weeks after talking to Joel he had enlisted in the army. Whether with guilt feelings, or a mature man they were not told. Indeed who could say—who knew?

CHAPTER 32

"Let's be up and at it," Joel said, as he arose from the breakfast table. He spoke to the boys who also seemed ready to leave the table. It meant they would cut wood that day.

It was Saturday. The two boys had hoped they would have little to do. Phil was not out of school yet and wood cutting on Saturdays was to him an affront, even as he knew it was necessary.

Shandol and her mother would be busy cleaning house, Shandol's job, while Audrey cooked, including baking bread.

Ardena and her mother came to visit in the afternoon. Glenna, as she preferred to be called, rather than Mrs. Ruleton, sat in the rocking chair holding Karen. Because of her bad foot she was afraid to carry her, but she could "nuss" her in the rocking chair. The word "nuss" meaning simply rocking, had at first shocked Shandol. She thought the correct word was nurse and meant breast feeding. But there were certain words she had heard only here and that was another one. Most older women used it, younger ones sniggering.

Shandol and Ardena talked about strawberry picking time and when it would really start. They decided to try as they could make some money of their own.

"Now, I ain't done much of anything like it before," Ardena admitted. "I may be awful at it. Yuh know, slow and awkward."

"Don't worry," Shandol told her. "We'll just do what we're told. I've picked some in our patch but it won't be the same pickin' for someone else. These are big patches and need pickers, so why not us?"

"Wonder what Mom would say to it," Ardena mused.

Shandol knew her mother wouldn't mind and doubted Glenna would. Shandol had picked strawberries and she supposed this year would be no different, if she stayed at home. She kept hoping she would be able to find a job somewhere, doing something to help out rather than a drain on a low family income. It was her own private thought. She was not made to feel anxious about it, she just felt she was old enough.

Ardena was visibly disappointed that Phil would not be picking. "He'd be a help tuh me," she explained. "He already gives me nerve enough tuh try."

"Well school's not out until the twenty-first of this month," Shandol told her. "Maybe he's already told yuh. They go on a picnic the last day too, I understand."

Dean came Saturday night and they went to the movie at Waiton. Shandol had long since learned to enjoy the cowboy shows and also enjoy the singing of Gene Autry and Roy Rogers, especially. And because it was a double feature there was the bonus of a love, adventure or detective show which she also liked. Shandol was sure she would always remember the Saturday night movies, going with Dean Leonard, all her life. Because she had enjoyed it; even the aroma in the car of her chewing gum mingling with his cigarette smoke would stay with her.

Dean also came on Sunday and Shandol went out with him. They saw their friends briefly and Shandol talked to everyone or anyone about picking strawberries this week, the first time for her.

"Oh, don't get bored with me," she once admonished Dean. "I'm a little nervous about it as I've never worked at that before, so I just have it on my mind is all."

"Don't be a-scared of 'em, they ain't a-gonna bite," he teased.

Ardena came early Wednesday morning to go to the patch. There were others besides themselves, which was just as well as they scarcely knew the way. They walked the almost three miles and still arrived at the patch early.

Shandol learned she was a good picker, and could, as they were admonished, "take care of the vines." When they first arrived the few low weeds and berry plants were still wet with dew. There were several other pickers as the patch was large and they picked only the ripe ones. There were still green ones and even blossoms left. There was also another patch some distance away almost as large and separate from this.

The berries grew on a farm owned and operated by immigrants from Germany. Industrious and always busy people, which they no doubt had to be, to make the Ozark farm pay for itself. They had first come to the United States and gone to the city. They were now getting up in years, but they had a large family and they had somehow decided to leave the large city to buy land in this area. They had not only bought land but also built houses and made improvements and made a living off the poor rocky soil.

There were two young women whose husbands worked in city jobs now in some type manufacturing plant. One was in Chicago and one in Detroit. They had their own farms and worked as men to keep them in shape. They dressed like men usually, and were seen in Greenway either walking, riding horseback or in an oldish red pickup truck. They were large-boned, muscled, with frizzy short dark hair. Though they were not ugly, their faces were not fine featured but somewhat manly. One had a blond-haired son who would go to school in

Greenway next year. They all spoke with the German accent.

There was a young man at home with his parents and a great help to them. He hauled the berries in crates from the patch to the house in the truck. There was also a younger boy who helped in the patch.

The older girls helped in that they kept track of the pickers and numbers of boxes, which were quart size, each picked. The pickers were paid by the number of boxes they picked, at so much each.

There were other children Shandol did not know. Some were perhaps members of the family; others neighbors or picker's children. There was a heavy-set woman Shandol knew on sight who had children there. Even while they kept busy picking there was also visiting. Shandol preferred to keep busy. She and Ardena picked close most of the time.

Outside of being startled by an occasional shriek of "snake!"— usually false and to frighten everyone as a gag, everything went peaceably and smoothly. The children were kept out of the patches, though they sometimes "forgot." And actually they saw only one small ground snake which was promptly stoned to death.

There was friendly competition as to who would get the most boxes, but Shandol had no intention of trying to race because of the vines. The large woman, who was constantly brushing at her sweaty forehead and unruly hair in her face, was fast but she was cautioned several times to be more careful of the vines.

The mosquitoes were bad, as the day wore on. There were also chiggers and ticks, but they made their presence felt later.

Shandol and Ardena worked two days. Joel worked at a cemetery one day for the Allsup family—three of the brothers were active in The Church. But he, too, picked berries the balance of the week.

They were taken back to Greenway by the young man, who drove the red pickup. The berries had all been taken to the house and unloaded by the time the pickers pay had been figured up and given to them. They drew their pay each evening, all figured and in cash.

On Friday Ardena and Shandol went to Plainesville for a shopping trip. With money to spend they could hardly wait. Their excuse had been to get something more suitable to wear to pick berries. Skirts and dresses were unhandy and Shandol dared not show up in the old faded overalls she wore to pick blackberries. The boys had none better to spare and besides she couldn't wear what they wore now.

She and Ardena bought identical styles of bib-style overalls of a heavy cotton, resembling denim yet not so heavy, and softer being more feminine. They were a deep rust color trimmed with bias tape of blue and yellow. Two strips of blue trimmed each shoulder strap with a row of yellow between. Around the torso top was a row of each, the blue finishing the edges. The front was high enough to be worn without a blouse, but the back was made quite similar to overalls. So Shandol did not consider that possibility as modest enough. Instead she wore her old standby, the blue satin, long sleeved blouse with hers, and realized she likely would not wear them to the berry patch lest they got torn or stained. Ardena had a yellow blouse to wear with hers, but she planned to wear hers to the berry patch anyway.

There were others picking berries the day the girls were not there, however. But as it would turn out Shandol was not to go back to pick berries anymore—though Ardena did.

The next day was Saturday but Shandol stayed at home to help her mother get the washing and ironing done. Joel and the two older boys went to pick. Lester and Jane came late in the afternoon.

The next day all went to Sunday school except Joel who picked strawberries. Shandol knew everyone would understand why he was not there. They knew he would need the money. They also knew such crops couldn't wait and must be taken care of when the time was right. The same dilemma was faced at fruit harvest time, which some of them knew about. Yet the Sunday school was never closed for any such reason.

Shandol went with Ardena to visit her Sunday school class, which was not the first time for that at the church-in-the-holler. The other was closer, but she knew more people, some relatives, at this church.

Ardena came to see Shandol in the afternoon. She was dressed in the slacks they had bought Friday. Shandol decided to wear hers also, as they had decided to do that afternoon. The yellow blouse looked good on Ardena, Shandol thought. On me it would make me almost olive skinned, though since the school picnic and ride in the truck she had acquired a very even tan. She rarely sunburned, but her nose peeled occasionally. But not that time. She wasn't sure if it had been sun, wind or a combination. But now she supposed it was Ardena's lovely green eyes. The blue satin was a better color for Shandol.

They got tired of just sitting around talking and went for a stroll. Ardena elected to go toward the meadow where a ball game would be in progress, as the boys had already started playing when the weather was fit. Shandol suspected Ardena wanted to go to see Phil. She was not subtle about her crush on him, and cared little who else played, though in this case it was just town boys choosing up sides. There weren't always two full teams but it made for tougher play.

The girls watched the game awhile but then wandered off just walking in the pasture. They discussed boys, dates and their separate backgrounds. They had not gone far when there were yells from the ball grounds for Shandol.

Shandol was surprised as she turned around to see where the call came from. A young boy, Tommy, outside the ball "diamond" was pointing. Then she could see the front-end of an automobile, one she did not recognize, near the three-strand barbed wire fence. She supposed it was Dean with a friend so they started toward the fence, she and Ardena, walking briskly, swinging their clasped hands between them.

Ardena's yellow blouse seemed to deepen the sun's rays while the full sleeves of Shandol's blue blouse, caught the breeze, and made her light hair seem fairer in the sun. The clean strands mirrored the sun to sparkles.

When the girls became near enough to see they saw the occupants were not Dean, but a couple with children in the back seat. She did not recognize them and could not imagine why they would want her in particular. She said so to Ardena. Shandol went to the car window where the woman sat.

"I'm Mrs. Brown," she introduced herself, smiling uncertainly at Shandol's questioning gaze. "I have a job for a girl who can milk. You see my husband here," and she nodded toward the driver of the car, "works in St. Louis and is home only on weekends. This leaves the children and I alone during the week. Besides help with the milking I'd expect someone to be useful around the house.

"Well, I'd like to see what my folks think," Shandol demurred. "Where do yuh live?"

"About six miles up the highway," she replied. "You turn in at a gate just past the county farm houses."

"Oh, yes," Shandol smiled, which changed her face into the pretty girl she was considered to be. "A boy named Brown got on the school bus there."

"My husband's brother and he's in St. Louis too now." she replied nodding her head. "And—uh—we already saw yer folks. They have no objections to your working for us if yuh like. In fact I think your mother is all for it and your dad too. They thought, since I'd like you to start tomorrow, you could ride that far on the school bus. It still comes by there."

"Well, all right," she agreed.

"We had quite a long talk with your parents," Mrs. Brown said. "And I'll expect to see you tomorrow. You and I will be there by ourselves with the three children." She motioned to a blond curly haired girl about three and a brown haired blue eyed boy of five in the back seat and she held a sleeping baby whose bottle had fallen from his mouth to beside him. "My husband will be home on Saturdays and you can be at home on weekends. You can come back on Sunday night or on the bus again Mondays, as you and your folks decide."

"The pay will be five dollars a week and you'll help milk. We have three cows. Help wash and iron, otherwise just helping with usual housework as you probably do at home."

"I see," she affirmed. "And I'll be there in the morning then I suppose. "I'll talk it over with Mama and Daddy."

"They will let you," the lady smiled, "and I hope yuh don't change your mind and I see yuh, because I need someone. Bye now."

They turned around in the unhandy place and drove back the way they had come down the unkempt lane, with the deep grass, weed cluttered, and dodging a few saplings of the former street.

"Now that was fast work," Shandol muttered, but smiling. "Here I've a job all lined up. But milking? I haven't done that in sometime. Oh, well, and I used to feel sorry for the Winsch girls who had to milk. But they had more to do than I will."

"Who told 'em about yuh?" Ardena asked.

"Yuh got me there," Shandol replied. "She didn't say, did she? Maybe they told Mama. Let's go see."

And they started walking that way almost before she finished saying it.

Misgivings began stirring in Shandol's mind as soon as she was alone to think about it. Also there was dread and the sense of inadequacy she always felt when facing something new and different. She almost hoped that at the last minute her mother would change her mind and say she needed her, but she wasn't counting on it. Shandol knew her mother seemed to take for granted she was going to leave home sometime, and she would have to do without her. Besides, with Joel's depleted income sources, it seemed sometimes, Shandol might need the money as Joel could allow her little now. It would be awhile before berry picking time and Joel didn't much like for her to do that anyway.

"It won't hurt to try it," Audrey reasoned. "If yuh decide yuh don't like the people or the work yuh can come back home."

"It isn't somethin' yer startin' that yuh can't get out of simply by quitting," Joel added. "Yuh may get homesick before even the week's out, but I think yuh can make it. If I didn't I'd veto the whole idea."

"Wonder if I should pack?" she asked no one in particular. "Prob'ly won't hurt to start," Audrey replied. "Yuh won't have much time in the morning."

She invited Ardena up to her room to help her decide what to take. She decided she could take what she would need for the one week. Then perhaps she would have an idea of what else, if anything, she would want. She had no idea if she would have a room to herself.

She laid out on the bed what she considered her house dresses, anklets, slips, and other necessities.

"I'm gonna take a better dress in case Dean should come. Wonder what he'll think of the idea."

"Oh, he'll prob'ly be up there," Ardena replied. "I wouldn't doubt that."

"Well, I'll make it clear to Mom that's to be part of it," she replied firmly. "But I see no reason why it will matter to him or Mrs. Brown or Mama."

She didn't question his chances to use it to his own, he hoped, advantage.

CHAPTER 33

—At the Farm—

The next morning Shandol was up early. She ate breakfast with the family quietly and thoughtfully, actually dreading the day. She bade them all a rather stony good-bye lest she burst into tears.

She went to the school bus with Phil and got on ahead of him. She sat down near the front, though he went farther back "so not so many would climb over" him. Shandol was sure it was the same bus, just new faces she noticed as they rode back into the hills over country roads. She felt rather than saw, them staring at her, and except for occasionally looking ahead she stared out the window.

The driver stopped just past the county farm cottages, which were set back from the road with small yards. She could see the red barns on the other side of the highway. After the bus pulled away, she crossed the highway with her flour sack of clothing and few cosmetics. Then she crossed a cattle guard at a wide gateless opening and walked down a long lane to the yellow frame house she could see set back in a grove of pines. The lane to the house was across a meadow and at her right the county farm barns were soon left behind. A wood area seemed to surround the back of the house.

It was all quiet and she wondered if she was too early as she knocked timidly on the front door, though it was after seven o'clock.

The plump, round-faced woman opened the door, her blond curly hair in disarray, almost immediately. Shandol recognized her as the Mrs. Brown of the day before despite her lack of makeup and uncombed hair.

The first remark she made was that she opened the door without delay before the children, who were still sleeping, were awakened by the knocking.

Shandol looked around her as she entered the house. The first impression was of clutter and crowdedness, perhaps because the boy was sleeping on the couch which had been made into a bed. She was shown the baby in the crib in the bedroom, just off the living room to the left, and the tousled-haired small girl, with perfect features, including long dark eyelashes, slept on the full-sized bed in the room. With the chest and dresser it too seemed crowded.

Mrs. Brown combed her snarled, blond hair into some semblance of order, making a face now and then as she tugged at a tangle. Then she invited Shandol to go into the kitchen with her where she went to a wood burning range and began to kindle and build a fire in it.

"Your mother said you are pretty good at about ever'thing about housework except cookin', and you don't like to cook?"

"I'm just not a good hand at it," Shandol told her.

"I can't understand anyone not being a good cook," Mrs. Brown told her. "It just seems to me anyone can learn to cook who can read."

"I don't get much chance to try," Shandol replied. "Dad and Mama are both pretty good cooks, and so when Mama can't cook Dad just does it. Mama always says about teaching me, she had such poor ways that she'd rather I learned to cook right, not always scrimpin'. But I'll be glad to help yuh, if yuh'll tell me what tuh do. It's the responsibility of it I don't really like."

The fire was built and rapidly warming up the stove.

"I'll need you to do this sometime I expect," Mrs. Brown told her. "I'll just sort of go ahead and show you for now. Now we go milk."

She had large buckets and smaller pails to use for the milking, handy, and they set off across the wood lot, which included a pile of ashes on down from it. There was a chicken house and then the barn.

At the barn Shandol was introduced to the four cows. "They're all gentle and easy to milk," she assured Shandol, "except that young black over there. We call her Jenny, but she is a pill."

Shandol had to milk her. She was the test. "If you can milk her *you* can milk," she said.

"Is she dangerous and mean?" Shandol asked, wondering just what she had gotten herself into.

"Oh, no, not really," Mrs. Brown conceded. "She's mostly just fidgety. She'll spill the milk if she can or just put her foot in your bucket. She just can't stay still while she's being milked."

Shandol had never actually milked any but gentle cows, almost family pets, on the farm. And that was sometime ago. But when she was on the farm, from the time she was eight or nine years old she had milked two cows night and morning. She had learned to milk when she was six or seven because of a very gentle cow they had. The children fought to milk her and all sometimes did from both sides, and even behind her.

Somewhat warily now, Shandol took a three-legged stool Mrs. Brown handed to her and sat down to milk, expecting anything and scared and nervous. If only the cow doesn't know, she thought. The cows head was in a stanchion. As she went closer to the cow, she spoke to her so she wouldn't be startled.

"Saw bossy," she soothed, low and in her most coaxing voice. "Saw." She passed her hand over the cows stomach, patted her side and brushed the udder for dirt, in case she had been lying in the hay or barn lot.

She put the milk pail between her knees, half-way wondering if she could hit the bucket, which she kept out of the way. It was all so new to her and she was very nervous. But she started milking determinedly. She braced her left arm against the cow's leg nearest her, and began with the teats nearest her. Maybe, she reasoned, I can control this leg, and when I get one side done I may have a lot of milk in the bucket. But if she kicked or stepped on the other side it would miss her bucket.

But that cow seemed as determined and stubborn to keep that right back leg too far forward. She'd step, sway, stretch forward and fidget. But only managed to splatter the milk. Shandol had made it! She had milked that mischievous heifer, though Shandol was sure the cow had tried to buffalo her. She also realized that although she was a hateful thing, she produced an abundance of milk, and she must be careful now that she not spill the milk, which would be sold, now that she had kept the cow's foot out of it.

Shandol then milked another cow, a gentle jersey and finished in much less time. Her hands were stiff and cramping when she finished, as were her arms, from the use of muscles that hadn't been used so much in sometime.

"I'm glad I don't have to milk anymore right now," Shandol told Mrs. Brown, smiling and flexing her fingers, and in turn, massaging the muscles of her arms. "My, I didn't realize I had so many unused muscles. I'm not used to it but I will, I'm sure."

Mrs. Brown had milked one cow and "stripped" the fourth, after a young calf had been turned in to eat his fill.

As they collected the filled pails of milk and went back to the house they discussed the black heifer Jenny.

"Do yuh think you can manage her now?" Mrs. Brown asked, in concern for them both, Shandol supposed.

"Well, I'll try it awhile," Shandol replied, then added, laughing nervously. "I think I had better trim my fingernails before tonight though. I was so worried that they would cause me to pinch her and get kicked. I had to be so careful!"

"You're prob'ly right," Mrs. Brown agreed. "We'll try it for a week and if we can't manage there's no need to keep on with her."

"I was glad you were close by," she admitted.

Back at the house Mrs. Brown strained the milk into a tall milk can and set it in water to cool. A crockful was saved out for the family's use.

By then it was time to start breakfast. The stove was hot and Mrs. Brown added a few sticks of wood. She prepared scrambled eggs, bacon and toast from the oven, coffee for herself and Shandol, and milk for her children. The two sleepy-eyed children were called to the table. They yawned and rubbed their eyes.

Shandol watched them pick and nibble at the scrambled eggs. They turned down the toast for cereal flakes, which they covered with fresh small strawberries, a thin dark syrup and sweet cream. As Shandol watched them enjoy the fruit and cereal and ask for seconds, she thought of K.C. How he would have loved that! The sad, lonely feeling swept over her. For a moment she thought she might cry and wished with all her heart she were at home again.

Mrs. Brawn noticed her watching the children and thought the longing look in her eyes was for some of the fruit and cereal herself.

"Shandol, try some of the berries and cereal if yuh like. I never thought tuh ask what yuh'd prefer."

Shandol batted her liquid brown eyes, lest they show tears, and smiled. "Yes, thanks, I will," she replied. "But I was really thinking of the little brother I lost not so long ago. I was thinking how he would have loved to eat that too." And she decided the syrup did add a delightful flavor to the already flavorful fruit.

After breakfast they began the day's housework.

"We'll do the dishes and straighten up the house, and then I must show you where your room is so yuh can take care of your clothes. Is that what yuh brought in that sack?" She looked surprised at such a traveling bag.

"Yes," she replied. "I only brought what I thought I'd need for a week, and we have only a large, rather battered old suitcase, which seemed too big to carry so few things. I can make do on these things and I thought next time I'd know more about how it would work out and everything. I hope it's all right."

They picked up the baby's bottles. There were a day's bottles, some already in the kitchen, but others were where they had been left—in the floor, in bed, under the couch. They were put to soak awhile and washed. She prepared the new day's supply to show Shandol. The milk was sterilized, as were the bottles, and a thin cereal, which resembled cream of wheat, was added. When the bottle was empty and dried it made it hard to wash, even with soaking. And the bottles were left to soak while they made the bed and rolled the things on the divan where the boy slept. Shandol made the bed and Mrs. Brown showed her how she expected it to be done.

Shandol had to be shown how to miter the corners over the mattress at the foot of the bed. Shandol had made beds only with feather-ticks on them so knew nothing about mitering corners on mattresses.

Then Mrs. Brown showed Shandol her room upstairs, and told her she could have a few minutes to take care of her things.

Shandol was dumbfounded to see the upstairs of the house. There was a large room, with a large window, so it was light enough, but the floor was completely covered by magazines of at least three feet high, and not in neat stacks at all, though it appeared it had been tried but they had fallen to one side. Shandol wondered what type they were and greedily surveyed the mass of possible reading material. She noted how the futile attempts at stacking them had resulted in the stacks leaning this way and that. It gave the impression of a hopeless mass, and the fact many looked backless suggested they had been handled a lot, perhaps roughly. Backless, she could not identify them except at closer scrutiny which now she hadn't time to do.

The thought of them being a fire hazard caused her heart to beat rapidly and she wondered if she could sleep for worrying about it.

She was led along a narrow hall-like path, which kept her clear of them near the stair railing, that led to a small room to the left as they arrived at the top of the steps. It was scarcely larger than a small bathroom or large closet.

It contained a twin-size bed and a night table. A string to the bare bulb overhead turned on it's only light, and was tied to the bedstead to be handy to find quickly if she needed the light in a hurry.

"I will ring a buzzer to wake you up. Here, I'll show yuh." Mrs. Brown left to go to the foot of the narrow stairway.

So while Shandol hung her dresses on hangers and also nails, Mrs. Brown rang the buzzer so she could recognize it. Some of her things she had to leave in the sack as there were no drawers in the night stand; there was no room for a chest.

Mrs. Brown also showed her a long string over the stair steps, which switched on the bare bulb light over the stair rail side of the steps, so she could see to get to her room. She was told to turn it off as soon as she had turned on her own light.

When they finished this chore, and before they went back to where the children were, Mrs. Brown said, quite seriously: "There's something else I usually tell the girls who work for me." She paused as though to let it soak into Shandol's mind or for emphasis.

"So," she continued, "under no circumstances do I allow anyone to lay a hand on my children. I feel, and pretty strongly, that it is for me to correct them, no one else."

Shandol wondered what had happened for her to make that stipulation. Perhaps someone had slapped one of them.

"B-but the thought hadn't even entered my mind," she replied defensively, and it was true. "I know I'm not here to take over your family—only to do the work yuh ask of me."

As they cleaned the large uncrowded kitchen, Mrs. Brown explained that the rounded front glassed in china cabinet was her pride and joy.

"The last girl who worked here before you, lost the key to it," Mrs. Brown explained, as though the girl had mistreated one of the children. "We found it in the ashes, where the trash had been burned. So I'd appreciate it if yuh'd take care not to repeat that."

"I'm glad you told me," Shandol replied. "I sure hope I don't do such a thing and more so since it means so much to you." She wondered how she had kept the children from breaking a glass accidentally at play or scuffling over something.

An electric refrigerator was the one real convenience. The water was pumped from the well just outside in an enclosed back porch. The stove was a smaller version of the large wood burning cook stove Shandol was used to at home; and she recalled how much space it took compared to this one. The kitchen was large, with no built-in cabinets, but free standing as those they had at home.

After the house had been gone over to Mrs. Brown's satisfaction it did look transformed and now neat and tidy, the living room quite respectable. Next came the baby's bath and he was put in his bed for a nap.

By this time, as the work had gone slowly, due to Mrs. Brown's showing Shandol how she wanted things done and they had actually made the bed three or four times to be sure Shandol could suit her, it was time to think of lunch.

Lunch consisted of a few fresh vegetables, lettuce and radishes, canned peas, potatoes, meat chops, gravy, and strawberries and cream completed it. Supper would be leftovers.

After they ate and the kitchen in order once more, they went to the small garden strawberry patch to pick more strawberries. It was not a large patch but seemed to supply them with what they could use. They ate some, Shandol also ate a few luscious ripe ones, but the boy who was called Rodney, ate several. At lunch he said his name was Basil Rodney just as his father, but he was called Rodney so they would not be getting them mixed up.

Shandol had, of course, learned the children's names by then, as they gabbed and picked strawberries. Then realized she had forgotten them, but believed she would remember them now. The little girl was Joyce and a sweeter child could hardly have been wanted. The nine-month old infant, who was in a baby carriage "for the fresh air" was Brent.

As the day wore on Shandol realized she was expected to do most of the work, except cook and care for the baby's bottles, though she washed them before they were sterilized. She had also come to another conclusion: Rodney was also his mother's absolute pride and joy. She saw him only as perfect. Shandol simply could not understand why she would forbid any correction of them. How that boy needed teaching a few things. She would like to see him in the hands of her father for a short while!

He nearly teased his little sister, two years younger than his five years, to death. He pushed, interrupted and bothered Shandol, sometimes deliberately undoing what she had done so she had to do it over again. He wanted to be played with, especially pulled in his wagon. Shandol was quite put-out with him. His mother, though she could surely take it all in, said nothing. Shandol decided he was a spoiled brat, but she kept the opinion to herself. All she did when he misbehaved was to threaten to tell his mother, which had little impression. It certainly had no effect.

Joyce, on the other hand, was a pretty little blond with curly hair, fair features and violet-blue eyes. The baby was good and unless uncomfortable or hungry played or seemed content. He was either in his bed, put on a quilt on the floor, which he could now manage to get off of easily; or sit in a swing hanging in a stand. Once a day, if weather permitted he was bundled up and taken outside in the fresh air in the yard. Shandol sometimes held him for the sheer joy of it and missing her sister at home. He was not spoiled and demanding of attention.

The day had been a full one for Shandol and time had gone quickly. She was learning the ways of a new household and her part in it. There was getting acquainted with the new family, their own ways which made them uniquely themselves.

When it became time for bed, Shandol felt the outsider, and alone. Mrs. Brown made up the boy's bed on the couch. It seemed the signal of bedtime. Then she dreaded going up stairs alone. How lonely it felt to know there was no one else through the door across the hall.

The huge pines outside in the quiet moaned in the wind, whistled and creaked, as their branches rubbed together or against something, perhaps the roof.

Shandol fought tears of homesickness as she pulled the string at the stairwell for the light in the large room, which also lit her way. She went into her small cubby-hole bedroom and turned on the light, then remembered to pull out the other light. She felt lonely and discarded by her family, both at home and the one below. She felt the lowly servant in an attic room. She sniffed, brushed at her eyes determinedly and settled in the firmly soft bed. She realized she was tired; and that milking that cow twice a day was to be a drain on her emotionally, but she soon slept.

403

The buzzer sounded the next morning, and Shandol considered it a novelty, though startling when one was sound asleep; it was effective. She got up immediately. Mrs. Brown was again building the fire in the cook stove. Shandol supposed if she ever had to build a fire it would be for some other meal or another week? As it warmed they again want to milk.

As the weekly chores and days progressed, the time seemed to go rapidly. More so than she had supposed anyway. In fact, she began to think it was such short intervals between milkings! She dreaded the black heifer, because it was such a chore to milk her and Shandol felt so responsible. That was new to her. But she had to keep the cow's foot out of the milk, dodging her almost constant movements and busy tail. Outside of that and the mischievous boy, she decided it was not a hard or undesirable job.

It was on wash day Shandol learned Rodney's weakness. It was midweek. He had pulled his wagon through the clean clothing on the line, when she had pleaded with him not to do it. He even dumped one basketfull she was preparing to hang, which had to be re-rinsed. He wanted her to pull him in the wagon and was showing his displeasure at not getting his way. But Shandol was doing the family wash and knew she did not have the time then. Still he did not let up. He continued to torment her to play with him. His mother said nothing. She merely put the baby outside in his buggy as they were in and out to see to him.

When the wash was finally done and lunch over, there was a lull in what was to be done until time to gather the clothes before suppertime. The baby was taking a nap and Shandol was glad to sit down to rest.

But then Rodney came up to her with a handful of comic books and wanted her to read to him.

"Read to you?" she asked, unable to keep exasperation from her voice. "With all that extra work you caused me? Rewashing already clean clothes and bothering me when I tried to hang them out? Rodney, I'm much too tired. But if you'll be a good boy for me, then I won't get so tired and I'll read to you."

"Promise?" he asked, looking at her skeptically.

"I promise," she replied, and wondered how the girls before had handled him.

Thus she learned to reward him to mind her. And she did read to him, whatever he asked, at anytime she had to spare. She read comic books, child's storybooks and stories from books. It was boring at times, because at times, he would want to hear what he liked over and over. It was worth the effort, however. She took the time because she had promised and it also made a change in him. His mother remarked about it approvingly, and soon after asked Shandol to call her Sybil.

Though Mrs. Brown had the car, the only place they went was to the mailbox, perhaps a half-mile away. It was not at the highway near their driveway but east on the highway to a corner, Shandol supposed at least a quarter of a mile. It was a brief ride but the children looked forward to it. Sybil did not consider it necessary to go everyday.

The first company Shandol had was Cal, who came Tuesday evening, a cool rainy one, but he asked her to go for a ride. Shandol was glad to see him and went. They went to Plainesville, ate a sandwich with soda pop. Cal had also gone to pick up a friend, which he did after that and they started home. She thought it even nice riding in the rain. It was hardly more than nine o'clock when she was let out at Mrs. Brown's. They did visit briefly in the car and sitting on the porch swing, but that was all. Cal hated to keep his friend waiting. He had introduced him as Mel Sandler, a cousin to Rod and Bucky; he lived west of Greenway. Shandol did not worry what Dean would say, though she knew he would find out and very likely say plenty. Shandol could hardly believe she had only been away from home two days. It seemed like a week. She could hardly believe it as time seemed to go so quickly each day.

Dean came Wednesday, which was the day they did the laundry. It was a reasonably pretty day. Dean, however was in a wretched mood and Shandol was tired.

Dean's mood was the result of his having had time to think about Shandol's job. She had explained on their Sunday night date that she aimed to try it. And he lost little time in letting her know what he had decided. That being he could see no reason to it.

They went to a movie but it failed to help his mood. Before he took her back to Mrs. Brown's he tried to reason with her.

"If yuh have tuh do housework and milkin'," he pleaded, "why not your own home with yuh husbin'?"

"Yuh know you do have uh point there," she replied, thoughtfully. "But the thing is I can quit this. My own, and yours, I suppose you mean, I couldn't quit. There I'd be. And I'm not sure about that forever commitment yet. Oh, I wish I could make you see."

"But you—I'd not want yuh to quit," he replied, sweetly. They were parked at the roadside just before the turn into Mrs. Brown's driveway.

"I really must go," Shandol told him. "I don't know what Mrs. Brown will say if I stay out too late. She might not let me inside, or I can't even get her up!"

"Somethin' else," he remarked, "I don't want you goin' out with nobody but me, hear? Oh, I heared about yer goin' ridin' with Cal. I thought I made it clear to 'im."

Shandol could see he was furious. He kissed her possessively and grumbled, "I cain't share yuh with nobody."

"But I only rode to Plainesville and back with 'im. We ate a sandwich and had soda pop. He had some friend tuh pick up—a cousin to Sandler boys. He aimed tuh take him on home. We weren't gone long and I was glad to see a familiar face. Just a friendly car ride."

It was nearly midnight when Shandol got into the house. Shandol missed her sleep next day, and seemed less energetic. She was disgruntled at Dean.

She explained to Mrs. Brown why she had been late. That her boyfriend pointed out if she aimed to do this kind of work it might as well be in her own home.

"But I can't make up my mind if I'm ready or not, so I tell him I need time to be sure, which makes him angry so we quarrel. Sometimes I wonder why he puts up with me, so I suppose he cares. After the movie we had a bit to eat as usual and then the discussion. Time gets away—" She paused, wondering if Mrs. Brown wanted to know or believed her.

"Yuh know," she said, looking at Shandol in approval, "yuh're right tuh wait until you're sure. Yuh are still plenty young. How old's he?"

"Just a few months older than I am," she replied, "but he has older ways or something, in some cases. He's been around more, yuh know what I mean? But I've been kept pretty close tuh home, chaperoned and goin' tuh school. I don't know what I do want yet. I hope tuh get married sometime—but I feel if he's right for me I'll know—in time anyway. Well, better get up and at it. Whatta we do today?"

"We're goin' to paint the woodwork," she told Shandol. "Not only the baseboards around the rooms, but the floors around the rugs as well, We do this and the bedroom today."

There had been a new linoleum put down in the living room she had noticed. And Sybil had told Shandol they planned some new decorating as part of spring house cleaning.

"Have yuh ever done any paintin'?" she asked Shandol, who shook her head negatively.

"No, we've not done much paintin', and besides the boys and Dad would do it. I helped put up wallpaper once, dabbing paste. Mama's good at that but we didn't paint a thing."

"Well, my husband washed it for me last weekend," she said, "so there won't be that delay. We'll just have tuh dust it all including the floors. Yuh can do that, I guess. And perhaps, with my help, yuh can paint some. I want tuh get it done. I haven't done a lot of paintin' myself, but we'll get it done."

They moved furniture to the middle of the rooms, on the rugs and started. It was quite a job for two inexperienced women. Lunch consisted of cereal, fruit and a sandwich.

The children wanted to help, but Rodney she gave the job of helping with the baby and helping to amuse his sister. She bribed him by promising they would go to town on Saturday while their daddy was there and they could get whatever they wanted.

They were finished by night and had a late supper after milking. So with the smell of wet paint over everything else they went to bed early, hoping the next day it would be dry.

However, it didn't dry overnight and Sybil was surprised and vexed that she couldn't get on with straightening up for the weekend when her husband would be home. It left her not knowing what to do but wait for it to dry. She tried opening the doors and windows but decided it was too cool for the baby. It had been a cool month anyway.

Shandol spent a lot of time reading to Rodney, as there was not much to do but what housework they could manage. She also spent time with the boy outside pulling him in the wagon, just riding around. She got quite bored with it and was always glad when Sybil called her for something to be done, such as putting the baby to sleep. It seemed with things different and crowded he was more demanding and often had to be rocked to sleep. She was glad when the day was over.

Dean came that night. Though they only went to Plainesville to eat and spent time talking she got home at a more decent hour. He took her home to spend the weekend with her family, as had been the arrangement.

"That you, Sis?" Joel called. "Th' door's not locked."

"Yeah," she answered. "I'll be fine, Dad. I'll just see yuh in th' mornin' I guess, huh?"

The week hardly seemed gone, but seemed ages to her. She wondered if they would ask about her week and wonder what she had done. She knew she wondered what they had done.

She washed her face as usual, got matches from the dispenser, as was her habit, and climbed the stairs in the dark to her own room. As she sank down in her soft featherbed she realized how good it was to be in her own bed.

The next day she chatted and babbled on about what she had done and about the family to anyone who would listen. She in turn wondered what the week at home had been like and the answers to her questions she considered short, to the point and inadequate. It was so piecemeal she only had a vague idea of what had gone on and felt she wasn't told all she wanted to hear. She wanted to know about *everything*.

She didn't go deliberately to her mother's diary. She hadn't thought of it but she did pick it up off the floor where she had accidentally knocked it off the tea table not ever realizing what it was until she looked. She idly flipped through its pages, bringing her mother to her mind as she recalled her mother had always kept a diary as long as she could remember. Then, as she glanced through the small book, as though fascinated and forgetting to put it down, saw what her family had done in the brief lines her mother put down in the yearly space of the "five year diary."

It seemed to have been a busy week. More garden had been plowed and beans planted. This was one day after they had gone berry picking. They had had to return home as there weren't enough berries for too many pickers.

On Tuesday they had gone to Plainesville with John Ballen. It was "relief" day. They sold rags and papers. They tried to see if Joel qualified for help with the younger children from the State. No answer. It had rained as Shandol knew and Bobby got new shoes. "Cool," Audrey had added.

The next day, Tuesday, there had been too much rain to pick strawberries, but Audrey had taken the two younger children to see Lester and Jane. They had ridden the school bus. They bought a grass hook in town and used it.

Thursday was the last day of school for Phil and he was on that picnic. The washing and ironing was done and there had been a shower of rain in the morning hours.

As so, their week had gone picking berries and other outside work. Audrey washed for the baby between times. She always thought it best not to let it pile up, as well as the fact it was necessary sometimes. Apparently Karen had been a good baby.

Sunday morning Shandol slept late again. No one had awakened her. She had barely been up long enough to have breakfast, help with the dishes, as Audrey would also, give Karen her daily bath, when Dean came. He was early. It was barely eleven o'clock.

"I want tuh spend time with yuh, " he explained. "If yuh'll get ready we'll drive around awhile."

As she hurriedly did so she hoped her mother might object and ask her to stay awhile there, at least eat dinner with them, but perhaps she supposed it was no use. Or perhaps it was Shandol's place to do it, but she couldn't face a disagreement with him now. She knew it would be awhile before they would eat dinner, so she went.

That night she went back to Mrs. Brown's after her date. It was rather late, and Shandol was unsure how Mrs. Brown felt about such late hours. In fact she might have to go back home as she might not be able to get in. She wondered why he acted so. He didn't seem at all worried.

Did he know her parents had wondered and worried about her after all? They had asked her to stay at home? That Audrey hadn't realized how much she would miss her?

"But I didn't bring everything home," she had pointed out. "I'd have to go get them anyway so I'll try it another week and then we'll see."

It had been good visiting at home. Mrs. Brown had paid her on Friday and she had stashed away her pay.

The week, Shandol supposed, would be much like last week, but then found some changes had been made. First of all the black heifer was gone! In fact, all four cows were! She'd not have to milk. What a relief! She was somewhat hurt and disappointed at first that they had decided she couldn't handle her, but relief outweighed it.

"A man has been wanting to keep the cows for the milk," Mrs. Brown explained. "He'll provide us with the milk we need and sell the rest. He has several cattle of his own anyway."

Mr. Brown decided to take the offer. He knew his wife would not go near the black heifer, she was so scared of her. Yet he knew she felt the responsibility while he was away. Mrs. Brown had explained how small and defenseless Shandol had looked beside her and they decided they couldn't take the risk of her getting hurt.

Mrs. Brown explained it all to Shandol with obvious relief. "Yet she's such a good milker we hate to get rid of her just yet. We hope in time she will be more settled."

Shandol was not sorry she was gone. It would make her stay seem almost enjoyable, though they would delete two dollars a week from her five dollars a week pay. There was still work to be done, and she knew Mrs. Brown, with no real close neighbors, was glad of her company.

Shandol looked around her. A fire was already made and heating so they had talked; now warm enough to start breakfast. Mrs. Brown prepared scrambled eggs, oatmeal, toast and coffee. She had not rung the buzzer quite so early as there was no milking to be done.

As Shandol's eyes took in the disorder still evident, only more so, she was sure, Mrs. Brown explained it.

"That paint's not dry yet," she said, with an audible sigh; meaning the woodwork they had painted last Thursday. "I'm so disappointed," she went on. "I had supposed it'd dry practically overnight, but even now it's still sticky. I'm really put-out by it. My husband says I must have used linseed oil to mix it instead of turpentine for inside. He says it will finally get dry, but it's sure a nuisance not to be able to straighten things around."

Shandol noticed and commented on the new furniture which had been delivered while she was gone. There was a new divan and chair for the living room and a daybed for Rodney, who had slept on the old couch.

"We went to town Saturday and got it," Rodney was first to explain.

"It'll be a nice lookin' room when th' straightenin' up is done." Shandol agreed.

But the sticky paint was delaying that. The room was large and there would be enough room when everything wasn't left in the middle of the room, with just ample walkways. It was all on the new linoleum which was put down and still protected by newspapers as when they had painted.

That night Dean came. He kept her out late. Shandol pleaded with him, but it was no use, even to pout. Then it came to her that despite Dean's bluster and show her father had been the factor in her getting home at a reasonable hour after her dates with Dean. Here, he felt, it was just her by herself and he didn't have to take her home until he was ready.

He must have been afraid of Dad after all, she thought. At least he had avoided any confrontation. Shandol resented the thought yet didn't know what she could do about it.

"You always took me home at a reasonable hour," she stormed at him, "when I was at home. You were afraid of Dad!" It was an accusation. "So you're not so brave after all."

He tried to kiss her, she refused to respond. He must have felt the prick to his pride, as he bit her mouth. "Ouch!" Shandol jumped, dumbfounded. "That hurt," she pouted. "I'm only thinkin' you'll get us talked about, Mrs. Brown, too."

"I only want us together," he said, "but sorry to hurt yuh. Oh, I wish yuh had tuh marry me!"

"Dean," she exclaimed, horrified. "My stars, what a thing to say. I sure don't. You're impossible."

"I knowed what yuh'd say," he nodded. "But it's a idea and it ain't no new one neither."

"Here I thought it was girls who made such—such terrible gambles to get a guy tuh marry 'em," Shandol taunted. "Anyway they sometimes lose. I have not made up my mind yet, Dean, about marriage. Can't

I please make yuh see? If I won't one way, why should I another? You—you,—you take me home now or I'll never even go out with you again, that I promise."

Shandol was frightened, but she hoped it didn't show. He was so different now, so determined or something. Why?

Were they reaching a dead end again where he'd make the same ultimatum? Surely he knew that didn't work. She was becoming confused, and more undecided than ever. The impatience of him. Did she really know him after all?

She arrived at Mrs. Brown's at one-thirty. It was so terribly late for just a car ride, Shandol thought, and wondered what Mrs. Brown must think. She was actually disappointed in Dean. She had supposed Dean would want to protect her more than that—even her reputation. She was so overwrought she was almost in tears when Mrs. Brown let her in. She managed to murmur sheepishly, "Thank you," and went on to her room. Mrs. Brown said nothing.

It was brought up the next day, however.

"You'll get us all talked about," Mrs. Brown reminded her. "And you came well recommended, too."

"I think Dean is just throwin' his weight around," Shandol replied. "And I agree with you. At home Dad always insisted I be in at a decent hour and I had no trouble with him. But up here I guess he thinks Dad won't know and that makes him boss. We had a spat. In fact we quarreled and I don't see why we stayed out so late just for that. I'm not sure what I can do about it. It seems so childish to threaten to tell Dad."

She couldn't confide further to Mrs. Brown about his impatience for them to get married. Not yet anyway. Shandol decided Dean was acting like a child pouting because he couldn't have his way and was frustrated. Shandol felt a maternal urge to smile, and as the smile flickered she saw Mrs. Brown was studying her face.

"He's just the willful sort," she added quickly, "and I guess I'd better have an understanding with 'im before I go out anymore." She turned away thoughtfully.

But she felt exhausted all day. She had had little sleep and the emotional drain made her tense, even after she went to bed that night. *Have to get married* kept going through her mind. Oh, how could he? Her father would be horrified and exceedingly angry, she knew. She was seriously wondering if they shouldn't split up before she did finally drift into marriage, because there seemed little else for her to do now.

But it did little to settle things in her mind. Oh, how she needed to get farther away from him to see if it would help her make up her mind. But how on earth could she manage that? She had finally drifted into uneasy sleep from sheer exhaustion of mind and body.

She wondered how she would manage the next day. Perhaps she could take a nap later in the day—even if she had to read to Rodney to give her a few minutes of peace. She could promise to read more after supper. The sleep she had had seemed not restful or sufficient. She tackled the morning chores determinedly. There was the housework, baby bottles and straightening up. Then they went to pick strawberries again from the garden patch. The morning passed quickly.

But she was not to take a nap in the afternoon. Not that she even wanted to, as it turned out. Audrey and Mrs. Bright came by in the early afternoon and asked her to go to Plainesville. Mrs. Bright had heard of a camp for girls the government provided, where they worked for their keep, yet there were classes in a number of subjects, including, she was told, shorthand and typing. Mrs. Bright suggested they look into it. And here was Shandol's chance to leave Greenway—maybe. That became the highlight of the trip for her, not just the getting away for a few hours.

Shandol had never heard of the National Youth Administration camps before. It seemed her mother had, but that was about all. She had never thought of them in connection with her daughter, at least. They apparently weren't as numerous as the CCC's had been, and that there were some for girls was really something for Shandol to contemplate.

Actually, NYA had helped Shandol through high school, somewhat. But because she rode the bus she couldn't get in the hours some other students had. In fact some had been able to get it who hadn't really needed it as badly as she had. It hadn't seemed fair, but the school seemed to favor the town students. There had been no actual issue made of it until it was learned the principal's daughter had been given one of the best paying jobs! It had caused quite a stir and she was immediately taken off. But not until she had drawn it for a whole year; taking it away from someone else who needed it much more than she possibly could have: Perhaps looking down her nose at them, yet it was not her nature to be snobbish. She had many friends.

As Shandol learned about the things offered at the camp where she'd go, she wished she had heard of it before. She knew her parents would hate for her to leave home. They probably don't like the idea much, but she supposed because of Dean they were encouraging. They just didn't consider him a suitable prospect for her husband. He was young yet, but was so sure he knew what he wanted.

412

Perhaps they have heard he's been keeping me out late, she thought. *Mrs. Brown may even have told them about her in the first place. Perhaps it had been Mrs. Bright.* And Shandol knew what her father thought about girls being out late. He had made that clear enough times.

"There's just no decent place for a girl to be after midnight," he had told her. But since the New Year's Eve party he had amended, "except in specific cases—maybe."

Shandol sometimes felt her mother knew the stress she had been under lately and Audrey was sure Dean was pressing Shandol to get married. She knew her parents worried she might just get married to get away, hoping to settle down, and especially if she had nothing better to which she could look forward.

Audrey guessed her mind see-sawed in turmoil and Shandol was left uncertain and dangling on loose ends.

When she signed up to go the camp she learned there would be a station wagon, which came from the camp to pick up any girls who signed up, early in June. And "early June" was just around the corner. She was told perhaps the fourth. That would give her time to get ready to go.

Later that day she and her mother shopped. Audrey purchased much needed shoes for Tommy. But they mostly just looked and "finger shopped" while Mrs. Bright attended to her own affairs, whatever they were. When they became tired they went to Meyer's hardware store's waiting room to wait.

Audrey and Shandol discussed the latter's going to camp. "There's nothing compulsory about staying there any length of time, even though you're signed up," Audrey reassured her.

"I wonder what Dean will say?" she wondered aloud and realized she had not considered him before about that. Just being away from Greenway. "Guess it's too late for him to say or do much of anything. I've signed up."

"Let him stew," Audrey agreed. "Don't worry about it." She looked at her daughter. "If he really cares he'll wait. He'd want choo to be sure if he's the right one for yuh. I think this may be to the good. You can get away from his influence and take your time about making up your mind. Marriage is for a long time—" She sighed.

"I must plan what tuh take and if I have enough clothes and good enough to wear "

"Just remember what I'm sayin," Audrey said.

Shandol, who would now prefer a nap to a sermon, realized the excitement was wearing down and she was tired—but probably too excited to really sleep.

"Mama, please, no preachin'," she grinned, however. "And here in public besides? I know whatcha mean."

Just let me make up my own mind, she wanted to scream. *Just give me peace now to think, to plan and reason.*

"You must tell Mrs. Brown as soon as you can," Audrey reminded her.

"Yeah, and I'm gonna dread that," she agreed. "She's been pretty good tuh me." *I also have to tell Dean too,* she thought, but said nothing.

Shandol told Sybil her new plans the next day. She found it harder to broach the subject than she had thought. It made her feel she was letting Sybil down. Yet, with the cows gone, she sometimes felt she wasn't needed very much, except for company. It occurred to her then how little company Sybil really had, and how little she went to see any of her neighbors. Perhaps the distance between the farms made it unhandy. And farmers, in most seasons, were busy. Also, as her husband was gone all week, few neighbors cared to stop by. She did not know if they had company weekends or not.

Shandol explained the trip to town, the camp she had heard about and even mentioned the fact she hoped to improve her typing and shorthand skills so she could get a job doing that kind of work. She hoped Sybil would understand.

"This may give me a chance for a real job," she exclaimed, brightening. "I've liked it here and you have been swell to me, but it is not what I want to do all the time. I mean it isn't what I went to high school to prepare for, and besides, I could help at home that way. This way I'm just one less mouth to feed, so to speak. You understand?"

"Shore," Sybil replied, heartily. "But you know we're gonna miss yuh around here." She smiled warmly. "But I can't blame you at all. And don't worry about it. Now that there are no cows to milk it will be easier to find someone else if I decide to. And I'm not sure about it yet. I wish yuh luck."

"I'll prob'ly need it," she replied. "Thanks. But as Mama told me there's nothing compulsory about it. If I don't like it, or just want to come back home, I can. Because we only know what we've heard about it."

"What's the boyfriend gonna say?" she teased.

"Oh, him," Shandol sighed. "I really don't know. He'll prob'ly be against it—maybe surprised and stunned that I even want to go. But I feel it's simply the only chance I'll have to see what I want. I'd really like to work awhile before I get married, and settle down, just for the experience I guess. He may can't see that, but he'll have to accept it, that's all."

It was breakfast time for the children then so the subject was left there. Shandol then tried to go on with the work as though there were no other plans in the offering.

The children were told later, however. Rodney was terribly disappointed and became emotional about it.

"I don't know who'll read tuh me," he moaned.

"Maybe your mama can sometimes, if yuh help her get things done and help with the baby and things. She won't be so tired." Shandol soothed. "Or there might be someone else come to take my place if your mother can't do it all. How's zat?"

Shandol tousled his blond hair so like his mother's and realized she rather liked him. He was just a boy, trying to be the man of the place, yet needing attention too. But when she read to him he was himself and reminded her of K.C. The thought was a stabbing hurt sometimes at the loss of K.C. And it must be worse, she supposed, for those at home where there were more reminders. But when Rodney was read to he was likeable because he chose to be.

Dean kept his midweek date, as Shandol supposed he would, yet dreaded that too. She couldn't prepare herself for his reaction because she wasn't sure what it would be. Perhaps he would be glad she would have a chance to be away to make up her mind. He would be disappointed, she was sure, as she would be disappointed if he didn't worry about her going, somewhat. However, she could assure him there were rules and regulations and the girls must meet standards or they would be punished with extra work or someway—perhaps kicked out.

But she was not prepared for the fury he showed at his first reaction. He had planned to take her to a movie, but as they drove along to Plainesville Shandol started to talk about it. She supposed she might as well get it off her mind as he would have to know sooner or later.

As she talked he decided they must just go somewhere and discuss it. He was so hurt, Shandol saw. She was surprised that he would show it. Also it showed how furious he was, but she saw he was trying to hold his emotions in check.

"Tell me," he said forlornly, "how kin yuh wanna go? Why? We orter git married I tell yuh. Yer not gittin' any younger, yuh know."

"Or wiser either," she hedged and added. "I don't know why but I feel I've got to get out somewhere. I feel I'm missin' somethin'. This small existence, except for school, is all I know. It's not enough. As long as I feel like that I won't be satisfied with you or anybody—includin' myself. It's somethin' I wanna do before I settled down. You don't understand because you can go, if it's nowhere but a sale or drivin' a truck load uh hogs. Yuh see people, sights. But I've done nothing. *Nothing.* So—" she mused almost to herself. "I feel I'm missin' out on life itself. And I need tuh know how, why or just how I could be otherwise. Not this nothing. *Nothing!*" She exclaimed the last word, emotionally.

"Is that what high school did to yuh?" he asked, taunting her. "Jest makin' yuh so's yuh cain't be happy doin' what women is supposed tuh do—marry, have kids and keep house."

"Don't blame goin' to high school," she retorted, her voice raised. "Women are people with feelin's. I know what you think I'm supposed tuh do. I don't expect it tuh be an always thing. It may turn out it's not what I'll want tuh do after all, tuh be satisfied. I realize it and I wish you would. But I don't want to have tuh do it just because that's the only thing there is, when it ain't. I don't know. I don't know, yuh hear? I wanna find out!"

"When yuh git tuh be a old maid," he taunted, "then yuh'll 'preciate what yuh've missed and intended tuh be."

"It's no use talking," she replied. "I'm already signed up. I'm goin'. I promised Mama I'd not get married yet, that should give yuh some comfort anyway. She says I'm much too inexperienced where men are concerned to know what I want. She's sure going away will help me see objectively," if he knows what that is, she thought. "She and Dad want me tuh go, because we are supervised, which helps set their minds at ease. I can come back whenever I like. It may be a week—a month or longer, they've told me that. And I actually can hardly wait!"

"Please don't go," he begged. "What'll I do without yuh? And all you're doin' is what Mama wants—what Mama says! What about me? What about us? Shandol, lissen to me fer this once."

She sat silent for awhile thoughtfully. He thought perhaps she was considering and was silent also.

It may be true what he says, she thought. But how could she be sure? Was she just being selfish? But how could she admit to failure—or was it failure if one went into what might turn out for her a loveless marriage. She found it exciting and was glad to go away, awhile anyway. Still it hurt Dean, she saw that. Was it love when you hated to hurt someone? But she had promised her mother; she had signed papers. She would even soon have a social security card! And if Dean really loved her he would give her this time, this chance. If she realized he was what she wanted she would return with contentment to be with him, and the urge to be away and see the big wide world satisfied. Perhaps she would find it wasn't all that great, being "out in the world" on one's own. But for her there was only one way to find out and this was her chance. A small one, but a start.

Suddenly she realized Dean was talking to her.

"—it's been done before," she heard him say, and it didn't occur to her she had been so deep in thought she hadn't heard what he had actually been talking about. But she supposed he had been thinking the same as she had.

"Of course," she agreed, brightening with a smile, which showed her white even teeth, not realizing what she was agreeing with.

"We'd both be satisfied then," he went on in a change of mood, much to the better she realized.

"Why, yes," she agreed again. The smile broadened. "Oh, Dean—"

"Let's go then," he said.

They left town then, where they had eaten and just lingered awhile; as long as they supposed was allowed. Then they were in the car soon, heading south toward Mrs. Brown's. They were silent occasionally looking at and smiling at each other. Shandol even moved closer to him. She didn't question his change of mind and heart, she was just pleased. A week might be all she would need; she was almost in agreement with him. Perhaps a month at most. She knew it would be so different than when she saw him every few days. And she wouldn't have anyone where she was going. The loneliness could be too much for her.

At Mrs. Brown's gate, where they should have turned in he drove on. Shandol looked at him and he smiled confidently back at her.

"I thought you were taking me home," she said. "We should've turned in there."

"We can't tell her," he replied, "it won't be elopin' if'n we tell anybody."

"Oh, but we can't elope," she protested breathlessly.

"That's what yuh agreed to back there," he said.

"Elopin'? I couldn't have," she gasped, incredulously. "I had no such thoughts. I just thought you'd decided to be more reasonable about the whole thing."

She realized she hadn't been listening. She had been so caught up in her own thoughts she knew now she hadn't heard what he had been talking about.

"I'd be reasonable if we'd be married," he replied. "Yuh kin still go. No one'll know we're married fer awhile. Yuh kin stay a week—even a month—come back and we let ever'one know we're married and start livin' together. Happy ever after I hope."

Shandol let out her breath audibly and realized she had been holding it. Her shoulders sagged in a deep sigh. At the corner of Mrs. Brown's mailbox he stopped.

"We kin leave her a note," he said, his old self-confidence back. "Here I'll find somethin' tuh write on."

417

He opened the glove compartment of the car and found a store ticket which was plain white on one side.

"Use this," he said, handing her a stubby pencil from the same source.

"What'll I say?" she asked.

"That yer goin' home fer th' night, but yuh'll be back tomorrow as soon's yuh kin make it. She'll think yuh've learned there's somethin' more to attend to. She won't know th' difference."

The note was written and placed in the mailbox. Sybil would think Dean had brought a message. She hoped, but she hated lying about it. Her parents in turn would suppose she was at Mrs. Brown's home.

"I'll stop by my house to change clothes," and he looked at his clean khaki colored pants and shirt, which always looked freshly starched and ironed. His black slippers shone.

"Well, so will I then," Shandol said.

"We're not goin' back there fer yuh tuh change," he stated flatly. "She'd ask questions and we'd never git started again."

"But that's not fair," she objected.

"Ain't necessary yuh mean," he replied.

"It's not for you neither," she challenged. "I could stop at home, yuh know, sayin' I needed somethin' or other. I don't have all my things up there. No use. I don't see nobody much."

My heart should be singing, she thought, but here we are practically quarreling. And I wanna tell Mama. The thought was a revelation. She did not believe in what she was going to do.

"The plan is this," he said, to take her mind from anything else. "We'll go into Arkansas tonight. It'll be late when we git to uh county seat, so we'll have to wait til tuhmorrer."

"WHERE do we wait?" she wanted to know, suspiciously.

"Oh, in the car, where else?" he mocked. "All decent. What difference does that make?"

"Every difference if we're keepin' this marriage a secret," she replied. "Just no tricks, huh?"

"Trust me, my dear," he said, leaning over to kiss her cheek affectionately.

"I can't do it," she moaned. She was near tears and her voice was choked as she tried to hold them back.

"Stop! I tell you, I simply can't do it!"

Dean slowed the car, glancing at her. They were nearly to the state line. Dean had decided not to go home after all. Dean glanced at her. He pulled off and onto a side road.

"Take me back, please," she sobbed. "I promised and I can't do it and I *won't* do it. If you go on it'd be kidnappin' or somethin'.

Don't try tuh make me go through with something we might both regret later. You will if I do, for I will make you. Not on purpose," she hurriedly added, forgetting tears in her hurry to get it said. "But because I couldn't help it."

Shandol looked at him, but through the darkness she could not make out his expression. She steeled herself to firmness.

"You really made up yer mind to this whole thing," she reminded him, stonily. "I didn't. I didn't hardly realize what we were talking about. I hate to admit it but I must not a been listenin'. I was thinkin' and I thought your thoughts the same as mine.

He was still silent, and she supposed sullen.

"All I need is time," she said, "just time. I haven't made up my own mind and surely yuh don't think you can do it for me. I can't, my mother can't. Now can you?"

"Nope," he said quietly, "But I don't promise tuh wait years for yuh tuh make up yer mind neither."

"Mama wants me to go to meet more people," Shandol reasoned. "To broaden my perspective, too."

"Tuh meet and go with other guys," he interrupted, "tuh see if yuh like me or somebody else better. Shandol, it's yer life, live it!"

"I intend to," she replied quickly, pointedly. "Now let's go. We're gonna be late again."

"What if I have to go to the army?" he asked.

"Write to me," she answered sweetly.

"Yuh're such a baby," he mused almost to himself. "When yuh gonna grow up? Beats me."

But he took her back to Sybil's.

"Oh, we have plenty a time," Shandol sighed, glad it was over. "Let's take the time. I want yuh to want me for a wife, but—"

"Yeah, but," he repeated sullenly. "But we wait. Guess I'll see yuh Friday, as usual."

Shandol was surprised, but realized she was glad he was coming.

"I'll be here," she smiled, warmly.

It wasn't as late as she had supposed it would be. Dean had driven faster than usual. She hadn't said anything, but she was tense and preoccupied.

She laid awake awhile thinking about what she had almost done. To think of it even now frightened her. It might have been fun, she thought, at the time, but what about later. She'd have broken her parent's heart. They were so against him. Just let her be gone awhile and see how he acts, is all they wanted from her. It had been a narrow escape. Why hadn't she been listening? How had she convinced him she would not go through with it? She couldn't have said. Perhaps because he wanted to be so sneaky about it.

She always wondered why he bothered with her at all, and did now. She decided perhaps he did love her, at least he thought so. But she asked herself shouldn't it follow that she must love him? How do I know? How do I find out?

Dean, as he drove hard and fast going home, had a look both solemn and grim, his mouth pursed.

"I know why," he muttered. "She's just too sure uh me. But would it matter if she wasn't? I dunno. God, I don't know. And me—hm –m–m I won't be sure uh her till she's mine. She's just gotta be mine."

In helplessness he bore down harder on the car's accelerator to quicken his already fast pace, perhaps to help tear down the urgency that tore at him.

CHAPTER 34

Dean kept the Friday night date with Shandol: As she had not seriously doubted that he would, she was ready to go. She had also packed all the things she had at Mrs. Brown's, as she would not be returning.

It was an easy-going date. Dean again voiced his displeasure at seeing her leave, but he had not pressured her.

"We won't have many more dates, and I don't wanna spoil 'em with us fussin' all the time," he told her.

"That's prob'ly best. I'll have good memories to think about when I write," she replied. "That is if you want me to write."

"Of course we must write each other," he said. "Gee whiz, don't get the idea I don't wanna hear from yuh."

It was late enough when she got home she went straight to bed, because everyone else had already gone. Her things she brought from Mrs. Brown's she decided could wait for tomorrow to be put away.

She awoke that Saturday morning so glad to be in her own bed in her own room. It had seemed so long since she had been there, yet it had been only a week. A week? If the weeks at Mrs. Brown's had seemed so long, she wondered how she would be able to stand being so far away from home for very long and not being able to come home every week. She looked at the ugly familiar walls, the gray plaster cracked and scratched full of initials and other designs and lines. It seemed plaster particles sifted into the window ledges, around the floor and even from the various cracks in the walls, less from the ceiling. It had only a round crocheted rug on the otherwise bare floor, made of wide planks, and her meager furniture. She looked at it all with affection. Grandpa had made all of it at different times. Her bedside table was made of broomstick legs. There was an eight-inch square shelf, perhaps eighteen inches below its top, which itself was only about sixteen inches square. She kept her lamp on it, and a Bible, which she realized she had been neglecting lately. She had taken only a small New Testament with her to Mrs. Brown's.

The smallish mirrorless dresser was painted white. There were three drawers on one-half and a door with one shelf made the front. On one side of it, in the corner, was a glassed-in shelf cabinet, not quite as large as the medicine cabinet downstairs. It had once been a large clock. At the side of it a small mirror hung on the wall. What would happen to it all when she left? Perhaps it would be left alone until they found out if she could stand to stay away.

No one had awakened her so she wondered what time it was.

Her watch showed after ten o'clock. No wonder it was quiet. But how had she slept so soundly so as not to hear anything earlier?

Feeling wonderfully refreshed and wide awake, she threw back the quilts, stretched her well-shaped limbs and petite body lazily and got up. Surely, she thought, she needed that complete rest and she was glad she had been allowed to sleep. Yet she felt rather timid, docile and ignored as she went downstairs to the quietness. It seemed there were no sounds from anywhere in the house. Where was everyone?

She went on into the kitchen to see about some breakfast for herself. She realized she was hungry. Yes, leftovers had been placed for her in the warming oven over the stove. While she put food on her plate, the gravy and fried potatoes looked and smelled good to her. Her mother came into the dining room, apparently from another part of the house. Shandol took her plate and added a small dish of rice cooked with plump raisins, and put them on the dining table to eat. Audrey brought her a cup of coffee, still hot because the stove was kept with wood in it, even though the bright sunny day gave promise of plenty of warmth. Audrey planned to iron, she told Shandol. In fact, she had to, and grinned.

Shandol wondered where everyone was. It seemed so quiet.

And no one seemed to have been there to greet her or realize she had been gone a week and hadn't seen her. Of course she realized they couldn't just sit around while she slept either.

As Shandol ate Audrey checked on the baby, in the bedroom, where her crib had now been moved, and Shandol realized the ironing board was there and her mother had already done some ironing.

"Has Karen had her bath yet?" Shandol asked, hoping she hadn't so she could do it herself.

"Yes," Audrey replied, "and is taking her morning nap. "She's been good while you've been gone or I don't see how I could have managed."

Shandol thought her mother looked well, and not as tired as she feared she might. Shandol, chewing her food, thoughtfully, was quiet though aware her mother was ironing.

She wants me to go this time, Shandol thought. To keep me from Dean awhile. From making a mistake, as they had termed it. How did they know? Why were they so sure? Perhaps they aren't. They know they cannot choose my husband or the way I choose to live my life, for that matter. And so they give me the option of returning at any time I choose, and if I choose.

"The trouble with me," she muttered aloud, pausing long enough to sip at the hot coffee and place the cup back in the saucer with a muted clatter, the aroma lingering, "If ever I do make a mistake I can't blame nobody but myself. I can't say I haven't been brought up right, or warned. Still it is hard to know what is right all the time, except where it's so definitely spelled out, of course."

"Don't be so serious right now," Audrey laughed. "You look so wretched and defenseless. You'll be in a state of nerves to go to this new thing you're goin' to. Don't try to be perfect, but as nice as you can. Don't change, I guess I mean."

"But that's just it," she blurted. "I want to change! For the better I hope. But gosh, I feel so nervous and inadequate sometimes. Just a hick I suppose. So countrified and—and simple. What good is training if I stay the same shy, timid little rabbit I know I am and can't seem to help it. I've always been so, remember? I even had problems in school reciting in class, yet doing good on my written work. It mostly got me through. So many of my teachers I do believe, actually understood."

"Oh, you weren't a bad student," Audrey protested. "yuh couldn've worked harder, but I remember—" she broke off as though her thoughts went back, too.

"Anyway," Shandol went on, "I just don't like being that way. I know how kids can be after going to school in Plainesville. Dean thinks that's my problem. I should be just content just to marry *him* and be a housewife. But I just gotta see if that's what I want."

"Now," she went on, "I must clean up my mess here and, if I look so bad, maybe tidy myself a bit—at least comb my hair and brush my teeth. Do yuh want me to iron, or anything else especially today?"

"Well, yes, Shandol," Audrey answered. "I'd like for you to look over your things upstairs and sort them out, and put away the things yuh want to keep. And then arrange them so the room up there will be easy tuh clean; the stuff sorta outa th' way. That way, if anyone comes, I can still use the bed as an extra. Of course, dear, it's yours and you'll still come first with the room, if it comes to that. But maybe I'll need it in a pinch."

"I think I understand, Mama," she replied, thoughtfully.

"But it's gonna be a job."

"Don't throw anything away if yuh want tuh keep it awhile yet. Just pile it up in boxes in the next room if you like—some of it at least, so it will be easy for me to clean and dust. Only Shandol," she added sentimentally, "leave something out to remind us of you. Don't make it so bare it will seem you're gone forever. Maybe the doll, nobody would bother it. Leave a dress or two hanging on the hooks and a few things on the dresser top. We're goin' tuh miss yuh so, child."

Shandol felt her mother was thinking of the small son she had lost forever. She wondered if she should say something but then suddenly realized it was not needed to bring his precious memory back to her mother. She felt helpless because she could bring no comfort to her. The pain had perhaps lessened, but a scar, which was tender and sensitive, would always be there. Instead Shandol talked of the things she had to put away.

"Will yuh keep the boys outa my things?" Shandol asked. "I know you've always taught them to respect my privacy and things, which kept 'em from snoopin'. But when I'm gone they may think it won't matter anymore, so will need to be reminded. There's nothin' awful they can't know about, it's just that they tease me and it embarrasses me about somethings. They'd figure or change it somehow—maybe."

Shandol meant no malice in her request. It was as much a stated observation as a request. There was trusting faith in her eyes as she looked at Audrey and a smile rather frozen to her lips. But Audrey was not fooled by the forlorn look and realized Shandol only wanted to be happy, even if she must go away. Audrey knew she was glad to have the chance to leave Greenway. Shandol knew Audrey understood. Still there was a lost feeling that made her heart ache at the thought of leaving those so dear and so close to her.

"Uh course," Audrey replied. "Yuh'd hardly have to mention that. I don't want the things mussed through and scattered about."

By the time she had finished her breakfast, washed the dishes and had the conversation with her mother, it was nearing eleven o'clock.

"Yuh may have ta help some with Karen," Audrey added. "I'll have dinner to fix and I won't get done ironing this morning. Karen has so many little dresses now. But your dad and boys are gardening—that is hoein' and cuttin' weeds around the place, so they'll be in hungry at dinner time. Maybe yuh won't care to get started until after that."

"Okay," Shandol answered. "But since Karen's still asleep I'll go up and have a look anyway. I've the things I brought from Brown's to put away. I'll keep my ears open for Karen and if she wakes up I'll hurry to see to her."

Shandol went to look at her sleeping sister and went on upstairs. "I wish we were more the same age." Shandol muttered to herself. "We're too far apart to ever wear one another's clothes and really be company to one another."

It was her one regret that she had no sister. I wish I could see Margery, she thought. Wonder if she's heard of my plan.

Upstairs, she surveyed the room. With only a little rearranging it would be neat. Many of the clothes she would take; the rest she would put away.

424

But there were the boxes in the next room, which faced the street and had two large windows. What did they all contain, she wondered. She would certainly have to find out. However, she decided she had better wait until afternoon to tackle it. It would be quite a job, but mostly only time consuming. She determined to dispose of most of it.

Shandol was concentrating on the room when Karen awoke and Shandol heard her fret. She went downstairs for her, made her comfortable with a diaper change, got a bottle in case she might need it and reascended the stairs, back to her room. She laid Karen on an improvised pallet of the round rag run at the foot of her bed on the floor and a folded quilt.

"If I put you on the bed, you'd be sure to roll off," Shandol explained to her baby sister. "Let's see," she went on, aloud, as though Karen would appreciate the conversation. "I'll leave that in there until later and concentrate on these things in here. Some of these extra clothes I must take care of and remember where they are in case I want or need 'em. The winter things I'll have Mama put away. Oh they look hot—and I'm hot!" She looked at her sister.

"Oh, dear, Karen, I gave yuh nothin' tuh play with. Will yuh get bored? Are yuh old enough? You're company tuh me anyway, yuh know? But I must find yuh somethin' tuh look at."

She went to the baby and caught her small baby hands in her own. "Yuh're so sweet and so pretty," she told her impulsively. "I hope if I ever have a daughter she's as pretty as you. Just be my luck—no daughter—no nuthin'. Just nothin'. I will be lonesome for yuh then, but yuh won't always be a baby. Anyway, wish me luck, little darlin'," she cooed, softly, her eyes soft and brilliant. Her voice throaty, as she couldn't seem to avoid a lump there.

Shandol gave her a small, empty face powder box, an empty face cream jar containing buttons, she was sure Karen couldn't open and an old rag doll which sat on her dresser.

"There now; we'll see if you can be a ladybug," she said.

Shandol first boxed some clothes for her mother to put in the downstairs closet for out-of-the-way keeping. It was under the stairway and went back someway for extra out-of-sight storage. Her coats could hang there also, except a light jacket which she was sure she should take. Such a job, she thought, and I supposed I had so little!

It was not long before Audrey called dinner and Shandol, carrying the baby descended the steep stairs; Shandol very carefully with her precious bundle.

In the afternoon Shandol helped with the dishes and Audrey decided Karen could stay downstairs. She would be satisfied for awhile and Audrey was about finished with the ironing. Tommy could help if necessary.

Shandol looked around the room next to her bedroom again. Most of the things there were hers, but not all. Her eyes fell on her "doll box," a large black hat box her aunt Ruth had given her. It contained small dolls and clothes she and her mother had made for them. A large doll lay on top of it. Shandol still liked to make doll clothes.

There were papers in the room, mostly schoolwork. Here in another box were newspaper clippings, some in scrapbooks. These were of movie stars she knew only by the pictures; a scrapbook of the quintuplets, the historical beauty aids she found interesting, or otherwise had some appeal for her at the time. I must destroy them, she thought. It is silly to keep so much stuff.

But then she didn't. I can always do it later when I have had more time to think about it. Though her mother had supposed that without Karen to distract she could concentrate better, Shandol found it wasn't easy. It was a time of reminiscence. There was a wooden box of schoolwork. Some of it good, some not; some in workbooks, some notebooks and some on yellowing paper. She had kept it all. There were writings and drawings, tests and maps. Shandol glanced at them all.

How they had piled up, she thought.

Then there were her notebooks of scribblings. Poems and happenings in journal and brief note form. There were school notes and letters. She spent sometime reading through, or sometimes only a glance and she could remember the times and circumstances.

She recalled Phil teasing her about a poem she had written: "Who Cracked the Acorn?"

"How 'corny' can yuh get?" he'd mischievously asked.

But she would have been hurt if he hadn't appreciated it or, as he did, treated it lightly. She remembered how important that she really had the answer! Yet trying to make of it a mystery of nature she had discovered deep in a wooded place she had sometimes frequented. And how like Phil to tease her when he had found the notebook carelessly laid on the dining table.

Then, too, she sometimes shed real tears sentimentally, for the past and because she was leaving.

"But I'll be back," she muttered, scolding herself, brushing at her eyes and nose. "One'd think it was a final leavetaking, yet I'm afraid when I go so far things will never really be the same again. I just feel it. And even Dad has said so."

426

She had hugged her father then. "But I'll always feel like I'm comin' home," she replied, "as long as you and Mama are around."

"But visits and short stays will only make you feel the removal from the family, because they may not always be here either."

It was that removal from the family to some other place and environment that disquieted her. It was hard to think about, to talk about or to put into words.

The afternoon passed. The mound of the things she would be disposing of didn't grow as she had supposed.

"I mustn't toss things out, then wish I hadn't," she defended it. "I'm in a 'to much of a hurry' mood."

She had the things boxed, and as neatly as possible placed in a far corner of the room, so her mother could tell what was hers. She knew she could have discarded more, but no hurry as Audrey had warned. She could still feel she belonged here.

She put the wadded paper in a dilapidated cardboard carton to carry downstairs to the stove. As she lifted the box to the stove door level she heard the car; and while she stuffed paper into the large stove in the dining room Lester and Jane came in.

"Shandol greeted them warmly: "Hi, you two. Travelin' or goin' somewheres? No, really. We sorta looked for yuh."

"Whatta yuh doin'?" Lester asked lightly, "buildin' a fire?"

"Nope," she replied. "I've been upstairs sortin' my junk and puttin' stuff away outa Mama's way. So I looked through it and thought I'd throw away a lot of it, but this is all.

They'll get burned when we need enough fire to break the chill, like when it's damp and rainy, because of Karen."

"Gettin' ready tuh go, huh?" Lester asked. "You're really goin'?"

"Uh course I am," she replied firmly. "I'm all signed up, so I feel it's settled. I go next week."

"Do yuh really wanna go?" asked Jane, watching her.

"I think so really," Shandol answered. "Oh, I'll miss being here and miss everyone terribly, I know. But I want to go just the same. To get away awhile. If I don't like it I can come back, yuh see."

Phil, who held Karen, handed her to Jane.

"Don't do that," Shandol said aghast. "Can't you see Jane has on a new skirt? It is new, isn't it?" She looked at Jane. "It's such pretty material," Shandol complimented her and secretly wondered if Jane's mother had purchased it. It was blue and of a fine material; she wondered what it cost. But Jane always managed to look neat. The short sleeve blouse looked in season and fit her so well.

"But I want to take the baby," Jane objected. "She can't hurt it—not really. Anyway someday I hope I have a baby of my own and I'll surely be holding it." She glanced at Lester and grinned, then winked at Shandol.

Dean came and Audrey asked him not to take Shandol anywhere. However Dean said he came to talk to Shandol so they went for a snack with soda pop and talked. Dean again wondered why she must leave and tried to make future plans for them, but Shandol was simply not in the mood. He tried to be surly and snarling, but he realized she was paying no attention to him. Shandol tried to turn it all into a joke. She was gay and alluring. Her spontaneousness, happiness and sweetness to him seemed contagious and his mood improved.

She had so much on her mind. And as promised, they got back before Jane and Lester had gone.

Shandol caught Jane and Dean just inside the kitchen door talking earnestly, but when Shandol came near they hushed. Dean had gone to get a drink of water and Jane had stopped him before he could go into the dining room. Shandol missed him shortly and wondered if he were ready to go home and too embarrassed to ask her to see him to the door. Perhaps he thought her too busy to do so. But she was puzzled because that was unlike him.

"Anythin' else I kin do jest let me know, now," he told Jane, which added to her puzzled expression. "A wonnerful idea."

"What's a wonderful idea?" Shandol asked, smiling, but somewhat confused. Surely, she reasoned, *these* two would have no secrets from her.

Jane laughed. "Let 'em tell yuh. If he don't I will later."

"But, Jane— " Shandol began.

"Oh, he will," she grinned, "but I can't do it now, I must go see if Lester is ready to go."

"I'll jest let 'er sweat," Dean taunted, "she's good at that, so I'll take my good ole easy time too. Oh, boy!"

"Meany," she pouted, but he left it at that despite her coaxing.

x x x x

Sunday was "Decoration Day Sunday." Actually "Decoration Day" had fallen on Saturday but the closest Sunday was observed at the cemetery and church west of Greenway. It was observed at the closest Sunday unless it fell in mid-week, in which case it was observed the last Sunday of the month.

It was actually a big day. People came from far away, and even out of state, to attend the memorial service for loved ones who were "laid to rest" there. For some it was actually placing flowers and wreathes, mostly homemade of crepe paper, or bought from someone who did a beautiful job making them.

Luckily, Greenway had such a person, a widow who spent weeks before the actual day preparing flowers for herself and others. Her name was Annie Wittevers and she loved doing it.

Others sometimes came the day before and stayed over if possible. Phil had had Cal to take the Sonnett family out Friday afternoon to decorate K.C.'s grave with some of Annie's flowers. Annie had given them to Audrey, though the Sonnets had protested they should pay her. But Annie insisted she had done them for that purpose and the flowers were not for sale. They hoped the weather stayed pretty because of the decorations.

Audrey was sure she couldn't manage to spend the day out there. It would be a sad time for her and she felt she wasn't up to it emotionally, and Karen had to be considered. A way to get there was a hassle too, she knew; and she would have to come and go when the other fellow was ready, so she couldn't know what time that might be. Joel had ruled the trip too much for her to attempt.

Shandol had never gone to the all day meetings, and, as she had already been there and expected Dean to come, decided against going also. It would be strange now, and sad, and she wouldn't have wanted to stay very long either. She went to Sunday school with Joel.

Actually, Shandol was preoccupied. She would like to see Margery. She wished she knew if she were at home or at the cemetery. As it turned out she met her on the way home from the church. Margery had come in to the post office and laughingly told Shandol she hoped she would see her.

"Have yuh heard about me going away?" Shandol could hardly wait to ask, her eyes merry, and dancing, made her face seem animated.

"Not only heard," Margery replied, "But I'm goin' too."

"Who told you about it?" Shandol wanted to know.

"Mrs. Bright. She came out here tuh tell me about you and wondered if I'd be interested. Boy, was I! I feel like I could do with a change of scene too."

"Are yuh all ready?" Shandol asked.

"Not really," Margery replied. "But I'm goin' tuh town Monday to buy some things."

"Oh, so am I," Shandol exclaimed, almost jumping up and down, "we must get together."

"I'm goin' with Della Bright," Margery said. "She said she'd be goin' and I could go."

"I am too," Shandol said. "Yuh know, she may have figured it and planned it this way. Be just like her. So now I won't be goin' away alone, Margery," and she grabbed her. "I'm so glad. And glad it's you. I hope we can have fun along with the rest."

"Watcha doin' this afternoon?" Margery wondered.

"Oh, I suppose Dean will come by," she answered. "Otherwise I'm still packin'. I'm sure I'll forget something I'll want, but I do things as I think of them. Lester and Jane will prob'ly be back, to bring Phil at least, so I'll just be around and help Mama. She's rather upset. She wanted to go to the graveyard, but knew she couldn't. Dad didn't want her to this year anyway. She still has sad times about it all."

"If yuh weren't goin' I couldn't go," Margery said, "so I gotta go help Mom. They still have doubts about it. I've never been away before for very long—just a few days with relatives is all."

"Me neither until I went to Brown's," Shandol replied. "But I made it and that may help me a little."

Margery soon declared she'd better get going and Shandol's father had long since gone on to the house so they soon parted with glad shouts of "be seein' yuh," to each the other.

Shandol had supposed the afternoon would drag. She knew what went on on "Decoration Sunday" from reports of past years. She could just barely as she had never really gone. The boys went, by invitation usually. Lester would look so nice in spotless white pants and light blue shirt. Phil went with Lester and Jane this year. Jane's father was in charge of the service, as well as the cemetery. He introduced the speaker of the day, both before and after noon. And it was up to him to set the date of the actual program and let it become known.

A basket dinner was served at noon. It was a carry in dish affair where each family seemed to try to outdo another so there was plenty of food.

In the afternoon Dean came by on horseback to talk awhile. He expressed doubt that he would get the car that night. He wanted her to know why, if he failed to come, and, as their times together were growing short, he decided to ride over. He said he aimed to go on to the cemetery if she hadn't been at home, though Shandol had said she doubted if she'd go.

"Too many strangers," she had said, "and I've never gone before. Now that K.C. is buried I can't go milling around those people. For some it almost seems like a family reunion. It's just a time to get together."

Dean did, however, come later in the car.

"As a special favor to you," Dean said, "'cause yuh got me to go tuh church."

They went to a movie in Plainesville. Phil and Ardena went along. Phil had not waited for Lester and Jane after all. He rode home on the back of a truck with a family who could not stay long. They kidded Phil about going for a good meal. He admitted it was worth it so they could make little out of it. The truck had also brought Ardena and her mother home, being relatives, and considerate of her crippled foot. She rode in front with the driver and small son. Ardena, Phil and one or two others, Shandol understood, had decided to return also.

Dean still tried to dissuade Shandol from leaving. But she had made too many plans and felt she needed time away from him and his influence over her life. Anyway she hoped to better her circumstances and decide her future.

* * * * *

The first three days of June were to be the last days Shandol would have at home before going away. She knew she would be leaving on Thursday, the fourth, and there was still so much to do.

Monday she and Margery spent in Plainesville as planned. They were in a gay mood, and they went from store to store for the best bargains in what they wanted and needed. They talked and they planned—and even dreamed, as they confided their plans and hopes. They were laughing, but footsore by the day's end.

"We don't have a lot to worry about, I keep tellin' myself," Shandol said once, seriously, "except gettin' on our way and of course learnin' to manage on our own. I've already been warned we'll get homesick and get lonesome for home. But I try not to worry about it. But down deep I sometimes get so scared, do you?"

"Yeah, don't I?" Margery laughed, agreeing readily. "And we've a lot of family to get lonesome for and miss, don't we."

"And we're gonna miss 'em," Shandol agreed. "But others manage so why not us, huh?"

"Shore," she agreed again.

Shandol was glad she had some money she had earned and saved to buy some things she thought she needed. It was fun to shop when you had a reason, she decided.

The girls chose shoes just alike, patent leather pumps, low heeled, trimmed in soft leather, with a wide grosgrain ribbon bow on top. There were also skirts alike of tiny red checks, with four gores, slightly flared, which fitted them perfectly. Margery also chose a blue pants and top set, which Shandol decided was prettier than her own pink one, because it had white bands of trim on the front. But Shandol was sure it and the overalls she had was all she would need, because Joel didn't like for her to wear them. They also bought dress material, unalike, however, which they hoped they could get made up before they left.

All in all they were satisfied with their day in the town. It had taken them nearly all day. They also used some money to treat themselves to a hamburger at a small cafe, at noon, and had loved spending the day even though admitting they were tired. Rest could come later. There were things to do.

Dean came that night also. Audrey asked them not to go anywhere so they spent the evening there. Dean wanted to go for just a car ride, but Audrey objected, and Joel gave Shandol the look she knew so well: The "do-as-your-mother-says" look.

"Tell yuh what," Dean said, "we'll go for a short drive and bring back nuff soda pop fer ever'body." It won him his case of course, but they must be home early. Shandol had busy days ahead.

The next day was wash day. Shandol knew she was expected to help her mother get caught up on as much work as possible. They were up early, and, as it was a pretty day, the ironing was gathered as soon as it was dry enough to iron, and the ironing was finished in the afternoon. But everyone pitched in to help. Even Tommy helped with Karen.

But Wednesday was busiest of all. Because there was the house to clean and Shandol's dress to make. Shandol had done some cleaning upstairs, which helped, but the floors would need to be gone over again. Audrey lamented to Shandol she would miss her help and with Karen she was sure it would be awhile before she had managed a routine to get things done by herself.

They cut out and sewed Shandol's dress. With both working it had gone smoothly. By noon it was done, except for a few finishing touches. It was made what to her seemed a little fancy, with two wide ruffled tiers attached together to form the skirt. The sleeves were short and she planned to buy a white collar of lace or lace trimmed, in Plainesville before going next day. She would be there early, and she could later attach the collar herself. So it was one more thing done.

Shandol lost no time in beginning the housework; she knew what had to be done. The floors gone over and mopped. Papers and any other straightening up necessary to make the place appear neat. Also dusting the furniture and replacing the clean, freshly ironed scarves.

Just when Shandol decided it was suppertime she saw no preparations.

"Isn't it about time to start supper?" she asked Audrey. "I'm famished. I've been almost too excited to eat, but now that everything is about done, I'm tired and hungry."

"Why don't yuh rest awhile while I build a fire and get things started," Audrey told her. "I can rest tomorrow but you may have another big day. Yuh'll have tuh get up early anyway."

432

"I'd better take a bath though," she said, "then I might lay down a minute. But Dean will surely be here tonight of all nights—at least he's supposed to."

"Yeah, prob'ly," Audrey agreed.

Shandol had gone to her room where it was quiet, after she had bathed downstairs. She would try to rest awhile on her own bed, as her mother had said everything would be looked after. And, despite the fact she had meant to lie down awhile to rest and relax, and feeling quiet and refreshed after her bath and even looking for Dean anytime, still she soon fell asleep. Blissful, restful sleep which she had hardly realized she needed.

She was awakened sometime later by voices, muffled voices from downstairs, some almost distinct enough for her to hear what was said. She knew she must get up. Dean may be down there. Perhaps her brother and his wife would want to visit with her on her last night home.

She got up, ran a comb through her hair and wished she had some cool water for her face. But she already had makeup on, so she could go on downstairs. She hadn't aimed to sleep. Why hadn't someone awakened her? Surely she had missed her supper.

Dean was there as were Lester and Jane, who were there before Dean. Also Margery and three of her sisters. Shandol greeted everyone in turn.

"What're you doin' here?" she asked, when she got to Margery.

"We've come to church," Margery answered. "But there don't seem tuh be any yet, so we came here to wait awhile to see if anyone comes. Maybe we're early."

It did not surprise Shandol to see these people here, but soon others began to come in. Then she realized there was a different smell in the air. Something was being cooked.

"Hamburgers!" she ejaculated, aloud, and rushed to the kitchen.

"What's all this?" she wondered aloud to no one in particular.

Tommy crowded through. "Looks like a party sure 'nuff."

A party? Of course. But Phil said how had he said that? She went to find Jane.

"Know anything about a party here tonight?" she asked, as though she had been done a wrong.

"Yuh aren't mad about it are yuh?" Jane asked, in genuine concern.

"Of course not," she hugged her sister-in-law.

"Looks like they've did it again," Margery laughed, her violet eyes merry and shiny. "Church indeed? Just one way to get me here."

"We talked it over," Jane explained. "We thought it might be a good excuse for everyone to get together—an excuse—you know."

"I said I wish't someone would give one," Margery said.

"All the best parties are here, everybody says so. More people come and seem to go away very happy and sayin' they had a good time. Uh course I only said it at home."

"I, too, tried to give hints," Shandol giggled, "and now I realize there'd been vague hints by Tommy about one, but I didn't catch on. In fact I asked Phil. He said it wasn't for him to decide, besides he supposed ever'body thought we'd only be gone about a week and then be ready to come back. Same with Dean. And when I asked Mama she'd said not unless it's to be a surprise. I supposed she'd meant to herself too!"

"So Phil acted like it's unimportant?" Margery mused. "Yeah, Shandol said. "Too unimportant just like that. And I considered it an absolute turning point in my life—one way or the other."

"Me, too," Margery agreed. "Notice how many are already here."

"And her about to sleep through it all," Dean taunted, coming to join them.

This was going to be real nice, Shandol thought, as she watched preparations, almost stupefied for awhile. Just like Lester's birthday party—a hamburger fry! With real buns. There'd be cake, cookies, coffee, as usual and other sandwiches and food. There were other women in the kitchen helping Audrey assemble it all.

"It was partly yer boyfriend's idea," Jane confided. "And a lot of the plans—particularly to surprise yuh—was his. Of course yer mom and dad had to say it was all right, and helped. But the meat and buns are his doing mostly, I mean." Meaning she and Lester had helped but she would not mention that. "He loves yuh so, Shandol. Dean, I mean."

"Don't know what love is," Shandol whispered, her face going pink. She had carefully left off a pronoun so Jane could only guess who wasn't sure what love was. And seeing Shandol's obvious reticence to talk about it, Jane said no more.

She just doesn't care enough yet, Jane decided, thoughtfully to herself. Is she blind—or is it love is blind, heartless or just unawakened, as Lester said? Now I know what her mom and pop mean when they don't want her to get married yet. She's not ready or she'd know it. No one could stop it!

But the revelation was momentary and Jane's thoughts became centered once more on the party and the large crowd for the small town it was. It took all hands that were willing to work and she must see what she could be doing to help her mother-in-law.

Besides the meat to fry there were plates of other sandwiches to be made and put out. There were cakes to cut and put out, cookies to be arranged neatly on plates. Also cups and glasses and a fruit flavored drink donated from the store. Also someone to stand guard at the table so the children would not be tempted to poke their fingers in the cake icing and eat it.

The sandwiches were made of cheese or a lunch meat; some of the two combined and cut in triangles. Also there were the hamburgers. They hoped to have enough of the latter to go around once, and there would always be those who would come back for seconds—perhaps thirds.

Margery and Shandol were almost too excited and busy visiting with different ones to eat. While the food was being prepared there was music played, party games outside, the inevitable checker game, even dominoes were started, but for the most part the young people wanted to be more active. Shandol had gone in and out. Inside to hear the music and visit; then outside to see that the games were being played and everyone enjoying himself. Although it was unplanned and rarely mentioned it was taken for granted that Shandol did watch the games to see that enough played to keep the game going or if tired of it to see it was changed. She kept an eye on whether the couples were being away too long or not, which was rare as they knew she would notice. Sometimes she joined them briefly, but everyone knew if she were gone long Dean would come looking for her.

Dean stayed close by Shandol as he ate. In fact she and Margery were going to have only one-half each of a sandwich but he told them if they didn't eat he'd personally poke something down them. They good-humoredly gave in. They especially wanted a piece of Mrs. Bright's cake as she said she had made it for them.

Margery also kept an eye on her sisters. They played with the younger ones, schoolmates, tagging, and sometimes joining other games or teasing those who were. But when the food was ready they waited in line as ready as any of them. They had to eat standing, sitting on what chairs there were, on the floor, divan, back porch, wherever they could. But the music went on. Those who played went to eat also, and there were less efficient musicians singing, picking or playing, though not so loudly or assuredly as they were timid about their playing. One of those was Steven Fullerson, though he wasn't all that bad. In fact Shandol loved to hear him sing something about a Rancho Grande.

Freda Horn was there. She was good help in the kitchen. She was also showing her small flashing diamond to anyone who would look and hear about it. She was engaged.

"We'll get married on his very next furlough," she told Shandol.

Now that she was engaged she talked to Jane about it, too.

At other times she had always carefully avoided confronting Jane.

She saw Jane as the triumphant rival after Lester had married her. Jane, of course, had no idea she felt that way, but extended good wishes to her in her marriage. Shandol thoughtfully watched. *Dear, sweet Jane*, she thought. *Why must it have been her only brother who was one of those lost on the ship, Arizona, at Pearl Harbor?* How bitter Jane's mother had been for awhile.

Of course Shandol and Margery were kidded about staying away a week or two. Hadn't Shandol stayed at Brown's only two weeks and came home weekends at that?

"Don't yuh bet on it," Shandol challenged Dean lightly.

"Nope, couldn't," he agreed. "Cain't say 'bout you."

It was a good party. Friends and neighbors had gathered, partly perhaps to have somewhere to go, but most had actually wished to see the girls and wish them well on their new venture. Some were curious, but there would be little gossip.

Karen received her share of attention. Once she stuck her foot in her mouth and laughed with them when they laughed. She was played with and carried around until she became worn out and fussy and so was put to bed and soon slept.

Grandpa fiddled, despite his apology about his stiff fingers; and even danced a little jig to the delight of everyone. It was also something he had done for years. He was still a spry old gentleman for his years. He and Steve Werst discussed a fiddle tune. They played it together. It sounded almost as though they had rehearsed.

"I've sometimes had trouble with that 'fine' part," Grandpa said, "but I made it then."

"Yuh mean after th'—"

"The chorus," someone else replied.

The women took their turn last eating and visiting. The checker game seemed never to stop, but the dominoes were mostly a mess to be played with, rather than a game. And as the evening wore on the younger ones were outside teasing more and in the way of young couples who were paired off in their own games. The nearest thing to dancing allowed was singing games. One of the favorites was the couples in a circle facing the couple in front, going forward, round and round, right hands clasped in front, left in back, singing:

"Johnny was a miller boy who lived by the mill—
The wheel turned around of its own free will—
One hand in the hopper and the other in a sack—
The ladies step forward and the gents step back."

It was varied, as they could just turn around, perhaps, and go the other way, if they had their correct partners.

436

And so on. There was usually a leader—dissatisfied, and wanting to change. Then another would undo it.

Tomorrow they would all say what a good party it had been. What a good time they had had, and perhaps talk about it until the next party came up.

But Shandol and Margery would not hear. And Shandol thought that while her mother cleaned up the next day, ostensibly to keep from being lonesome, Shandol wouldn't be there to help. She would be on her way.

And Shandol hadn't heard what her parent's discussion had been about her going away. She suspected they talked of it, but had no idea of how they worded their comments.

"She just must get away from that man," Joel said, decisively. "He monopolizes her completely and no other young men have a chance. I'd rather she'd have a chance tuh meet other young men. I don't think he's the right man for her. Spoiled and selfish and a bit overbearing. I wonder she can't see it!"

Audrey silently agreed, and added: "He's so possessive. She's beginnin' to depend on him."

"Exactly," Joel said. "He's tryin' to hurry her into marriage I believe, and prob'ly anyway he can, which also bothers me. No principles."

"But I do so hate to see her go," he said ruefully, after a pause. "I'm afraid she'll never be content to stay at home anymore. She'll be gone for good."

"But she had to grow up," Audrey reasoned. "She can't stay a baby girl all her life. Won't be so bad—we have a baby girl anyway. She can help with the feelings of loss."

"But, never, her place. But the camp is a God-send," Joel mused. "And I guess the baby too, so we will have a little girl around the place with yuh."

Shandol only wondered what it was going to be like, away and alone, except for Margery. Was Margery having doubts and worries too? But she knew she must rest. Tomorrow was the day.

CHAPTER 35

Shandol awakened early. She was in familiar surroundings she knew that. Yet she had awakened with a vague doubt and unease that made her pause and wonder what day it was. And as she became fully awake she realized today was the day she was leaving home again. This time farther away. Much farther away.

A gnawing dread swept over her as she lay in the early morning quietness. The thought of facing the day made her wish she could go back to sleep. But the gnawing inside persisted. She was sure it was caused by the uncertainty, unsureness and self-consciousness at facing the unknown. It would not be quieted and so she could not go back to sleep. It made her feel cross. She had been up late at the party the night before also, and thought she should get, and probably needed the extra sleep.

While these doubts and fears were assailing her sense of well-being, she tried to picture in her mind what she was getting into. What would it be like? But there was no way she could picture herself there and know what all she would be doing.

She wondered if she could measure up with the others. Who were those others? Those blank faces of which she pictured many, and now strange and unfriendly. She thrashed uncomfortably in her bed.

She did have the comforting thought that her family hated to see her go in some ways. But why? She sometimes felt they were pushing her to go with one hand, and yet trying to hold her back with the other. She supposed her parents were afraid for her. They were fearful of things that can happen to girls away from home— even good girls who became too trusting. Were they afraid she would become different? She was hoping they would miss her but were just not resigned to the fact she was going. Did they love and appreciate her, knowing she had to go sometime?

But Dean wanted her to stay. He wanted her for herself. Or was it for himself? He had let his feelings about it be known. But it was left up to her to decide. Would it have been easier the other way? Yet it was partly because of him they had accepted her going away. Would it help for her to be away from Dean for awhile to sort out her feelings? Just to see other people and get a glimpse of another side of what life might have to offer. Dean was possessive, and so she had no choice here, even while he had been away working in the army camp construction. And the controlled, structured environment appealed to her father. She would not be turned out into the world alone without rules and regulations, and perhaps guidance. That had somewhat set Joel's mind at ease. No more was likely to happen there than at home; and it was all she could look ahead and back objectively. This is what they reiterated that she needed, and she had readily agreed. Her world was indeed small, but she had books and she knew there was more to it than the small area in which she lived and moved about. In fact had not Lester joked—if off-handedly: "Is Dad really letting her out of her cocoon? Incredible!"

Still she could not quiet the uncertainty. She tossed in the bed. She ran her fingers through her hair and held her head. Surely it would burst. She must think of something else. What about Margery? Was she feeling the same or was she exuberant at getting away from the near drudgery and work she was expected to do every day. She got up early every morning to help with the household and farm chores. And with the large family there were always things needing to be done. She worried as it was that her mother worked too hard. It was discovered she had a heart condition before the birth of the last baby. Yet they were allowing her to go also, hoping she could better herself. Besides she would be with Shandol, which they thought would be a good influence on her.

Shandol realized it was better that Margery was going. At least, she would know one person and not be thrown alone into the company of the strangers feeling alone. After all, Margery was perhaps seeking and searching for a more broadening view, even as she herself was. It would also be a learning experience, and Joel insisted a place made up more or less like themselves. But is anyone like me, Shandol wondered, in an illuminating flicker. After all she hardly knew herself. The merry-go-round of thoughts was tiring her mentally, physically and emotionally. She was becoming depressed. She must get up and move around.

She began hearing stirring around downstairs. From the sound it seemed the fire was being built in the cook stove.

"I won't go down yet," she muttered, low. "I wouldn't be able to do anything, and I doubt if I'm expected to anyway. And, bug-dust, I'm muttering to myself again. I must quit it. M-m-m." She closed her mouth firmly.

She would check again the things she had to take; and gazed at the things she was leaving behind, with heavy heart and loneliness, as though parting with old and fond friends. It hurt, she realized, this going away; this growing up and wondering what was ahead. And so she wept emotionally, her head on her hands resting on the door facing. She was taking a last long look at her makeshift storage boxes; and then the dresser drawers. The drawers held just odds and ends. Nothing tempting, she thought. Letters and papers in one drawer she hadn't packed away, but left her old under clothing and some doll clothes over them. She doubted they would ever be detected or searched for.

Then she suspected it was time to go downstairs. She must take a bath. There were indications it would be a hot day. The warmer weather had just seemed to descend after a relatively cool wet May. The first twenty-four days of May it had been necessary to put fire in the heating stove to break the chill. While the warm-up had been welcome, it had come suddenly and the general consensus was that it became too hot too quickly, and would take getting used to.

Shandol looked back into her room as she prepared to leave it. Outwardly it looked as though she might return anytime. She had left the few, mostly faded, dresses hanging in their usual place along the wall, hanging on the hooks on the painted gray plank fastened along the wall, as Audrey had requested.

"It won't seem so lonesome with just a small reminder such as a few dresses hanging where they belong. It won't be like you're so completely gone. We are going to miss yuh you know that."

She could put it off no longer. She must face this new day.

She left home at eight-thirty that morning to catch the bus at Leggitts garage. Phil and Joel had gone with her to help with her suitcase. She said her good-byes, her mother with tears in her eyes, at home.

"Don't cry Mama," Shandol comforted. "I'll be back sometime." Her own eyes were near tears.

In Plainesville she took her suitcase to Carol Middleton's apartment until she would be ready to go. Carol, her parents and a sister lived there and it was close to the square. As she went up the stairs to their apartment, she hoped they wouldn't mind. But she was greeted warmly, after all, and she told them how grateful she was to have somewhere to leave her things.

She met Margery at Meyer's Hardware store, waiting. She had managed a ride with a relative from a short distance past their place. She was earlier. There was time to spare though they were to leave shortly afternoon. Shandol bought a plain white, lace-trimmed voile collar for her new dress. She had remembered to bring thread, needles, thimble, writing paper, a few stamps and envelopes as she packed. It would help her meager funds last longer.

Shandol and Margery ate dinner after the shopping and looking. They were tired walking and it was good to sit down. They bought two hamburgers each and orange flavored soda pop. Later they had ice cream from Yokum's. They knew a girl from Greenway, Gloria Dahle, who worked there. Shandol also saw Douglas Lindersilt but had no chance to speak to him. She was surprised that he was riding a bicycle.

About noon, or shortly after, the girls had gathered ready to go. There were some who had come from counties adjoining Plaines county.

Their transportation was to be in a dark green station wagon, which they could see; and wondered why they couldn't get started. It was actually one-twenty before they finally left Plainesville, Most of the girls were quiet and reserved.

"They're prob'ly as nervous as I am," Shandol whispered to Margery.

"And me too," Margery smiled, shyly.

Just outside Plainesville they picked up a hitchhiking soldier, going home for a leave, he said. He went as far as Maple Hill with them. The girls all eyed him curiously, but he sat up front near the driver and talked to him or was silent.

There were eight girls counting Margery and Shandol so there was plenty of room. It was learned later there were two from the same county who had not met before. One was a slightly tall girl, with prominent teeth, brown hair and oval face who finally broke the ice. She had suggested getting acquainted, as the girls would be going to the same place, and no doubt be seeing each other. She gave her name as Nancy Rayford, and told where she was from. She even gave her age, seventeen. She looked at each girl in return and asked for the same information. Thus she met Edna Barkers.

When the girls learned Margery and Shandol were from the same town and had known each other a long time, Nancy remarked how lucky they were.

Edna Barkers, a short dark brunette, whose very dark brown eyes commanded attention, and were set in a small pleasant face, suggested they sing. The singing started out straggly and draggy at first, with only Edna and Nancy keeping it going. Soon the others joined in and they sang and laughed together over the song or forgetting the words and having to stumble along or just hum.

They drove into a shower of rain, which came and went, or they passed through it in a short time and soon the sun shone. But the girls were hardly aware of the beautiful Ozark countryside as they rode along. Wild roses were in bloom at the roadside and daisies nodded to them as they passed.

Shandol and Margery learned all the girls were curious as to what they were getting into. There was talk of what they were interested in doing. Five of the girls were going to take shorthand and typing, including Margery and Shandol; two were going to do waitressing and one sewing.

As the afternoon wore on they began to wonder how much farther. They were getting tired and hungry and some grumbled. They pointed out cafés to the driver.

"We'll make only one stop, to get gasoline and a rest stop. It will be brief. There's no time for anything more. We're expected at the Center for supper," he told them.

"But when do we get there?" asked Diane, a tall blond, whose hair looked artificially blond. She had a baby-doll face.

"In due time," the driver replied. "Soon," he amended. The "due time" turned out to be six o'clock.

* * * * *

The long ride was over at last. And as the dark green station wagon came to an abrupt halt, the girls were surprised to see it was in front of an impressive large stucco, with stone trim, structure. The girls looked at the building in awe, completely missing the large well-tended lawns, it's lawn chairs and benches conveniently placed around the area, or the large trees to the north which resembled a park. There was a neatly kept area at the south in which a court for games such as tennis or even volleyball could be played. And there seemed to be huge trees everywhere.

They had known when they were coming near their destination. They left the highway nearly a quarter of a mile and traveled on a graveled lane. The crunch of deeper gravel for a short ways and they had soon stopped.

Wildwood was actually a large sprawling stucco structure, with a large stone-trimmed enclosed porch around the front. It looked modern and well-kept, and was situated on the banks of the Merrygo River, though the girls were not ready for that fact either. From the outside Shandol sensed it was meant for luxury living yet she had come here to work. She had no doubt that her life would be changed by it, and she hoped, enriched. If only there were someone to teach them the art of living as people would in such a setting, which seemed so grand to her, what a self-confidence builder that would be, she thought. But it was no such place. She was expected to work and go to a class, but not that kind. Hopefully, she dreamed that in time she could do well enough to qualify for an office job.

442

The girls, one by one, stepped out of the station wagon door to the white pebbled driveway, which made a circle around a rock-walled terrace, with a tall iron posted sign proclaiming in a glass covered plaque: "Wildwood Hotel" in large letters. At a glance Shandol noticed the benches and thought perhaps sometime later they would look inviting, and the girls would climb the concrete steps to the velvety green of the neatly clipped grass of that portion of the lawn; but as of now the girls were weary from travel. They seemed to stumble and wobble on half asleep, uncertain limbs, due, they knew, to the slowed circulation from sitting so long. They were dizzy and giddy and giggled feebly as they mocked their situation, and the nervous excitement of starting something new. They were apologetic about, and self-conscious at the wrinkled, disheveled condition of their clothing, which as they weren't aware, felt worse than their actual looks warranted.

The girls chattered nervously in small groups, wondering what to do next. They did not know where to go so hung back nervously. They could see the driver getting out the suit ases. He had already told them he was referred to by everyone as "Pop" and was the man for manly chores around Wildwood.

Pop pointed to the entrance. It was necessary to descend a half-dozen or so steps, and Pop, with a suitcase in each hand led the way.

"I'll bring it all in, girls,"he said, and added, "follow me."

The outer screen door was opened by one of the residents who, along with the rest, anticipated their coming. The door was held while the girls entered, and she smiled warmly at each. Shandol could never recall if she returned the smiles or not, but she sensed a friendly atmosphere. The door opened onto a wide built in porch, which went the entire front of a spacious lobby. Open double doors led on into the huge spacious lobby, which seemed sectioned by large pillars, spaced so they added charm to the room. The lobby was light and airy and there were two wide windows on each side of the double doors.

Inside the lobby the girls noticed girls sat around the lobby on some of four or five sofas and upholstered chairs, against the walls. The rugs in front of the sofas were room sized on the shining hardwood floors, yet looked like mere scatter rugs in the spaciousness of the room. There were girls looking from hallway doors, on the two stairways, and although the "new" girls were unaware of it, eyes were watching from overhead from the mezzanine guard rail. The girls could not take it all in at once, but were impressed and almost overwhelmed by it all. They knew one thing they must try to concentrate upon the business at hand, which was, to be sure, mostly keeping quiet, and from making comments to keep their attention centered correctly so as not to miss any instructions when they came. And they came soon after they had entered the lobby, though time had seemed to lag. Soon Pop had all the luggage inside which seemed to be the cue to the next step. Each girl must claim her own.

"Girls," a woman's voice came from behind the lobby desk. "I'm Mrs. Lockney, your head supervisor, or the superintendent here. First, I must call the roll to see if I have all your names. As I call your name, please come to the desk here, so I can see you and meet you personally. This is necessary to be sure I have all of you accounted for."

Mrs. Lockney was a soft-voiced, short and rounded, although not overly plump, who appeared to be in her mid-forties. Her hair, the salt and pepper mixture color was worn in one roll, with waves about the roll around the back of her head. A soft wave at the top right and soft curls framed the pleasant round face. Her eyes were a soft blue and crinkles shot out at the corners when she smiled as she talked to the girls.

Each girl was called to the desk in turn and all were accounted for except one whose name had been inadvertently left off the list. Her name was quickly placed on the roll and "the details would be worked out later," Mrs. Lockney smilingly told her.

"Now, we must assign rooms, Mrs. Lockney told the group. However, first you get to eat supper. You must all be very hungry. We've already eaten, of course, but then some of the girls have been waiting to serve you. And while you eat, we will talk about rooms, some of the other girls and I, here. Let me remind you new girls, you may be thinking about that. We may have some doubling up to do. If you have a hometown friend or schoolmate, you could talk about it and decide if you'd care to share a room. And you older ones—those of you who've been here longer, rather—may help out on that, too, in case you could share a room to make some rooms available. All right, girls, show them the dining room. Let's show these girls how we do things around here and start getting acquainted."

A short crippled girl, who they later learned was president of the girls' council, led the way through double French doors, which were opened on cue, almost ceremoniously, into the dining room.

The room was spacious; a many windowed, cheery room, with white sheer curtains blowing faintly as an evening breeze seemed to stir them. There were square, café-style dining tables, which seated four. They were arranged in rows. The floors were the same shining hardwood as the lobby.

444

"I'm Evelyn Watts," the crippled girl, who had limped to the front of the room, told them. "Just follow right on in girls and choose a table—just anywhere. Food will be served you from the kitchen by girls who are learning that—to be waitresses, I mean—and some cooks also. Any questions you have just ask. The girls here are friendly and helpful. So welcome to Wildwood, girls, and now to your good. Thank you."

The girls had come in orderly and quietly, somewhat hesitantly and seated themselves. Shandol and Margery who had stuck pretty close sat down at a table across from one another, and were the only ones at the table. They glanced at the other girls scattered around the room, at the tables in groups of two and four. Mrs. Lockney came in and stayed until each girl was served. This was a plate of food from a tray, which also held a glass of milk, salad and dessert, and deftly handled by the waitress. Shandol and Margery, making themselves at home began eating.

"Isn't this a nice place?" Margery beamed.

"Nice? It's positively lovely," Shandol replied. "I never imagined anything like this. What is it—or was—I'd guess was a first class hotel. And this service! Bringing in our food, why, we'll be spoiled!"

"Yeah, and no dishes to do," Margery added. "I mean unless we choose. I believe I'll like it don't you?"

"I hope so," Shandol agreed. "Anyway here we are and Margery, let's try to get a room together. Well, we may as well since we may have to share a room with somebody anyway. We'd be better company for one another since we've known each other so long."

"I was just thinkin' the same thing," Margery nodded. "If only we can choose. And we still can get acquainted with the other girls. Shandol, let's truly try to enjoy ourselves here, too."

"Of course, Shandol agreed. "I don't care if I could just change my whole personality, to be different a little—you know?"

"At least yer folks won't get a say in ever'thing yuh do, will they?" Margery asked.

"How 'bout yours?" Shandol countered.

"Yeah, mine too," she conceded.

"Don't eatin' different food and eatin' different make a difference?" Shandol asked, thoughtfully. "I mean, I'm enjoyin' this meal, Margie. I mean truly. I guess we'll give it all a try. Everything's so pretty. And I wonder if I packed enough etiquette among my things," she giggled lightly. "I guess I'm forgettin' these are just simple girls, mostly, like myself. Still we were served properly, I bet, so maybe we're supposed to eat just so too." She sighed. "I'm always worried about such stuff," she added.

"I'm too tired to care much right now," Margery declared. "I wonder what we do next? I suppose wait until everyone's through."

"But will we be finished by the time everyone else is?" Shandol wondered. "We've talked too much."

At about that time a girl wearing a waitress's uniform, including cap, was at the left of Shandol asking if she'd care for "seconds" on any food.

"Thank you, but I believe not," Shandol answered truthfully, hoping she had replied correctly. Margery also dissented and the pretty petite waitress went away to another table.

"I was so hungry," Margery said, thoughtfully, "but I guess we've just had too much excitement for eatin'. But it was a good-sized meal anyway and I ate everything." She pointed to her plate.

It was only a few minutes later that the others seemed to rise, look around and all were soon leaving the tables, so that Shandol and Margery followed suit. They glimpsed the girls with the trays coming to get the heavy dinnerware and silverware, to carry back to the kitchen.

The girls went back to the lobby and seated themselves as close to the desk, built in an arc shape, as possible. Some sat on their suitcases, Shandol and Margery sat on the stairway, which was nearby.

Then the wait began. It seemed to Shandol it would never end. More of the staff had joined Mrs. Lockney. They talked and reasoned among themselves. There were plans offered and rejected. It seemed there were only two available rooms for eight girls, so more would have to double up. The two girls from the county adjoining Plaines asked for a room. Shandol and Margery quickly volunteered to share the other.

This was accepted. In fact they were made to feel they had done a favor by speaking out. Two other girls volunteered to share a room with other girls they knew, which made another room available. Two other girls volunteered to share that room. Two other girls offered to accept a girl in each of their rooms. Soon it was all settled. It had taken some thirty or forty minutes, but had been tiresome and boring and the time seemed endless.

Before the girls could leave, then, a few directives and rules were handed down. One concerned the incoming mail: It was handed out every morning at nine forty-five at the desk. Outgoing mail must be left in a small special cardboard box to be taken to the post office. The girls were responsible for their rooms as to neatness and housekeeping; and were inspected each Monday. The laundry takes care of all the washing except personal things. There can be dating, but the supervisor must meet each date. The girls expected to take the fellows to be introduced to her.

"There'll be other instructions," Mrs. Lockney added kindly, "concerning work and study, but we won't go into those now as I'm sure yuh feel you've had a full day. Now, girls, neighbors of the girls who must be shown their rooms, please help the girls, find the rooms. She called out the room numbers again, with the girls' names who would occupy them, and the moving activity began once more.

Almost immediately a large, heavy-set brunette approached Shandol and Margery, and behind her was a smaller girl with fairer hair.

"We're tuh be your neighbors," the brunette told them. "We have th' room next door. I'm Betty Drews and this," pointing to the large brunette, "is Mary Fraise. We're the room next to yours just down the hall."

"Now, we'll help yuh move in," Mary offered. "Which things are yours?"

Shandol and Margery chose their suitcases, even checked the name tags to be sure. Theirs, like the others were black, new and cheap, except for a nice two-piece set, and an older one which had been fairly nice at one time. Margery and Shandol started to pick up their own, but the girls took one each and explained:

"We take them up for you. So just follow us and we'll take yuh to room thirty-seven."

"Thanks, girls, a whole lot," Shandol said, surprise in her voice. "It's nice for yuh to do that for us, right Marg!"

"Oh, gosh, yes," Margery agreed. "We weren't exactly expectin' it."

"By the way, maybe we should introduce ourselves, too," Shandol said, as they climbed the wide stairway to the second floor. "I'm Shandol Sonnett and this is Margery McNeely. We're from the same town and have known each other for quite awhile. Are you girls?"

"No," the one who was introduced as Mary told them. "We never saw one another until we got up here. I was here first and when Betty came I just took her in, as another girl did me when I first came. She's gone now though. She got an office job."

"She was so swell," Betty said, meaning Mary. "So yuh see we know how it is tuh be new here. And here we are at number thirty-seven."

"Now we'll leave you," Mary told them. "We'll go next door. The beds are made and extra blankets in the closet. There're hangers there to hang your dresses and whatever yuh have to hang up. And the dresser drawers are for the rest, such as stockin's, undies and the like."

"We'll be back in a few minutes, now to see how you are making out. Maybe show yuh around some if yuh like."

"Okay," the girls agreed and added, "Thanks."

Almost from the time the door to the room was opened, after following the girls down the wide hallway, with a carpeted runner, which wasn't quite wide enough, Shandol studied her surroundings. It was modern, she supposed, though not quite as grand as she had expected. Yet she wasn't sure what she should have expected as she had never been inside such a place before to compare it.

They tried the dresser drawers first and found them empty, except for one stray silk stocking, which was dropped into a waste paper can nearby, after a few words of deliberation. There were two beds, actually iron cots, neatly made and a blanket folded at the foot of each. A gray wool rug covered the floor. It had a dim design of blue and rust flowers in each corner, and no doubt even bright and pretty at one time. The dresser had a clear mirror and there was ample closet space for their things. There was a sink with two faucets, and another door, which didn't open when they tried it. A rocking chair, a straight chair and towel rack, with towel and washcloth, constituted the furnishings list, as each mentally took stock.

They tried the faucets and were delighted there was both hot and cold water.

"This sure ain't bad," Margery exclaimed. "Hot water, closet space; it's all so handy and *private*. Wonder if that's a bathroom," as she pointed to the door which wouldn't open. They had learned the rest rooms were at the end of the hall, which they'd passed on their way to the room.

"Yeah," Shandol agreed. "Anyway let's get to putting some of this stuff away like we're goin' tuh stay awhile. Let's see, let's save these small top drawers for pencils, writing papers, stamps, envelopes, and, oh, purses and things like that. That will leave one each for other clothes and stuff."

"That'll do all right for now at least, since stuff like that will need a place for sure," Margery agreed. And she took a dress to the closet, brought out some hangers and began hanging things on them.

"That's good," Shandol suggested. "You do your hangin' while I'm at the dresser and then I'll hang up mine while you put your stuff in the dresser. We won't get in one another's way so much then."

"I'm gettin' 'em on hangers and puttin' up," Margery said. "I'll take one end of the closet, Shandol, and you the other and that way we can find our own things easier."

"Hello, girls," after a brief time there came the greeting from Mary and Betty. They put their heads through the door, which hadn't opened for Shandol and Margery.

"Hello, yourselves," Shandol beamed. "And how'd yuh get that door open, may I ask?"

"Sure thing," Mary laughed. "Yuh see in there is the shower and the door was hooked from the other side. It's really a wonder though, for that shower don't work, anyway. We use the one across the hall. Just go tell Agnes in that room across from us yuh want tuh take a shower, and if she ain't usin' it herself, yuh can be sure she won't mind. She's uh rather big redhead, yuh can't miss what she looks like. She's nice, too."

"Well, I see you're about done unpackin'," Betty observed, surveying the room quickly.

"Oh, it don't take as long to unpack as to pack," Shandol replied, putting her suitcase in a corner of the closet out of the way. "There that just about does it, but I packed for days, don' it as I thought of it. I figure I forgot something as it is."

"Well, we really come to show you gals around," Betty told them. "Let's take them to th' river, Mary. The Merrygo River flows right below the hill." And she pointed toward their one window. Shandol thought it must be the longest window she could imagine. She had thought those at the Old Hotel were long, and as Audrey often complained, hard to fit, at least those downstairs. Upstairs they were more a normal size and Audrey used curtains she had for those. But this long window was covered with a maroon colored drapery of a heavy material. The girls had no idea what it might be.

Margery was still arranging a drawer, rather preoccupied and indifferent to the two girls who had come in.

"You're hesitatin'," Mary accused her. "If you're too tired we can go another day. This has prob'ly been a tryin' day for yuh. But it is rather pretty this time of day."

"And maybe we can get some of the other girls to go too, if they'd like to. It's just up to you girls."

"Oh, it'll be all right with me," Margery answered, looking at first one then the other. "It'll take me a minutes to finish here. We have tuh take turns openin' our dresser drawers. When one is open it makes it hard on the other to see hers—you know? So we took turns. I hung things in the closet while Shandol was here. So its my turn here, even if she is finished hangin' stuff. Sure, I'll go. I feel pretty good now that I've ate."

"And I can make it, I think," Shandol added. "In fact I think it's nice of yuh to ask us. It's still fairly early, after all and we'd sorta be at loose ends. Not knowin' where to go or what tuh do. Just anytime I'm ready."

"Put that thing away!" Mary shrieked, as Margery slung her now empty suitcase over her shoulder. "I nearly got hit!"

"Oh, sorry," she apologized, and strode on over to the closet, smiling at Mary's reaction, and placed the "weapon" on end in her corner of the closet.

"Still plenty room in there," she muttered.

"They're nice-sized closets, ain't they," Betty agreed. "And the 'hotel' room I had at home wasn't this big either,"

Shandol laughed, looking at Margery. "Nope, guess not," Margery agreed.

"We live in—that is my folks and us kids—live in a supposedly former hotel. Actually now it just looks like a big old unpainted house. It's still called the Old Hotel. I can't remember it ever bein' a hotel, it's been so long ago. And, gee, it's sure nothin' like this. It seems rather crude compared to this."

"Are we ready to go, girls?" Margery asked. "I'm finally ready—not to change the subject—sorry 'bout that."

The girls filed out of the room one by one, and turned down the long hall the way they had come, toward the lobby.

"The toilets are there," Mary reiterated, as they passed the last door before the stairway.

"Seems somebody told us— but it'll help us remember. It seems a long way but I guess I'll get used to it. No worse 'n goin' outside at night," Margery giggled.

"Let's see," Shandol spoke lightly, "I know our room number and that the numbers go downward as we go this way, which is to the lobby. Yuh know, I do believe I'll be able tuh find my way back to my room. And that's something. I get turned around in strange places sometimes."

The three other girls looked questioningly, even Margery, and it occurred to Shandol that Margery might not know that either, so she shouldn't have spoken. She tried to explain as they walked slowly down the hallway.

"I shouldn't think out loud, should I?" She looked at them. "I was and laughin' at myself really. And I forgot Margery wasn't with me this morning when I made my blunder. Yuh see I left home early this mornin' to go to Plainesville, our county seat, to come up here. I ran into a friend I know who wondered why I was carrying a suitcase. She invited me to leave it at their apartment until I was ready for it. I was glad to find a place to leave it as I'd wondered how I'd manage. In fact, I was gonna ask them anyway. I was supposed to meet Margery later and go back to town. Anyway, when I went back to get my suitcase to come up here, instead of openin' the way to the stairway, which led to the street from their apartment, I opened a closet door! I didn't the first time though. But I was so mortified I wanted to crawl in a hole

450

right there. But they were nice about it, as I was so embarrassed and apologized. They were always nice tuh me but I bet they had a laugh about it later. So I don't want tuh blunder into anyone else's room by mistake."

The girls by then descending the stairs, having passed the first landing and were almost to the lobby.

"Oh, somebody say somethin'," she pleaded. "I know it was silly."

"Glad tuh meet someone with my trouble," Mary, the dark- haired one spoke. "I know just what yuh mean."

"You're Mary, aren't yuh?" Shandol asked. "I hope I remember names better 'n doors and get yours right. But that is something else I'm not so good at—rememberin' names."

"Yep, she's Mary," Betty said.

"And I've got yuh straight, too," Margery said.

"I think I have you girls straight, but I can't remember her name," pointing to Shandol, but turning to Margery added, "you're Margery aren't yuh?"

"I'm Shandol," she replied. "It'll grow on yuh. And I'll tell yuh the story which might help. Briefly, I was named by my dad because he dreamed the name. I'm surprised he remembered it. But he once said the dream stuck with 'im. He's got a surprisin' memory anyway. It didn't matter to Mama. In fact, she said the name grew on her too. Oh, I get teased about it and all that. Does that help?"

"Well, it may," Betty said, looking at Shandol directly, smiling and then around the room.

"Oh, we'll straighten it all out in time," Margery assured Shandol, as well as herself Shandol suspected. "Name and all the rest—wait and see."

"There's that girl that helped start the singin' on the trip up here," Shandol pointed. "Let's go ask her."

"That's what we're huntin'," Mary spoke up, "the other girls that came today, mostly. Isn't that another too?"

"Let's see their names were—what?" Margery faltered.

"I forgot too" Shandol replied. "Let's just go ask 'em. They've prob'ly forgot our names too."

They went to the large sofa where the girls were. They were quiet, just looking.

"Are you girls already unpacked too?" Shandol asked.

"Not exactly," the tall one answered. "You see, there are three of us in this one room, and I told them to go ahead and I'd see how the closet space and all held out. We may have to use our suitcases some, or one of us anyway. So I'm waiting until later. I just hung up some things. Same with her," and she pointed to the small brunette next to her.

451

"Are yuh gonna be so crowded yuh'll be unhappy, reckon?" Mary worried.

"Oh, no," the tall one spoke again, "we volunteered. And it may be only temporary if we don't like it. This other girl decided she wanted to be with us, because we had come together, and we wanted to be together," indicating the small brunette. "We're from the same county and don't really live very far apart. We just went to different schools and never met. She went to a country school."

The tall slender girl doing the talking was smiling by the time she had finished speaking; her eyes almost closing as she did so. She had fair skin and her light brown hair was worn in a short pageboy; her eyes were a deep blue. The girl beside her was decidedly opposite. She was tinier and darker complexioned. Shandol tried to remember anything she might have learned about the girls on the way, but if there had been anything special it eluded her then.

"These girls are taking us on a short walk or tour of the place—" Shandol began, "if yuh'd like tuh go. I mean, well, there's so much getting acquainted to do and all, we'd like for as many as can to come along."

"Sure," Mary added, "yuh see, we'll learn names, and where we're all from, and we'll try to tell yuh more of the routine here—that is if yuh want to hear it now."

"We know you are from our group," Margery added. "I wouldn't trust my memory to get the names right, so we'll just have that to do over. There are so many to try to remember and I don't remember anyone."

"We'll learn by repetition," Betty suggested.

"Let's do go," the small girl spoke, brightening, "maybe we should ask Eileen if she wants to go."

"Yes, I'll go ask her," the tall girl replied, and went down a nearby hallway.

"You're on the first floor!" Shandol exclaimed. "Is it better than the second, I wonder."

"I'm glad we're down here," the small girl replied. "Well, soon the girls will be back, but let's introduce ourselves. I'm Edna Barkers, the girl who was with me is Nancy Rayford and the girl she has gone to get is Eileen Rotherall. Oh, here's Nancy now. Where's Eileen?" she asked Nancy.

"She didn't want to do anything right now," Nancy replied.

"She had her shoes off and was lying down already."

"Oh, well, let's get goin' then," Betty said.

They went out the front doors and on outside the way they had gone in. Betty and Mary were pointing out lawn, calling attention

452

to the park, like the beauty of it, with the large trees and completely deserted area. Then they went on around to the rear of the north wing, which would direct them to the back of the river.

There was small talk as others introduced themselves again. They discussed home towns, their schooling and what they each hoped to accomplish at Wildwood. There were questions about the kind of work they would be required to do, but such a question could only be answered generally, because it was a changing thing. Girls changed their minds. Sometimes, the girls admitted hearing the staff say, it was a job planning for positions the girls could qualify for.

There was talk about the staff members, which from these girls was quite favorable. Pop was a dear, they learned, and showed no favoritism.

They discussed the activities and recreation; fellows for dates, and they were reminded that the army camp wasn't too far away. (It was the one Shandol's father had hoped to help construct.) It was already in use by the army.

The girls worried about their personal laundry, but they were assured it would work out.

"And don't forge to write home sometimes," Mary said, firmly. "The girls here are expected to write home and they can write whatever they wish. I mean the letters aren't opened or read. It will help set the parent's minds at ease. Also they must want to know your address."

Mama gave me strict orders to write," Shandol said. "Hey do yuh mind if I ask yuh a question? I hope yuh won't get me wrong—but how about the conduct of the girls here? I suppose they are mostly all right aren't they?"

"Yeah, " Margery added, "what it amounts to is that in a place like this it would be easy for everybody to get a bad name and I mean just because of a few."

"Sure," Shandol agreed. "In fact I think they have it already and have to prove themselves. Of course that's what my boyfriend said, but he didn't want me to come. So he was prob'ly terribly biased and wanted my folks to change their minds about letting me come."

"Sounds serious," Nancy smiled.

"That's what I'll find out," she conceded. "My folks don't care much about him. But I don't wanna talk about 'im."

She understood Dean. He hadn't wanted her to come, to realize there were lots of other men around. And he tried to picture them as not fit to tie a lady's shoe, especially the one he had chosen for himself.

"Mother told me to write home about anything that wasn't nice," Edna was saying. "I don't know how I ever could, but—" her voice trailed off.

"My folks said the same," Shandol and Margery said together, and looked at one another and smiled.

"Most do," Mary conceded, and Betty nodded. "Most of the girls are nice though yuh'll see, and came to learn. There have been rumors, I admit even some wild ones; wild parties, drinkin', but it's always been quiet up where we are. It could be just hearsay, so we can't say. But just about all the girls are good-natured and helpful, I'd say."

"Oh, I suppose it will work out," Shandol replied, thoughtfully. "It's just that we don't know what we've come into, so how could our parents? Wish mine could see where I am. But yuh do understand, don't choo?"

"Of course," Betty smiled. "We felt the same way at first. Some of the girls yuh'll like, some yuh may not—just like anywhere else."

"There are some we'll warn yuh about now though," Mary giggled in anticipation. "We do have our characters here, so let us tell yuh about the two main ones."

But they were descending a hill, which was so steep it seemed to Shandol it might be more correctly referred to as a bluff—only perhaps it wasn't high enough.

"You mean we can go down here?" she asked. "I mean upright or do we tumble?" she laughed.

The girls laughed, as at a joke.

"Sure we go down," Mary smiled. "There's a regular goat path down. By that I mean a goat really made it!"

"But I'm not sure I'm the mountain–climbing variety," Shandol quipped, and added, "then how do we get back up?"

"Looks bad but that's just the Ozarks for yuh," Agnes, who had silently joined the group and introduced as the one with the shower in her room. Her red-gold hair shone in the waning day.

"Of course we go slow and easy," Mary directed. "We better go first because we've been down before. Hang onto the bushes, roots or scoot on yer fanny, because it is steep and easy to lose yer footing."

They took a slanting path that was at times parallel to the river. It was farther but safer, they thought. They soon came to a narrow plateau shelf—a break in their descent. There was a weatherbeaten park bench leaning precariously against two good–sized oak saplings. The brush had been sparer above and outside the path had been a rank growth of grass and weeds. Below the shelf were more trees, undergrowth and weeds. The shelf was narrow and they could rest only a moment and went on downward toward the river, but not before Margery tried the bench.

"That's a spoonin' bench if ever I saw one," she said, as she tried out for size or safety the now weathered bench on the bluffside. "Do yuh suppose it's ever used? Down *that* path?" She mused almost to herself.

"Hey, you gettin' ideas er somethin'?" Nancy asked, closing her eyes in her broad smile.

"Do the girls come down here very often?" Edna asked. "Not as a rule," Betty admitted. "But most of them have been down here to see it at least. It's quite a task as yuh can see, not that much to see once you're there—*and* there are prettier places on the river."

"Oh, we understand," Margery said, "and it must be handy bein' a goat. Where are any goats by the way?"

"There's not any here now," Agnes laughed. "The path *was* made that way, but kept open by such as our own curious selves."

The girls sometimes squealed in delighted daring at their precarious predicaments, as they made their way carefully down toward the water. They slipped and sometimes were on all fours going backward while others laughed at them. However, they were never in any real danger.

"If we get started tumblin' can we stop before we hit the water?" Shandol asked.

"I'm sure of that," Mary assured her.

And in a short while the girls were standing on the narrow sandy, rocky beach of the Merrygo River. The sand was moist but firm and not at all marshy. They walked a short distance downstream. An abandoned building, they assumed to be some kind of boathouse, obstructed the way. To go around would be impossible because of the bluff and brush; and the other way was too close to the water. It was not very high above the water and only a narrow, muddy, sloping strip separated it from the water. It seemed to jut out over the sand, perhaps in case of higher water.

There wasn't much else to see, it was just the trip down; the wild beauty and peace of woods around them. The water barely rippled along in the shady protected area. The water was beginning to look dark and forbidding, even mysterious, in the now fading hours of the daylight. The sun had already gone from sight behind the hill which arose across the river. For another bluff rose more densely wooded and higher than the one they had descended and ascended directly above the water. It was the bank. There was no sand patch there.

They stared at the lazy water, threw in a few stones to hear the "ker-thomp" for some idea of the depth of the water. Even so there was disagreement. It sounded deep, Shandol insisted, yet the girls said it was not considered to be very deep. Still no one cared to test it personally, as there was a chance they could get in over their heads.

"How it all contrasts so completely," Shandol sighed, gazing around her at the relative wilderness. The wild woodiness of this in contrast to the up-to-date, modernistic development up there where they were staying. It is a wonderful, beautiful place, she thought.

Then, with Betty, Mary and Agnes in the lead, they started back. Almost in one accord, they decided they must climb back over the steep trail to the hotel. It would certainly soon be dusk and they should be in by then, they supposed, so no one would worry that they had wandered off somewhere, in this a new and strange place to the newly arrived girls.

The path upward was slower going than downward. At times they almost had to pull themselves upward by branches and bits of brush. However, they enjoyed the challenge of the climb, yet had to wonder how Mary and Betty seemed to make it seem so much easier than the rest of them. They would pause, smiling, as they waited for the others to catch up with them. Best even the beginners had their luck and they were soon at the top once more.

"Before we go in," Betty said, mysteriously, "we must warn yuh about two people here. So just sit wherever yuh like, as on the grass here."

"Carrot?" Agnes cried.

"Yes, but Perry, too," Mary added. "But first let's sit down here, catch our breaths and marvel at our mountain climbin'."

"Well, one at a time," Betty said. "The first is this boy. Is he ever red headed! He's real short, about four feet and eleven inches, and not very big anyway, and he's a pest if there ever was one. He thinks he's some kind of Don Juan, so don't give him any encouragement, or he'll worry yuh silly. He'll think yer crazy about 'im. Some of the girls have had to learn it the hard way. They'd just go along with his teasing and think he didn't mean a thing by it. But give him an inch—well, he thinks he's the most popular thing around here. And he's made them miserable, just hangin' around and wantin' to go wherever they went. So just sorta leave him be, outside uh what yuh have ta."

"Betty knows first hand," Mary went on, lightly, turning toward her friend affectionately. "I don't mean t' tease, now, so don't say nothin'. Yuh didn't know then, no one tuh tell yuh." She turned to the other girls. "But you can't say you've not been warned."

"Then there's a girl yuh won't want tuh have much tuh do with, either," Betty said. "I know what yuh're gonna say. Yuh can't be rude tuh people or shut 'em out in a place like this, but she's different as yuh'll soon see. Not very smart either. She's a big blond, with steely gray eyes. Her hair's not pretty. It's kinky and frizzy with too many permanents which her hair don't seem tuh hold good. It's all broke

456

off at the ends and it's real short. It just don't seem tuh grow. But I'll tell yuh what happened—one thing she did. She got married to an army lieutenant! Both got drunk—he was out for a night on th' town and picked 'er up. When he woke up the next morning and had sobered up and found himself married to 'er, he wouldn't even touch 'er, and the marriage was annulled just as fas' as he could. He was apparently from a very nice family and he didn't want the likes uh her. She talks baby talk and is *so cheap—*"

"Oh, tell 'em the other," Mary interrupted, impatiently. "It's th' real part."

"I'm gonna get to it," Betty replied, "just gimme time. Well, yuh see she already had a child—before the marriage, I mean. And I'll tell yuh how she says that happened. It seemed some guy she was out with told 'er all she'd hafta do was eat carrots and she wouldn't get *that way—*"

"She told it herself," Mary exclaimed, interrupting again. "She looks just that dumb too."

"Just eat carrots?" Edna repeated, incredulously, then cupping her mouth in her hand in an embarrassed manner.

"She thought eatin' carrots would keep 'er from havin' a baby?" Shandol asked, thoughtfully.

"Are yuh gettin' ideas?" Nancy teased, smiling broadly, her eyes not quite closed.

"Oh, go on, you," Shandol pouted. "I know it's not that simple."

"She should've remembered the rabbits," Nancy announced gleefully. "Maybe it's th' other way around."

"I think it's almost unbelievable," Margery piped up throwing away a piece of grass she had been nibbling. "That's really being dumb. D— U—M—B, dumb!"

"We'd best go in now. We can sit in the lobby, go to our rooms or visit someone else's. It's just to wait and see if anything develops in the meantime. Ha, ha."

The girls got up from their sitting positions on the grounds and went into the lobby. The lights were on and music was being played rather loudly.

"A nickel machine," Margery exclaimed, when they were inside and realized the source of the music. They had supposed it to be a radio.

"Oh, that thing goes about all time during off hours, which seems nearly all time for someone or other. And anyone and everyone can play it."

"Somebody's who's made uh nickels, yuh mean?" Shandol asked.

"Hey, huh don't know. Silly me," Mary replied. "It used tuh be that we used th' same nickels all th' time. They'd be put in and then taken out over and over, and it was a lot of fun that way, but tiresome. Yuh see only Pop could take th' nickels outta th' thing and sometimes he wasn't around and he just got tired of it, too, I think. So he finally just put a wire on it tuh trip it with instead of usin' coins. See that wire at th' side there?" She pointed and it was no trouble seeing it, as they had ambled that way as she had talked.

"Yuh just pull th' wire when yuh select your song and it's tripped. No coin needed."

"Well, now, ain't that clever?" Margery marveled aloud. "Woultn't yuh say?"

The girls waited for the song to finish to see how it was done. It was already turned on so they had only to pull the wire. As the song died away they decided to sit in the lobby. The six girls sat on sofas near the fireplace. The sofas faced the desk rather than the fireplace. There seemed to be several girls there. The music began again. Some of the girls danced.

"Aren't they good?" Margery whispered to Shandol.

"I think they are too," she answered. "They're so graceful even doin' that 'jitterbug' dance."

"Maybe we can learn it," Margery suggested.

Pop came through then and he took turns dancing with some of the girls on the smooth shiny floor. He did not try to do the "jitterbug" at first, just two-step and waltzes, and to the slower smoother music. But with the one girl he did do a slowed version of the dance. She was the one girl they had seen so far who could do it extra well. Even Shandol admired her dancing. She had lovely honey colored hair, which waved slightly and was thick and it gave promise she was a pretty girl. But she had a prominent nose, small eyes and a tiny mouth. She had't a very pretty face but she never lacked a dancing partner, especially among the girls. Shandol secretly thought they hoped to learn from her and probably did.

"Her first name's Betty, too," Betty said, looking at her, but she has a very difficult last name. So we just call her 'Wally'. She's lots of fun too."

Later Eileen, one of the group who had arrived that day, did what she called a tap dance. Of course she really hadn't the shoes for it and she did only some simple steps, but the girls seemed to enjoy it. Her dimples showed deeply as she smiled, her gorgeous complexion enhanced by the lighting, her fair curly hair moved as she did, yet never seemed to look rumpled. One girl, lacking appreciation got up and left.

458

"Not even a good jigger," she was heard to mutter as she went into the hallway, and presumably to her room.

Shandol soon left to go upstairs, followed by Mary, Betty and Agnes.

Sometimes we play games," Betty told them, but tonight I guess no one was in the mood. I wasn't, was you?"

"No," Shandol replied. "I really wouldn't have been. I better go write to my mother I think. She will be wondering where she can write to me. How long will that thing—the music—be playing?"

"More'n likely until lights out," Mary told them. "And when they say lights out here, they mean it, don't think they don't." She added. "They have one of the girls on the floor do it. A new girl is chosen every week. Can you girls find your room okay now?"

"Yep, it's number thirty-seven," Shandol said. "We just keep on this trail till we find it."

"I remember too," Margery agreed.

"I don't think I'll ever forget it," Shandol laughed.

"I should write home," Shandol repeated, once she and Margery were in their rooms. But I'm so tired I'm going to write a card and go to bed."

"I think I'll just skip writin'," Margery yawned, and started getting ready for bed.

But Shandol did write the card and even made some notes of the events of the day in a small spiral bound notebook she had purchased that day. She could hardly believe that only last night she had been home, and had awakened that very morning in her own bed!

CHAPTER 36

The girls were jarred awake the following morning by a seven o'clock buzzer. They had been warned to expect it, but awoke with a start and sat upright in bed as though by an unseen force.

Breakfast was at seven-thirty, so this gave the girls time to get ready, perhaps do any needed eye-opening rituals, even take a quick shower if desired. But Shandol and Margery, not wanting to be late, straightened up their beds, got dressed and washed, their faces, and made a trip to the end of the hall, though not necessarily in that order, for each.

"I'm wonderin' what'll be comin' up today." Shandol said. "I'm not sure I understand it all." She had stretched sleepily, dreading as was her usual reaction to the unfamiliar and unperceived.

"*I* wonder what's for breakfast right now," Margery replied.

The girls were served, as the night before and marveled as they finished the good breakfast of buttered toast, orange juice, eggs and bacon, with coffee.

They were instructed by a voice in the room to go to the lobby as soon as breakfast was over and further details would be announced.

There was a lady who soon came in to explain again to the girls they would be doing work in the mornings. She assigned each girl, or sometimes a team if it took more than one, to the exact task or tasks they were to do. The first thing Shandol did was clean the rest room of their own hallway. This consisted of cleaning the sink and sweeping and mopping the floor. Then she swept along the sides of the long corridor to and beyond their own rooms. It seemed a mile long. Someone else would vacuum the narrow, faded maroon carpet runner, she was told. Margery had dusted in the lobby, emptied ashtrays and in general attempted to tidy it. Then she and Shandol carried out some comforts to air on a line at the back of the building. That day they discovered their back stairway. While the comforts were airing they were directed to an area, a sort of back porch, to hull peas to be canned. The peas had come from the garden, which other girls had helped plant. There were perhaps half a dozen there now hulling.

They quit the work when it was time for the noon meal. There had also been a fifteen minute break at nine forty-five, which was mail time, but could hardly interest Shandol and Margery. They couldn't

460

receive any mail. The noon meal was referred to as lunch. They would need only to wash their hands, they were told. At breakfast and at noon the girls would go into the dining room to eat in whatever they wore for work. But they were required to dress presentably, though not elegantly, for the evening meal. This meant they could not go to the table at the evening meal wearing shorts, for instance, unless they wore a skirt over them. It was not allowed. Of course, this did not affect or concern Shandol or Margery as they had no shorts to wear. Neither owned a pair, and said so, admitting their parents hadn't approved of their wearing them, so no use getting them. Besides hardly anyone wore them in their small town.

It was a gray day. Rain finally fell. A mist had hung over the river and hills as a shroud, and Shandol wondered if that was like mountains would be. It was the dampness of it which brought it up in conversations. It seemed to penetrate everywhere.

Classes began at one o'clock. After eating Shandol decided to write a letter to her mother. She wrote of the work she had done that morning from cleaning the restroom to hulling the peas. That their work would be every morning from eight o'clock until noon. Margery, at the sink washing, had spattered the first page, but Shandol explained about it in the letter and that she couldn't take time to do it over.

The buzzer rang for the shorthand class and cut her letter writing short. The class lasted from one o'clock until two thirty; then there was a thirty-minute "recess." Shandol resumed her letter writing. She tried to describe the places, and made note of how glad she was she and "Marg" had a room together. (In all her correspondence, she explained, the Marg was Margery, saved writing the whole name and they'd know who she meant.) She told of going down the bluff to the river and the girls dancing and how in demand, though for a short time, Eileen's tap dancing was, and that she wasn't very far along in the learning of it.

I hope, she wrote, Marg gets to bring their camera so we can send pictures of the surroundings. The skyline or looking into distance is hilly and the mist hangs in the air like a mountain— well, I've seen pictures—

We get our books and paper furnished for shorthand and typing. I didn't realize I'd forgotten so much shorthand as I realized when I went to class.

This is later, the letter continued: In typing test, which is ten minutes, I made eight words and twenty-five errors! But isn't that why I'm here—to bring it all up? Typing lasted from three *until four-thirty.*

I guess Marg and I will go to town tonight. It's date night but of course we don't know anyone, and only girls are here. Two other girls are going just to show us the town, though some of the girls say the place here will be surrounded by soldiers. Whew! What a temptation to see, eh?

Today we had an interview and learned we have to have another physical exam and a dentist to examine our teeth. Marg is scared she won't pass a physical and I may not. No dental work will be done but any that needs to be done will be pointed out.

I hope you can make this all out. I'm hurryin'. Marg has written to her folks and boy friend (I didn't know she had.)

Boy-dee, some of the girls here even smoke and do they ever' darn' and bang around (in speech)!!

And do we ever make a 'mob' to eat. We eat at tables of four. Girls who are taking waitressing and cooking do that kind of work.

We have to be vaccinated for smallpox and get three shots for typhoid.

Well, you must be tired of this so I'll close.

Write.

Love, Shandol

P.S. When you can spare it send me some stamps, etc. money. I have thirty-five cents to my name. S.S.

Shandol confided to Margery after classes she hadn't realized her skills could have dropped so low in the year or so she had been out of school. However, she had had no way to practice. And, though she had kept her books, she hadn't tried to work on the shorthand much either.

But Margery was evasive: "Yuh got more words than I did," she pointed out, "but I didn't make that many errors. Anyway let's just say we got work t' do there, and no classes tomorrow—Saturday— though we do have to work."

The shorthand Margery discussed less. She seemed preoccupied and worried about it, and she admitted it was fairly new to her. Shandol understood how completely baffling it could seem at first, but if she would apply herself she could do it. But Shandol wondered if she would. She still lacked a year of having her high school diploma.

Shandol changed the subject: "Wonder why we have to have another physical examination."

"I wonder too, and if I'll pass." Margery groaned again.

462

"Yeah, I know," Shandol sighed, "and I might not neither. Then there's the dental exam. I just wonder why." "Beats me," Margery brightened a little, and added. "Let's just not worry about it. They won't do anymore than send us back home at the worst. If we can't help it we can't, that's all."

Yeah, I know," Shandol admitted, "but I did so want to improve my typing and shorthand and get a job and be on my own. But you're right of course. May as well be optimistic until the worst comes to worst."

"I feel better about that," Shandol went on talking. "Gee, but I'm glad yuh're here with me. I'd be scared prob'ly to be able to discuss such things with any of the girls here. They are still all really strangers; a feeling that mayn't surprise huh. But you can take things so in stride. I make myself miserable dreading things I don't know about or understand. The nurse seemed nice at the interview, didn't she?"

"I thought so too," Margery replied, and shrugged. "Maybe it's all just routine," and added with some mirth in her voice, "to see if we are healthy enough to take all this—maybe."

* * * * *

Shandol debated about whether she should confide in Margery what had happened or not. She decided against it. It was Saturday. They had been up since the buzzer and, as the first thing to do was the work assigned them, that's what they did—except Shandol. They had been assigned to housekeeping chores again. Shandol had been asked to vacuum the large rugs in front of the desk and where each of the large divans were located around the lobby. She had asked where she could find the vacuum cleaner and was shown where it was and even had help carrying it to the front desk; There was usually no one in the lobby when it was being cleaned until the nine forty-five mail time, and this was no exception, except another girl or two dusting and doing their chores.

Shandol looked at the tangle of wire, hose and tank of the vacuum cleaner and knew she would have to be shown how to manage it. She had never used one in her life and the only one she had ever seen was at her uncle's. He had paid for their transportation to visit a week when Shandol was perhaps thirteen years old. So Shandol asked one of the girls to help her and where to plug it in. Apparently she had known little more than Shandol because she only told her where she would find the socket to plug it in.

"But I don't think I can put it together," Shandol admitted.

"It fits together easy enough," the girl replied. "Just takes a minute to do it."

But Shandol hadn't known how or where to begin. So she had fussed over it awhile, spent sometime in the bathroom and her own room, thoroughly ashamed of her ignorance and wondered what they would do to her when they found out.

At mail call she was at the lobby with all the other girls. The vacuum cleaner was gone, and all the reprimand she received, though it was not directed to her was: "Whoever uses the vacuum cleaner from now on please put it away and not leave it for someone else to do."

Shandol felt terribly guilty the rest of the day. She had hardly done anything, not even put the thing away, where it belonged.

Oh, I'll never do that again, she vowed to herself, if I have to kick up some kind of fuss! But it was during the break that Mrs. Green had asked for volunteers to work in the garden the next two hours. Shandol and Margery were among the first to volunteer. Shandol had asked Margery to go along too. They planted beans and dropped garden corn.

There were no classes in the afternoon so they washed and did their hair. Margery had little to do to hers with it's natural wave, but Shandol pinned hers in pincurls around her face and across the back. Not that it would do a lot of good. It was getting so long, but it did help so she took the time to do it. There was humidity and threatening rain everyday, so it would soon fall to below her shoulders once outside, especially at night. Margery's dark hair was only an inch or so below her ears.

It was date night so the girls decided to go to town after supper. As they came back they were offered a ride by two young men in a car. The girls wouldn't get inside but did ride on the fender back to Wildwood. The two men did not leave however, but hung around to talk to Margery and Shandol. At first they were bothered about it, and wondered what they should expect next. But then, they learned, there were "regulars" at Wildwood and so far they had behaved as gentlemen. They begged Shandol and Margery to go to a nearby town to a small carnival and they decided to go. Clyde Middleton, who seemed to have eyes only for Shandol said he was from Eagle Roost Ranch, which wasn't very far, and was a dude ranch. His friend and fellow worker was Art Weagler. The carnival was a small one. Shandol was given the ridiculous looking clay pipe from a game Clyde won. She promised to cherish it as a souvenir.

The four got back to Wildwood in plenty of time for the Saturday night curfew, which was twelve midnight. On Friday night it was eleven p.m. The men did not leave until it was time.

The next morning the girls were awake before the buzzer sounded. However, breakfast on Sunday morning was not until eight-thirty.

They learned Pop always took any girls who wanted to go to church in the station wagon, which belonged to the Center. There were only three denominations to choose from and so they chose the Baptist church, where most of the girls went, "because we have the sweetest lady for our Sunday school teacher." And indeed Margery and Shandol also found her so.

After Sunday school, Shandol and Margery walked back to Wildwood. Shandol and Margery always went around by the highway unless they were with some of the other girls, as they weren't quite sure of the way or the short stretch of timber, with its fallen rotting logs, deep dead leaves and quiet desolate seclusion, almost sinister feeling it gave them.

As they walked along deeply engrossed in their own thoughts and conversation, they were hailed by who else but two soldiers from the nearby army camp. They had only walked a short way with the girls until they were introducing themselves. One, a husky looking, tanned guy with dark eyes and brown hair was Leon Harvey. His buddy he introduced as Jack Oaky. He was slender, blond, with a ruddy complexion. Leon seemed to take to Shandol and also seemed the leader of the two. Jack was also easy to get acquainted with, according to Margery. They tossed away cigarettes as they walked along with the girls.

The conversation began with getting acquainted questions and answers. Where are yuh from? How'd they like the army, their ratings and goings on of the war. The men were both from Michigan.

They waited outside patiently on the grounds while the girls ate. Then they went with them to town so they could eat a lunch. Leon insisted upon giving Shandol a silver ring—a simple band.

"It isn't gold or a wedding band," he laughed at her hesitation. "Only a souvenir yuh'll remember a certain guy on a certain day." Their stay at the camp might be terminated by a transfer to somewhere else he told her.

Shandol and Margery were required to be back for supper. In fact they later learned they were not supposed to have left the grounds at all. The men did not return to the Center after supper. Shandol was surprised. But it made no difference to Margery. Another army boyfriend of Margery's came to see her that night. Shandol was so lonesome and hurt that she had no one, she went to her room and burst into uncontrollable tears. She went into the closet among her dresses to cry, because she didn't want anyone to catch her. She realized it was loneliness and homesickness and when the storm was over she felt better.

She looked into the mirror to see the damage she had done to her face. She wanted to go back downstairs to see what was going on and not just stay in the room and cry and brood. She had sobbed bitterly and long and she supposed her eyes must be swollen. They were red. She bathed her face in cool water for a few minutes, repaired her makeup, and saw no tell-tale signs. She went to the lobby.

Nancy was by herself also and Shandol surprised herself by asking if she would mind company. She sat alone on one of the large sofas. She smiled warmly at Shandol's offer to sit beside her, and promptly admitted she was looking at the guys. She hadn't realized, she said, there'd be so many on Sunday night and she marveled and watched them dance, or some of the bashful ones just eye the equally bashful girls.

Nancy looked neat. She had nicer clothes than Shandol had. She was well-groomed. Only one thing marred her otherwise pretty face was prominent teeth, which fascinated Shandol. Her smile was always ready and intimately warm, as though for only one person at a time.

They eyed "army guys" awhile, as the men were referred to generally, and one had caught Nancy's eye.

"Let's go for a walk and see if he follows," she whispered to Shandol. They got up and went out to the spacious porch.

It was Shandol he had had his eye on, for no sooner had they left the room then he caught up to them. He was young and very handsome in his uniform, which he wore without flaw. "What'd you say your name is?" he asked, "Marie?"

"I didn't say," Shandol replied. But then she told him as he had guesses she would. More getting acquainted questions and answers.

And when he was embarrassed or they were, he took the blame and pretended remorse. "Shame on me for thirty minutes," he'd say.

He asked Shandol for a date for the following Saturday, after introducing himself finally as Johnny Halleron. She was so tickled. She couldn't help it. She knew Nancy wanted to be with him so badly, but he promised to bring a buddy.

Now Shandol had two dates for Saturday night and she wasn't sure which one she would rather keep. She knew which one she wanted to go with, but Leon, after all, had asked first. And he reminded her so much of Hugh Burdette, more in actions than actual looks though, she decided.

On Sunday night the girls could not go anywhere except to church with Pop. As it became time for church to be over the soldiers began to thin out. They were due back in camp also and had a drive of some duration. They had no desire to be late either.

Shandol wrote to her mother, or rather finished a letter she had started the night before. She wrote of what she had been doing and about the men she had met. She even wrote what she had had for supper, which had been pork chops, potatoes and gravy, corn and peas, salad, cookies and an orange, which she had taken to her room to eat before going to bed. She also admitted being blue and crying, but how impressed she was by the soldier boy she had "caught" and over some competition. Shandol decided Nancy simply came on too strong. And he seemed so young to be training for war. Shandol was genuinely drawn to him.

"Oh, it beats Greenway up here, anyway, wouldn't you say?" She ended her letter to her mother.

The weekend was over.

CHAPTER 37

A week soon passed. The girls were becoming accustomed to the routine and regulations. At least they thought they were learning what was expected, required, and allowed.

Then the first Monday had presented something new. It began the same. They got up early and worked in the garden; they went to class as usual, they had heard Monday nights were known for something else: Council meeting. They supposed, however, that whether they attended or not was optional and they chose not to go. They hadn't known to reckon with the fact the roll was called and anyone missing had to be accounted for. So they were sent for by the girls next door, who explained, "Everyone goes to council meetings!"

Later Shandol was hard-pressed to recall what it was all about. There were minutes read, old business and new business which certainly meant little to her. She actually hadn't had her mind upon what was going on. She began to wonder why it was so important she was there. Margery had a bored expression as she and Shandol looked each at the other. Shandol wondered why a crippled girl, whose face was badly pitted by acne scars, had ever made president. Later she was to become better acquainted with her and learn she was compassionate and helpful, had a good personality and a husband in service. She had come to Wildwood to learn skills to help somehow in the war effort to speed her husband's return home. But she hadn't known it that night. She hardly knew she would feel guilty about her first impression and unkind thoughts that night. She consoled herself she resented being there and it perhaps only reflected her mood at the time.

But Margery's and Shandol's boredom was dispelled as the matter of a dance and party, which was to be held later in the month came up. It was for a company of soldiers from the nearby base. It was then Nancy and Edna came to sit near them. And then Shandol and Nancy learned it would not include company F and Johnny Halleron. But instead the solders would include friends of two women on the staff. One of these women had never been married, one was a widow with a six-year-old boy. Some of the newer girls resented this, but many more favored that particular group. There was no pleasing everyone. But as time went on, and the girls talked about it and prepared for it, excitement would grow—even at the council meetings. Those who were so exuberant could always console the others with "there'd be other times other parties." Even Shandol and Nancy decided they might enjoy it.

"Margery," Nancy bantered, "has two soldiers to write to, so she won't care. She has nothing to lose." Of course, neither of Margery's friends would be there.

Shandol finally heard from her mother on Tuesday. Margery had received two letters; one from Madge Middleton, a school friend of them both. Shandol had walked to and from school with her at lunchtime. She usually smelled of onions. She was younger than Shandol, nearer Margery's age. Margery also heard from one of her solder boys, Chilton Hawkins.

Shandol's mother's letter was dated simply, "Sun eve" and began:

Dear Shandol:

Guess its my first letter I've written you. Was expecting a card yesterday. Guess would have been disappointed. Kept watching every mail train, no letter or card until the train came from the south.

I hope you like your habitat by now.

Shandol wondered why she had chosen that word. Guess she couldn't stand to write "home" and it had come to her mind first.

You will have "blue spells," the letter continued, but guess we all have them. You'll meet lots of nice girls as well as some bad ones."

Went to church this a.m. Mrs. Ruleton and Ardena to dinner with us. Mrs. Lindersilt and Douglas went to Horn's for dinner. Said Horns were so good to come to church up there. We all went to Grandpa Brights after dinner. Mrs. L. and Douglas too.

Looks sorta rainy this eve. Truck's supposed to go to town (Plainesville)but don't think it will.

Karen is fine. Seems to be doing fine on her "cow diet."

Lester and Jane were here last night. They're okay. Lester brought his questionnaire so Dad could look it over.

Phil and Dad drew twelve dollars a piece Sat. eve. Phil was sure proud of his. Will get some clothes and the like Tuesday when he goes to town. They have to do some clearing this week. That means the old cross-cut saw.

Dean and Jr. Bright were in town Friday. He went west

yesterday about four-thirty when he came back the car was full, guess he got the Martin girls.

Was too rainy for Young People"s meeting Friday night. Looks as if it might be again tonight. Dad was supposed to make a talk about the Devil tonight."

We had a hot time the night of the party to hear Alva Parkley tell it. She said a bunch stood out in the street and mocked the folks at Kaspers having a prayer meeting for him. I asked Mrs. Colmay and Mrs. Kasper and Mrs. Pipkin and they never heard anyone so it must have been pretty close to (her) home. No one heard it but her (or them). Need not worry about it just skip it. Can't hurt us. While they got us on the block they're sparing someone else (gossips I mean). Just study hard so you will get away from here as soon as possible. Maybe you can help us get away too.

Mrs. Kasper about as usual. In bed most of the time.

Harriett Dolphus come by to see if I had heard from you girls. She said you girls had better stay. You won't get another chance like it. If you get too homesick we'll try to get you home some weekend.

Mon. a.m. Just finished reading your letter. Should have gotten it yesterday (Sun.)but for some reason they didn't get the mail, We were at church. Talked too long, post office closed.

I'm sorry you've forgotten so much but it will soon come back to you. Won't be so bad as having to start from the first. I'm sure you'll have fun. Just be careful who you go with. Go ahead and date. Don't set around up there and mope. Might as well enjoy yourself. Don't neglect your lessons though. Those supervisors have their eyes on you (all) just be the Shandol you have always been then I'll have something to be proud of. You will have a better moral rating than those who hang around. Still preaching!! Karen is cooing at you while I'm writing.

The truck went to town last night. Not much rain. About enough to lay the dust.

Dad and Phil are working today at Moelmans. Bobby is still asleep. Mildred, postmistress, came said cow was in tater patch. Had a big stick of wood on her but she manages to drag it around.

Must sign off. 9:15 as usual nothing done. Baking bread and want to wash some for Karen after awhile. May hoe some more. Bob and I hoed the onions and cucumbers Sat. Didn't have much to do in house. Wasn't very dirty.

Maybe we can get a way to get some pictures.

Write often if it's nothing but a card. I think of you the last thing at night and the first thing in morn.

Yes, I could make your card out. I guess I can read between the lines. Ha. Am enclosing dollar now. Will try to send some along.

Must quit.

Tommy wants to write some. He caught a little bird has markings of a canary but its beak is too long for that. Pretty yellow breast. Wants to tell you about that. Well here goes. Karen says she wants her bath so must quit. Be good and write.
Your loving Mom.

P.S. Excuse grammatical construction.

P.P.S. Yard is full of Colmay kids again so Tommy says he'll write this eve. Told him didn't want to wait. Lester came to get Mildred, at post office to fix questionnaire.

Shandol and Margery did two hours gardening work in the evening at six o'clock—the cool of the day—in the early morning and evening. They set out cabbage and tomato plants. It was either that or washing dishes for one hundred girls!

Margery wrote to Madge Middleton, while Shandol wrote to her mother and to Carol. She told Audrey the collar she bought in Plainesville didn't fit the neck of the dress and wondered if she should get another. She also asked her mother to help her save so she could get her long hair cut and a new permanent. She even hoped to save a part of the dollar she had been sent. Shandol did not realize how lovely and young she looked with her hair down long with it's few curls and waves at the end. It was shiny clean and invited many eyes to wish they dared touch it. She also asked her mother to send her old tennis shoes she had worn in "phys. ed." in high school to work in the garden, and thanked her for the money.

On Wednesday Shandol received her first letter from Dean.

It was a nice letter for him. He wrote how lonesome he was without her and that he still loved her. (What was she to believe? He wasn't acting like it!) But his loneliness got through to her. She realized one didn't have to be alone to feel lonely. It was the matter of being with the right people. And even then the feeling might come. So she wrote. She also answered the card from Leon Harvey, but only a short letter. He had written he was sure he'd be leaving there sometime in the "not too distant future."

At night Shandol and Margery put on slacks and went to a carnival being held there in Strawsville. It was small. It had only a Ferris wheel, four or five stands, including a picture-making one and some small cars for the children. The girls had their pictures taken separately, looked it over and went back to Wildwood. They were real pleased with their pictures at least.

They walked home at night by way of the highway, as they were more frightened of the woodsy shortcut at night. They were offered several rides but weren't interested in a "pick up," as Miss Lockney called them, making them sound almost criminal.

"She's so nice, and we don't want to break anymore rules by next council meeting," Shandol ventured.

It was true they hadn't known not to leave the grounds on Sunday afternoons, and the other rules they had inadvertently broken, including being on time. It seemed Shandol was always hurrying Margery, or the other way around. But they must realize this wasn't play school or working at play, it was grown up and serious. And it was up to every girl to do her part because it was for her own good. Shandol wondered if many of the girls had, for awhile at least, considered it a holiday from home routine and had to come to the same realization and adjustment.

The girls were encouraged by smiles and unspoken bond from the girls who had come up with them, especially Nancy and Edna. The way their rooms looked was their problems, for instance, and they talked and understood some had never spent time away from their parents and would have other adjustments to make.

"And we're all believin' you girls can do what we're here to do," the president had smiled at them warmly that first day. Both Shandol and Margery felt they had done better since then.

Then it was Thursday and the first week was over.

It was a rainy day. It had continued to be a wet and gloomy time, but it never dampened Shandol's or Margery's enthusiasm or spirits.

Shandol received two letters from Audrey and the package with the tennis shoes, for which she was thankful. Shandol enjoyed the letters from her mother. She wrote about everything—whatever or whoever came to mind, in a rambling, ungrammatical, natural way, abbreviating some words.

One was dated "3:30 Tue eve." And began:

Dearest Dear:

Received your letter at noon. Guess you got mine today.
Had a hard rain last eve. Dad and Phil went to Plainesville

472

today. Relief day—not much, just flour, oatmeal and cornmeal. Help some.

Washed today. Haven't swept the dining room as yet. Bobby helps me lots, swept the front room. Not as good as you but we manage. Karen hasn't been so good or maybe 'cause I had so much to do. Had twenty-four diapers, seven dresses for her, two or three for myself, shirts and four overalls. Didn't get started until late—put water on nearly nine o'clock.

Freda Horn and Orville Brack and Ambert Horn and Melba somebody were married yesterday. Ambert has to go back to camp tonight. Will *charivari* Freda tonight. They aim to stay at Horns until the men are transferred to Texas, then they will go there (Freda and Melba). Melba is only sixteen years old.

Ardena is here with Tommy and the two little Alston boys. Looks as if it might rain again. I mailed the shoes on north bound train. Guess you received the dollar.

Go ahead and have a good time (behave yourself tho') and forget about Dean. I won't tell him anything you say, but if I was you I wouldn't care if he found out. You'll find the world is full of them as good as him and better.

Lester stayed for dinner yesterday. You remember when he walked in before? He was sorta blue. Guess the Mrs. (meaning his mother-in-law) keeps on until she causes something desperate.

Wish you could see me. I look like a 'glamor girl'?? Have your old blue skirt on and a white blouse. All my everyday dresses were dirty or had the back or rear out. Ha.

The handsome young preacher hitchhiked to Iowa yesterday. (Shandol knew she meant Mr. Colmay, who was neither young, handsome, nor much of a preacher.) Reckon he'll be any account when he gets there. I set the birds up housekeeping in their big cage. It's rather handy.

Shandol could just see her mother using an oatmeal box or some small box, sometimes she had to sew small pieces of cardboard together to make a box to put bits of cloth and stitch it down for the bird's nests.

Same old Greenway. You know I wouldn't be here if I didn't have to be. A fellow gets blue once in awhile and a good cry does him good. If you should get a job you would be far better off. Cheer up!!

What did your interviewer say to you? Did you have your dental exam?

Club this week don't know whether I'll go or not. Out to Beatrice Freedman's, so guess I won't walk. Mrs. Freedman is going to teach in Louisiana this fall so I hear. Some talk of transporting the H.S. here if they can't have some more applications soon.

Shandol could recall Mr. Freedman. She had gone to school to him also.

Must get this mailed or p.o. will be closed.

I've the beds to fix, sweeping to do as well as other things that will pop up.

Be good, have a good time, study hard in between times. Do you have any idea of how long you'll have to stay? It isn't too far if you get too blue maybe some of your soldier boys might bring you home the 4th. Spend vacation with us here. They get pretty blue so far from home and friends. If it was Michigan where you were you would have something to cry about. Margery's aunt said her brother couldn't come no matter how homesick he got, so you can. Here goes.

Bye Love, Mom

The other one also began "Dearest Dear:" but was dated Wed. p.m." It read:

Received your letter at noon. Glad you have plenty to keep you busy. I pulled weeds, got dinner and cared for baby this a.m. She's awfully good lately. Lays in bed and plays on floor.

Not much news as it still rains. You surely haven't had any rain. Would mire a saddle blanket in our garden.

Harry Bright came after Dad a few minutes ago. There was a high school teacher at the store.

Rained them out didn't work today. If it don't keep them out too long maybe I can help you get a 'frizz.' I won't get any now until the moon fulls again last of May. You need not pay any attention to no one if you don't want to. Just when you get the money.

Shandol knew her mother thought hair grew slower if cut in the "dark of the moon."

The letter continued :

Do you just get mail once a day? Is Strawsville on a R. R.? Didn't cheverie Freda last night. They all took Ambert back

474

to Fr. Woodman so they aim to tonight.

Gerald Thelby is going to Wyoming to work on a railroad. Dad had a chance to go but didn't want him to. Too far away. He can do pretty good here as long as he can stand it. Rain's out there he'd have to pay $1.10 to $1.30 a day for room and board so might not have so much after all. Didn't get a grocery order yesterday. The lady had gone on vacation.

Dean said he'd come by before he left but hasn't yet. Don't know whether he's gone to Kansas or not, do you? Hope you can forget about him somewhat. Why would you want him if he drinks? Oh, well, no use to preach!

No, Mrs. Lindersilt & Doug didn't come to house. They brought us home from Sunday school. Maybe Madge can come when she returns.

Night I read the diary? Yours? ? ha ha

What is council meeting? You'll have to tell me better. Have to watch out. Hate for you to have to be punished.

If you can't sell the collar to some of the girls or trade it someway, keep it and get you another. We might use it somehow. How do you manage about your washing? Do you go 'dressed up' in your classes? Who does the ironing? Bobby is writing. I think Dad aims to write sometime. I'll quit now and get this mailed. Be good and write.

Love, Mom

Shandol wrote to her mother to answer the two letters and to thank her for sending the shoes. Having received two letters, she felt she had had a "visit" with her mother, and because they were rained out of the garden work and came in at nine thirty, she had the time:

Wildwood Hotel
Strawsville,
June 11, 1942

Dear Mom,

I got two letters from you this morning. Also the package containing the shoes. I'm glad you sent them promptly, thank you. I had to work in the garden this morning barefooted—all the girls did. It sure was raining too. We set out cabbage and tomato plants. I'd rather do that than work in the kitchen for Mrs. Prine. We work for Mrs. Green and she's so much nicer. Not so sharp tongued—even if Mrs. Prine doesn't mean to be.

We quit this morning at 9:30 because of the rain.

Then the nurse met us at the door and we went to the dentist. He merely tells us what is wrong. We have to have our teeth fixed, which I need, but will have to wait, eh? Did I tell you I was vaccinated for smallpox and given one shot for typhoid. There will be two more for later. My arm sure is sore. The smallpox vaccination of course hasn't taken yet.

So the Horns finally married, eh? Well, I guess that's what they wanted. I wasn't much surprised.

I must say I'd like to have seen you in the 'glamor garb'? ha

The interview was a checkup. About like what we'd had when we signed up. She didn't do a thing to me. I still have a blood test to take then I guess I'll be more settled where that's concerned.

A regular term up here is eight weeks. But some have been here as high as nine or ten months. I think I'll get out as quickly as possible. My typing keeps coming up. I made 38 and 32 words. I'm going slow and gaining accuracy too. Don't you think that's better? I'm taking more pains in learning shorthand, too.

I'm answering your two letters together, but I'll write again soon. Don't wait for me to write. And tell the kids to write. Letters to the girls here mean a lot, "more the merrier." ha

Rain? I believe it's the name of the place. It rains every day. It even rained on us some coming up here.

Does Dad still play checkers? Or is he too busy?

I'm really 'crazy' to get my hair fixed. Margery has written to her brother for money for herself. But really no hurry I suppose.

Margery and I went to this 'two by four' carnival last night. Sure was small. Just a Ferris wheel, some shooting stands (4 or 5) a picture taking place and some cars. Not much to it, eh? So we had our pictures taken and came back. We came back by highway, we were afraid of the shortcut. It's woodsy and wild. But before we got out of town we were offered a ride. But Marg and I won't go with just a 'pickup' as Miss Lockney calls them. She's the superintendent here. Say, she's nice too. Before we got home three more cars stopped to offer us rides. They were fine cars too. But I think it best not to get in cars. We can talk to the army guys right here on date nights. Yes, I'll try to be good.

I'm going to send you the pictures to see. Select one and send the rest back. Be sure to, please. I think they're pretty good. But they show how long and impossible my hair is. I had on my pink slack outfit. Marg's pictures were good too.

Tell Ardena to write. Glad she still comes. She helps too, doesn't she, especially with Karen? I'll write her a card.

Boy—de—e—e something sure smells good cooking. I am hungry. Lands do we ever eat. This morning I had two pieces of toast. They feed well here.

Write.

Love, Shandol

P.S. Note new address. Instead of putting NYA Center put Wildwood Hotel. All the girls do it. Keep forgetting to mention it. S.S.

At the end of the first week Margery decided she had better drop shorthand. She was sure she was falling behind. Most of the girls had had some in school, as had Shandol. And Margery was afraid she wouldn't be able to catch up as well as keep up, with all the interruptions and work—and activities. She decided to take Home Nursing instead. Shandol hated to see her make the change and was nervous in class. She made mistakes in typing and in shorthand made only seventy words per minute, which was so much behind what she could do when she left school. Even she was discouraged.

In the later part of the afternoon the girls tried to iron. However the cord on the iron was frayed and shorted so the iron wouldn't heat. Shandol got shocked by it twice before they finally gave up. They decided they would just have to find out from some other girls how they managed to get theirs done. They might borrow one. They left the things dampened and rolled, and knew anything that is damp could "sour" quickly up here, so they would have to make that temporary.

"Must be this damp climate," Margery had observed. "Yeah," Shandol agreed, and added, "so much rain and it seems the misty fog over the river just creeps inside. The washcloths actually sour before they dry over the sink! I can hardly believe it!"

That night the girls went again to the carnival with Nancy and Edna. They wanted to get their pictures taken. They had seen and agreed the ones of Shandol and Margery had turned out so well.

Shandol asked about the ironing.

"We went to the construction room where they told us an iron and ironing board would be, but it shocked me and wouldn't heat. How do you girls manage?"

"Lucky us," Nancy replied. "Eileen brought her own. So she lets us borrow it. I'm not sure we were supposed to tell, because she can't

477

let everyone use it. But she might let you if you come to our room."

"We may have to ask her," Margery replied. "Can't leave the clothes damp long or they will smell sour and terrible.

Ain't it a sight how damp it is here?"

"Yeah," Edna agreed. "I see yuh've also washed your hair today. Uh—huh, date tomorrow and guys tonight."

"If it dries," Shandol replied. "Ain't this rain something. Hey, we also got our blood tests today, did you?"

"Shore did," Nancy replied, "and I understand that ends all that stuff."

"Let's hope," Edna muttered.

Shandol eyes took in the room. It was crowded with a somewhat cluttered look, as suitcases and a box or two were in sight. They had already told Shandol and Margery of their crowded circumstances, but they laughed and said they didn't mind.

Shandol and Nancy were really concerned whether Johnny Halleron would show up Saturday night from the army camp for the date. Leon Harvey had already written Shandol he couldn't make it after all.

Saturday was a workday and the girls were up at six to go to the garden. Mrs. Green told them they had to pick two bushels of lettuce, which they started to do. But it began to rain harder and they had to quit.

"Because it's a Saturday, I'm giving you the time anyway," she told the girls.

They were back for breakfast at seven-thirty.

At mail time Shandol heard from her mother with a letter from Bobby and a card from Ellen Garfield included.

The card from Ellen was a short acknowledgment of a letter Shandol had written to try and see her before the Thursday she was to leave. However, Ellen had been to her sister's visiting and hadn't received the letter. She wrote she hoped Shandol got to go to Strawsville and wished her the best of luck.

Bobby's letter was also short and concerned mostly with their disappointment in not getting to charivari Freda Horn and her husband. His letter was dated and began:

"Dearest Sis:

I will try to answer your letter I got this morning. We tried to charivari Freda and Orville, but they wasn't there. Mrs.

Brack said and that they were 25 years to late. Three shots were fired. And Mr. Brack said to go home and go to bed. But we didn't for awhile and he got a gun and said the first one to stick his head in the door he was going to let him have it and leave him lay. So we went home and went to bed, Ha. We tried to charivari them again last night (Thu) but old man Brack come and got them and went to Plainesville.

Just wait they'll want a shower. Phil and Dad are working today. Well, guess I will close for this time.

I'll remain,

Your bro
Bobby

Audrey's letter contained her welcome gab. She sent the pictures back and made note it was a hard decision to make. Shandol read the letter:

Greenway
June 12, 1942

Dear Dearie:

Missed your letter yesterday but guess we can't write every day?? I dreamed about you last night. Tho't you came home. I asked you why you were home and you said you're supposed to come home as much as you can. I thought you were with Dean. It's fair today, now at least. Sure been rainy here too— out of the blue sky it seems sometimes. Day before yesterday even the neighbors all went to Pres Sandler's cellar. Cloud came from SE didn't scare me so much. Pulled weeds out of tater patch this a.m. Am getting supper and baking bread. Now am going to get ready to go to club but can't walk—but just in case someone comes by for me. They hired the high school teacher. You remember hearing Lester talk of a one-eyed teacher at the CCC camp? He's the one. Was a mistake about Mr. Freedman going to La. to teach. Phil and Dad are working. Dad started to write but didn't get it finished. I'll have to boost him up. You know how hard it is to get him to write. He's as eager to hear from you as the rest. Wish you could see Karen. She has found her feet. Sticks them in her mouth. She's so sweet. The pictures were all good. You surely need a permanent. Won't get much of a check this week but I'll see what I can do. Can you get it there? No, don't ride

with everyone. They'll think you cheap there at the 'hotel'.
Bobby says not to write all the news so if I don't you'll know
why. Not much to write about anyway. Haven't been anywhere
since you left only church Sun. Phil got a reed for your old
clarinet and does he play. I get a kick out of it don't know how
about the rest. Am mailing the card received from Ellen today.
Don't need to look for paragraphs—or do I know better? Ha. I
haven't time to try to write such a (business)letter, couldn't if
I tried but maybe you can read between the lines too. Cotilda
is here guess Tommy won't write this time. Will try to get Dad
to write. *Do you get mail on Sun?* Must quit and get to work.
Be good—

Love, Mom."

Johnny Halleron was late. So late in fact Shandol and Nancy
had about given up on them. Shandol couldn't imagine what had
happened. But an hour and forty-five minutes after the six o'clock
he had hoped to arrive, he made it. Shandol was happy and flattered.
But it had been a matter of getting there.

They had planned to show the girls Eagle Roost Ranch. They went
in a green sports Plymouth roadster belonging to the "Rooky"—the
only name they were ever to know him by.

All the outstanding features were pointed out to the girls, proudly.
There was another couple, "Jerry and her boyfriend." The "Rooky"
was from army camp also.

There was a rain and electrical storm there. The lights all went out
so they got a very dim view of Eagle Roost Ranch. There was little
they could do—not even look around. It was a super place, it was
reported, but Shandol and Nancy could not see in the rain. Yet, later
as they recalled it it was certainly a memorable occasion! They had
even drowned out the motor trying to cross a flooded creek, which
had no bridge only a concrete floor where the road went through.
They had to call for help to get out. Shandol got her back wet. Don,
who got out of the car to help, slammed the door when he re-entered
the car and it splattered the creek water inside. Don was with Nancy.
He was a soldier, dark and handsome, a settled type, yet Nancy
seemed drawn to Johnny.

But the girls were to remember the occasion fondly as having been
a fun time. It was all so completely off schedule and unexpected it
seemed an adventure to the two girls. They were to giggle about it
later and recall what a close call it was, as they returned not a minute
before midnight. However, in time they were told, as they had car
trouble. Mrs. Lockney signed them in, in fact, at one minute past

twelve. The girls were terribly disappointed as no future dates were made.

Johnny had been so nice and Shandol had begun to feel sure of herself. It was somewhat of a let-down to her. Nancy teased them singing "Oh, Johnny" to her—perhaps he resented it.

Earlier in the day Shandol had had the letter she had written to her mother that morning after ten. She wanted to report the doctor's finds. She was surprised she had written :

My eyes are weak. Nothing but some astigmatism or eye strain. He said it will cause headaches later. My ears are okay. A scar on one eardrum, probably caused, he said, from a throat infection sometime. My tonsils are bad, he added. Otherwise I'm okay. I have a few bad teeth in the back. The nurse said I had pretty teeth, they are so even. Got my blood test or did I tell you? I hollered when he drew blood from my arm. I was so nervous about it all anyway. Marg admitted being scared, too.

Talk about 'glamor garb', you should see mine. It's a dark blue, white speckled cotton coveralls. We can wear them to work in and saves washing our own clothes. Mine are a size thirty-two, the smallest, which must be the waist because they are so baggy. Marg and I could almost fit in one pair. We can wear them to breakfast and dinner, but not supper.

We don't go to bed until about eleven p.m. The jukebox downstairs is going most of the time. There's a radio across the hall we can hear and girls gabbing and talking, yelling and hollering back and forth—upstairs and down so it's impossible to try to sleep. But all is quiet by 11.00 p.m. I do mean quiet.

CHAPTER 38

To Shandol and Margery it seemed there were simply no two days alike at Wildwood. Constantly the new and different things to them, cropped up. Sometimes they were so completely unexpected, sometimes merely by the natural turn of events, following a never ending changeable pattern.

For instance it was the second Sunday they were there before there was a day in which there was no rain. It was a bright and beautiful day. There was freshness in the clean air warmed by the sun. There were the trees and grass washed clean and shiny green around Wildwood. And for once the mist did not hang over the river and bluffs.

Shandol and Margery slept late, but were up in time to eat breakfast at eight-thirty. They had started to help clean the lobby but Mrs. Lockney was taking any of the girls who cared to go to church. Pop was taking a weekend off. The two of the girls, with others who chose to go there, enjoyed the lesson at the Baptist church.

In the afternoon a soldier Margery wrote to came to see her. They strolled about the grounds, taking pictures and visiting all afternoon. She was disappointed when he didn't return after supper. However he telephoned his regrets. When Margery was called to the telephone to talk to him, she turned as white as a sheet. She was almost afraid to go down and see who it was, for of course she had no idea. All she could think of was that something had happened at home. Who could be sick or hurt? Or what could have happened? She was so relieved when she heard Arnold Welch's voice, she got tickled and could hardly talk. She had to explain to him she was so happy it was him and not that something was wrong at home; she was laughing nervously with relief. He seemed to understand, as Margery told Shandol as she confided her day.

Shandol told Margery she had been with Nancy and Edna all afternoon. They had gone to town. Shandol spent ten cents for an ice cream cone and a package of gum. Nancy and Edna also got ice cream. They had also taken a walk to the river, and sat in "porch" swings under trees, on the grounds.

"There were two guys talked to us," Shandol added, "but we didn't care for them. One was a curly haired, baby faced guy who was so conceited he was obnoxious. The other seemed nice enough, but also wanted to talk only about himself and the convertible they were driving. Anyway they weren't in uniform and were really unkind in their remarks about uniforms." She went on to explain they decided they had missed the draft for physical reasons, though no flaw was apparent. Even the flattery they tried seemed forced and an invitation for flattery in return. They were glad to see them go, though, they had talked for sometime, in fact, until supper time. Again it had been Shandol who had received the attention. They did compliment on her "nice even tan, which was so becoming." Shandol was embarrassed. She knew that came about while riding the truck on the school picnic. That she did not explain.

Johnny came after supper to the delight of Nancy and Shandol. At first he stood around much like a whipped puppy too afraid to make a move. It only added to his charm. But he finally ventured over to the sofa where the girls sat waiting and wondering. He and Nancy were soon engrossed in reading and writing shorthand, Nancy hoping to crowd Shandol out. Shandol knew shorthand also, so was not after all. He gave Shandol a picture of himself, Nancy had to coax one from him.

"He's so cute," the girls told one another and the other could only reply, "yes, he is." And Nancy would add: "Shandol, you're so lucky!" Shandol wondered how Nancy could be so "crazy" about him when she had met him only the few times. Was looks all that mattered to her?

Monday morning was quite cool for June, but the girls went to the garden. They were there by six to pick peas but quit to eat breakfast a seven-thirty. Margery decided not to do garden work that day, complaining her legs hurt. After breakfast, Shandol went back to the garden to pick beans until ten o'clock, when their workday was finished. Shandol was somewhat resentful of Margery for not going along. By now Shandol was friendly enough with the other girls not to show it or to feel alone, still she failed to understand it. The girls kidded among themselves about it. Perhaps Margery couldn't take the wet and cold, and found an excuse to play hooky. It was good-natured and Shandol laughed along, and added perhaps her legs were just sore from all the walking she did with her soldier boy.

Shandol asked Margery about her legs when she was with her alone after dinner in their room.

"Not much better," Margery replied, rather sheepishly Shandol thought.

"Tell me honestly, Margery," Shandol couldn't help asking, "does your legs really hurt, or are yuh faking a wee bit?"

"Shandol!" Margery exclaimed. "I'm tell'n the truth. If yuh won't tell I'll explain it better."

"Oh, I won't," Shandol promised. "Really. You can tell anyone else what yuh want 'em to know—if there's somethin'."

Margery let the final insinuation pass.

"I hurt myself yesterday, Shandol," Margery said. "Let me show you." She held up her dress to expose a huge bruise mark, black and blue and indeed wretched looking. "I fell," Margery continued, "when I was with Arnold. I was so embarrassed. He was good though and wondered if I was hurt bad and have myself seen about or somethin'. At the time it was painful, but I supposed it would be all right in awhile. But today I'm so sore and stoved up, though I try not to let on, I can hardly move without pains."

"I'm sorry," Shandol replied, humbly, "for being so silly as to doubt you. You've had to work hard all your life almost, I should have known yuh'd not shirk here." And she remembered the bruise which was as large as her hand on her left leg.

"I admit I feel like it sometimes," Margery confessed. "It's this place. It overwhelms me sometimes. I'd just like to enjoy it all, ha, ha."

"I know what yuh mean," Shandol replied. "Now, it's gonna soon be class time."

"I think I pulled somethin' in my back, but I'm just glad I could go on yesterday."

"Yuh must've had quite a spill," Shandol observed, almost muttering to herself.

"Walkin' too close to the bank and lost my footing," Margery explained, "and of course I tried to catch myself. Almost pulled Arnold along with me. He really helped me—maybe from gettin' a harder fall. Oh, well, I'll just be sore a few days and then I'll be all right."

"Be all right when it quits hurtin'," as my mom always says," Shandol retorted, lightly, but added, "I *am* sorry you're so sore and glad it's no worse and all that; *and* that I know."

Later Shandol wrote to her mother :

Wildwood Hotel
Strawsville,
June 15, 1942

Dear Folks,

I'm just out of class and have come to my room. I'm in the bed too. It's so cold up here we have to go to bed to keep warm. They have a fire in the fireplace in the lobby, but who could write there? This morning at 6:00 I was in the garden

484

picking peas and the dew in the vines nearly froze my fingers. You should see Marg and I! We're both in bed. She has a fit on laughing about it, so don't mind my writing. By the way if it stays this cold you may have to send my coat for the Fourth of July!

It's still rainy here, too. It didn't rain yesterday, the first day since we've been up here. But it's at it today again. The Merrygo River is fairly raging. The garden supervisor, Mrs. Green, is afraid of the flower garden, which is on its banks, will be submerged. We're on a bluff so it can't get to us.

How'd you like the card of Wildwood I sent you? Don't you think it's pretty? Some of the most beautiful scenery. By the way it is hilly here.

I got a letter from Ardena today. She told me about Grandma Dahle. Too bad. Did you go to the funeral. And also did you go to club?

Marg and I sure need to wash our clothes, and do some ironing. Not serious yet, but will be.

Yesterday I went to Sunday school. Dad, there's really a good teacher there. She was a substitute for us and the regular teacher was absent (which may explain the subject). The lesson was on the resurrection (!), but she began by discussing the words of Jesus on the cross. Several lines when you count them. Really interesting to me. The teacher ordinarily taught the young matron's class.

Saturday night went to the Eagle Roost Ranch.

Yes, Johnny came. The girls here can't go anywhere by themselves so they must always *double date*. Therefore there were two couples besides us—I sure think Johnny is nice. He's just 19 years old, be 20, 22nd. I have a picture of him I'll send to show you, if you'll be sure and send it back. I guess he's coming back Saturday. Listen, don't tell everybody though.

Marg has caught her a soldier boy, too. His name is Arnold Welch. He has relatives in Plainesville, he told her. He's nice too. They took pictures Sunday, but it was after supper before Johnny came. We'd seem to rather go with them. Guess you're rather tired of this by now.

Write soon. Tell kids to write whether I answer or not.

Love to all,

Sis

P.S. There's to be a big dance here Sat. night for soldiers. Don't think my Johnny will be able to come to that. So I won't dance. Write. S.S.

After supper there was the usual Monday night council meeting. Shandol got more out of it, though she wasn't able to add to or say anything. It was just as well. She was still timid with the large group. The small groups she could open up and be herself completely. Thus it did seem the council meeting became drawn out. There were still plans to make for the dance, and committees organized to see that the plans were carried out. The dance was something they were all enthusiastic about. Even the members of the staff. But it was a major highlight for most of the girls as it was a monthly event.

Later Shandol added a confidential note to her mother.

She wondered if reports concerning herself, and where she was, were being kept straight.

The letter was dated simply "Mon. eve."

Dear Mom.

Guess you'll think something's up by me writing to you separately, but don't. Just a spell to be confidential. Ha.

Besides, Dean asked me if I could write to him what I did to you. He wrote he'd talked to Phil. Tell him (Phil) not to 'air' too much. I'd hate for Dean to be angry by my mentioning it.

Would you like to hear what I did. I told you in the other letter about going to the Eagle Roost Ranch. There were two other couples with us, all guys in the army. Johnny is in the army, he's only nineteen. He told me he'd had two years in college. He does know shorthand, and he writes the prettiest handwriting. I bet you wonder why I think so much of him, but he's really cute. Just like a little boy or something, compared to Dean. There's a girl who came up here as we did who is sure trying to steal him too. That's griping me to death. Sunday night we were sitting in the lobby on a couch. She'd *just sit so close to him* and read shorthand. She's going out with a friend of Johnny's but she's really crazy over Johnny. She wants him to moon over her instead of me. Only one thing she has over me is pretty clothes. I don't think she's so very pretty, but so neat. I guess to the dance, by the way she talks, she'll really be dressed up. I'm going to wear my new blue with pink flowered dress. I've not worn it yet. I think her dress will be silk or something like that! After all he may not look too much at her lovely clothes. But if she just throws herself at him—and you know how I am—backward. Oh, well, here I'm grumbling, but I'm far from unhappy.

The kid who drove the car we went to Eagle Roost in was born in Africa. His dad was in the army there. He's so much like Pluto back there.

I'm about ready to go to bed. Went to supper and council meeting. Washed some panties, socks and slips. It's now 8:45 and I'm thinking of going to bed. May write in diary, ha. Write.
                    Love, Shandol.

However Shandol could hear the jukebox and she and Marg went downstairs to watch the girls dance. It was not unusual to find at least a few dancing. Their partners were girls, but that beat nothing. Some were such a delight. They were so good, so smooth and rhythmic even doing the jitterbug that Shandol envied them. How familiar the tunes were becoming. She was sure she'd never forget them: Jersey Bounce, Moonlight Cocktail and the others. Shandol and Marg danced only in their room. They felt they weren't ready to be observed as yet.

x x x x

When it was too wet to work in the garden the girls had to work inside. The next day was one of those Shandol was supposed to vacuum again, but couldn't as she had no one to show her about that vacuum, so she swept. There were others helping and they washed the woodwork and windows in the lobby. They killed flies lest they be let into the dining room through the French doors.

At mail time Shandol received a letter from home, and seemed a family affair, as other members had written. She read each hurriedly and took it to her room to go over again when she wouldn't be so busy. There was also a letter from Calvin Horn.

Shandol and Margery, joined by other girls, were given their second typhoid shot after the shorthand class. Shandol asked to be excused from typing because her arm hurt and she had a toothache. She learned she had gained two pounds!

In the evening she and Margery went to town to get some aspirin. Shandol also got a Father's Day card to send and readied it to be mailed.

Later she was able to let Nancy give her some dancing instructions. She and Margery laughed at their rate of progress. They were slowly improving and Nancy coaxed them to dance some in the lobby as it was virtually deserted awhile. They were still so self-conscious there.

Before going to bed Shandol went over the letter her dad had written. She had not quite known what to expect from him—if he ever did take the time to write, and here he had. And she read it again. Tommy had also written a few lines, as had Audrey. But she considered her father's letter first. How familiar his rather old-fashioned way of writing and even of expressing himself, she thought.

487

Dear Shandol,

If you will keep right still, not sing too loud or shake my desk, I will try to spring a surprise on you with a short epistle. I note when reading your letters you solicit all the kids correspondence, but leave *Pappy* off the list. No doubt you don't think of hearing from me only about midnight something like this: *Sis, Get In Here, Bedtime.* Anyway I'm taking the liberty to write. I wrote the other night and did not mail. I wrote with ink and spoiled a sheet or two of this pretty paper trying to write you a pretty letter. I even bought this bunch of paper on purpose to write you and when I got it written I found I'd spent all my money and couldn't buy a three cent stamp. Had a payday yesterday so I hasten to write to you before going broke. The week you left Phil and I made twelve dollars each. Phil spent his for clothes which he badly needed. Mine went for rent, insurance, groceries and so on. Last week was all rain. Rained everyday. We made only five dollars each.

I believe you wrote it had been raining back in your retreat, that you had been working in the garden, that your Mrs. Green boss rousted you out about six in the morning to hoe and pull weeds. I'd think that early in the morning you would get those oversized coveralls wet plum up. Do you wear blisters on your palms? And are your fingernails long? And I wonder how long polish lasts pulling wet weeds. Seriously, you girls must have a good time—a bunch of you gardening. What if your dad called you that early a.m.? Ha, ha.

Phil and Bobby just came in from somewhere. They are discussing the moving picture *Gone With the Wind*, the boys saw last night.

Young folks here are bitten by the marriage bug.

Ambert Horn and a Mamony Yokum, Freda Horn and her Brack and such like.

I have shifted positions and have moved myself and thinking apparatus from the front room to our bedroom. Now, I find Bobby lying in here. He is apparently asleep and so not interfering. I don't know if I can pick up my trend of thoughts again. Do you know that two and two more make four? Haw,

Haw. How are you getting along typing and short-handing? I am thinking about writing about the devil and if it's any good I'll get you to type it for me.

The Colmays are still friendly. The old gent hitchhiked to Iowa to work. They say he had a job when he got there. They gave us some cabbage for dinner.

We are glad you write often and hope you enjoy your work even more than you pretend. Mix with it all the fun and enjoyment you can. And of course be alert. Your mixing with nice young men and girls is a part of your education. Those nice young men I would discourage their flirting and flattery and appear disgusted at their mushy stuff. I do not intend to do much advising.

Your going away was like Lester going to the camp. I get awful lonesome when I come in.

Your Dean, I hear, is very solicitous about you. Thinks you in a tough place. I suppose he thinks you are safer with him than with anyone else.

That's the way with men. I'll close now on account of lack of space. Just write to Mom and I'll read your letters.

Your Cranky Old Dad

Tommy's letter was short, but precious to Shandol. His large, uneven scrawl, which was not hard for her to read, looked what it was, a letter from a little brother! He wrote,

Dear Sis,

Did you know that Mrs. Grandma Dahle died. I have $1.40 cents in my bank.
The baby has gain 1/2 lb.

Brother Tommy Sonnett

Audrey added a few lines:

Sissy,

Rest have written, I will wait until a later date. Helped make some flower sprays for Mrs. (Grandma) Dahle this a.m. As usual don't have anything done.
Raining again. Cool. We're about to freeze. Bye till morning.

Love, Mom

That night Shandol began a letter to her family.

Wildwood Hotel
Strawsville
June 16, 1942

Dear Folks:

I am in my room and ready for bed, but as the jukebox is going and I can't sleep I'll drop you a line. Got Dad's letter this morning. Glad you all wrote. I'll write one letter and it'll be to all. Is that ok? But I like to hear from each one.

Now, Dad, don't feel slighted because I didn't ask you to write. I didn't think you hardly had time. But I was *very* glad you did.

Listen, I go to the garden because I prefer to do that. Imagine washing dishes for four hours. Or even working for Miss Prine. Mrs. Green is much the better boss to work for. I'd actually rather get up at 6:00 than 7:00. Because if we work from six to ten, then I have two hours, besides lunch hour, to do what I want to. I usually write letters or wash my clothes. Otherwise I do these after supper or between 4:30 and 5:30 (suppertime). It would have seemed funny indeed to have gotten up that way at home, but I'd have felt better, I believe. You know what?! Marg and I have both gained two pounds since we've been up here. (Can't tell it.) We're going to weigh again Thursday and see if we gain this week.

Of course, we have fun and are growing healthier, too. We sometimes have to go to the garden barefooted. I had to before I got the shoes. But lots of the girls did. Just got shoes too dirty to wear in the wet weeks and mud.

I guess I'm progressing okay with shorthand and typing. I'm still slow in typing but I'm gaining accuracy. I'm really learning shorthand—by studying.

I have to pause each time I hear the song that just played, the name of it is 'I Wrote You a Card'. It's so pretty. I have the words to it. I'd send them to you, Phil, if you could hear the tune. I also got 'Daddy'. It's pretty. I saw the show that it was sorta a theme song. Was pretty good. Phil, I knew you'd like *Gone With the Wind*. I thought Clark Gable fascinating. Wasn't Vivien Leigh good as Scarlett O'Hara? Glad you got to see it.

My how does Greenway manage without Mr. Colmay? The handsome young preacher? Ugh!

Now, Dad, I'm not making eyes at or listening to flattery but from one boy that's up here. That's Johnny. Lots of other boys stop or encourage talk, but they don't long. One day one old blond chap sat with Nancy Rayford and I on a porch swing that is in the yard under a tree. He was sitting closest to me. Soon I said some ants are biting me and got up. He soon left then. Cold shoulder, eh? But he did compliment me on my even tan, which I got on a certain picnic, right?

I got another shot for typhoid today. Boy-dee, is my arm sore! I tell you that hurts me. Some of the girls can even watch. Not me.

This is no tougher than going to a large school or living in town. There are possibly some *undesirables*, but you are told of them. I think for it's size this is a nice place. Several girls smoke, but according to a bulletin at Washington, D.C. they will have to have a smoking period to avoid accident. Several dance too. But otherwise most seem to be quiet girls.

I bet you are nearly ready to throw up (?)by the time you've read some of my letters, aren't you? But I just write home—especially to Mom—just what's on my mind. I wonder if I'd read them now I'd blush.

Tell kids to keep writing. After all they are all different. Besides you probably keep tab on young people. But all write soon.

Tell Tommy he writes a nice letter. Write again, Tommy.

Love,
Shandol

About the time the girls supposed they had settled into a routine of going to the garden, classes, doing personal things such as visiting, writing letters, studying, watching the girls dance in the lobby or doing their personal laundry, there would be a change. Usually with good reason.

The next day was again rainy and wet and so the girls weren't even called to go to the garden. But there was plenty to do. They cleaned up the large kitchen. It was not for punishment but to get in their work time. They carried dishes from the roomy cabinets and cleaned shelves high and low, and washed dishes which weren't used regularly. There was the huge cooking range to clean, which Shandol helped do. She was sure it was the largest one in the whole state and the oven a huge yawning gap, to her eyes. She almost had to crawl into it to reach it all. But somehow the washing, scouring and scrubbing was finished. Even the floor scrubbed. Several hands working under a precise and demanding boss probably helped. Surprisingly, Shandol and Margery still had time to carry wood and swat flies.

Shandol was happy at mail time. She heard from her mother, who had sent a dollar bill. Shandol had only twenty-four cents left. She also heard from Johnny Holleron and Dean.

After classes, Shandol, Margery, Nancy and Edna walked to town. They went the shortcut, but came back along the highway. Shandol bought fifteen cents worth of stamps, of which she "loaned" Margery two, and also bought a laxative. The girls kidded her about knowing where to go for something.

They were offered a ride by a bus driver, but they declined, as they did all other rides by "a pickup," as it was called.

At night Shandol wrote to Dean and Calvin, and a card to her mother. Her mother had raved about the environment Shandol was in, or as she had written, she had heard, and Shandol was astounded, but a letter enclosed from Phil was to even the score. It was written in his familiar mannish handwriting, which wasn't bad for a boy. He wrote:

> Greenway,
> June 15, 1942

Dear Sis

Your having asked me or us kids to write I will scribble a line or two. Everything is going well for me down here. Still working at the Germans.

Last Saturday night I got the wish of my life. I went to see *Gone With the Wind*. Boy it was good! Cost 50¢. Bobby went with me. Do you remember where all those wounded men were out in the street or whatever it was, well if you do, Bobby says to me says he let's get out of here.

I kinda felt sorry for Scarlett O'Hara. She was sure fit for that part. Clark Gable isn't as good as I thought he was although he played his part well. Cried most of the time and laughed the rest.

I guess I'll close for this time. Time for lunch.

> As ever, Phil

Shandol reread her mother's letter. It was dated simply, "Tues. a.m." and she read:

492

Dear Dearie: I'm wondering why I didn't get a letter off this train. Are you wondering why we don't write. Or are you broke, ha. I forgot to send the dollar yesterday so will today. Phil spent $3.00 over weekend. Can't let him spend money like that. They just made $5.00 each last week and of course couldn't ask Dad for any this week. Looks as if it might be as bad this week. Work three hrs. Mon. Didn't go to work all day today.

House and yard full of kids as usual. I've two more now that come. Chester Parkleys drive the car for Mrs. Colmay.

The ship that Hugh Burdette was on was sunk the 18th of May in that Coral Sea battle. He's coming home. Said he was wounded. Don't know how bad.

Lester and Jane hadn't got your card Sat. night. Maybe have by now. They were ok. Dean was through here Sun. horseback. Said he was going to harvest field Thurs.

I'm catching it all around about you being in the 'hoar house', so I'm counting on you don't let me down. Calvin Horn said two girls from Plainesville came back. Dean told Phil and Bobby, Dad and I would be sorry we let you go. Lester said you'd have to be careful. Verda Kirby has two babies now. SO BEWARE.

The hotel looks inviting. Looks like might be some level country around there.

The wedding bells rang again. Wanita and Druce Connal were married. Arvin Jarred married them. Steven is back. May ring some more? Still rains. Arvin Jarred is going to harvest fields tomorrow. Hadn't heard anything about Julie Allsup getting married. Jane didn't say anything about it Sat. night.

Karen is fine. Just gained a half pound last month.

She was cranky yesterday, so cold we nearly all froze.

She's so 'raw' again, makes her cranky. Don't know what I've been doing to her. Have 29 diapers on the line now. She rolls quite a bit now. Won't stay on a pallet. Just cross and scolds all the time. Real good when nothing hurts her.

Had so many things I wanted to tell you but seems I'm blank. Insurance man just left. Paid it up for a month. A new one again. Buried Mrs. Dahle yesterday in the rain. Didn't go—was so rainy. I was at the house the eve she died but didn't see her. Said she looked natural at funeral. Didn't care about seeing her. I'll just remember her as I saw her last. Don't know what Mr. Dahle will do. Guess he can't stay there. The Basher woman is expecting the stork, don't know when tho'.

Your improving in your shorthand and typing. Just be patient. Don't try for speed as much as accuracy first. Do they help place you or are you to get your own job?

You needn't care how you look when you're working. Just be clean and neat otherwise. Be careful your clothes will mildew, won't come out. The feather bed mildews sometimes where Karen sleeps. So damp.

Am going to have vegetable soup for dinner. Um-m.

Mrs. Colmay gave me some cabbage. Have green beans, lots of taters.

I must quit if I get this mailed. I'll try to send a dollar along as I can spare. I must have some teeth pulled soon.

First good payday Phil has I'll try to send enough for a permanent. Harry played checkers here last night and Sat. night.

Must quit now. Write. Be good. Tell Marg I said to behave herself. Ha. Ha.

Love, Mom.

Shandol read some of the gossip, as she told Margery it must be, to Margery. Then added :

"Just what do yuh think uh that? I always told Mom most of the girls I've known seem all right to me. Of course I may not know all they are or do, but what's it to do with me, and those of us who came here to try to learn and maybe better ourselves? Makes me mad!"

"It'd only take a few to give the place a bad name," Margery reminded her.

"But if they're gonna be bad their gonna be wherever they are; and be what they are wherever they are. They don't come here for that. I bet, even if it happens. There was that type girls before this place became what it is and also where they've never heard of it. So why do they pick on it so? They could cause it to close or something, do you suppose?

"I hope not," Margery remarked. "Let's just say there *are* all kinds here. Well, there are everywhere else, so it all goes back to either those who will worry about us, don't want us here," she looked meaningfully at Shandol, turned her hands expressively and went on, "or jealous they aren't here! I doubt if they could take anymore girls since it seems pretty near full up to me."

"I wonder if your mother hears all that gossip, Margery," Shandol sighed. "Would she write it if she did?"

"She or aunt Harriett one," Margery laughed, uncertainly. "But aunt Harriett's out of town so Mom prob'ly hasn't, and may not."

"Well, lucky you," Shandol said. "I know Mom worries about me. She's a worrier. But to take all the sins of everyone and blame it on this place isn't fair. Just isn't. I'll write and hope I can ease Mom's mind some. Oh, I'm tired. Let's get some sleep."

"Now yer talkin'," Margery replied.

Among the girls the party was discussed on about everything. Even as they worked in the garden, hulled peas the next day. It also seemed to add zest to do the things they had to do.

In typing Shandol was still making only thirty words with one error in a five minute test, not quite so good in ten minute tests. She wondered if she'd reached a plateau and how long she'd be on it.

Shandol started a letter to her mother right before noon. She needed to get something off her chest. Her talk with Margery had helped her get over some of the anger, but she knew she would have to try to reassure her mother.

Strawsville,
June 18, 1942

Dear Mom:

I will now answer your letter. I won't get it all done though as it's too near class time. I worked in the garden this morning for awhile, then I hulled peas. Marg too. We didn't get to work four hours. We'll have to make up the 1½ hours. But while we were off Marg and I cleaned up our room good.

Is Hugh B. home yet? Wonder if it's be okay for me to write him? Tell me when you write. Especially if you see him. Guess he feels lucky he got off the ship alive.

Mom, stop worrying about the 'environment' I'm in. I'd like to know where and *how* you get so much information. What did Lester say? I just doubt if he writes to me. Reckon? Anyway at the dance I'm going to keep my eyes open! Perhaps I'll see some of what's being told. Don't you think that should open the truth to the matter if anything will? These girls seem to be a pretty fair lot to me. Is Verda Kerby married? (I assume not) Who said she had two babies and not? Has she been to a resident center? Even so, look in her family. She's not the only one of the girls. 'Tuff' was born out of wedlock, so I've heard. Where is Verda now? I suspect the reason that talk is out is because the army camp's so close. If some of the girls are going to *be tough* they can't help that here. Do you see what I mean?

We had a chance to write to the army camp for civil service papers for a call to take the examination, but requirements are for 35 words for a jr. typist and 80 jr. stenographer (shorthand) so I decided I'd wait as I don't have any such average.

I've had the toothache today. Got me some aspirin for it. By the way my smallpox vaccination didn't take this time either. Remember? It didn't the other time either.

I started this letter this morning. It is now after my typing class, which is 4:30. Still hoping to improve.

I haven't heard from Lester yet.

Miss Lockney has gone for a vacation. Sure will miss her. She's nice and the main 'gun'.

I got a card from Dean today. He's in Kansas.

I'd just wrote to him. But I guess his mom will send the letter to him.

How's Mrs. Kasper? Does she ever come to see you? So you have Chester's kids now Guess them and the Colmays are thick? Marg is washing her hair. I'm going to do mine as soon as she's through.

Do you feed Karen that Pablum? Isn't she growing all right?

I must close to wash my hair. Can't mail this before morning anyway, so may write some more tonight. Soon be supper time.

Am sending Dad a greeting for father's day. Hope not too soon. I'm going to attend a Father's Day service at the Baptist church Sunday.

Morning : Marg and I washed and ironed too yesterday. I still have a voile dress and two cottons that need washing. I'll do it some spare moment. Time for breakfast so must close and mail this.

Write soon tell kids to write.

Love, Shandol

The girls were still counting down to the dance. Two days. Would they never pass?

On Friday they picked beans in the garden. Then they had to string them.

Margery missed her class to finish ironing, but Shandol attended classes.

At mail time Shandol received three letters. One was from Carol. She was surprised but happy to hear from her. It wasn't a long letter but so like her. It was dated "6/15/42"—but she surely hadn't mailed it right away.

"Kid," she wrote, "I was really glad to hear from you and to know that you were liking it so well up there." She apologized for not writing sooner, but had been busy. There was the Emily Joan Allsup bridal shower. She, Emily, was married two weeks ago, she informed Shandol. There was a farewell party for a girl in church who was leaving and she had to help as she was on the entertainment committee. On top of that," she wrote, "it was her full-fledged duty to keep the house clean and run her mother's errands. Then there were the recordings they were having fun making with her brother-in-law's recording machine and "you should hear my solo of 'Johnny Doughboy'." She assured Shandol she had never heard anything like it. She repeated granny Dahle's death and wondered why Margery hadn't written. "Tell her if she don't I shall warm her little ——!! the next time I see her." She invited comments on their activities and another letter.

Shandol, allowing for her bragging, which was part of her personality, enjoyed the letter. But she had learned how Granny Dahle had died. Everyone had written about it but not much details. She must tell Margery.

Margery and Shandol went to town about seven o'clock that evening and she had the chance then. Shandol bought a new collar for her dress. It was somewhat lacier and prettier and later she learned it fit. It was attached to her dress. She also rolled up her hair. It would be the last chance before the dance tomorrow night.

After that the girls watched the other girls dance in the lobby. However, Shandol's mind wasn't always on the girls dancing and the music. She went back over the events of the day and the letters she had received. Even Ardena mentioned Grandma Dahle.

She wrote that Bobby was cutting weeds for them, but rained them out. Phil and Joel had gone to work for the first day this week. The rain was from the north and was cold for "this time of year." They had their lights put in and she would iron. She praised *Gone With the Wind* about as Phil had. Wanting to laugh at times—others, to cry. She wrote she had seen Calvin and he had written. He has to be examined for the army. She wrote Lester and Jane were at Sonnetts. Young People"s meeting was held at their place last Sunday. But she wasn't there. She and Phil had gone to town on the truck. *It will be at Sonnetts tomorrow night and a marshmallow roast. I'll go if Phil's not*

497

there. Confidentially he hadn't talked to her since Sunday. She had painted her bedstead white and green and around the windows green. Her curtains are green and white. She thinks it will look "pretty good when I get it done." She too hoped for an answer soon.

The tidbits Shandol could piece together from the different letters almost gave her an idea of what was going on in Greenway. Of course Grandma Dahle's death had seemed news. She was not only old, but well-liked and she was "gittin' up in years." Too bad the children hadn't been able to come back for her funeral. It was perhaps financially impossible. There were marriages, the activities, neighborhood gossip and feuds, which weren't nearly so important as it seemed. It seemed like Greenway.

She wondered about Dean. Would they eventually get together again? How lonesome it made her feel that he wasn't there even if she should want to see him. Did she? Yes, of course, she decided. But was it any different than any of the others she would like to see? Her family would come first, of course, and the others, because they were friends; and she would like them to know she was fine and not in such a bad place as they may also have heard.

Shandol was so glad Lester and Jane each wrote short notes.

She opened Lester's first. It was headed Greenway, and dated June 18, 1943.

> Dear Sis,
>
> Read the letter you wrote the folks. Glad you like it up there. Watch those soldier boys and all boys and don't get into trouble like some of the girls did at Plainesville. I happen to know some. (some advice).
>
> I'm going to Cheyenne, Wyoming tomorrow to work on the section gang—Union Pacific R.R. I get 53¢ per hr. time and one-half for overtime, living quarters are furnished, but have to cook for myself.(May starve, ha).
>
> Jane will have to stay back here for 90 days, until I get my seniority rights. I know it's going to be lonesome. But I'll never have anything here. Jane is okay except for everything that goes along with—shh!
>
> I don't know much to write, so I'll close for now.
>
> Will write more when I get settled.
>
> Love, Lester

Jane wrote a page also, headed and dated as Lester's.

Dear Shandol:

How are you anyway—fine I hope. We all feel okay so far.
Sugar (Lester) is leaving and boy am I ever going to miss
him. It sure will be lonesome, but he has to make the living
somewhere so it might as well be out there. I can go after he
gets settled I hope. I think I will like it out there or anywhere
he is so I can be with him. We don't like the farm.

I'm glad you like it there. Have all the fun you can. You're
not young but once and take the good advice Sugar gives you.
As far as I know there is going to be an increase in our family.
So much for that. I'll close. Maybe more next time.

Love,
Jane

On the back of Jane's letter Audrey scrawled: "I'll write tomorrow.
Lester and Jane are here stayed overnight last night—Mom."

Shandol soon after told Margery she was going on to bed to try
to get some "beauty rest" for tomorrow. But there was the whole day
before the dance at night.

They got up early the next morning and went to the garden awhile
to hoe. Also they scrubbed the "lower" kitchen. By then they had
finished their work, except to wash some dishes to make up the one
and one-half hour they had to make up. Some of the other girls were
decorating the lobby to give it a festive air. There were crepe paper
streamers and bows, and mock lanterns.

At mail time Shandol heard from her mother and a solider she had
met named Dean, of Carthage.

Shandol and Margery, because there were no classes in the
afternoon, had time on their hands and slept some before time to
dress for the dance. They had not intended to do so but just plopped
down on their beds, soon were quiet and asleep. Both were surprised
they had fallen asleep and it was almost supper time when they
awoke. They chatted awhile, washed their faces, in turn, to look wide
awake to go to the dining room.

As they weren't sure just how each one of the girls would manage
taking a shower, or how many used the one they used, they did that
as soon after supper as they could and were first. They were sure all
the girls would plan to do that before the dance.

In fact they got ready early, and wondering what else to do, went
on down to Nancy's and Edna's room. They still shared the room
with Eileen, as they had grown accustomed to the company. And

even though it was crowded none of them cared to even try to find another roommate, though they had heard another girl had left for a job.

When Margery and Shandol knocked and were let in they discovered the girls in various stages of getting dressed—none complete. Eileen was lying on the bed in her white lace-trimmed slip, her face covered with a white face cream and she had balls of cotton over her eyes, which she had wrung out of ice cold water. (The cubes were still in the bowl on a stand nearby.) She had such a beautiful complexion, Shandol wondered why she thought she needed to do it. Her skin was fair, delicate looking with almost a translucent quality about it. Shandol also wondered if the care she was giving it helped.

Eileen was a pretty girl anyway. She had deep dimples when she smiled. Her teeth were white and even and they showed also when she smiled. She had dark blue eyes, with naturally dark eyelashes making a stunning delicate fringe. Her ash-blond hair, thick with a natural wave, seemed easy to manage and was always neatly turned under on the ends, and not quite shoulder length. She was neat in appearance, average size, trim and shapely. She had told them she would rest ten minutes with the cream on her face, and wring out the cotton in the cold water a few times. So there was no use to hurry her. Yet with all her care in grooming she was not "boy crazy." In fact she was only friendly, smugly reminding them, or anyone, of her special boyfriend in her home town.

The other two girls were excited and fumbling, also in their slips, fresh from the shower by now, also having to take turns. They rummaged in their suitcases, giggling and explaining, chatting as they searched for hose, makeup and sat down soon after Shandol and Margery entered.

"We're so excited we just go in circles," Nancy laughed.

"We've plenty of time. Maybe we should be like Eileen and just relax for ten minutes."

"Go ahead," Margery replied. "Don't let us bother."

"Oh, no, we can go," Shandol added. "Perhaps we should."

"No, don't," Nancy said. "But you can see how cramped we are in here. We'll just have to go one by one to keep out of each other's way. No—you're not in the way, just sit on the bed." Shandol wondered if Nancy had read her mind. She was about to ask if they weren't in the way.

"Just talk to us," Edna said. "I wish we knew more about these things. I don't know what to expect."

"Just so two guys from battery "F" are here is all I'm interested in," Nancy looked at Shandol for agreement.

"Well, Johnny said in his letter he'd see me Saturday," Shandol replied, knowing who Nancy meant. Don is supposed to be along also, but Shandol suspected Nancy was more interested in "her" (Shandol's) Johnny.

But they were to be disappointed. They did not show up. The girls learned only the "company" invited attended, and to all others it was off limits. They weren't invited.

It left Shandol completely at loose ends. Several soldiers came, many wanted her to dance. But she demurred, admitting she couldn't dance. Some offered to teach her, but she refused. She just knew she would stiffen and make an enemy for life. Why ruin their fun, she reasoned. She sat and talked to one soldier who begged her to let him teach her to dance. He talked about his family and how he missed them. He showed her pictures of his wife and two children. At least he hasn't tried to be a cad, she decided.

But she also talked to other soldiers, timid also about their dancing and how to approach a girl. Shandol pointed out some good dancers, perhaps he could have a chance with one of them. They would be nice and understanding, she was sure. He could certainly try. Shandol wanted to see what *really* went on.

There was a nice crowd, everyone had to admit. There was the inevitable, it seemed, thunderstorm and the lights went off briefly, which threatened the party. But luckily the lights were not off long. Amid shrieks of "what's happenin'," and "what kinda lights can we rig up," they were on again.

Punch was served, and no liquor of any kind. There were also sandwiches and cake. And everyone boasted of it's success—except Nancy and Shandol.

They "boo-hooed" in mock dismay on each other's shoulders, even when the dance was over. Yet they giggled at better times hoped for and sympathizing with their own disappointment.

Margery admitted she had dared to attempt to dance. She hadn't done too bad, yet she knew she wasn't good and wailed at being a disappointment.

Well, next time they'd know, they vowed. They would learn more. But how then were they to know there would be no next time?

CHAPTER 39

The third Sunday they spent at Wildwood was Father's Day, and almost a holiday, it seemed to Margery and Shandol. The girls had not been allowed to sleep late just because they had been to a party the night before.

Shandol and Margery helped clean up the lobby, and it didn't take several girls very long to get it in order. When it was time to leave for Sunday school and church those girls were excused and those remaining finished anything that still needed doing, though it was not cleaned as on a regular cleaning day. But it had to look neat as there would undoubtedly be company during the day, if only solders from the army camp.

Margery and Shandol chose to go to Sunday school and stayed for church. Shandol and Margery were surprised to find the church they attended decorated with flowers and a "Happy Father's Day" sign, edged in flowers. It was, all agreed, real nice and "oh's" and "ah's" could be heard. During the church service, also, the pastor was presented with a wristwatch as a present from the deacons.

The girls were in for another surprise when they got back to Wildwood. There was a birthday dinner for those whose birthdays fell in June and December, which meant Shandol and Margery both could sit at the reserved table, nicely decorated—even place cards had been constructed of simple design. It was a long table, actually three of the small square ones pushed together, but covered with tablecloths, it could hardly be detected.

Because it was Father's Day, Pop sat at the head of the table, though his birthday was not one of those being celebrated. He was given a present which the girls had chipped in money to buy. He was well liked and appreciated by everyone there.

The girls learned a birthday dinner was held each month, in this way, or sometimes for two months at a time if necessary to make enough to celebrate.

Shandol and Margery were delighted, yet somewhat self-conscious by all the attention; and were dumb-stricken by surprise. Yet as they talked with the others they relaxed somewhat. They realized they had a very fine meal capped off with ice cream and a decorated birthday cake. Shandol and Margery were never to know quite by whom or how it was made possible, possibly the cook.

502

After the meal and everyone had left the dining room, Shandol and Margery went to their room to marvel at their luck at their birth month just happening to be one that came up at their first month there. They both thought it an excellent idea; and for that matter, to have come up with the idea in the first place. Shandol would have something to write home about.

In fact she decided to start a letter to her mother when she was called downstairs. She had company. She had misunderstood the girl who called up to her to say Francis someone to see her, but it was Leon Harvey. It was a let-down, but he was a soldier so she tried to appear happy to see him. He was friendly and amusing sometimes, Shandol thought, sometimes to the point of foolishness. Then there were two others who joined them.

"What a pretty girl, Leon, she's everything you said—even golden hair," one of them flattered her.

Shandol was rendered speechless at that. No one had ever called her hair golden before, but it did bleach in the sun, just as she tanned easily, even by the wind on that hazy, partly cloudy day. Entertaining all three kept Shandol on her toes. They were nice to her, not even a hint of rough talk. She wondered where Margery and Nancy were. Probably asleep or with company of their own. Shandol didn't encourage the men to come later so she did not see them after supper. Leon insisted upon calling her Sally Ann, but she wasn't satisfied with his reason why: "Because you look like a Sally Ann," he'd say, "and I do so love that name."

"You're impossible," she retorted, smiling a final smile. Perhaps he found her name hard to remember. Yet the afternoon passed quickly. They walked around, sat in the swing, anything to pass the time, as Shandol couldn't leave the grounds with them. Later, she, Margery, Nancy, and Edna walked to town, but came back soon. Neither girl had company or a date at night.

Shandol supposed she should write to her family. She re-read her mother's last letter to see if there was anything she needed to answer. Then she realized it was in answer to ones she had written before the dance. She re-read it all.

Fri.11:30

Dearest Shandol—If Karen will behave long enough I'll try answering some of your letters. Guess you got Lester and Jane's letters. Sure hated to see him go but guess couldn't do anything. Mrs. Chaldon wouldn't let them alone and Jane wasn't satisfied either, so made it hard on him. Worked like a mule all spring nearly ready to harvest his sowing but just couldn't stand it any longer. We told him the last time he was here if he didn't want to stay on their farm not to.

Thought you may have gotten tired of hearing me 'preach' u didn't write so often. Ha ha. (Had to stop to get Karen's bottle) Just write what u think we get a kick out of them.

Dean shouldn't expect you to write to him such as you write home. Guess he's gone now. You'll surely meet lots of interesting people after you get away from old Greenway. Never mind the 'silk'. Just be yourself. 'Clothes don't always make the man'. Here's hoping you can have some prettier clothes. Be careful and don't be a wallflower at the dances! If you like him don't be afraid to show it but don't be mushy. (Something keeps bothering me, can't write. Teddy Colmay just came for the hammer.) (They got some more chix today— Colmays.)

Rained everyday this week so far. Looks as if it might be fair today. Phil and Dad haven't worked very much again. Hope they get in these two days. Be careful and don't commit *sewer-side* in the river. Guess it has subsided by now.—

Yes, Mrs. Davis came by for me and I went to club with her. Not so very many there. Mrs. Milcher, Elma, Mrs. Davis and her mother, Margo Dell, and Mrs. Aubine and myself. Beatrice served sandwiches and coffee—was real good. Guess the club will finally fizzle out.

Going to try to have some amusements here in the 'Big Town' for the young people. Beatrice said alls they did at their parties was get Sam and some of them to make music. The young folks got tired of it. She can't make it any better!? Think?

Got letter from Lafey and a pretty birthday card. Am sending you the letter. Save it. Not too much to answer but might want it for reference sometime.

Washed Wed. rained all p.m. hung it out in eve stayed out all night got dry yesterday, ironed this morning before breakfast.

Young People"s meeting here tonight so you know what that means. Decided we didn't want to be responsible for light bill. Mr. Butler didn't come anymore. Della went home with Marsha so we thought we could meet at each other's homes.

Last Friday night not many came to church. Mrs. Colmay tried to get Silas to bring them to her house. He wouldn't. Do you wonder? (*Yep, she's dirty*, Shandol thought as she read it.)

I'm glad you are feeling well. You may have to reduce if u get too fat. They told me the other day I was getting fat as a bear. How fat is that? I've been barefoot too. My old shoes are so crooked they make my feet so tired.

Do they take a funny paper up there? I could send you the comics if you care for them. Mr. Borsek's grandson Bobby is here—he and Buck. Tho't if there was anything worthwhile in Heartbeats I'd send them to you, but nothing much lately. That battle at Coral sea about all—("Heartbeats" was a column in the paper Shandol knew.)

Got your pretty card today. Must have some beautiful scenery around there. Yes, you'll meet all kinds of people everywhere and anywhere. One has to know how to handle the good as well as the bad. You'll have to destroy this letter so no prying eyes will see it. Lester told me I might be grandma. Ha. Don't even tell Margery. I must get to work. Have to mop, clean the lamps as well as a 100 other things. Lester brought the little black dog back home. Did I tell you the old cat had three kittens. Mr. Kasper is about the same. Such a pitiful site.

Mr. Dahle moved to Milton Monroes. Leah and Jab didn't come.

I asked you before if there was a R.R. thru' Strawsville. *Now tell me* and *do you get mail on Sun.* Good-bye now.

Am so lonesome but guess it will wear away. Don't see why a fella has to have kids and them leave?? Karen sits up now alone. Tommy got a big *pasteboard* box she sets in that pretty well. She's had diarrhea (sp?) for two or three days. Am going to put her back on canned milk diet.

Study hard so you can get u a job somewhere. I'll quit now.

Love Mom and all the rest.

Shandol had been delighted to read Uncle Lafey's letter. It was dated June 15. He wrote he was not going to let his "delinquency keep me from sending a birthday card." He wrote he had bought it several weeks ago but was kept busy with music lessons and funeral participation that his time "goes like all get out," He'd planned to send it but was called on to sing and other things, "besides making out school records for the Supt. while he is away." He hoped she'd forgive him for being late.

He related they were both all right except Ruth had been "under the weather" since they were expecting the stork around Christmas. She was bothered by her stomach but supposed Audrey could sympathize as having experienced the same thing. They had thought of adopting a boy and girl but there were those advising not give up having one of their own. (They had lost three children as Shandol knew.) It explained her condition now. There were those, he conceded, who thought they should be content without children but they saw it differently. He must hurry as time to give music lessons. And he hoped all well and Phil found work soon.

Shandol soon had a letter written to her mother.

The next morning Shandol got up early to clean up the room. Mondays they were inspected as to housekeeping habits. Only once had Margery and Shandol been reprimanded about their room. Of course they had aimed to straighten it up early that morning but had gone to the garden instead. It was in one "horrible shape" as the girls shamefacedly conceded. They had left clothing everywhere, including the floor. Their beds weren't made. Shandol hadn't wanted it to happen again; and was sure it had never looked so awful before cleaning at any other time!

However, Shandol couldn't get Margery up. She was so sleepy-headed she only muttered she'd get up but didn't. Shandol reasoned she wouldn't have been much help anyway. She did make it for breakfast, but just barely.

They helped do the morning cleaning of the lobby and other chores as directed. Then classes, which was a routine day.

After classes Shandol and Margery went to town. Margery bought film, stamps and a birthday card for her oldest brother.

There was still time so the girls of the "garden gang" went to the garden, dressed as they had worked, to take pictures with Margery's small camera. They wore their oversized coveralls, had hoes and were barefooted. Nancy just had to have her picture taken with Shandol because of Johnny and their dates.

Shandol later wrote to her mother and Johnny Holleran. She had received letters from Margery's brother, August, Calvin Horn, the latter in the evening. Shandol wrote a short letter to August as Margery was sending him a birthday card with a letter also.

Then at night there came that fateful Monday night council meeting. All the girls were dealt a blow. It was a low one, they thought, because it was unexpected. *Wildwood would be closed as a resident center.* They were saddened, sick at heart, angry, surprised and incredulous, some emotions all at once, others in turn, as realization dawned. Mostly they were regretful that their pleasant times and holiday setting were to be terminated.

They were then told of one up north, which was composed of all boys, but they had decided to open it to girls also. It was training for specific defense jobs. A man had come to explain it to them.

506

Wildwood could not be considered a defense-training job resident center. He had gone on to explain the rent, which the government paid was three hundred dollars a month, and the milk bill was over two hundred, as examples. This was needed for the army and defense. They were told they could all help their country by training for a job in the defense of it.

Still, truth though they recognized, there was not a girl there who would not hate to see it close. They would be leaving Thursday, exactly three week's stay for Shandol and Margery, and those who came the day they had. It had opened a new life, insight and perspective to each of them. But how well they had kept it all secret, to have it worked out so exactly to spring it upon them.

Tuesday was as much the same as any other day as moods could allow. They were up at the sound of the buzzer. The garden girls went to the garden to gather cabbage to be cooked for dinner. Pop had aimed to get the girls but they had walked back to the hotel. He waited, so they had to go back for him. He said he supposed they were behind some bushes where he couldn't have a clear view.

They also went to the lower garden to pick beans. Then they had to wait a long time for Pop, at least it seemed a long time. They finished their work duty snapping beans until the noon meal was announced.

Shandol had received a letter and one dollar from her mother.

At the dinner table Nancy, Edna and Eileen chose to do some foolishness, much to the surprise of Shandol and she supposed Margery. They were actually trying to turn one another's stomachs. It is a wonder any of them could eat a bite thinking of "scabs on smashed bugs" or "fly and snot soup." Shandol thought it vulgar but knew it would not do to let on. She would never have any peace from being teased. So though she nor Margery contributed to their conversation, Shandol did at once exclaim in mock disdain: "How can you dream up such awful stuff. Ugh!"

The girls, for the most part, stayed out of class. It was the last day of classes anyway. Shandol went to several of the girls with the autograph book which she had brought with her. Of the girls who had come with them she had lacked only Diane Witcliff's and she went to her room. They talked with heavy hearts, as did all the girls, when the subject came up. Those who planned to go to the "other place" (as it was referred to, usually) hoped it would be as well liked. But the boys! It would be different. Shandol wondered what her parents would think. What would she tell them and how? The truth, she knew would be the only way for her. It was also time to think of packing.

This was mostly done Wednesday. There were no classes, but they did work at packing and sorting things at the Center to leave Wildwood in order for whatever was to be done with it later.

Shandol and Margery also packed their suitcases. They, and all the girls going to Midhill were ready by eleven o'clock the following morning, but it was about two when they were loaded and they themselves got into a tarpaulin-covered truck, with benches along the sides to sit on, almost army style, they grimaced.

They were on their way. Their stay at Wildwood ended and some dreams and hopes were left behind as ghosts to walk the corridors in their minds. Most left with tear stained faces. Those who chose not to go to Midhill were allowed bus fare home.

What lay ahead? Shandol wondered. Had the man said? She was so shocked at his words about all she could recall registering was, "No more Wildwood Resident Center."

CHAPTER 40

Off to the new destination at last! But only after the seeming interminable wait. The girls were all already tired, nervous and wondering what lay ahead. They were worn-out because of the uncertainty and delay in going. They were told to be ready by eleven o'clock; they were, and then little to do but grumble, fidget and complain about being held there. They were nervous because they weren't sure they wanted to go to a boy's camp and unsure as to what their training would really all be about. How did one train for defense jobs? What defense jobs and what would they do? They were wondering what lay ahead, somewhat apprehensively, because they had been warned not to expect a place such as Wildwood.

In fact they had heard rumors that the living quarters would be crude compared to where they were. They would be masculine because they had been made so.

Some of the girls were going out of curiosity, as well as no promise of anything better. Shandol and Margery frankly admitted to each other they weren't ready to go home yet and aimed to give it a try. There was nothing compulsory about staying if they preferred not to do so.

It was a bleak day weather-wise also, the girls lamented. It had poured rain in the morning and most of the time as they rode along having finally left at two in the afternoon. They could see only out the back entry as they rode, because the large truck bed was covered in dark canvas. Was it an army truck, they pondered. It was such a rainy, gloomy day no one really bothered to see the rather narrow band of scenery that seemed to be floating from around them, yet ever changing. They took note of the towns, as they became visible and even tried to figure out how far they were from their destination. How long was it going to take?

The streams were full, as they could see as they crossed various bridges. The river near Capital City was out of it's banks. There were people lined up on higher ground to see the flooding of homes and land though it did not affect the road or hinder their journey.

They arrived at their destination at six p.m.

"We should have known," one wag was heard to say. "Just leave so we'll make it in time for supper." It was true.

Then they were shown their living quarters. "Barracks," they called them. One had been vacated for the girls. It had been cleaned—but such a disappointment to the girls.

They were first shown into a large center room in this "barracks," which they were told was the day room. There was a table with a small radio, gray wooden chairs, which looked homemade, and, in fact, had been made in the wood shop there. There was a desk-like table with a chair. They were encouraged to write home; and that sometimes it was even quiet there.

The man chosen to show them around gave them a brief description of the place:

"There are two things in these long rooms you'll see. Each side is divided into two sides. There are five two-tier bunks. Both sides are identical except a portion of each side has been petitioned off for rooms for the two supervisors who came with you, Mrs. Crocker and Miss Morris here. You will see there are bunk beds and some will have to sleep on the top bunks. The bath facilities are directly behind here, though they are entered from the wings. Each side has separate facilities. There are basins, showers and even a washing machine, ironing board and iron. If you have questions just ask and someone can help you. If it concerns rules and regulations ask your supervisor for your wing. If they don't know they will find out for you. Guess that's it, girls. Good luck."

"Okay girls, go find your bunks," Mrs. Crocker said.

Shandol and Margery went south because they were closest to that door. They took the last bunks (and farthest from the restroom, as they later observed) on the side facing the street. There was a linen closet at that end of the room, and each girl was required to make up her own bunk. There were no bedside tables or mirrors except in the bathroom and certainly all the girls couldn't use them at the same time. It was soon realized other arrangements must be made.

Shandol and Margery came up with one solution. Shandol's suitcase was put on a stool-like table, covered it with a folded flat sheet and had a "vanity table." A smallish framed mirror would be added when they could purchase one. All the girls then used washcloths, towels or handkerchiefs, whatever appealed to each individual, to cover a small table to use at the bedsides. Shandol even put the picture of Hugh Burdette on hers. He had given her one in a folder. He looked quite nice in his Navy uniform, or what she could see of the bust exposure. She also laid a small New Testament there so it wouldn't look so bare until she decided how it would be used.

Shandol also sat on, and spoke first for the lower bunk. Margery wanted it also, but agreed to take the upper one so they could share the same small closets and the two drawers under the lower bunk— one drawer each. The small closets were at the head of the bunk or near the wall. The bunks were perpendicular to the walls, leaving a passageway at the end of them. A row of windows faced the outside, theirs the street.

It could hardly be made to look homey, but they laughed at the crudeness and decided to see how long they would want to stay. After all they hadn't seen the shops yet.

The camp was laid out in a sort of elongated semicircle.

There were the barracks from the north side of a town street called Grealy and went south past the five barracks, then the building at almost the center where the food was cooked and meals served (referred to by the boys simply as the "mess hall.") A corner of it had been made into a mail room, with alphabetical pigeon holes. In front of it was a counter with a chair behind it. It was not always occupied. Just east of that were office buildings and the entranceway from the main highway, which went through the town. On past, with a roadway along it all, were the three shops. The first one was woodwork, the second the machine shop and the next the sheet metal, by day, and arc welding by night.

The next thing, after the girls had taken in their luggage, chosen a bunk, added personal touches and made up their bunks, was to be taken to the mess hall to eat. They were told by the supervisor they would be segregated at meals, the boys using one end, the girls the other.

On one note the girls were harmonious: That compared to Wildwood, the place was a "dump," and the sooner they could get their training over and out the better.

The next few days were spent in getting accustomed to the crude living quarters, orientation as to what was expected of them at work and their free time privileges and obligations.

The next day was Friday and it had been planned that they should look over the workshops to give the girls an idea of what was taught so they could decide which would interest them most, that they'd prefer to train to do. However it was pouring down rain and they went into only one and were then sent back to the barracks. Everyone was soon soaked to the skin by the rain and it was decided, rather than risk exposure and illness, they'd wait until the next day. So there was little to do but write letters, which Shandol did, watch it rain and actually go to eat between rain showers, which began to slacken in the afternoon.

Saturday they did go to the shops. Several girls had already decided to take welding, including Shandol. But that was firmly ruled out for beginners. Shandol decided the whole idea was just too new to take any chances.

That day Shandol and Margery decided to take machine shop. It seemed to offer the best bet for future job use. As there were boys there to demonstrate what the job was about. They were shown the lathes turning and the micrometer, which measured the size needed "to a hair's fraction," and the way the gauge was set to be sure they could be accurate. It was explained some boys had been trained and gone to work. They were shown each shop in turn and the function of each. The wood shop kept the chairs and tables in the living quarters and "mess hall" repaired, if any became broken, and they did. There was other work which was used by other departments having it done. They would learn of these as time went on.

Margery and Shandol checked out to go to town that very afternoon, to look around and just missed being caught in a shower.

Sunday, Shandol and Margery went to Sunday school and church service. They were put in the young adult class in Sunday school. They got little out of it as they supposed the young people were college students and they felt out of place. But they did stay for the church service.

As Shandol and Margery were walking along to the mess hall they were joined by a young man who said his name was Dean Karr.

He asked Shandol for a date, after they had eaten and on the way back to the barracks. She hardly knew what to say, but Margery poked at her with her elbow and so they were together that afternoon. They sat under a tree on the grounds and talked about the camp and their backgrounds—getting acquainted talk. The date was for after supper and Dean Karr had a friend who had a car and the girls went to town with them.

They first drove around: There were the all men's and all women's colleges to see. They went by a hospital and country club grounds. They got ice cream and tried to find the park, unsuccessfully, so ate as they parked on the girl's college campus. School was out and it was deserted.

They saw the movie *Ship Ahoy*, which Shandol considered rather silly. However they had a special feature newsreel of the sinking of the Lexington and Arizona ships. Shandol watched it in mute fascination. Jane, her sister-in-law's only brother had perished in the Arizona. It had taken the family awhile to adjust and accept. Jane's mother had even blamed his girl friend's mother, saying if she had let them alone they would have been married, he would have had a safer job and alive now. Her grief had abated only a little but life went on. Because there could be no real funeral, people found it hard to express sympathy. Yet there were prayers and silences in the churches in memory of those lost in that attack.

Jane had thought it so unreal and that he was merely away. She ached for her parents and her own loss, but she thought she must not be moody because she was glad she still had her "Sugar," She could be thankful for that.

After the movie they went into a small café and played the jukebox and drank orange soda pop. They made it back in plenty of time, though they were stopped by the night watchman to be sure they belonged on the grounds, but that was no problem.

Monday was their first workday. They were up at four forty-five to eat breakfast, get ready and be at work by six o'clock.

Most of the girls went to the machine shop. There were simply not enough machines for all those who decided it was best. It seemed the machines were a first come, first served basis, and those fortunate or aggressive enough to grab one would not relinquish it. There was only one answer to the dilemma : Some would have to choose something else. Shandol and Margery, who had vowed again to stick together if possible, became very bored in the machine shop. They grumbled that there was nothing to do and so time passed slowly. It was incentive for them to decide to make a change along with others, who had done nothing all morning either. They chose to go to the woodworking shop.

The girls, with willing help, made two handles, which might be used for tools and thought it great. It was considered practice.

There was a break for the noon meal, and the workday was over at two p.m. Shandol and Margery washed some clothes, took showers and felt refreshed.

Shandol soon realized she was not as well satisfied as yet as she had become in Wildwood, and she suspected Margery felt the same. Some of the girls had even voiced doubts of sticking with it. Shandol was homesick, she knew it. But what had she really to look forward to if she went home. She and Margery had discussed it and couldn't decide. They would wait to make up their minds.

To take her mind off her misery and indecision. Took some letters she had received while at Wildwood and read them. One from Calvin almost matched her mood, yet had a message for her about Greenway. It was dated the twenty-first.

Dearest Shandol,

I am answering your letter I got the other day. Sure was glad to here from you. This leaves me fine and hope you are the same. I am glad that you like it up there, seems like this place is dead since you left. I sure would like to see you kid. I went to church four night last week and I guess I will go this week. I wish you was hear to go to church with us. Well, kid Wanita and Druce got married last Monday night. Looks like all the kids are getting married down here, but I guess I will have to go to the army. I got to go to St. Louis now soon for the rest of my examination then if I pass I am going. I hope you come home before I go. I want to see you. It rained almost all last week and I sure hope I get to work more this week for if I go be examined I will have some money. Kid has Dean left yet. I haven't seen him in a long time and hope I never see him again. You are the one I want to see. Well they are getting up a dinner next Sunday for my uncle and me at his brother's. I will be 21. I guess they will have a party too—if not I will go to the show. Well I will close for now. Answer soon from your love one to mine.

Cal Horn.

Her mother's letter had been postmarked the day after. The only date was "Mon morn."

Dearest Shandol: Today is relief day so am going to town. Bobby and I, Dad and Phil have gone to work but it's sorta cloudy today again. All are well except Karen's bowels are some bad yet. Some better. Put her back on canned milk. She sets lots now. She's awfully nice. Has found and enjoys her feet lots.

Had a card from Lester yesterday. Was in Topeka, Kan. Said he didn't know where he'd be sent to possibly Oregon. Can you imagine him being gone that far away and maybe no telling how long. I could cry about it every time I think about it but won't do any good. Dad can hardly forgive Mrs. Childon but guess he'll have to love her if he goes to heaven. Lester said he was sorta enjoying himself so no use to worry about him. Shandol I'm not worrying so much about your environment, but when that's all I hear I sorta become skeptical. *I still have faith in you.* You know the old saying all said words of tongue or pen the saddest are these it *might have been.*

How did the dance come out? How's Johnny? Did the other girl get him? Ha. Hugh B. was here a few minutes Fri. night and said he was coming back to see us but hasn't. Don't know how long he aims to stay. When I see him again I'll ask him why he didn't write to you. Said he had been on land since Dec. But he received your letter u wrote in Oct. or should have so you do as you feel about writing to him.

Had a marshmallow roast at Ruletons after Young People"s meeting here Fri night. Went up there on account of Mr. Kasper. Had young p. here last nite.

Phil, Bobby and Ardena went to see *Tarzan* last nite on truck. Mr. Kasper about as usual almost past going. I don't go much anymore. Keeps me humping to get anything done. She doesn't come much either. Just enough to keep posted, ha. Had a community singing yesterday didn't go didn't want to take Karen. Dad aimed to write but as usual put it off. The card was pretty. I'm glad you sent it. I'm sorry to have to hurry but will write again soon. Have to be ready to go by 8 o'clock, now 7 so will have to hurry. Be good.

Love, Mom Write

P.S. If they get a good week in this week I'll try to send enough to u for permanent next week if u haven't got enough.

By the next day Shandol received a letter from both her mother and Dean. The one from her mother was in answer to Shandol's letter about the Center closing and her safe arrival in Midhill. It seemed she had known about it, according to her letter, which was marked "Sat.12:30."

Dear Dearie

Your letter just come was glad to hear from you. Sorta worried read about the water being out between Midhill and the river. Got the NYA slip before we got your letter but didn't look for you much before I heard again. Haven't heard anymore from Lester so you see I had a double worry. Phil has missed two days work went today don't know how he ll make out. Had that bowel and summer trouble that's been going— Grandpa Horn died last Sun. Dropped dead as Mrs. Dahle. Buried him Tue.

Maybe I told u. Tommy's soaking his foot was afraid he'd have infection but seems better. He stepped on a nail.

Didn't go to Young People"s meeting had to stay with him. There's a party at Ardena's tonight. Guess will have to go I'm sorta tired don't sleep very well at nights. Have so much to do today. Have the kitchen cleaned, bread baked, part of dining room mopped. Bobby swept front room.

Hugh B. went back the 24th. He sure was disappointed. Dad told him you'd be disappointed too. Said he sure was. Said "I sure loved that girl." Said if he had had longer to stay he would have come to Wildwood to see you. Thinks he'll get to come back so if he does maybe you'll get to see him. Mrs. Borsch came after your address yesterday so sent it to her now. Said for you to write to Hugh. Said he would write to you but maybe u won't get it now since u've moved. If I get his address before you do I'll send it. He's sure a pitiful sight. Fell off 20 lbs. just a slender pole now. Said for 15 days he lived on beans and rice, went barefoot almost a week lost his shoes. Jumped from the ship and started swimming shoes got too heavy pulled them off in water everything went down with the ship $25.00 in his billfold lost it too. Said he could have saved everything but thought they had the ship saved towed it half a mile but exploded from below burned out then.

They (U.S.) blew it up to finish sinking it. There was installments in the daily news read just like Hugh told it, only one could get a more vivid picture. Awful. Bobby, Tommy, Karen and I ate dinner with Ruby Fargon last Mon. got relief that day. $8.oo gro. order. Had fried steak for dinner sure was good. She had done a big washing. They were all ok. Her baby pulls up to things. Karen has been cranky today. Think she'll have some teeth 'ere long. She sits alone now. Said to tell you she got some pretty white shoes. She gets a kick out of chewing on them! Rained yesterday p.m. first we've had for quite awhile. Garden is weedy. Don't know whether Dad'll clean it out or not. Saw Orvin was at home didn't harvest much don't know what was the reason." (Work too hard, thought Shandol as she read.) "I'm not paragraphing this. I'll have to hurry just write as I think. There is lots of money in that welding job maybe hard too. Take something that will do you good later too.

Sorry you have to be so far away but guess we can expect that sooner or later. Hope you like your new job. You're not out for a good time now that must wait until later. Don't sit around and moon but don't slight your work. How long will you be there? Is Margery old enough to be on a defense job? You'll see lots more Johnnies. Ha. Do you still write to him? We went through Midhill when we went to Lafey's don't you remember? Is that girls school still there. Aunt Ruth went to school there. That's where Joe W. went to school. You may get a chance to visit all those places. (The later was at the School for the Deaf, Shandol knew.) Don't know if you can make sense out of this or not. I'll have to sign off if I get this mailed. *Tell me when you git this*. Harriet just left so will have to hurry. Write again soon. Be Good.

Write Love, Mom.

P.S. Your prospects look good better study hard I get a kick out of Phil teasing him about his money. I'll tell him I want something. He'll say 'how can I get anything u shipping it all to Sis'. Ha ha. I'll try to send some the first of the week.

At work that day Shandol used the jigsaw. She sawed out tulip designs and painted them. She was fascinated by it as it worked so much like a sewing machine yet sawed just any shape one was able to make it do. There was also demonstrations and sandpapering to do.

That day the girls learned Miss Prine, who had been head cook at Wildwood had come to this Center.

In the afternoon the girls took their inevitable showers after the dust of the shop. Then went to town with Nancy and Edna to the movie. They mostly wanted to see the newsreel, as it was the same show they had seen earlier. Shandol still thought *Ship Ahoy* silly and this time she had had to pay her own way. She also purchased candy and popcorn as the other three girls did.

At night there was a "baseball" game with the camp and town teams. The Center team won. Shandol and Margery went, but didn't stay. Shandol said she had such a headache she wasn't enjoying it. She took some aspirin and laid down awhile. Margery ironed. Shandol did some also later, but the lights were out by 9:30 during the week so she didn't finish.

x x x x

On the first Monday she was there Shandol wrote her mother a more detailed letter of her new home away from home.

Midhill
June 29, 1942

Dear Mom,

Do you reckon I can write you a letter in thirty minutes— with noise and all? At nine thirty the lights will be out so guess I'll hurry.

517

If I hadn't gotten your letter today, I was going to write to see if you were ever going to write. The first day or so I was here I thought I'd die. Lands, these old bunks to sleep on! We have to go a half quarter mile?! (more or less) to get anything to eat. To the 'mess hall', only we girls call it cafeteria.

I just saw the movie pictures show last night of the sinking of the Lexington and Arizona ships. That was in a special feature. Yes, I went to the show Sunday night—awful ole me. It was *Ship Ahoy*. Just silly. Marg and I had double dates with a couple of boys here in camp. The boys here, for the most part, are nice. Makes them feel so important I think, because they do give over to us girls. We get our work shift of a morning. They have to take evening and night shifts. Well, to get back to the show and the boy I went with, I met him walking to Sunday school and church Sunday morning? Well, I did go that morning. I think I'm trying to tell everything at once because I have such a few minutes.

The church I went to was like ours—communion every Sunday, except it has a pipe organ and piano. They used the organ in church service. It's a nice church.

Sunday eve before the show we drove about town. The reason we did was to find the park. The boys were new, too, but we had ice cream and never did find it. So we just went past the country club, parked and ate. (Later they were to learn the park was across the west to east street they had traveled.) I'd like to see lots of this town. I heard it's called a retired farmer's town as that's what started it. Do you remember reading about the fine new court house the government built? It's pretty. I believe it was here that such a grand courthouse was built, wasn't it?

Yes, I saw the college. I suppose it's the one you mean. You know what! Downtown we stopped at a 2 x 4 place to get potato chips. One man asked if we were from the deaf school!! Some people resent us being here—as in Wildwood. (Did I tell you of one time a fight broke out between some town and Wildwood girls? Over boys! They broke it up. I wasn't there I just heard the girls fuss and fume over it.) Anyway we'll have to build and guard our reputation.

I think I'm going to take up woodwork after all. Mr. Mallery, Supt. said he wouldn't advise a beginner, girls especially, to start out on welding. So it wasn't allowed. I really like woodwork. If I could do it real well. I'd get a job in St. Louis in the glider factory (supposedly). They are crying for over

1200 girls we heard. Hope I can do it. I'd take machine shop but it's too slow and crowded. Marg and I made two handles that looked like this (a terrible drawing.) We sandpapered them and oiled them. The man in the shop said we did real well for beginners. Besides, here they take interest and help students who try and take an interest themselves. Boy-dee, we thought we'd done something great, too. We put wood in a machine that turns very fast—a lathe. We hold the chisels and cut the shape we want. Some of the machines though are very complicated—even dangerous—and I will never need learn about them as they involve heavy work—says the boss.

Tell Dad I learned to read those numbers on a square in order to find number of board feet. They are offering pattern work too. Guess I'll *try* some of that.

Sure too bad about Hugh B. I wish you'd save me those clippings, will you? Send them to me so I can read them. I don't get to read a newspaper. The one radio we have always has something else on the string when I'm around.

Tue., 30th—Well, the first thing I knew last night all went black. With no warning they turned out the lights. I'm now off work so I'll finish. We get up of a morning at 4:45! Eat breakfast and start work at 6:00. Then we're off at 11:30 to eat and then we get off at two for the day. If I'd stayed on in machine shop I'd have gotten off at noon but work on Saturday. This way my week ends Friday. I believe I like this better.

Today we sandpapered laths for venetian blinds. We also cut out some flowers on a 'jigsaw' machine. It's like a coping saw blade but it runs like a sewing machine—only no peddling. Ha. A boy from the shop gave me a round box he'd made with a lid and all. He's called Hi-ho—says just call him that everyone does. Marg also got a box. One boy is making an ashtray on a stand and for himself.

Do you know I couldn't come home if I wanted to? Can't hardly cross the river. Have to go way round.

Dean is still in Kan. He wrote like if the rains quit they'd have work to do. However, they work for a specific farmer each year.

I got your letter Monday, June 29.

Is Phil okay now? Don't work too hard.

I have on my old overall slacks. Does Ardena still wear hers? Tell her to write to me. Are the young people that just got married still in Greenway?

I think we'll get a check this week. Don't know what it'll

be. Just now signed my time card. We have number buttons. Guess Dad knows about that. Ha ha.

I'm worried about the first of this letter. I'm hoping you can make sense of it. Guess I'll close now. Tell all hello. Would love to see baby. Tell boys to write.

Love,
Shandol

P.S. By the way did Hugh say where he was going? Back to war I suppose. Why shouldn't I get a letter if it's sent to me here. Is his aunt going to give him my address—I hope? S.S.

CHAPTER 41

The first week soon passed. There was no doubt but that the girls being in the camp had made a difference, both for themselves and the boys. The girls had to make adjustments to the living quarters, the new morning hours of arising and the new type of work they did.

But there were also orders that had been given to the young men on the project. The girls learned by bits and pieces of conversations of some of the orders they had been given. One was to clean up their language, if they used any foul type, and that they were to treat the girls as ladies as well as they knew how. They were not forbidden talk or contact; indeed, some were chosen to as teachers-helpers by showing them how to do certain work and to acquaint them individually with the machines. This was a great help to the foreman and the girls knew it. It also allowed the boys to become more friendly even while knowing it was work and not just flipping around for attention. This the girls were warned about though there was innocent, clean-perhaps it could be called guileless flirting.

There were also drawback to having so many in one room.

They had to learn how to cope with that, mostly by ignoring what they didn't want to hear, see, or know. Both Shandol and Margery had to learn to take showers before other girls without nearly dying of mortification. Though Shandol had had physical education in Plainesville high school, showers afterward had not been mandatory. It was not only the showers, they would grumble, but brushing their teeth—everything was so open there was little privacy at all. But there was a washing machine, iron and ironing board, possibly from Wildwood, though they never thought to ask. As at Wildwood they were responsible only for their personal laundry.

On July second the girls had been gone from Wildwood a week. They were still having adjustments to make, but were becoming more settled and at ease about their new conditions.

Shandol received three letters. One from Lester, one from her mother, who had sent Lester's letter to her, and one from Dean.

Her mother's letter was dated, "Tue. eve."

Dear Dearie:

Enclosed you will find M.O. for $2.00 for permanent. Was afraid to send bills.

What's the matter? Will I hear from you in the gulf of Mexico? Too much water? I'm sorta worried about u. Canned beans for Mrs. Borsek today.

Went to town yesterday got me a permanent!

Mr. Kasper's real bad. Mr. Strasser is about to pass away. They came back last week. I must hurry want to mail before p.o. closes. That's where I am now.

Had letter from Lester. Said to forward to u his address. It's on back of this paper.

Good-bye now, be good. I'll write again soon.

Write. Love, Mom.

Lester's letter was short and moody. It was dated,

Somewhere in Oregon,
June 23, 1942.

Dear Folks:

Well, I finally got here after four nights and days of h--l. I sure don't like it here and don't really care who knows it.

Tell Phil he can have all the dang west he wants, but I'll take ----.

I got a bad cold and feel like thunderation. Maybe I'd like it better if 'Ducky' was here. I didn't realize I'd miss her so much.

I'm not worried and they treat me swell. I'm just blue and lonesome. Sand and sage is all I see. Will write when I feel better. Send this on to Sis.

I'm too sick and tired to write anymore now.

Love, Lester

Shandol thought he was somewhat perkier in his letter to her. But still terribly homesick and realizing he was far away. Her heart went out to him. He missed his wife and the family so much.

Shandol and Margery kept busy. Shandol washed her hair, took a shower, tried to dance some, wrote home but actually went to bed early. Margery wrote to her soldier boyfriend, whom she had met while at Wildwood.

The two girls had talked awhile low, Margery beside Shandol in the bottom bunk. They criticized some of the loudmouths they had to listen to, and especially one. She seemed to consider herself very popular and the boss of the area. Actually a show-off, inconsiderate and merely showing her ignorance, the girls smugly decided to themselves.

"But I wish she'd leave off reading the letters to the boys she writes to," Shandol complained. "They're pretty silly I think."

"Do yuh suppose she'll send 'em?" Margery asked, wondering, as Shandol did also. Not that it mattered. Perhaps they knew and were used to her or as silly as she was.

They discussed how they missed Nancy and Edna, who had by now gone home. The place was simply not good enough for them. They admitted it. But Shandol and Margery knew they would miss them. They had left Shandol and Margery souvenirs, which made Shandol and Margery more sad, because they could not reciprocate. Nancy gave Shandol a small bottle of perfume and Edna gave Margery a fancy lacy handkerchief. They promised faithfully to write, but Shandol wondered if they ever would, really. They would have gone home sooner but the high water had left them stranded a few days. There were tears in the girls' eyes at parting time. How close they seemed in so short a time!

Then they remembered the flies bothering all afternoon.

"No wonder Nancy and Edna left," Shandol moaned. The flies seemed everywhere even in the cafeteria. There were no screens on the windows, which had to be open at this time of year. Such few there had really been at Wildwood in comparison! Always there was that comparison of Wildwood and "this place." Soon Margery climbed up to her own bunk to sleep. They had to get up early.

Shandol had taken the time to write a long letter to Audrey.

Midhill
July 2, 1942

Dear Mom,

I got your letter and the money order this noon.

Thank you heaps. I have four cents to my name! You just can't imagine how it'll (money) fly. So many little things that I need that don't seem important. Soaps, stamps, paper, I want to get some starch, and I've been buying a laxative.

I'm glad you sent Lester's letter, but I got one from him when the mail came in this evening. He's sure homesick, isn't he? Poor boy. I know how he feels, but I *do* hope he stays, as it seems to me he's doing pretty good. I'm going to write to him soon, because I know how a letter helps. How he misses Jane! I do hope they can like it out there if he can get settled. I just can't hardly feature him so far away. Where's Jane? I asked you before but you never said. I'd like to hear from her. Don't believe she thinks the West half so romantic, eh?

Don't worry about me and high water. Going to bed so late and rising so early 'it'll not catch me napping'! Seriously, no rivers close enough to flood here. The River is twenty-some miles away. The girls who've been stranded here and couldn't go home, after coming this far, went home today. So the river must be going down.

What kind of permanent did you get? I'll tell you of mine when I get it.

Too bad about the elderly men in Greenway, guess it won't seem like Greenway when I go back. All the kids will be gone—married, gone to war or to work somewhere else. The older people dying. Oh, my, doesn't time pass?

Oh, me, some people here! A girl in an upper bunk a little way from mine is reading aloud a letter she's writing. She thinks she's some letter writer. Therefore I can't hardly write. They're writing to boys—a few with her—and of all the crazy things. Don't be surprised at what I write.

Oh, yeah, I got a letter from Dean today and is he ranting!! Quoting him here's what he said : "You have traded the witch for the devil when you went to Midhill. You know I don't want you to stay in that h--l hole." Whew! Said if you wanted me to come home I'd better go. But he's just crazy because it's me or something. This is ok. These boys are nice up here. Funniest thing one boy kept on the morning shift to help girls get started, has his pick for me. He has helped me make two candle holders and I've varnished them. They're nice. I made all but puttin' the 'last minute' finishing. They're so easily ruined on those lathes, I let him do it. Marg and I make little trinkets (for practice). Those things made of scraps we can keep. We made a book back of plywood for photographs. It's right cute. Has my initials and word 'photographs' on front. I made a tiny rollin pin today but I forgot and left it at the shop so guess it'll be gone by tomorrow.

Oh, yeah, I received a letter from Carol Middleton.

Said she took care of Karen while you and her mother canned beans. Here's exactly quoted what she wrote of Karen. 'Your mother brought her cooker down and helped Mom can beans and I got to take care of her. She's honestly one of the sweetest kids I have ever seen. I think she's the very image of you! Quite nice eh? Lands, how I miss her. She's going to be all grown up from me.

What's the other kids doing? I guess Bobby's the same mama boy who can see what needs to be done.

Don't tell him but I've envied him his initiative in the house. He was actually better help I know than I. Tommy may take after him. Hope Phil's feeling better now and working again. This place might appeal to him. He likes to make things— progress or something. But I'm no fortune-teller.

Funny isn't it? Remember how the fortune-teller said I'd have a brother in another state. We thought it'd be Phil in Iowa. (But she probably had in mind the army—a guess, eh? She did make some odd predictions which were true anyway— however she knew or guesses.)

Tell Dad when I wrote in his letter about getting to bed late I meant 9:30. The lights are out then. We can only stay out until 11:30 on Saturday and Sunday nights. In the day room, or sitting room (?) lights go out at 10:30, but in bunk areas it's 9:30.

Marg says we've got an iron so guess we better iron. I borrowed some starch but I'm just going to have to get me some. More stuff to buy.

I believe I'll write Lester tonight while Marg irons some. Must write to Carol too.

Some people are here who I think are some kind of bosses of the place. They're talking so I can't think.

Lands, the flies are bad here. We've no screens on the open windows.

Write and tell all to write.

Love, Shandol

"I just can't believe Nancy and Edna would leave," Shandol told Margery the next day, as they were sandpapering a large door. "It's lonesome with them gone."

"Yeah," Margery agreed. "I hoped they'd change their minds at the last minute. Wonder what they'll do."

Then, the girls became abuzz about Claude making Jean a better box. She was a petite brunette whose dark eyes and even features only made her large mouth distinctive. The boxes considered were supposedly face powder boxes. They learned Hi-ho's real name was Claude. He promised to make Shandol one also.

Claude was young, good looking, fair, and with eyes too large for his face. He was not very tall and of small, slender build.

* * * * *

525

At the shop the next day they watched an army convoy going along the highway in front of the shops. They were near enough they could wave and cheer them on. At the sound of the motoring trucks and other vehicles there was no keeping any of them inside the shops.

In the afternoon the girls went out on the grounds to idle some spare time. They discussed the ballgame of the night before.

The girls, however, because of the early hours perhaps, soon fell fast asleep. They awoke, soon learning they were "full of chiggers." It meant taking a second shower, then washed clothes. They ironed and wrote the inevitable letters. It sometimes seemed to Shandol she was always writing letters or feeling guilty if she didn't. She had written to Lester and Dean last night. She had tried and hoped she could soothe his ruffled feathers.

Then, too, whenever they could privately, the girls still tried to dance. After all they had brought the jukebox along.

But they felt they weren't very good so hated for anyone to see them.

They also marveled, as many of the girls did, at the sight to see, when mealtime neared and the boys and girls left the various barracks—which the girls were trying to make sound better by calling them dormitories or "dorms"—to go to meals. There were paths made, though some went the graveled road which connected the buildings. There was a boardwalk from each wing door to the street. A small concrete porch and sidewalk connected the street and the day room. On a clear day when about everyone went it seemed like a young army.

On this day, going to supper, Margery and Shandol were going the shortcut, a path beside a huge oak tree, and dusty now, and when muddy the grassy area was used. So it had become quite a wide path by now. Margery and Shandol were giggling and mumbling low, then laughing hilariously. They were quite surprised to discover they were not exactly alone. Not very far behind them were the two dorm supervisors. The girls giggled nervously, then.

"They must think we are telling dirty jokes or something," Shandol said, uncomfortable at the thought. "We'd better say something to give them an idea."

"Yeah, how about the truth," Margery laughed. "It's silly but not bad."

"You do it," she coaxed.

Shandol turned around and, stepping backward slowly, smiled at the two women.

"See if you can say 'rubber buggy bumper' right fast a few times," she said.

526

They tried and realized it did not always come out as they expected.

"Where'd we hear that?" Margery suddenly asked.

"Oh, I suppose it's some of the foolishness of Buck Sandler," Shandol answered. "I'm not sure, but he'd go on foolishly like that sometimes."

"But no rough stuff around you, right?" Margery teased.

They were again talking among themselves.

"You're so right," Shandol conceded. "I guess I wasn't grown up to them—still in my 'cocoon'. I wonder if I'm out yet." She was pondering seriously, Margery saw.

"What?" Margery exclaimed, looking at her questioningly.

"Oh, nuthin'—just a private joke of my own," Shandol assured her.

By then they had luckily reached the "mess hall" and no more was said on the subject.

Shandol's letter from her mother was dated "Fri. 11:45, Greenway,"

Dear Shandol,

Rec'd your letter this morn. Began to wonder what was the matter with *you*. I wrote two letters to *u* didn't hear from *u* so quit too. Thought the high water was hindering. I'm sorta under the weather today. Felt real bad last night. Have Phil's *besease* (the besease for disease dated back to Lester's babyhood, Shandol knew.) I'm so afraid Karen will have to have it too. Hasn't nursed me since night before last. She doesn't care whether she nurses me or not.

Been canning beans this week. Canned 54 qts for Mrs. Borsek, 20 for Mrs. Jarred. I'm quitting now. Should have canned some for myself but felt too bad today. Haven't washed this week only for baby guess I won't now just a few pieces. Had another letter from Lester Wed. He likes it better.

Jane wrote me a card. Said to tell you 'hello' when I wrote to u. Did you get the M.O.? I hope you make good on your woodwork. How long will you have to stay there? Want you to come home before you go to work anywhere. Would like to make you a dress but fear it wouldn't fit! Maybe when u get ur check u can buy one. Had a letter from Nona today. (Shandol's cousin). Said Granddad okay was still at her mom's.

I'm sending Hugh B. address you might write to him. Don't know whether Mrs. Borsek sent ur address to him but she got it from us. Karen's fine wish you could see her. I'm wanting another picture of her—seems she's so sweet. Guess it's 'cause my other girl is gone. She acts up now tries to crawl. She manages to get where she wants to go especially if she sees something she shouldn't have.

Mr. Kasper's about the same. Mr. Strasser too. Under an opiate all the time.

Colmay's have a cow now. Sold a strip of land in Iowa $100.00, Silas said bought one from Mr. Freedman. Freeman's are selling sows and chicks going somewhere (she said). He didn't have a school to teach as yet. Phil and Dad are working don't have much of a week this week. Lost Mon. Are you going to work in garden tomorrow (July 4)? Remember what we did last 4th of July—pulled weeds out of onions. Onions need pulling now.

Bobby fixed fence for Mrs. Ruleton yesterday. Dug taters for Mrs. Wolken this a.m. He washed dishes, swept this morn for me! I got up and made biscuits, Dad finished putting in pan. Got sick had to go back to bed.

Ardena is wondering why you don't write. Did u get her last letter? Was ur mail forwarded to you from Strawsville?

We've an icebox now. Got Mrs. Borsek's. Bot 50 lbs. ice today. I think I'm going to like it fine. Bobby has fixed some Kool-aid and put it in icebox for supper.

Sam came back Tue., I believe. Was here Wed. *nite* fiddlin'. Sat. eve Bobby, Phil, Buck and Hollis was on porch playing. Bessie Wittever came over asked them to quit bothered her dad. (Mr. Kasper). Wouldn't have griped me so bad but they weren't out there five min. Oh, well, guess I shouldn't feel that way, but sorta grinds. If it was every *nite*, all night and day wouldn't have thought so much about it.

Did you get your permanent? I sorta like mine. Miss you to help me care for it. Ardena came up to me fingering my curls said, 'you look so much younger since you got your hair fixed. Your hair is so pretty and black and shiny.' Should have got some towels and dresses. I'm nearly naked. One old dress has completely fell to pieces but maybe I can manage.

Don't seem to find the paper installments. Guess I've put them away too good. Maybe don't have them at all. If I find them I'll send them too. I'll mail funny papers and some other clippings soon.

Did I tell you we might have to move? U remember Mrs. Laughlin's last letter she wrote that a man wanted to buy the place. Well, next time she wrote she told us who it was. Guess who! (Get the smelling salts) Oran Kasper! Ha Ha Ho Ha.

I'm not ever figuring on moving as far as he is concerned!

She still struts around like she was worth a million.

Harriet came to see me this a.m. Midhill must be doing something to you and Margie. Her folks haven't heard from her either. Said Margery had always wanted to go places and see things now she was doing it. Ha Sh! Sh! I must quit thought I'd get another letter but didn't. Train has gone. Runs 12:06 p.m. now. Guess we can't write every day but don't wait tooooo long.

Must write to Lester too. Did you get my letter that had his letter in it?

Must quit, Write and be good.

Love, Mom

Shandol hurriedly wrote to her brother:

Dear Brother,

Mom forwarded your letter to them onto me. I got it in the morning and yours in the afternoon. So you might say I heard from you twice in one day.

So it's lonesome in Oregon? Boy-dee, I sure was lonesome too until I became acquainted. Now it's not so bad except I'd just like to see them all at home. Where is Jane? I ask Mom but she never says.

Lands, if you get that much I think that's pretty good. It's better than where you were. I hope I can do well here. By the way, guess you've noted my new address. Yep, I'm in Midhill in that Boy's camp. There are about 160 boys and 33 girls. The boys sure are nice. This is training for defense work. The Center at Strawsville closed. It cost a lot to run and the rent and food bills were all needed to be used for defense. We're here in a "bunkhouse," Marg sleeps over me. Guess it's sorta like CCC camp. Sure is odd. What's funniest (?) though, is the eating. We have to go to the mess hall—'cafeteria' and line up!

Is that like CCC? We eat on one side, and boys eat on the other. But we work together. I'm taking woodwork. I started taking machine shop, but this is definitely more interesting. You remember the kids used to make in Plainesville—round boxes, smoking stands, etc., thats what I'll learn to do. A boy helped me make some candlesticks. They're nice I think. Today, tho' we sandpapered big doors. Boy-dee, my hands are rough! Some job. I have also helped sandpaper venetian blinds. The machinery used here is very powerful and swift. Somewhat dangerous maybe. The head man says, 'don't go to sleep!' And we do get up early! at 4:45, eat and are at work at 6:00. But we'll get off at noon. We'll work six hours all time after this week.

I have dated one boy from camp here. He's from north of here. We went to a show. I've gone to church, and seen some of the town. I want to see or hear about the deaf school. Remember John Wesley B. (cousin) was here.

From your letter I gather you're lonesome. Let's buck up! I can't see any good in Greenway. And if I went back as soon as I'd visited I'd be ready to go again. But I'd love to visit them. I am when I get a chance. But you're a long way from home. Do you ever think back? Now, remember you're an old "married man"? Ha.

I want to comb my hair before supper as I've just taken a shower. Please write. If you think of it tell Jane to write. I expect she's lonesome for you too—guess? Hope it's not too long before you see her and she's o.k.

Your Sis
Shandol

P.S. I heard from Dean. He certainly don't like me to be here, but—— S.S.

The Fourth of July fell on Saturday which meant no work for Margery and Shandol, whereas some in other shops were required to work. Both girls got up to go to breakfast, as a special "cook" had made biscuits.

For awhile Margery and Shandol remained in the "rec. hall." This was the part of the mess hall where there were no dining tables; just open space and the jukebox, which had soon been moved from the 'girls' dorm. The two girls, being alone danced to the music. There was nothing else going on and no one to make them feel self-conscious.

They had learned some kind of "head man" was visiting the camp that day. They did not see him—only heard he was there.

Breakfast had been early and the morning might've seemed long except they had so much to do. They did some washing and Shandol ironed Margery a dress and herself a slip. She also swept their side of the dorm wing with a push broom.

They went to lunch at noon. In the afternoon Shandol took a nap, bathed and put on a fresh clean dress to go to supper. She and Margery did their brand of dancing again. They could do fairly well together, but were fearful to try with anyone else.

They decided to go to town later. They saw no one there and there didn't seem to be much going on. At any rate they had no money to spare if they had thought of something. And, later, when they came from a small café where they had had a soft drink, they noticed a black cloud forming in the southwest. The reason they went to the café was because it had records on the jukebox which they enjoyed hearing. One Shandol liked was "Sycamore Lane" sung by Gene Autrey. But this night they gasped at the black cloud coming so hurriedly and knew they must head for camp and hope to make it before they were caught in a downpour—perhaps a storm. They barely made it. In fact they were on the grounds when large drops begun to fall. They had hurried, were exhausted, but missed the eventual electrical storm and rain.

"Ain't that lightnin' terrifyin'?" Margery stated rather than asked, as a loud clap of thunder boomed as though the lightning had detonated an explosive.

"Oh, I hate storms," Shandol admitted, "but yuh know there's not much yuh can do about 'em—except get out of their way in as safe a place as possible.

"Yeah, but how safe is this?" she wondered.

"There's no wind to speak of, so I guess we're safe if that lightnin' don't stick it's fiery finger in here somewhere and score a hit," Shandol replied, startled visibly as just such a light seemed to fill the sky outside, but hit somewhere else, the loud clap of thunder reassured her.

Soon the storm passed over, and as it was leaving the thunder rumbled farther in the distance, a more reassuring sound.

"Let 'er rain, but darn the thunder," someone in another bunk was heard to say, as even the rain became more gentle.

It had, after all, seemed a long day. Shandol had received a letter from her mother and it had made her lonesome and homesick and feeling she just must see her family. She realized that the novelty was indeed wearing off. How could she ever hope to get used to this? She thought of the cafeteria—or call it what anyone cared to the rectangular gray tables in there, which were meant to seat six people, three on each side, and the odd looking chairs, which were turned seat down on top of the table when the area was scrubbed, were also painted gray. Why was everything painted that color? Was it cheaper? Or for identification purposes? Shandol doubted anyone would care for them. It also made it more lonesome when she realized she had no money and her parents couldn't spare it, so she could hope if they did, or she did, she could go back to see the family.

But Margery, who was in a better mood, wrote to her mother and volunteered she and Shandol to work K.P. early the next morning, which was Sunday. They decided they were much too sleepy to attend church that day.

They got up late and washed out a few pieces. In the afternoon they sat under the tree, not so far from the dorm. They took a blanket on which to sit to discourage the chiggers. Margery had a date. She had made it during K.P. The boy Shandol had dated had gone home for the weekend.

Later the four went to town. Margery, her date, Shandol and another girl from their side of the dorm. She was Loretta Sheane. She wore thick-lensed glasses, which almost blurred her eyes. She had dark wavy hair, which was shoulder length and she made no attempt at a particular style. She was taller than Shandol, quiet, and of slender build. She was good company, Shandol judged her, as the time passes. They walked to Lover's Leap, as Margery's date had no car, a boy from camp. They walked around town. Shandol and Loretta went back to camp as Margery and her date went to the show. It was *Tortilla Flat*. Shandol didn't hear Margery when she came in.

The next day it was up early and back to the shop, after a morning ritual of dressing, brushing their teeth and getting their hair combed. Hi—ho made another lovely powder box, but would give it only to one who would promise to let him take her to the ball game that night. Trudy made the promise. Many of the girls thought it unfair of her, as they were sure it was unlikely she would really let him take her. He was a small youth, less than average height. He had a large nose and prominent upper lip which ruined his looks. His neat brown hair was his one redeeming feature. He kept it combed so one small wave showed on one side.

Trudy was a petite brunette, more cute than actually pretty. She had delicate features and trim figure so pretty or not seemed not to matter. Her thick dark brown hair hung to her shoulders in a (straight) pageboy style.

Shandol made rolling pins for Margery's sisters, and did some sandpapering. There were other girls with them and they began to sing. They realized they could harmonize and soon everyone in the shop could hear them sing. A Mr. Smith heard them. He told them he might be able to get up a singing group certainly a quartet and they would certainly be included. The quartet of girls were even asked to sing some more.

At the dorm after work they cleaned some for the inspection of dorms, which would be held the next day.

At night, as was usual on Monday, was the council meeting, the same as at Wildwood. But there was little to consider and the meeting did not last long and seemed less dragged out.

Shandol started a letter to her mother.

Margery wanted to go to town so Shandol decided to go along. They had no dates. There was a car stopped and two guys offered to take them riding perhaps to the airport, but Shandol declined, later explaining she thought they acted too silly. She looked greedily at the car, however, as it was a nice one indeed. Elsie Harple and two girls she was with did go with them.

Margery and Shandol noticed a couple of guys making eyes at them at the ball game. They even lost interest in the game, looking at them to see if they were really being noticed. The girls soon left. The one who had eyes on Shandol, followed.

He stopped the car before they had gone very far up the highway. The girls declined again to be picked up. The boys gave them tiny flags, the driver told Shandol his name and that he would see her again. His name was Rory Wheaton.

The supervisors, Mrs. Avery and Miss Morris, had seen the girls leave and the car stop. They had supposed the girls got in the car to go to camp and they, too, left immediately. How relieved they were to find the girls had come on to the dorm on their own and found no problem! Shandol and Margery had not realized they would be followed home. They were glad they did and apologized for not letting the supervisors know so they could have stayed at the game.

"We've caused you to miss the game," Shandol wailed.

"Our jobs aren't watching ball games," Mrs. Avery, whose room was on their wing, reminded them, "but seeing to you girls. It's all right. We saw the car stop and weren't sure what it meant is all."

"Oh, that was just a guy from town. He asked us to ride, but we knew how you'd feel about it," Margery said.

"We're sorry if it caused you to be put-out," Shandol added. "We had no idea it wasn't all right for us to come on to the dorm. The seats get so hard there and we were just tired and left." She gestured with her hands, palms up, and shrugged her shoulders. "That's about it," she added feebly.

We're relieved yuh didn't get in the car," Mrs. Avery smiled. "At least there's nothing to worry about. Thanks girls." And they went on into Mrs. Avery's room and closed the door.

The next day Shandol finished the letter she had started to her mother the day before, but it was not until her workday was finished. And being Tuesday, it turned out to be a different Tuesday in some ways.

First, it was Margery's and Shandol's turn to stay in the "office." This job was to check out tools and see that they were checked in again by the ones who used them. It was considered the only way to keep track of the tools, and to know why—and who last had it—if one was unavailable. They learned this respect for the tools they worked with for their own, as well as everyone's sake. So the girls stayed every day. They took turns.

At eight twenty-five they were sent to the dorms to finish any last minutes cleaning as it was also dorm inspection day. There was a large banner for the cleanest dorm and a small one for the cleanest wing. It began shortly after nine a.m. and lasts as the inspection team goes through each dorm. Each girl stood by the bunk where she slept, one on one side, one on the other (as one slept on the upper bunk).

The girls had been warned the inspections were thorough, and so had done their level best to have everything clean. They touched areas for dust, looked in closets and drawers for untidiness and anywhere some unsightly speck might be. The bunks had to be made up just so, though they were required to be made every day.

The girls won the main pennant, which meant both sides and day room passed. Oh, but they had tried hard and it had been worth it. How could they stand it if the boys beat them at housekeeping! But the girls were soon to learn the boys would be stiff competition, and as in every game, could not always win. But they were triumphant that day! They were back at work shortly after ten o'clock. They saw Mr. Smith again and he again promised if he could start a quartet they would be in it if they liked.

And they were glad when the day was done. In the afternoon Shandol finished the letter to her mother she had started the day before. She re-read what she had written to catch her train of thought and so she would not repeat herself.

> Dear Mom,
> I hope this finds you better than when you last wrote. Are you better yet? Hope Karen didn't have to catch it. Would love to see her if she's 'getting around.' Wish you could get some pictures and send me one of her. But how can you do all that canning for those people if you've been sick. I wonder that Dad doesn't like it.
> I think I told you I heard from Lester the same day I got your letter. Yeah, I think he'll like it better as he gets more used to it.
> Sometimes I'm somewhat discouraged about the woodwork. There's a boy been here for nine months.
> He's really good too. They say he's been taken out twice to take jobs, *but his mother won't let him go.*
> I think two no three months—possibly longer for a girl—

says the supervisor—for the average job in a factory. Isn't that a long time.

You know before I got your letter I wondered what I did last July fourth, but couldn't think of anything. The shops went on—we worked as usual.

As it happened though our shop hadn't started to work Saturdays. However, we'll have to work next Saturday.

I don't understand about Ardena's last letter.

I was certainly thinking I'd written to her last. Tell her I'm sorry and to write. I wrote her one day last week to renew our correspondence. I just thought perhaps she was neglecting to write like sometimes I do.

Say! Are you splurging? An icebox indeed! That makes me want to come home—to help get some good out of it. Do you blame me? I know how handy they are as I've been where they were. Where do you have it? Did it cost much?

I haven't my permanent as yet. I'm just wondering if I should borrow money for a stamp. Our checks won't come until the 15th after all. They were supposed to—at Wildwood—come early, but here they won't. Oh, me! If I have to spend some of it guess I can make it up when it does come, can't I?

Since I wrote the above I have attended council meeting, seen a baseball game (Monday), and have worked six hours. It is now 1:25 Tuesday. It was my day to work in office at shop—two girls each day. Today Marg and I kept 'office.' We just check out tools, etc. And in spare time we're to learn names of different tools and uses. By the way—when you get looking through a book like that it sure 'bumfuzzles' you. I saw a *whole book* today on the desk on the frame square (like we have at home). Book with how to file and 'set' a crosscut saw in them, etc.

Guess you've moved?! Ha. Is Oren still working in the army camp or wherever he was?

I think Harriet has to keep in touch with Margery through you! Not so long ago Marg wrote to her mother and said she was going to drop her Great-Aunt Harriet a few lines. On a card Marg received from her mother recently, said, 'don't you do it. I'll tell you why in my next letter.' I may get to find out why! I wonder. Did you know Marg gave her a good whipping one time? I didn't know it until she told me up here. I suspect Dad knows it, as she said Harry Bright called her 'Joe Lewis.' Ha ha. I guess she knocked her down and pounded her until she yelled 'enough.' Poor Harriet—how Marg's mother dislikes her. Marg's dad was going to the wheat harvest in Kansas with Dean, and Sloan Houver, but Dolphus said not to. But Marg said Harriet thinks it's okay for her to be up here with me! Marg told me herself that Harriet thought me a lady and that she wanted Marg to be like me! Was I surprised! Sh—h—h.

I'll tell you the truth of the matter, they've only sent her one dollar since she's been gone from home! Now! How do they expect her to write? She's gotten six or eight stamps from me. But what can one do? I hate to tell her no when I have one or two in my drawer (all but now). Don't say too much about it in your letters. Oh, I guess it would be okay except I like to be able to tell her the news. She doesn't read my mail if I don't want her to, I'm sure.

I'm ready to go to town to get the money order cashed. Couldn't do it Sat. p.m. Mondays we can't go to town, so I'm taking it today. I will have to take 25¢ from it I guess to mail this letter and get some stamps, etc. Maybe not that much. I can make it up on my check the 15th.

This morning our 'boss' asked Marg and I as we were in the 'office' if we thought we could hold a job in eight weeks. My lands—if in eight months—not quite I hope. I told him I was still awkward with the tools! And did he ever laugh. He said that's one thing to learn good use of tools and we've not even been here very long.

Write real soon.

Love, Shandol

P.S. You're not answering my questions. What'll I do with you? S.S.

Then Shandol realized she had not given her mother any description of her "boss" or the "office." He was a tall slender man, with fair hair and complexion, and blue eyes. His face was handsome in a rugged sort of way. He was perhaps younger than Shandol's mother, but he seemed old to her. The shop was a small anti room petitioned off for that purpose. There were drawers and places to hang the tools very handily the girls thought. It had a cluttered look in spite of it, actually, of books, manuals and a few handmade tool holders placed about. The unpainted desk top was carved with V's and initials, perhaps by bored boys who had had "office duty" before them. There was a businesslike book to write down names of persons getting tools and the name of the tool. There was a place to check it when it had been returned. There was also a low stack of thin plyboards, and Shandol and Margery took turns stretching out on it chiefly to "study." Yet it was very difficult to concentrate and study a book when it seemed they could hardly grasp what it said. Shandol slammed the books in frustration many times, as did Margery, only to go back determinedly, to become thwarted, baffled and bored again. Wasn't there any help for them in the study of it, they wondered. They felt it all needed to be explained, perhaps demonstrated. Or, they reasoned, perhaps as they saw the work done, that was demonstration, but for now it was no clearer than trying to read a foreign language must be. The words were there, but hard to make them make sense.

In the afternoon they went to town. Shandol took the money order to the post office to be cashed. She was asked for an identification card, but had none. It was cashed, however, and though it had been sent so she could get the permanent wave put in her hair, she purchased stamps and a penny postcard with twenty-five cents of it. The postcard was for Margery. She had word from Arnold, who had written he would come to see her Saturday, but that he wouldn't be able to get the car. He wrote he might try to borrow one, in which case he could take the girls home for the weekend. The girls hardly dared hope. It probably wouldn't be that easy to get a car—to borrow one, that is. But the girls did plan some and hope. Margery wrote the card while they were in the post office. Shandol did not read what she wrote, perhaps not much if she expected to see him on Saturday.

Wednesday of that week there was an open house in the afternoon. Margery and Shandol made no special concessions for it. Shandol wore a blue print cotton dress and sandals; Margery a navy, polka dot dress of thin material. In fact the girls rather ignored the open house and relaxed under the tree.

Later that evening they went out walking around the grounds. In their strolling went by the workshops. There were two fellows from the machine shop who talked to them.

They had never met either one of them before and so had to introduce themselves first. The boys introduced themselves as Elroy Sprunks and Harley Lensing. Elroy Sprunks had a picture of himself in a folder, which he gave to Shandol. He was not handsome but it was a good picture. He was dark, with small eyes, sharp features on a slim face. The girls also talked them out of some snapshots—one Shandol thought adorable was a speckled pony, which Elroy said was on his father's farm. They soon walked on slowly and were back by ten-thirty. They told the supervisor what they had done.

She told the girls she was glad they told her, because she was sure they had broken an unwritten rule. The shops, except for their own shift, was more or less off limits to the girls—and particularly at night. The girls took showers and went to bed. It was not until the next day their supervisor had been asked about the girls being in the workshop area. In the afternoon, as they were cleaning up the dorm for inspection the next day, Mrs. Avery mentioned it again to Shandol and Margery.

"But girls, I was so glad I could tell them I knew it," she told them. "That way I could add I was sure you hadn't intended to break a rule, that you had just been out walking and, out of curiosity went by there."

"We didn't suppose or just didn't think about seeing anyone," Shandol told her.

"We won't plan on doing it anymore," Margery added, with a smile and twinkle in her eyes, which she could not always control.

"I can even see how it could become a nuisance," Shandol said, thoughtfully. "I really hope we didn't cause you any trouble. We really didn't know."

"It's all right this time, but remember it's not to be repeated." She smiled at them as she said it.

The girls worked hard to clean up the place for the inspection. The boys had told them they weren't going to let the girls get by with winning. So the girls washed windows, scrubbed floors and woodwork, dusted and whatever they could think might help them win.

Shandol received letters from her mother, Dean and Ardena. Shandol was always glad to get letters. The letter from her mother was long and newsy, and Ardena's added to it. Dean seemed to feel she should be at home where he could look after her.

Audrey's letter was dated July 7, 1942.

Dear Sissy,

While the beans are perkin I'll answer your letter of Saturday. Aimed to do it yesterday, but you see I didn't. Canned 20 qts. beans and made Karen a pretty pink voile dress yesterday. Will have 18 qts. today if none broke. Mrs. McNeeley came by this a.m. They have a cute baby. He's real pretty!? So chubby and fat and such a lot of pretty black hair. She and the children were going to Plainesville to have some typhoid shots today. Didn't any of us go don't think very much of them myself. They were free but had to pay transportation up there. Jeth Ballan took them. Looked like several went. (Thought the old hen saw a snake but couldn't find any.) Guess you got your frizz? I got rolls this time in back with waves at top back of head, three big curls on side and four on top and I like it fine. Guess she did a good job. They had a girl in there really knew how to put the finishing touch on. She shampoos the hair. You can tell I'm *whee whawed* today look how *crooked* I'm writing.—

Had a letter from Lester yesterday ranting 'cause we hadn't written. Guess his mail has gone haywire. We registered one yesterday surely get it 21¢. He said it was 126° in the shade out there? I'm afraid he'll get too hot. Believe if he had "Ducky" there he'd feel better. Haven't heard anymore from Jane, guess she's at home. Ben Childon and Grandma were in Greenway Sat. eve but Jane didn't come here. Yes, I hope he makes good so he won't have to ask anyone for anything. We miss their Sat. night visits, but as long as he's okay, maybe I can be. Have to??

I don't think Lester was ever so crazy about the west, but maybe he'll like it better as he goes along. Did some of the kids go home? Why? Mr. Kasper is better. Up not going. So is Mr. Strasser. Mrs. Strasser was here Sun. eve a little while. Said we had a pretty baby. Looked like Shandol. She always thought Shandol was so pretty. Ha. Ha. Don't tell Shandol tho! Ha. Tried to put Karen to sleep—no luck. Guess you are getting used to Dean ranting by now. I don't want you to come home UNLESS YOU WANT to. If you're satisfied that's all that matters. Understand. I'd like to have you home the best in the world, but what's here? Maybe you'll be our salvation getting out of here. Dad went up yesterday to sign up for a farm loan, but they haven't received any money as yet. Said maybe about Aug. 1st. Let Dean rave! He'll quit when he unwinds. You'll meet all kinds of boys. You'll have to make the best of them all. I've two nice candles. Might make me two holders. Ha. You know I love pretty things like that and if you made them they'd be even nicer. (Karen finally went to sleep sucking her thumb.) Carol Middleton simply had a fit over Karen. Might have been put-on. She's terribly sweet we think. Wish u could see her crawl. I had just given Karen a bath when Carol saw her and she was sweet and clean and I kept her that way. Makes lots of difference (when Carol had her). Tommy is writing and wanting to know how to spell so you may have some things spelled out. Tommy had decided he wants to be saved. Wish he could hear some good sermons. Glad you go to church. Just keep on going.

Did I tell you Arlene Konnrad and Claudie Bevinson

(Shandol's friends from last two years of school) were here a few minutes the other eve. I didn't talk to them. Bobby saw them. Of course when they found you were gone they didn't stay.

Two of the Colmay children have been staying with Nora Kasper since their daughter has been at her in laws. Enid Colmay was real sick Sun. Mr. C. has had something the matter with his ear. Wanted her and the saints to pray over a handkerchief and mail to him?!

Phil has been complaining with his ear today. I'm sorta worried about him. Bobby feels bed too. We all have colds in throat, Dad has been dragging around too. Not working today. Pulling the onions. Aims to clean out garden too. We need some rain now! The ground is hard and dry. Have made 4½ gal. dill pickles. Have nearly 2 gal. churn salted down. Will make sweet pickles out of them.

Signed up for sugar today. Got 48 lbs. Guess u don't ever see your card anymore. Do you miss sugar there?

Its 4:30 if I'm going to mail this again this eve I must get busy. Insurance man just left. Haven't swept dining room today so here goes this time. Hope you are ok. Write. Love, Mom.

P.S. If you're homesick to come home maybe we can get u the transportation.

Ardena's letter was short but she did send some pictures which she asked Shandol to send back. They were of herself and Phil. The letter was dated July 8, 1942. She wrote she had a permanent, but her hair was cut shorter than she liked. She said she was anxious to see Shandol and couldn't wait for her to see the pictures. She promised to have some more made like them so Shandol could have them. She wrote she bought a new bathing suit though she couldn't swim. Was hoping to go to the river and expected to when her aunt visits, "next week sometime." She wrote of the late hours she and Phil kept. Apparently they were at home. By midnight, which she wrote soon came, she got sleepy too. She had done a wash the Fourth, she wrote and Phil worked so they didn't do anything special that day. She made mention of Karen as growing "and the sweetest little thing you ever saw." She had other letters to write and hoped Shandol wrote back sooner than she did. She hoped to receive the pictures soon to get more and Shandol would get her choice then. She signed off, "a friend, Ardena Ruleton."

Friday in the workshop was a slow time. One lathe was "somewhat

540

out of order," they were told. Shandol made a handle, however, and some initials.

It was also the new inspection day at the dorms. The girls lost the large banner for their building. Dust was found on a high shelf. However, Shandol's and Margery's side kept the wing banner as no fault was found there.

Margery and Shandol slept in the afternoon then later tried to get a special pass, which was denied. Only three were allowed in a week besides Saturdays and Sundays.

Shandol then wrote to her mother but the only mail she received was a letter from her pen pal in Indiana, who was continuing her education to become a nurse and be a missionary in a foreign land.

The next morning Margery and Shandol were up early. It was their day to work K.P. There had been a change made so that everyone was required to work at least ten hours K.P. unless they could get someone else to do it for them. Shandol and Margery didn't mind as they had even volunteered once when they wouldn't have had to. They were up at four-thirty, as required and Mrs. Avery was unaware they were to do it. Later when she got up and found the girls gone she was mystified and frightened. She just supposed they had slipped out. *But when*, she wondered.

She immediately began asking around trying to find out if anyone might know where they had gone. It wasn't hard to find out. The girls at the next bunk told her they were working K.P. Relief flooded her attractive face.

To Shandol and Margery it was a busy time. They dipped apricots into dishes for breakfast. At serving time Shandol placed bacon on the plates as the trays came by. She was too busy to see what Margery was doing on down the line.

After the meals the girls washed dishes and swept. There were two boys also helping, but who scrubbed the floors, which was a job for strong arms and backs. Even the mop pail could hardly be moved by the petite girls.

One of the boys called Shandol "Blondie," because he couldn't remember her name. Shandol had had such problems before.

And not to be outdone, she called him "Dagwood." Once he tried to kiss her, but Shandol was sure he was married, though as she had learned later he wasn't. Margery also began calling him Dagwood and he called her Daisy (after the comic strip pup). So it had not been all work and no play. They had kidded around and talked and been helpful and thoughtful; and slipped out extra rolls to eat and considered it hilarious.

In the afternoon Margery's army boyfriend, Arnold came, which left Shandol to herself. She decided not to try to learn their plans.

Margery, however, did not wish to leave Shandol out the next day. It was afternoon when he came, as he had supposed the girls would go to church. They had planned to go and started but ended up riding around with Rory Wheaton, who had eyes for Shandol. They were back in camp by noon.

Shandol had herself planned to go with two other girls, only one of whom had a date, but was after all with Margery and Arnold. Loretta Sheane, who was Wilma Harris's good friend, was with Shandol who had no date.

Wilma was a natural blond, with curly hair. She had a cute baby face, blue eyes and a walk as if she was sure she was worth a million. She dressed neatly, if not expensively, Her boy friend, George, had come to see her from Strawsville, and Loretta suspected they would rather be alone. They said they planned to go to the swimming pool.

But Shandol and Loretta were talked into going with Arnold and Margery because they wanted to take pictures. They went to different places, which included the town's Lover's Leap. This was a rather steep rocky bank or seemingly small bluff. A narrow rock jutted out from the main part of it.

They could get on another protrusion of rocks, which was less narrow and take pictures there. They took several and included them all in one way or another. Margery was mostly included in those including Arnold though she took one of him alone.

Lover's Leap had the legend told about it that two hopeless lovers had jumped to their deaths from the high bank. Most people took it for just that—a legend—but reasoned it might have been. The young people supposed it had been in the long ago when such a thing might have happened, if indeed it had, and what a tragedy to be or feel so hopeless as, or talked into it by someone else who was. In fact, they speculated, the fall might could be survived with the small brush and other foliage to break the fall. No matter about the practical side, they supposed, just which might have been.

At night Shandol had a last minute date with a boy at camp, who had asked her a few other times to date him. He was also from the south part of the state and she decided why not? They made it a foursome with Margery and Arnold. His name was Leo Eaton and he was a short sandy-haired, somewhat immature looking youth. But he had surprisingly beautiful even white teeth when he smiled. He took care of them, he laughed. Shandol enjoyed the movie and visiting with him. They exchanged small talk of their separate home towns and schools, which were small on his part. (Shandol considered Plainesville a large one.) The town he was from was smaller than Greenway Shandol learned.

Her mother was right. This was a place to meet different boys, and many different types.

CHAPTER 42

Shandol worked in the "office" with another Margery, last name Black. She was a tall, attractive brunette with a self assured air about her, which almost intimidated Shandol. But soon Shandol realized she just considered herself one of them. It was her statuesque look, Shandol decided, which made Shandol self-conscious.

Shandol was completely at ease so far as the job was concerned. She even laid down and slept on the plywood boards. She hadn't intended to do so. The girls tried to even the work checking tools in and out and Shandol had had her turn.

But it was a hot day and easy to fall asleep once one was comfortable. In fact Margery slept, too; and Shandol slept nearly thirty minutes, she was sure. The "office" seemed hotter than the rest of the shop, because there was so little ventilation which could reach it.

It was soon noon and the girls were finished. The last ten minutes were allowed to sweep and clean the shop for the next crew, who also had to clean for the next group, and so on. Those in the office were exempt from that except by choice, and there usually weren't enough brooms as it was. But there was straightening to do in the office; the most important, however, was to be sure all checked-out tools had been returned.

When the girls got back to the dorm the news was on the radio. It was unusual to hear the news, but it hardly registered. A man had come and repaired the jukebox they learned.

Shandol and Margery finally got permanents in their hair that afternoon. They went to Dolores Kerr's shop, because Mrs. Kerr was a friend of Mrs. Avery's. They were pleased with the results. And how glad Shandol was to have her hair short in the heat. While Shandol was in town she bought Dreft (brand) 'washing powder' for Agnes Drake; also a Coke, and forgot soap for herself!

Shandol wrote to Ardena. She received a letter from Audrey.

Shandol and Margery did not go to supper. They each had a leftover hamburger they had taken to the dorm from their noon meal. The girls had done a wash and hung it on a line behind the barracks. They also somehow managed to miss council meeting they were so tired.

Before morning they heard the thunder and saw it lightning, so they clamored outside in their nightclothes to get their clothing off the line. No rain fell, but it did turn cooler.

544

The next day at the shop was a busy one for Shandol, Margery and two other girls. They put together—that is, nailed plus glued, about one hundred frames for screens for the dorm windows. Four of them made that many before the "related training," which was the reading and studying the printed materials about tools, and constituted the last two hours, minus clean-up time, for them. Shandol found a comfortable spot and was trying her best to concentrate, but she fell asleep again! She never knew when the book fell from her hands. She did not hear the usual talk and silencing of the machines, and no one awakened her when it was time to go.

She slept until after twelve o'clock noon, five minutes or so. When she finally did awaken the new shift had come in and stood watching her. She was so mortified she ran to the cafeteria, wondering why Margery hadn't awakened her. Forcefully she asked her.

"How could you leave me for those—those boys to glare at?"

"I didn't see you," Margery reasoned, "and I thought yuh'd gone on ahead." Margery could stifle her laughter no longer. "Sorry kid, but it's funny. Yuh'll prob'ly get teased."

"Oh, no doubt," she agreed, chagrined. "And it's not that funny to me. I don't see how I coulda done it. Oh, I'll never live it down. How can I face anybody again?"

"But everybody has fell asleep," Margery reminded her. "They all know how boring those books can be. Yuh just got caught after hours is the thing. In fact if it hadn't been for you I might uh done the same thing once. Remember?"

"No, but why couldn't yuh a returned the favor?" Shandol moaned. She ignored any stares and ate.

The girls went to town at night. They went by the mental institution to watch the patients, who were able, dance and enjoy themselves. Outsiders, they were told, sometimes went, if only to watch. However, they were told the dances had been discontinued for the summer. They then stopped by the ball game, but a town team was playing an out-of-town one, and they could not tell one from the other. They became disinterested at seeing no one which interested them or they had seen before. The girls were accustomed to all the walking and hardly noticed.

Shandol wrote to her mother. But first she reread what her mother had written in the letter she had received the day before. It was dated July 10, 1942.

Dear Dearie:

Here another day has gone and I'm still aiming to write. Just seems I can't get anything done anymore. Washed yesterday, canned 15 qts. blackberries and went to town. The day before that I canned 14 qts. beets so have I been doing anything or not!

Went to club this p.m. at Elma's. Ironed and baked bread a.m. Next month club meets here. Will I miss you! I'll have to manage somehow. Had iced tea and cake. Mrs. Ruleton went with me. I think she will become a member next time. Druce Connal is working at a Lovilace place (or was). Wanita is still home. Freda is at home too. Ambert's wife was there awhile but think she has gone back to her mother's again. The Pullips boy burned the marriage license (he and Emily Martin)and has skipped. Don't know what they done about it. Mr. Martin was up on his ear about it I hear.

I'm feeling okay (except mentally). Had another letter from Lester today wondering why in "thunder" we didn't write, says he was going to quit too. Will send him a telegram the first of week if we don't hear more about it. The letters aren't coming back so don't know what to do about it. Will give the special delivery letter time to get there.

We've all had colds. Dad has felt pretty bad.

They haven't worked any this week. I've had a cold in my bronchial tubes. Dad coughed last night. I couldn't sleep either.

Lester said he loved the mtns. I believe if Jane was there he'd be ok. Heard from Jane this week again. She said she hoped to be with him soon.

Next time Phil gets some money we'll get some pictures. By the way have the old banjo going. Just four strings but sounds pretty good. He got him a nice new $2.95 hat at Monkey Wards (black).

Shandol, I don't know what to tell you about your job. If you were somewhere you could be working now. Gertrude told me today Yvonne was in St. Louis working (not in a defense job tho', she's not old enough) but if I was you I'd leave in eight weeks if I thought I could hold a job. It isn't that boy's fault if his mother won't let him go. You need not be discouraged about that. What sorta factory is the glider factory? Don't believe I'd sign up for any defense work you might have to go to Pearl Harbor! If you could work in one without too much red tape would be ok. Phil is banjo-ing: "You'll never Miss Your Mother Till She's Gone" so don't worry if you have a few stray words or notes.

Ardena wrote to you. Guess you'll get going again.

Yes, the icebox is ok. rather expensive. I'm wondering? It's along the north wall where the table was. It belongs to Mrs. Borsek. She wouldn't sell it just loaned it. I'd love to have it though. It's a good one.

Yes, Oren Kasper and Ambert Wittevers are still at the army camp. Come home every weekend. Nora came after some flower slips today. Guess she thinks when she gets moved she'll have some flowers. Ha.

The yard is full of Colmays again. Two or three here last eve. Got up and went to Mrs. Borseks. Oh! While I think of it Hugh B. has moved, said not to write until they heard again. Mrs. Borsek said not to pay any attention to go ahead and write to him. (I mean about him not writing to you.) Said they got letters sometimes but couldn't send any. So don't write now until I hear or if you don't hear before I do I'll let you know. He's moved but don't know where they sent him.

No, I hadn't heard about Margery and Harriet. Dad said he'd heard it. Oh, yeah, Harriet don't find out much about Marg from me. I'm careful. Sh! Harriet told me all she could find out about it was thru the little girls, so now what and who? Well we've tried to bring you up as a lady, why shouldn't she think so? Harriet and Dolphus says that's the place for Marg. Guess he hasn't become reconciled but for the two. We didn't get any relief this time. Bobby said he'd guess Dolphus had been up there. Did I tell you about mine and Harriet's experience? She came by after some pepper plants one morn. I didn't have any then she started on that same old story hard times and 'Roosevelt'. Said she never had as hard a time as she had now. I told her she didn't know what hard times were at the peak of the depression she bought two properties here. She walked out didn't say anymore, I wasn't sore but had promised myself I'd head her off. Sh-h-h. Bobby just laughed at us. Came near telling more but thought I'd better not??

The other day Teddy Colmay went to the store after something. Clive said, 'I'd just as soon wait on a bunch of hogs?? Do you wonder? Boy was the Mrs. mad. If he hadn't had room—don't you think. Ha. It's okay to share somethings but I want you to quit doing without things to accommodate somebody else. Let them go awhile without a letter to show them how it goes. You won't get any thanks for it nor anything in return. I'm sending 25¢ in this letter to help you buy stamps. Just can't send anymore—if you don't get your check next week let us know.

Don't believe I'd sign up for defense work, might send you no telling where. I'm not trying to discourage you if you think it will help you in the long run! But want you to hurry and get enough money to finish your business course. You don't have to work only long enough to send yourself to school.

Wish you could see Karen. Crawls flat on her stomach. Boy does she get dirty. Everyone says she's such a pretty baby and looks like Shandol?? Ha. Lester always writes, kiss Karen for me. Must write to him whether he gets it or not.

I think I answered all questions this time. I believe do as well as you do at that. Tried to rain last night or this morn. Wish it could rain a good one (slow and steady). Dad talked to Dean last night.

Dean said he didn't think your woodwork would do you any good? Said he believed you'd have been better off to stayed and took exams for teaching again. Dad said he was afraid you'd get homesick since Dean came home? He's going to help put up hay at home then go to Neosho again. Must quit—if I start another page no telling when I'll quit.

Write.

Love, Mom and all the rest

Shandol began her letter:

Dear Mom and all,

Maybe with noise and jukebox I can drop you a line or two. How s everyone?

It's five minutes till ten p.m. I went to the State Hospital for the insane to watch them dance, but a lady at the information desk said they were having no more dances this summer. That's my luck. We didn't stay there long, but the buildings and grounds are rather pretty. Grounds almost like a park. Last Saturday I went with Marg and her army guy to the girl's college campus. We sat out there awhile. There was another guy along but he was engaged, so we talked and I enjoyed the scenery!

Sunday we took some pictures, I hope they're good. My hair was still stringy. But, oh, yeah, I got my permanent Monday. I got a real short one, my hair grows so fast anyway. I like it fairly well, Marg got her one too. It's not so short, but looks better on her.

Tonight was a ball game but not camp connected. We went but didn't stay long. Marg and I went uptown and heard some songs—that made us think of home, (especially Folks Consent—the coffee shop there, Kisses Cafe).

Too bad about your colds. Hope you are all feeling better. I'm ok. Sleepy all time. I must tell you what I did today. It's so very, very ridiculous!! I went to sleep in the workshop & the boss wouldn't allow anyone to wake me up—just to see how long I'd sleep. Well, I awoke at 12:05 p m. (about).

Did I ever feel small? Marg couldn't find me, said she'd have awakened me (somehow), but she just supposed I'd gone on to dinner. We're off at noon for the day, so the next shift of boys had come in. I think I shall be able to stay awake from now on. Lots of us have gone to sleep. I bet every girl in the shop has napped at one time—and another. But why did he have to pick on me? (Or I made it so easy!) Oh, me. But I had helped put together plus gluing about one hundred frames for screens for the dorm windows. There were four of us girls made that many. After we finished all I had to do was read. I don't remember laying down my book! By the way two hours are "related training" to read and study about tools and machinery. That was not my favorite type of book.

Do you know if Lester got the special delivery letter? I haven't heard from him either. Yeah, I think he can become accustomed to it out there enough to like it. I hope—hope—hope. Hope Jane writes to me. Did you tell her to? If not then do.

I'd love to hear Phil pick the banjo. I bet you all enjoy it. Does Bobby take to it? Hope Tommy will. Be so cute if he'd learn to chord. Tell Phil I like his hat—looks good. I saw the pictures Ardena sent. Gee, but I sure hated to send them back. But she wanted to get some more made.

Don't you be like Marg's mom. She just doesn't write like she should. I get two or three letters from you to her one. But Marg just can't hardly stand for me to write home and she not. So she's writing 'home' too. You're not like that so don't start.

I had to sign that paper to get my check. I think I have one I'll just send it just to show what it's like. I only had to sign my name. Don't send it back. Just burn it or something, anything. So I got the check. I think I told you.

Gee I bet Mr. Martin is raring about Emily. What can he do?

Does Karen really look like me? Hug her sweet neck for me.

Marge and I washed yesterday eve. We had to get up in the night to get them as they were hung outside. Didn't rain after all. Just turned cool. Was a terrible cloud though. Time for lights out. May write more at five in morn—if I'm not too sleepy. Or can get up in time to do it and go eat breakfast. Until then goodnight.

Love,
Shandol

P.S. Addressed card by candlelight 'Twas in Marg's candle holder.

I'm afraid I can't hold a job in eight wks.

When is Dean leaving? Must close. Tell all hello. Tell Tommy I'll write to him soon, but I want this mailed in the morning. Please write soon.

Love to all,
Shandol

The next day Shandol was kidded some about going to sleep but not as she had supposed. Actually there wasn't a whole lot most of them could say. They had just been lucky enough not to sleep past the clean up time. Shandol had never tried to renege on helping clean the shop. It was possibly the first time she had not been able to do at least her part of it. It was considered facetious, absurd—but a lesson. No one else wanted to be caught napping! Even the boss explained he didn't mean her any special harm or embarrassment so much as that he didn't want it to get out of hand. They would have to work to accomplish what they came to accomplish in a reasonable amount of time.

Shandol, in turn, admitted she was not blameless and it had seemed strange. First she was reading in a book and next she was staring at a new boss and a shop full of boys; though later she could not have identified any one of them. She must watch about getting "comfortable" to read. And she wasn't the only one. If one's best friend forgot or overlooked one, then anyone could find herself in a similar predicament.

Shandol had no future trouble at all keeping awake.

There was a new girl to come to the Resident Center, Shandol and Margery learned when they returned from town in the afternoon. She had arrived, but they hadn't known, and so met her later. While in town Shandol bought envelopes, eight three-cent stamps and postcards.

Shandol was with Rory Wheaton. She giggled to Margery how cute she thought him. He drove his own car, though he was near

Shandol's age. His father's a mechanic, she learned, and he too was out of high school. Shandol walked in front of Jonny Hyman, who saw her with him. She didn't know whether to yell, "Hi Dagwood" or not. He didn't speak first so she decided against it. Shandol enjoyed the show at night with Rory.

Shandol wondered why she had received no letter from Dean.

She heard from her mother the sixteenth. She and Margery sent off the film and spent an unusual day in a somewhat usual way. They did things as they did many days: Danced to the "beetle organ" (jukebox) in the rec hall, which was what they sometimes called the day or sitting room. They washed, using the machine; took showers. Shandol and Margery each received letters from their respective mothers. There was cleaning to do for inspection the next day. And there was time to take a blanket into the yard under a tree and Shandol jotted notes in her "diary." But then there was a lull and there seemed nothing to do.

They wondered if anyone ever broke the rule and left the Center without signing out.

"Looks to me like it'd be easy tuh do." Margery observed. "No fences and here we are almost out of sight of the dorms and so often no one thinks anything about if we're really here or not.

"They assume we are!" Shandol reminded her. "The thing is if one tried and got caught they'd never be trusted again."

"Maybe so, but who'd know?" Margery smiled, a daring mischief brought the twinkle to her eyes.

"We would!" Shandol replied. "And if anyone saw us they'd tell on us."

"They'd not know we slipped off unless we told," she reasoned.

"Gee whiz," Shandol replied," yuh'd think we was plannin' tuh go any minute. You're not serious?"

"I didn't mean to be, but suppose we just snuck on down through Bear Cave Holler there and came back. I bet we'd not even be missed."

"I don't know about it," Shandol replied." Maybe I'm just not as adventuresome as you are."

"Oh, come on. We got our purses, so let's do it. We might just get more K.P. and bawled out," she persisted.

The girls folded the woolen blanket and stashed it out of sight, and walked as far on the Project as they could and then slipped across the road. The area there was wooded, with houses beginning farther on down the street so no one would bother in that respect if they had known. But it always seemed spooky in the woods and there was a branch to cross, which was too deep and the bank too steep to walk through even though it was dry. So they had to cross it on a sewer pipe six or eight inches in diameter. It was a precarious walkway as it was six or eight feet across. But they had done it before and decided they could again. They soon left the wooded area for less rough ground and, after a short way, was on a street that went near uptown. They had come the shortcut, which was often used by the girls—and boys—during the day.

They crossed the creek bridge, looked at a huge lake of water made by a stripped fire clay mine, which was a lightish cream murky color, and, they had been told, quite deep. They walked the three blocks to Jackson Street and up two blocks to Bert and Carrie's, a small café. They listened to songs on a jukebox, got an ice cream cone each. Shandol spent twenty-five cents, Margery only ten for the ice cream.

"Let s go," Shandol said, nervous now. "I'm so scared someone will come see us, or be looking for us at camp and start a search."

"I'm ready," Margery admitted. "Now if we can only get back as easy as we've made it so far."

"Yeah," Shandol replied, "and besides it will be time to go in—if we were just out under a tree."

They retraced their path and arrived back where they had left the blanket. By then they were ready to go inside. They had made it, but they weren't going to brag about it to anyone. They never did.

The next day Shandol answered her mother's letter she had received the day before. She went as far from the dorm as she could, and still be on the Project, sat down under a tree in the shade to write. She had her mother's letter along to re read in case there was something she wished to refer to or a question to answer. Audrey's letter was dated "July 14," and began:

Dear One:

I'll proceed to scribble a few lines this hot day. I've been aggravated with Colmay's all day. I sent them all home Sat. eve. Looks like they'd take a hint. Can't do anything with a sucker??

We're all very well. Dad is feeling pretty bummy yet. Been trying to get him to go to Dr. but he won't do it.

Canned beans for Mrs. Borsek yesterday, 18 qts. Made $1.00. Been canning a few qts. blackberries along. They're real good this time, sorta scarce tho'- started bailing here but didn't get enough.

How's K.P. Ha.

Haven't heard anymore from Lester. Am sorta worried about it. Guess you got my other letter. Believe I ans. about all the questions in it. Haven't heard anything from Jane lately.

Know she'd write to you if you write to her. Lester makes about $110.00 a month after his board and room, ins. and security. Don't know about the future of it. Seems men are pretty scarce. He may have a good job—can't tell. Am afraid about the next thing he'll be in the army.

Karen s hair is a pretty glossy light brown. Has real pretty eyelashes. She's so sweet. Got so she squalls after Dad. He carries her around after supper. Makes her so mad when he walks out on her.

Dean and Jim Brown were here last night. I didn't see them. Jim wanted to see Phil before he went to the army. Guess you wouldn't be in any better company if you were here with Dean than you are there if what I can hear is true. I'm going to find out more about it. 'Fraid you wouldn't be satisfied here anymore. Study hard at your woodwork if you think it will do you any good. Get out of there as soon as you can. Make them think you can do it! You can learn the craft. Whats to hinder you? Just study hard..

Don't know where Arlene Konnrad is but Claudia was working at the overall factory in Plainesville, the last account I had of her.

It might be a pastime to go to the dance. Who could dance at a sanatorium like that. Suppose others go to make the crowd.

Joe W. Bradson went to the Deaf School there. I'd like to see that. You might go there to look if you can.

I didn't get your letter until Mon. morn. Seems it takes three days to get your letters or else boys didn't get mail Sun. Dad and I went to German's and made cheese Sun. Had a real nice time. Such friendly folks. Hedda came and got us and brought us back. Our cheese (theirs) was nice in texture. Hope it's good.

If the truck goes to Plainesville we're going to church too at Christian Church as you do, just to see. Phil says, "why don't you go to Church of Christ?"

Told him I've never been there, so want to go there. Yes, this is an ever changing world. Seems some times I'm living in a dream but guess it's reality.

Had a party at Freedman's Sat. night. Didn't go tho Phil went. Freedman and Arvin Jarred have gone to St. Louis for work. Beatrice stays with Mrs. Jarred. She was to have set my hair today but I didn't wash it as she said she was going to wash and go to town. Guess I'll have Ardena to do it tomorrow.

Mr. Kasper is better. Walks around in yard. Karen is awake now. It's 4:10 if I get this mailed I'll have to quit. Not much of a letter but maybe help chase the blues away.

Boys are eager to read your letters but they don't stay home long enough to write. Think Phil was at Ardena's every night last week but Friday. If I was Mrs. Ruleton I'd run him off!!

I'm going to can Della's beans tomorrow. She hasn't come back yet but Mrs. Borsek will pick them and bring them to me here.

Must get this mailed. Write and be good.

Love, Mom & all

Shandol wrote:

NYA Center
Midhill.
July 17,1942

My Dear Mother;

I am out under a shade tree as far as I can get from dorm and be on project. How is everyone by now? What is wrong with Dad? I hope he's lots better. Are he and Phil still working?

I guess I'm still coming along. Only I can hardly write with my paper on my knee.

I feel sorry for you and the mess you must put up with—for instance the Colmays. Does she still gad about! Every time they came if I didn't like it I'd send them home. Don't guess you'd have such good luck as making them peeved. Reckon? They re to be pitied though after all aren't they? The kids I mean.

We've been sandpapering venetian blinds in the shop. Do I ever get dirty. I have worked some on the lathe this week. Gee, seems to me it's very slow learning. But I'm just awkward. Takes practice to make perfect, eh? It's so easy to hit the wood, as it turns, with a tool and just ruin it (wood).

Beats me! I haven't heard from Dean since he's been home. He hasn't written to me. What have you heard? Will you tell me? You can tell me later how true or false it is. Does he come to Greenway? I can't imagine why he doesn't write. Guess I'll just wait and see if he does. Who else does he run around with?

How was church at Plainesville and Christian Church last Sunday night? Did you get to go?

Last night Marg and I slipped off and went to town. For land sakes don't tell anyone that. It was easy to do and so far they haven't found out. We took a blanket and went to a shade tree and started to write. We hid the blanket and went to town.

We got 10¢ worth of ice cream each. Marg had a stomach ache. Now don't worry. I don't think we'll do it anymore. We felt too guilty to have a good time. Weren't gone long. It was just Marg and I.

I'm now in my bunkhouse (dorm). I'm ready for bed. By the way I've been "entertaining" a boy from camp. We have quite a good time. It's here about like a public school. Can't you imagine? I didn't go anywhere tonight.

And you still haven't heard from Lester? Marg said for a long time her brother didn't get their letters, but when he did he got fifteen or twenty.

I'm anxious to see Karen as I've written so often. Do you manage to keep the house clean? I'm coming home the first chance I get. You mind?

It's ten forty-five! Tomorrow is tool-check day. I'll write again real soon.

Love,
Shandol

CHAPTER 43

The next letter Shandol received from her mother the mystery of Lester's whereabouts was cleared. He was at home again!

Audrey's letter was dated, July 16, 1942, Greenway. She wrote:

Dear Shandol Dear—

I guess I'll start you a letter as it's no telling who'll come by before I get it finished.

Received your letter on the noon train. Thought you'd better write! Lester came home yesterday. He lost his job on extra gang. A car ran over his toes. They laid him off because of that. He then got a job in an engineer outfit (gov't) but couldn't hear—good enough for that. it's a shame how hard of hearing Lester is. Maybe he'll be better now. May have been the climate affected his hearing. They examined him before they let him go. Oh, well, he's better off perhaps. He's pretty low in spirits but I told him he wasn't any outcast he still had two good hands. He "could cut wood, 'spect" as Tommy used to say, remember? Lester went to see Jane today. Said he might as well have it out with his mother-in-law and get it over with. Said he'd be back tonight. He's so thin and felt so bad I told him he'd better rest, but he wanted to see Jane.

I have four little Colmay girls again today. They were here all day yesterday. She's planning on going to a sale tomorrow—But! I'm not keeping her brats. She never asks me to go anywhere with her. I'm expected to stay and keep the kids?! I'll strike one of these bright days.

Mrs. Colmay is jealous of Mr. Borsek and I. She asks Mrs. B. to go with her lots. Dennett (her grandson) drives the car now. Don't know what got the matter with Chester Parkley.

Canned 13 qts. of beans for Della Bright today. Canned 17 qts. cucumbers. The German's gave me ½ bu. Have the two gal. churn down in salt yet and that'll be about all I'll get. Been watering the vines but too near dried up when I started. Have had roasting ears. Pretty good! I'll eat yours. Ha.

Shandol if I was you and that close to your Aunt Clara and Aunt Maud I'd go see them if could. I suppose they'll transfer you to your job and they'll be anxious (there) for you to get started working. Otherwise you'll pay the transportation?

Harriet just left. Wanted to know about uns. Said Rita Bright told Mrs. McNeeley that Margey was just crazy to go to that NYA outfit & Rita was supposed to come and stay all day with me but she hasn't showed up yet.

Oh, yes, how's Johnny? Do you still write to him? What's the matter with your dates? Have you gone on engaged list too?

Better stay awake. A Jap might get you napping. I'll bet the boys had a laugh at you.

Phil is sorta particular with the banjo. Wants to keep the head pretty and white. Bobby and Phil have been trying to 'second' since they have the violin at home. Tommy took the guitar out on the porch the other evening stayed a long time. So *important* trying to play. ha

Haven't heard anything more about the Martins. Guess there isn't a lot he can do.

Ardena set my hair last night. I didn't get up there until 9:30. Mrs. Colmay came and talked and talked. Didn't want to sleep without it so went anyway if it was late. Phil was there or they might not have been up. Honestly I don't know what we'll do with those kids. If he isn't up there she's down here. Sh-h-h.! Think she's swell though. Drops in several times a day anytime. Lots of company that way.

It's 3:30 train just now going northbound. I'll have to feed Karen now will finish SOMETIME.

While I'm waiting on Lester and Bobby to dinner just fed Karen, I'll finish this. You'll notice it's Sat. p.m. Aimed to send it out yesterday but Dad forgot to leave me any stamp money.

Karen has begun to da-da-da so cute in her. The kids think it's funny. I think Lester aims to drive Mrs. Colmay to town (Plainesville this p.m.).

I've the dining room and kitchen mopped will clean the front room after dinner. Want to patch some too.

Dad and Phil have worked all week—some days just eight hours.

Joe Balleran hauled four loads of poles up this a.m.

Dad and Phil get the wood and 20¢ pc. for cutting it.

Mrs. Borsek bro't me a dress today. I surely need it too.

Whee, I smell vegetable soup. Wish you were here for supper. Tho't Jane might come in. Don't know whether her dad will bring her or not. Lester will write when he gets better settled. He's sorta discouraged and blue but guess things will work out.

I must quit if get this mailed on northbound train. We're all o.k. Dad still coughs but feels better. Hope you're ok.

Write. Lots of love,

Mom

Just got your card. The building is beautiful.
Old fashioned but pretty. Must quit.

Shandol had sent a picture postcard of the college buildings.

x x x x

As a new week began Shandol realized she had been gone from home only one and one-half months. Had it really been only that long? Yet sometimes it seemed she had been gone for ages and at other times only a short while. But there had been so much to do; such new things to learn; new places to be and see; so many new people to meet she was somewhat amazed at it all too. How had she crammed so much in so little time?

The week was a routine one for them. It was Friday when Shandol again heard from her mother. It was dated:

Wed. 1 o'clock, July 22, 1942. And Audrey began it as she often did.

Dear Dearie:

Just read your letter. If I hurry I'll have time to write a few lines. Aimed to write anyway. Been trying to sew some. Don't get much done only cook, eat and wash dishes.

I guess I told you Lester and Jane are here.

Lester has gone to Waiton with Mrs. Colmay. Phil drives some for her too.

We'd be tickled to death to see you but be careful—don't be out with a batch of drunks. Ha. I'd be uneasy about you until you got back. It will be okay if u invite some boyfriend over the weekend with you. Let Dean rave!! I don't want him to monopolize all your time anyway!! He's talking about going to Salina, Kansas don't know when tho'. Lester thinks he might go too but won't until his hearing gets better.

I'll try and contact Mrs. McNeeley hope she can come and eat with us. I'll drop you a card if I find out anything for sure. Anyway you make your plans for home we'll manage.

Phil and Dad are working for Hedda now. Got through with Jacob. Paula's hubby started home about ten days ago. Haven't heard anything from him. She has gone to see about him.

(This was the German families, Shandol knew, who lived west of Greenway.)

Sam is going back to Peoria, Ill. Joe Middletons are going to move in Noah Parkley property. Mr. Borsek said he'd give Sam his money back for the property (Sam's) so guess he'll sell out.

The Pearl Harbor tragedy may come home to all of us. The outlook is mighty gloomy now.

If you should come or if you don't let me know more about it. I'll try not worry about you, but you drop a card if you don't come. If you write Dean, don't expect to go to any picture show or anything, 'cause we want you home. HEAR!!

Karen's sweet as ever. Mrs. Borsek gave her two or three little dresses·. She gave me a new dress too. Don't you think she's nice.

I'll be wishing Sat. night would hurry and get here so try not disappoint us if you can help but be careful.

I'll quit now. I'll try and write again this week. Bye now. Dinner's ready. Hope you can eat with us 'ere long. Be good.

Lovingly, Mom

Couldn't plan a party very well unless I knew about when you'd get here. You tell me when you'd start if you know then I'd know about when you'd get here.

Shandol thought about what her mother had written about Pearl Harbor coming home "to all of us." She thought of the tragedies certain families had already known. Jane's brother was only one of those she had heard about. Arlene Gallmire, who'd been engaged and told Shandol about it so happily in church one night, had learned her fiancée had lost his life there. She was so terribly hurt, so blue, bitter and almost ill about it for awhile. She swore even if she married sometime, he was the only man she'd really ever love. Would she get over it in time? There had been other casualties whom the children had gone to school with who didn't live quite so near to Greenway families. But their hearts went out to them as they could sympathize with them for their loss and heartbreak. Would any more from there have to go? If so how many would come back?

Shandol, Margery and all the young people of the project were concerned about the war. It was true they knew what was going on mostly from hearsay—what someone else heard or read—they were still certainly thankful they were no closer to it than they were. How awful it must be to live in Germany, for instance. They knew what was to be gained: It was their very way of life which was threatened. Their freedom and that of the country. Shandol wondered, and assumed others did too, why there must be these war mongers raised up to threaten other people and countries so the greed for power certainly could get out of hand; and in this case one man's? One man the cause of so much misery, degradation and ruin? What a trying thought. She must answer her mother's letter on a brighter note when she wrote. The idea of being away from home in such an uncertain, frightening time gave her pause and made her blue and somewhat gloomy. "But we keep on keeping on," as Audrey would say.

Jane's letter was dated July 24, from Greenway.

Dear Shandol, she wrote,

How are you fine I hope. I feel pretty good but nothing extra. Sug' has gone to Waiton today. He took Mr. Colmay down there to a stock sale. No telling when they ll get back.

I'm glad you like it up there. I know just how you and Margie feel. We'll all be glad to see you again. You'll get to see Lester if he isn't gone. He's talking of going to Salina, Kansas to work. I hope if he does that he will get a job that he can do, without being laid off. He is doing the best he knows to. He is a swell kid don't you think. I hate for him to be so hard hearing. I'd hate to see him go to the army. I don't think he'll have to go. I sure hope not.

I don't know anymore to write so guess I'll close for now. Answer soon and tell us more about yourself.

Love, Jane

Monday nights were still council meetings for the girls. It was finally and definitely decided there'd be a party—dance on Saturday, July thirty-first. There had been talk of it at other council meetings, but now there were more definite plans, more commitment. There were a few volunteer committee chairmen selected to form committees, and individual to assign certain tasks. The refreshment committee chairman, the activities, also, for those who might want more than just dancing. They decided the boys must help and might be included on committees, and help with the organization of it. It would be theirs, also. One of the first tasks would be to move the girl's jukebox to the main rec hall—a now vacant part of the mess hall. By now the girls and boys were sharing one eating area; could

560

indeed share a table if so desired. They would need a clean up crew and on and on. Shandol and Margery so far weren't asked and hadn't volunteered. They had felt so cheated at Wildwood.

It was intended to be for those on the project, the girls decided, but each one, boy or girl, would be allowed one extra invitation for an "outsider" if a boyfriend or girlfriend didn't happen to be a resident there.

Most of the girls were enthusiastic about it. They could remember Wildwood and the soldiers. Yet this would be different. In fact this, they were later sorry to admit, took mostly a wait and see attitude, though they decided to do whatever they were asked, if anything. But the girls who had had "experience" at Wildwood were the most essential, prominent and useful.

Later, Shandol wrote to her mother. The time for "lights out" came before she was finished and she was invited by Mrs. Avery, the wing supervisor, to finish in her room. She would be in Mrs. Morris room awhile. The door to her room was near Shandol's bunk and handy. Mrs. Avery could close her door at "lights out" and it did not affect her. She could stay up longer so long as she could do her job, but it was usually out before eleven p.m.

Shandol dated her letter July 27,1942:

Dearest Mother,

Maybe I can stay awake long enough to scribble you a few lines. By the way scribbling it will be as I've been working K.P. today. I'm really tired. I'm off now until 4:45 so maybe I'll have a couple hours sleep. K.P.'s okay I guess only I'd rather go to the shop. We get all we want to eat, however. I ate two oranges, (when cook wasn't looking). I'd hate to say how many cinnamon rolls with white frosting on them, besides cake, meat, etc. We had a swell dinner, but I was too full to eat On my plate I had potatoes, steak, slaw, dry beans—um-m. Cake for dessert. A man brought seven big cakes about two ft. by eighteen inches, chocolate. And were they ever good. We always have bread and butter.(Milk to drink for breakfast.)

Were you very much worried because I didn't come home? When I wrote the card I had my doubts. Hope you didn't worry. The kid who was going to take us was going to borrow the man's car, that he's under (in the army).Well—he was transferred. Besides he was in a wreck, which didn't keep him from coming up here to see Marg Saturday night any-way. Marg was with him. Last night I went to the show with a boy here in camp. He's a swell guy if he is two years younger than myself. He would pass for twenty-one in looks, size and actions. He's out of high school and taking welding up here. He was too bashful to ask me for a date, ha. But he told a girl here on the 'wing' he wanted to date me some.

He knew he was younger than I am. By the way I have a hard time making kids believe my age. "Lucky" says I don't look a day over fifteen. He's a friend of the guy I was with Sunday night, although we weren't with him and his gal. I really don't crave the company of his (Lucky's) gal even if she is on our side of wing. The boy I was with is Harley Lensing from Lorrah. His dad is a contract carpenter. The boy himself could be working under him for $1.50 per hr. he said. Odd. He has true blue eyes (sky blue almost) and wavy black hair. He's manly, and not bad looking—average height.

I went to Sunday school and church yesterday at the place on the picture card I showed you. Don't you think it's pretty? It has rooms for every class. A student from college, who is studying for the ministry is our teacher. I believe he's genuinely interested too. Quite nice also. I wanted to call something to Dad's mind that was discussed, but I can't think right now what it is. I just want to know if Dad had ever heard of it. I never had. it's not a religion, just an organization.

We got some pictures today. They were fairly good. I was going to send two of me but a kid working with us on K.P. took the best one from me. It was so good. He may give it back to me, just teasing me, but it sure makes me mad. He took my key ring and never gave it back. I do wish you could have seen that picture though. It was taken in front of the sign at Strawsville. It sure was good, too. I don't see what he wants with my picture. He doesn't date much I don't think. He calls me Blondie, I call him Dagwood. Last time Marg and I worked K.P. together we called each other that, and an old red headed guy called Marg Daisy (after the pup, ha ha). We have quite a bit of fun.

This morning when we went to breakfast there wasn't any. The cook had passed out, some said an epileptic 'fit'. Must not have been. He's just a kid too, by the way. (Young). He felt better later. Came to dinner. They found him when we K.P.s went in to help serve. He was as limber as a rag when they took him out. (It's about all I saw.)

Maybe you think I wasn't disappointed when I didn't get to come home. I still have suitcase packed. I just can't stand to unpack it, but of course I will—maybe. Marg says she's not going to be here long. If she leaves guess I will too. I'd just like to come home on a visit, because I'm afraid I'd never be satisfied to stay. Reckon?

Well, I'd like to rest a few minutes, so guess I'll close for now. I'll write soon again. You write soon.

Love,
Shandol

P.S. Mom, see about getting me a play suit (shorts?) All the girls up here wear them of evenings to lounge in. Size about 12.

Tell all hello.

Save the pictures. Send them back. Show them to Dean if he comes in time. S.S.

The next day was what she considered a routine day except Shandol went to the show again with Harley Lensing. She was flattered by his attention and words of how pretty he thought she was. She was also flattered that he had to take off from his job to date her. He was taking welding and it was only offered on the afternoon to midnight shift. She enjoyed the date and told him so. He replied he was the one pleased and that he would like to spend more time with her.

Ardena's letter, received the following day, was dated July 27, 1942.

Dear Shandol,

Will drop you a few lines to let you know I'm just fine. Sorry I haven't written sooner.

We sure got a good rain last night. I sure was glad. Sure was disappointed when you didn't come home. They had an ice cream supper at Mrs. Davis. We sure had a good time. Also they had a speaking at the community house. I saw Dean Sunday. He was riding his horse.

Your mother is giving me piano lessons and I'm trying to get Mother to get me a guitar and get Phil to give me lessons on it.

My cousin, Marlene, is trying to get a transfer to St. Louis from D.C. Said it didn't look much like she'd get it. The boss was helping her all he could, she said. She said if she didn't get to feeling better she might have to come home. Ambert is trying to get her a job at Fort Woodson. Don't know if he can help her or not.

Calvin was called to St. Louis for his final examination but he didn't pass. I almost knew he wouldn't.

Phillip took some pictures a week ago Sunday. I think he will get them today. Sure hope so. Me and your mother haven't sent them pictures off yet but we will before long.

Well, Mother's griping so I'll quit and get to work so answer sooner than I did. Maybe I'll write more next time.

From Ardena Ruleton

At night, Shandol wrote to her mother, dated July 29.

Dear Mom,

I said if I didn't hear from home in the evening mail I was going to write, so here I am. I didn't hear from you. I suppose, as I'm writing, I'll just about get a letter tomorrow. I'd better! Anyhow I can hardly think for the "beetle organ" in the 'rec' hall.

By the way the "beetle organ" will be moved before Saturday to the main rec hall in the cafeteria. There will be a dance Saturday night. It's for the boys here in camp, however, we are allowed one invitation for an outsider. I don't think I'll go as the boy I'd be with is on the serving committee. Yeah, they'll serve refreshments.

I washed my hair today. Feels so soft and nice. I used Dreft soap (comes in a box in a fine beady-like powder), and rinsed in vinegar. You can't imagine how hard the water is here. If ordinary soap is used, it makes one's hair just plain sticky and gummy! (Many a girl wailed in learning it the hard way.) Marg also washed her hair and of course I fixed it up for her.

One of our supervisors—she's on our wing—has a little boy up here. He's about seven years old and as sharp as a tack. His father and her are separated—don't know who keeps him, grandparents most likely. Anyway just last weekend she married a soldier from Fort Woodson. Something was said in his hearing about his mother being married again. He looked up at her, she said and said, "Again? Mother, were you married before?" Yet he knows about his dad but doesn't remember him. Guess he's about K.C.'s age and—

Once a group of us were around near his mother. He piped up saying he knew a joke. "Yuh know why popcorn is so scarce? Well, the reason he said was all the kernels (colonels) were in the army.

Oh, did I tell you my Johnny boy in the army I met at Strawsville has been transferred? I don't know where yet. He's supposed to come up here this weekend—but—

Why don't you tell me the news? Ardena tells me things done in my own family that I don't know about. Phil took some pictures. Your helping Ardena with music. Guess you can't think of everything, but I'd like to see the pictures.

I've a blister on palm of my hand from driving nails. Another girl and I made 'duck boards' for the shower baths. We used oak lumber and finishing nails. Really. When I laid down in the afternoon to nap I could see those things before my eyes. Ha. Anyway my hand is sore. That was yesterday. Today I helped make some steps and banisters for a tower to be used in Duncan county. Wouldn't it be fun to climb them and say I helped make them. Not very likely. We wrote our names on them underneath.

Tonight is dorm open house. Therefore the house and project are full of boys. Why am I here?? Johnny (I pick John's don't I?), the kid who snatched my picture isn't here. By the way he took my letter to you to the mailbox (in town) to mail. Hope he did mail it and you got it. It had the pictures in it. The kid I went to the show with last night, however, works tonight from 6 p m. to midnight. I see him at mealtimes.(Did I ever tell you the segregation lasted only a short while?) Last night he took off from work to go to the show. Had a good time, Marg went with us but she had no date.

Nine-thirty. Lights are out, but I'm in Mrs. Avery's room (we still call her that tho' we know she's married).

By the way, tell Phil there are the most boys up here from around Plainesville. Some of them graduated when I did, so he may not know them. But Russell Perkins, Sanford Tankers, "Beany" Walters, Melvin Varner, Clifford Harpel to name some.

I just aimed to write a note? so guess I'll quit. I got a long letter from Dean tonight.

I really don't think Marg will stay long. What'll I do?

Do write. Tell all hello. Hug baby for me.

Love, Shandol

The next letter Shandol received from her mother was dated the same day she had written: "Wed. morn. July 29, 1942.

Dear Sissy

Here it is Wed. and nothing from u since Sat. How do I know but that u might be up-sop-size (which had been Bobby's way' of saying upside down when he was learning to talk, Shandol knew) somewhere? What's the matter with u? Got *your* pretty card Sat. Maybe I'll get a letter on this noon train?

Well didn't see u Sat. Somehow I didn't look for you. No such good luck! I didn't let myself look too much. I'd only been disappointed more.

Just got thru rolling Ardena's hair. I'm not so good but manage. I've been giving her lessons on piano. Middletons are moving it tomorrow, guess they have been kept informed? (Never heard why they left it when they moved and now want it.) Ardena ordered a guitar so guess Phil will take over from now on. Ha.

Jane is still here. Don't think she feels so well today. Lester is at Paula's today working on a barn. Phil too. Phil mixes cement Lester wheel-barrows it. Am afraid Phil will work too hard. Dad isn't there. He's still at Hedda's. Paula's hubby was sick, too sick to write. She's still there with him. Adora is caring for her c hix and the like.

The kid question is a problem. Don't know what I'll do. No, I make them stay out of the house. I can't stand them in one door and out the other—bang, bang. Mon. she was gone all p.m. Yesterday she was gone 9 till 5. Think she aims to go to Folks Consent today. Chester Parkley is driving her again. Dermont Borsek is at his dad's. With Lester working she had to go back to Chester.

Don't know whether Marian (Bright) would go up there. I think she'd like to get from under Rita's claws? Saw Laura Middleton and Marian at Penny's store last week in Plainesville a few minutes. I was to have gone to town yesterday to see about a grocery order but didn't feel like it. I just can't take Karen.

I washed a big wash Mon. A quilt too. Had lots of good rain water. Rained Sun. eve about an inch. Wasn't enough but will help things.

The old cow's about dry. Dad thinks she'll be fresh in about a week. But you see we don't know so are still milking her. I just can't use the milk, been doing without. I'm about to starve for milk and butter.

Dean was in town Sun. eve., Bobby said he saw him, his head lying on Beth Cumberlen's lap and his feet across Frances Dahle. Yet, his wife must not even smoke!! Oh, well such is life. They're more suited to him than u ? ? U don't worry about him, let them have him.

(Then, Shandol noted there was something she'd written and erased, as she wrote in pencil, as did Shandol. Her letter continued.)

I guess I'd better leave this out someone else can tell you!! I sorta promised Phil I wouldn't. Phil drove him to Folks Consent and Dad really got on to Phil. Told Phil he wanted him to leave Dean alone drunk or sober. Guess he'll tell you someone has lied again but he can't do such low-down things and get by without someone knowing it. Supposing u had been with him? Oh, Shandol, it makes me shudder every time I think of you. My heart goes out for u if u marry him. Guess I've already ruined one of my kids life domineering. I'll try not interfere again. But! But! Still preaching. Ha ha. Guess no wonder you don't care whether I write!

Did you go to church Sun? We didn't go. Truck didn't go Sun. night rained them out. It went Mon. night and aims to go Fri. night again. Zane Gray's *Union Pacific* or something like that.

Phil took some pictures Sun. July 19. Send back what u don't want. We didn't get the films back guess Buck has them so save what u keep until I see about the negatives.

Mrs. Colmay took Karen again this morn. Wish you could see her. She's sure sweet. She fell off the bed again just now. She'll get up before the mirror just hollers and laughs so sweet. But dirty, oh, me. She crawls over the floor she just gets awful. Used to I could set her down she'd stay put but now she can get down to crawl can't keep her anywhere. I could cry when I pick her up so dirty. She loves to eat. She pulls up some now, wouldn't take her long to start walking but hate to have her in the floor getting so dirty so don't allow her on the floor as much as I should. I'll make her some creepers. Her diapers get so dirty too.

Frances Dahle told Ardena she was to have had a date with Dean Sat. night. Don't know whether she did or not. I'll try and find out!

Phil bought a 22 pistol from him Sat. eve. Guess he had to have money to celebrate Bobby just now told me. Oh, yes, did you get Hugh's letter I forwarded. What did he say? Jack (Tommy's friend and Hugh's cousin)told Tommy Hugh would be there for the rest of the war. Did Hugh say? I'm forwarding another letter from Ellen Carfield today. Has she quit working in K.C. ?

Got your letter just now. The pictures were good. Look like you. I'll send them back next time. Dad, Phil, Lester and rest will want to see them.

Is Margery thinking about getting married? Ha. Yvonne Hockley is working in St. Louis in a cafe for $17 a week and board. She won't ever be able to do anything else tho' can't climb any higher.

You'll soon be gone two months. You do as you feel about coming. Would love to see you the best in the world but better stay a little longer and make some good out of your last two months work. You do as you feel.

If we could get on a farm might try raising chickens and turkeys. We'll see farther.

Be good. Write.

Love, Mom

Shandol then read Ellen Garfield's letter. She was at home as was evident by the heading of her letter.

Folks Consent
July 27,1942

Dear Shandol

I've been thinking of you for sometime so guess I'll write a few lines.

How s the world treating you? I'm home to stay for awhile now. Lora and Chester have been home. Lora went back last night and Chester is going tomorrow. (It was a large family and Shandol hadn't met them all, but felt she knew them and the mentioned brother and sister because of Ellen and the closeness of the family.

Are you still planning to go to Strawsville? When I was in K.C. my roommate and I were talking of going there but Dad didn't much want me to. So now I'm home. I have been having quite a lot of trouble with my knee and I can't work for awhile.

Guess you know Shorty has gone to the army.

(Ellen called Jim Brown that; Shandol smiled in recollection.)

Week ago Thursday night as I got off the train he got on. He went south somewhere.

Kid, I have to go to supper now so I'll finish later—having fried chicken. Ha.

Gosh, it was good!

How's your little sis? Is Phil still home? If he is tell him 'hello' for me with a capital H.

I saw Dean L. in Folks Consent Saturday but I didn't get to talk to him. Do you see Margie often?

Kid, how are we going to get together? I would just love to see you. If I knew when Dad was going to Plainesville I would ride up with him. He doesn't go so often anymore though.

Well, I must sign off and help mother with the dishes. I'll write more after awhile.

My sis Ruby came up today and helped us wash and iron. So we don't have anything to do now until Fri. (this is Mon). Then it's wash day again. I may go to Pallan's sale tomorrow.

Do you go to church often? It's been so long since I've went to church that I've about forgot what it's like.

We all went on a picnic Sunday to Cave Bluff, our whole family was together. I sure hate for Chester to leave. I wish you could see him in his uniform. He sure looks nice.

Shandol, I'll bet you wouldn't know me now. I weigh 134 pounds. Everyone says I have changed in looks.

Well, Kid, I'll sign off now. Here's hoping I see you soon. If I don't write me and tell me all the news.

Lots of love,
Ellen

If only Ellen knew, Shandol mused, where I am and the circumstances and the set-up here, she would really be surprised. Shandol did wish she could see Chester before he left and was sure he was handsome in his uniform. He was a handsome farm boy.

And Ellen weighing one hundred thirty-four pounds! She's getting fat, Shandol thought. *She was much bigger than I am though—of chunky build. Pretty little blond Ellen, with the slow but friendly smile and cute nose. But she gave such few particulars about Dean. Wonder what she's heard and could tell me if I could just see her. Perhaps nothing if she doesn't even know I'm gone.*

How worried Mom is that I'll marry Dean, Shandol's thoughts continued. *I wish I could reassure her. If I really loved him I'd be heart broken at the things said, wouldn't I? All the strange and tender emotions, what were they? It does bother that Dean tells me things, and others write differently. I don't doubt my family,* she decided.

She knew he kept her away from home to stay. She was not ready for him to take possession of her as though she was his property either. No one else had a chance. They knew they would have him to contend with—most likely fight! She could not pinpoint her feelings for him. He would mean more to her if he would behave himself as he would expect her to do. But she couldn't fault his going with other girls. She was going with other young men. She and Dean were not engaged. Yet she knew he wanted her to be his girl and his alone. She was flattered, she supposed, on one hand, but had no desire to be engaged yet. She was not ready. And certainly not with him acting so reprehensible and irresponsible. He would wind up in the army next thing he knew. This was always a cloud over everyone's head. The war must be won first. It was everyone's war. The soldiers fought it but everyone was concerned and wanted to help in whatever capacity they could. It was so crucial the United States win! Everyone said that or knew it.

So Shandol felt that Dean could wait. She would make up her mind later if he was still interested, yet she wasn't worried. She had learned she could attract boys and didn't have to worry about him being the only chance she would ever have of finding a husband. She decided that had been worth being away from home to learn. But her mother would worry, only because Shandol was so undecided. There was no use of her dwelling on it. Perhaps it was just as well she was learning what kind of person Dean really was. How could she even respect him if he didn't want to act decently? There was no hurry but she wished Audrey wouldn't worry. But there were always things taking Shandol's mind from him. Sometimes she thought she only wondered about him as she did many of the friends, classmates and people she knew—both boys and girls. It didn't mean she was in love with the boys and girls. It was just that she had been around them so closely they were closer than most of her blood relatives She simply cared about them. Besides, Dean hadn't been her first love. There was Steven. What about him? She never heard much from him. Was she still in love with him? Or had she ever been? His kisses had been more thrilling than Dean's, if possible. He had awakened the emotion, the ecstasy of the promise of what love might entail. How could it all be erased? She must find it again or it would not be a love she would be satisfied to hold to forever.

CHAPTER 44

The Saturday night party had been an unqualified success.

So much so in fact several voiced the opinion it should be done more often, at least once a month. And the boys had helped immensely with details. As they all worked together and the boys admiring the "woman's touch" plans worked out to the last detail seemed perfect.

Shandol had, until almost the last day, made no specific plans to go. She was sure she would be a wallflower because she couldn't dance and therefore not enjoy it as an outsider. In fact she didn't think she could stand it if no one paid any attention to her.

Margery, on the other hand, had planned big on going with Arnold, her soldier. She had been allowed to ask an outside guest and she knew she would be proud of him in uniform. She wouldn't care what the others were doing, she would be seen with her soldier boy.

During the noon meal, however, Shandol had talked to Harley Lensing. He asked her if she had planned to go, and he seemed surprised when she told him she hadn't planned to go. Then he asked her to go. In fact he pleaded that it would ruin the night for him if she didn't show up. He wondered, of course, why she had made such a decision.

"I don't dance very well," she admitted. "Just Marg and I dance some, but I can't be relaxed with a male partner."

"Don't worry," he grinned, "you won't be alone in that. I'm not much of a dancer myself."

"Then I won't be the only wallflower, will I?" she asked, forthrightly. "I mean if all there is is dancing?"

"You a wallflower?" he sighed, incredulously. "No one will mind if you dance or not. Least of all me. How about it?"

"Alright," she had agreed. "I suppose I can always leave if I feel like it."

So her heart sang as she showered, put on the small amount of makeup she wore and put on the same dress she had worn at Wildwood. It was the only one she had which even suggested a party style. The material was soft, printed, the skirt flowing and the lace collar in place. The short puff sleeves made it cool-looking for the summer season.

By the time Shandol was ready to go, so was Margery.

Shandol hated to leave her but it soon became apparent either

Arnold wasn't coming or he would be quite late. Shandol tried to get Margery to go without him. After all, he would know where to find her. Besides it was time to go. Shandol had supposed she would be the one who would be lagging and dreading to get started. But she knew Harley would be wondering about her,

"You must go on, Shan," Margery told her. "But I just can't and won't go unless Arnold comes and goes with me. I have a date and he's going to find me waiting whatever his excuse."

"But Margery—," Shandol began.

"Just don't wait on me, please," Margery interrupted. "I'm gonna wait for Arnold," she added flatly.

"I guess I'll see yuh, then, but I hate to go and leave yuh," Shandol replied. "I can't see how I'm goin' to enjoy it, but Harley wants me to go. But dancing—," she threw out her hands hopelessly.

"Yuh could really," Margery told her. "But yuh think that way and just stiffen up. I don't know how to break you of it—only you can by trying with somebody else.

Shandol supposed it was true, but she also supposed it unlikely. She had been brought up to believe it wrong and she wasn't sure how to rationalize it. Because everyone did—almost. Perhaps if just unmarried people? She wondered. Or was that hypocritical? And so perhaps it was true. She had never tried hard enough.

Shandol reluctantly went on without Margery. It was almost nine when Arnold and she had arrived.

Though Shandol hadn't danced much she enjoyed herself. Even her brief attempt at dancing had been successful and to her a minor triumph. There were refreshments and dozens to talk to. She and Harley had danced, and he proved not bad and considerate of her problem so that she did relax. They also watched the dancing. There was a group called CSC (Christian Student Congregation). She wasn't quite sure how she should judge them (if indeed at all) as they danced also. They were a group, principally of college students, who had been given honorary guest invitations.

Margery also had enjoyed and praised the party. She was somewhat disappointed Arnold had been so late, but he had a good excuse: His means of transportation. He admitted to her he was lucky to have made it at all.

"Who'd have thought it?" Margery mused aloud, after she had climbed to her upper bunk to sleep at the late hour.

"What?" Shandol asked, sleepily. She too was in bed.

"That we'd have so much fun and everybody else too, and it was such a good party."

"Yep, it was that," Shandol replied, briefly.

The next morning they slept later than usual, but went to church. They were too late for Sunday school. That is, Shandol went to church. Once the two girls were in town Margery decided she would wait for Arnold. She was never able to locate him that morning but went back to camp with Shandol as she was supposed to have been to church.

Margery returned to town in the afternoon and found Arnold with another girl. He left her to go with Margery, as they had a date. Had he tried to evade it?

Later Shandol could see Margery had been shocked and hurt.

"He did ditch the other girl for me," Margery's laugh seemed forced. "But he better not do me like that anymore."

Shandol was at the dorm all afternoon. In fact she had sat under a tree with Harley Lensing, near the dorm. They were on a blanket but later complained of chiggers anyway. In the evening she went to town with two other girls. As they were on the way back to camp they were caught in a sudden downpour of rain.

"A regular cloudburst," she had told Margery. "And not a dry thread on any of us."

They were unprotected and were drenched as though dunked into a pond. Shandol took a warm shower, pin curled her hair and went to bed.

Audrey's letter was dated, "July last, 1942"

Dear Dearie:

I guess you received my letter and card. How do you like the pictures? I wanted to surprise you with the pictures. I sit down to write next thing I know somebody comes and bothers, then it's near train time and I'm blank. I guess I'll have to get me a *day book* (not date ha) and write down the happenings so I'll remember them.

Trying to rain today. Bobby and I picked a peck of beans. Got the little washtub full. They (beans) didn't do any good.

Dad, Phil and Lester are still working. Lester got his money today guess he'll be taking out for a defense job 'ere long.

Wish you could see Karen. She has the sweetest squeal you ever heard. When anyone laughs she'll holler and laugh great big too. She's pulling up now. Have to watch her so close, fear she will fall and make her afraid to walk.

Read your letter off the noon train. Glad you're working hard. You might climb a tower and say it, who knows?

Carolyn Parkley was soliciting for Mr. Kasper some pajamas yesterday. Several gave something, but didn't feel like I was able. Dad has just been dragging around, still coughs some. I felt like their kids all had jobs if they wanted to make him comfortable they are plenty able. If they had been destitute I would have been willing to tried at least to have helped a little. But we have our own debts to pay. Sometimes I can't see how or where it'll come from, but does somehow. I get sorta blue when I give things a good think (as "Skippy" used to say in paper) but don't seem to help any. School coming on, books to buy—for Bobby this time. Better *give it a good think* before you come out. Let Marg do as she feels. If you think you'll ever be able to do any good with it, if not and you want to come home, why just come on. I hardly know what to say. Can't you find another pal for a little while? Mrs. Colmay said, "if she was my girl I'd have her come home before she had to sign up for a defense job and be sent no telling where. Don't know what to tell you. You do as you feel. I'd love to have you home, but fear you wouldn't be satisfied. Think it over!! Just don't know what to advise.

I know how hard water is in north part of state. Your not telling me anything. My hair needs washing but have to get someone to do it up for me so put it off as long as I can.

The little fellow there must be witty. They're cute at that age too. Miss K.C. when I think of such things. The lady that stays at Grandpa Brights has a little boy 8 or 9 I'd judge. Tommy says he'll be nine same as him. Dale something. He and his mother go to Colmays lots.

Do you still hear from your Johnny boy or just through someone else. Lots of troop trains now. Also tanks, cannons, cars, trucks and the sort. Makes me shudder to think about it, Germany is sure pouring it on to Russia. Wonder why the United Nations don't do something. Maybe we can't see everything. Mrs. Colmay's son is in the hospital. She hadn't heard from him for five or six weeks. Something dropped on his leg. She didn't learn many particulars.

Bobby has written. He was telling me what to write, I told him to write himself then you wouldn't always hear me preaching about it. Ha.

Wish you could see Karen now. She's holding to my chair by the window, 'member? Squealing with delight. She's so sweet. Costs 10¢ a day now for milk for her. Don't care. We'll feed her somehow. We've turned the old cow dry. She has a nice bag guess she'll be fresh 'ere long.

Jane has to eat bread and jelly for dinner sometimes. I don't cook three meals a day. Have to cook supper, it's like old times. Bake bread every other day. They all nearly eat us out of house and home. Phil says if you don't fix me more dinner I'm going to eat the dinner bucket. Ha. Sure hard to fix lunches, nothing to fix. Lester has been buying peanut butter 40¢ qt. I want Dad to go up tomorrow and sign up for a farm loan but guess he won't.

Margery's three little sisters were here the other eve a little while. Mr. McM. had gone to a sale and they had gone too and he hauled some things for Mrs. Colmay. They rode home with her and came here.

Tommy says "I want her to write to me separate. I don't get to read what she writes to you" (meaning me). Think it's just as well he doesn't too much, don't you??

I'll close now. Dining room hasn't been cleaned today. It's terrible. So be good and write. Just do as you feel about coming then you'll be satisfied.

I'm returning the pictures. I sorta hate to. The two of you are good. The other looks like you only funny. Yes. I *laffed*. Its good of you but you look funny in those clothes you wore to garden at Wildwood. The surroundings—the field of corn and the hoe reminded one of the labor you did. Your teeth showed so white. Both real good of you. Maybe I can have one later?

I still have your old blue dress hanging on a chair in the bedroom. Trying to kid myself you'll be home. Also the "step-ins" and an old ragged petticoat. Seems like it helps me.

I'll have to get this mailed. Does it take three days to get you a letter? This is Fri. Tell me when you get it. Write.

Lots of love,
Mom

Shandol wrote to her mother in answer to the letter. She had received the letter August third, and so it was the date of her letter.

Dear Mom,

Sure enjoyed your letter, guess because I wasn't really expecting to hear from you. I got a letter from Dean today. Sure beats me about him. He writes so innocent-like. Guess I'll hear about it if I ever do come home. He talks as though he'll have to go to the army sometime soon.

I went to the cafeteria to the dance (party) after all even

though I didn't dance much. I had a pretty good time. I was with a kid from camp here. The same one, Harley Lensing. Marg had to wait for her soldier boy until nine or so. They served sandwiches, ice cream and punch. I ate two ice cream cones. I had a good time and I think the whole thing was such a success that they've decided to 'do it more often'—maybe once a month if allowed. The CSC (I told you about them Christian Student Congregation) came. They danced too!

Yesterday I went to church. Got up too late to go to S.S. at 9:30. The pastor was absent so the man in charge only talked very little. Marg didn't go. She was on the lookout for her soldier boy. She didn't find him in the morning, but in the afternoon she did with another girl! Ha ha. He ditched her for Marg, however.

Last night I just went to town with some girls. Did we ever get rained on. We were already too far out of town to call a taxi when it just literally poured. I didn't have a dry thread on me when I got to the dorm. I doped up with Vicks like someone with pneumonia, after taking a warm shower bath, and went to bed, tho' I had to roll up my hair. You remember I told you I had some cold. (miss coal oil grease, ha). But my cold is no worse today.

By the way I'm still doctoring the poison, but it's pretty well cleared now.

Last night a girl had an attack of acute appendicitis. She was in the other wing but the girls there said she'd just lay and groaned and moaned about all night. Sort of a sob-like too. Sure pitiful. If I'm not mistaken she was operated on this morning. Sometime one of the cooks was operated on for the same thing. She has gone home now though. The nurse was in here to see about the girls and I don't remember it. I do remember waking up and sometime this morning to doctor my poison with the remedy you sent me how to fix—and I could hear her taking on. They said the nurse came about 2:30.

I was 18 minutes late for work this morning. Everyone was. We just overslept. We were allowed to go punch our time cards and then go back to breakfast! Therefore, this has been a fairly short day. I have slept some this afternoon, and it's now almost 'chow' time again. By the way I don't have my ironing done. I had to iron a blouse yesterday to have something to wear today.

I don't especially want to come home now to stay. But

sometimes I wonder if I'm doing any good here!

Wish I could see Karen too. She must be sweet. Do people still make over her so much? When I got the picture I showed it to the supervisor here. Told her I'd love to squeeze the baby.

Marg heard from her folks today. Thinks they are about all under the weather. Marg is wondering if her mother is able to stand the strain. I certainly hope Dad is better now. Does Jane feel any better?

Well, I think I will write to Tommy. Maybe to Bobby. Whether or not they write right back, tell them *I said* I certainly enjoy their writing to me. Must also write to Dean.

Tell Jane and Lester 'hello', if they're still there. Tell Bobby to write some more. Is that really so?? Do tell me about seeing him. I'll write to him soon. Guess Bobby knows who I mean! *Dean.*

Tell Phil 'hello.' That I'd like to hear him sing. Ask him if he knows the songs I hear on the jukebox up town and tell me what he says! "Sycamore Lane," "I Wonder Why You Said Good-bye," "I Wrote You a Card," and "Tears On My Pillow."

Write soon.

With love,

Shandol

The next day the girls went to town to "celebrate," as they called it, because they had been away from home two months. Shandol also needed some letter writing paper. But they each had a hamburger to eat and some orange soda pop. Shandol told her mother about it in the letter she wrote home later that day. The letter was dated Aug. 4, 1942.

Dear Mom,

I have just returned from town. Yeah, I had to buy something to write letters on. So I got this stationery. We also ate. We had a hamburger and drank some orange flavored soda pop. I weighed too. I now weigh 107 lbs! (When I went to Wildwood two months ago (note date) I weighed only 100 even. I can hardly wear my pink checked skirt. I burst the button off Sunday. Ha. So I can tell I've gained weight.

I learned today that last Sunday when Marg was supposed to go to church and didn't she almost got some extra duty. They sat on the grass of the courthouse lawn; also they were supposed to come back for supper and they didn't. Mrs. Crocker (was Mrs.

Avery) gave them a sound talking to. Marg was with another girl and the army guys. It wasn't brought up at council meeting this evening. I didn't leave the project *that* afternoon.

While we girls were in town this afternoon, we visited the girl from here who was operated on. Said she felt pretty good but was somewhat sore.

Mom, the first of September a number of girls will be sent out on jobs I hear. We would go to Curtis-Wright glider factory in St. Louis. I don't know if I'll be far enough advanced to go or not. Lands, but I hope so! I believe I could stay up here that much longer. However, I'm not building up any (false)hopes, and don't you!

Ask Dad if he still wants me to type his talk on "The Devil." How did 'some people' like it? Hope the right ones heard it. Did Arvin Jarred agree with him?

Today was election day, eh? How did it come out in and around Greenway? Tell me what you think would interest me. Up town a man in front of the newspaper building was giving returns. Made me wonder about home.

Guess you knew, likely Dean told some of you, that Brad Lawson had to go to the army. Gee, but don't you feel sorry for Fran? She's expecting too. Know what I told you? She'll feel bad about it I'm sure. Guess I'll be like Marg says, "Ain't I glad I'm single?" Ha.

Mom, don't say anything about the factory at St. Louis until I know if I'm going or not. Now, hear? They say they are 'just crying' for girls to work. Hope I can go, do you? As I said, though, I'm not going to count on it yet. So don't tell now.

Hope everyone's ok. Yeah, my cold is getting better. Still have some runny nose.

By the way what hospital did you mean—about Harolds? What about it?

Tell all 'hello' and kids to write.

Love to all, Shandol

Shandol also received a letter from Ardena. It was dated Greenway, Aug.2,1942. She wrote:

Dear Shandol,

Will drop a few lines to let you know I'm real fine. Kid, since you asked me to tell you about Dean I will. He was with Frances Dahle a week ago Sat. night and then on Wednesday and I saw him with her today at the bus depot. He was with her a week ago Sunday evening too. He was drinking also for he was up in the yard talking to Bobby and one Colmay. Kid, Bobby told me, I didn't get close enough to tell.

Your mother said she sent the pictures to you. Yes, she showed them to me as soon as they come. The two pictures of you, kid, I can't imagine you out there that away. Kid, Maida took the piano home. I won't take anymore lessons I don't guess. Phil hasn't taught me any guitar yet but I think I can get him to.

Kid, I sure wish you was here. I sure miss you. Well, Shandol I went and got vaccinated. My arm is so sore I can't hardly write but I'm trying to take the soreness out of it.

I started this letter Sunday as I guess you can tell. I saw Dean in town last night. He was with the Hower boy and they picked up Frances just on the other side of the tracks.

There is going to be a show up on the highway Thurs., Fri., and Sat. They are going to show the bombing of Pearl Harbor. I sure want to see it.

Cal said he was going to take us kids to the creek Sunday if nothing happens. Hope he does. He was supposed to take us last Sunday, but he stayed in Plainesville with his grandma.

Is there many army boys out there. I saw quite a few in Plainesville Saturday night. Well, I guess I had better close for it is hurting my arm so answer soon.

From Ardena Ruleton
P.S. Mother said tell you hello.

The next day Shandol received a letter from her mother. She had just received Shandol's letter and wrote a letter in stead of a card. It was dated Mon., 1:20, Aug. 3, 1942.

Dearest Dear,

If I'll hurry I might scribble a few lines. Aimed to send a card but just now got your letter so will send a letter.

Have the four Colmay kids again. Dad went to town, brought another application for farm loan. Guess that's all it'll amount to. He's not overly enthused.

Phil drove the car for Mrs. Colmay to Plainesville. Lester is working for 'big Adora'. Will have work most all winter. Said he'd try it awhile. Got his money the other day. Has $25.00

now. Trying to save for her hospital bill?? Jane is fine. Her parents and grandma were here a few minutes Sun.

You may keep the pictures. I meant Mrs. Colmay took Karen's picture. No, emphatically no, she's not taking Karen!

The old cow has a steer calf. White one. Came yesterday (Sun). Nice and big.

Saw Mrs. McNeeley yesterday. I wish you could have seen babies. I had Karen she had her baby. We held them pretty close together and they would just scold each other. Was sure cute. We laughed and laughed about it.

We didn't get to go to church at Plainesville. They've changed the Sunday night going to Sat. night. Went to Young People's Meeting last night. 23 there. Dad spoke about the 'Devil'?

No, I'm just the same old shaggy outfit as ever. Had that old blue silk dress Rita Bright gave me. Not sure it looked clean at that.

Shandol, I'll just send you a long letter Wed. Haven't time to write and can't think now as I'd wish. Too much banging the doors.

I've always liked Hugh, but you might in the meantime decide he's not for you. You are the one to be satisfied. No use to be in a hurry about it anyway. Better forget Dean. I'll write you more. Dad has come in. Wants his dinner and it's train time.

Hope your cold is better.

I'll write soon. You write and be good.

Love, Mom

Shandol was glad, as usual, when it was mentioned, her mother did not try to push her and Hugh together. She was sure his family had hopes they would make a match. But he was so much like the other town boys, as she so often thought, who were closer to the family than any of their relatives. How could she fall in love with them? Or with Hugh? How could she know if she loved Hugh? He was a good friend, she liked and respected him. And she had adored watching him play basketball in school. He was good and usually taller than the other players.

That night Shandol was in town with Rory Wheaton, who was from town. He was bashful around girls, but had now learned how to bring the girls back to camp and on to their dorm "on the grounds." He had hated to face the officials at the office, where all incoming cars were checked and granted permission to enter or not, as they deemed suitable, but, after the initial daring on his part, now accepted it.

The next day Shandol received a letter from Dean. He wrote that his mother had said to tell her hi. Shandol was indeed surprised. Could it be she too saw a difference in her boy since she had been gone, she wondered. But Shandol had always felt timid around her and in turn she seemed stand-offish toward Shandol. Of course Shandol recalled the pie or cake she had served the few times she had gone there. But that had partly been Dean's idea too. Perhaps she had not realized Dean was so serious about this girl. Dean was still young. Shandol knew she could be married to him by simply saying the word.

Shandol received a letter from her mother again on Friday. She also wrote to her. In fact she wrote several letters. Besides her mother she wrote to Ardena, Dean and Cal Horn.

She reread the letter from her mother before she wrote in reply. Her mother's letter was dated Aug. 5, 1942, and Shandol read :

Dearest Dearie:

Jane and Tommy have gone to the garage on highway for something—just foolishness I guess—ice cream or something. I guess I'll try to scribble a few lines.

Lester and Dad have gone to work. Phil didn't go today he felt bad. Dad was a judge at the primary yesterday. Guess a fellow is never too old to learn. Elma Butler was clerk.

Why do you wait until everything is dirty 'ere you wash? Ha. Guess Mom isn't there, eh? I washed. Jane helped some yesterday. Had 27 diapers. Don't know how many baby dresses. Washed 26 dresses for her last week. She's been feeling bad. Mon. night she cried a lot off and on all nite. She must be cutting teeth. Had a pretty high fever. She's some better not well yet. She was awfully 'raw' again. Seems when her bowels get bad it just seems to 'scald' her. I'll wash the bedding this week later. I was too tired today. Rained yesterday. Have plenty of nice soft water.

I promised myself I would quit carrying tales, but since you asked me this time and I found out from a different source I'll write it to you what I wrote and erased. Dean went out to Beatrice Freedman's drunk that night. She asked him to leave five or six times. Madge Middleton had her shorts on; he (Dean) had quite a bit to say about that. But the other boy that was with Dean (as well as I can find out) Nevin Hower said he was cussing and talking awful. Don't know if he too was drunk or not. I promised Phil I wouldn't tell so felt sorta conscience stricken. But have since found out more and from another source so don't feel I've broken my promise to Phil. Yes, Dean is dating Frances Dahle regular. Dad saw them Sun. eve.

Harriet just left! Seems I can't sit down and write without someone bothering me.

Dean has been to the house here (not in the house) two times since he came back. He sees the boys at the store and talks to them. I don't care for my part whether he comes to the house or not. Shandol how can you tolerate him? He stooped low enough but when he goes out with that kind its enough!! Dad says they're more "his type." Ha. No, don't preach at him that's what he wants. But don't believe everything he's telling you because I know better. I'm not spying or having it done it's just plain enough to see!!

I suppose if Hugh loves you he'd expect you to wait on him, but I'm not going to encourage or discourage you about him. You just do as you feel. I'd sooner see you go with him if he is a Burdette as Rita said than Dean Leonard. You've known Hugh a long time. No bad habits such as drinking or smoking. Don't believe you'd have to worry about the "other woman" but you figure it out. Nobody knew I got your last letter, so didn't erase it. Jane likes to read your letters so if you have something write it separate. You can tell me anything.

(And in fact Shandol usually would, as there was no one else she could confide in.)

Did you get Phil's letter with the picture! He told me to send it to you but never could find it when I wrote. He said you may keep it.

I hope your cold and poison are better. How was the dance? Did you foxtrot? Ha.

Della Bright came back Sun. She looks so well. Brought 13 baby dresses so Karen has quite a supply now—30 altogether. I try to keep her nice and clean, too clean I guess. It'll make an old woman out of me. Ha. She pulls up to everything she can. So afraid she'll fall some of these days. I don't let her on the floor as much as I should. She gets so dirty. She's beginning to find out there's a way to get around on her hands and knees but can't quite make it work yet.

Mrs. Colmay bought 2 bus. peaches at Folks Consent $1.50 a bushel. Awful faulty and wormy. She should have worked her peaches yesterday but went to town with Della. Gone till five o'clock. Those kids went all day without anything to eat. Mon. she sent them over here, never said dogs about them. Was gone until three o'clock, came home, stayed about 1 hr. went to Folks Consent, came back, and went to prayer meeting. Never gave kids their supper. They bought two loaves bread and something in a snack. I'll declare! I don't know what'll become of those kids. Poor little ones. Are so poor and thin. Little Norma, as she calls her, is really poor. I'd be uneasy about her if she was mine. Oh, me. No use to lecture you but I wish I didn't have to see them and worry about them. I just can't help it though. You must be careful about that cold!

Phil and Bobby were on the pond (on Phin you know). Parkleys kids go tell Phins about it. So Floyd and Vernon came down with a sign. Don't know what it says. Will see soon. Guess they fear they'll shoot their good cow. Oh, me! The nerve of some people. But that's all he's got to do though is sit around and mind somebody's business.

I must get this mailed. Five after one. Train goes 1:51 so here goes.

I'll write later.

Write and be good.

Love, Mom

Shandol answered the letter. She dated it Aug.7,1942:

Dearest Mom,

I've just washed and did up my hair. I also fixed up Margery's too. I'd like to sleep some today too, but, oh, you should see the letters I must write! Margie and I are going to wash some too, this evening. It's been so rainy that we've not done any washing. We don't wait too long to wash Mom, but just about as long as we can. We have some uniforms now that we wear. They certainly do save our regular clothes a lot. Lands, at the clothes Karen has! Too bad we can't wear each other's. Ha. Hope she's feeling better.

I received another letter from Hugh Burdette this week. And guess what! He sent me the nicest picture of himself. Seems like being nearer home to be able to see a picture of someone I know. I keep it on the table beside my bed. I'm glad, too, that I didn't have to ask him for it. I sure was glad to get it. I answered his letter yesterday.

583

I got a letter from Dean today. I don't think he'll be around there to bother you much longer. He thinks he will be called to the army anytime. He sees too where I used 'my head' or was it Mom's head, in not getting married. He told me so. Said Fran cried when Brad found he was sure he'd have to go. He, Dean, may think he's feeding me a line. He admitted he was with Frances just driving. But that he didn't take her home *as a date*. I don't see why he writes such lies. But he swears the person who told me he was drunk was mistaken. But when so many tell me otherwise, well, it must be so. I'm going to tell him though that he's not feeding me that line. The Beatrice's outfit he pulled *WAS* awful! Is he dating Frances Regular (capital R)? He can't be seriously. You don't understand do you? It's to make me jealous—to bring me home, I think. Or don't I understand?

Yes, my poison and cold are better. I'm still digging at some chigger bites though. Ha. Sat on the grass (on a blanket) Sunday, but I just got covered with them anyway.

I'm so glad you can keep the baby sweet and clean. I just love a sweet and clean baby. Wish I could see such an assortment of clothes& wish I could see her too. She may be walking before I do see her, however.

Do you ever feed the Colmay kids when they're there so much? I think someone should make a complaint. Poor things. Do Parkley's kids ever come or have anything to do with Tommy, Phil, or Bob? That's all Chester can think of! Maybe it'll make him fat!

I'm writing to Phil a few lines separate about the picture. Gee, it's so good of him. Did you know I've written some letters to Cal Horn? By the way Dean knows that too. Just to hear from down there from anyone. There's a girl here whose brother is in the army and has come to see her. She lives only 24 miles from home and has never gone! Doesn't that seem odd? I can hardly imagine it, and she seems like a swell kid too.

Well, I can't start another page so better ring off. At that I haven't told you of my good times. Was with a kid from town Wed. night. I met him and have been with him lots. He's swell.

Tell Lester and Jane hello. In Dean's last letter he wrote his ma said tell me 'hello'.

Feature that! Maybe she knows a difference now.

Love to all,
Shandol

Shandol received a letter from Ellen Garfield. Her letter was dated from "Folks Consent, Aug. 5, 1942. She wrote:

Dearest Shandol,

I received your very nice letter and sorry I haven't answered sooner. Sure was glad to hear from you and that you're having such a swell time. Wish I was there. Never can tell maybe when you come home I'll go back with you. No, I can't go that soon but I'm thinking seriously about it.

Kid, do you mind me asking a few questions? No, I don't think you would.

Well, first I want to know if this is defense work you're doing now or just a place to learn and wait for defense work later. Do you wear uniforms? Are your expenses very much? What hours are you on duty? When you are not on duty can you go anywhere or do anything you want to?

Yes, kid, I was just 18 years old in July and I would like all the information I can get if it isn't too much trouble.

Tell Margie "hi-ya" for me and I'll write her next time. I have four letters here to answer. So you see I'm quite busy. Tell her to write me anyway.

Do you girls have lockers to put your clothes in?

Kid, I really don't know what Dean has been doing. I saw him Sat. in Folks Consent. He was with Nevin Hower. Mrs. Leonard told mother he was filling out his questionnaire.

Elmo said "hello" right back at you and he remembers the opossum grapes, ha.

I went to Plainesville Monday and looked around all day. Sure was tired.

Oh, yes, something else I want to know. How far is it to Midhill and how much is train fare or bus fare?

Well, Dearie, please excuse this writing. I'm lying on my tummy and it isn't a very good position to write. If you don't believe me try it once. Ha ha.

I must sign off now. Write me again real soon.
                                        Sincerely, Ellen
P.S. How many girls are there in the camp?

Shandol received a letter from her mother the same day. Both letters bore Aug.7, 1942 dates, but were received the ninth. It was not a long letter and seemed to rehash things they had already written about. Audrey wrote:

Dear Dearie:

I'll proceed to answer your last two letters this cloudy day. Rained a pretty good shower yesterday eve. Looks as if it might rain some more. Wouldn't hurt. Might sow some turnips and plant more beans.

I see you're still asleep. Better wake up. Ha. Must go to church and S.S. while you have such a good chance.

Hope your poison and cold are better. We've all had colds. Dad is better of his cold but is almost down in the back or hip. I can't do anything with him. Have to just let him go until he gets past going then I'll go ahead.

The German's don't want us to leave for the country. They want the men to work, but we have to look out for ourselves too. Dad got an application but as usual guess that's as far as it will go.

Better watch out you'll have appendicitis. Must put rocks in the grub?? Ha. Too bad, seriously. I hope all are better.

What did you do about being late? Have to lose it or make it up? Still sleepy?

Karen's fine, sweet as ever. She sure likes her daddy. It nearly tickles Dad to death. That old woman that stays at Bright's had her the other day. She said that's the sweetest little thing I've had in my arms for a long time. She sure cut a caper at church Sun. eve. She saw Madge and would just scold her. Was cute, but had all the kids laughing.

Phil didn't know the songs. If he heard them once he'd know them. Wish he'd take more pains with music. He'd be so good if he would.

I don't remember saying you wrote a card. I said I aimed to write a card but did better with a letter?

(Shandol smiled. She had made reference to the name of the song and Audrey had misunderstood.)

Jane is ok. She and Lester, Bobby, Phil, Ardena and Tommy went to show last night.(Thur.) Nearly in rain. They have the Pearl Harbor bombing tonight. Costs 21¢ and 27¢ instead of 79¢. Dad asked me if I wanted to go. I told him I didn't want to see it. If I imagined things that was bad enough. I have two boys I may have to worry about being bombed.

Cheer up! You'd better be glad you're out of this place. I went over to Mrs. Kaspers this morning and told her her chix were eating my tomatoes. Did she ever get mad? Whew!! She just flew right off the handle. We had it up and down for awhile. Poor old soul because it's her she thinks it's okay

586

because it's her chix. But she's struck a snag this time!!

I could have tears on my pillow because I have to stay here. I miss you too. Been gone two months now. Wish you could come home to visit. Dad said he might help pay your transportation one way—if you could get off to come home for a visit without it interfering with your work.

Yes, since you have to be gone from home I'd be glad if I could go to St. Louis. Don't stay because Marge has to if she does. You could do it. Just make up your mind and go ahead!!

Better watch out! Those supervisors can't let those girls loose to do as they please. Wouldn't do. That goes down on your record so be careful. Haven't heard anything about election. Clyde Garther and Orson Downey were running a pretty close race for collector. Don't know who won. Arvin Jarred didn't hear Dad's "Devil" talk. In the Little Mission church and Arvin won't go there. He paraded up and down in the road, don't know how much he heard.

No, wondered about Brad and Fran the other day. Too bad. She should be in school yet with out the responsibility of a family and to have to go it all alone.

Your boyfriend and Nevin Hower double-dated last night. Guess he'll write you all about it. Ha. You wouldn't believe us if we wrote about it, so why?

Can't you read in between lines better than that?

I told you sometime ago I'd be grandma!! Don't you remember? She aims to go to the hospital so thus Lester's hospital bill.

I've some clippings I want to send. Don't amount to much, but will help while a few minutes away.

I'm on the bed. Karen just climbed over me.

So I can't write grabbing left and right. I'll quit now. Be good and write.

Tell Marge I said to be good. Her mother was sacrificing a lot so her lot would be better. So will quit now. Write soon. Hope you're ok.

Love, Mom

P.S. You'll be getting a check soon? Shandol, I keep forgetting about the play suit! I'd thought I'd try making you one but I'm afraid it wouldn't fit. So will send you money next time and you can see about one yourself. I hardly go to town. Can't since Karen came. Mom.

It was after work the next day that Shandol wrote to her mother. She had eaten and though she and Margery had discussed somethings they could do, they weren't sure what they would get done. But Shandol determinedly set about writing to her mother. She also wrote to Ellen Garfield to answer her questions and tell of some of their other activities and in particular, their personal ones. Her own as well as Margery's. But she also wrote much of the same thing to her mother. The date was Aug.10.

Dear Mom, (she wrote)

Finally got your letter. I wrote a few lines yesterday as I couldn't think why I hadn't heard from you. It's afternoon now and I'm going to write to you and then go to sleep—if I can stay awake *that* long. I know you'll think what terrible writing, but I wish you could see the position I'm in. So don't think too much of it.

Marge and I thought we'd wash today, but we're too sleepy. Too close to the weekend. Ha. So we're going to rest and sleep. I went to the show last night with a boy here in camp. The name of it was *Tarzan's Adventure in New York*. I certainly got a kick out of it as did my date.

In the shop today I sanded mostly. Still sleepy. Ha.

I got a letter from Dean today but he didn't say anything about a date. Tell me about them, Mom. You know I want you to do it. I mean it. Tell me all you can find out! Of course it's not that he's dating, I do that too. But who he goes with and does.

Too bad Dad feels so bad. Guess boys will have to do just that much more to help.

That girl who was operated on is back here now. Just six days in the hospital. She's up walking around, even goes to the cafeteria to eat meals. She was operated on a week ago today and came back yesterday. Just seems she should be taking things easy yet.

Do you have lots of tomatoes? Lands! How I wish I could take a salt shaker and go to the patch and get me some (not one) to eat then and there. Boy, I love them and we only get a slice or two—when we even have them.

I'd love to see Karen. Know she's sweet. I just look at the pictures every day. Wish Dad would have put his "head" in some place. Why didn't he? Guess I told you about the swell tinted picture I got of Hugh Burdett. How many times? I'm right tickled over it.

Guess I'd better close and go to sleep. Marge and I are going to town tonight so guess we'll mail them then. And get some more stamps. We had to borrow some money for that, but we don't mind and they didn't either. We can and will pay it back when we get our checks. We'll get them I think about the 20th.

No, I won't stay because Marge does. But sometimes I wonder. Are there any hopes. Marge heard from her mom today. They think Arthur is gone from the states. She (Mrs. McN.) says she walks the floor at night!! They can't hear from him is why.

I go by Blondie a lot here, in fact mostly. Sometimes Sue. Sometimes I even say my name's Sue, they can't remember Shandol anyway. The guy I was with last night calls me Sue. I told him that was my name, but told him differently too.

Tell Jane and Lester "hello." Give my love to the whole family.

Oh, by the way I may get Ellen Garfield to come up here. I wrote her today too. Do you reckon she'd like it?

Do write soon.

Love to all,

Shandol

Shandol received no more letters from her mother until Wednesday. It was also dated the tenth, the same day Shandol had written. So many times their letters were dated the same day, so it was hard to decide just which one owed the other a letter. So each one wrote to the other as time, activities, or mood allowed. Audrey wrote more regularly however.

But this letter was in answer to one Shandol had written Aug.7, 1942, though she had not mailed it until the next day. It had been a Saturday afternoon when the girls had gone to town. While they had done their walking to town, going by the post office, and just walking along window shopping and even having gone into one store. Actually they had been looking at play suits, as both girls did so wish to own at least one.

"It's not much use lookin'," Shandol told Margery, "when we've no money. But I need tuh know the price in case I can talk Mom into gettin' it for me."

"Don't cost nuthin' tuh look," Margery rejoined, light heartedly, as she was in her more natural, for her, jovial, good moods.

"I think things are high here," Shandol complained. "or maybe it's because I've so little to spend. But I just believe it'd be cheaper at Plainesville."

"Oh, yuh're just partial," Margery decided, "but then so am I." She squenched up her nose. Her eyes shone merrily.

They rarely missed spending some time in the dime stores, whether they needed anything or not. As they came out deciding they may as well go back to camp, they were startled at the change at what they could see of the sky. It had grown quite gloomy and a closer look revealed why. A dark threatening cloud loomed to the southwest, which they had not noticed coming up. There had been so much rain lately, they were sure it meant more rain was imminent, perhaps a drenching downpour.

"We'd best make a run for it," Margery suggested. "We're gonna get wet and we've no money for a taxi."

They discussed if they should go up the highway in hopes someone they knew might happen along and pick them up, or if they should take the shortcut to get to camp quicker.

Shandol decided she was afraid there might be lightning and she wasn't sure the wooded area was safe. Margery considered lightning being a treat, a vague possibility, but they decided to go the highway. If they got wet, well they had been before and it hadn't hurt them. Once they had been lucky and beat the rain, they recalled, and were only sprinkled on slightly. That time they had had a chance to ride home. An imposing looking, new looking car and two more mature young men, in contrast to most of those at camp anyway, had stopped and asked them if they would care to ride wherever they were going.

Shandol and Margery had looked at one another, each thinking the same thing: "It's a pickup; we can't do it." But it was Shandol who had decided to level with them.

She explained they were girls from the camp and being picked up by anyone they had never seen before was not allowed.

One had insisted no one would know anything about it unless they were told.

"But we're not in the habit of doing things we're not supposed to do," Shandol replied. "At least not deliberately," she amended, remembering some of their botches and blunders.

"Oh, cheese," the one on the driver's side said, sounding surprised.

"Sorry. Nothing personal," Shandol went on to explain, glad she had heard the way to express it, though she knew not where, nor from whom. She was looking at the driver, wondering who he was and what he did for a living to drive a car like that. "Just rules and regulations of the camp, which our parents sort of agree with too, I might add."

"Well, I hope yuh don't get wet before yuh get back out there at least," the one next to the driver said.

"So we'd better hurry on." Margery spoke up.

Shandol wanted to linger feasting her eyes on the driver but she realized the wisdom of Margery's words.

"Suppose we'll ever see 'em again," Margery continued as they walked on, but turning frequently to watch the shiny maroon colored car move on around the block out of sight.

"Be sorta funny if we did and could talk a few times, then we'd know 'em," Shandol said.

The dark menacing looking clouds were moving in and the girls had walked as fast as they could, even ran down hills. They entered the Project at the nearest corner and hurried up the last grassy hill which seemed endless. The first splats of large drops of rain seemed to meet them at the boardwalk leading to their dorm, and it didn't actually rain until they were safely inside when it poured down rain. It seemed a secret sign to the girls they had done the right thing.

Later they had seen the car again and spoken to the men in it. Actually they had learned by now where it would be parked if the driver were home. The owner lived with his cousin, who had a husband and four children in a walk-up apartment almost downtown. His parents were both dead and he had been on his own a long time. His friend lived with his parents, who had a cafe in town where there was also a bar. There was loud music, food and drink. Their home was actually out of town a few miles. But the girls soon became curious about whether the car was there or not and often went by close enough to be able to see.

Shandol had to admit she was interested in the driver. He had curly dark hair, blue eyes, a smooth even-featured face with a high square forehead. He was thin in build, as far as she could tell. But the other was frankly fat for one so young and good-looking in his pleasant face. He had straight black hair, combed back, slicked down. He had a plump face and his dark eyes almost closed when he smiled. His was a ready smile, and a double chin was becoming evident below his round face.

When the car suddenly appeared beside them in their stranded situation, because it had already started to rain quite hard, the girls looked at one another and back at the maroon shiny car, and looked again as though to be sure it was not a mirage they were merely dreaming. A ride—any ride was what they needed. Shandol had hoped Rory Wheaton might happen along. But here was this chance again. Should they consider it they were wondering when, "You girls get in this car," the driver said, looking at Shandol. "We'll take yuh to the camp, or the nearest road to it. We won't bite," he grinned a crooked grin.

"And it's a-gonna pour harder any minute now," the other added. "And yuh can't say we're strangers now. We've already introduced ourselves all proper like, and talked, so now we can be your friends and get yuh outta this rainy walk."

"Let's do it," Margery said. "We'll get some more acquainted that way. It's the way we got acquainted with the boys in camp. We just talked and exchangin' stuff about ourselves."

The driver, Nicholas, as they'd learned his name by now, said something to his friend. He promptly opened the door, pushed forward the seat and climbed into the rear seat.

"Get in," he told Margery, motioning, grinning.

"Come on in," Nicholas told Shandol.

Though Dwayne was the name of Nick's friend, he went by Derry and seemed not to mind. Nick called him that of course. They were told his young sister called him that, completely giving up on saying his name.

The car was cozy, and the couples talked on the way back to camp, as the rain fell, the slap, slap of the wipers on the car kept the windshield clear in rhythmic time.

It seemed Derry lost no time in discussing a date with Margery. Derry asked Nick what he thought of it.

Shandol gave Margery their "you would" look and grinned at Derry.

"Will you go too?" Derry asked.

"I've not been asked," she replied, shyly.

"Oh, but I was goin' tuh ask before yuh got out," Nick assured Shandol. "We was talkin' of other things—" his voice just trailed off.

I've been babbling really, Shandol thought, and knew she was nervous. She had talked about life in the camp and was just asking him about his work when she was interrupted.

"Come on, Shandol," Margery pleaded, "Yuh know how they are about us girls datin' alone."

"Oh, all right I'll do it," Shandol replied, reluctantly, wondering what kind of date it would be called if she only went so Margery could go and if Nicholas had really intended to ask her, if the others hadn't rather forced the issue. They made the date for the next afternoon.

Shandol had read the letter from her mother headed, Greenway, Aug. 10, 1942.

Dearest Shandol,

I received your letter this morning at 8. Does it take three days for me to get a letter from you? Your letter was

592

postmarked 3:30 p.m. Aug. 8. We don't get mail off the north bound train on Sunday anymore. She doesn't open up.

It's been trying to rain. Showers everyday or two. Sorta warm and close today.

Lester went to Plainesville today. Dad aimed to go but thought he'd wait and see what kind of luck Lester had. There's a big timber job at Ft. Wood—? I wonder! So Aubrey Wittever said. Greener pastures? Dad said he was going if it was true. I would like to get away from here, but I'm not going to jump from the frying pan into the fire.

Did you get your washing done? I was afraid you was sick when I didn't hear from you.

I'm glad about your letter from Hugh. Guess he's happy as a lark too. Did you send him a likeness of yourself?

Dean was at the store nearly all day yesterday on horseback. He doesn't bother me at all now perhaps not so much as if you were here. Ha.?? But—he was with Frances last night at the show whether it was a date call it as you wish! He was with her three nights last week—so what ?? I hate to have to see any of the boys have to go to army, but we're in it. May have one or two myself.

You give credit to anyone you please (you're not married) but I'm glad it isn't done anyway. Plenty of time after this turmoil settles. All people can't be so mistaken—when so many tell the same thing about Dean must be something to a bit of it. Beatrice told him they didn't want any "drunks" around there. If he can make you believe something even if it's a lie he thinks he's smart!! What will it be later? I'm afraid its you that don't understand. He's just telling you a mess of gripe and getting away with it!!

Karen's as sweet as ever. She's cried quite a bit the last three or four days. I think she's just spoilt. Phew! Her gums are swollen that might have something to do with it. Maybe cutting teeth. She stays clean the biggest part of the time. She pulls up now in the little bed. Stands up to screen on window and pulls up too. I'm so afraid she'll fall.

Mrs. Colmay has gone to town again this a.m.

Dermott drove the car. (Karen got hold of my paper). I'm sitting on bed trying to watch her too. She fell off the bed again this morning.

I fed the kids last Mon. I feel like complaining but sorta feel sorry for the outfit. Mrs. Pierce went to the store the other day and asked Harry if she was crazy. Said she came over there the other night talking crazy. Maybe that's the solution? I wonder.

I could hardly wonder about it tho'. I believe if I had to put up with what she did I'd go crazy too. She hasn't let kids bother so much lately. She'll send one after one it'll stay until she sends another. Bobby and Silas are quite cronies. The Parkley kids don't come so much only when they want something. Bobby don't care about them anymore. Yes, Cal was down one night last week asked me about you? I knew you were writing to him. Why not?

Phil did Ardena dirty over the weekend. We had a picture show here Thurs, Fri. and Sun. nights. The Pearl Harbor bombing was a fake. Dad went but I didn't want to see it. Phil wanted to go up on the truck. I told him no use spending 30¢ for transportation when there was a show here. He got with that Kink Ballan outfit and Megan Jamish. Lost $2 somewhere or spent it—which ?? Last night he went with Shorty's at Plainesville to show. I don't know what will become of Phil. I'm still praying that something will save him.

We went to church across the tracks last night. First time I'd been to church there since I don't know when. I had to play piano. Played "Camping in Canaan Land," I think it's pretty. They were all new songs to me but I managed them.

Guess I've told you all the news this time. I don't go anywhere as usual so don't know much. I'll let you rest now. Be good and write.

Love, Mom

Shandol answered the letter the next day. Many times Shandol was hurt by the things her mother told her about Dean. And Shandol wished she could make her mother understand it wasn't as though they were engaged or anything. After all couldn't she see Shandol went out? Perhaps it was the company Dean chose to keep. Why *did* he pick on a girl of such doubtful reputation? Was that to embarrass them all, or couldn't he do any better? Was he considered to be still Shandol's boyfriend except by Frances and her kind who could not care, only think they were putting something over Shandol? That was a laugh to her! But it was true many of the young men had considered her his steady girlfriend, and had been told the consequences if they'd try to go with Shandol. This separation of Shandol and Dean was perhaps doing what her parents hoped: Showing Dean to be immature, morally irresponsible and certainly doubt provoking as to the type husband he would make. Shandol had too much to look forward to to brood or be depressed by any news concerning Dean Leonard. She was much too busy. Perhaps her mother became depressed about it because she herself was so tied down. Audrey needed to get out more, Shandol reflected. But it would be hard to convince her of that. There was Karen to consider and she simply had too much to do and too little money to really consider it. In fact it probably never occurred to her or to any of the family for that matter.

Shandol wrote in her usual bantering, chatty vein. She was never quite satisfied with her letters but she sent them anyway as she was afraid it would be awhile before she recopied them, or be in a mood to do better, if she could.

She answered the letter, captioning it, as all the others, the same: NYA CENTER, MIDHILL, with the date, this being August 13, 1942.

Dear Mom

You started off your letter of the 10th asking questions, so I'll begin mine by answering them. I suspect it does take you three days to get a letter from me, mostly because I mail them at night (in eve). Besides there's no train through here. They have mail cars (automobiles)to take the mail to Capital City. I think is where the mail goes. At any rate mail goes out of here by car—or so I'm told. One freight train comes here twice a week (I'm told) and then goes only to Milton which is about thirty miles away. In fact it's only a spur-line and mostly to carry stuff to make firebrick or take them from a plant here or something like that.

Yes, I finally got my washing done. Marg too of course. I even did three uniforms. The NYA would do that only I have found some that fit me so I wash them myself. Had about all my socks, underclothes, etc. to wash. Had three skirts to wash (you've seen them all) and as many blouses plus a pair of slacks and blouse. That's most important part of it besides three handkerchiefs. Ha.

I wrote to Dean a "heck" of a letter, told him I knew about it and for him to tell me about it all. So he had—in his way. I don't know if he was telling the truth or not. I told him he might as well tell me, after all I go a few places myself. I have a boyfriend here in camp. He has a picture of me and I of him. I told you about him.

I also like to go with a certain one up town, too. I've been with him twice. He drives a swell car. Makes $160 a month. Just yesterday he passed the examination for the army. But said he would go to the Navy instead. Construction dept. It'd pay almost as well as above. He's now head of a fireclay pit something or other, runs a shovel, a huge mechanical thing. I've seen the plant in Milton where it goes. Sure a large place. His name is Nickolas Johnrow. But back to Dean. Don't think he's feeding me a line and I'm swallowing it hook, line and sinker. I'm not! I'm making allowances for what he tells me!

That Colmay outfit! What'll become of the crazy outfit—the poor kids especially? Oh, my, maybe that woman is bordering insanity. I'm like you I wonder. Guess she can't help it.

Is Phil still asleep? I wish too he'd wake up. Ardena is a swell kid. I haven't heard from her this week.

No, I didn't send Hugh B. a picture of myself as I didn't have one.

Today is cleanup day so I had to quit just awhile. I also helped Marge write a letter to her boyfriend. She's "canning" him. Reckon it'll bring me bad luck? Oh, I'm not superstitious.

What do you mean you may be "closer St. Louis than you think"? By the way tell me if the timber job at Fort Wood is still open or a fake, eh?

It sure surprises me at the "date bait" Dean picked on, eh? I'd have thought he'd have gone to Folks Consent and some of the girls down there. A lot of them are gone though. Guess he has a habit of being in Greenway. He already has his call to be examined for the army. He was to go the 13th today. Brad tomorrow! Or so he wrote.

Mom, are you bothered yet by hay fever? I just wondered. A girl up here has hay fever which is bothering her.

Hope everyone's ok. Oh, by the way K.P. was so terrible the other night. I had to mop the whole kitchen by myself. The cook said I "sure knew how," that I was "getting it clean." Also my boyfriend watched me. Imagine that! I also had to wash pots and pans, did that first. There were only three of us girls and the other two were cleaning the long dining hall—mopped it, cleaned off tables and washed dishes. There's a dishwasher for that. The tables are the same painted gray as the chairs, and made here I assume. They seat six and are oblong shaped. Hold three trays and a little over in width and a little longer than three trays long—long way of tray. They are rather rough and crude, but not bad, and serve the purpose. The chairs defy description. They have one board to form back and "legs" with a slender board across the top. The legs are wide boards front and back and braced under the seat of boards. We got to eat during K.P. tho'. Had some good peach cobbler "like Mom makes" almost. Anyway sure tasted good. Also a glass of sweet whole milk and a hot dog sandwich. Then to bed! Well, that was worse as I was so full. 'Twas midnight when I got back here. By the way I dropped my watch while on K.P. won't run now. Another $2.50 to fix. But I really am going to have it fixed when I get paid. I miss it so.

Mom, if you want to hear from me again send me some stamps. Lands me, aren't I awful? But it's that bad!!

Please write soon. Tell kids "hello" for me.

Give my love to baby and always tell me how she's 'doin'."

Tell Tommy to write. How's Jane. Say "hello" to her and Lester if they're still there.

Do write.

Love to all,
Shandol

Shandol received a letter from Dean, which came after she had finished the letter to her mother. He was mad because he wouldn't get to see her before he left to go to the army.

The girls were all also made proud that day because they won both dorm pennants. Shandol's wing got the wing pennant and the dorm, the dorm pennant. They had worked hard for it, all girls cooperating. The only thing wrong was dust under one table, but it was still the cleanest one. The "judges" looked very closely for dust on window sills, doors, under the beds, in the ventilators, etc. The girls stood more relaxed now as the "judging team" went by the bunks. At first they had stood rigid, nervous statuettes, suffering pangs of uncertainty and inadequacy almost as though their lives were at stake. Now it was another part of the routine. They tried to do their best and could now take the results in stride.

The next day Shandol received two letters from her mother. Audrey had written her usual letter in answer to Shandol's, and then she had answered a card, which had come "on the noon train."

Greenway
August 12, 1942

Dearest Dearie,

Received your letter off the eight o'clock mail.

The letters have been coming on noon train. I should have written sooner but we did a big wash. Jane had seven pairs step-ins—seven pairs men's pants, seven shirts. Karen had eleven dresses, two gowns, don't know how many diapers, five sheets and pr. pillowcases for each and on and on. So am sorta tired. Just had what we could find for dinner. Have to cook supper anyway.

Friday is club day. I dread it as usual. Wish you were here! Haven't seen Dean lately. Did I tell you Kurt Butler was at home? Well, it was Leon Martin instead. Elma Butler is moving to Plainesville. She's working at the Currin Hobart hospital.

I canned three coffee jars tomatoes yesterday. I often think of you eating tomatoes. But lots of things I think about.

Mrs. Colmay has gone somewhere. Don't know what she has done with her brood. Silas is here. I sent Freddy home this morn. I aimed for Bobby and Tommy to help. Couldn't get anything out of any of them otherwise. They all have been scarce around here lately. I got so I've quit going over there. Every time I went two or three followed me home so I just don't go.

Karen pulls up to chairs now. Gets around fast. Funny to watch her walk along Tommy's bed in bedroom. She knows how to get down now. She used to cry when she wanted to sit down again. But she manages, now. She's sweet.

Went to church across tracks again last night. 10:30 when we got home. Don't think I'll go again soon. Don't seem to hear much of anything.

Marg's sisters Iris and Lorene were here yesterday trying to buy some wood. Didn't have any to sell though. Iris has the nicest figure if she can just grow up that way.

The men're all working today. Lester couldn't get in employment agency until Fri. He still has Saline, Kan. on the brain. Guess he'll spend all he's saved running around. I guess I haven't the right to say anything?

Yes, don't get discouraged. Just play like you're capable of doing a lot if you get the chance. Sometimes that's all it takes to do it—just think you can.

Mrs. Kasper has quit cutting through our back yard when she goes to town. But why should I care? Ha. The longer I think of it the less I think of her. Guess I'll have to love her?

I was afraid you were broke. I'm not half through but I'll have to get this mailed or you'll be longer getting it. I'll write again soon. You do so too.

Love, Mom

P.S. I'm using this paper because it's all I can find. So rather than wait I'll send it. Phil is too busy to write. Always gone or someone here. Buck and Hyman Sandler were here last night.

(They were cousins Shandol knew but weren't usually close. Hyman lived with his grandparents; and his grandmother was an incorrigible gossip.)

The night before it was Hyman and Dermott.
Mr. and Mrs. Borsek have gone to Ark. to can peaches. Della Bright (her daughter) is looking after the old grandma, Mrs. Burdett. Have you heard anymore from Hugh? You didn't tell me about the play suit!! So what about that?" Mom

The second letter was dated Aug.11, 1942 but had Thurs. 1:15.

Dear Dearie

Just received your card off the train. I'm sorry you're so broke. I'm sending a dollar. Tell me if you get it.
Ardena is here now. She and Mrs. Ruleton were here a few minutes last night. Then Phil was up there until 12:30 a.m.!
All are working today. Tomorrow is club day. As usual busy as I can be. Nothing really done. Karen's fine. Just stretches her little mouth from ear to ear. When she smiles, the black eyes sparkle.
Gertrude Jeffany is staying at Wise's. Don't know where Cloynes have gone. Since Mrs. Kasper doesn't talk to me I don't "heerd" anything. Ha.
Robbed a beehive of bees Sun. eve, maybe I told you? Got lots of nice honey. Such good color and tastes so good.
Ardena is going to take my big basket of ironing up there to do. Isn't that nice?
Sorta cloudy. Guess it'll rain tomorrow. Remember how it rained the last club day we had. I'm going to have cherry tarts and coffee.
I must get this going or I'm "afeared" you'll starve for ice cream.
Love, Mom
P.S. Had to borrow 3¢ from Bobby to mail this.

Shandol decided she'd share the one letter she received from Dean with Margery. They did not ordinarily read one another's mail but discussed portions from them they supposed would interest one the other, or concerned a member of the family and such. But because Shandol had received letters telling her positively the opposite of what was in the letter, she wanted Margery to see it and understand why she was so bewildered and yet marveled he could have the gall to write such to her. The others who wrote she considered more trustworthy, because she believed they simply would say nothing rather than invent lies. Could it really be he expected her to distrust her own family and friends, who'd really not gain anything?

They certainly wouldn't do it to make her feel bad.

When Shandol mentioned this to Margery she asked, "Shandol are yuh sure you want me to see?"

"Well, it's not going to interest you much, his writin' is awful, words misspelled and he writes all over the page. The margins and all around as well as where he should I mean. He repeats himself so maybe I should just pick through and read lines which I wonder about. I mean he's makin' my folks out liars—somebody *is*! I mean I just need to let you hear—you say who you'd trust if you were me."

"Shoot. I'm all ears," Margery replied, and sat on the lower bunk opposite Shandol.

"The letter's dated August 12, 1942, Folks Consent and the Route 3. 'Dearest S.H. of mine'(spelled 'myn') he begins it. 'Well, deer I am got your letter this morning.' Says he was glad to hear from me, 'but you say you can't come home before the 20. Well it maybe too late to see me hope not you can come before that I know you could come if you would only do it I have go to go be examined tomorrow 13 so it won't be long if you want to see me you had better be home by Saturday night.' He goes on..."

Shandol read looking at the letter and straightening it out more as she went along. "He goes on that they say he may have to go about Monday or Tuesday so if I want to be sure I see him I had better come on home. He says he wants to see me so bad and if I wanted to see him as bad as he did me I would come home. And if I don't want to see him why don't I say so. If I don't want to see him why don't I act it and write him the truth. One more time he will tell me to come and told me when he'd have to go to the army, so if I don't come right away I had just as well stay up here the good it will do me. It's his last time to tell me to come for he is leaving. And after that a few lines he says don't write and ask him anymore when he is leavin'. I won't know until he's gone. He will write when he is in there. Maybe that's the way I want it, he put. Says not to answer in a letter but to his face.

"But here's where I really want to start. He goes on writin' that he answered my questions in a letter he wrote yesterday (which I received before this). He says I can believe whoever I want—him or my mother. Says she don't know what he does. She sees him in

Greenway she thinks he is with someone if someone rides up to the station with him. He's not datin' anyone or doin' any drinkin' and that is all he has to say about the deal. If I want to believe my mother, he says, what she hears, or him, do as I wish but he is telling the truth and I can take it or leave it. But, he writes, not to be mad at him for what I hear. He says to tell the truth there's a lot of fellows around that *big* (Hah!) town that likes to talk and I should know that as well as he does and to believe *him*. And if I will come home I will see he's right. He repeats to remember what he said about coming home and for me to please come soon so he can see me before he goes to camp.

"Then he closes because 'dinner is ready' and writes, 'all my love to you from me. I am a true sweetheart' if I will treat him right and come home. He also puts love and kisses and writes around the margins to come home, to write, to answer soon.

"He also writes he saw Ellen and she talked like she might come up and she was a good girl, which I know. At the end is 'love and kisses Dean.' Some love letter huh? But then I don't guess I write such lovey letters either. But you see what I mean. What about that guy?"

"Shandol, I don't believe you care that much for him. If yuh did, you *would* want to see him," Margery replied. "I'm with yuh. I'd not let him feed me a line either. Just wait. Time'll tell. I get letters sayin' same as your mom. So, don't be a dope and let on you're believin' it."

"Mom says let 'im go. I'll learn what he is," Shandol said. "But, Margery, I know my folks. They wouldn't lie to me. I know it."

"Maybe the army'll make a man of 'im," Margery soothed. "He's young and he can learn a thing or two yet. If yuh ain't in love yet yuh ain't. So don't worry about it girl, huh?"

"Sure, Marg. You're a pal, yuh know it?"

"I'm glad yuh think so. And we do get on don't we?"

"I don't know how I'd manage without you!" Shandol exclaimed. "It'd be so lonesome I couldn't stand it. I just know it."

"Me neither," Margery agreed.

Shandol wrote to her mother the following day. She began the letter as always:

NYA Center
Midhill
August 15, 1942

Dear Mom and all,

I got two letters from you yesterday. One containing the

dollar. Thanks a heap. Boy, I was needing it. So yeah I got it.

How did you make out club day? Be sure to tell me about it. Were there many present? Did it rain?! I bet they made a big fuss over Karen didn't they? Just think last time you were hostess we had no Karen baby. Ha.

Was there really so much honey? I believe anything "at home" would taste good to me now. I'm so hungry for fresh tomatoes, onions, etc. out of the garden. We have raw vegetables—but only two slices of tomatoes when we have them, which is about once a week. We do have celery, cabbage, lettuce, and once in awhile onions. Once this year we had corn-on-the-cob. But you know what. I'd really like some fried taters. Ha.

Today in the wood shop I made an ashtray stand on the lathe. The boss said I made a nice finish job.

The wood was somewhat rough to begin with, but I made it all by myself, so I'm rather proud of it. The boss bragged on me and others stopped to stare at what I'd done. I was so 'flattered.' Marge, however, got in a corner and slept. Don't guess the boss caught her. She just feels she can't get a job so why be in a hurry to learn it.

Oh, by the way, Dean wrote he was talking to Ellen Garfield and she said if I came home she was coming back with me. I'd sure love for her to. I believe she'd like it. But it might be too crude for her.

Last night I was out with the guy who lives uptown and drives the nice car. It's a wine color VK '40. But I think I have some competition!! But I have another date with him tonight. Marge goes with us with Derry—another guy from town and Nick's friend. They seem really swell. Tonight we're going to a picnic. Don't know if it's a carnival or not. By the way Nick got deferred from the army again. I told you he passed the examination remember? The job he's on is classified 90 defense. He's six years older than I am.

What do you want to know about the playsuit? Do you think it's too late in the season? Are you going to need to make it or let me? Or buy? What do you need to know?

Why, Mom, I can come home when I please. I can't miss but three days of work. If I do I have to sign up again and have a good excuse for being gone. So mostly of a weekend is best to come as we'd have Sunday plus three working days, I think. (I bet you didn't think I'd see that note on the envelope flap did you?!)

I received a letter from Dean yesterday. Is he ever mad because he won't get to see me before he goes to the army. I haven't had time to hear from Hugh B. yet.

Oh, yeah, on this week's cleaning we got both pennants. Our wing got the wing pennant. The only thing wrong was dust under one table in sitting room, but still we were best. Boy, do they ever take close notice for dust anywhere—windows, doors, beds, closet shelves, under beds and ventilators—counts against us. We work hard for it (pennant) too. Or did I tell you?

Hope everyone's ok. Are Lester and Jane still there? By the way don't Dad ever think about me or what? You've hardly mentioned him in awhile. Just so he's ok.

Guess the kids are beginning to think about school. Are they enthused? Where is Phil intending to go? To Plainesville or Folks Consent? Has he money saved to go? About like me, huh?

Well, write soon. I think I've received three letters from you.

Love to all,
Shandol

The next day was Sunday but Shandol could not get herself in the mood to go to church. She didn't much want to go by herself and Margery was expecting her soldier boy, Cpt. Arnold Welch. She waited, and waited for him. In fact she waited all day. He never did show up.

"Well," she sputtered in fury, "it's the last time he'll stand me up!" Her left eye squinted so Shandol knew she was not only angry but also hurt, disappointed, and frustrated. Her eyes could give her away every time. She was even embarrassed, which added to her anger.

Shandol did not know what to say so kept quiet. There may have been a number of reasons why he couldn't make it, but she saw Margery was in no mood to rationalize.

By the middle of the afternoon she gave him up and when Nick and Derry came in the early evening she and Shandol went with them. Margery was soon lifted from her low mood of earlier in the day. It was better to date a guy when in a car, even if not with the driver of it.

It was Tuesday when a letter came to Shandol from her mother again. Audrey wrote a long letter, and as usual, Shandol was happy to hear from her. The letter was headed "Greenway,—Aug.17, 1942. She read;

Dear Dearie

I've snuck off in the bedroom to drop a few lines to you without being bothered. I've three Colmays again. I felt so bad I told her I'd keep them awhile. I'll have them here until five o'clock this eve. I'm not feeding them.

Mrs. Chilton came by after Jane awhile ago to go see Mrs. C.'s brother at Folks Consent. She never said beans to me. Guess it doesn't matter. She's married and 21. Sh-h. Lester has gone to Springfield. He went yesterday eve (Sun) to see about some farm work. A piece came out on front page of Sunday's paper about help being so short. He went to Ft. Wood to see about work. Plenty of work there but no place to stay and no way getting to and from work. So guess we're Greenway bound for awhile.

The rumors are now there's going to be a bomber factory go up in Colver. (You remember up the tracks about six miles?) Don't know how true it is nor where the rumor started. Only Della was telling us about it. Would hire 2,000 men so if that's the case I may be running a "Hotel" here yet. You see me? Ha. Greenway will boom if that's the case.

Here I've been chasing cows. Colmay took their calf to town this morn. Old cow saw it and she went through the fence. Dad and Phil are working. Aimed to go to town but didn't get their pay Saturday.

Saw Dean horseback riding with some dark haired girl yesterday. Didn't pay enough attention to find out who she was. It's getting to be such a common affair we just don't pay any attention. Wasn't Frances, she's blond, but she's (Frances) sure snooty to us all, especially the kids. Bobby went out there to a marshmallow roast the other eve. She mouthed so at him, he said, he finally told her "to kiss my ankle!" Old Dean's "date bait" don't have to be so grand!! Grand?? Ugh! Bobby didn't stay long. I don't wish her any bad luck but she can have Dean so far as I'm concerned. Seems his aims don't run very high—yet he told Phil he "wouldn't give Shandol for a hundred Franceses." Don't know why he acts so possessed!? Too bad all the Johnny's go to war. This world is just full of Dean's type.

Dad said if he could get 55¢ an hour at Fort Wood he was going, so I thought perhaps we might get to leave. I finally told him he could go and we'd stay here, but he said he wasn't going by himself. Didn't want to sell the cow and maybe have a job six weeks.

We can *kinda* bob up and down here without sinking for awhile, so think we'll hang on awhile. I don't see how?! When I think about H.S. books to buy, clothes for school I sorta feel down and out. I don't have half enough clothes, just have to get by the best way I can. I sometimes wish I was away from it all!

Guess I'm laying down on the job. I should be thankful for a lot. I have so much to do I sometimes have to neglect Karen to keep things going. When you cook and wash dishes three times a day for this mob (sh-h) besides a dozen other things that pop up you feel like when night comes you're ready to go to bed. Nearly ten or eleven o'clock every night before we go to bed.

I didn't sleep a lot last night. I felt so bad this morning. I'm going to have some teeth pulled tomorrow *IF* my heart don't fail me. I think when Karen sleeps I'll nap too, but I'm so far behind with my work I have to make good use of her nap time.

I don't have hay fever much yet. Only when I'm in the weeds too much.

How often do you have K.P.?

Della Bright is having something up there tomorrow. Something about the Bibles. She never told me just Tommy, so guess I won't go.

By the way the club was a howling success. About the usual were here. Della, Mrs. Milcher, Mrs. Davis, Mrs. Ruleton and Ardena and Mrs. Millie Middleton were here. Had a good time tho'. Got lots of compliments on my cherry tarts. They were real good—the pie crust too. Baked them in the little pan like I used for Dad's lunch. Crust was real *short* and flaky and had whipped cream, coffee and graham crackers with a filling too. I'll try to get hold of a paper if I can to send you.

Myra (Connard) Shipley is home. She's ill. They took her to Dr. Said one of her lungs was affected.

All the rest are okay in Greenway. Mrs. Kasper is sure *bowed* up at me. Oren and Nora have gone to St. Louis. When he gets rich guess we'll have to move?? Ha. Mrs. Kasper is telling it around now "wonder what Mrs. Sonnett has in her garden" she had to keep her chickens up. I'm going to remind her some of these times when she's passing thru (yeah, she does some now, why doesn't she tell people her chickens were eating my tomatoes instead of telling that.) I'm paying for my garden and I'll do as I please.

Chester Parkley is sawing the wood (poles)Dad and Phil cut. They sawed a little Sat. eve but belt wouldn't stay on saw rig. They'll finish 'ere long.

You'll have to get "time off" to read this if I don't quit.

Hope you are well and working hard.

They tried to get Lester to go to NYA there at Midhill when he was at Plainesville Fri. at employment office. Said in an eight week course he could draw 86¢ an hour as a machinist. So wouldn't you feel funny if you'd be drawing that 'ere long? Dean's eyes would bug out too! Guess we'd all take notice. Well, anyway work hard you'll be drawing something before long.

Karen's fine. Climbs up to chairs going and coming. She can smack her lips and is so cute. She learns so quick. Beginning to crawl on her hands and feet. Sure tickle you to watch her.

Here I'm rattling again. Here goes for this time. Good-bye now. Tell me if you need any money before you get your check. Don't have lots but will help you all I can.

Be good. I'll declare I must quit. Write soon. Bye till next time.

Love,
Mom

CHAPTER 45

It was late that night, or early in the morning as the case actually was, when all was quiet, all the girls seemingly having escaped to the land of Nod, in the arms of Morpheus, or just plain sleeping like the proverbial log that Shandol was awakened suddenly, startled. She sat up in bed, feeling the presence of someone standing near her bed. She could not see a light from the supervisor's room, a small night light strangely comforting when awakened feeling the strangeness of being away from home.

It took her awhile to become completely awake and assure she wasn't having a strange dream.

Then Mrs. Crocker spoke. She was standing near Shandol's bunk.

"There's a man in my room, girls," she stage whispered with terror in her voice. "Psst, girls, did you hear? There's a man in my room." she repeated.

As the girls aroused from sleep, Mrs. Crocker repeated again that someone was in her room.

Shandol, Margery, and nearby bunkmates began to get up, dressed in various sorts of nightwear, and ready to gang up on and do battle with whomever had entered. They were told he had come in through her room's private entrance on the back side of the building. He was perhaps halfway into the room when the girls could see the shadowy figure of him. Mrs. Crocker, thus reinforced, switched on the light. She could then see it was a young man, so she spoke to him, by then reasonably sure he was from the camp.

"What're yuh doin' in here?" she scolded in a forceful voice.

"Tryin' to find my bed," he muttered, slurring his speech.

"You're drunk," she admonished him. "Get out of here. Yuh don't belong here, now get out!" Her fear had sped and she was angry.

"Wrong barracks," he hiccuped, and staggered out the door.

"Oh, that—that *brat!*" she exploded. Her long blue night-dress of some flimsy material became her in the light as she stood partially shadowed. How pretty she looked to have been roused from bed. Perhaps she hadn't been in bed long. Shandol was watching her. She rubbed her forehead with her fingers. She appeared also slightly embarrassed.

Mrs. Crocker had had a good look at him and promised herself she would turn him in when morning came, her mouth straight lipped and determined.

"I'm sorry, girls," she said, "but he scared me. I was half asleep too. And wouldn't you just know no night watchman around. Let's go back to bed. I'll take care of it in the morning."

It took the girls awhile to settle down again. There were some ifs and wonderings as to why the door was not locked. Perhaps she would not forget anymore.

"He was really harmless," Margery reassured. "Wonder what they'll do to 'im."

"Wonder if many have drunk around here," Shandol remarked, as it was so frowned upon in her upbringing. "Wonder if he'll get sent home, extra duty or what. I hope they stay away from us."

"Guess the rest'll know to be more careful," Vera Brunt giggled. "Oh, me, good-night girls. It was just a Saturday night drunk comin' home."

It seemed the signal for silence, but Shandol was longer going to sleep. After all it had been right beside her bed she had seen the frightened supervisor, she hadn't known what was going on and, trying to awaken from a sound sleep had been frightened.

It was the talk of the camp the next day. All the girls could learn, however, was that there would be a meeting of officials and supervisors to handle it the next day. And their imaginations: "What if it had been someone from the state hospital, or needed to be there, who could have hurt someone!" Yet they saw humor in it too, at all the sudden excitement and horror they had experienced at a mere boy, too drunk to do anyone any harm.

"Yeah, yuh coulda prob'ly knocked 'im over with a feather," Margery quipped.

A new rule was circulated during the day—an actual coincidence though. Everyone would have two hours of K.P. a day.

There would be several working together, but everyone thought it fair enough. Margery and Shandol learned they would be on from four o'clock to six o'clock p.m.

Shandol, in the afternoon after work, wrote a "special letter" to her mother, but there was also the usual one they could all read. She had just washed her hair and was letting it dry. She wrote:

NYA Center
Midhill
August 19, 1942

Dear Mom and all,

Got your nice long letter yesterday evening. Was so sorry to learn you are feeling so poorly. Hope you are better by now.

Was I ever disappointed this last week! The station wagon from here was in Plainesville—and again today! It went as far as Maple Hill yesterday! Can you beat that? We tried, Marg and I, to ride down that far, but they wouldn't let us. Two girls from Maple went, however. There were also two girls from Waiton who wanted to go so they said that would be too much vacancy in the dormitory. Maybe it will go again sometime. That would be at least a one-way ride. The two girls from Waiton have spoken to go next time. Reckon we'll ever get to come home for a few days? We were all sure disappointed and blue for a few hours. I swore as soon as I got my check I'd come home and stay, but I have decided to buy me some clothes instead. After all "Nick" (for his middle name) isn't going to the army yet! Ha. Sure love to see you all however.

Did Jane go home with her mother, or is she still there? Hope she's ok. Lester will just about end up in the army. Do you suppose he'll stay in Springfield? Have you heard from him?

Wouldn't Greenway boom if a bomber factory went up there (so close)! I believe I'd be tempted to help run the "Hotel"!! Ha. Do you reckon such good luck could be in store? Have you heard anymore? Be sure and keep me informed. And answer my questions!! Some you didn't answer: Where's Phil going to school at? Hasn't he helped himself (financially) to go to school?

The other night Marg and I were in town. Johnny's ex-girl friend saw me. She didn't do a thing but get in his car, get his car keys and just sit!! Was she ever cursing Marg and I. She got so mad at Marg's boyfriend that she started on her too.

She said, "I thought the blond (meaning me) was good-looking and she is! But the other one I don't think is a bit good-looking!!"

Was that girl ever stubborn! She sat in that car until 11:00 o'clock p.m. so they couldn't go anywhere.

Last night we fooled around town—them and us. They got a big watermelon and we ate it. They also told us then about that girl. So, oh, do you know what Marg said—even terrific guys, too—well, she said that she'd heard many a girl curse me behind my back. She said "Shandol, I've been with the girls in Greenway. They sure envied you. Even the boys would talk about you and compare you with the girls they went with. Even Frances' boyfriend. Yeah, Shandol, he's asked me to make dates with you for him! I heard Randolph Gilmore say one time, 'she's a perfect doll'. Mom, do you know why? They said my character was above reproach!! She said they envied me my good looks too. Marg said this; "Shandol you were considered by far the best looking girl in Greenway." She said when Wesley Kampkel was home he'd given his right arm to have gone with me! Also Ralph Gilmore. But they were afraid to ask BECAUSE THEY DRANK!

No wonder I had no real friends in Greenway—too much jealousy. She even quoted Madge Middleton saying to one of her boyfriends after he'd said something good about me, "You've never said anything that good about me"!! They also wondered (!) at Marge's associating with me and even envied her my company. So am I ever hearing things. Marg has told me this. She said she has had many a boy try to get her to make dates with me for them. Could I ever have guessed that?? Never! Some must have wondered at Dean. Did they ever! No wonder he was so jealous (or possessive of me, eh?) I wonder if he had ever heard stuff to that effect. I almost wish I had never seen him. Aren't I wicked? I guess I am. Even Marg says I've changed! I don't know how though. I was so tickled that she told me—not so tickled either only just so surprised, it's a better word, that I couldn't wait to tell you. So I had to write it. She also added she had seen Frances and Madge M. turn away many times when my name was mentioned. But I guess they looked up to me. Marg said her aunt Harriet and uncle Dolphus thought I was the ideal. And I used to feel so sorry for myself because I had so few friends. I'm still glad it was that way. I thank no one but Mom and Dad. And I'm going to try awful hard to continue to be that same good girl when I come back too.

It's rather hard to, because here on every hand one hears a "d--m," "God dern," "sh--," etc. Imagine all this. Guess I could have talked better than I have written it, but you can get the general idea. (And I supposed I had not one conceited bone in me! ha)

But it's like a window Marg opened to me! Even she envied me a little, she admitted (sheepishly).

I've heard so much about Frances, I don't admire her even a little bit. Marg knows her because she said she's helped take care of her when she was *drunk*. Yes drunk! She smokes also. Yeah, Marg said herself she had walked her many times in wee small hours of the morning to sober her up. Slapped some boy's hands to make them leave her alone!!

I feel like a kid beside Marg, almost. She's been "around" so much more. But she's not been bad. She told of a spiked 7-UP she drank once. Her big brother was along, however, and she felt so sure with him along. Don't tell this around now. I'm just getting it off my chest before it bursts. Ha. Maybe I've not been so bad after all? But I never saw myself like this—but rather just a self-conscious stick-in-the-mud.

Marg is in town this evening. I am so lonesome. I guess this will be a rather drab letter.

Guess I'll write about last night. A boy who was drunk came into Mrs. Crocker's (supervisor, our side) room. She saw him in the door shadowy. She was really scared. But he was merely lost. She finally just drove him out. Don't know yet what punishment he'll get for it. When he came in she was so frightened! No night watchman around. But he was too drunk to do any harm. But we were all very frightened for awhile. She came in through the door next to my bed when she was so scared. Woke several of us up. Ugh! Sort of funny now anyway.

Washed my hair just now. Need to wash some clothes too! Always something to do here too.

We have two hours of K.P. every day—from 4:00 to 6:00 p.m. I think I like it better that way.

Don't just keep yourself worried sick over that Colmay outfit. If she doesn't worry why should you? Did you have the teeth pulled?

If Karen walks on hands and feet she's a genius. Remember we read that in some paper? Wonder if it's true?

If I'd allow myself I'd never stop writing. Won't you dread my coming home with such an endless chatter?

Hope you're all ok. Kiss the "darling" for me.

I must take a shower and go to K.P. Do write soon. Send me some stamps if you can get them.

Our checks will be ten days late we heard today. Hate to borrow money up here. If you can't you can't so don't worry about it (if you can't send some).

Love to all,
Shandol

Shandol also received a letter from Ardena, who wrote a different type of letter from Audrey's. It was more youthful and revealed her interest in the younger set. She wrote:

Dear Shandol:

Will drop you a few lines to let you know I'm just fine only kindly lonesome.

Yes, Shandol I think Dean is going with Frances steady—or I would call it that—he is up every Sat. night, Sunday night and two or three times through the week.

We have been having some rain—sure helps the gardens. The tomatoes are getting ripe one by one. Can't get any to can don't look like.

The truck went to town Sat. night it was sprinkling but we went anyway and had a nice time.

Your mother had club Friday and I helped her Thursday. So please forgive me for not writing sooner. And I've got to help Della Bright at 1:30 this evening clean house. Yew!

Phil and me are just fine—he comes up about every night. If he can't come he sends Tommy up after me. So there is where part of my time goes. I like for him to come though he don't stay long.

Kid, Della and Harry Bright are trying to get me in the ninth grade—sure hope they do.

Phil made a talk for us at young peoples meeting.

Sure was good—he's going to talk Tuesday, too—he's naturally a good boy, ha—or anyway I think so. I think he looks good in his new hat.

Well, kid, I'll close 'till I get back from work and I will write more.

Well, here I am again—we had to clean up Della's whole house and yards—there is going to be over forty there tomorrow.

I think I'll go up to Plainesville tomorrow and get my last shot for typhoid.

They have been sawing wood at your place with the old buzz saw—sure sounds like home to me.

No we haven't got to go to the creek yet. Cal hasn't had time to take us.

Jack Alahle passed away a day or two ago. Rose got the telegram and was afraid to open it—she thought it was about her brother.

(Shandol thought. Yes, he was Frances' uncle.)
  Well, kid, I had better close and go to bed—think I'll go to Plainesville tomorrow—don't know for sure. bye now.
  Be good and if you can't be good be careful.
                          Ardena Ruleton

It was Friday before the next letter from Audrey came. And such a letter! Shandol was sure her mother was terribly put-out at her. It was dated simply, "Wed. noon."

  Dear Dearie:

  Today is letter day again. It's past train time don't know if I heard from you or not?
  No news as I know. I'm sorta blank. Karen's had an awful cold in her head but she feels better today.
  Don't you think it's chilly for Aug? We just shiver around here in the early morn. All are working today. Didn't get to go to town. Dad went Mon. after all. Came home from Hedda's about fifteen min. before train ran. I didn't go. I'll try to go sometime this week.
  Teddy C. is here. They have been shy for awhile. The baby (Jimmy) has had an infection in his mouth and glands. Has been pretty bad—took him to Dr. last week. Bobby griped about the kids being here holding Karen so guess she tho't she'd keep them in her own yard—suits me! Dr. said that was the third case he'd had in a week.
  Karen's bothering me till I can't write. She climbs up and hangs on to me, snatches everything she can get her hands on.
  Yes, I got your letter, now I'm blue! Shandol I can't understand you! Why you would like anybody that made such a spectacle of himself as he did. If you just will I can't help it. I've tried to warn you—but you won't listen. No use to preach but you'd better wake up before it's too late. If you was younger, I'd turn you up and spank you real good and say NO! Only consolation I have I've *tried* to make a lady of you. If you come home Dean *can't* come here. I'm not going to be ashamed of him. Don't want him around me. Beatrice Freedman can't high-hat me with that kind of trash. Oh, well—

As though Beatrice even had any right, Shandol thought. *She's not been all that perfect herself. There was talk of her and—boys—!*

You come home if you wish and marry him if you must—
don't think you are doing any good there anyway.

Somebody's tales don't jibe. That Nevin Hower said Dean
had gone to his brother's in Ill.—believe I told you before.
Another one of his lies. Just you go ahead and he'll lead you
a merry life. Before I cried I'd have something to cry about.

You can do with your money as you wish it's yours.

Guess you got the picture?

Jane is ok. Ardena was here awhile ago.

Karen's hollering so I'll quit now.

Write when you have time.

As ever, Mom

"As ever, Mom"? Shandol was stunned at the tone of her mother's
letter. What had she (Shandol) written? Her mother must think she
and Dean had set their wedding date! Nothing was farther from the
truth. Shandol was fighting tears, her eyes were bright with them.
She was rubbing her cheeks as though to wipe moisture away, when
Margery came to her. Shandol, ashamed of her emotions, turned and
started to the dorm, and Margery followed.

"What's wrong, Shandol?" Margery asked, a puzzled expression on
her face. "You turned pale up there. Now you look like yuh could cry."

"I am," Shandol admitted. "It's Mom's letter. I don't understand
why she's so hostile in it. And that's the word hostile. About Dean of
course. And and yuh'd think we'd set our wedding date or something."
She sniffed and wiped at her eyes, where tears gathered in spite of
her brave attempt at self-control. She looked young, defenseless and
quite helpless, managing to look desirable. "She misunderstands the
whole thing. I'm so miserable. I bet they think I'm worthless and a
nuisance anyway."

Shandol thought of the letter she had written to Audrey containing
all the compliments she had been paid. Still Audrey's last letter had
been long and chatty too.

Marg, I know she thinks I'm just being stubborn," Shandol
continued, as they walked slowly. Shandol wanted to talk about it to
someone, and Marg was handy right now. It was either talk or have a
big cry. Usually it was her mother to whom she went.

Strangly, to Shandol, it was about her mother that was now the
problem! Well, perhaps there would be both, but the crying would
come later.

"As I've told you," Shandol went on, "I am disappointed in Dean.
And I think he's acting like a little boy in a tantrum because I won't
come home. Maybe I flatter myself there," she shrugged, "but I feel

he thinks he's breaking my heart by his capers. My heart? He's hurtin' himself and his chances with me. He's—he's embarrassin' and hurtin' my family, because his name has been linked with mine. He just wasn't like that with me. So why does it make me feel so dirty?" The last erupted in a sob, but she controlled herself after weeping briefly.

"Yuh weren't secretly engaged or somethin' like that?" Margery wanted to know.

"Oh, no, not really," Shandol quickly denied. "He did consider us goin' steady, but he knew I'd be goin' out with others if I left. No one else had a chance down there, which is one reason my folks wanted me to get away awhile. He acted like he *owned* me, and he'd fight if anyone even looked at me good, let alone go with me."

"I know that, too," Margery confirmed. "But why do you feel so bad now?"

"Mom's letter helped. But it's my feelings for him. I don't know what they are." Shandol stopped under the tree between the mess hall and dorm. It was a large spreading oak and near their shortcut path. She leaned against it, her usually bright features morose, her eyes bright with unshed tears, her mouth a line of visible emotional effort at self-control, which she wasn't sure was intact.

"He was so different with me. Nobody understands this not even Mom. I wish she'd listen to me. I'm not ready to marry him that's for sure—yet. I'm not sure I ever was or ever will be in love with him. But I've hurt him. I know it. I've prob'ly led him on, as they'd say here. Maybe just to have a way to go, or because he was different—or both. I don't know. And so it's that too, that makes me miserable." She was quiet, thoughtful a moment. Margery was silent but studied her friend and saw the misery there.

"I wonder," she went on, "if I'd done more dating, if I'd ever even have gone with him so much. But I see now so many of the guys were so stilted with me—except Cal and Hugh. And I really wasn't serious with them. Mom and Dad like Hugh so well and his folks (well, aunts and cousins, perhaps his dad is neutral)would like us to get together. But he's so much like a relative. I always liked Steven when I was younger. I guess he was my first love, but that's all different now. I think more of him than Dean really. But Dean was himself. Let's go on to the dorm." They began walking on. "Once in awhile he'd say "G-----m," for instance, and then cup his hand over his mouth, realizing he'd made a slip and apologize as having said something not fit for my ears. But he didn't drank. So it's so hard to see him as they're seeing him now. I can hardly get it in my head it's the same person."

Shandol wasn't sure if she were talking to herself or if Margery were listening. It didn't matter. She was just giving vent to her thoughts anyway.

"It's your mother's letter that's hurt though?" Margery ventured.

"Well, it didn't help." Shandol conceded. "I ll let you read it. There's nothing in it but a verbal whipping for me." She laughed, hollowly. "I feel homesick right now and homeless," she sighed, which ended in a sob, but she went on talking. "Dean told me he was going to the army. I guess he thought that would get me home. He went to his brother's in Illinois. So he told a lie. So I've learned he can lie. I hate liars. It's like an insult to my intelligence, especially when he should know I'll find out about it. Oh, I must be boring you to death." She smiled wanly at Margery. "Thanks for listenin' anyway. You're a friend to me here. What do you think?"

"I don't think he's worth it all," Margery said flatly. "I know his family are supposed to be a fine one. He has a good mother and father—hard workin', God fearin'—as they say—but he's the youngest and a spoiled brat. Oh, I've wanted to say that a long time!" She grinned sheepishly to take away any sting it might bring to Shandol in her present mood. "They're just too many others to be so concerned with it," she added.

"If it turns out he mends his ways and loves me enough—and that will take some time to prove now—and I decide I love him enough, in time it'll work out. If not then perhaps it was never supposed to be, right?"

"That's the spirit," Margery patted her shoulder affectionately. "Maybe your mother just had a bad day and that was only the part that concerned you."

"Maybe so," Shandol agreed. "The neighbor kids nearly run her ragged and she has a lot of work and worry to cope with. Never enough money and school starting again. She gets discouraged I know. Maybe I should be there to help, but they don't want me to be unless I want. After all I stayed the year after high school, as they point out, which was a sacrifice they call it. I've always told Mom so much, it just seemed that in the letter she was slinging it all back to me, so it threw me. See?"

"Yeah, caught yuh off guard," Margery provided. "Looky, if we're gonna go to town to cash our checks and shop we'd better get goin'."

"Yuh're right. I shouldn't be feeling as though the world's on my shoulders. We've money to spend." Her endeavor to put spirit into her words was succeeding.

The girls showered and ready to go into town. Their minds were soon on going, anticipation of what they would buy. They knew they would have to choose carefully to make the small amount go as far as possible and still be practical in what they chose. There was one thing though they agreed on and that was each needed a nice dress

616

to wear. Their others were looking older by now and seemed at times quite inadequate. This especially when some of the other girls had nice things to wear even if they made them themselves.

As Margery and Shandol walked to town they were discussing the latest rumor making the rounds at camp. A couple had said they planned to get married sometime in the near future.

She was Vera Brent, a brunette, who was petite in size, with an outgoing personality—completely unselfconscious, as Shandol often thought. Her manner was coarse sometimes, yet about everyone liked her. She was so natural, so herself. She was not pretty. Her coarse facial features, including a large mouth, suggested a more mature person, almost mannish, which defied, and almost overwhelmed her tiny size and girlish figure. The guy was "Lucky" Jones, as he was called, and only a few knew his name was actually Charles.

But to Shandol she was a source of wonder and Shandol's assessment of her character was judgmental. She made coy remarks about sexual desires, which Shandol found as offensive as off–color talk. She thought no lady should speak in such a way. And the way Vera had broken the news of her approaching marriage was in her light-hearted bantering, offhand way: "We *better* get married before something happens." She saw the innocent questioning eyes upon her, and the blushes slowly rising to some faces. She amended the thought. "We love each other so it just sorta follows." There was a group of girls around her bed in the dorm as she had told them she had some news to tell. Curiously, all who knew came to hear.

"There is a problem," she conceded. "I don't quite know how to break it to my parents. And Lucky says I'm too old for him to ask them. At twenty-four he thinks I'm one of the grandmas of this place." She laughed light-heartedly and affectionately.

It had seemed, upon reflection, Margery and Shandol agreed they had seemed serious, but that they would wish to marry at such short acquaintance would take some time to accept. Their combined incomes were so small. How would they live—in camp? Apart?

"I'm wondering if Vera and Lucky can make a go of marriage," Margery said, the two vertical lines appearing between her eyes, and almost as if to herself. Shandol looked at her. She had come to notice the vertical lines, but not quite read them. Questioning perhaps now.

"They've certainly grown close here," Shandol reasoned, "and they're together ever'day and have close contact—maybe they got acquainted and feel they know each other in the short time."

"Yeah, together all but sleeping together," Margery laughed, and Shandol blushed, but couldn't resist her friend and also laughed at the joking remark.

"Anyway I think I'm falling in love myself," Margery added coyly.

"Marg! Shandol ejaculated. "Who on earth with?"

"Derry," she said simply.

"Ole Derry? Are you serious?" She saw her friend's serious face and it answered her question.

"But Marg, how does he feel? I mean I didn't expect you to go serious about anyone here," she was groping for words in bewilderment.

"It's not that bad yet," Margery amended. "But he does fascinate me somehow "

"That's better," Shandol sighed. "I don't want your folks to blame me if you do something rash. You hardly know him."

"Oh, I know that. Maybe it's just that he's so different. So hard to pin down to a certain type. And—so good natured. He treats me like a little lady, so I just can't help liking him a lot. You know what he calls the full gathered skirts we made? Our *windmill* skirts. I get tickled at him."

"But that's how I am about Dean. I like him a lot and we had some good times together, but I'm sure not yet so in love that I want to marry him. And just as long as these doubts are there I'm not gonna hurry. Something seems to press me to wait."

"You're smart there," Margery conceded. "I mean the way he's turning out and all."

"He's young, too," Shandol pointed out, "just my age. So why should we hurry? I'm not sure enough."

By then the girls were in town. They had taken the shortcut through the Bear Cave Holler, but had hardly been aware of where they walked. It was becoming so familiar now. Even the homes which lined the streets.

They went to the bank first, feeling it would be the best bet in getting the checks cashed. They assumed they would have been required to show their NYA identification cards but were not. The cards were small rectangular cards, which the two girls usually carried in small coin purses. Margery's small coin holder was made of an oilcloth—like material with an envelope snap closing. Shandol's was one her mother had crocheted of fine variegated pinks and white thread. It was round with a tiny (used) zipper. All residents were issued one card each month and the numbered days of the month bordered them. The days they checked out to leave the grounds were "punched" out, using a paper punch, by the supervisor. This was because they were allowed only three passes a week, plus Saturday and Sunday.

Shandol and Margery knew about what they wanted so went to those stores to find the merchandise. They bought dresses alike. They were black, but had white trimming which brightened them.

618

Shandol hoped it would make her look older, and they were within the amount they felt they could spend. They each bought a pair of practical walking shoes. Shandol had her old black pumps for dress-up. They bought black and white saddle oxfords. Shandol also found a light sweater for one dollar. She bought some ribbon for her hair, what cosmetics she thought she needed, two pairs undies, postage stamps at the post office and had some money left over. They both felt they had spent too much on only one shopping trip. Margery's purchases were only slightly different. She bought tooth powder, it was her time to buy laundry powder and she bought postcards. She had more money left over than Shandol and it must last longer. It was just as well it was time to return home, as they called it.

"Isn't it awful not to have more money?" Margery sighed. "So many pretty things to choose from but we have to be so *practical*."

"I know," Shandol replied, "but Dad says if you're liked only because you can wear fine clothes you'd never know if you'd be if yuh couldn't. Then maybe it won't always be so."

They seemed to lapse into silence, each considering this possibility in her own way.

"If only—" Shandol said, significantly.

"The jobs here work out," Margery finished. "Well, let's hope it's a start in that direction anyway."

Early Sunday morning Shandol wrote her mother a letter, dutifully, before going to church.

NYA Center
Midhill
Aug.23, 1942

Dear Mom & All,

As I am going to town to church I've decided to write a letter to take and mail. I haven't as yet received the letter you were supposed to write to me Wednesday. Last night, however, the mail wasn't brought in. I doubt if we get any mail today either.

It's barely rained here last night again. But it is so pretty and sunny today. The sky is a true sky blue and warm, but so far not too warm.

Last night a girl from town, who goes with a boy out here, stayed in our dorm all night. She came back where I was and said, "Do you sleep with your earrings on?" I said no that I just hadn't taken them off yet. She blew her old breath in my face and I already knew she'd been drinking. Guess she wanted to remove any doubt. Whew! Her old stinky breath nearly knocked me down. I don't know if the supervisor knows that or not. One of our supervisors goes home every weekend, leaving the other in charge. This weekend the one on our side went home. She's the one with the little boy. She will leave him with his grandparents this time. Here's another one of his "wise cracks." Do you know why Hitler sleeps on the third story of his home? He said it's because "his bed's up there!" Cute, huh?

Marg's army guy is here already. She is going to give him the works—brush-off—today, too, she's decided. He stood her up last Sunday. Anyway she has another date today. But I'd sure like to see her tell him off.

We both had dates with the guys in town. Went to Milton and had a swell time, including a good meal. The guy Marg goes with sure enjoys good food. I can't eat much out like that and never could. But they insist on it. As Nick has the car, Derry pays for whatever we do, including eating, show tickets, etc. It's sort of an unwritten rule. I noticed that down there too though, as I've probably told you.

Guess I'll get ready for church. Hope all're ok. Tell Lester and Jane hello; Hug Karen for me and do write soon.

Love to all,
Shandol

The day turned out to be a very nice day for the girls. One they could certainly write home about.

Monday Shandol received a letter from home.

Fri. A.M. Aug.21, 1942

Dear Dearie,

Today is letter day again. I'll have to hurry as usual. I laid down and slept, and slept too long.

I washed a few pieces yesterday. Karen had 17 dresses, 2 gowns, 18 or 20 diapers.

We went to a show last night. The picture show was a sorta sermon. Was pretty good. They sang, Shandol, and the songs were on the screen. Saw pictures of scenes as we sang "I Love to Tell the Story," "Old Rugged Cross," "Let the Lower Lights Be Burning," and they sang some booster songs such as "My

Little Light Will Shine" and some one verse songs. They had the kids who all had Bibles up there hunting up scriptures. That was who was behind it. That "free tract" institution, Pitts or some such a name. It was a man and his wife. The woman just loved on Karen and kissed her. Karen was so sweet tho. I'd sure love for you to see her. Bobby is her idol. She likes Bobby. He can do almost as much with her as I can.

Just read your letter. I decided the other one got you down. Ha. I know it costs lots to write every day but that don't keep a fellow from wanting to hear. Well, anyway, I've decided two or three times a week will have to suffice.

If you get a chance like that you mentioned (the station wagon?) come home for a little while anyway.

Yes, Shandol, I've detected a change in your letters. I hope you don't change too-o-o much—just as you've been will suit me. You are old enough now to begin to see. I'm glad you are. I saw Dean last night driving around the block, 1st by himself and then with Beverly Connards and Frances Dahle. I just made up my mind then I *wasn't going to let you go with him* if you came back. He's sporting Beth now. It would be just as well if you didn't write to him, too. I guess people thought I was too nice to associate with them (or vice versa) and that's the way I felt about a lot of them. (I feel I'm as good as anybody, but don't have so much in common as to associate with everyone, or have the means to put up a proper front as they might expect.)

I believe I answered your questions in my last letter (Wed.). Jane is still at her mother's. She'll be home sometime Sat. or Sun. Lester is working at the German's (Adora's). I believe he's becoming sorta settled now. Phillip is getting more serious now about school. Guess he'll go to Folks Consent. He and Ardena went to a show last night together. I was glad too. Megan Janisch was there and Evalene Ballan, Madge Middleton too.

Ardena swept upstairs for me yesterday. She's a swell kid. She said I don't like the looks of Megan. Ha. Ardena sure idolizes Phil.

Yes, Greenway would boom if a factory went up but haven't heard anymore. I'll keep you posted.

I've had more than one tell me you were the best looking girl in Greenway, and Allsup girls lived here too. The scripture says, "character is better than rubies," so that makes the man. I hope I can bring Karen up to be like you. That's my prayer and aim. If she'd just be like you. Bobby got through reading your letter. He said, "she's a darn good kid." (meaning you). Anyone can't help but say anything else. Dad says he guesses he was too hard on you, but I think sometime you'll see. He said you disappointed him a little, but I told him you were a darn good kid. I'm proud of you!!

Ardena asked me yesterday how you ever *met up* with Dean. Shandol, my prayer, each night is, "Where ever you are you're in his care. I believe He'll still care for you. Go to church. You'll be rewarded in the long run. Don't be a *sport* because somebody else is.

Yes, I'm glad you wrote. Eases the tension to me too. I'm sending you some stamps. I'll have to quit, Karen's time to be fed so will quit till next time. Write and be good.

As ever your best pal, Mom.

P.S. Mrs. Colmay came and bothered me again. So I hope to write more next time.

Shandol felt better about the letter from her mother. She was happy, if somewhat embarrassed to read the nice things her family thought about her, which her mother had written. It made her feel good about herself. What she was not ready for had been the idea of being set up as a model for her baby sister.

Perhaps Karen's life could be improved, because there wouldn't always be so many children around as she grew up and she would have more advantages. Shandol hoped so anyway.

And Shandol faced the possibility her dad was disappointed in her, and often wondered. After all she was so old to have to write home for money. Both ideas rankled somewhat. Besides Joel Sonnett expected such perfection from his own children, while he had more tolerance for the antics, failures and mistakes of other people's offspring. What had Joel expected of her, Shandol wondered. Always the Belle of the Ball? He was so strict how could she ever know what a "Ball" of the kind implied actually was? Had he still perhaps the idea she should have been an "old maid school teacher"? She supposed that even an unkind thing to call them, and she had not known one until she had gone to Plainesville to school. They were hardly pitiful, in fact she admired them. But somehow she wanted to be more as her mother with children and a husband to shoulder the responsibilities as her dad always had. But it seems he had had his hopes. Could he still? She did so want his approval and praise. But it was so seldom she measured up to what he wanted. It had always been so. Because she valued his opinion it often contributed to her lack of self-worth, though she could not have expressed that as a possibility.

How hard it seemed trying to plan one's life when everything was so unsettled. She was unsettled. The country's freedom was threatened and upset everyone's life, What was her part, Shandol often wondered. If only there were selections, even teaching, life would seem less complicated. For now she hoped she had found the means to the end of all the indecision and speculation.

CHAPTER 46

Shandol and Margery were virtually alone in their dorm. All was quiet. The sun came in their open window. It promised to be a warm day. A persistent cricket mocked them. The smell of clovers and summer baked ground filled the air, except for Shandol's talcum or tooth powder, depending upon where they were.

The girls were discussing their date of the night before. They had been up at their usual time, supposedly doing their usual morning chores. This included their daily grooming procedures as well as seeing their bunk area was clean and tidy. There was the bit of chatter which very often accompanied these times together, and particularly the morning after a date, which was the case today. There were other topics of course. These included reminiscing of other days and some of the unusual, or usual with a twist, of happenings at the Center.

One such unusual at the camp was Margery telling Shandol of the three girls who wore long skirts with a ruffled tier around the bottom. It was as though that was intended to make it longer. Shandol had noticed them and knew they were two sisters and a cousin. But they kept to themselves and were almost impossible to get acquainted with. They had stayed three days only. Shandol had not heard why but Margery had: They were simply too modest to live in such an open, no privacy situation. They could not take a shower if anyone else was around, even one of the three. They did not undress to go to bed. Shandol had been shocked at this news. That anyone could top herself in such matters she could hardly fathom. Yet how her heart would have gone out to them. Their only recourse had been to leave. Then Shandol recalled, what the girls called, flounced skirts, their timidity, their reticence at even speaking to the girls. How they must have squirmed inwardly at some of the chatter at their end of the row of bunks, Shandol had pointed out. They chose to leave with no intention of trying to adjust.

But today was their date of the night before. Margery had a large smile evident and her eyes twinkling in satisfaction and merriment, as she recalled the evening before.

They had had dates "with the men from town," as they often referred to them still. They had voiced amazement that the men, so far, were not the type whose sole interest was to park, to kiss and "pet." There were the many places they had gone and things to see. Interesting things that the girls had thoroughly enjoyed, and the men seemed to also as they saw them through the delighted eyes of the girls. It was as though the men sensed, or could obviously come to a correct conclusion, there were many things they had not experienced, and places they had not seen, particularly this place where about everything was new to them.

But after last night they decided they were decidedly going with men, not inexperienced boys. However, they treated the girls, perhaps they had not revealed their minds.

This morning Shandol was miserable! She was embarrassed, and all because of last night. She was not sure if it had been her ignorance or the shame of having learned of "such things" in the first place, or her innocent, but indiscreet questions, and Derry's obvious enjoyment of her discomfort, was the cause. It had probably been his idea, Shandol hoped. So it was to Margery she would turn to settle her mind, or "talk it out with," She had to learn if Margery had learned the reaction of either of the men, though of Derry's she was fairly certain. He would enjoy it!

"Margery," Shandol got her attention, "about last night—" she went on straightening up the bunk. "I'm so embarrassed at being so ignorant. What on earth got those men into taking us where they did?"

Margery could not have controlled the way her face lit up merrily, nor the broad smile, with a trifle of superiority thrown in also. "Oh, Shandol, I couldn't believe you and neither could Derry."

"But—" Shandol would have interrupted.

"No, wait. They realized you were sincere," Margery went on talking. "And Derry got a big bang out of it."

"He would!" Shandol mocked, "but I didn't!—I felt like some ninny. How was I to have known of such a thing? And how did you know, by the way?"

"Guess just dumb luck I knew," Margery replied, unruffled.

My brother is a few more years older than I am, than yours is to you. Besides he prob'ly couldn't tell you. But you were cute, Shandol, and funny. So—so uncomfortable and all."

"And ignorant," Shandol finished. "A red-light district indeed! I bet I never forget it again. What do yuh suppose Nick thinks of me?"

"Oh, he'd be crazy about you no matter what. He was probably impressed! Why, do you know, he once told me to go with Derry so he could go with you? He didn't know—and I didn't either, or even guess—that I just might like to go with Derry anyway. And one reason I like to go is they have an interesting place to go or idea of something to do which appeals to me. I think last night was Derry's idea of a joke. He knows how you are, easy to blush, you know. Bet on it. And he just did it for fun. Don't be mad at us."

"Well," Shandol softened and let her somewhat ruffled feathers droop. "But I wish there had been someway you could have got me word so I wouldn't have made such a fool of myself. My profound exclamation of what's a red-light district? I don't see much but houses and buildings, must have been a scream!"

"Oh, live and learn," Margery cracked, the smile still on her pleasant features. "I realized such already and then some—awhile back that is."

"But why?" Shandol persisted. "They didn't think we wanted any part of such a thing, or were hinting or something, do you suppose?"

"Heaven's no, girl!" Margery exclaimed. "I told you Nick cares more for yuh than that. It was just one of our new experiences to them, and as I said Derry got a kick out of it. I guess we're something different to them."

"Well, I should hope so," Shandol said, reflectively, "if they know about stuff like that." Shandol pouted.

"From their reaction we should be glad," Margery soothed. "I only knew what I had overheard, which was just the barest of facts. I wasn' much ahead of yuh. Let's just wonder what's next, Shandol. No harm'll come to yuh, I betcha, if Nick has any say."

"Oh, really, well, that's something anyway. As Mama said I'd just hafta be myself, so that's what I was, I guess—my old ignorant self."

There was a pause.

"Oh, I'll tell yuh how Carol Middleton told me once how she was embarrassed with a guy," Shandol continued the conversation. "One time she was at a party with a group, of course, and somehow the subject of cesspools came up. The young people there had sort of paired off, so to speak, and Carol asked the boy she was with, as quietly as possible, so as not to reveal her ignorance, I suppose, what cesspools were. He explained. She said she nearly died of mortification because she hadn't known. She said her face turned red and she just knew he was overheard when he told her. So we small-town girls don't learn some things very early do we?"

Shandol, after rationalization and realization anyone could have an embarrassing moment was at least somewhat placated, and less ill at ease. She supposed she could even face the men again. No doubt she was expected to.

"Guess I'll write Mama," Shandol added. "But some things I just can't put in this letter, can I?" And she laughed at herself.

Shandol pulled the writing paper from the box of inexpensive stationary from the drawer built under, but into her bed. There were two such drawers. One Margery used. Shandol also had pencils there, selected one, and sat down to write her mother a letter.

626

Dear Mom,

I'm just back from work and dinner. Guess I'll answer your last letter.

Today at noon I got the derndest news—a letter from Dean again! He's left for the army! He just got my letter and wrote back on one sheet that he was leaving in about ten minutes. So he's gone by now and I didn't get to see him. Boy, that's what hurts me! Of course you think I'm silly but—but—well, I might never see him again. Well, I do like him—or did—I'm not so sure now. Anyway the news makes me blue, but it won't last long. I can think of the good times we *had* anyway.

Yesterday, Marg and I went to Capital City with Johnny (or Nick) and Derry. We were just out driving around. I was with Johnny. The day before—evening we were in Columbus just driving and such.

Yesterday we were out gadding again. We drove to some dam out east and south—or whatever, in the afternoon; the day before too, about 25 or 30 miles from Columbus. We took pictures there. Marg and I had on our "windmill" skirts, as Derry calls them. Then we went by one of Johnny's aunt's and his brother and family were also there. I and Johnny posed in a picture with their 15 month-old daughter, Joy. By the way, the dam is on the Cedar or some such name creek.

Don't let anyone feed you any lines about the Ozarks being rough country. Some of this around here is as hilly, rocky and rough as the Ozarks are—especially the river hills. We fairly covered lots of ground yesterday. Had supper in Capital City. Had fried chicken. The boys are really swell to us, so we enjoy ourselves.

Marg gets as undecided about going home as I do. She leads me to think she may go home right away. Arthur may get a furlough and she wants to be there while he's home. Listen, if she goes I'm not likely to stay up here long afterward. Ellen Garfield would probably come up here if I did go home and back. Marg too, if she gets tired of staying home.

I've got my check, I guess I told you that. Well, I've spent it. Most of it at least. Here's some of what I got: A pair of shoes—

627

yes, again—for $3.05. A new dress, $3.06. Some ribbon, cosmetics, a sweater, $1.00, and some undies. I also bought some stamps too.

Today in the shop I made picture frames. They're 5 x 7 inches, I have a picture of me for one of them. I don't like it though too good, so if you don't, I'm going to give it to Marg. I don't like it but I want the frame. They look real fine.

Wish I could see everyone.

My new dress is black and white. Marg has one just like it. My shoes are also black and white, oxfords. We have to have that kind as we walk so much.

Wish I had some of my junk home. You can't imagine what all I've accumulated. I got me a nice big mirror, which I get lots of good out of. It's all mine. Marg has no interest in it, but she does use it.

Do write right back. I'm so blue or something today. I can hardly write. Maybe when I have a good cry I'll write again in a different mood.

Tell all hello—write soon.

Love to all,
Shandol

Shandol received a short letter from her mother. It had been written Saturday and was short and to the point. Shandol read:

Sat.1:25

Dear Lil Birdie:

I'll hurriedly scribble a few lines. Rainy and cold today. Should have written sooner but thought you might be coming home.

What would Marg do about coming home? If you *are sure* you want to *come home* and *stay* I'll mail you the money next week.

All are well. You write right back then. I'll do whatever you say. I'll answer your letter later. Dad wrote. Aimed for me to mail it yesterday, but didn't hear from you until north bound train—too late then. I'll quit now. This'll be a little news. We're waiting for a yes or no. Write.

Love, Mom

P.S. Send picture of Karen back. Isn't she sweet?

Dear Dearie:

If you'll notice I started this letter last night but Karen wouldn't behave while the rest went to church, so I went to bed too. Just got through washing. Had a big one as I didn't wash much last week. Ardena helped me and Jane. Thought I'd go to town today, but Dad didn't quite get the well done so he went to help finishing plastering. Guess I'll go tomorrow. I'm about all in. Don't know what I'll do. I'll have to quit working so hard?

Did Dean come by? He has gone to Illinois to visit his brother. Guess he thinks no one will see him and know what he does there!

Why in the world don't you sleep enough? You better stay home a night or two and sleep!

I don't know how to take you. One time you write you wish you'd never known Dean, the next time you wish to see him. I think you'd be just as well off if you never see him!?

Yes, you may send the letter if you wish. What interests you interests me. You wish not even Dad to see it? I'll not let anyone see it.

You better watch out. You'll be given double K.P. Yes, I love good mutton. I wish I had a big bite now.

Who do you call "them"? You said you ran around with *them*.

---- I'll see about the playsuit tomorrow. May just try to make one. Rather you had your own things as one might get a *besease* (as Lester used to say).

What do you want to do about coming home? Do you want to wait and see what Hugh Burdette does? Mrs. Borsek (his aunt)said if Hugh came home he'd help you with your bus fare? Ha. You tell me. I'm not so excited about him coming and helping you!

Guess *he* (is it Nick) is like the Alden boy and thinks everyone out to do the chasing. Just let him go. That's what he wants. But after he finds you won't then he'll do the chasing. Guess the $160. a month job has gone to his head?

Yes, I'd like to see the picture. I might like one. I'm sending Karen's picture, but you'll have to send it back. It's Mrs. Colmay's. I'll have some made. You should see her. She's beginning to wave bye-bye so cute. She has a tether (?) chair now. Hedda's. Dad wanted to buy it but she said "you know I might need it again." Guess no prospects anyway.

Maudy Thelby is great big. Guess she didn't let that big kid suck long enough. Ha. Mrs. Thelby is at Pipkins now.

Jane came home yesterday. Lester worked Sunday all day. All but Phil are working today. He went to town on school bus, but I know no such good luck as him going to Plainesville to school. Mrs. Borsek came to talk to him but he didn't happen to be here. I wish he'd go there (Plainesville).

Dolores and her hubby came back yesterday. They think Loyd Parkins and Grover Downey will get to come back on furlough. Have Macs heard from Arthur? Don't see any of them to talk to them. Harriet has quit coming I guess! I don't go anywhere though. It's one o'clock. No dinner for us washer women so I'd better quit. Ardena said she wrote to you so she has probably told you all the news.

Karen opened her mouth real big and let out a big squeal, just as I snapped this picture. I think it's cute though, don't you.

Jane is writing now. You write her a line. She always likes to read your letters. I'll quit till later. Be good and get enough sleep once and you'll feel better.

Love, Mom.

P.S. Send picture of Karen back. Isn't it sweet?

The same day Shandol received the letter from her mother she made time to sit down to answer it.

NYA Center
Midhill
August 25,1942

Dear Mom,

I'm very much awake now and I think I'm in the mood to write—but we shall see?

I just now got your letter. I really wasn't looking for one until at least tomorrow. Sure was a sweet picture of Karen. How she must be growing! She looks so nice and healthy. Sure love to get hold of her. I'll send the picture back (as bad as I hate to!!).

Who on earth wrote such a letter to Phil? And where did he get it? I mean did it come in the mail? Does he have the least idea who wrote it? Boy, it is a "whizzer." What does he make of it? I'd call it almost fan mail like Clark Gable might get or something wouldn't you? A beautiful redhead wanting him to marry her and go off somewhere, with a lot of sugary words and flattery thrown in. Hah! Hah! Or was he mad about it?

I think Dean had better make up his mind where he is going. He said he'd go to Jefferson Barracks then into the army. Said he'd write to me in a day or two but I bet he doesn't. Especially if he's gone to Illinois—and after his telling me he had to go to the army. He was really in a hurry when he wrote. Just wrote he'd gotten his "card" and was leaving in about ten minutes. It is somewhat vague.

What did you mean when you wrote in your letter, speaking of Hugh B., "I'm not so excited about him coming and you"? Did you mean me being excited? I doubt if he comes myself. Yeah, I'll wait until I hear from him again. Guess *maybe I can* wait until almost time for my next check when I can use part of it to come back on. I said maybe—ha. Sometimes though I think I can't stay up here another minute. But I think of the soldier boys who must have the same feeling but not the same freedom to leave if they want to.

The "them" I run around with is Marg and her boyfriend and Nick. If I didn't go some I'd be in the "bug" house. (I shouldn't write that really. Sometimes jokes are made, or concocted probably: about the insane asylum being here.)

What would you do without Ardena's help? I haven't received her letter as yet. Some of the mail I don't get for sometime. (Maybe three or four days.)

No, Dean didn't come by. (I guess you can tell I'm going through your letter and answering questions to be sure I get them all.) His actions beats me too. I know you dislike him, and I do too—because I liked him so well and he let me down being as he's been drinking and wrong type girls. Do you see how that can be?

I stayed home last night and slept. We've a "new rule." We always have to, from now on, Monday as that's council meeting night and every girl must be present.

But this week I'm getting up at 4:00 o'clock. K P. of course! After Saturday that'll be changed (probably to worse hours.)

I've told you what I wanted to do about coming home. But I may write anytime to come. I still like it up here all right, but I'd just like to see everyone so badly! I hope Lester doesn't have to leave until I can see him.

Yeah, Mrs. McN has heard from Arthur. he's wanting them to send him a $45.00 ticket to get home. He's wanting to see home folks too. I bet they try to get him too. So if Marg takes off, you know I'll come too later.

A girl up here married a boy here. (I mean both in NYA.) She is trying to compose a letter home. Ha. Mrs. Avery said she's sweating blood. She's 24 and he is 26. That makes two married couples here. Another just came about a week ago. The girl who's married bunks on my side of wing. She smokes, "damns" around and has a weakness for beer and "such" I'm told. I've heard some wonder if they'll stick it out—if such a marriage can hold?! But back to the newlyweds. Don't know why she's so concerned. She's of age. But she's so afraid they'll resent "Lucky" and that would hurt her so she says.

Don't you remember every person has a blood test and physical examination up here? I might not get a disease anymore than anywhere else.

(The bugaboo of an awful disease of "that" kind had been drilled into Shandol until her fear of them was very real.)

What's a teter-chair?

When does school start? Guess the boys are waiting anxiously. Is Bobby glad to be in H.S.?

Tell 'em all hello for me.

Tell Jane I'm so happy she wrote. I enjoy it so much when the rest drop a few lines. Tell her this can be her letter too. I'd just have to write her about the same thing. She may not care to read all this stuff. Do you? Sometimes I wonder. I'm glad she's doing well.

Time to go to supper. I'm going with another girl and she's ready to go, so I'll close.

Give my love to all,

Shandol

Jane's letter had been little more than a short note. Shandol knew Jane supposed Audrey wrote the news. She always began a letter "how are you fine I hope." She wrote she felt ok. She had gone for a week to visit her parents. She mentioned Lester still worked for the "German's." She and Tommy had walked to meet him, which was quite a walk. She was worried Lester would soon be drafted because his name was up for "next call." She repeated Dean still liked to hang around. Spent a lot of time in Greenway. She wrote she would try to write more next time.

632

The rest of the time the girls considered just routine at camp. Their three passes for the week were used for dates with Johnny and Derry. It had just recently been working out that way. Some of the fellows at camp had remarked about it as they had asked for dates, and accused the two girls of going only because they had a good car in which to go.

"Is that a crime?" Margery asked, once, neither admitting nor denying the charge.

Of course, it was partly true. They didn't really know the men very well. But they were always shown a good time, and could think of places and things to do, and didn't expect to park and "try them out" yet. Not that they weren't affectionate, but the moments were so natural and open, of which Shandol approved. She felt her parents would also. Yet the camp boys had done the same. They hadn't tried to take advantage of their situation there—at least with them. And the two girls were inclined to believe in the other girls with whom they were in contact each day. If it were looked upon as unsophistication or their being slightly naive they would hardly have been able to consider it. It was neither in their upbringing, nor experience except to give the other girls the benefit of the doubt unless hit with a distinct truth otherwise.

They had truly been shocked, for instance, when there had been rumors of one of two girls making money, in a questionable way, for clothes it was considered she did not have money to buy, but buy she did. She was not able to afford them when she came. The two girls had come to Wildwood when Shandol and Margery's group had. They were from the same general area, but had not known one another either until they met on the trip. One was a blond, curly haired girl with an innocent baby face. She was not pretty, but rather comely. She carried herself importantly, and was quite apt to attract a second glance. However, her good friend was quite the opposite, who was a blue-eyed brunette, who wore thick lens glasses and her teeth were prominent and seemed large for her mouth. She was the first girl to make the skirt of the plisse material (later dubbed the "windmill skirt" when worn by Shandol and Margery). She seemed not to mind when they copied hers even to the exact color and type of material. That was the blue background with large white flowers and leaves print. Somehow the rumor got back to the supervisor and the blond could only date when her friend went along. Whatever truth or rumor that remained was squelched. And she suddenly realized she didn't need more clothing, which could very well have been the case as space to put them was limited anyway. The rumor, of course touched the other girl. She gained the same reputation, and the rumor persisted awhile. In fact it was added they would not be there long because they would not be recommended for jobs. But if time could take care of such things both the girls and those at the camp could only play a "wait and see" game. Shandol could not repeat these rumors.

On Friday Shandol received a letter from Nancy Rayford, who had come with them from Wildwood, but had stayed only a week. She and her friend Edna Backers had gone, hoping to go elsewhere. When Shandol opened the letter she found it was to Margery also.

It gave the address, date and they were both surprised to learn it was a St. Louis address. It began:

Dearest Shandol and Margery,

Well, kids, how goes things? Don't tell me you are still with it. If you are I've got to hand it to you.

I really miss you both and all the rest of the kids. We had a lot of fun didn't we? But I'm not sorry I left, because I really hated that place.

Edna and I got home and we decided we were going to St. Louis the next week. You know, we thought I was the one that would be held back by my folks, but my folks didn't care and Edna's wouldn't let her come so I came alone and I've been here ever since.

It's real easy to find work if you've had any experience in anything and if you're 18. I was neither, but I found work after so long. But, kids, if you all have stayed in Midhill this long, stay until you finish, because that machine experience will really help and I don't mean maybe.

Boy, I'd really like to see you both. Say, does any of the soldiers ever come over? Shandol, do you still hear from Johnny? I hear from Don once in awhile. He said he was coming over payday, but whether he will or not is a different story. I'll tell you who'd I'd like to see is Fred Lewis—the guy that was with me at our Ft. Wood dance—remember?? Margery, I'll bet Arnold is the one that's been truest of all—you lucky girl.

I meet soldiers quite often. I met the cutest one last weekend from Jefferson Barracks—he was a doll. Kids, I really have a lot of fun up here, but like every place there are times when I don't like it.

I wish you both would come up some weekend. I board with my girl friend and her husband, and can go and come when I please. Bring some Ft. Wood guys and we'll have fun.

Kids, write me and tell me everything.

How's Mrs. Avery and Morris coming along? Do you ever hear from Edna?

All for now.

Lots of love and stuff,
Nancy

"What a nice letter," Shandol told Margery when they'd finished reading it.

"Yeah," Margery agreed.

"We must answer it sometime," Shandol vowed. "Wouldn't it be nice to be able to go to the big city, be on your own and do as you pleased, work for what you want and need. But it is completely out of my dreams. I'm lucky to get away from home at all. Even this place is better than nothing. Somehow it gives a ray of hope."

"Yuh said it all," Margery assured her.

Shandol's and Margery's weekend started out as most of them did now, because they were expecting dates with Nick and Derry.

They came for the girls earlier, however, and they were given permission to miss their supper there as they would be having supper out. They went to a good spot north of town, perhaps seven miles, where another interstate highway intersected the one on which Midhill was located, and had a good meal at a "truck stop."

After the leisurely meal of good food and friendly gab, some teasing and jokes, though none of the latter caused Shandol to blush, they got into the car again and wondered what they could do besides go to a show or drive to the next town. "Let's go to the fair," Derry finally suggested.

"Tonight?" Margery asked.

"No, we'd go there and stay all night in the car and be ready first thing next day," he replied.

"I doubt if they'd let us," Shandol said. "That doesn't sound so good to say when askin' to stay overnight."

"Tell 'em we're takin' yuh home," Derry suggested.

"It won't hurt a thing," Margery replied. "Nothin' 'll happen."

"My folks 'ud have a fit," Shandol proclaimed, "if I mentioned that."

"Don't tell all yuh know," Margery suggested.

"But stay all night?" Shandol persisted. "Even the guys in camp might hear of it and get the wrong ideas."

"Yuh could really take us to where we live," Margery goaded Derry.

"Yeah," Shandol added, suspecting joking, "to the other side of nowhere."

"How far is it?" Derry asked.

"Somewhere between 150 and 200 miles." Margery's tone deliberate. "We've never really tried to figure it out," She added. "And some of the highway is really crooked."

"Yeah," Shandol added, "some of those curves are almost 90 degree angles. You know like a perpendicular corner." She made a T with her fingers to illustrate.

"You girls 'ud really like to go, wouldn't yuh?" Derry smiled at Margery.

"In the worst way," Margery admitted. "But we could never get down there and back in a few hours."

"We do have a curfew out here, even on weekends," Shandol added.

"Let's see if we can get permission to go and you stay overnight," Derry finally joined the conversation.

"Listen, it's nothin' to kid around about," Shandol remarked, seriously. "We get homesick enough without you guys goin' on with all this talkin' and teasin'."

"We're not teasin'," Derry said, firmly. "Are we Johnny? Whataya say?"

"Why not?" he replied. "Do the girls good to see their folks. Maybe they'll stay around longer."

"What about the State Fair?" Shandol asked.

"Oh, we go there every year," Derry shrugged.

"It ain't that we wouldn't like to go," Margery said. "But it really's not practical."

"Let's go ask the lady in charge how we get the permission," Derry said.

They were soon on the way back to camp. They asked the supervisor on their side of the dorm. She led them to the day room and sent for the other supervisor. They conferred briefly, the one finally deciding to go along with whatever Mrs. Crocker decided. At first Mrs. Crocker demurred, as though there were too many questions and possibilities. The girls knew she was weighing the odds as one possibility could be they merely wanted to be gone overnight. How could she really know whether the men actually aimed to take them home or not?

"Who's driving?" she asked. They pointed toward Nick.

Mrs. Crocker turned pointedly toward him. "You do aim to take these girls home?" she asked. "I understand it's quite a ways."

"We're not goin' to get them in any trouble here, if that's what's worryin' yuh," Derry interrupted.

"We plan to take them home," Nick said.

"Okay, girls, I'll give you the benefit of the doubt this time," Mrs.

Crocker smiled. Shandol thought she looked so pretty when she smiled. Her dark brown hair waved around her face naturally, in a rather fluffy manner. Her regular features, good facial bone structure, white teeth, she was a true brunette and a truly handsome person. She shook her finger at the girls. "Don't you let me down. Perhaps you'd better bring a note signed by your parents—or one of 'em."

"Oh, good." Margery exclaimed, and grabbed Shandol's hands, looking into her smiling face.

"When'll you be back? It should be by eleven tomorrow night remember," she told them.

"Oh, we can make that easy enough—unless somethin' really bad happens to the car or something. In which case we'll let you know," Nick promised.

And that is how it came to be that Margery Kay McNeeley, Shandol Joy Sonnett, Johnny Nicolos Norman, and Swayne Johnrow Woodley began the journey to the south part of the state Saturday night in late August. It had all taken time, the talk, the decision to go, and asking the supervisor and it was growing late (to the girls at any rate). They figured it would most likely be past midnight before they could hope to arrive at their destination, but as they set out the exuberance of the girls was so evident the men could scarcely miss it and it proved to be catching. Not even Derry's sheepish comment, they could still go to the State Fair and fake the signatures, dampened their spirit.

Shandol was secretly horrified at the thought, but knew she could never do it and get by with it. Suppose they checked? They must by now know her mother's writing from her letters. Margery treated it as a joke however, and goaded Derry with "we wouldn't dare—you wouldn't dare give us such a disappointment tonight."

When the girls had dressed for their dates that afternoon they had no idea they would be doing anything special, so they had decided to wear the simple gathered skirts they had made, and Derry affectionately called their "windmill" skirts, because they were so full of gathers making them wide at the bottom. They were of blue plisse (to save ironing)with large white flower and leaf design. They had added white blouses and otherwise casual and unpretentiousness. Now they were glad they had worn the skirts for their mothers to see.

They had also prepared for their weekend pretty much as they usually did. Each girl had washed and "done" her own hair to a shiny cleanness, they were fresh from their shower baths and a bit of makeup only enhanced their happy faces, which now seemed redundant. Their faces were flushed with excitement and expectance.

Shandol, as they were driving out of town, seeing a bright star in the west, as they had headed south, muttered under her breath and barely audible to even herself, the childish wishing upon a star: "Star light; star bright—" she went through it all and wished they would indeed make it home all right and then back again. Then promptly put it out of her mind as foolish and was just because she was a bit nervous, going so far with almost strangers. Though she tried to have complete confidence in them she wondered if they expected payment. Of course, they had strongly denied any such idea, but the State Fair having been mentioned by Derry made Shandol wonder about him. But at the rate they were going and the direction they were headed, there could be little actual doubt but that they would make it home in a few hours.

Shandol and Margery worried about and voiced their thoughts wondering what kind of shape things would be in when they got there. Would the house be a mess, each wondered. There was no way of getting word ahead of themselves now. Shandol especially worried that it might be a bad time. It just might turn out that lack of enthusiasm or some circumstances had kept Audrey from worrying about the house. Perhaps there would have been a group of people there and any evidence of the muss let go until morning. The next day, for instance, Jane or Ardena might help.

So the girls worried as they discussed it, and Shandol learned Margery had the same worry. Her younger brothers and sisters could make things look mussy, if not dirty. After all weren't they younger and more of them.

"Don't let it bother yuh," Johnny told her. "Just be glad you're goin' to get to see your folks."

"Yeah," Derry added, "women worry about the silliest things. We're not goin' to inspect the housekeepers, yuh know, we're on a trip of seein' you girls so happy at goin' home."

"Yuh know, you look so pretty tonight," Johnny told Shandol. "Your eyes are so bright and shiny, yuh look happy, you're cheeks are so rosy and your hair shines in every light that touches it."

"Hey, John," Derry mocked, "I didn't know you could talk pretty words."

"I ain't much for it, am I? Anyway you're not supposed to be listen."

And so they were a close-knit group as the darkness enveloped them, the headlights of the moving car slit the dark curtain always ahead, though it was a star-bright night. The car was their haven as it moved them smoothly through the night.

They made a late stop at a café outside the largest town between their starting point and home, and a little less than the halfway mark. It was at an intersection of a major highway going to points southwesterly and northeasterly. The intersection was referred to as

638

the Wye as the intersection resembled a Y, rather than a crossroad. The café was a popular one it seemed, as there were several still there, including many servicemen who were not with dates, and no doubt from the nearby army post.

The men ordered a "plate" meal for each of themselves and the girls, including soft drinks, though Derry, because he was not driving he said, ordered a beer.

Shandol squenched up her nose when the beer came before the food order.

"What's wrong?" Derry asked, looking across the booth table at her.

"I smell that stuff," she grimaced. "It's terrible. How can yuh drink it?"

"Never thought much about it," he replied. Guess I just learned it like smokin' or somethin'." He was not a heavy smoker, but he did smoke a cigarette there. Johnny, on the other hand, rarely smoked. He smoked a cigar once in awhile Shandol had noted, or rather it seemed to her he chewed on the end of one, as he was forever trying to get it lit and to stay that way.

As they waited the girls went to the ladies' room. In turn the men also vacated the booth. This way there would be someone there if the food was brought.

While the men were gone the girls glanced around, passively curious about other patrons of the place, wondering what kind of place it really was. Shandol knew Johnny had become acquainted with the place when he had worked for awhile as a truck driver while the nearby army camp was being built.

As Shandol gazed around, one serviceman caught her eye and winked. She was embarrassed. She saw he was handsome (and knew it, she assumed) dark haired, yet a serious-eyed young man. She was not close enough to be sure of the color of his eyes, but she was sure they were a dark shade of blue because of his fair complexion.

When Johnny and Derry came back Margery was teasing her friend about it. "Don't let Johnny know it," she said, and it seemed to Shandol she hoped he'd hear.

"Let Johnny see what?" He had heard.

"That soldier guy winked at me and she's teasin' me," Shandol laughed.

"What soldier boy?" he demanded, immediately incensed. "I'll punch 'em one, pickin' on my date to flirt with."

"Here's our food now," Shandol replied hurriedly. "I won't even look at 'em again. I know yuh think girls have a weakness for uniforms, but we don't want to see no fights in here and he don't mean nuthin' to me. I'll never see him again most likely and wouldn't remember him if I did. So there."

As she ate Shandol hardly dared look at anyone in case Johnny was watching. She certainly kept her eyes off the uniformed men.

"These plate dinners really make a big meal," she said, conversationally.

"And, um-m so good," Margery added.

They had fried chicken, mashed potatoes with gravy, vegetable and salad, even desert, which she was sure was extra. It was delicious and thoroughly enjoyed by the girls as they had had an early supper, eaten hurriedly. As they prepared to leave, when finished, Johnny still hadn't forgotten the winking incident.

"Just show me that soldier and I'll call 'em outside."

"I just won't do it," Shandol said. "I'm sure he meant no harm—just a lonely guy away from home. He could even be engaged to marry—how'd we know. It isn't as if he touched me or even said anything."

"Aw, fergit it," Derry agreed. "Poor devil—even if he would like to have your girl."

"Don't say that," Margery scolded. "Say, I don't even see him. Guess he's not interested when he found she had a date and don't change 'em in the middle of the night."

She punched Shandol secretly with an elbow. But Shandol refused to look around in case Johnny's eyes would follow hers and somehow she gave it away if she saw him and recognition flashed over her face.

When they were in the car Shandol apologized. "I'm sorry about the whole thing back there," she said. "I want yuh to know I didn't wink back. I realize you guys are doin' us a real favor takin' us so far and I'm certainly not interested in being picked up, yuh should know that!"

"Johnny wanted him to know it," Derry interposed.

"I don't like brawls anyway," Shandol continued. "I think they're disgustin'. That is what few I've seen or heard about."

"I'd felt better beltin' 'im one," Johnny insisted.

"Oh, you men," Shandol sighed, resignedly.

"Let's not let a soldier with good eyesight ruin our trip," Margery rejoined. "Tain't worth it."

"A level-headed observation," Derry smiled at her.

Johnny was quiet after that for awhile, as he kept his eyes on the crooked, unfamiliar, dark blacktop road ahead, stealing glances at the girl at his side from time to time.

Shandol was also quiet, though she heard Margery and Derry exchanging small talk of small incidents of each her or his family. Margery hoped her oldest brother would be at home, though she doubted it.

And so the miles and minutes were ticked away, and long before they arrived at their destination Shandol and Johnny were also talking amicably again. When they passed through Plainesville, Shandol explained she had finished high school there, so that brought back memories. They drew attention to the one-way street circulating the county courthouse, so different from Midhill, which had intersections at each corner. Plainesville's entered the center of the block. As they passed on through and on down the highway Shandol could point out certain landmarks even in the dark. These included Deadman's curve, a sharp, blind curve in the highway, a "bent-elbow" curve, which had indeed been the scene of several accidents, many fatal. It was one which could fool the driver unfamiliar with it, or a careless driver, who, as one wag had attested, "tried to straighten it out." On farther was the county farm, on to the bridge, which was the railroad overpass—and always referred to as the "overhead bridge" by local residents.

Then loomed a modest sign, "Greenway," and Shandol pointed the way to her own home. At least there would be room for them all, even if she had to give up her room to the men and she and Margery sleep on the floor on a feather tick.

When they arrived it was after one o'clock, Shandol knew she must arouse her parents. First Joel because he could hear them, then Audrey so as to introduce the company. It was also she who would decide where they should sleep. As Shandol suspected it turned out to be no problem. Bobby was aroused to sleep with Phil and Tommy went downstairs to the cot in that bedroom. Karen still slept in the baby bed.

Audrey made up the bed across the hall from Shandol's room, and the first door to the right at the top of the stairs, with clean sheets, pillowcases and even quilts saved and kept clean for company, and which she had made herself. Shandol's room was quite as she had left it, except all the bedding was freshly laundered in case company came. Shandol and Margery shared the bed. It was not the first time the girls had spent a night together. In fact, they often had. Shandol had also spent nights with Margery but less frequently of late. Again she was accused of having ulterior motives and had gone to see Margery's brother! The bothering, nosy gossips! The memory flooded over her again. This would be different, with Joel Sonnett as chaperone, there would be not a feather ruffled. The girls bid the men shy good nights and thanks.

The girls talked awhile of their memories, the trip, the resident center and what they hoped to get out of it. But they were also exhausted after all the excitement, the journey, and lateness of the hour, which was nearly three a.m. when they settled to get some sleep.

"It's so good to sleep in my own bed again," Shandol had sighed, sleepily, the moment she had settled down.

"I bet," Margery agreed. "And I'm so near home I feel good too."

"Too bad we must sleep," Shandol observed. "But I am sleepy and we don't want to sleep all day tomorrow."

"You're so right," Margery agreed.

After it all, their brief good-night was "see yuh in the mornin'." All became quiet.

x x x x

As the girls were settling to their night of rest they were completely unaware that two very concerned women at the camp had, only a short time before, also settled to sleep, realizing the "die was indeed cast" and they could do nothing about the situation now.

Because hardly had the girls had time to be taken out of town when the two lady supervisors looked at one another in sudden, but almost simultaneous dismay.

"What have we done?" Mrs. Crocker spoke, a look of incredulous wonder on her face.

"Have we thrown them to the wolves?" her companion asked, her hands on her face one on each side of her mouth.

x x x x

As Sunday was not a day the family got up as early as week workdays, Audrey had breakfast ready shortly after eight o'clock. She had made to have hot biscuits, scrambled some eggs, fried potatoes and made gravy. She also had rice and raisins, in case someone might want that, as she prepared it often for her own family. She did not usually prepare all these at one time, in fact to save money, one or more was usually all. But she hoped with this variety everyone could find something they liked for breakfast.

Joel showed the men where to wash up. Though Shandol and Margery had fallen into their habit of washing before going to bed, last night had been no exception. So a hand washing and face splashing to look wide awake seemed adequate.

Shandol hoped the others enjoyed the food as much as she did. She felt she overdid it somewhat, but it all tasted so good!

But she hardly expected they would, except perhaps Margery. As it was remarked by Shandol, even though she disliked drawing attention to the "country-type meal," it turned out to be more than the men

642

were accustomed to having. Sometimes Johnny felt he hadn't time and stopped for coffee or had dry cereal and coffee at his cousins where he stayed. Derry had remarked his mother made him a hot breakfast sometimes—even if at the restaurant.

The first thing after eating was to go to Margery's so they would know she was home and how happy she was to see them. They seemed surprised and unbelieving that they had truly finally made it home, even for the short visit this would be. They visited awhile so they could meet every member of the family, and they could see the company Margery kept. Margery would hope her parents approved, though of course they approved of Shandol. They too were just finishing their breakfasts, the younger ones still in sleepwear, so shy they barely wanted to show their faces until coaxed by Margery, she must see them as she hadn't in a long time and she just had to hug them and have them see her friends and they couldn't stay long, which was true. Johnny went to work early on Monday morning.

Audrey had told them she would look for them for dinner shortly after noon, so they visited at Margery's, drove around to see Greenway, explaining bits of history, legend and pointing out interesting people or homes. It did not take long. So they then went to Sonnetts to wait for Joel, who would go to Sunday school as he still taught the "Bible class."

Audrey prepared a good meal of fried chicken, home grown vegetables, mashed potatoes and gravy, and especially green beans. Shandol suspected in her honor. She so loved them. Her mother had opened a large jar she had canned, to save time and Shandol enjoyed the way she prepared them, with onion and a slab of "fat back" in the iron skillet. Also Shandol loved sliced tomatoes—she could eat them right off the vine also, and recalled how she had often taken the "saltcellar" from the table, gone to the patch and eaten her fill. Again Audrey had prepared a variety, as she wasn't sure if the men were finicky about their eating. She told them, had she been sure they were coming, she would have made light bread buns, though she usually didn't bake bread on the Lord's Day, except in such cases. But there was homemade light bread, and an un-iced cake, faintly warm, she had "hurriedly stirred up," she told them, with canned peaches for dessert.

It was such a treat to Shandol to be eating at home, that her exuberance created a genial atmosphere and it would have been hard for the others not to enjoy the meal.

Shandol, in her excitement, even hailed the canary for his concert. "Timmy bird, I know that's you," she cried happily, watching him sway on his perch in the familiar way he had of seeming to put his heart and soul into it. He had a dark dot on his head, a few gray wing feathers, otherwise he was a rich yellow color. "Right, Mama?" Shandol asked. "He's such a good singer Mama sure has no trouble selling his—uh—offspring—" she blushed, looked at Joel, who promptly became engrossed with his food.

Audrey had already told them, even before they sat down to eat, not to worry about the dishes. She had told Shandol she wished they could just sit and talk, but realized it was impossible, as she had her friends along, and she knew it was exciting and that they could do whatever they liked.

Shandol did point out she was wearing the skirt she had made.

Audrey told her she had thought so and aimed to ask. She wondered if Shandol had had any trouble doing it.

"Findin' the time was the big problem," Shandol laughed. "But a girl at camp had made one, so we got some pointers from her. You'll see," she sought among the soft folds of the skirt for the opening. "It's only a snap fastener placket, with a button band. I had to show Margery how to make a buttonhole. But all in all it was nice to know we could do it, as well as having an extra change of clothes."

The girls, Shandol and Margery, wanted to go where they had had good times, and even thought the men would be interested to see. They drove to Folks Consent, as Margery had gone to school one year there. Otherwise they went by the cheese factory, its only industry and which set it apart from Greenway and many other small towns. It did not take long to show the town, but it brought back memories to the girls, only a few of which they mentioned.

Shandol did not care to bring her boyfriends into any conversations, except casually as she was not sure what Johnny's reaction would be. They did reminisce about the small café and dance hall, though Shandol had never been to that part of it where they danced. Shandol had referred to Dean as a guy she dated some and he didn't dance and she couldn't either. The Saturday night movies, cowboy for him and a love and adventure story for her, though she liked both kinds. How could she help liking the singing cowboys?—but double feature night was that and a double treat. The town they had gone to these movies was next down the highway, a larger town. The highway did not go directly downtown and they knew so little they only saw the west edge of it. The next state was only two or so miles and they wished to see Titan Springs.

It was beautiful to see at any time of the year but especially in summer. There was the park area beside the spring where the reunion was held each year, church groups, schools or certain groups or grades and even family reunions and picnics were held there. It was also busy because of boat riding, dancing and a general playground area.

But back of this was a more formal park-like area, where there was a "fish hatchery" so-called. There was a building which was comprised of a roof and sides of wire such as was used for chicken fences. In this enclosure were aquariums and the fish were visible. Fresh water bubbled in and water flowed from various glass tanks at all times.

Outside were symmetrically placed shallow pools, supposedly with fish in them. And indeed some were visible in most of them. They were placed in well kept, landscaped lawns, with shrubbery; flower beds and weeping willows shaded the pools.

Shandol and Margery sensed and could even see the men enjoyed seeing the place. It was certainly different. There was a bridge crossing the lake and also a walkway across the dam. A powerhouse was located across the walkway, but so far as the girls knew no tours were allowed. It was hardly that big anyway. They walked across to see one side the deep blue waters, the other a splashing, playful spillway making a large waterfall. The water then joined Eleven Point River. They went to the water's edge, where others had come to rest and let children romp. There were weed and rock formations that were formed as only nature can blend them to perfect harmony with the setting. Even fallen logs added the rustic touch.

It was a warm, vibrantly clear August day. More agreeable weather could hardly have been ordered. Pigeons perched on the bridge and powerhouse. Others flew across the lake into the wooded area along the river. The air seemed so pure as to lend light-headedness in its freshness. It was a day which would chisel itself into Shandol's memory never to be completely eroded by time, of that she was sure.

The men were so impressed with the spring and dam they wanted to see the town bearing the same name. It was small, which surprised, and, perhaps, disappointed them. But there was hardly time to regret the fact as they had to start thinking of getting back.

As the girls had decided to take some things back, mostly clothing, and having asked Johnny's permission to do so, they went to Margery's first. She not only picked up what she wanted but after a short visit bid them a final "until next time" farewell. There were tears and mixed feelings in the good-byes and abundant thanks to the two men for bringing the girls home, which the men thought much overdone, as they could not know the proportion such a gesture could take for someone not used to having such lavish favors bestowed without some compensation. It took some doing to convince them they had done it for a date and it seemed nothing to them. However, the men had not been so confronted, though they had somewhat expected Margery might come home this way, they had supposed she might ask for help with the gasoline to go back. Such was not the case. If it was all right for Joel Sonnett's girl it was certainly fine for theirs also!

But what they, nor any other family member or visitor knew was that Joel had spoken privately in the kitchen, having made it a point to do so.

"How many cigarettes yuh smoke?" he asked his daughter.

"Oh, I try to limit it to half-pack a day," she replied flippantly. But the look of horror, mixed with a whipped dog expression she realized he was serious. Could he think she did that? No, he was asking. He knew there were pressures. She pulled him by the neck and raised to her tiptoes to kiss his tanned, as yet unwrinkled cheek. "Dad, I'm kiddin'! I've not done a one yet, honestly."

It would kill him, I believe, if I drank, she thought. He still worries about me. I'm still his Li'l Birdie; still part of the nest, not completely flown away. "Please Dad, believe me," she pleaded.

She saw the ripple in his jaw, his mouth's familiar movements showing emotion, his face so expressive in relief and gladness.

"I'm glad Sis, really glad," he managed.

Shandol took time, hurriedly to take a sponge bath, in her parents bedroom. She changed her dress and put on a long sleeved one, as she had brought no sweater. She and Audrey had made the dress of blue gabardine material. It had shrunk some, as it had been washed a time or so, and was a bit shorter than she liked, and Shandol could tell she had gained weight. She took a few other dark or fall dresses, and even included her winter coat, as she explained she didn't know when she'd be back. It surprised her brothers.

"I know I prob'ly shouldn't," she admitted. "But I might need it before I get back here. And maybe not. It could change my luck. Here I'm prepared for anytime and it may mean—just my luck—to have to cart them home again! And anyway I can somehow. But it's soon goin' to get cooler if this trend keeps up, so just don't you make fun of me until we're shown."

"Oh, don't be so defensive," Joel told her. "If it helps you feel more at home take more."

"No," she said, "just what I have, which I can carry on my arms. Even Johnny might get the wrong idea and he don't care about these—I asked him."

Shandol took time to confide to her mother to forget the playsuit." Johnny don't like to see girls wear them anyway, he said."

"I don't either really," Audrey told her. "But I just didn't want you wearing anything besides your own things."

Margery had also changed and this helped convince the supervisors they had indeed been home. Each girl also had a note.

Joel had composed a note, adding his appreciation, but Margery had not trusted her mother to do it, so did it herself and they both signed it for her.

Though it had not at the time entered the minds of Shandol and Margery that they might do other than go home as they had said, they learned there had been speculation and suspicion. It seemed Margery had mentioned they had thought of going to the State Fair over the weekend. So the supervisors were quite obviously relieved when they came in about nine-thirty that night.

"We're sure glad to see you girls," Mrs. Crocker smiled. "After you left we had second thoughts. We thought what if those guys were lying to you and had no intention of taking you home, just away too far for you to get back. But we know you did and it's a relief." She audibly sighed.

"I worried what my dad would say coming all that way with those men, which we've not known long," Shandol told her, and musingly added as if to herself, "but sometimes I feel I've known them for ages."

"And oh, we did enjoy our trip," Margery spoke. "But I am tired and sleepy," she yawned.

"Well, so am I," Shandol replied. "Only thing, wasn't a long enough visit."

"Oh right yuh are," Margery readily agreed.

The supervisor smiled and the girls began putting their things away, so they could bathe and prepare for bed and work the next day.

"Wonder if we'll ever do it again," Shandol mused sleepily. "Yeah, and when," Margery added.

How completely unknowing they were of future trips—

CHAPTER 47

Shandol and Margery were soon aware there was something in the air that September morning before they had been up very long.

In fact, they had barely finished dressing when the supervisor came in, as they went back to their bunks to put their toothbrushes combs, etc, away from the bathroom.

The sun shone through the open window brightly. A slight morning breeze came in and with it the faint smell of freshly cut grass.

The girls made up their bunks, thinking that was what she was waiting to see was done, though why that morning puzzled the girls. They did that chore, as required, almost without conscious effort.

"When you girls finish will you go to the rec. room, please?" Mrs. Crocker finally said. "I need to tell you something."

Shandol and Margery exchanged questioning glances. She was decidedly upset at something.

"Yes," Shandol answered. "We'll be right along."

They traced her steps along the passage at the end of the bunks, after only a short time.

"Wonder what's up?" Shandol put it into words first. "We haven't done anything have we?"

"Not that I can figger out or remember," Margery replied.

But soon the girls were seated in the large room, vacant except for themselves and the supervisor.

"Don't be alarmed," Mrs. Crocker said, and tried to smile.

But she could not cover the tiredness in her eyes. Shandol's eyes, questioning before, showed fright now. Something was wrong. And where was Mrs. Morris? They usually handled things together.

"Girls," she begun. "I hardly know how to begin, but last night one of the girls was missing all night. We've been up all night. She finally came in about five o'clock." She paused and looked at them. How, she wondered, could she give the details to these two sensitive, seemingly innocent, girls? She turned away, rubbed her forehead with her thumb and forefinger, and looked at them again.

"You're going to hear about it anyway, more than likely." She went on, "so we're trying to find out who she was with."

"Why don't you ask her?" Margery asked.

"We did," Mrs. Crocker replied, calmly, "but we're sure she was given a phony name. The police are sure there's no one around here by that name."

648

"Where were they all that time?" Shandol wanted to know.

"They spent the night in a motel room. Apparently her sister knows nothing about it either. She was here all the time. Jody came in with a story about them being married." Mrs. Crocker sighed. "Did you girls see them in town last night?"

The girls looked at one another again.

"Where's Jody and Cleo now?" Shandol hedged the question. "They've been sent home. Mrs. Morris and Mr. Jackson have gone along with the driver to explain what happened," she explained painfully.

"We saw them just a minute from a distance." Shandol admitted, unsure of whether she was doing the right thing. "She was getting in a car, but we don't know who with."

"What kind of car?" Mrs. Crocker asked.

"Uh—a black, Model A type—I-uh-think." The "I think" was added hesitantly.

"Yeah," Margery agreed, "but we honestly didn't pay much attention to it. We couldn't see who was in the car really."

"Thanks girls," their supervisor said. "Those girls were underage, and the police will investigate."

"Poor Jody," Shandol breathed, using her imagination for the worst.

"Yeah," Margery agreed, a glint in her eye, meaning she suspected them too, and punched Shandol with her elbow.

They'd been sitting at a long table rather like the ones in the cafeteria where they ate. The supervisor on one side and the girls on the other.

"D—did anyone else see them, or anything?" Shandol asked, shyly. After all they'd been brought into this, who else, she wondered, had been questioned and what had they learned?

"Yes," Crocker answered. "Another girl saw the man, and described him. In fact the police are almost sure they know who he is, but they need proof. Every little bit helps."

"Then who, and shouldn't the other be warned?" Shandol asked, incredibly.

"Aw, he uses a phony name, remember?" Margery reminded her.

"Just know who you're getting into a car with." Mrs. Crocker reiterated. "Perhaps we've been lax in advising that lately, we've had such good luck with the girls who've come here. Most are here to better themselves and have no wish to cause anyone—including themselves—trouble. I hate to say it but I don't believe these girls were very bright. Or at the least easily led astray as it had to be. Still I'm not saying it isn't sad. But I don't want another night like last night was."

The girls could see her tired eyes, and how dispirited she was.

"Why don't you take a nap?" Shandol suggested. "Things will likely go on as usual today."

"I'm tempted and may do that," she smiled agreeably, "but I think of Mrs. Morris, but perhaps I can give her time to catch up on her sleep. She won't sleep until the girls get home. It's over sixty miles there, I think. Anyway that's all now girls, though you maybe questioned again, I'm not sure."

She got up and the girls followed. She seemed headed for her room and Shandol and Margery followed, because their bunks were next to her door.

"But that's all we know, really." Shandol said, and looked at Margery. "Don't seem enough to go on or much use. There are lots of cars just like it around."

"Jody must be dumb," Margery observed offhandedly.

"It's likely to give this place a bad name—girls doing such awful things," Shandol remarked, firmly, "and it's not fair."

"Like one bad apple spoilin' the whole barrel," Margery added.

"Something like that—only there were two. Too bad her sister gets the same name. Don't you wonder why some girls get into such trouble. And it sure happens."

"Yeah, it's a wonder it don't happen more." Margery said. "Take yourself—everyone thought you'd be wild—almost once you got away from home. In fact, one old woman said you'd go 'hog wild'."

"Me?" Shandol almost shrieked. "But I want to go back. You don't know my dad. He'd not be very sympathetic or easy to forgive me. Oh, I hope nothing like that ever happens to me. Besides, I thought people liked Dad. Do you think he just rides herd on us and that's all? He's not like that. I think lots of my dad and I'd hate to hurt and disappoint him anymore than I already have."

"Have you disappointed him?" Margery wanted to know. "For goodness sakes, how?"

"Oh, you know," Shandol answered. "They all supposed I'd have a job by now. But he really wants me to be an old maid school teacher—only that's not the way he puts it." she smiled. "He just says he wants me to be a teacher, and only implies the rest."

"Teachers get married," Margery replied.

"I suppose so," she admitted, "but it's harder. You'd be so closely watched and need to be so "above reproach" in conduct, and in a new place—well, see what happened to Jody. Dad may be right. Perhaps I should take his advice, I don't know. But I needed to try something anyway this summer. I hope to get married sometime, too. There, I said it!"

"Ha, ha," Margery laughed. "You're so serious. But I know what you mean," she added, knowingly, the twinkle back in her dark blue eyes. The long fringe of eyelashes shading them made them look darker than they were.

Later, as they went to the cafeteria they realized the camp was a buzz with the news—mostly talked about in an undertone. The dorm, where the girls were, had been almost empty as they worked during the morning. Those few who weren't were busy or gone into town, the girls just weren't aware of anyone else.

Some of those who talked of the girls who were expelled were saddened and pitying—almost unbelieving, as Shandol and Margery. Others mocked their lack of caution in being caught. But *would she have helped herself* haunted Shandol. Suppose Jody objected? There were others who thought the whole thing a huge joke. Those were mostly the boys, Shandol noted.

They all wondered if there'd be new restrictions or harsher demands made because of it. There'd been no word such was the case, but a few were ready to show angry feelings at the possibility. But as the day wore on the girls decided there would be no change, at least until after the next council meeting.

That night Shandol and Margery had gone out on a date with Johnny and Derry, and had a surprise for them when they returned to the dorm. They were met at the door, and informed the police were waiting to talk to them.

"What on earth for?" Shandol implored nervously.

"Just to see what you know about Jody and the man who picked her up," Mrs. Crocker told her. "So I'm glad you're here in plenty of time before curfew."

"What luck," Margery grumbled.

"But we've told all we know, which is practically nothing," Shandol insisted.

"Tell it to them," Mrs. Crocker smiled. "It's just a routine thing so far as they're concerned. You may be a witness they can use."

"Gosh, I don't like it," Shandol went on. "I'm so—so nervous."

"Don't be," Mrs. Crocker soothed. "Just answer the questions they ask truthfully. It only concerns what you might know, not you personally."

"Oh, of course," Margery sighed.

But to them it was nerve-wracking and they were frightened at the two men in uniforms who looked as official and earnest.

The girls could add no more than they had before: That they'd seen Jody get into a black shiny car. They thought it a Model A, like dozens of others anyone might see, but they really weren't much on the makes of cars, except they were so common.

They wondered who the girls were with and if they'd had had anything to drink, which made Shandol's eyes blaze in disapproval.

"Of course not," she replied, meekly.

"But this Johnny's married? Seems I read in the paper he'd been issued a license to marry." One policeman spoke to her.

"No, he's not married—I—I mean I don't see how he could be. I wouldn't go with him if I thought—"

He put up his hand. "I'm not sure, we'll check that later," he replied, pleasantly.

"— For your sake," Mrs. Crocker added.

"I thought this was going to be about Jody, not us," Margery said, when she was asked about her boyfriend, but she told them his name.

"Yeah, we know him," the policeman nodded, and seemed to dismiss the matter.

The girls faced one another. What a letdown Shandol felt. By the time it was all over, if she could have gone off somewhere by herself she would have cried and cried. She shed a few tears as she and Margery went back to their bunks.

"I can't believe he's married," she choked, her voice ending in a sob.

"Don't cry, Shandol," Margery urged. "He admitted he didn't know for sure anyway."

"Well, it's going to be settled before I go with him again," she said, firmly, and tears came again. "I can't believe he'd do anyone that way—with a wife?" she shuddered. Almost as much to herself she muttered aloud, "I just *can't* believe it!"

The next day Shandol received a letter from her mother, but she re-read her mother's letter before she wrote. She wrote of her experience, except the possibility Johnny was married. She couldn't bring herself to bring such a worry to them. She wrote:

NYA Center
Midhill
Sept.19, 1942

Dear Mom,

I have decided to answer your letter separately.

I don't feel so well this morning. I was up last night until 12:30. I'll tell you about that and get it off my chest.

Thursday night a girl from here in camp left on a pass and was gone all night. She stayed in a cabin with a man! She came in at approximately five o'clock Friday morning with a tall tale about being married. Of course, she could produce no certificate, and in tracing it all down found it wasn't so at all. But they had policeman from uptown, Mr. Jackson (our head man), the nurse, and our supervisor out hunting them. Mr. Jackson and Mrs. Morris (our supervisor) took she and her sister home yesterday. In other words, she's expelled from NYA. Everyone thinks it's so awful especially as the above mentioned were up *all* night.

Guess you wonder why we were up so late and what that had to do with it. Well, here goes. They are trying to trace the man. They think they know, but they want to be sure. As Marg and I saw her get into a car in town the night before, they *know* (nearly) it was the same one and we were called before police for questioning. (We'd gone on a date so was after that made us later too.) But we didn't know anything except we saw her get into the car. They hoped we could identify either the car or the man, but we couldn't— just a Model A like one would see a hundred of anytime. I saw no man. One girl, who did see him says he's about 35, is married and lives with his wife. She (the girl) told he was getting his divorce that day. Anyway the NYA took (meaning sent) them home. (She had a sister here too.) Now don't worry about it, as Mrs. Morris said we'd not be connected with it in any way, only if we could help find that man. (She, the girl, is underage!) So don't worry, and don't tell anyone.

We hate that girl for doing that. We'll all have to be so careful, so the place won't get a bad name.

It made me very nervous to go before the law men.

I just got up about ten this morning. Didn't go to breakfast.

I'd like to go to town this evening if we get our checks. Yes, I'm about broke. I have a dime, but our checks will come today or Monday. Don't want to be broke when I get my check so I won't spend my dime. Ha.

I'd like to have seen the folks, Clif and them, I mean.

Isn't Phil a nut? He may wish before the term is out he'd have gone on to school. Didn't he plan to try for basketball— at least when it gets started? What will he do? He's too young to be up here I do guess. I haven't decided what I think of NYA. Just right now I wish I'd never heard of it! I really feel terrible— spiritually I mean. Maybe that's what's wrong with me. I don't go to church like I did. Even though I go to Sunday school, I'm in class with the college boys and girls and it just isn't the same. Can you understand how I mean?

I don't know when I'll be home. But when I come I think I shall stay. When I was questioned last night I told Mrs. Morris I was going home. She seemed hurt and said, "Now listen, girls, you'll not be affected by this, only tell what you know." Of course, she hates for girls to leave—except poor little Jody who was taken home. She was a small girl, with dark hair and pale blue eyes set close together. Not really very pretty, only her mouth. She had a cute, almost cupid's bow mouth. Her sister looked like her only she had pretty eyes and an ordinary mouth. They had small noses.

We got the pennant for the cleanest dorm. The boys had it last week. They would! On the big day—open house and flag raising last Sunday!

I washed my hair yesterday and did it up, but it's rainy today so guess it won't be so pretty after all.

Are they having many parties there?

Well, it will soon be time for lunch and go to work.

Tell Dad he shouldn't have mentioned helping me home— he may get to do just that!

Well, write soon.

Love to all, Shandol

P.S. Please tell folks if they read this to keep it quiet. It was just that girl's fault what she did. S.S.

Shandol's letter from her mother, which also contained one from her father was dated Wed. p.m.

Greenway
Sept.10,1942

Dear Dearie:

I'll prove to drop a few lines tonite. Tomorrow is wash day. Have to hurry so I'll try to do it tonite. Would have written today but the train was late so didn't get your letter until one o'clock. Went to Freedman's today p.m. The club had a little affair—a cheese making demonstration and some other business. Jane went along. Had cheese, cookies, coffee and iced tea. Tomorrow nite they are to have a hanky shower for Mrs. Elsa O'Brine. She and "aunt" Dot are leaving for Calif. Fri. Mr. & Mrs. Closh have bought that place as you know.

Alvin and Louise are at home. He goes to the navy 26th. Don't know what Louise will do. She seems to be ok?? Steven came in today. Guess you knew he was in the navy? I didn't until today. Lester came and said, "some navy boy got off train, must be Steven." Didn't know before he was in navy. Lester passed his exam today. Thornton examined him. Told him his left lung didn't open to the bottom. Don't know whether that'll keep him out or not. Lester has the war jitters. He's so nervous and worried too. He thinks the big event will be in Feb. Sh-h-h. She don't look like it. She goes to Dr. Huger ever ten days. The hospital bill will be $85.00. She says there won't be any more ?? Ha.

Now for the letter:

I'm glad your to-do was a success, but I think I'm discouraged with the NYA. If you're ready to come home it would suit me ok.

Dad is writing too so don't be surprised if we write the same things.

Shandol, you know how I feel about Dean. No use for me to preach about it anymore. I haven't any use for him, don't think I ever will have. Yes, he'll hand you a line and may get away with it! What do his promises amount to? If you want to marry Johnny and are sure just go ahead, but don't do it IF you think I want you to. I want you to be satisfied. Everyone liked his appearance, that's more than I can say about Dean. Mrs. Ruleton won't let Ardena go with him in the car. Remember you have a lifetime job ever-which (as Buck says) way it goes. Better come down and I'll go with you and cry. Ha. Ha.

I would be glad if you came home if it wasn't for Dean. I guess I'm jealous? I'd just like to have you to talk to like we used to do last winter, remember?

Oh, by the way, the nursing course starts next Wed. p.m. for 10 weeks. Hope you're here so you can go too. I want to go if I can hear it.

You should have gotten my letter before Carl's. Sometimes I think our letters are held up somewhere, I wonder?

I got a letter from Ivy Walters. Things're about as usual in north part of state I guess.

Wilda weighs 108 lbs. She's shorter than you (about 5 ft. 1 in. I'd guess). She's pretty, tho'. Wears glasses.

Thurs: Rainy today. didn't wash. Karen's okay today. Wish you could see her play. She climbs—just like you did.

Better think before you swap Johnny for Dean! But you be

satisfied. Do you know anything about Johnny's past, present and future? Ha. *Just be sure you don't have any war babies!* Do you reckon he'd have to go?

I must quit now and get to work. 10:30 now, must get dinner. Am baking bread today.

Shall we look for you home soon? Dad said many a good girl had gone down the downward path in a shoe factory. SO BEWARE!

Write.

Love, Mom

Shandol unfolded the letter from her father. She never knew what to expect, his somewhat serious nature, banter or a mixture of both. His letter was dated, as her mother's and written in what she thought of as his old-fashioned handwriting, which was good and legible for a man's handwriting. He took pride with it.

Greenway
Sept.16, 1942

Dear Shandol:

I started a letter to you Mon. night and was interrupted with company. Clifford Plyne. They stayed only a little while.

I was glad to get your letter and I'm really in a hurry to answer it, being the first letter you ever wrote directly to me. I have nothing interesting in the way of items. Mom will take care of that.

First I want to say I am not at all pleased about your treatment at N.Y.A. Center. First a commercial course offered and you got well started; then a transfer and woodwork training until you are about finished, and now sheet metal. I suggest you quit the outfit. I don't think you are strong enough to stand it. And if you could, one that is trained as well as you can get something else. There is lots to do now, and jobs are not hard to get. I'll help you if you want to come, just write Dad. I told you when things didn't work right to come home. In fact I didn't encourage you to go away. I don't doubt your experiences are profitable to you however.

I like the appearance of your Johnny pretty well, if he brings you home and gets you here alive and well.

I liked Dean pretty well, but I have found he is everything but what he should be. Had I known what I now know he would have traveled the same route with Landon Drawlson and a few other unfits, and he's worse than any. He is a drunkard and a fool. He tried to force Phil to drink, I am not going to have him coming to my home anymore. Well, so much for that.

If you want to come home we will not be disappointed, but glad. We will as soon as we can move out of this hole where you can stand better chances. My paper's gone. Hope to see you Sunday.

Dad

Typical, Shandol decided. Of course, he worried about her. And he never thought of her as strong enough for anything outside the home. Some of the girls Shandol had gone to school with had had to help saw wood, but Joel Sonnett would not allow his daughter in the timber. There were enough boys and she was needed at home. As a child, on her grandfather's farm, she'd milked but that had started because it was a game. Then it was a help and not hard work when the two cows she milked were gentle. She was less than ten years old then.

Then when she had to ride to school on the bus, a long rough ride, they had about decided she couldn't stand it, when she finally began to adjust. The ride almost made her carsick and she got off the bus pale and almost faint and wobbly for two weeks or so every night. Then it seemed to wear off. But it tired her so at first she was hardly able to do any home study. She'd read and study awhile and go to bed rather early. She had to make it. Little wonder he questioned her ability to do hard work, lifting large sheets of metal. She had never had to do it.

The next letter Shandol wrote to her mother on Monday, her spirits were once again soaring. She had thoroughly enjoyed the day before and she could hardly wait to write and tell them about it. She knew her up and down moods must baffle them and she thought it was a wonder that they didn't become more impatient with her. Her wanting to come home, and being on the brink of it it seemed, and then being content to go on with the day to day routine and seemingly somewhat content. They recognized the home sickness, yet she wondered if it ever wore off and how long it would take. Not that she would ever be where she would not want to see her parents and brothers and sister.

With Margery commenting on her always writing; and knowing Margery hadn't been able to have shared the day with Derry, hardly dampened her enthusiasm about sharing her happy experience in a letter home :

Dearest Mom,

I have so much to write I don't know where to begin.

First I'll say we haven't our checks, but we are looking for them today. Or at least we'll probably have them before you receive this letter. At least I hope so.

Next I'll say I had the grandest time yesterday. It was Sunday you know and I was with Johnny Norman. Guess what we did? You can't, so I'll tell you. I went with him to take his brother back to St. Louis, where he works. Imagine, I was actually in St. Louis!! The first thing I saw in outside St. Louis was the streetcar. No, I shall never forget them. Have you ever been there? Well, some of the buildings are sorta *High*!

I think Johnny's brother stays on the same street as Nancy, a girl from here (rather Wildwood, as she wouldn't stay here. We write to her. We are going to write the two an introductory letter, I think. He's twenty and just as cute as he can be—almost girlish looking. We told him she would be fun—and she is, not bad, though). Marg went with us to St. Louis of course. She rode in the back seat with Johnny's brother. What will Dwayne say? He don't know it. Marg thought him cute too. He has the prettiest black hair you've ever seen. He wears it combed back and it lays in tiny waves, just right.

The only time we got out of the car was at West Lake Park. Not so much going on there, but seemed plenty to do. With Marg wanted to see the Mississippi River, but we were afraid we'd not have time enough to go there and get back to camp in 'plenty' time. We left here at 1:30 p m. and got back about 8:15 p.m. We drove around there a lot, too. It's a little over a hundred miles. But I was plenty thrilled to see St. Louis. I didn't get to look Nancy up, as I'd didn't have her exact address and couldn't remember it. She'll be disappointed too. So much for that.

No, I didn't know Steven was in the navy. How long will his stay be in Greenway?

I just now heard from Dean. He was in a hurry. Had twenty

minutes to write, eat breakfast, and go to work. Said he'd seen you folks to talk to you. Wish I could. Ha. He's also looking for me very strongly, or so he wrote??

Will you write me more about the nursing course?

I really don't know when I'm coming home. I may, then I may not! I'll write by the time I get my check and tell you about it. I can say this, tho'. I want to get me a suit with my check! I've always wanted one.

So Dad may get to send for me, if he still thinks it worth it? I'd really love to see you all. Tell Dad to depend on it (if he will consider it, ha).

I actually can't write. The radio is on. Don't be surprised if you read "Farther Along" or now it's "Golden Slippers" Ha. I want to write to Nancy Rayford and tell her I was on the street where she lives yesterday.

Do write soon.

Tell Dad I'll surprise him again sometime and write again.

With love to all,
Shandol

Shandol wrote to her mother before she heard from her, because she wrote in the morning and her letter came early afternoon. But she felt she had plenty on her mind she wanted to share and it was so cool there wasn't much else she cared to do, so she wrote without a letter to answer.

NYA Center
Midhill
Sept.24,1942

Dear Mom,

Here it's Thursday and no word from home. Are you all froze up? Boy, it's real chilly up here. One morning a slight frost was on, they said. Not a killing one, but sure cool. I can see my breath today. As yet we have no fire, so I'm in bed covered up. Well, there is a fire in the fireplace.

Last night there was a wiener roast in our dorm in the fireplace. But Marg and I were with our friends uptown, Johnny and Derry.

Guess I'll tell you how I spent my check. Yeah, it's mostly gone and I'm not home yet, am I? Well, first, I got a nice plaid skirt. (I realized I couldn't afford a suit after all.) I like it fine.

Marge has one like it. Next I got what cosmetics I'll need this month, including 25¢ size of tooth powder.

Next, I got me a slip, purse, and a nice pair hose. I also got a housecoat. I'm so proud of it. You remember I've always wanted one, and almost all the girls up here have them. Marg got her one, too. She wore her skirt, slip and hose last night, but I didn't. I think they will be out tonight, or are supposed to be.

I didn't tell you the last time when I wrote of going to St. Louis, about St. Charles. I'll tell you that place has more justices of the peace than you can shake a stick at. Johnny wanted to stop at one (to get married, of course), but sez I, "No." Ha. (I'd be in a good humor today if I just weren't homesick. Is that it? Anyway I just want to see you all so much.)

Margery got a letter from her grandpa yesterday, telling us about Mr. Kasper. Poor old fellow. What's she do— never stay at home? She will be lost won't she, without him?

We're on yard duty this week instead of K P. I'm not sorry either. Being in the kitchen ALl time is a gyp. I've been washing the supper dishes. Is that ever a job? Makes my dates late, too, working until 8:00 p.m. Of course the dishwasher does the dishes in very hot water, but there are the pans to scrub in the real large sinks. Sometimes it's necessary to change water, it gets so dirty. And someone must clean off the stove and wipe up tables and scrub the floor so it's a team job. Yard duty is also tough. We pick up trash, paper, bottles, and anything unsightly on the grounds and carry trash, paper and whatever else in trash barrels from the workshop and kitchens. Then we get a ride in the truck to the dump. It's a scramble as to who gets to ride in the cab with the driver! Ha.

Something else, though, I didn't tell you was that when the police were questioning us one of them (Borton was his name) said Johnny was married! Whew! He asked me about it and I said he wasn't. The policeman thought he'd seen his license notice in the paper. Then the funny part (now anyway, it wasn't then), Mrs. Morris just kept asking me if we were married!! She just kept asking. Not only not taking my word but asking Marg also. I was afraid to tell you that until I was doubt sure, for fear you'd worry. We laugh about it now. All the boys in camp think we're married, but we're telling them differently. Hope you don't worry as it's all over now. Gave me some bad moments, though. But I was just sure no one would do a new wife that way so openly, I mean.

Hope you can read this. I'm on bed lying on my back.

How is everyone? I went to the dentist this morning, but he didn't get done with Marg in time. She had eleven teeth filled, including some in front. Sure looks better now. Not a cent cost to her either. I hope he gets to me too, though I don't have any in front that shows, anyway.

I went to sleep few minutes before ten o'clock.

Hope I get a letter from you today to answer.

Love to all,
Shandol

P.S. Write soon.

Shandol did receive a letter from her mother that day, which included a note from her sister-in-law, which she was happy to receive. But it was to her mother's letter she turned to first.

Greenway,
Sept.22, 1942

Dear Baby Mae

What do you think now we've forgotten you? Well, I guess we were looking for you home strongly! Also kids said Dean said he'd "heared" from you and you were coming home Sat. So we thought you were. Your so-called 'true' sweetheart was drinking at Elsa Closh's party the other night! Don't that sound as if his promises would stick! He didn't act as if he was looking for you Sat. night. He and Beverly were together, also Sun. night. Figure it out! Don't bother with him!

How did the girl scrape come out? Did they find the man?

Better go to church. Have your Johnny boy go along! The college boys and girls may have it over you in some subjects, but I doubt it in the Bible. Don't be that way. Study! Adams from Folks Consent is holding meetings until Wed. night. We've been going. Sorta like to hear him preach. They buried Mr. Kasper Sun. He died Friday about four o'clock. I went to the funeral. Imagine me going! I didn't go to the house, so thought we should go to church to funeral. He was laid away nicely. Kerr from Waiton conducted services. It was a sad funeral. Mrs. K. took it real hard, as did Bessie. Edith got peeved about something, or someone made her sore. Don't know what it was all about. She was plenty hurt at funeral.

No, not many parties anymore. Too much booze. Omar got drunk at Elsa's. Jess Parkley was drunk. Dean was drinking.

They danced there. We didn't go as we thought it might turn out like that. Ardena danced. Phil played guitar too. Phil didn't like it a bit 'cause she danced. He left, when she got through, he was gone!! She went outside to hunt him. Mrs. Ruleton said she began crying, said, "wonder what Mom and Dad (us) would think about it." She didn't come to the house then until Sat. When she came I felt so sorry for her. She said, Mrs. Sonnett I finally came. I said what's the matter? She just laughed and her face turned red. I just laughed at her and said, "I never did hurt you." She really did hate to come back. I didn't say anything then, she was so remorseful, but I'm going to tell her sometime she's too nice a girl and pretty to start dancing. Merabel comes home Fri.

Ardena, Phil, Jane & Lester went out to Chilton's last night in Mrs. Colmay's car. Lester got his stove. We'll have to put it up. Are you shivering? We're about to freeze to death!

Had dinner. Had beans, cornbread, carrots and taters stewed together, milk & butter. Old cow doing nicely. Have lots of milk so been making plenty of butter since it's turned cool.

Got your other letter so that I am answering them both. Jane is writing too. I'm glad you got to go to St. Louis. I've always wanted to see it.

Surely you got your check by now.

Don't know whether Steven has gone or not.

And I don't know much about the course, but I hope to find out more tomorrow. (Karen woke up. Gone back to sleep in my arms.) I'll write you more about it when I learn more.

Shandol, I wish you'd hurry and decide what you want to do. If you want to come home Dad will send you the money.

Rained three days, didn't work so we're sorta pinched, but if you want to come we'll send you the money as soon as Hedda pays them. Phil went back to work today. What would you do if you stayed there? If you want to come just say so and we'll send for you.

Want you to be satisfied.

You may have to pay extra postage so I'd better quit. Might send you money next time. I'll talk to Dad tonight. Be good and write.

Love, Mom

P.S. Mrs. Mack is looking for Marg too. Ha.

I'll try not wait so long. Haven't time to see if I made any mistakes. Must get this mailed.   Mom

Shandol knew her mother would be surprised she already knew about Mr. Kasper, as she had just written about it. Also that it was cold where she was too.

Then she read her sister-in-law's letter. The news was about as her mother had written, but she had such an individual way of expressing herself. She called Lester "Sug" (short for "sugar"). She reiterated her mother's comment of the cold and added she'd almost froze. She also told that she and Sug and Ardena and Phil had gone to town Sat. night and had lots of fun. She thought Phil and Ardena about as she and Sug when they were "sparking," but added they were still sweethearts. She hoped Sug didn't have to go to the army, though, he'd taken his first exam and passed. She hoped he wouldn't pass at Jefferson Barracks. They had gone to her folks she said, got their heating stove and put it up, but had made no fire in it as yet.

She wished Shandol would come back to have lots of fun. She mentioned Dean and wrote he was still running wild like a stray hog. She couldn't see what Shandol could possibly see in him: that he was just as "two faced as he could be."

She also hoped Shandol was close when "little Lester junior" came, which the doctor thinks will be about the seventh or eighth of January, and they were all looking forward to his coming. She wanted Shandol to write soon, but come home very soon, as they all wanted to see her.

She's such a dear, Shandol thought. Just right for Lester. At least she adores "even the ground he walks on." She had always been "crazy" about him, so Shandol well knew.

CHAPTER 48

When the weekend came the girls dressed for their dates, and Shandol noticed Margery dressing up in her very best. Shandol wondered if the difference was because of her teeth being made to look so much nicer. So Shandol wondered about it and decided to make light of it.

"Just because you get your teeth fixed doesn't mean you have to be so finicky how you dress, does it? I mean you've been wearing your very best, I'd say, with hose and the whole bit. And we won't be going anywhere to merit that. Or so I feel. After all the men aren't all that dressed up. Or do you know something I don't?"

She was surprised at the answer she got. It was Saturday, and there had been some changes made the day before, as Shandol had taken time out to write her mother.

NYA Center
Midhill
Sept.25, 1942

Dear Mom,

Well I'm moved, or at least almost. Anyway I'm taking time out to write to you. No, I'm not moving uptown! Ha. Ha. But we have changed our dorms around. The girls on the side we were on (south) are all on the morning shift; the afternoon shift on this north side (where we're moving to), and the girls who are on the night shift, that is six p.m. to midnight are in the north side of the infirmary. Therefore, Marg and I had to move. I still have to clean my drawers but most of the things are at least off the floor. I really didn't realize I had accumulated so much junk and stuff. How'll I ever get it home?

This morning I watched the sun come up (and then go behind a cloud!) from the dentist's chair. I had five teeth filled. They weren't so very bad, but he said they needed to be fixed. The one (that aches sometimes, remember?) he didn't fill, nor would I let him pull it. He said it was too far gone to fill. Land, how that drilling *nearly* got to me! No wonder people hate their dentist visits so much, eh? But I'm glad the works done and it didn't cost me anything except some cold shivers when the drilling hit a certain spot. Wonder what you think about it?

A kid from sheet metal wanted me to go to the show with him tonight. He's really nice looking and I was flattered at his asking me, as a girl thinks and looks at him twice—but I didn't have a pass! Nope, Johnny takes all three of my passes (I already had a date). Would he ever "die" if he knew I talked to the NYA boys. Not really, but just tease me. You know what I mean? Johnny does get after me for talking to them, but he's not like James! Not at all. But I can hardly refuse to talk to them altogether, which I hope he can understand.

In the Sheet Metal shop we've made (I helped) a molasses pan for the State Hospital, to make molasses in of course. Don't see how it will be done and yet maybe I do, too. Sometime I'm going to make a special drawing like ones we make to learn sheet metal. They're used too, to send. I believe you'll find it interesting. Surely I can learn it. Some of the girls are going out on jobs Monday for $140.00 per month, I heard, so I may stay awhile. That sounds rather good to me! Eh?

Got a letter from Dean the first of the week and I haven't answered it yet! I guess I will but it will be very vague. He *is* a rat!

I haven't heard anymore about the "girl scrape"! Guess they were just that kind. Some said they 'sold' themselves here! Yes, they found the man, but don't think anything will come of it. They are gone, so doubt if we hear anymore about it.

Tell Phil to 'stay in the buggy' about the dancing I mean. I bet I can realize how she felt though. Hope he'll always feel that way about it and booze too! I'm glad the kids, Jane & Lester and Ardena and Phil are having fun. Does Phil ever wish he were back in school?

Tell Jane I was so glad she wrote. Sometime I will write to her—maybe soon, no telling. What's Tommy doing? Still entertaining his company?

Really I must close as I must wash some underclothes, and I must get at them.

Here's hoping you write soon.

Love to all,
Shandol

The moving had been accomplished and the girls laughed at themselves and one another over the amounts they'd had to move and how they had tried to make things appear as before. However, this time Shandol and Margery had taken the first bunk from the middle room, instead of the last bunk in the row as was the case now.

They all agreed it was a better arrangement this way, as they could get up as necessary, and not bother anyone by coming and going while others wished to sleep, having different hours.

But as the girls dressed for their dates Shandol looked at Margery quizzically as she questioned her about dressing up.

"No, I don't know something you don't," Margery replied, "about the date, I mean. It's just that if Derry asks me to marry him I'll say yes, the sooner the better and besides I'll be ready!"

"Margery McNeely," Shandol ejaculated, "are you serious? And don't answer that way—'the sooner the better'?" It was quoted as a question.

"Oh, I won't," Margery replied, smiling, the dark eyes twinkling. "I just wish he'd ask me, darn it. And I meant the sooner he does the better I'd like it."

"Well, he wouldn't be ready, would he?" Shandol asked. "Wouldn't you need to make plans?" she added.

"He'll suit me," Margery replied firmly. "I can't do any better for clothes anyway. He'd understand."

Shandol was thoughtful, her bright eyes questioning, puzzled. Margery was in love with that big lug. But was he that serious about her? It seemed so unlikely.

"Well, I haven't made up my mind so finally and surely," Shandol told her. "I don't know how you can be. Too bad he wasn't with us when we went to St. Charles that time!"

"Yeah, I've thought of that," Margery replied. "But then he might not have since you wouldn't agree to with Johnny."

Perhaps he knows, Shandol thought. Johnny may have discussed it with him. Yet he seemed sincere, but passively unconcerned when they were unable to find him.

Shandol still thought the idea incredible on Margery's part and thought about it at times as the evening and evenings they were together. There had been no hint from Margery that he'd proposed or given her reason that he would. Once she thought she'd confide in Johnny, but she wasn't sure he would know or how confidential it would remain. Anyway she didn't want information if it might hurt Margery, and she couldn't tell her and she'd hate herself for letting her hope if there was little hope; though any hope at all would leave her undaunted in her affection for Derry. Shandol decided it was nothing to write home about—yet. It seemed it was always time to write, which she felt she had to do to receive regular mail from home. Never mind the help she often needed and requested and she was thankful she could do this and they were as helpful as they could be.

666

Perhaps they made some sacrifices, though she was not to realize that fully until later. The last letter she wrote during September was dated the 28th and headed by usual address.

NYA Center
Midhill
Sept. 28, 1942

Dear Mom,

Guess I'll start this letter and aim to finish it.

I started one yesterday and thought I might hear from you, so I didn't finish it. I'll probably hear from you today, as I'm writing. Ha.

Is it ever cool up here! Is it very cold down there? I just wonder if its as cold there as here. I mean if even that much farther south and at the "foot of the Ozark Mtns." make any difference.

Is Ardena sick or dead—or what? I haven't heard from her for two or three weeks. Guess they all think I'll be home sometime, reckon?

We didn't go anywhere yesterday, Sunday. We were with them last night however, and got in early.

I'm really blank today. Is the revival meeting still going on at the Little Mission Church? (Pentecost). I didn't go to church yesterday. It's so very cold.

It's time I was getting ready for K.P. I'm on yard duty this week. Right now I'm still in my housecoat and I must get my work clothes on.

I'll let you know how I make out on the pipe I'm making in Work Shop. I'll finish it today.

Here's hoping I get a letter from you today. Write soon.

Love to all,
Shandol

P.S. I'm broke. Have only one stamp. At least need stamp money. Thanks. S.S.

Shandol did not realize it, of course, but her mother was also writing to her that morning. Shandol received it, however, the last day of the month, as it took them that long en route.

The letter was hurriedly dated simply, "Mon. morn." 9-28-42 and continued:

Dear Shandol,

I'll scribble a few lines this morn if Karen will let me alone. Mrs. Colmay is going to town so Dad and I are too. They have taken off this week to cut wood but Mrs. C. wanted Phil to drive her to town.

The 'old' nurse didn't come Wed. Have never 'heared' anymore about the first aid.

Freda (Horn) Brack was down to see us the other morn. She's expecting. Don't know when. Ardena told me she was so I knew. But she said, 'I just love to hold a baby. I'll be glad when mine gets here.

Mrs. Kasper stays at her daughter's, Bessie.

Aubrey is at home now. Don't know whether he quit or what?

Lester and Jane are at Chilton. Clifford Rinard came after Lester yesterday (before I got up) to cut cane. So Ben's came after Jane later. He took Tommy too. They will work out there for $2.00 a day and board. He has to build a shed or something. Mr. Chilton said he'd have work for him 1/2 the winter. Then he could cut wood the rest of the time and use his rig to saw it. So don't know how long he'll stay. Sure miss them. They got Ben's car and took most of their things back out there. So you can write them there, c/o Chiltons if you write Jane.

No, Phil is too dumb to know what he's missing about school!! I was so in hopes he'd change his mind, but he hasn't.

So you've decided to stay again?! I wonder. I'm going to let you decide then you won't say it might have been!!

Dean is a rat! He was parked at Connard's yesterday afternoon (Sun). I wouldn't waste 3¢ on him!

I couldn't understand about the license. You better find out—maybe Johnny is married.

Marabel came Fri. I've never seen her as yet. Mrs. Ruleton's sis (Elberta) is there too.

Guess church closed last night. Don't know so cold I didn't go. Went to S.S. yesterday, all gone but Dad and two boys and I, so didn't cook much.

Did you mean you had to move over by the infirmary or in another bunk?

Wish you could hear Karen talk. She talks to Tommy and looks so serious and concerned while she's jabbering—so cute. She's a case. She cried some off and on last night. Did I tell you she's sleeping by herself? She won't sleep in our bed. She cried last night, I took her to bed with me thought she'd go to sleep, then I'd put her in her bed. But, no, she wouldn't have it that way. I put her in her bed she went off to sleep without a whimper.

Dad is hurrying me so I'm blank now. I'll try to do better this week. You write and be good.

Love,
Mom

The cool of September lingered until the end of the month. At least it was not uncomfortably hot. Shandol and Margery worried about their lessons in the shop as they drew angles, squares and lines into patterns to be put on tin, so they'd fit. At first it had been awkward learning to use easily even the square, but as time went along they became more accurate and surer of themselves. Sometimes too sure, because they'd have to do them over.

They mingled with the young people around them. It was impossible not to as they met on the grounds, on the way to the cafeteria, to eat, get the mail or dance to the "jukebox." They met going to work, going to town and sometimes girls from the one side visited on the other side, particularly, after hours. Yet no one seemed to worry about his possessions. There was no trouble about things missing from where they should be, someone appropriating "that which was his own." Not that things were not loaned. But they asked and the girls sometimes might share with another anything from enough toothpaste for a brushing, to laundry soap or even some article of clothing but they had permission. Any thievery would not have been tolerated, of course; and so far as either of the girls knew only one boy was sent home because of it and that was before the girls had arrived. Perhaps it was fairly evened out. None had a whole lot more than the next one, and only about what he needed. There was no place for things of value—if anyone owned such. Once Shandol had left her watch on the wash basin and was much relieved to find it still there when she returned for it.

October came in just another day. In the morning there was the two hours of yard duty. But all the girls liked the large, heavy-set man who drove the truck which hauled the trash and the girls were fairly eager to please and worked to keep the grounds in order. The driver was a mild-mannered, middle-aged man, with a mop of unruly dark hair showing gray, a full face and a bulbous-tipped nose. He was usually smiling and jolly, though Shandol never learned much else about him.

669

Shandol wrote her mother that day also:

NYA Center
Midhill
Oct. 1,1942

Dear Mom,

I'm still not ready for K.P. but I want to get your letter mailed. I'm already late writing as it is.

I was a good little girl last night and didn't go anywhere! What's going to happen? And on Wed. night at that! Some kids saw Johnny in town and said he was asking if I was in town. He's to come out tonight. No, I stayed home and washed some. I washed my red jacket—yeah, I'm still wearing it— and was it ever dirty! Also washed my sweater and of course underclothes. So even though I stayed at home, it was time for the lights to go out before I went to sleep. Besides that there was a picture show (free and educational) at the "cafeteria" which I didn't see. I hadn't planned to go anyway.

Margery has gone to town. Poor girl she must see Derry. Ha. I didn't have a thing to go for so I just stayed here. Both Marg and I went to breakfast this morning, and that is something. We hardly ever go to eat. Rather just wait until noon.

Well, Freda surprised me—but not much at that? Already pregnant and all. Did she ask about me. She wouldn't? (I don't mean she hasn't had time to get pregnant. It just doesn't *seem* so.)

Should I just write to Jane and Lester at Maple Hill, or what? No route number, box, just in care of Ben Clyborn, or how? I should write to Jane. She's written to me a couple of times. Is Tommy missing school? He will have the time of his life, won't he?

I bet they're tickled as he'll amuse them so much.

I still haven't written to Dean. I think that's as easy to quit him as to write a letter full of adjectives I could use to describe; he'd probably not understand. Ha.

No, Johnny isn't married—yet! That's all straightened out now. Why, Mrs. Mayor just out and asked him if he was. Then she explained why she asked. We just laugh about it now.

Ardena is at last thrilled, eh? Merabel is there!

Is she going to stay very long?

Has Mrs. Kasper taken her things out of their home there?

I have moved to another side of the dorm. Yeah, to another *side* and *bunk not* another building.

Karen must not be so very much like the rest of us kids! Sleeps by herself, talks and jabbers so young. Does she take steps by herself yet. She will soon though, won't she? Guess it's being by older people, (and children) may make a difference. Too bad Grandpa can't see her. By the way, do you ever hear anything about Grandpa? Guess he's still living. Where? Do you reckon he'll ever go back to the Ozarks?

I thought I had so much to write about when I started, now I can't think of anything. Just ask questions.

Hope you are sending me some stamp money at least if you can't spare so very much. I had that much saved out, but unless I go ahead and buy stamps, I'll spend the money every time.

Well, time to comb my hair and go to work.

Write soon.

Love to all
Shandol

It was the next day when Shandol heard from "back home." Her mother wrote:

Greenway
Sept. last

Dear Dearie:

Here it is 12 o'clock and no lines written. Mrs. Colmay came over this morn, left after 11 o'clock. Didn't have anything done, just got dining room swept, birds fed and watered. Was aiming to iron but do you wonder? I'm baking bread but it has risen so slow have it in the front room. Will bake it when I come back from First Aid.

There was a misunderstanding about that before. Seems Mrs. Milcher didn't set any date with her, so guess she'll be there today.

Mr. Colmay has gone back to Iowa. She hasn't heard from him but once since a week ago this past Mon. She's sorta worried about him.

I washed some yesterday including a quilt. Had a line full of baby clothes and overalls and shirts. Had an awful time getting it done. Put my water on early, thought Tommy would take care of Karen before he went to school. But Mrs. Follerson came after a pepper relish recipe. Then Ardena came awhile. Took Karen home with her. She hadn't got gone good when Mrs. Colmay came and sat and sat. I finally had to get up and finish with dinner. Dad and Phil was to have cut wood but they and "big Addie" couldn't agree on the line. The man told them where to cut and cut a tree for a mark. They're cutting wood out by Freedman's—on a German's place today.

Mrs. Colmay wants Phil to drive her to a sale tomorrow, but I'm afraid he won't. Dad wants to go to town Fri. to see about employment. The office is just open on Fri. now. She'd like to get a big farm with two houses on it. One for them and one for us? Ha. They're going to get a gov't loan too.

Shandol I dreamed you married Dean! I thought I just cried and cried. You may, who knows? Guess I wouldn't be surprised at most anything, but I certainly hope not.

Ardena had a party last night for Merabel. Same old Merabel. She is bigger than I thought. Has real pretty black hair, eyes and eye lashes. Her hair is long. The permanent grown out, comes well on her shoulders. Several there. Mrs. Ruleton's sister is there. She's a big rough somebody. Smokes and swears like a man. You wouldn't believe they were sisters.

Church ended last night. They were to have a "hen" shower for the preacher. Don't know how it came out. We were there awhile, but Karen cried and we left before he finished. He preached on book of Revelation. Nearly bit off more than he could chew.

Harriet just left.

Well, I must quit. Karen is hollering. Thought I might get a letter from you today but didn't. I'm sending some stamps and two dimes. Dad didn't have any more change. I'll mail you a dollar soon.

Be good. Can't help but think about my dream.

Write.

Love, Mom.

P.S. We've all been looking for you home, too.

It was on the following Monday before Shandol wrote to Audrey again.

NYA Center
Midhill
Oct. 5, 1942

Dear Mom,

I'm ironing and dabbling out wash tonight, but in between times I'll drop you a line or two. All I lack is my collar to be ironed. I'm going to iron it dry, as I've just washed it. Sometime soon I'm going to use the machine and do a very large washing. I said sometime, tho', ha.

I got a short letter from Ardena today. Mostly about the visitors and school. I don't think she likes school so very well, does she? Or do you ever hear her say? Yes, I remember Merabel's very black hair. It is coal-black! Pretty.

I have still not answered Dean's last letter he wrote to me. I wonder what he thinks! Do you suppose he misses me or will ever miss me again?

Sometimes I wish I had answered it, but I guess I won't. He'll be married next thing I know. Do tell me about him, because I don't hear from him, will you? (His versions anyway)

It rained over the weekend. And it poured down too. An awful lot of mud around here, can't you imagine?

I saw a good picture show yesterday. Tell Phil. The name of it was *Sergeant York*. It really was good. Ask Phil if he's seen it. I remember seeing the previews at Plainesville. Good show. *Gone With the Wind* will come here soon. Marg wants to see it and so do I—*again*. Marg went with Johnny and I to see *Sergeant York*. Her boyfriend wasn't to be found. At least he wasn't with Johnny. So we went without him.

Ask Tommy why he hasn't written to me. He must have so much to say about school. How does he like Della Bright for a teacher? Seems so odd that I'm not there to hear them chatter about school.

Soon be time for Council meeting, so I must be ready to go. I've some cleaning to do around my bunk. We're looking for the Regional Lady anytime from Topeka, Kan. By the way we must work either this Sunday or next. From then on we may work one Sunday every month. Makes the week seem so long, but outside of that I don't mind.

Write very soon.

Love to all,
Shandol

In Ardena's letter she'd written she'd write a few lines to let Shandol know she wasn't dead. Shandol decided she had used a poor choice of words, but was meant lightly. She wrote her aunt, uncle and his brother had come to see them. And that Merabel would have to leave on Monday 5th, which was today, Shandol reckoned in her thoughts. She had added Cal Horn was taking her and Phil to town that night, which was Saturday when she wrote. And that that was better than going on the back of the truck.

She wrote Merabel was fat as a little pig. Also that she, Ardena, had missed school since last Friday. She planned to go back. Wrote Phil wanted her to finish high school. (Well, what about himself? Shandol couldn't help thinking). She asked Shandol about Johnny and then wrote it was nearly noon, so she would close and hoped to hear from Shandol soon, but see her sooner. Shandol liked that thought.

The next day Shandol heard from her mother. She was surprised to learn a letter from her father was also enclosed.

Greenway
Oct. 4, 1942

Dear Dearie:

While I'm waiting for company I'll scribble a few lines. Who? Well, Rita Allsup told Tommy she might come by. Douglas Lindersilt preached this morning. I should have gone but Karen has had the croup the last two nights so thought I'd better stay at home with her.

I missed out entirely on my weekend letter. I'm sorry if you think I told you a *lie.* But Dad went to town Fri. and I forgot to get a dollar. Saturday morn he and the boys went to cut wood early and forgot it again. So I'm beginning in time this time.

You must quit going without your breakfast!! You'll get as thin as a bed rail.

Yes, Freda asked about you. Where you were and what you were doing. You know since she's married she is getting better looking or something. Wears better clothes maybe that's it.

No, dear, Lester and Jane are on the farm west of here. You know Mr. Chilton has been transferred to Plainesville. He drives back and forth now from the farm.

Lester and Jane were here last night a few minutes. Don't think he'll stay out there long. No, Tommy just went for that day.

Yes, that's as good as anyway. Just quit writing to Dean. He isn't worth any consideration. Just save yourself a lot of heartache later on.

Merabel is going home Oct. 5, tomorrow (Mon). She had a permanent since she has been here. She's sorta pretty. She just does something to you in an appealing way. You know she's part Indian. She came down here a few minutes the other evening.

No, Mrs. Kasper stays at Bessie's at night and home in the daytime. Says she's going to keep her own home. She told Mrs. Colmay she was going to try for a raise in her pension. I still don't talk to her much, but speak.

Did I tell you Karen has a tooth—lower one. She's feeling pretty bad. I'm sorta worried about her. She has such a cold. Colmay kids have all been sick. Missed nearly all week of school. Mrs. Colmay came over Thurs. p.m. And told me Morna was feeling so bad, had a high fever again. Asked me if I would be afraid to come and look at her. I told her no and I went. She was a sick little girl. Had an awful cough. I asked Mrs. Colmay if she believed in mustard drafts. She said she had prayed and hadn't got a victory so she thought it was time to try something else. I put a draft on her chest and she seemed to improve. Dad got some grapes at the store and you should have seen how greedily she ate them. Phil bought a sack of popcorn, I took her some of that. Mrs. Borsek asked her if she wanted some ice cream, but no she didn't want ice cream or soups.

I went back then to ask her if she could eat some cream pie. She said yes, so made her a small pie that night when I cooked supper. She ate it all. So Fri. night Mrs. Colmay wanted me to make another plaster to see if she couldn't get rid of that cough. I felt sorta funny working with Mrs. Borsek & Mrs. Colmay, but I honestly believe if we hadn't put that plaster on her she would have had pneumonia.

I sometimes have a feeling about Karen that I maybe shouldn't. She's so sharp just nearly walks. She can hold to your finger and walk. Maybe the Lord will spare her though. I certainly hope so. She's so sweet and such a treasure, she must be sent to console us about K.C. Of course she can't take his place. One child simply can't replace an other child just like that, and we loved him for himself. But we enjoy her as much as we've missed him. Don't misunderstand—we love her for herself too.

Yes, I'd love Grandad to see her.

I guess you got your stamp money. I'm glad you got your housecoat. I've always wanted you to have one.

Dad is writing. I'm sending your birth certificate so you may have to pay extra postage. Be good and write.

Love, Mom.

Joel wrote only a note, in comparison to Audrey's letter to his daughter. But Shandol did so enjoy receiving a letter from him. It meant he was taking time for her and thought of her even in his busy day. Yet, with a smile she reasoned privately, how could he help it, with her letters to her mother reminding them she was broke between monthly checks. Her father wrote :

Greenway
Oct. 4, 1942

Dear Sis

Mom's writing you. I have been intending to for sometime.

Fine weather after a brief cool spell. Frost but not damaging.

Your birth certificate came yesterday. Lester's will have to be made. You'll see your Dr. signature.

I was disappointed when you didn't come home. Had your money for coming in hand. I have spent it now. I am thinking of hunting a place where I can make more. I am sending a dollar to help you until you get your check.

We won't send your birth certificate for the Dr. marked it male instead of female and we will have to send it back.

They are gabbing in here until I can't write.

Mom wrote lots.

Dad

Shandol's intentions good, started a letter in answer at night. Her mood wasn't very conducive to a long letter, but she knew she must get at it. She felt obligated, almost, as they'd been so sweet about her endless stream of demands on their time and resources, she felt. She sometimes wondered if they didn't consider her something of a nuisance. So she began to write:

NYA Center
Midhill
Oct. 6, 1942

Dear Mom,

I've made up my mind. I am going to write to you before I go to bed tonight. Before I think I waited a day or two? Yes, and you'll be wondering if I got the money so I'll answer right back. Thanks so much for sending the money. I was sure needing it. Yes, I got the stamps and stamp money you sent. By the way it came in handy as I had to have some paper to write on and some envelopes.

Did Rita Allsup come? If so guess she gave you the family history (as though she'd never done it before!). How are they all? Where's Mariam?

Does Douglas Lindersilt have a regular appointment at Greenway? I would liked to have heard him preach. Did you see him?

Oh, my lands, Mom, I'd rather sleep than get up at 5:30 to eat breakfast. I could go back to bed I suppose, but I usually don't wake up. I won't starve, so don't worry about me.

Well, you can see when this was dated. I didn't get to finish it after all. My intentions are good, but it seems I'm slow or something.

About the birth certificate: Are you sure it is a *photostatic copy*? It must be. It will probably cost 50¢. It will be black with white writing. The white paper is *birth registration*. You probably know but just in case you don't. It must be a photostatic copy. Was it?

How did the party come out? I would love to have been there. I want to finish sheet metal, but, gosh, how I'd love to come home. Sometimes I think I shall come home and stay awhile, then have them transfer me out of the state. I would still be in NYA. I think when I get my next check I will. What do you think?

Last night Johnny and I had the awfullest quarrel. Maybe that's why I'm so nervous. I doubt if we ever get together again. Such is life? Tonight there's a circus in Capital City. We were going, but guess instead I will go to the show. It is *Beyond the Blue Horizon* in technicolor. I saw the previews, and I think it will be a good show. One thing though, I think John thinks lots of me and he knows I'm going home, so he rather exploded and said he didn't give a d--m. Yeah, that's the way he said it.

Seems to me Karen is smart, too. But that should be nothing to worry about. You should be glad!! It was tragic about K.C. It hurt us all so, one wonders why. He was such a lovable little guy, really. Only the Lord's reasons and we can't understand, I guess.

Doesn't Dean ever come to Greenway? Guess I'll lose all interest in him.

Yeah, Marg is Sheet Metal. And I'm not sure she'll ever make it. Sh-h-h. In the first place she wants to go home, and she doesn't care much for it. I'm ahead of her on the lessons at that, which isn't saying much.

The poor Colmays. Is the old man still gone?

Guess it's too much for him! I hope they're better.

I will write to Lester and Jane. I didn't know her dad worked in Plainesville. I'm glad I didn't write to Maple Hill.

I'm sorta blank today. Probably I'll think of something I wanted to write when I have this sealed. But I've been intending to tell you about the birth certificate for a long time. Do go ahead and get it, as I said.

Soon be time for K.P.—rather yard duty. Yup, I'm still on yard duty. Today we go get ice, which we consider quite a treat.

I remember Merabel and I thought her looks arresting. She was pretty except her deep-set eyes. Yet they added a certain charm, because you didn't really notice them as a flaw. But she'd be beautiful otherwise nearly.

Well, I'll write again soon. I'm really sorry I wait so long as I just have to wait that much longer for an answer (though sometimes we write the same days, eh?). I try to write three times a week at least. If I think of something I'll write before I hear from you.

But write right back.

Love to all,
Shandol

P.S. Marg and Derry have had a fuss too. But it was not just last night tho'.

Tell Dad I'll write him sometime also.

Write, all.

The next letter she wrote was before she received another letter from "home." She wasn't particularly interested in the conversation around her right then.

Dear Mom,

With the very old discussion among the girls, I'll try to
write a few lines, or at least start to. Some girls! They think
they are getting by doing questionable things, like Frances
sorta. They smoke, some do, not all, and are course in their
language. They try to get me and Marg to smoke. One girl said
this is mentholated (I think is the term), but I just said still
had tobacco behind it. Can't understand, when they're rather
scarce. The servicemen get first consideration, it seems.
Anyway—

Today, we had a meeting of all the boys and girls. The head
man, of the place had intended to say a few words, which
turned out to be a sermon almost. It was about the war; how
clean we kept ourselves and quarters (no criticism) and the
fine work and impression we made when the regional head
lady came. Now they are trying to get all the youth they can
so they're offering a prize of $5.00 for the one who gets the
most to come here. Of course I won't try for the prize. Don't
know that many girls.

I went to Capital City to the circus after all. We didn't stay
as we got such a late start. When we got there the elephants
were being lined up to leave. There were 42 of them! They'd
chained them in twos and they marched off the grounds
a-foot. Sure seemed like several. Wish we could have gotten
there sooner. Had we gone on inside we'd have gotten to see
about 25 or 30 minutes of the main performance. But we
mainly watched the elephants, and looked at other animals
(ponies mainly). We had a swell time. We were with Johnny
and Derry of course. Johnny wasn't mad at me, after all. Just
a misunderstanding on my part. We sure had a nice time. We
got a twelve o'clock late leave. The first one we'd had. We were
on the dot coming in—11:55! We got some trinkets, of course;
and I'm now finishing a sack of popcorn, which I didn't eat
last night. It's too bad they're rationing tires, gas, etc. By the
way, the 35 mph speed limit is in effect. A patrolman stopped
us and told us that! Not last night however. It's for everyone's
own safety, tho' isn't it? They know how everyone's tires are—
or getting to be!

679

I just washed my hair. Did it ever need it! So oily. I washed Margs too and rolled them both up. I also washed some clothes too. I just had to!

I'm so glad Karen is better. Hope you are all ok.

I think we got the pennant this week. We had it last week at least.

It's not so cold is it? I may go to breakfast in the morning—if I wake up, that is.

So Dean still runs in and out of Greenway, does he?

I wish he'd go on back to Folks Consent, but he never will. Who does he go with now?

Oh, I'm lying in the most cramped position now. Can hardly write so don't mind the writing.

I finally wrote to Lester and Jane. I'll try to write to Ardena in the morning. Sometimes I get behind on my writing, eh? I like to get letters though.

Marg got a letter from her mother today *telling her to come home!* Don't know how she'll decide. Sometimes I don't know? Marg's mother said if she didn't have the money to come on to let them know immediately. She may go. If she goes I may (will!!) too, but maybe I won't stay. Anyway, what shall I do? Tell me. Dad used to say, "Sis, go to bed" or whatever and I'd know. So I'm in a quandary trying to make up my mind. I really am. Do write real soon.

Love to all,

Shandol

P.S. Tell Dad not to think anything about me saying he said "go to bed." Just brings back old times when I had guidance. Remember? I was also glad to get the clippings.

The next day Shandol received two letters from her mother. It was dated simply, "Wed. A.M." and began with the nickname they sometimes used in the family:

Dear Shan:

There was a farewell party at Jr. Porter's Mon. night. He's going to the army. Had to bring hankys, towels or anything usable in the army. We didn't go. Karen was broke out with something. Thought it might be contagious. She's okay now tho', guess it surely was the hives.

So you want to come home!!? Well, I'm sorry, but right now we're sorta broke. Dad and Phil are cutting wood (poles) this week. Aim to saw some Sat. They are thinking of going to Iowa to shuck corn and want to get some more wood up. However, I'll see what I can do and soon about the money. I'll send it as soon as I can get it.

Dean was drinking at Jr's. Mon. night, and was with Frances. That sounds like a true sweetheart!!

Shandol, if you come home I don't want you to have anything to do with him. You've shook him off—or have you? So let it go at that. Sam Wolkens said he wouldn't be caught out with that son-of-a-B----. Said you were too good for a thing like him. That's just one man's opinion. About everyone has the same opinion, only haven't expressed themselves.

Lester and Jane were here a little while last night.

Today is first aid again. Got my report ready, but maybe too scared to have sense enough to give it!! Ha. I'll be glad if you come home. Maybe you can take it too? I'm baking bread today. Guess I'll keep Bobby home with Karen. He wanted to stay out yesterday to work for Della but I said no. Dad's talking about keeping him out one day to cut poles, but I don't want him to as next week is exams. (Selfish aren't I?).

Fine weather we're having.

If Phil could help us any we could have sent the money. Don't know what he does with all of it. Dad doesn't seem to care. It's 12:15 a.m. have to take a bath. Might have to take one up there. Ha. Don't want to be *dirty*.

Don't be too downhearted. I'll see what I can do.

I'm glad you and Johnny are patched up. What will he do when you come home? Get him another like Dean? Ha.

I'll write again soon. Be good and write.

Love, Mom

P.S. If you could get money somewhere else we could get it back to—you go ahead. Shall we look for you?

The second letter was shorter and was dated simply, as was often the case, "Wed. noon"

Dear Babe

What's the matter, are you dead or what? Thought sure I'd get a letter just now.

We're ok. Karen has some cold in her head, but apparently her croup is better.

Today is first aid again. I don't feel so very good but guess I'll try to go.

I got my wires crossed, thought "the passenger train" had gone, went to the post office, no mail, but when it did go I got a letter. I was sorta worried.

I cooked three chickens for Mrs. Colmay today. Got ½ of them so we'll feast once. Ha. They're clean. I helped clean them myself. The wiener roast was good Mon. Made coffee too.

Harry Bright came too. There was a farewell party for Otis Sandler's at Dahle's too, so the grown-ups went there. No more there than at wiener roast though. They aimed to have the Young People"s party there but Della decided it would be more centered here.

Phil just now came in. He's been out to Hedda's. Dad's there. Been out to Jacob's cutting cane Mon. and Tue. Phil stays up every night until midnight no wonder.

Dad said he saw Dean the other night. Since it gets dark earlier we don't see him. Just forget him. There isn't any principle about him. No use to preach, but you know how Dad and I feel about him.

I must hurry. It's 1 o'clock, have to be there by 1:30. No news. I'll write later. Wish I could talk to you a week. Hope you're ok.

Write more. Did you get the dollar? You can write even a card would do. I'm so very busy I neglect writing I but don't get too busy to think about you.

You've been gone four months now. Seems a long time.

Here goes. Be good, Write.

Love, Mom

Shandol wrote to her mother the same day, and acknowledged it in her letter. She had mailed the letter written the day before that morning.

NYA Center
Midhill
Oct. 10, 1942

Dear Mom,

This will be one of the biggest surprises you've ever had! Or at least for sometime. I told you Marg's mother had sent for her? Well, Marg has told her mother to send for her. So she will receive the money sometime real soon. The way her mother wrote as soon as they could hear from her and back again. Marg won't be satisfied, but I think her mom will let her come back, or at least do something else, as she'll never be satisfied. (No wonder Harriet said she didn't think she'd stay long up here). Yeah, I just now got your last letter—that's had time to get here, I mean. Now back to what I was writing —I know you've guessed it. I would like to come too. *For sure this time!* I doubt if you'll be in the notion now (or take one seriously?). But will you? Guess I should have come when Dad said he'd have the money. If you can't spare it, for goodness sake don't worry. But you see if I want to come back up here I can come sometime when the station wagon is in that part of the country. It comes quite often. Whatta ya say?

Well, anyway I'll be glad to stay awhile in Greenway. I think Marg wants to go and come back, too. Anyway answer right back, please.

Perhaps I should answer your last letter while I'm at it.

Yes, Marg is taking Sheet Metal.

The first aid course sounds interesting. Marg took that at Wildwood instead of shorthand.

How was Club? Who are the new officers? Are there still several who attend the meetings?

I'm sorry about Karen's upsets. Hope she's better by now. Must be her teeth. Does she eat very much at the table?

I'm glad Bobby likes school. I must write to Tommy.

I just mailed a letter this morning. Not much to add. I'll try to write the first of the week.

Love to all,
Shandol

Shandol's letter to her brother was what few lines she could hurriedly finish. Anyway he'd owe her a letter.

Sat. eve
Dear Tommy,

Well, I'd forgotten you had written to me last.

I'm so sorry I didn't remember to answer. But most of the time when I write Mom, I just suppose everyone will read it, and you too. I bet you do, don't you? Or is it sometimes too much.

How are you and school coming? I know Della is a swell teacher. I thought you'd have written to tell me about it. You will, won't you?

I've got to think about going to supper so I must stop.

Do write soon.

Love,
Sis

The letter from Audrey, Shandol had received that day, was a surprise. Not so much in content, but what was written. She could hardly keep things straight. Sometimes their letters were dated the same day, which meant they received each the other's about the same day. Sometimes Shandol could hardly tell where they were in their correspondence. But the surprise was it was dated only the day before. Usually there was a day between the time written and received. Shandol had answered it and marveled over it later, even rereading it. Sometimes, as she read them, she could almost imagine herself looking over her mother's shoulder as she wrote. Other times it seemed she had. This was the latter.

At the top of Audrey's letter she'd explained some smudged places, which she'd had no doubt added after the letter was finished. Shandol read: "They're going to Folks Consent to play ball. Bobby came in so excited he got milk and butter all over this." But Shandol couldn't see it was so bad. She read on:

Greenway
Oct.9, 1942

Dear Dearie;

For some reason I've not 'heared' from you but once this week. Harriet came by awhile ago, said Margery said not to be surprised if she came home. So what?? What is she doing? Is she taking Metal Sheeting (or whatever you call it) too?

I was supposed to have gone to help Mrs. Ruleton today but Karen is nearly sick. She was real sick yesterday. Vomited and bowels are not too bad. She's feeling better though. Guess it's her teeth.

Today is club day, officer election. I don't care much if I didn't go. If it wasn't at Mrs. Ruleton's I wouldn't go. She's going to have chicken salad sandwiches, cookies and coffee. I cooked her chicken in the pressure cooker *done*. Ha.

Mrs. Colmay got some beef yesterday. Gave me some as I

cooked hers for her too. Made her some noodles. She hasn't any wood, or at least none cut. He didn't cut up what poles they had on woodpile. She came over here a day or two after he'd gone and wanted 50¢ worth of wood. We didn't let them have any because it was already on woodpile and didn't want to sell any of it anyway. I told Dad it looked too bad when we had so much wood and them freezing, but with the gas rationing we may not get more hauled. Anyway we didn't agree to look after his family.

I told Tommy what you said. He said "I wrote to her last." Ha. He doesn't say much about Della one way or the other. Bobby likes Mr. Knight real well.

Bobby stayed at home Wed. p.m. and cared for Karen. The first aid is going to be grand. Learning to take temperatures with fever thermometers. Never could read one before. Next week we have to learn how to make beds. Next week after that Wed. we're going to give somebody a bath! Everybody's scared, 'afeared' it will be them. I wouldn't be surprised that we don't all get baths??

The first day I was sitting on the very front seat. Mrs. Ruleton and I, also Mrs. Follerson, but I happened to be nearest. Our leader put a thermometer in my mouth. They all laughed at me but I got to laugh last & longest. Everyone had to have their temperature taken. I think it's going to be nice—if I could only hear better!

Train was late. Don't know whether I'll get a letter or not. I must quit and get this mailed.

Be good and write.

Love,
Mom

CHAPTER 49

Margery seemed to become less and less satisfied and preoccupied as she and Derry seemed to drift farther and farther apart. He had begun to show up less and less as Johnny came to see Shandol. And though they had sometimes asked around about him they did not find him. Since his dad owned a small café with a bar, they did not expect him to be at home, so Johnny usually did not think it worthwhile to go there.

Once Johnny confided Derry did some gambling. He explained that upstairs, over the café, small "card and crap games" were played and he would get in on them. They were illegal and were supposed to be considered "small and secret." But there were those who knew and wondered, and even when "raided" by the law there was a warning code they had allegedly worked out all they would find was an "innocent" card game, with no money visible and, conveniently, no "proof" anyone had any.

Margery was aware of this fault of Derry's, as well as the occasional drinks he admitted having, as did Johnny admit to the latter. But Margery did not seem to feel these were important. Outside of driving a truck occasionally, Margery could not see that he had a steady job. He also helped out in the café he said. Yet, he always seemed to have money to spend, and was generous with it. She was sure she loved him. And she was miserably disheartened when he did not accompany them. Margery always paid special attention with her personal grooming, and wore the best she had to wear.

She decided to go back home. It was either to forget him, or try to make him realize how much he would miss her. But it was apparent to all except Margery he wasn't really interested in getting married or even serious, so far as anyone could tell. At least, not in the immediate future. In fact, he had dated another girl from camp, they had learned. And by the next time, after hearing it, Shandol wrote to her mother, the couple had double dated with Johnny and Shandol.

Shandol learned more about her one Friday night on one of their dates. They had stopped at a small café, which was also a bar and dance hall with a jukebox. Johnny had had a beer or two also, the girls soft drinks, and he went outside to get some air as he didn't feel like driving yet he said. Shandol learned so much of it made him

686

drowsy. And anymore made him sick and he'd pass out. That night he was drowsy, he explained, and wanted to get some fresh air through the open car window before driving, which was fine with Shandol. Though he wasn't his usual talkative self, Shandol talked as he leaned his head against the door (glass) frame and she was as close to him as she could get.

In the back seat Shandol suspicioned another story. There was "heavy petting" going on Shandol soon realized; and not only that but the car seemed to be rocking in an unusual motion. She could not see clearly what was going on—only guess. It gave her funny feelings inside herself. New strange ones. She wanted to know how Johnny felt and yet she was afraid he might guess she herself was aroused in a new way. She was frightened and wondering if she were in control. She was sure Johnny slept. Or was he faking it? For her and himself?

Shandol knew the girl was from Plainesville, and her name was Freda, but she preferred to be called Fredie. Shandol was shocked, and a reaction set in later. She was ashamed then, as though she herself had become dirty just by being there; and by having the feelings she had had only a few times before. That was when she went with Dean and even Steve, when she was being thoroughly kissed. It was a certain way they kissed her, she recalled. But was that love: If so was it Steve or Dean she loved! Johnny did not try to probe her emotions in that way—not yet anyway.

The next day Shandol had been cool toward Fredie, as she had asked Shandol if she had a date with Johnny the next night. Shandol looked at her, her mouth pursed, and from the corner of her eye. Fredie must have detected mistrust, discomfort, and animosity in Shandol's dark eyes, because she was soon apologizing profusely.

"I promise *that* won't happen again," she finished.

Shandol sighed. She thought of the two girls who had been sent home. Fredie hadn't been there then. Had she heard about it? Shandol decided not to mention it. In fact, Shandol hadn't been sure. She had questioned herself in case she imagined it, or just been mistaken. Now there was no doubt.

"Please forgive me," Fredie pleaded, and sat down on the bunk beside Shandol. "If we're going to double date we can at least pretend to get along, or the girls might ask questions. I'd rather we kept it between just us out here, Shandol."

"Oh, I agree," Shandol answered, quickly. "I'm sure you wouldn't want anyone to learn of *that*."

And I wouldn't want anyone to know I was in such company, Shandol thought to herself. She would not tell Margery either. Perhaps Derry would be disgusted with such a girl and realize what a favorable contrast Margery made. But Shandol would not soon forget it, and wondered what kind of girl Fredie had been at home. Perhaps she was freeing herself of imagined parental pressures. After all, hadn't a few predicted Shandol would "go hog wild" when she left the strictness she had been brought up under? Yet, Shandol had long since learned she preferred to be able to tell her parents what she had done (because they invariably asked). She could especially talk to her mother about almost everything. And she certainly hoped she never got into any trouble which would disgrace her family. She felt she would be completely, perhaps literally, ostracized by her family. Perhaps Fredie was only a strong, self-willed girl. Shandol did not know. Fredie's actual best friend was the girl who had claimed to be Hugh Burdett's girl friend from Maple Hill. The two girls had met on the station wagon coming to Midhill and sat close together, talked, and just seemed to take to one another, as neither had anyone else to chum with and the friendship continued in camp.

Fredie was a slender girl with wavy brown hair, shiny, yet inclined to look frizzy when mussed. She had large blue eyes, classic shaped face, her chin inclined to appear pointed. Her skin was not so pretty as the pores were enlarged, but she dressed tastefully and assumed an arresting appearance.

Her friend was almost the opposite. She was plump, with dull blond hair. Her almost round, plump face was ruined by close-set, small gray eyes. Shandol would thought Hugh would have been more discriminating. Yet, Shandol sighed, she herself looked plain to some people too. And that was the word for Winnie Redlour. Shandol had nothing against Winnie, felt no hard feelings toward her simply because she was Hugh's "other" girl friend. Shandol decided she was likeable and did not write to him anymore. She did receive a letter from him after knowing about Winnie. She was sure he would learn, and understand, why she chose not to write anymore. She was rather disappointed in Hugh. He wrote her love letters. Did he to Winnie too? Wasn't that rather two-faced? She could not reconcile herself to it.

It was Monday when Shandol wrote to her mother, following that weekend with Derry and Fredie. It was still on her mind and she wasn't sure how she should handle it. She knew she could not write about her feelings concerning it in a letter home because everyone read them. And Shandol didn't want anyone there to know. She wanted no scandal started about any girl in camp. There was plenty for her to write about if she wanted to just concentrate on it. What Fredie did was her own concern. Shandol could do nothing about it.

So she went ahead with an attempt to write.

Dear Mom,

I expect you have my last letter by now. I'm just wondering what you are thinking. Well, anyway, I'm not taking back a thing.

Yesterday I went to church. I bet you wonder what'll happen. Well, my intentions are each Sunday to go and do what is right, but people's intentions can, and often enough, are broken, eh? Too bad I had to set it off by going to the show last night. It was: *Pardon My Sarong*—a comedy, and the funniest thing. I thought I'd die laughing. But it was good.

Oh, I forgot to say I went to the Baptist church. Heard a good sermon. It was about "The Forgotten Teaching," which was, the way I got it, *giving*. His text was taken from II Corinthians and the eighth chapter. I remember it because it has in it the Golden Text we used to *sing*. It's the fifth verse of that same chapter: "...but first gave their own selves to the Lord." Do you remember?

Well, council meeting is now over, so I can proceed with my letter.

There are some more girls up here from Plainesville. The ones I know of course were some that went to school there when I did. Some of them I was study hall pals with. Others I never knew.

We took some pictures yesterday. I sure hope they turn out good. Maybe I can get them tomorrow, as we took them to the studio here in town, and we're going to check in the morning. If they are good, I'll send for you to see what I think you'll like. I bought the film (one roll) and another girl took another roll. We still have some yet to take, and we're going to take all of them of the camp and scenery here. Our shops—all of them, our dorm—and the rest of them too; the cafeteria will be included and I even got a picture of all the people in our shop standing in front of it. Of course I got the boss in it too. A girl from another shop took it so I'm in it too.

I sure enjoyed myself yesterday evening and afternoon. In the afternoon I was with some girls here in camp. We just walked around and took pictures. In the evening I was with Johnny. He took us and showed us one of the gasoline driven shovels he operates, and even showed Marg and I how it worked. Very interesting. I took his picture and I hope it's good. I also had taken another picture of me by his car and *he* was in it. We won't get them tomorrow however, as they're not in the group we sent off.

Margery got a newsy letter from her mother today. Was she ever thrilled over it. She gave me "some" of the highlights of it.

Sometime real soon, Mom, I have something to tell you. I'll probably wait until I can talk to you. I can't mention anything now, without you drawing conclusions, and I know I can't tell it all in a letter. Maybe you'll think of it as a whim of mine to talk about it. It's not so much about me even! Just how I have to live. Who it's with now. No, I'm not married. Now wonder, eh? No, don't. It's really past now. I'll write it sometime in distant future or tell you. You'll see why I'm ready to come home.

Tonight I've read in my New Testament. I've seen the queerest experiences and I think I'll take the Bible in mine, as 'they' need it. Don't be guessing now about 'they'. Mostly the girls here are ok. Is my ear ever burning! What's that the sign of? Someone talking about me—but good or bad? Ha.

Today in the workshop I finished another lesson for related training. It all fit nicely—the pattern I made and the finished work, I mean. It was another pipe of four inches joined to a six-inch pipe. I lack six more lessons. It'll take me possibly two weeks to finish them. Then some actual experience here in shop—if I stayed. Some more girls are going out of the machine shop next week. Lucky gals. I think we could 'go to Kentucky to work. (Sheet metal girls, that is.) Imagine that! Also some welders are going out too. I just wonder if Phil would like that.

It's nearly time for lights out, so I must stop. Perhaps soon I'll get a letter but I thought I would today.

Hope all are well. Karen too. Do write soon.

Love to all,
Shandol

What Shandol could not know was that her mother had written to her that morning, so their letters would, as was frequently the case, cross in the mails en route. Shandol would receive it the day after tomorrow, as her mother should hers, also. The letter began with the by now common, "Mon. Morn."

Dear Shandol,

I'll proceed to drop you a few lines if Karen will let me. I
have her in my lap, head on a cushion in the hickory rocker.
She feels very bad. All broke out this morning like measles or
something.

Don't know where she could have gotten anything. We
had her to Plainesville the 7th of Sept. but didn't hear of any
disease. She will sleep in your lap but won't lay down. If you
were to come now you would say "how come the house is
so dirty?" I wish you were here now so you could help with
her. Also help me with the fall cleaning. Oh, well, I guess I'll
manage somehow.

Mrs. Kasper moved over in the yellow room at Otis Sandler
house. Lora and Mr. Dahle stay in the other part. Don't
know who will move in the other house across the road. Joe
Middleton moved in the Lewis Parkins house. Millie was at
club Fri. and she was so *sour*castic I was amazed at her.

Today is achievement day at Plainesville but we couldn't
go.

Leola Shiller (Follerson) is our club president; Mrs. Milsher,
vice-president; Mrs. Ruleton, secretary–treasurey. Don't you
imagine the club will boom now! Ha.

Mrs. Colmay is in bed, went to bed Sun. She was still in
bed this morn when I went over there. She's nothing but skin
and bone. I fear for her sometime. I told her she'd have to get
some nourishing food.

She said she'd have to have wood to cook it first. But she
expects you to wait until she gets ready to pay for it. Dad and
Bobby went over yesterday and sawed a few poles. Guess we'll
have to take them to raise after all. He's in Iowa getting $3.50
a day. Will shuck corn when it's time.

Dad and Phil have gone to town today.

Lester and Jane were here Sat. night and Sun. They all went
to the show Sat. night so guess it set old Phil back a little
money. Guess I can't do anything about it. No use to nag at
him. He spends about a dollar a week on Ardena. Ordered her
a locket the other day $1.75. She's a swell kid though.

Yes, I think Douglas L. will preach the 1st Sun. You knew
he was turned down for the army? Was ruptured. No, I didn't
go. Karen had too much cold.

We got the birth certificate but the sex is marked male.
Don't know what we'll do about it. It was the doctor's mistake.

691

Yes, it's a photostatic copy. We already have it. Lester has to have one made. His isn't on file.

Shandol I don't understand why you'd want to be transferred out of the state! My advice would be if you aim to finish sheet metal do it now! You're acquainted there now, know several girls. If you want to come home to visit awhile that would be ok, don't know why you'd want to be transferred. You do so you feel.

What's the matter with you and Johnny? Did you ever patch things up? Guess there's always a do or don't, so if you can't give him any encouragement it might as well be one time as another. The world is full of Deans, Johnnys and the like. That's life though. When one gets someone who thinks lots of them they don't appreciate it. If he'd do you like the "skunk" (Dean) did maybe you'd appreciate it?

Oh, by the way he and Frances were at church last night. Guess he's getting good? Shandol wake up! Forget him! I've been hearing some things about his mother, so maybe he just didn't 'happen to have his bad qualities.' You'd be far better off if you hadn't known there was a Dean. I guess I might as well give up! If you come home you'll marry him... you see if I'm right. If you think you'd be happy I wish you well. But I'm going to be somewhere else so won't have to hear about it. The farther away the better. No use to preach, but—but—but. No need to cry. I love you as ever. I guess that's why I'm so concerned.

Frances is cook at school now. Costs us 2¢ a day for Tommy's lunch but I haven't time to fix it and he hates to come home. Bobby comes home.

Nice and warm today. Cool at night and early morning.

A Mr. Montgomery preached at the Little Mission church last night. I was afraid to take Karen.

A Warden or some such name preacher at Church of God. He lives in Neal Parkley house, preaches every Sat. night, Sunday and Sunday night. Have never heard him unless I heard him before. Seems we have. His wife takes 'first aid'.

I never got that third letter last week. Kids said they heard from you. I'm making some cheese. I'll send you some and some cookies one of these days unless you decide to come home. You can tell me.

Have you heard from Hugh Burdett lately? Mrs. Borsek heard from him the other day. It had been so long, but she didn't know where he was the letter was *censored* so bad.

Kurt Butler is at home now. Lewis Perkins gets a 15 day furlough.

I must quit, don't reckon you got this far! I'm writing on the arm of the chair. If Karen don't feel better soon I'm going to take her to the doctor. Don't worry about her. Some think it's a "teething rash" so don't think it's serious. Makes her feel real bad. Have to hold her about all the time. Ardena came down Sat. to help me. Had to wash for her.

She had a diarrhea last week. We got her a new pair black patent leather stiff-soled shoes maybe I told you? They're so clumsy on her she can hardly manage.

I must quit. Hope you are ok. Be good and write.

Love,
Mom

Go home—stay here: While the indecision rolled around in her mind, Shandol's days followed one the other in mostly the regular routine. Margery was in the same dilemma, except she had decided to go home. The question with her was when. Shandol hoped she would wait until she too could go. However, Margery had the money and could go anytime, whereas, Shandol did not. That is until she received a letter from her mother on the following Saturday. It was not a long letter but contained the necessary amount of money for her to go home. She realized it was also in answer to one of her letters. They had been speculating about what Shandol had written about talking privately to her mother. She wondered why they thought the worst when she had written it didn't concern her only indirectly—at least she had intended to get that across. Hadn't she? Her mother wrote:

Thurs. noon

Dearest Shandol,

I'll proceed at last to drop you a line. Also send you the money to come home. If you don't come home send it back. It's just the same as borrowed money. The rent is practically due, but thought it could wait awhile.

After reading your letter Bobby says "What's this all about?" He said, James might be right after all." (You know he said it was tough). This morning he said, "I'm worried about Shandol. She says 'I'm not married' that's what gets me." I'm hoping it isn't *that* bad. If so you'd better get married. Ha.

Mrs. Colmay just left.

Learned how to make beds at first aid yesterday. Margo Parkley and Jane Lavenson will take baths next week. Ha.

Shandol, if you come home you better get sorta of an extension in case you should decide to go back you would still be eligible. You use your own judgment. Now if you're sure go ahead. We'd like to have you home.

Phil says, "Mom needs you." I wouldn't care if you'd decide to stay home this winter, (but I'm afraid that's asking too much) until I could get the diaper wash over at least. I have 3 bu. baskets of clothes piled up! Can't sleep at night when I wash. Should have washed but so late when Bobby got around I hated to start. Will have him get water this eve and start early in the morning.

We've a chance to go to some four or five counties in that area to work on farms. $50. or $60. per month, house, garden, meat furnished. I'd rather like it but don't think Dad's much enthused. They transport you there.

Karen says enough. Can talk better'n I can write.

Be good. Write.

Love,
Mom.

Shandol told Johnny of her plans to go home and that she'd received the money that day, as they were on a date that night. But he could not understand her wish to go home, especially as she was so undecided as to whether or not she wished to stay there once she was there and had her visit out. As they talked and Shandol told Johnny she hoped to finish her training and she would probably be only awhile.

"I hate to start something I don't finish," she told him. It was something her father had often said of her. When Shandol started something she'd stick to it. Whether it was going to school, helping in the garden, doing the washing or playing some game, she liked to see it through to the finish.

"Let me take you home again," he said. "Derry and his girl might go. She lives in Plainesville anyway."

So they talked it over. They made tentative plans for the last of the month. As it happened the Halloween party would be held the next weekend following the one just coming up. It seems there were several using the Halloween theme as an excuse to go home for a visit.

On each of the following three days Shandol sent a postal card home. The first she dated "Thurs. morn."

694

Dear Mom!

Just a few lines this morning. How are you all? I'm ok. Well, guess what I've been doing?

Well, here 'tis: I've been fixing a box I'm going to send C.O.D. I sure hope that will be ok. Be sure and get it as it has lots of my clothes in it. You know summer skirts and things that I can no longer use. It will probably come to no more than 30 to 50¢. Will that be too much? It's a big one! *Remember, I'm sending it C.O.D.* You can imagine what's in it!! But I won't mind if you open it just so the things aren't misplaced. It has a lot of old letters. Don't destroy them. None there except what you and others write, ha. I will probably sent it out tomorrow. Hope that is ok. Hope Karen's better,

Love, S.S.

She certainly wasn't going to send home letters from Dean and other such friends. She was sure their curiosity would get the better of them! She hoped they would understand that.

The next day the card she prepared she typed, It was dated "Oct. 16,–42."

Dear Mom

Please try to bear with me— I'm going to type this. I got your letter yesterday, but to stretch out my stamps, I'm writing a card hurriedly this morning. (P) I'm so glad Karen is ok. (P) Were you that surprised that I wanted to come home? Just don't worry about it. I will get my check Monday or Wednesday. (P) I got a letter from Dean yesterday. I hadn't heard from him for about two weeks. Well you know what I told you. (P) I haven't heard from the kids as yet. Guess they are looking for me to come home too. They at least could write a card. Tell them I said so, will you. (P) Yes, Johnny came to see me last night. I had just gotten off yard duty and I didn't even change my dress. Imagine that. By the way I had on a uniform. He didn't seem to mind though. (P) Well, Mom, I got to eat dinner. Then it's work time. Play like this is a long letter and do write to me soon. How did your report come out in first aid?

Love to all
Shandol

Saturday Morn
Oct. 17, 1942

Dear Mom,

I received your letter that contained the money yesterday. Was sorta surprised to get it. I'll let you know when I'll come so don't go meeting every bus. Ha. I'm waiting on Margery. She's looking to hear from her mother any day. (P)Yesterday in shop I finished one whole lesson. I made a blueprint on paper then on tin. I have copied a print to show you. They must be saved for the board of education. We are supposed to paint today. (P) I was with John again last night. We had to wash some when we got home. We are already through on yard duty. Now there's some swell music on the radio.

Hope everyone is ok. I don't have your letter here so I'll answer it later. Look for me when you see me coming.

Love to all, Sis.

Though Shandol, in the postcards, had acknowledged the money to go home, it was the next week when she wrote home the plans they had made.

Dear Mom,

I'm not out of bed yet, but that's no sign I can't write to you, is it? I miss getting letters, but of course I don't expect them when I don't write. I got your card yesterday. Also a card from Jane.

I think I can tell you when I'll be home. Look for me a week from this Saturday. If something comes up that I'll come sooner I'll let you know. That date will soon be here, as the time will fly.

I think this weekend we are having our Halloween party. So many will want to go home over the next weekend.

We had to work again last Sunday, and will have to one Sunday of each month. It's not so bad but I lose all track of the days and it does make a week seem rather long. Our boss doesn't like Sunday work either, even though he doesn't seem to be a particularly religious man. So we just went ahead with our drawing. Marg and I also painted the license plates. We did okay on them. They're for use here, mostly.

696

I was with Johnny last night. Went to Kolver City (mostly just a small, but busy place where the two highways cross). Not so much to do here except go to a show and we missed it. We were too late. Lots of kids do go dancing after 8:00 o'clock but after all we can do that here in camp. We went to Kolver to eat and just fooled around. Johnny still says he's not going to let me go home. Ha.

I have some more new pictures. Guess I'll bring them home to show you. I have one roll that has not been developed. Waiting for my check. Today is Wednesday. We'll surely get them today.

Gee, am I hungry. No, I didn't go to breakfast. But Marg and I had a small bottle of milk and a candy bar each to eat, here in camp. For supper last night I ate two hamburgers, a serving of corn, some salad and dessert, part of which I didn't eat. The dessert I hardly more than tasted. It was bread pudding. I believe I've eaten that at home, don't you? I sure like it, but got too filled up to finish it. Besides we had candy, pop and potato chips last night.

In the shop I have made and painted a metal box. It was my first one. In order to make a lid for it I had to make three. One was too large, one too small and one that fits fairly well. We painted them orange and silver. Well, I'm ahead of some and up with all my lessons, and that counts as related training anyway. Today I can put another lesson for tin. (It's put on paper first.)

I'm sending back the letter you sent from Aunt Callie. Guess you'll be wanting to answer it. Does Uncle Lafey write. Who do you hear from Grandpa from? Was sort of surprised to hear of Nona's son, weren't you? Does Ivy write? I'd have thought she'd have told you.

Dean finally wrote me again. I hadn't answered his last two letters to me. He's supposed to go to the army today. He says he may get to come back in 14 days, but I don't know.

I must dress for work. Still do yard duty at ten o'clock. So I must get ready.

It's sorta cool today. Do write soon.

Love to all,
Shandol

P.S. Guess the baby is ok? Tell Tommy it's not my time to write now. Also guess I won't mail the box as I'd thought I might bring it. Sorry I wrote I would then not do it. But I can save that much bringing it. Write soon. S.S.

It was by now that both girls had the money to go home on. Margery became less satisfied than ever and more determined to go home. Shandol supposed she'd had her convinced to wait so she could go with her. In fact she had told her Johnny was supposed to take her home the end of the month and she thought if she possibly could she would wait that long. Of course that would be for only a weekend. But Margery insisted her mother had practically sent for her.

"Before you go," Shandol told her, "please let me know as I can tell Johnny. Maybe I can get him to come get us or something."

Margery had half-heartedly agreed, but she became more withdrawn. She complained of headaches and hardly ever went on yard duty. She was behind and mostly using Shandol's patterns at the workshop. Trying to be cheerful, but an act as Shandol realized later.

Yet, Shandol was surprised that Friday morning when they had finished yard duty early to go to their bunk and discovered Margery packing. She was leaving on the afternoon bus.

"But Margery," Shandol pleaded, "you know I wanted to go when you did. But I can't possibly get ready in time now. If you'll just wait another day I'll go too, I promise."

She shook her head, fighting tears she waited a minute to answer. A long one it seemed to Shandol and her heart went out to her. She was truly showing her unhappiness now.

"I can't. I just can't, Shandol," she finally said, dejectedly. "You have Johnny. All I have is to see Fredie going with Derry. I can't stay around to see it. If he must, I suppose he must, but—just try to understand. I just want to go as quick as I can."

"I should have known—" Shandol started.

"But, I'm letting you down, is that it?" Margery finished for her, as she folded clothing and went from closet to bed and picking up her things and placed them in the suitcase she had brought with her.

"Oh, no, I didn't mean that," Shandol hurriedly denied. "I meant I should have seen how unhappy and dissatisfied you'd become. But I was so wrapped up in my own feelings and doings I just supposed you wanted to go as I did, and still do. But I'm just not sure about staying away yet, that's all. Are—are you coming back?"

"I may come back with you," she replied, brightening somewhat. Perhaps Shandol's company had helped some. She could still count on Shandol as a friend, she knew.

"But that's over a week," Shandol said. "Will you be allowed to come back?"

"Yeah," Margery said. "My folks have sent for me, haven't they? It has to do with family affairs, which are only minor it's true and my brother is due home—sometime and so on, I think I can come back. Mom feels bad with us both gone. It is a worry to her. She's bad about worrying anyway."

"So is my mom," Shandol nodded. "She's sure Lester will be drafted in only a matter of time. He's worried and so Jane is worried too about that. I sure hate to see you go without me. We've been good buddies I thought."

"I feel like that, too, Shandol," Margery assured her sincerity in her unsteady voice. "But I want to go home. I need to go home. Maybe I'll feel better about the whole thing after awhile. I hope so anyway. Maybe Derry will even miss me and wonder, too." She laughed, shakily and mirthlessly.

"I'll feel so lost," Shandol groaned. "I don't see Johnny all that much, and I'm sure Derry's new friend can't take your place. I hope they don't give some stranger your bunk; oh, my goodness, you'd better come back," Shandol took her arm and shook it gently.

Margery, meantime, went ahead with her packing. She wouldn't be going to work as she would leave that afternoon. Shandol still felt cheated that Margery hadn't finally confided earlier she would go home. She hadn't known until she was practically ready and time to go. Perhaps Margery hated Shandol because Johnny was still "interested in her," while Margery and Derry had not been together.

It had been almost the same as when she had started going with Dean. They'd had gone with Jim Brown, double dating. Then he had started dating a redhead, who wore lovely clothes. She was tall and sophisticated and Shandol felt terribly shy when she was around. She had told Dean she felt like a child beside her. So they had started going by themselves after only two dates with them. Dean used his dad's car, a not so new one as Jim's, and a small car, Shandol had never seen one like it. But he called it his old Chevy, so she assumed that's what it was.

Now, Shandol wondered if Margery had liked Jim or if she had only gone so Shandol could go. She had never said one way or the other, and had never said a word against him—only the fun they had had; it had been at times when they would be reminiscing about things at Greenway. But then Margery had obviously made other friends and gone with other guys. So perhaps she hadn't felt so left out after all. It may have been she supposed she and Dean were going alone and it was up to Jim to come get her. If he ever did she never mentioned it, except for one date they had after that and they were by themselves. She never mentioned why only one; or if they had drifted apart by mutual consent. Shandol and Dean had gone with him and the redhead only the two times. Shandol told Dean she would rather not go anywhere than go with them. She had dreaded that more than being with Dean alone. By then she had lost most of her timidity with him and self-consciousness and was more at ease in his company. He'd treated her with respect and decency—in fact devotion—as she had no fear of him. She felt she knew him. Now she wondered.

In her letter to her mother following Margery's leaving, which was early the following week, Monday, in fact, Shandol asked about Margery and what she had said.

NYA CENTER
Midhill
Oct.26, 1942

Dear Mom,

Well, we've finally got our checks, even though I don't have mine cashed. Some of the other kids do though, as I borrowed 3¢. Ha. Yes, I still have the five, but I will not break that even for a stamp. It's too tempting to spend some here and there when in change, don't you think?

Guess you've talked to Marg by now? What did she have to say? I told her if she'd wait another day, I'd go with her, but she wouldn't wait. She was packed before I knew she was going, all but some last minutes stuff. I'm still scheduled to come Saturday, if I can wait that long. But I'm going to try. Maybe I'd better tell you what I didn't intend to. Johnny will be with me, or at least he is supposed to, if something doesn't happen. If you mind tell me and I can say I can't wait till Saturday, or that I can stay for awhile, see. But he says he's coming too. (Wasn't sure it was important.) If Marg comes back she'll come back then. Guess she told you I said tell you to write.

I hope I hear from Marg today. She said she'd write soon. I just wonder if she wishes she were back up here, ha. Oh, by the way, if I come with Johnny, I'll be there only for a weekend. I'm going to try to finish this course, but I wish I had someone from down there up here.

"Yesterday, I went to Capital City with Johnny. I'd sure be lonesome if it wasn't for him. The night before (Sat.) I was there too. Last night, however, we went to Columbus. We'd aimed to go to the show, but some kids that run around with us wanted to go there. We had a swell time.

A girl from Waiton is leaving to go home today. She is getting a seven-clay emergency leave. Her mother is bad sick in the hospital and on top of that their house burned. She's terribly torn up. Also one from Maple Hill is going down that way tomorrow. No reason why I should travel by myself is there? The one from Maple Hill is going to see Hugh Burdett. She really likes him and she was jealous of the picture that I have of him. (It just showed!) I guess I didn't write love letters to him like he did to me. No fooling, I couldn't have. He was too much like "one of the boys"—my brothers. He's too good for her though. She will drink and smoke if she's with kids that do. I don't write to him since I found out about her. He wrote me some swell letters anyway, which I shall keep.

Do you hear from Dad often? Where is he? I hope he gets a job, don't you? If Phil and Les have to go you will feel lost won't you? Where will Jane stay? Tell them to be sure and come Sunday so I can see them. If, however, I can't get someone to come here from down there, I may go back to stay. It's too lonesome up here. It works out because almost everyone that comes has his own chum (or soon does) so one feels alone. I think thats better too. I hope Marg comes back.She just must!?

I can hardly get my thoughts collected. This will be a long week. And so much excitement. Getting to come home and all. Guess you won't have much time to answer this letter, because I'll be there Saturday whether Johnny comes or not. If he doesn't I'll start from here Friday evening. But if he does, I'll be there sometime Saturday evening or night.

Well, it's time for yard duty, so I must go.

I'll be seeing you.

Love to all,
Shandol

P S. No yard duty, I found out and didn't even ask. I'm sorta glad too.

I have moved again. Boy, this place is really filling with girls! We moved to a different dorm now. It's No. 3. They are numbered from Cafeteria 1, next to it 2, etc. We have two dorms of girls. All of us on the evening shift are in one dorm. There are a few girls who go to work at night. They are still in the other place, though. Hope you write so I can hear before Friday. Don't write so it will be any later.   S.S.

There were questions to Shandol about Margery. Only a few in the nearby bunks had had any inkling she had gone.

But other excitement kept her from being the topic of conversation. That very night another of the girls took what was described as "deathly sick" during the night. She too had been rushed to the hospital and her trouble acute appendicitis, for which she had an operation early the following morning.

Another girl on their side the day before, who had decided to descend from an upper bunk by sliding off the end of it, had sprained her ankle, which caused her to hobble around, seeking sympathy.

Still it was Friday before Shandol heard from her mother. Of course she had had time to answer Shandol's last letter, and she was glad to have it. It would be a help as she waited to go home. It was dated 10:00 a.m.

> Dearest Shandol
>
> That's as far as I got. Ardena came and just left a little while ago. Now I'm blank!!
>
> No Marg didn't come to see me. I saw her at the post office Sun. noon. I went over to talk to her. She was with that old gang—Frances and the likes. She didn't say much. I asked her why you didn't come and she said you didn't want to!
>
> Why didn't you intend to tell me Johnny was coming? I can hardly understand you. Mrs. McN. told me the boys were coming with you so I guess I sorta looked for them—or him rather. It will make it cheaper on you, or will it?? $10.00 is lots of money. Would buy you a nice suit. Phil was surely disappointed when he found out you were just staying over the weekend. Oh well, he'll be glad to see you even for a short time. I can hardly wait! Marg did say she and you intended going back together. She didn't tell me anything only what I asked her so I didn't talk very long. I believe she's just as two-faced as ever? She was out with some drunk last night at the pie supper. Didn't know him. Didn't ask Phil or Bobby. Shandol, I'll be glad when you get through there. I've been scared what might happen to her while you two were together. Mrs. Colmay said she was disappointed in Marg. I told her I wasn't. I knew her. She's just whatever the crowd is! No wonder you've about quit writing to me, I'm always preaching, but I hate to see you done that way!
>
> No she didn't say to write. I had just written to you anyway. She (Marg) said you just had five weeks yet. That won't be

long if you get to come this weekend. I would advise you to finish now. You'll be drafted for labor?! Lester has to go Nov. 5th for his final exams. How will we ever stand to see him go?! A fellow strives to raise his family so he'll be proud of them. Then along comes something that bars your plans.

Hugh Burdett's here now. Going to be sorta funny he'll have that girl on the string, and you Johnny. So what? Ha. I look for Dean to make a fool of himself again. I'll write to Lester & Jane and have them come Sat. night and stay over Sun.

No school the rest of the week—teacher's meeting. Phil and Bobby have gone to town with Mrs. Colmay. I kept Laura and Jimmy Mon. all day. When the rest came home I still had them till 8 o'clock. Got supper. I was sorta put-out about it. She repaid me tho'.

I got a letter from Dad yesterday. He was shucking corn in Iowa. I'm sending you an envelope with a stamp and address so you sit right down and write to him. He was terrible homesick. But said he was determined to stick it out six weeks. That's a long time. But if he stays well it will soon pass away.

Karen has two teeth. She's growing nicely. She misses Daddy tho'. If we get the store bill paid I won't care whether he stays that long or not. Just seemed like we couldn't pay any debts, just live. You know I didn't can very much last year so have so much to buy. (Won't eat what I have). Phil is awful finicky about his eating.

Guess there's not much news. I'd send Dad's letter to you but since you're coming home you can read it here. He said for you to write to him! I've sure made a few pennies stretch this last week. Dad left a week ago today (Wed.).

I must quit and get to work. Don't forget or put off writing to Dad.

Hope I'll be seeing you.

Train late thought I might hear from Dad again.

Love, Mom

The letter from her mother gave Shandol pause. She was standing by her bunk, and after reading it, sat down, her hands on the crude boarded end, with it's X bracing the frame, and lay her head against her hands in a thoughtful mood.

Shandol thought her mother was a little hard on Margery. Margery had no intention of getting herself in trouble. She was sly and crafty. She might lead a guy on, but she'd never go all the way. Shandol would bet on it, "if I were the betting kind," she added mentally.

But Shandol guessed Margery was going through a bad time now. Perhaps trying to forget. Shandol's heart went out to her. After all, hadn't she dressed up many times to be ready to marry Derry if he'd even broached the subject? She must not only feel remorse, but pangs of embarrassment that she was so serious and he apparently was not. Shandol hoped she didn't, or wouldn't, chase after him. He just could not be worth the tears Shandol knew she had shed.

Then, too, Shandol had not told her folks Johnny drank a few beers now and then, but not many with Shandol as he knew she didn't like it. Derry also drank, but one hardly knew it. He could be silly anytime. But once in awhile it was on his breath, which Shandol hated to smell. She had even said that to Johnny in reference to Derry, but hoped he would take the hint also.

Shandol wondered how Margery would cope if she came back up here. She hoped Margery wouldn't begin it around her, at least.

Shandol had heard from her the day before her mother wrote. The letter had been written Monday, but apparently hadn't been mailed until later on. She hadn't tried to be two-faced with me, Shandol decided. Yet, she hadn't mentioned talking to Shandol's mother.

Her letter had contained details of her trip home. She had left Midhill at 2:05 and gone to Capital City, where she had had to wait until about 5:35. While there she went into the Capitol building, she wrote. She left there and made another change at 10:30, with a shorter wait. Then into Plainesville about 1:15 a.m. She wrote that she had had to stay there the rest of the night; she sat in Smitty's café the rest of the night. But it was nearly 3:00 p.m. when she actually arrived home. She did not say why the delay in reaching home, but Shandol calculated it had taken her over twenty-four hours to get there, finally.

She wrote she was having a swell time. She'd double-dated with Dean Leonard and she'd been with Nevin Hower; also she'd gone out "gadding about" last night for an hour or so. Dean really liked Shandol yet she had reported, as he had told her so and would really love to see Shandol before he leaves for good. She decided not to tell him when or how Shandol was coming home. She didn't know whether to do so or not.

Of course she wondered about Derry. Wondered how he was doing and if he had given Fredie a ring yet. She wrote that she had written him an awful letter and mailed it that morning.(Perhaps she hoped it would help, getting it off her chest, Shandol thought.) She was so in hopes she could forget Derry at home but it hadn't worked out that way. Yet she thought it easier because she didn't have to see him with *her*. She also wanted Shandol to talk to him, and ask him to come down with Johnny and herself.

She asked Shandol to save the ninth lesson so she could get the measurements from it next week to make her own.

She assured Shandol she had missed her; even that she called her mother and other family members, Shandol half the time. Seemed she had been gone from Midhill much longer than she had, and was certain she would never go back to stay lest she go nuts after awhile, though so far she had had a swell time. She still couldn't get Derry off her mind.

She wondered if anyone ever thought or ask about her, particularly Derry and Johnny and those girls who worked with them or otherwise had become friends. "Tell them all hello," she had written, and added, "Kiddo, I must close and get busy. Answer real soon, as I sure miss you." And also hoped she'd see her soon also. She closed "Love, Marg."

Shandol was so happy to hear from her. She had received the letter that evening after work and as soon as she got through supper and back to the dorm, she sat down and reread the letter. How happy she was go get it. She decided she could write a card, since she would see her by Sunday, at least. However, as it turned out she had forgotten to mail it the next day and because she knew she would get there before a card or letter would, she would just wait and talk to her. Of course, she hoped to see Margery; even as Margery had indicated they'd be visiting when Shandol got home.

Shandol writing on the card had been small and neat so she could cram as much on it as possible. She'd dated it simply: "Wed night." and did not try to paragraph it to save space.

Dearest Friend, (she wrote)
I got your letter this eve. Sure happy about it. Since you won't get this until Sat. and I'll see you Sun. I'll just write a card. I just got back from town. Almost got wet. Is it ever raining: It's about 9:15. Can you imagine me home at that time! Well, I went with another girl and I didn't see Johnny. No! We didn't have a date tonight. Said he wanted to sleep lots so he could drive Sat. night. Saw the car. Bless Patty, it was where it belonged! I was glad. I couldn't find him in town either. Last night we saw the awfullest wreck out by Rod's Place. Two trucks collided. One was one of B. Brandall's (Johnny's boss) and the other an apple truck. We have moved to dorm three now. The bunk above me is reserved and you know why! It's fine here, too. I did finish lesson 9—just today. Was it ever

hard! But I'll try to help you. Mine went together pretty well. I'm on the last one now—oh, boy! But it's a corker too. Hard! My lands, old Coyne has been on it a whole week and has made it three times. Maybe by the time you're ready for it I'll have a pattern ready. Kid I can answer your letter when I see you, can't I? Space gone—Shandol

CHAPTER 50

Shandol was back in camp, but alone again. Margery had left the next day. She had received some mail and her check and was ready to go back home. She had tearfully told Shandol she simply could not stay around knowing Derry was engaged to that other girl. Shandol was lonesome that day, so sat down and wrote to her mother. Not only would it take her mind off the aloneness she felt, she also realized she should let her mother know she had made it back all right from their trip down there that past weekend.

NYA Center Midhill
November 2, 1942

Dear Mom,

I've decided to write and let you know we made it home ok. We got back here about 10:00 last night, which was in plenty of time. Lands me, was I ever sleepy! Guess what!! Margery came back too, but she's ready to go back. She was 'tight' I think when she left. I don't see why she doesn't stay but she won't. She just doesn't know what she does want. She had some mail and her check up here. She has them now and I declare I believe she'll go back today. I'm terribly blue about it, too. But as I told Margery I had that feeling too often to give up and go back today. Besides I couldn't get ready in time to go with her now.

We stopped at Ramey's last night, but I didn't look at anyone. Ha. Do they ever tease me?! (That's where the army boy winked at me the last time we came.) And we also stopped at Capital City. Marg is getting ready to go. I'm going to walk a ways with her. Poor girl, she's so dissatisfied. I feel so sorry for her. (She can't get that man off her mind. I doubt he's worth all her misery! But one never knows about the heart of another, eh?)

I aim to write to Dad soon, but I'll have to wait until I go to town to get some paper.

Hugh Burdett and the Maple Hill girl got married Friday night, I've learned. She's back up here and simply thrilled to tears. We're all happy for her—if that's what she wants. I guess he has gone back now. A rather short honeymoon I'd think. It was such a surprise he had another girl and never told either of us. At least he never told me about *her*. Wonder which of us was his favorite!

I declare I couldn't get up enough nerve to speak to Dean. I honked Johnny's car horn at him. He'd told Marg he'd like to talk to me. Johnny said he wouldn't have minded, but I wonder. Anyway Dean had that other girl so guess it doesn't matter now.

Fredie, the girl who came down with us, and came back, said her mother was terribly thrilled over her engagement. I hope nothing happens to them as to Marg and him.

Oh, I'm really blue, but it's because Marg is polishing her shoes now. I'm not going to spend the five dollars. I may want to go home again too.

I realize now why my visit home wasn't a complete success. *Dad wasn't there!* Of course I knew I'd miss him. Seemed so strange for him not to be hurrying around getting ready to go to church on Sunday. I really did miss him and I'm going to try to write to him real often.

Johnny apologized again to me for not staying there the rest of the night (or Sun. morning). I think it was because of Derry. He didn't want to stay this time. Guess he was self-conscious about what you folks would think. Anyway, I think Johnny likes you folks. And he didn't mind for Phil to drive the car but he was glad he didn't go very far. We were supposed to hurry, as you know. We weren't sure we could find where Fredia lived, it was so dark when we'd been there last night. But we finally did and we made it back in swell time.

Well, I'll have to close now. Do hurry and write. I have several letters to write. But right now Marg is in a hurry.

Love to all,
Shandol

While the girls made their way down the, by now, familiar shortcut, they were at first quiet. Shandol did not want to remind her of Derry, yet that was utmost in her mind as she was sure it was Margery's. But after awhile the silence became unbearable as they went sometimes single file because of brush and tree limbs, other times, side by side, and of course there was the pipe to cross the branch. They would certainly have to go single file there.

"Isn't this make believe bridge something," Shandol ventured. "I don't think I shall ever forget this shortcut."

"Me either," Margery replied, stonily.

"I just never thought I'd see the day when we couldn't talk," Shandol told her. "I wish I could do or say *something* that could make you feel better. You seem such a little lost lamb, not knowing which way to go."

Margery stopped and looked at Shandol. Her deep dark blue, almost purple eyes sad and filling with tears. Soon she was sobbing. Shandol awkwardly put her arm around her, as she let her suitcase drop and the girls embraced and both cried. Shandol in loneliness and Margery in heartbreak. Shandol still held to the letter she would mail to her mother, and would go on to town for paper to finish her letter writing. Margery would go on to the bus station. They were saying their good-byes there.

"I'm sorry, Shandol," Margery finally said, wiping at her eyes which seemed to fill each time she tried to dry them. Her voice was still unsteady, her mouth tight and she was trying to control her crying. "A good cry always did help us, didn't it?" She tried gamely to brighten, but her attempt at a smile still showed the pain she felt.

Shandol, I must say this," she went on. "I'd have married him anytime he'd asked, so I don't blame Fredie. So I'm embarrassed too, as well as hurt. Are the girls laughing?"

"No one knows that but us," Shandol said. "They may realize you were more serious, more settled than he, but that happens. They know you maybe hurt or maybe some just think you aren't that crazy about sheet metal." Shandol laughed, shakily, because she guessed that, at least, was a near truth, even if now the main trouble was perhaps Margery's lack of caring or being able to concentrate.

"I see what you mean," she nodded. "But I don't think I can concentrate on it just yet." She took the thought almost from Shandol's mind.

"At least Winnie's happy," Shandol volunteered, to have something to say.

"Were you hurt about that'?" Margery asked. "He was a good guy—better than Dean, I'd say. But Dean still loves you."

"Dean loves Dean, as my folks would say," Shandol contradicted. "He's too immature to know what he wants. Oh, he wants me now, but he's so spoiled, when he gets what he wants, would he be like a child with a toy—just want the next one that appealed to him? Maybe Derry needs some growing up yet. I wish he wouldn't hurry into marrying her. They haven't gone together long enough. How long? Two or three weeks and she already has a ring. One never knows, I suppose."

"Let's not talk about him," Margery eyes even made the appeal. Shandol realized it must be a tender spot indeed.

"Well, back to Winnie then," Shandol smiled. "I was surprised he had that other girl. Oh, I knew he had gone with other girls, but I had not known he was serious about anyone else. And I wasn't sure how really serious he was about me. His family was for me, I know that. They've as good as told my folks that. I wonder if they put pressure on him, and maybe he really loved the other girl, who knows? But he sure wrote me some nice love letters. I wonder if he did to her too! It sort of put me off him. But I don't think he sent her a picture. One thing she really wanted him and she wasn't going to give me a chance to horn in. Ha. Ha." Shandol laughed, almost merrily, thinking of it.

"Do you resent her at all?" Margery queried?

I don't think so, really. I wasn't involved enough or committed enough to be heartbroken or anything like that. I wish them happiness, and mean it. But it was a let-down to think he'd do that. I never did write to him anymore after I found out about her. He treated me like I was his first choice, but she was so insistent and all. She probably couldn't wait to tell him I had a steady boyfriend up here. Maybe added that we were likely to get married anytime—who knows? Anything's fair in love and war, as they say."

"Could be," Margery replied, gloomily.

"Oh, I shouldn't have said that," Shandol apologized, as she put her fingers to her lips.

"It's all right," Margery replied, "but here's where it seems we go separate ways. I hate to leave, but it's so bad to stay."

"I know," Shandol replied. "Oh, I'm going to miss you so. I don't know how long I can stand it."

She watched Margery disappear down the street as she went by the post office to mail the letter and on to Main Street, a block on and turned north to go to the dime store. It seemed so strange for her to be alone, but she was, so she got the paper she had come for, paid the cashier and hurried out.

She decided not to go back the shortcut alone. So she began the long walk up the highway, only a block from Main St., then to the street that led past the camp, where she could go in the nearest corner and not go to the road that went along in front of the dorms.

The morning then was practically gone, so the busy part of it would begin. She barely made it to yard duty. Margery had insisted on a rather early start. She had some thinking to do, she had said, and she might try to see Derry one last time if she could find him. If not she'd look at the town and recall memories.

"Sorry I can't go along," Shandol told her, "but guess I better go on back. I hate for you to be alone."

"I'm not very good company," Margery replied. "And I don't mind, really."

"Maybe we'll see each other soon." Shandol had answered, and their parting good-bye had been brief in what seemed like plain view of everyone.

x x x x

By Wednesday Shandol was writing to her mother in a different tone. She could hardly believe what Johnny had told her, but she knew he had no reason to lie. Anyway she just had to get if off her chest:

NYA Center
Midhill
Nov. 4, 1942

Dear Mom,

One reason I'm going to write is because I have something to tell you. Margery didn't come home after all, did she? Well, she's working up in town doing housework for Derry's sister!! I'm a bit put-out about it. Don't kid yourself, she's here for a purpose and I'm afraid it's to cause trouble. What kind? Well, she did make the announcement if she couldn't have one of the boys she'd take the other! Imagine that. Well, she asked Johnny to take her to Capital City to catch the bus home. He was intending to take her, he said, but she decided to stay up here. Johnny said he thought maybe she didn't have money to go home and he would have given it to her. Night before last she was with Derry! Went to the show with him! John was with Derry for awhile and they wanted him to go to the show with them, but he didn't. What I feel is she can put on the "little sister" act, like I won't care because she's my friend, or so she thinks. But I gave Johnny the understanding last night that a date was a date whoever 'she' was. Did I do wrong? I just decided to let him know how I feel. She would go with him in a minute, but he promised me last night that he would not go with her. She's changed, seems to me. I think trying to act 'smart'. Still smokes and drinks too. I know Johnny likes that (like a fish in the pickle dish). It seems plain she's just

711

throwing herself at them. Johnny said he told her he thought lots of me and didn't consider going with her. I'm not going around her very much. My friend indeed!? I'm sorry about it all. I liked her so much. Do you suppose she can 'throw herself at them' until they can't dodge? I believe Johnny when he said he wouldn't go with her. Oh, don't tell anyone, and make the kids keep still too, if they read this. They probably won't be interested, though. But it just has to come off my chest. Too bad I pick on you, eh?

I want to write to Dad again. I haven't had time to hear from him. I also have got to wash some. Always something, eh?

I'm reading a good book. You've read it and I may have. The name of it is *The Hound of the Baskervilles*. Sometimes I could scream! I'm not quite halfway through the book. By the way didn't we read *Jane Eyre*? I'm going to again. It seems I've read it but I can't remember how it comes out.

Marg's mother doesn't know where she is. She may go home before a week, but she is wanting her brother to come up this weekend when he's home. Well, so much for that.

I'll be looking for a letter soon. Hope all 're ok.

Love to all,
Shandol

Shandol heard from her mother on Friday. Her days had gone routinely and she had scarcely heard anymore about Margery.

Johnny hadn't seen her, and Derry would not talk about her when Fredie was along. Apparently, she had not left, however. If he did, it was to broaden his round fleshy face with his big smile, and deny knowing a thing about her—even if she did stay at his sister's. He had such a little boy, bashful way, which belied his actual assured attitude of one having been the worldly actualities—and possibly experienced some. But sitting in the back seat, when asked an unusually personal or a question he hated to answer, he could rub his palms together between his knees, appear embarrassed and probably was, and just shake his head negatively that he couldn't say anything about it, leaving the impression that he really had nothing to say.

Shandol and Johnny had had a date Wednesday night. They had been alone. It had been planned so, he told her, and it was later Shandol learned why. He asked her to marry him.

"I don't think it's a matter of if," he had added, "but when. I think we should set the date."

Shandol was silent for several minutes, until the silence became embarrassing.

"I—well—um—" she stammered. "I thought I'd be ready for some such question, but I don't know what to say now, really. I don't know what to do either," she added.

There was a lot she didn't know about the man sitting beside her in the parked car, she knew that. They had parked in a lane which went through the park. It was a shaded area. The air smelled fresh and crisp on the night air. By now a few crickets chirped and the other early fall night sounds were around them, including automobiles and the lights even faced them at times, but they could have hardly seen them let alone know their thoughts and topic of conversation. A slight breeze through the car window stirring at Shandol's hair, making a pleasant scene, even though almost deserted.

"I want to feel like when I get married I'll be married a long time," she said, almost musing to herself.

"It's true we haven't known each other long, but we've been together a lot," Johnny told her. "It seems I've known you all my life, almost."

"I know," she replied. "I've thought the same. But don't you see I felt almost like that with Dean. The only difference he was always in such a rush to get married. At least you aren't pushy. I believe that's why I've put him off. If I'd loved him I wouldn't have stayed away. But what he did interested me. It was just like wanting to know about anyone else down there. They were people I knew."

"I'm glad to hear that anyway," Johnny said, smiling at her, his large blue eyes tender. His skin, though tanned even on his face, was smooth and soft to touch, as Shandol suddenly felt the urge to put her palm along his jawline.

"The truth is," Johnny went on, "I'm afraid you'll want to go home and not come back and I just can't let you go."

"But what about the war? This awful old war?" Shandol asked, her lips pursed grimly. "You may have to go, so what's the difference?"

"I'd still want you to be my wife," he replied seriously. "I realize it's a possibility, and I'm not wanting to marry to keep out. That don't work anyway, and I couldn't do it in any case."

"Come to think of it I'd hate to be parted from you too," she said, and realized what a truth it was. She knew he had kept her up here this long or she would have been gone before. Yes, being away from him was painful to even anticipate.

"When did you first think you loved me?" she asked, coyly, "and would you have married me when we took your brother to St. Louis and went by St. Charles?"

"I believe I began to suspect it anyway when we took you home that first time and that soldier winked at you. I really wanted to pounce him. I realized I considered you my girl and I wanted no one to horn in. And of course I'd have married you that day. I asked you didn't I?"

"I just thought you were jealous of the uniform," she looked at him shyly. "And the marryin' part I wasn't sure we were serious enough. But we did have the witnesses, didn't we?"

"I know and I let it go at that," he replied, good-humoredly. "Maybe I was jealous of the uniform but there *was* a man in it! I had no cause to want to crumple a uniform. Besides uniforms don't wink at girls, they only get their attention."

"Yes, and I think I shall be jealous of you in uniform," she said, honestly.

"So no more about that day. We were trying to figure out a day when we got off the subject or around it."

"When would you like?" she asked.

"The sooner the better," he replied.

"Oh, don't say that," she replied quickly. She remembered Margery's flippant words and her heartbreak now.

"Can you be ready by Saturday?" he asked. "I can get off work early that day. And we can go to Capital City and get a license and I know where a justice of the peace lives."

"Who'll be going—" she trailed off. She knew the ceremony would have to be witnessed. She had seen her brother married.

"I think Derry and Fredie will go. They might decide to get married the same time," he said. "But I'll have that worked out, you just be ready."

"I think I can manage that," she replied, "but I will have to shop for a dress. Good thing Dad sent me some money to go home on, which I've kept. I hope it will buy something with what I have."

She didn't want him to assume she hadn't enough to get married and offer to help out. She would have just died of mortification. The truth was she had very little more to spend or she would be broke; and how could she write home for money after she was married? Which reminded her she must get it settled that she was to finish her training there in camp and she would be there awhile.

"We'll live—actually—pretty much as we are now?" she asked, shyly. "I mean I have so little time needed to finish my training and we've made no other plans, have we?"

"I understand that, sure," he replied. "Or we'll see how it's going to work out anyway. Two-three more weeks shouldn't make that much difference one way or the other. We can be together weekends anyway."

It sounded plausible and Shandol wondered how it would work out, but she was sure they loved one another enough for it to work out. They just drove around, mostly after that, talking or sometimes quiet, as though each one had to get this new idea established in his and her minds. But mostly their conversation was light and casual; wondering what their friends would say; and what about their families. Shandol's eyes shone and she smiled almost all the time, revealing even, clean white teeth. They also mentioned more about the day in St. Charles and how his brother had ridden along—just in case? Was it so incredible?

He looked at her, his bride to be, and when their eyes met Shandol realized she was having a great moment in her life. She loved this man.

As he took her home, he told her he would see her the next night.

Shandol decided to tell no one she would be married Saturday. She would not even write to tell her mother. Couldn't something come up that one or the other would have a change of heart? She wanted no embarrassment of being jilted or having to pretend she had made the decision. She was sure she would not change her mind about it. She was almost as sure of Johnny.

But it was touchy as she recalled Margery, and her enthusiasm and disappointment, even though the circumstances hadn't been the same.

But following the next night when he had surprised her by presenting her with a ring—a set, in fact, there was no way of keeping it. She didn't have to tell anyone. They guessed. Yet because she did not wear her ring all the time little was actually said to her.

They had gone by so Shandol could show Margery. She wanted her to know, as she still thought of her as a good friend and thought she would want to know. Shandol was not disappointed. She was all smiles and sincerely seemed glad for Shandol, and wished her well and even opened the door and the girls embraced, as though they had parted months ago. But there was no time to talk and no privacy, so Shandol did not ask Margery how things were with her. It somehow didn't seem appropriate, exuberating with her own happiness, even more than she could have realized.

So luckily Johnny whisked her away lest any strained silences fall. After all she had only wanted to tell her. Shandol could almost see the smile fade and hurt and despair replace it as they drove off on just another date, even though they were now an engaged couple. She had wondered how Margery was bearing up and if she sometimes cried in her pillow in homesickness, heartbreak and frustration at the helplessness—even hopelessness—of it all. But Shandol could hardly dwell on it for long as she was so much more concerned with her own affairs.

It was Fredie who went with her to choose a dress. They had gone on Friday, but by then Shandol had told her of her engagement, and Fredie told her she and Derry were not only going along, but were actually getting married that same night. They had decided it the night before. Fredie had more money to spend, which Derry had "loaned" her, she said, but Shandol thought her dress was about as pretty. Shandol's was a blue, street-length dress, buttoned down the front, with a self-material tie belt; and best of all it was on sale. The full price was the five dollars she had been sent to go home, plus eight cents tax. Well, could she consider she would be using it for that, only in time, to her own home. That had not been in the minds of her parents she was sure!

Shandol and Fredie had also already asked for the weekend off. Fredie tried to bluff it and say they were going home again, but the supervisor noticed the rings, which were by now no secret anyway, and smilingly asked if they were sure they were going home or getting married. So Shandol admitted she was getting married and Fredie also conceded.

"It didn't much seem to make any difference," Fredie apologized sheepishly (for her), we wanted the weekend off and supposed that was safest.

"You're both of age, aren't you?" Mrs. Crocker asked. The girls both nodded agreement.

"I've no objections then," she told them.

x x x x

The letter Shandol received from her mother that Friday was dated Audrey's usual brief way: "Wed. noon."

Dear Darling:
Received your letter this morning. Blue! I've had the blues so bad the last day or two until I think I can hardly stand it. Oh, how I wish you could come home and stay! But I know sometime I'll have to give you up, but how? Life's like that. Anybody looks at me and I cry nearly. Guess with so much on my mind and Dad being gone don't help any.
    Lester and Jane will come a little while tonight. Just can't hardly stand having him go. The old war is terrible! Dean has to go today. Yes, I know his mother feels as I do just like putting them before a firing squad. They're having a terrible

716

battle over there now. The Japs, seem to be pretty strongly fortified.

Dec. 4 isn't very long off now. I believe if I was you I'd stay my course out. Margery is just unsettled. So don't worry about her. One has to do for himself as best he can. But I want you to come home and stay awhile when you get through, job or no job, then you can tell me about Johnny. "Absence makes the heart grow fonder," I wonder!

We heard about Hugh Burdett. Maybe it's just as well.

Tell Johnny I've a crow to pick with him for not staying here!

Got a letter from Dad this a.m. Didn't say much. Corn is hard to pick. He has a good place to stay and lots to eat, but that isn't home. I guess I'm so dissatisfied as he. He sent me some money Mon.

Today is first aid. Just three more lessons after today. I'll be glad! The community house got on fire yesterday, but they weren't long getting it out.

Went to Mrs. Ruleton's yesterday to study.

Trying to rain today.

Phil has driven Mrs. Colmay to town today. Prof. Kinkle wants him to work but don't guess he will. Dad said he was afraid he wouldn't do any good there.

I'm sending your letter to you from Harley Lensing.

Karen has been cranky last day or so. She has some cold. I don't get much else done. I'm sorta blank.

Must get to work. 1:30 will be here 'ere I know it.

Cheer up maybe things will work out yet for the best. Here's hoping.

Write when you can.

Love, Mom

Then dawned Shandol's wedding day. No, it wasn't a long engagement, she agreed with the girls and just laughed that off. But she wondered how she would ever get through the day. And later, in retrospect, it was not sure how she had. The thought of her marriage never left her, yet make it through she must. It was supposed to be as any other Saturday. Johnny, she knew, had to work. It was not a regular workday for her. She was required to be on yard duty with the others. So Shandol supposed it had been a regular Saturday, as far as it could be when she had so much on her mind. It was an important step she was taking and she wondered if waiting were the answer. But it did not seem so to her, so how could it be? She thought the day would last indefinitely. She was nervous, yet she anticipated her marriage happily and dreamily. She was terribly shy, even jumpy, as she expected to be teased, or receive hints in snide remarks, and discouragement. But none came.

In fact, when it was time to get ready to go she felt the belle of a ball, she received so much attention. The girls wanted to help in anyway they could and couldn't seem to do enough, the atmosphere told her.

She later learned Fredie was treated the same way. When Fredie was ready she strolled to Shandol's side of the dorm, followed by her faithful subjects. Hugh Burdett's wife had practically taken over, since she wanted to be known as a new bride herself. Fredie was ready first and they came to where Shandol was having her hair combed by one of the girls.

"You must have something old, something new, something borrowed and something blue," someone quoted for the umpteenth time that day.

"So I've heard," Shandol replied.

"Do you have, Fredie?"

"I think so," and she began the enumeration.

Shandol, like Fredie, had a blue dress, which took care of that. Shandol knew a girl next to her own bunk with pumps exactly like her own, except newer, so she borrowed the newer ones. She would wear her "old" coat, which had been given to her second hand, and she had worn it to high school. It still looked nice enough as it was dressy to begin with. Her dress was new, but for good measure she wore a new pair hose.

Shandol could not think when she had received so much attention. The girls were excited for her, which added to Shandol's excitement and nervousness. She was reassured over and over, as was Fredie, because they both craved reassurance. It was comforting to have their moral support. Shandol was sure she would not have made it without it since Margery was gone and none of her family was anywhere near.

The girls gazed at themselves to be sure they looked their best. They were reassured over and over and told they looked like brides-to-be. Their eyes shone and they were so "dolled up" they were "a feast for sore eyes" and then some. They had each taken care to have their hair washed and clean. Fredie's was naturally curly and had only to be combed into its natural waves. Shandol had washed hers last night, pincurled it and left it up overnight and all day. That way she hoped it would not have time to droop. It was getting long again. The girl who was combing it for her had a knack, she was often told, doing hair and her own well attested to the fact. Shandol was happy to let her, she herself was so nervous and all thumbs, she was so grateful she hadn't had to ask.

They were getting close to time to go. They kept asking how they looked, and was everyone sure they looked all right or were they just saying that. Actually Shandol was quite pleased with herself, but loved the compliments.

The time by then was flying.

The grooms-to-be showed up on the appointed time, 7:30, dressed in suits and ties and looking handsome themselves.

They went to their supervisors, who were both waiting, as they had to sign out.

"You girls look lovely," Mrs. Crocker said. "Shandol, you look so sweet and pretty—and young."

"Just beautiful," Mrs. Morris added.

"Oh, your getting my goat," Shandol replied, embarrassed, hoping Fredie didn't feel slighted. But she was grinning broadly at Shandol's shyness and agreed. *Where's my manners,* Shandol thought.

"Thanks for the compliment?" It was almost a question in her unsureness. "I'm so unnerved I can't think straight. I just can't calm down."

"You'll be all right—just a slight case of jitters. It happens," Mrs. Crocker grinned knowingly at Mrs. Morris.

The innuendos were given at the send off. It was a sincere one, the girls had no doubt, and they seemed to fuss over them and followed them to the waiting car. There were shouts of good or best wishes for happiness, "loads of happiness," "best wishes always," and Hugh Burdett's wife, in jest shouted so everyone in camp must hear, Shandol thought: "Don't do anything I wouldn't do!" There were whoops and "careful now" until they were out of earshot.

The other two married couples had gone by now. One of the men had simply joined the army and his wife had gone back to her home town to hunt for a job. The other two had not aimed to stay—just long enough to get the money to leave.

They were soon on their way, emotionally charged. In turn shy, nervous, happy, scared and disbelieving it was really happening. There was joking, quietness, questions and nervous laughter as they made their way south on the now familiar highway. Just before getting to Capital City there was the Momundy river to cross. As they reached it they saw a growing line of cars waiting. They soon learned the bridge was "open" so a boat could pass upriver. So they too had to wait—and wait. It seemed a long time but was perhaps only fifteen minutes or so. No one thought to time it.

No sooner had they started moving with the traffic, when Johnny realized something was wrong. He voiced the problem incredibly, "I've got a flat tire! Of all times! Can't even move off the bridge—better not!"

But dressed up or not he had a tire to change. Derry got out, but the girls were told to stay put because of the traffic. Why had the tire gone down while they waited? Perhaps Johnny would learn later. As he inspected it by flashlight to solve the unfortunate mystery, he discovered a roofing nail had punctured it. It could be repaired.

Their first stop, once in the city, was a justice of the peace, which Johnny and Derry just happened to remember how to find. As the couples had no licenses he put in a telephone call to the Recorder of Deeds, whose secretary he assured them would meet them at the county courthouse.

Getting a license, they were to learn, wasn't to be all that easy for Johnny and Shandol. The lady would not believe Shandol was old enough. When asked her age she had told her the truth.

"I'm nineteen," she'd said, confidently.

"You only have to be eighteen, you know," the sophisticated, all businesslike lady behind the desk said, her eyes searching Shandol's face. She was not a pretty woman, but she could have been nice looking if she didn't seem so severe, Shandol decided. She could only see her upper torso but she seemed tall, and slender, well dressed and Shandol supposed she resented being called back to work at such a late hour.

"But I am nineteen," Shandol answered, realizing she wasn't going to believe her. Shandol looked at Johnny helplessly. The clerk did also.

"How old are you?" she asked.

"Twenty-six," he replied, his hand in his pocket, rattling coins nervously.

Shandol looked at Fredie who was only eighteen. How would she make out? And how were they to make her believe Shandol's age?

"Do your parents approve of you getting married?" she was asked by the lady behind the high counter.

"Of course," she replied. "But anyway I'm of age. Why do you doubt me?" The innocent eyes met the older one's head-on, but pleadingly.

"Is that your class ring?" she finally asked.

"Yes, it is," Shandol replied. If only she will believe that, Shandol thought. It had the year and school.

"May I see it?" Shandol handed it to her, from her right hand, now that she had the diamond ring on the other.

"You've been out of school over a year?" she looked at Shandol, who nodded affirmatively.

She looked at Fredie, who had her own class ring. "Well, it certainly wouldn't fit either of the men. I guess I'll have to let it go at that, then, but I declare you don't look like you could be a day over seventeen." She looked at Johnny. "If her parents come back on anyone about this will you take responsibility?"

"Yeah, sure," he replied. Shandol wanted to scream.

"They won't," Shandol heard herself say, she couldn't help adding, "I'm telling the truth."

"I don't have to issue this license if I don't think you're old enough," she was told.

"Sorry," Shandol said. "I was trying to help. I never dreamed I'd have to prove my age, but I see where it leaves you, if you misjudge—" her voice trailed off.

It didn't matter. She was going to issue the license.

Strangely enough Derry and Fredia had no trouble with their ages. They were believed. Derry had actually had misgivings.

He admitted to them he was actually only eighteen years old and he would have to lie about his age, since he hadn't wanted his parents along. Shandol had not known that, and she wondered if Margery did. Fredie had of course. He had told her, finally; though he had said he was twenty-one at first, she had laughed. But as they talked of marriage, he had had to admit it to her, wondering if it made any difference. Shandol had not been told. They had assumed Johnny had told her, she supposed, but it hadn't come up, though once he had said Derry wasn't twenty-one, she had supposed he soon would be. It had just not become an issue to ponder or go into. Now she wondered if he had confided to Margery. Somehow, she doubted it, because Margery herself was not old enough to get married without her parents consent.

They kidded Shandol about her looks, when no one else had had any trouble. She couldn't realize she could look younger than Fredie, who'd even been philosophical about it; "It's your bright hair and innocent look and baby face," she had said, lightly. The smile on her face happy and proud.

It was decided that because Johnny and Shandol had been issued their license first Derry and Fredie would actually be married first.

"I wanna get it over," Derry said. "I had some scary minutes when Shandol had such a time getting the license. I was sure they'd question me."

"Oh, it's not the same with boys," Fredie said. "Anyway it's not you look older, it's just that some people look young. Maybe that woman didn't want to go through *that* again," she finished, giggling.

"I believe she thought we'd back out," Johnny said. "I mean if you were underage," looking at Shandol and smiling, "but staying and keeping our heads helped—and the truth of course."

"And the ring," Shandol supplied. "I never guessed it'd do me a favor," she added, marveling as she looked at it.

After the brief ceremony of vows and nervous "I do's, " Shandol moaned to Fredie, "you got to sign your married name to our marriage certificate, whereas I wasn't married yet to sign mine so how was it, using a new name?"

"Legal," she laughed, "and fun, I think. We didn't do it for that though."

"I'm glad that's done," Shandol sighed, and was answered by sighs of relief and agreement.

"You could say that again for me," Derry laughed.

It was back to Midhill directly. They debated about eating, but no one was hungry. They settled for soft drinks and decided it was time to find cabin rooms for the night. The one they chose was one of a series on the hill, Shandol and Margery had passed many times going to town the long way round, on the highway, midway up the long hill going south from the main part of town.

Then Shandol was alone with her husband. She was nervous as ever and quite self-conscious. She wasn't sure what she expected and when she realized she had packed nothing for an overnight stay, she was mortified. She had no makeup except lipstick, though luckily she had a small comb with her. But she realized she and Fredie too, would be sleeping in their underclothing, which they did at camp. But this was different, she supposed, than being with a group of girls who did the same. In fact some only slept in bra and panty. But Shandol knew the watchman came through the dorm every night to see if every girl was in bed who was supposed to be, and in case the sheet and spread slipped she would feel more decently dressed. At first he had awakened her, though he was quiet, but the flashlight had caught her full in the face and she had roused out of fright. He had not aimed to throw the light in her face, only so he could see that the bunk was occupied. But now she hardly knew when—or if—he came through; though she was sure he did.

He had found Jody missing, hadn't he? And whether it was likely that would ever be repeated, it was intended as a routine thing. He also went through the boy's dorms.

Shandol and Johnny curiously looked the place over, to occupy some awkward moments. They could see the main room had a bed and dresser and two chairs, which looked more functional than for comfortably relaxing. There was also a small kitchenette, where they

722

realized they could prepare food if they had happened to have had any, which they hadn't; and of course, a small bath with shower.

But then they could not prolong the obvious indefinitely. Shandol must prepare herself to actually get into bed with this man she had married, "for better or worse." What would it be like? How could she possibly do it? But wasn't it done all the time? Johnny saw her agitation and remarked gently: "Don't be afraid. I'm not going to hurt you."

But she decided he was nervous. It was chilly in the cabin (as it was referred to) and he fumbled with the gas heater. Then when they smelled a strange odor, he worried about the stove, which they couldn't get lit anyway and decided they would have to do without it as it was so late. She wondered how Derry and Fredie were doing and voiced it.

"We'd better not try to find out!" he laughed good-humoredly.

"Oh," she replied, knowingly.

"Let's go to bed," he said. "Keep warmer anyway!"

"Uh—um—turn out that light," Shandol replied. "I'll be ready soon."

And she was. Almost immediately she was in his arms. He hungrily, it seemed to Shandol, found her mouth to kiss her. She realized he too was in underwear. But then as his kisses, more demanding and he found her responding, his hands slipped to her thigh, then to her utter surprised incredibility, they were shedding some clothing!

Then in love and mutual longing they truly became one.

Johnny was gentle, yet passionate, but he realized Shandol had things to learn, and he would be glad to teach her.

CHAPTER 51

They slept until afternoon Sunday. They hated to leave the only home they had even then, but knew it was necessary or they would be paying for another night. This brought a sadness, regret, and frustration as they knew they would not be sharing the night together, or until the next weekend. There would be their "dates" during the week, double dates, and their intimate moments would be restricted to just petting, kissing and unfulfilled desires. It did not worry Shandol, however. She would refuse to let any thought invade her happiness and contentment of the moment. In fact she felt marvelous. She had slept well; she took a shower before leaving the motel, once again wearing her wedding dress.

It was nearly two in the afternoon when they finally sat at a table in a restaurant for a meal. They had fried chicken, mashed potatoes and gravy, a vegetable and pie. It was a late breakfast or lunch but worth waiting for. They took their time over the food as they had learned Shandol was a slow eater, and she would not finish if they were all ready but herself.

Though Shandol had expected the rest of the afternoon would be spent as other afternoons, especially Sundays, she learned Johnny wanted her to meet another of his brothers. This one was in the army, home on furlough. Shandol thought he was very handsome in uniform. Johnny introduced him simply as Clay. He was tall, taller than Johnny. But the same blue eyes, dimples and pointed chin. In uniform he looked immaculate and distinguished. Shandol was becoming impressed by the handsome, good looking members of her husband's family whom she had met so far. But she still had some to go, as his was a large family. That is, larger than her own.

Clay rode around with them, visiting, discussing his army life, people he met and the trip home. Then they took him back to his sister's home, arriving expectantly about suppertime. The two couples went to a show, complete with popcorn. Then the girls had to go back to camp on time, which they were.

The next day Shandol received a letter from her mother. It was written the day before Shandol was married.

Dearest Dearie:

I have three pairs overalls to wash yet, but will sit down to write and get this off my chest. Sorta gloomy anyway so don't know whether I'll hang them out or not. Rained the last few days—or drizzled along.

Guess you received my other letter? Well, I feel better. Had a good cry that helps a lot. Lester didn't come Wed. so don't know anymore about him.

Received your letter today, dated 4th. I'm disappointed in Margery! Maybe I shouldn't be surprised. One thing it will let you know if Johnny is the sort of person who would do right or not. No, you did right letting him know how you felt! How he reacts will be the clue. The world is full of Johnnys or whatever tell him I said so!

What sort of person is Derry? I believe you'd be better off if you ditched the whole outfit. Derry must not be all that much, going with Marg—even to a movie. What does the bride-to-be think? Just read carefully. You know what's right and what's not. You can't do anything about them, so don't worry. But steer clear when you can't agree.

Tommy has written to you.

It's trying to clear off this morn. Rained every day but one last week. Phil and Bobby are going to town with Mrs. Colmay. I was going but she stays so long I decided to wait awhile. Didn't get started early enough to come back on the bus. Phil has been going to a serial show at three o'clock, then she aims to go out of town three miles to look at some cows. She never has to hurry. The last time I kept Jimmy and Laura he cried. I'm not going to keep them! That's her job caring for her family.

Don't know any news. Haven't been anywhere since Wed. first aid. Must get to work and clean up the house.

Write and tell me all the news. I've written this in a hurry—hope it makes sense.

Be good and write.

Love, Mom

As Shandol read it she thought of the letter she had written to her mother the night before and just got mailed as she had picked up the letter from her mother. Shandol knew her mother would want to know she was married and even expect details and Shandol's usual chattiness. Shandol had found it awkward, of course, because she hadn't told her before hand. But she hoped she would not be hurt or feel Shandol had acted too quickly, even though there was nothing she could do about it—should she want to. Shandol wrote:

NYA Center
Midhill
Nov. 8, 1942

Dear Mother,

(Shandol knew that would tell her mother something was coming:)

Tonight I'm very happy. Perhaps I should have told you, so you'd anticipate this letter, but I didn't know what might come up. I'll not keep you waiting, but I'll just tell you. Maybe you've heard or guessed already.

Saturday night at Capital City I was married. I can hardly feature it either (?) without you and some more of the folks. But that's the way we decided on it. Johnny and I, and Derry and Fredie were both (couples)married. We did not have a double wedding however, as we were witnesses for each others' weddings. I'll just begin and tell you from the beginning of when I really knew.

I have known I was getting married Saturday for sure since Wednesday night. Johnny gave me the rings (note 'rings', he wanted me to keep the other as was such a few days) Thursday night. I think they are a very pretty set and was (and am) so proud of them. You'll agree they're pretty.

By the way, I spent the five dollars you sent for me to come home on for a dress to be married in. It's really pretty, I think. It is blue. But that's about all that matters, except it cost $5.08 tax and all. I had on something old, something new, something borrowed, and something blue. I borrowed (because the girls insisted, due to that superstition) a pair of shoes which were identical to mine (black pumps), except they were newer looking.

We went to Capital City, leaving here about 7:30 p m. The funniest thing when we got to the river bridge it was open, as a boat was passing, so we had to wait. As we waited one of the tires went down. It had a roofing nail in it, so they had to change a tire, on the bridge—on our wedding night. Ha—ha.

We located a justice fairly readily as the guys happened to know where one lived. He telephoned for the Recorder of Deed's secretary to go to the county courthouse to get the licenses, as we didn't have them. They almost wouldn't let Johnny and I have one, because she wouldn't believe I'm nineteen years of age. My class ring saved me. She believed it. Said she wouldn't have thought I was but 17. She asked when I was born, etc. After we had the license, we went back to the justice of the peace who married us. Johnny and I got our license first, but Fredie and Derry were married first. So she got to sign her married name as one of our witnesses.

After the ceremony we came back to Midhill, where we stayed the rest of the night. It was late when we retired so we slept until afternoon Sun. Then we went to town in time for a good chicken dinner at a cafe at two o'clock. I met Johnny's brother, who is in the army, stationed in California and is now home on furlough. Is he good looking! I have a good folder picture of him he gave us.

I hope you aren't very mad at me for not telling you, but something could have come up.

I got your letter this morning. Thank heavens Margery has gone back to Greenway. She can't cause friction between Johnny and I even though she tried it. I didn't see her much. Wasn't around with a group I thought much of. But she left Saturday. I don't know if she's coming back or not. She even asked Johnny to take her to Arkansas again and she'd buy the gas. Imagine! Nerve or what? She'd seen my rings by then. Johnny makes light of it though, sh-h-h. (But couldn't it have gotten him in trouble? She's underage yet. Crossing state line with a minor—or something. Could get married or trouble?? Or do I have the wrong impression from somewhere?)

So Johnny won't let me come home, eh? Ha! Ha! Well, I'm going to finish my training—I told him that before we were married—then I told him I was going home for a week or so. Just so I come back, is all he said. Of course I'd have to do that. But that wasn't very nice of whoever said that. That sort of thing can't hurt us, though.

Yes, I'm planning on staying here to finish my training. That, too, is part of the bargain. Mom, please, just don't scold me now. I've done (do'ed) it and so far I'm not sorry.

I guess you'll have to write Dad as he's never written to me. I wrote to him twice. After all he might want to know he has a son-in-law.

What will Dean think? I told Johnny I was going to write and tell him. Maybe that'll make it final to him!

I really am proud of my rings! Be glad when you all can "admire" them. Guess I'll drop Lester and Jane a card, but perhaps you'll see them first. Dad too. Guess he wants me to do all the writing.

Have you ever had the birth certificate changed?

I'm very close to a transfer, but Johnny will never consider my going. My training, will be complete the first of December. I haven't talked to Mr. Jackson as I am supposed to do, as I must know about the certificate. I hope it can be corrected. It is supposed to be on file at the office, which mine isn't. Will you please see about it? If Johnny should ever go into the Navy that's what I'd do.

I mustn't start a new page and it's nearly yard duty time.

Write very soon.

Love to all,
Shandol

Shandol was only mildly surprised by the letter she received from her mother Wednesday of that week. She had certainly had dealt her mother no surprise in the last letter she had written, which her mother would not have had time to have received when she wrote. In fact it had been written the day Shandol mailed hers. Her mother wrote:

Mon. A.M.

Dear Dearie

Shandol now, Shandol ever, Sonnett now but not forever? Margery came back, said you were married or to be Saturday night? Guess I'll hear about it. She was spluttering around here again with her 'friends'. She's supposed to go back to Midhill—don't know when. Madge Middleton wanted her to stay until Wed. Don't know why. But Marg said if she did she'd lose her job, so don't know.

Lester has to be at Jefferson Barracks Fri.

Nearly breaks my heart, but what can we do but see them go? Clifford Rinard has to go Thurs. to Jefferson Barracks. There'll be 200,000 married men in army in Nov. and Dec. Sure too bad!

Got a letter from Dad yesterday. Said he'd heard from you.

Did you go to Kansas City? Why? Just driving or honeymooning? Ha.

No, I can't believe Dean still loves you! He sure didn't act like he was capable of loving anyone. Just forget him!

Lester and Jane were here yesterday. Guess he'll come back and see us before he goes. Heard from your grandad from Nettie and Leo (cousins, Shandol knew, of her mother's.) I was sorta surprised to hear from them but glad. Grandpa's at your Aunt Clara's and Uncle Wade's staying now. I'd love to see him, but don't guess he'll come. Maybe we were too hard on him when he was here.

Shandol don't bother about Margery. She might try to cause you trouble (if she comes back). I rather doubt her going back but one can't tell. If she tells her mother right I don't believe she'll let her go. The little girls told Mrs. Colmay their sister was working in 'tin', so I don't think her mother knows about her doing housework. But anyway don't let her bother you anymore. I heard Johnny wouldn't let you come home by yourself and couldn't leave you alone when you got here. Oh, yes, whom but that little mutt could start such lies. Shandol, people know your character is above reproach—or is it? I'm still hoping, so they have to tell something. But her 'friend' Frances was laughing at her going back without her clothes!!

No, you didn't do wrong giving him to understand where his place is—and stay with it! Makes my blood boil! Don't think Arthur has come home yet. They all met the train. I just hope she doesn't get in bad and Johnny or Derry get blamed. Doesn't make any difference if she's up there and friendless and wants to pull the 'good friend' act, she still has a home let her go back there and stay. She has a good mother.

I'm still at your 'service' if you want to lean on my shoulder and cry. I'll still listen. I'm still your mother! Makes one feel better to get things off their chest.

Seems I've read *Jane Eyre*, but like you, have forgotten.

Haven't heard anymore from Dad either. Guess he's ok. I answer his letters right back, but you know how hard it was for him to write.

I'll be wondering about you. If Johnny still runs with the crowd better watch out!

When you get through I want you to come home for awhile. Show the gossipers you can come home when you get ready and stay as long as you care to. Ditch the other outfit if you have to. Stay close to the Center.

These few weeks won't be long. Get as much out of your lessons as you can so you'll be prepared. The paper gave a list of occupations. Women and even children will be drafted for labor. I'll save it.

I still have faith in you. Don't let me down. Write soon.

Love, Mom

Shandol answered her mother's letter that day and also decided she would answer the short letter she had received from her dad. It had been about as her mother had written he wrote to her: That he missed being at home, his job wasn't so bad and he was glad to be earning some money which was as badly needed, he knew. Had a nice place to stay and nice people to work for. They were taking good care of him, Shandol decided. Said he was often tired and not inclined to write often, but hoped she'd hear from him through her mother. He also chided her for not even mentioning Karen. He missed her so very much. Shandol wrote him after a hurried letter to her mother:

> NYA Center
> Midhill
> Nov.11, 1942

Dear Mom,

Guess you weren't surprised when you got my letter, were you? About me being married at least. Don't know how Margery knew, unless Derry's sister told her. I think almost everyone up town knew Johnny was getting married, but I told no one here but Fredie, a few chums and the supervisor. I had to tell her to get a weekend pass. We at first said we were going home, then she saw my ring and asked if we were just going home or getting married. So I just told her. Everyone makes over my rings. I'll be glad when you can see them. The engagement ring is yellow gold with white gold trim. A solitaire, but has 'orange blossom' design on each side. The other ring has the white gold trim with 'orange blossoms' trim also.

Margery must be staying until Wed. Don't know about her and care less than I know. Did you see Arthur?

No, we didn't go to K.C. Johnny was going to take his brother-in-law up there, but he decided not to go.

Heard from Dad yesterday for the first time. He's sure anxious to go home. How do you suppose he'll take my getting married? Will you tell me what he says to you?

I got a card from Dean yesterday. Said he'd write to me when he was settled and could give me his new address. He may be surprised to know I've a new name! And of course can't write to him. Yeah, I'll forget him, which won't be much trouble.

Too bad Lester has to go *now*. How's he taking it?

Glad Grandpa is still kicking. I'd like to see him too.

Johnny tore up his car yesterday. As he was driving for his boss when it happened, his boss mechanic fixed it. He hit a big rock. Thought it was a big clod of dirt. Now laugh! Not so badly damaged though and it is now all fixed up.

So Marg's mother doesn't know where she's at? Someone really should tell her. I don't think she can cause trouble with me—but she might try to take things on herself.

I was with Johnny last night. Seems so odd to *date*, ha.(No more.) But he will come see me still—I hope.

I run around with Hugh Burdett's wife, Winnie, and Fredie. You should hear us talk. We're so dumb?! I knew I'd be, but I'm not by myself. Mrs. Burdett's really dumb. She seems a swell girl, even if she has some habits Hugh probably won't like.

I think I will write Tommy a few lines. He, at least, answers. Also to Dad.

Did Phil know the tune to words of song I sent? Tell him to put it with my other songs in the notebook—or does it exist?

Write soon. Kiss baby for me.

Love to all,
Shandol

To her father she wrote with pen and ink. She'd just used a pencil when writing her mother. Audrey almost always used a pencil so Shandol often did also. She used same white stationery she'd used to write her mother. She wrote:

NYA Center
Midhill
Nov. 11, 1942

Dear Dad,

Guess Mom has written or will write the latest, but you might feel slighted if you didn't hear it from me too. So I'll just tell you I got married, or had you already noticed my new name?

I was married Nov. 7. Hope you won't feel badly because you didn't know beforehand, because Mom didn't know either.

I didn't tell anyone except my new chums up here and the supervisor. After I got the ring then apparently several town people knew it and somehow Margery heard it and when she went home she couldn't keep still. Did she ever blab! She told Mom I was getting married, so Mom wrote and told me she knew before she had had time to get my letter.

I'm going to finish my training, however. Then I can do something if Johnny is called to the army, or if I'm drafted for labor. Besides I lack less than a month, as my twelve weeks are up December 4th.

By the way, you remember the five dollars you sent me to come home on? And—well, you know I didn't use it for that purpose as Johnny brought me home. But I used that same five to get me a new dress to get married in. It's blue, but suppose that's about all that you'd be interested in. Ha. I bet you didn't know you bought my wedding dress, did you? Hope you like Johnny, too, no fooling—well, you know, your son-in-law.

Did I ever miss you at home?? Well, I'd reckon. I told Mom my visit home didn't seem complete because you were gone. Boy, the rest sure miss you too. And as far as I saw the boys don't take advantage of your being gone.

I'm sorry I disappointed you in not mentioning Karen, but I was sure Mom would say more than I possibly could, as she says Karen's 'so crazy about her dad' and vice versa. Ha. She sure is worth mentioning, however, and I think she's about *it* too. She's sure growing and sweet. I'd just like to squeeze her right now.

I heard from Mom yesterday too. She said Lester passed the army and was to be in Jefferson Barracks Fri., Nov. 13.

Dean is a 'thing' of the past for me. However, I did get a card from him yesterday. Told me he'd write when he was settled to an address he could send. I shall only answer to tell him I am married.

I promised Mom when my training was over I'd come and stay a week or so, and I'm intending to do so. I told Johnny I was going to also and I don't guess he'll mind. Sure be glad to see everyone. Perhaps I can ride on the bus with you, if you don't go home too soon. Johnny, however, will buy me a round trip ticket—unless he decides to come for me.

I think I'd have a good chance to be placed in sheet metal, if what they claim is true. I sure like to do that kind of work anyway. I've completed my related training except one lesson, and now I'm helping build furnace pipes.

I'm about to forget to mention my pretty rings—imagine that. Have a set and I'm right proud of them.

Do write again when you can.

With love,
Shandol

Shandol looked forward to the next letter from her mother, when she would have had time to get her letter. Her days passed as routinely as was usual. There was her work, her personal chores, such as laundry and letter writing, and good personal grooming. She wasn't going to change the way she had been just because she was married.

There was no change in the attitude of the girls she was around and the boys were courteous and only one or two vague references she had heard about her still staying there and a husband somewhere. What kind of marriage was that? Shandol actually had no qualms about being married, and still only "date" through the week. They were given weekend passes—or would be. Her mother and father were apart, weren't they? Lester and Jane had had separations of necessity. Their marriage was new, yet she was sure Johnny understood as he said he would, and keep his word. Sometimes Fredie asked Winnie to go along, but their dates seemed no more stilted for her presence. They seemed to feel it was good for her to go sometimes; and felt compassion for her being so far from her husband.

She had times of concern and worry and she would be so sad when she didn't receive a letter from him she would sometimes cry, even though she knew he wasn't always able to get a letter going.

But it was Friday of the same week Shandol wrote her mother that she received an answer to her letter. In fact they had both written a letter to the other the same day. Her mother wrote:

Wed. morn

Dearest Shandol:

I'm glad you are happy! I hope you are always and have a prosperous married life. Yes, Margery told the boys you had the rings so guess you didn't tell us anything. Ha. I would liked to have been there, but maybe just as well. I hope you have chosen well. He'll be good to you and of course you to him. I don't believe you could have done any worse than the prospects here. I guess Dean will lose hope now. He'll get over it. If he doesn't no one hurt but him. Just as well be him as you.

Margery's dad bought her a new coat. She's not coming back to Midhill. She told Phil she didn't believe Fredie and Derry would get along very long? Ha. Sh-h-h. Marg is going to write to you today. I wouldn't waste any stamps on her. Just show her you are no fool either. Marg and the rest know they can't say too much about 'your character', that's what hurts. Gloria (Dahle) Downey doesn't act like a married woman. Perhaps she isn't now, who knows, but I wouldn't let my (soldier boy) hubby down even at that.

Haven't heard from Dad since I last wrote to you. He's too busy I guess shucking corn. Seems I still have to have a cry now and then. A daughter married and how can one send their darlings off to war with a smile? Doesn't do any good I guess. I bade good-bye to Lester yesterday. I'll tell you it was hard! They stayed for dinner yesterday. He's leaving Thurs. on that north bound train.

The happiest time of my life was when we were struggling along POOR to get you kids through high school. Didn't think then I'd have to give one or maybe two for 'cannon fodder.' I knew, or suspected you'd all get married SOMETIME!

Lester and Jane read your letter. Lester said he believed Johnny was a good kid. Phil is tickled to death. Bobby read your letter, said 'If she's happy I am too.' Tommy is already planning to visit a week with you. Ha.

Phil said for *yours* to bring forty cigars 'a foot long' when you came. Ha.

Said he knew the 'tune' of the song but not the words. Didn't have any so guess I'll hear him sing it.

Karen's fine. She's just full of mischief as her little black eyes sparkle it out. Nona said she looked 'devilish'.

Got a long letter from Ivy. Her sister passed away, was buried Oct. 25th. Said she hoped we'd go back there to live if my health would permit. We'd support things in the community that others wouldn't.

Today is first aid day. I want Phil to stay with Karen. Don't know whether he will.

No school Friday again, not on account of gas rationing.

I must quit. Hope you're always happy. Lots of ups and downs in married life but you get out of it what you put in it. It's a 60-50 proposition. You have to make lots of allowances.

Somethings I wouldn't tolerate is drunkenness, other women and abuse. All go together—but—but—I know you'll have other thoughts and things to occupy your mind but we will be just as glad to hear from our married daughter as ever. Must get to work. Write sometime.

Love, Mom

What? Shandol thought, no "be good and write?" Guess her mother thinks that's Johnny's problem now. Perhaps it was. Now when pressure was put upon her to smoke—or even drink—she could say her husband simply did not approve. And he would never buy her cigarettes to smoke. None of his sisters smoked. Or the girls who were yet younger than Shandol, and were the daughters of Johnny's cousin, where he stayed.

As Shandol learned more and more about where he stayed she was sure he'd appreciate having his own home. Although adequate, he had had no room of his own really, just a small space for a cot off the kitchen area. He had shared the other four rooms with the family in the upstairs apartment over a warehouse for a small grocery store next door. It had a section where sandwiches, mostly of cold cuts, coffee or soft drink beverage were served. It was referred to as the lunch counter. Some men bought lunch there and took it to work with them. But Johnny's cousin did not own or manage it.

Shandol answered her mother's letter the next day with a 'penny postcard'. It was hurried but she was so pleased with her mother's reaction to her marriage she wanted to tell her so. She wrote in part:

Saturday noon

Dearest Mom,

Received your letter yesterday. Decided to write a card as I don't have time to write a letter. Sure a swell letter you wrote to me. Glad you feel that way about me being married. You must have been feeling good when you wrote. Anyway I'm glad you're not mad. I wrote Lester and Jane a card. How is she? How'd she take it when Lester had to leave for the army? Probably hard on her too. Heard from Dean. He doesn't know I'm married.

She also went on to tell her mother the mother of a schoolmate in north of state had called. Was just passing and knew she was there.

Shandol was so surprised she wrote, and would loved to have seen her. She couldn't imagine why she was being called to the phone. And she had been nervous about the call. Actually Shandol had only room to report the call. Then it was more than the card held so she finished on back of the card, even if tiny writing. Shandol's card read:

> I've a card from Della Knoll in my lap. She was in Midhill one day and telephoned me, as Carla (her daughter)told her I was here. Carla has asked me to spend a weekend in Colombus with her. I'd love to see her sometime. I told Della over phone you'd like to hear from them. Was I ever surprised to hear or get to talk to her. Had I known she'd be coming to town I'd tried to have seen her.
>
> Love Shandol

The letter Shandol received from Dean was short and hurried and she thought almost impersonal, except as he ended it. No doubt but that he had sobering thoughts on his mind. He wrote:

Nov.14, 1942
Camp Stonemans

Dearest Shandol,

Well, here I am in California in a camp. It is a hell of a place too. We was told that we was going to be shipped acrost in two weeks. That makes me mad but there is not anything we can do about it, but go when we get our orders. It is pretty tuff by what they tell us. It will be two weeks before we go acrost then I will be a long time gone.

How are you getting along—fine I hope. I am feeling fine only my arm is pretty sore from my shots.

Where is Lester at. Write and tell me will you—I will do better next time. I am in a hurry.

Answer real soon.

Pv. Dean Leonard

Love and kisses. Dean

CHAPTER 52

It became apparent to Shandol and Fredie, after only a week, that only weekend romancing with their husbands was not their idea of a satisfying marriage arrangement. That week Shandol had finished her last related training lesson during a slack in work, so she was finished—unless it was actually required that she stay the full twelve weeks. That would hardly matter, why should it, when there was little chance of her going very far from Midhill to work and there were no jobs nearby for women to be needed in that type work!

It was the men who broached the subject that next weekend. They made it clear they were going to find a place to live, so each could have his wife near every night. Johnny had missed Shandol already and Derry thought they should have known better, to which they all agreed. The men had discussed it first among themselves, obviously, and said they hoped to find apartments close enough together that they would be company to one another. These apartments would have to be furnished because they were hardly ready to start housekeeping. They had no furniture and no hope of purchasing any, as their funds in the beginning were going to be considerably limited.

There was discussion in depth and breadth. It might be that one or both men could be drafted, they reasoned. Johnny said he hoped Shandol did not consider him reneging on his agreement to let her finish the twelve weeks. Derry was sure it was only a matter of time before he was drafted. However, he would wait to be drafted, he laughed, his grin wide and because he was married had no plans to join any branch of the service. Johnny was not sure, but knew it was a possibility even though his job was considered a defense job. His boss also considered him practically indispensable.

"I'll go to Washington if I have to to keep you here," Johnny quoted his boss as saying. "He does need me," Johnny recalled. "my boss said, 'My company needs you really, and everybody can't leave the country.' He thinks the draft board understands—so far."

There were to be complaints later from those whose sons and husbands had had to go. Their question was why was he a bachelor and so able-bodied and so on, not going when other men had to go." Even when he was married there were still complaints to the draft board. His boss did have to go to St. Louis once—or so he said—to keep his most important (to him) employee.

It was this here and now which brought the two couples—and doubtless countless other couples—to evaluate their situations and act accordingly.

"Well, we do hear about it," Fredie told them. What kind of marriage is it when the men live in one place and their wives another when it's not necessary?" she mimicked in a whining voice.

"We hear the same thing," Derry admitted. "In fact we get quite a bit of ribbing about not supporting our wives when we should be. Johnny here tells 'em he and his wife agreed she would finish her time there. But Fredie, you've hardly got yours started good, so that would be a long wait. Too long—*too long!*"

"Well, we must work it out ahead because I promised my folks when I finished I'd spend a few days at home. Johnny agreed to that too." Shandol looked at him for confirmation. He nodded his head briefly. "So I'll just do that when I leave camp and when I get back, or hopefully, when Johnny comes for me then things will be ready."

Shandol and Johnny discussed that more privately.

By the third weekend in November they had promise of a small house to rent. It was a three-room house, with only one bedroom, though the sofa in the living room made a bed. It was furnished and had everything they would really need—even dishes, towels, bedding and the utilities furnished. It was intended as a temporary arrangement of course. They were not sure how two couples could manage being together so much but they would have to give it a try. And they were optimistic that something else would turn up, if it proved impractical.

There was nothing for the girls to do but agree. The men would be gone to work during the day, and they could divide the housework and find something to occupy their time otherwise. Fredie thought she might find a job when they were settled more and a short amount of time had passed. She had no definite plans, but hoped she could find something. Perhaps in time they could move to themselves, unless Derry got his draft orders. Then she would probably just go back home.

Shandol though, was anticipating her visit home. Johnny had told her by then she could be gone only a week, so they could be settled. She had hoped to make it two, but there might be another time when her dad would be home also. It would seem strange for him not to be there anyway.

On November 23, Shandol, Fredie and Hugh Burdett's wife, Winnie, checked out for good. Their tickets were punched as though they were going on a date or to town. But in reality they were all going to each his own parents home.

It was a cold, rainy day. At times, it literally poured down rain and the drizzle in between never let up. Shandol's feet became soaked, her hair wet and in the chill of the November day she felt she would never be warm again. She was sure she would catch a cold. In fact she already had a slight cold, but it was just a snuffly cold, which everyone seemed to have had in turns. But wet, cold feet she was sure wasn't going to help any.

Fredie and Winnie had galoshes to protect their feet. Shandol had never owned a pair since they had left the farm. Then she had had to have overshoes to wear to school—"four buckle," as they referred to them. But in the south part of the state very few she knew had ever bothered with them, even during the snow. So when the ones she and her brother had were worn-out or outgrown they were never replaced. It had never occurred to her to change that now. In fact, the need had hardly arisen.

But they had to pack everything they had left. She was glad she had taken the box of extra things home when Johnny had taken her, otherwise she couldn't have managed. But she managed by adding a small suitcase Johnny had borrowed for her.

It seemed the time to go would never come. There were trips to the office, trips to the shop to see if they had left anything. There were trips to the canteen to have their mail sent to their new address there in town. Shandol doubted she would receive any as she had written her mother not to write until she got her new address, as she would be leaving the camp to move to town. She had sent a card and forgot to tell Audrey she would be home also. But perhaps Audrey would guess it as she had already said when she left the NYA Center she would be home to visit awhile.

They ate their noon meal at camp, though none of the girls felt very hungry. Shandol was anxious to get going. The rains had her wet from head to toe and there was still the walk to the bus station. The scarf on Shandol's hair was soggy and tendrils of wet, straggles of hair fell around her face, which she tried to keep pushed out of her eyes. Water squished in her shoes. They had walked through the grass at times instead of going all the way around the roads. Shandol was chilled. She hoped the bus would be warm and help her get dry because she had a long way to go.

The ride seemed long. At first the girls chatted about their trip up there, their reasons for going home, how they were going to find things at home and if they would be missed in camp, which of course they hoped they would be. Shandol pointed out how long she had really been there and she would miss it and being among those she knew and considered friends. Yet there was constant change as some left and others came. Some of the young men, who chose not to stay went on into the army or other branch of service or defense, if they preferred to wait for the draft—or didn't pass.

Shandol dreaded the stops and changes of buses, which seemed so often and the waits longer than they were, she was so uncomfortable. She was glad she had the other girls at each of these because she had never ridden the bus before and worried lest she get on the wrong bus, lose her luggage or just not make it and be stranded alone.

The drizzle stopped along the line, Shandol wasn't sure just where, but it was still chilly and she felt damp and she knew she was in for a seige of a bad cold.

It was six o'clock the next morning when Shandol got home.

As she knocked on the locked dining room door and her mother let her in, she said: "Shandol, I thought it'd be your dad," and hoped it I bet, Shandol thought and felt like crying. She was so tired and hungry. But mostly just tired and worn-out. She still felt damp and chilly walking down the long hill from the bus station carrying her luggage, stopping at intervals to rest.

Then her mother realized her soggy condition and told her she should go on to bed as she looked exhausted.

"I am," Shandol admitted, "but I'm glad to be here." Then she embraced her mother and was given a welcome kiss on the check in return.

"Are you hungry?" Audrey asked.

"Yes, a little, but just some milk will be enough. I don't want to wait for anything else."

Audrey brought a glass of milk from the kitchen, which was handy, because of Karen, in jars just outside the window and between the screen.

Shandol took awhile to drink it, not wishing to gulp it down. She explained the day before how wet it had been and rainy and drizzly, how she had been wet since, not being able to change. Even her coat had not withstood the dampness, and the damp chill had seemed to go to her very bones.

"You must go on to bed," her mother remarked. "Just go into the bedroom with me. Karen still likes to sleep by herself, though once in awhile she sleeps with me."

Shandol opened her suitcase for a nightgown and was glad to crawl into the bed under warm quilts. As soon as she was warm she slept.

* * * * *

Shandol slept until noon. She was called to eat then as Audrey had to prepare the meal for herself and the boys. Bobby would be coming home from school so it had to be on time.

Shandol felt rested but could still feel that she was coming down with a fierce cold. As the afternoon wore on she was sure of it. By late afternoon she began to feel bad. Audrey asked Shandol if she felt like going to prayer meeting, but she decided she did not. Audrey decided to go and leave Karen with Shandol.

"So you can become acquainted with your sister," Audrey had excused herself.

The boys left soon after supper to go to see Ardena. It seemed a habit, Shandol gathered.

Karen did not take to Shandol readily. Shandol tried, at first, perhaps too soon, or too enthusiastically. So she had to let Karen take the lead which she hoped she would do. *Perhaps she thinks I've come to take Dad's place,* Shandol wondered, but decided she would not bring that up as it wouldn't bring him and perhaps she couldn't make Karen understand what she meant.

By the time Audrey came home Sandol felt awful. Her throat was sore and she told her mother she was going to bed. By ten o'clock she hadn't rested. Her throat was so scratchy she could hardly breathe. She had gone to bed with Audrey again and she shook her and could barely croak out her problem.

"Mama, Mama," she said. "Wake up. Tell me what to do."

Audrey aroused and lifted her head to her hand propped on her elbow and asked, "what's the matter, Shandol?"

"It's my throat," Shandol choked out, holding it with one hand. "I think I have the croup, only grown people don't have croup, do they? Anyway, what's done in such cases?"

Audrey got up and went to the kitchen. First she added wood to the stove. She put kerosene, from a gallon can behind the large kitchen cook stove, in a saucer. She also got some meat grease from a coffee can from the warming oven over the cooking area and added it. She also added turpentine from a bottle in the medicine cabinet. The one Grandpa had made of walnut, which had the mirror in the door. This she mixed in and told Shandol to "grease your neck with it. I'll get a wool flannel cloth to put over it."

Meantime, the fire had taken hold and the water in the tea kettle was boiling.

"Shandol, come breathe in some of the steam," Audrey advised her, as soon as the steam began to come out of the mouth of it. Shandol did as she was told. In awhile, perhaps thirty minutes, her throat had eased and she took some aspirin and in time was ready for bed again.

"Thanks, Mom," She said. "I'm sorry I was such a lot of trouble. But I'd never slept feeling like that."

"You just plain had croup," Audrey said. "It was being so wet all day and the sniffles too, from the day before."

"It sure come on quick," Shandol said, still not clear-voiced, but improved. "And I'm glad you could help me out."

"Go to sleep," Audrey replied. "You need rest. Your throat still isn't clear. Leave on the flannel cloth."

"I will," Shandol grinned. *Even if it blisters, which it may though the grease will help,* she thought.

She was soon asleep and slept soundly the rest of the night.

Margery came to see Shandol the following day. Shandol's cold was some better, but she decided she would stay inside and rest and visit.

Shandol was glad to see Margery and told her she was glad she had stopped by. She was her same sparkling self, grinning and talking about the good times she seemed to be having. Marg didn't go into much detail, but Shandol gathered about like it had been at Midhill. The "gang" a little faster than their pace had been.

"How's married life?" Margery asked, out of curiosity or because she thought it expected. Shandol, however, wasn't sure of how to answer.

"Well, all right so far," she finally answered. "Of course we haven't moved to ourselves yet. I only checked out of camp to stay and came on down home. When we go back we're supposed to go to our own place, which I haven't seen yet. I don't think the men liked the idea of just weekend marriages. And actually I finished my training, but there was just no way I could expect to be eligible for placement."

"You got a bad cold there ain't yuh?" Margery asked after hearing her talk and Shandol's voice nearly giving out.

"Have I?" Shandol replied. "Last night I had the croup I think, though I thought only kids got croup. It was all the traipsing around up at camp in the rain and cold all day and not really getting dry until I got home. My feet got so wet."

"How long are yuh gonna stay?" Margery asked.

"Um—maybe a week or so, I really don't know," she replied. "I'd like for him to come get me, because I'd hate that ride back on the bus alone. Fredie might go back when I do. Winnie's not going back though."

After Margery had gone Shandol wondered that she still felt the same about Derry. She had let it show.

That afternoon was Audrey's first aid class. Again it was Shandol who kept Karen. Audrey particularly wanted to go as it was the end of the sessions and they were giving the nurse a shower. Shandol had no trouble with Karen. She had by now accepted her big sister and would allow Shandol to amuse her, rock her to sleep and feed her when there was no one else around. Shandol enjoyed Karen. She could walk now—having started only three or four days before Shandol's arrival.

The next day was Thanksgiving day and it was spent with Mrs. Ruleton and Ardena at their home. Audrey had prepared some food to take and they did not get up early, so it was practically mealtime by the time it was ready. Both Ardena and her mother had asked for them to come. Ardena had had to be reassured several times. Shandol wondered about Johnny. In fact, she missed his being nearby and wished he could also have been there. But she supposed he would be at his cousin's, perhaps go to her mother's. Or he might find some odd jobs at work to catch up on. She hoped he was not alone; and she supposed he was being kidded that they were apart so soon. It seemed strange to Shandol too, but under the circumstances it might be awhile before she could make it again.

The next day Shandol felt better and decided she should write Johnny a letter. She wasn't sure if she should, but surely there could be nothing wrong with it. She did miss him and wondered if she should have written sooner. He must have wondered how her trip had been. She wrote the letter and mailed it the next day. She decided she would not mention her cold. It would soon be all right as far as she could tell. Audrey was washing and Shandol was supposed to be caring for Karen, so she had to be satisfied to get a few lines going. Her mother hadn't expected her to help, it seemed, because of the terrible cold she had. She wrote:

Greenway
November 27, 1942

Dearest Johnny,

Did you think I'd come off down to south part of state and deserted you? Well, I haven't. I'm just slow this time.

How are you making it? Have you ever gone back to the camp. You know you'd better not.

I wrote to Fredie today too. Where's Derry and how's he making it? I keep watching the papers about the gasoline. Guess you can't come unless you do come this weekend. I wouldn't be much surprised to see you.

I saw Margery the day after I got here. I suppose from the way she talked she still runs around. She came over to see me and was telling me.

What did you do Thanksgiving? We went up to Phil's girlfriend's. That's the only place I've been so far.

It was sure nice to see everyone. Mom was certainly surprised to see me. Hope you aren't missing me too much and are being good. Be good, hear?

Lots of love,
Shandol

Shandol was glad to see her husband come early Sunday morning. She was not surprised, as she had stated in her letter, and she knew there had not been time for him to get it. She should have written earlier in the week.

The day before had been threatening rain, but, Shandol had gone to Plainesville with her brothers. She hoped it would not add to her cold, now more on the mend. Karen had been cross, Audrey told them, and she hoped she wouldn't catch Shandol's cold. But she had been happy when she had heard from Joel and he'd sent twenty dollars for living expenses.

But apparently Johnny and Derry had been watching the gasoline rationing, and had decided to get their wives. They had all gone out to see Jane. It was a cold, winterish day. Audrey had heard from Lester, but not Jane. She would possibly hear from him on Monday as Jane didn't get mail on Sunday.

Shandol and Johnny left about four-thirty that afternoon and realized she was ready indeed to go. Fredie had also decided she was ready to go back, as she worried what Derry was doing with his time, especially at night. They both wondered where they would be going for the night. As though anticipating or realizing they must be wondering they were told.

"We've rented that house," Derry grinned sheepishly, shyly? One could hardly tell.

Johnny could only glance at Shandol as he had to keep his eyes on the road.

"You mean the two of us are going to be living with the two of them?" Fredie asked.

"Well, yeah," he answered. "It'll be cheaper that way for awhile. And—"

"And it is for just awhile," Johnny broke in.

"It isn't easy to find a place on short notice," Derry went on. "Except sleeping rooms and we didn't want that. This will give us time to look around. Besides it was cheap," he chuckled.

In the days ahead the girls could understand why. It was small, only three rooms. There was a front porch onto which the living room opened. In the middle room was the bedroom and a kitchen next to that large enough for table and chairs. There were dishes in the cupboards, a sink, built in, but there was no floor behind the cabinet door, only bare ground. Shandol was surprised to find *that* in a 'house' in a town. Of course, there had been no sink where she had lived. There was bedding and also towels and tea towels to use. It was indeed ready to be lived in.

First, there was the question as to where each couple was to sleep. It was decided Shandol and Johnny would get the bed and Derry and Fredie would share the sofa, which made into a double bed. They reasoned Johnny would be getting up first, then they would be using the kitchen first each morning and should thus be nearer it, and would not disturb Derry and Fredie if they ate later. That night they went out to eat supper as there was nothing to eat.

It was Shandol's turn to be surprised when she learned just how early Johnny had to get up. She made coffee. He helped cook eggs and bacon and Shandol prepared a sandwich for his lunch, wrapped it in newspaper to put in a paper sack. But of course this was after they had gone shopping to buy some necessary things with which to prepare meals. This had been their chore the following day. It soon became a day to day thing. Having to go to town to get groceries for the meal. The girls were neither very much at cooking but Fredie decided she'd rather do it than the cleanup after. So it was decided she would cook supper (the men were gone all day and they could make out), while Shandol cleaned the kitchen. Each would be responsible for the bedroom they occupied.

They anticipated no problems.

But then after awhile Fredie was enticed into a small café, with bar and a room for dancing and booths around two walls.

Fredie enjoyed stopping, enjoying a soft drink and listening to the music and meeting the people.

Shandol did not like them. At the second or third stop she had had an experience which had ruined it for her. She wasn't sure how it happened. She had been sipping her orange soda, listening to the jukebox music and talking to Fredie and the girls she had met. However, a man, obviously, older than they were, came and sat in the booth across from Shandol. Then when one of the girls got up to put money in the jukebox, he had moved to beside Shandol. She had no idea who he was, and wanted out of the booth. Before he let her out he put his hand on her knee. She was horrified and in a shamefaced, determined manner made haste getting out of the booth, as though pursued.

"Who on earth?" she fumed, exasperated.

"Good looking, anyway," Fredie sighed.

"But I'm married," Shandol reminded her. "I don't care to carry on behind my husband's back. I'm going home."

"Yeah," Fredie agreed, "guess it's time."

They carried their purchases home. Derry was buying food that week. Johnny would next week. They had also split the rent cost.

There was one thing about the house which Shandol could not seem to understand. There were bugs everywhere! All sizes, and she was sure all the same kind. Then she was told what they were. Roaches. It meant nothing to her.

"But they get everywhere at night," she complained. "They're in the cabinets walking over the dishes we eat out of. We do dishes before and after we eat."

But with the bare ground there seemed little lasting thing they could do, though they did use a spray. Shandol even wondered if kerosene would repel them, but it was too dangerous she supposed. So the days passed.

The next weekend Derry and Fredie went to Derry's parents for dinner. Shandol and Johnny were not invited. This was a family affair. Later perhaps they would all get together. But Shandol was glad not to go. There would be drinking and she would simply not enjoy herself. The next day Fredie told her about it.

"Shandol! I'm ashamed of the meals I've been making for Derry," Fredie confided. "You never saw the like of food they served and how Derry ate—like he hadn't had a decent meal since he'd been gone! There was such a variety—it was like a feast. I'm going to have to do better. If you have any ideas, help me," she added.

It gave her more reason for shopping. But she spent so much time at it and visiting with girls that Shandol did not care for, that she often pleaded off. She had letters to write or she hadn't cleaned as she should, especially since Fredie had gone on about the lovely home Derry had come from.

One day Fredie had decided to invite the girls she had met home to supper. She asked Shandol if she would mind.

"Who are they?" Shandol asked. Fredie told her only their given names; Dolly, Eva and Norma, which was all she knew, Shandol supposed.

"The girls from the camp—you know," Fredie replied.

"But they ran away. They don't have jobs. I don't think they're very nice girls," Shandol answered, wondering why Fredie would want to feed them. "Where do they live, since running away from camp?"

"Wherever they can," Fredie replied, laughing hollowly, and shrugged her shoulders knowingly!

"You mean—?" Shandol started, and stopped. How could she put it?

"If necessary," Fredie went on. "But they're looking for jobs, really. They just didn't like camp. Neither did I, really."

"Fredie, we're new at all this. Please! Let's leave it all for another time," Shandol said, almost pleadingly. "I don't care for them and don't think Johnny wants me with them. So some other time, please."

"Okay," Fredie agreed, "if you wish."

It was that night Derry did not come home at all. They supposed he had gone to his parents, as sometimes there were late hours.

Then Fredie stayed out late a night or so later.

"All isn't right between them," Shandol and Johnny told one another.

Then Shandol wrote her mother about it. She could hardly believe so little time had really passed. It had seemed months. She wrote not quite the middle of December:

Midhill
Dec.14, 1942

Dearest Mother,

I'm going to sit down right now and answer your letter that I received just before noon. I had been wondering if you had forgotten me or was ill or what.

Oh, say, can you keep a secret? (Not particularly from the family unless they might let it slip to an outsider—gossiper?) Of course you can, so here goes: Fredie and Derry have separated! She is now in Plainesville working as a clerk typist for the Farm Loan—whatever it is. She aimed to take the job anyway, about the first of the year, as she's sure Derry will have to go to the army sometime before or (soon) after then, but she certainly hated to leave and be on the verge of a separation. Don't ask me what it's all about, unless I might say my opinion that he's too much of an irresponsible kid and now just seems to be *through!* I think she loved him very much; and Derry's folks liked her too. Derry's folks don't like it a bit. They were asking Johnny about it. One thing they did have a turn of stepping out on one another!! He started it. I wouldn't say that to anyone but you folks, however. Fredie was also seeing girls which I didn't. I just believed them to be rather undesirables. Fredie knew that too. She never seemed to resent my not being chummy with them, however, and once asked me if I cared if they had supper with us. I answered in these words (or to the effect), "Fredie, frankly I don't like the girls and wish you'd wait another time." (Hopefully when I wasn't around.) She agreed to do so. Johnny is glad that I don't like them and told me so. He added, "you'd better leave them alone." One gets taken as being the same kind when with them and I'm new here. The girls are here in town without jobs, expecting room and board from—don't ask me! Men? They have jobs now, I'm told. They left camp—that is—ran away.

I had a letter from Fredie today saying she'd written a letter to Joel Sonnett; and asking if he were my dad.

So if Dad remembers his last letter from the Farm Loan office in Plainesville, Fredie Woodley wrote it. Ha.

Mom, please don't inform Margery about what I said about Fredie and Derry. They may or may not go back together, who knows—but she has no business up here! And if she knows, she might draw some wrong conclusion, you know? I wrote her a card yesterday telling her about the pictures. I didn't give her my address, wasn't I awful? She was such a good friend to me until Derry hurt her so bad. But I may write her a long letter sometime. I wonder if she still carries on as she did?

If I heard from her she might tell me, especially if she thought it smart. But since Fredie isn't here, she might or might not.

What are other girls doing there? Does Madge Middleton still make eyes at Russ Balleron? She used to, remember? If I'd have seen more people or someone like that, while I was there it would have seemed more like home, and Greenway. Instead of I had such a cold I hardly wanted to see anyone. But I do think of the past and the people and times we had then.

Yesterday, Johnny and I spent the evening at one of his sisters' home who lives here in town. He has a terrible time getting me to go to his folks but I have a very nice time when I do go. She wanted to fix supper for us but we came on home. They all seemed to like me and as good as said so, especially his sister who is about twelve or thirteen—the youngest. She lives with this older sister who also has a boy. I like them too.

Last night Johnny and I went to the show. He doesn't care much for them but he did go with me. It really was good and I'd really hated to have missed it. The name of it was *Now Voyager*. Why it was called that I don't quite know as it was the story of a girl with an inferiority complex. It probably was an extreme case, but very well gotten up. Bette Davis played the main part. She's splendid I must say. I'd never heard of the show before though.

Lester's letter was certainly welcome. Guess he has mine that I wrote from here, by now.

Yes, I miss my cook, but where there's not so many it takes less cooking. Johnny and I mess together.

Truly, he doesn't mind as he and his brothers batched for awhile. If he happens to see some dishes to wash he does them. Makes me feel odd, but that's the way he is. A lot like Dad, eh? He was such a help to you. Johnny also keeps and builds fires; and usually carries a day's wood and coal for me.

We've had so much bad weather lately, he doesn't work as he'd like to. His last two weeks of pay was only forty-eight dollars. The smallest pay he's ever had since working for Wilbur Brandall. It would have to be that way right after he's married. Ha. But lands, that seems lots to me.

We still have snow up here. The last one fell Friday morning and was about two inches. We've lived up here about two weeks and in that time have had four snows! All two inches or over, too. Gets slick—I'd say. We've been using two dollars worth of wood a week, now! And Johnny says old man winter isn't even here yet. Ugh!

Mom, I bet you're tired of this babble. I would write to Fredie but I must talk to her husband first. She says send her the iron. It's his too.(His money bought it I mean.) Johnny and I want to buy it. It's a seven dollar electric iron and I'm sure a good one. So I'm going to see him, or have Johnny to. See, she has some clothing and things she couldn't get in the one suitcase which she had. She wants me to mail them to her. She owes me 50 cents so I'm going to send them C.O.D. She wants me to pay for it and insure it at that, but I'm not going to do anything about the iron so I doubt I do that.

Lester says Jane don't write. I'm going to write and ask her to. He'd love to hear from her, wouldn't he? Has she been to see you yet?

(Johnny has said I may come Christmas, but that bus trip, Oh, me!! Wears me out to think of it. Does Phil still say he's coming to Midhill?)

I meant to copy words to a song and let him rewrite it for my song book but I'll have to wait. Do write often. I'm up here by myself again, all but Johnny of course.

By the way, to set the record straight, Derry wasn't drunk

when he and Fredie were married. Who said that? That sorta burns me, but I was in the crowd so it's just not so.

One thing more then I'll hush. This is a sort of joke on me. The other day a lady came to the door and wondered if the lady of the house was in. I said, "No, she isn't." But who am I?! But at the time I supposed she meant the lady that lived there before us. It was the blackout Warden of our street. (is that what you call them?) She'd come to tell us a complete blackout tonight (Mon.night) from 10:00 to 10:20 p.m. Does that come in down there too? Surely does though as I understand its every rural section and everything.

Hope all're ok. We are.

Love to all,
Shandol

Shandol felt she'd made up for lost time with such a lengthy letter. She knew she would have to write more often.

They'd be so bored with such long letters. Her mother had written a rather long one too. She had only received cards from her mother and had been happy to receive the news of the past two weeks or so. She could have taken it from her diary, Shandol mused, or from what she had written to Lester.

Audrey told her that she and Mrs. Ruleton had made quilt blocks last week. It had been a cloudy day and she had also kept the two youngest Colmay children as their mother was gone again. Bobby was hobbling around for awhile as a result of a sprained ankle.

They had had winter too. She had washed and clothes froze stiff on the line, so had to bring it inside. Hung some upstairs. Snowed later there.

She had been sewing. Had made Karen two dresses, two under-shirts and there had been a wiener roast at Ruleton's all the same day.

Joel had come home so she was happy about it. He got there December sixth. He had rested a day or so, being so tired, but hunting work now. Cutting wood too. Thought he would work on a railroad bridge but apparently no job there either.

Phil had gone hunting and brought home a rabbit. He also helped paint the inside of the Little Mission church. She had heard from Lester, which she sent as Lester wondered why Shandol hadn't written.

She had gone to club on club day. They quilted. Apparently they tried to keep a quilt in the making all the time. Hoping as soon as one was quilted another could be started. It was sold to raise funds, of course.

And, yes, she'd try to write more regularly.

Shortly after Fredie and Derry left, Johnny had mentioned to Shandol they hardly needed all that room, and should try to find an apartment and cheaper place. Derry would not be there to share expenses. He began to think about an apartment, a small one.

Shandol had never lived in an apartment and she wasn't sure how she would take to it. But it seemed she was going to have little say in the matter. She wasn't sure she liked where they lived. She had no knowledge of handling the bugs and she hated them. They seemed to be a common thing in town if you weren't very careful where you lived, but she had never heard of them before. Never, she told Johnny. Some used sprays but their landlord seemed it their place to take care of the menace, which is what Shandol considered them.

So at the first of the month, when the rent would be due, they paid rent on the apartment and moved in. There were not quite as many things furnished at the apartment as at the house. They had to have their own bedding, dishes, cooking utensils, towels and other necessary things besides furniture.

Before they moved in, Johnny's sister and brother-in-law gave them a set of dishes and tableware. They had had to buy some bedding, a change of sheets and pillowcases, a blanket and Shandol's mother had let them take one quilt home as a wedding present.

But Shandol knew they'd need other things along and had written to her mother, hoping to get an answer as soon as possible.

When the package came Shandol sat down and wrote to acknowledge receiving it. Johnny had already had the mail address changed at the post office so there was no delay. She wrote :

905 Parkside
Midhill
January 4, 1943

Dear Mom,

I got the package containing the skirt, scarf, tea towels, etc. this morning and was glad they came. Thank you so much. Also I received the letter containing the birth certificate, the V-Mail (!!!) letter etc, Saturday. Guess I can look for the watch this week??

This is the first letter I've written this year. Ha. May come up missing too in many points—I'm sorta blank today.

Yesterday Johnny and I took one of his cousins to the country, which is to say to her mother's and Johnny's aunts. Johnny took them in our car and of course we stayed for dinner. We had a swell time, too. The woman we took had a daughter 14, also one 16, a boy 10 and a boy 7. Johnny's youngest sister also went. Of course she likes me and we were together lots there (we three girls). There was quite a crowd there. Another one of "Aunt Trudy's" boys was home and one of her sisters came. So you see there was quite a crowd of us. We had a very nice dinner and nice time. And as usual Johnny had a hard time getting me to go and he wouldn't have gone without me either. But Aunt T. was one of his aunts I'd never met. Her sister, who was also Johnny's mother's sister, I'd met before. She was real nice and wants us to spend a day with her sometime.

The roads to the country were very muddy. When we got to Aunt Cornelia's we could get no farther in the car—but guess what? Aunt Trudy's husband met us there in the wagon!! So more fun you see.

We all piled into the wagon to go on to their house. You know it'd been a long time since I'd ridden in a wagon. It was a high-wheeled wagon and sometimes we'd almost go to the axle as we crossed the low land. My the mud was deep. Still it was on bottom and not as many rocks as down there. Then we crossed this bridge over a fair-sized creek. The bridge had the overhead framework but just as we reached the other side it was concrete and on a curve and seemed to me straight up. Certainly a steep hill, though only about one half or less concreted.

When I got there someone said, 'How'd you think you'd like it down in these sticks, or something to that effect. 'About like I'm used to,' I said to about all who were listening. Uncle Ted (which is a nickname) said, 'I told the folks you'd feel almost at home out here if you came from near Arkansas.' Well, I did! High hills, covered with rocks, as down there. Several timbers with evergreen, but not pine, just cedar. But really there are several of them. Johnny told him that down near where I lived there were big pine forests. Of course they'd heard of them. We did pass a government park sort of once where there were pines that had been set out.

Yesterday our fair weather days ceased, in that it turned

cooler. The wind today is blustery and so cold, but the sun is shining. But it was rather airish yesterday riding in the wagon. We didn't have far to go in the cold though, and when we were coming back about five, the ground had begun to freeze.

Johnny's folks are all so spotlessly clean in their homes, and Johnny's Aunt Trudy was no exception. Even his sister is very clean. When she puts coal in her stove she takes a whisk broom and dustpan and cleans around it. They have nice things too in their house. But they can make anyone feel very much at home, and she serves a swell dinner.

Last night the picture show was the war story of *Wake Island*. It was supposed to be as near like the real thing as possible. Johnny as a rule, dislikes picture shows, but as it was a war story he decided to go. Isn't it awful? I'm so tired of war. How I hate those Fiends who could take over the Island.

They never did surrender—Americans, I mean. I suppose you followed it in the paper. It was a good show. The army is fairly taking its toll here.

Even some men from Johnny's job are going. I'm hoping Johnny's never called. Ever so many are going though. Johnny has three brothers in the army. What'd you think of the "V-Mail letter I got which you sent on to me? Of course it was from Dean. He'd never received my other letter. What shall I do? Write and tell him I'm married and to stop writing or ignore them so completely he'd wonder enough to inquire and me just trust someone else will tell him. Don't think Johnny wants me to write, but told me to do as I like. I don't suppose I'll write or would you? *Should* I?

Our rent is only two dollars cheaper but we think we have bettered ourselves. We like it better here than where we were. There's another family across the hall from us, but they both work. She at shoe factory and he at the deaf school. He's a "shoe repair and harness work" instructor at the deaf school. He's also a lieutenant in the local army. I don't quite understand about the army, but there's one here. (Missouri Guard or something is what they're called I think). Everything can be found in Midhill. Just name it, it's here. The two colleges, deaf school, state hospital for insane, the NYA schools— public and so on. The family are very nice folks though and leave us much to ourselves. So it's like living in a house by ourselves, as far as that is concerned. We have two furnished rooms, and the water, lights and fuel are furnished. All except the kerosene we cook with. We have to buy that. The people have a boy seventeen and a girl about fourteen. They have a parrot, Mom, and would you—individually you—get a kick out of one! Or at least I believe you would. Since you are carried away by the songs of the canaries, so would you be brought back to earth—and almost rolling in laughter—by the parrot. They seem so amusing and talk like a small kid. It'll say, "Mrs. Percy," that's the lady's name. And 'good-bye' and 'hello' and it'll say 'good-bye Polly'(it's name). The little boy said if anyone doesn't pay any attention to him, he will tell them 'go to hell'. When someone's at the door, whether there's anyone there or not it says, 'come in.' It can whistle. They're so amusing, I'd love to own one.

My pen pal in Indiana sent me two towels for a wedding present. My she was surprised when I told her I was married.

Uncle Lafey's have a boy now? I bet he composed that announcement himself, don't you?

About NYA!! I'm almost forgetting. For to work in, the NYA furnishes overall pants or coveralls. They will also launder them. There'd be naught for Phil to consider there. The boys usually have a good pair of pants or perhaps a suit for Sunday. These are for church or dates. Also just pants or overalls like they'd wear to public school or go to town, or just to clean up after a shower. Twice a week the laundry comes in and the boys (and girls too) check out the overalls, pants or coveralls. Those they had checked in. The night watchman takes care of that, however. The bedding, towels, etc. the NYA keeps clean too. I think Phil should do something as when the war is over employment may be scarce. Mr Percy's boy says and it's so, he could get a good job now but his dad is keeping him in school. As always, people who are the better educated, are preferred. If Phil could learn some trade *he'd like* why wouldn't he be better off. He'd never have to worry about clothes. He might do as I buy something every check. All he'd have to do with it is buy cigarettes, soap, hair oil, shaving cream and personal items like those—and stamps and envelopes to write home (and to Ardena).

The sacks you sent for tea towels will certainly come in handy. We had to buy some. So we got four and I have one of them on the stand table. Ha. I'll probably hem some of them and may embroider some too. By the way, Johnny got us a bedspread. It was only three dollars. It's blue chenille. Do you like them? I like ours, and still have my money. Ha.

Well, fan my brow! Thelby and Gerald have another—!

"What'd they name it? Uncle Lafey's picked a pretty name, didn't they?

Oh, gee, I mustn't start another page—and I said I was blank! I must quit. Do write.

Tell Ardena 'hello' and to write. Hope you don't have to pay extra postage.

Oh, yeah, did you see Hugh Burdett's wife in Greenway. She wrote to me. Said she liked it down there. I told her Della and them were nice and she'd love them. She said they wrote the sweetest letter to her. She likes them just fine.

Hope all are well, we are.

Love to all,
Shandol

Later in the week Johnny's sister and her husband came to visit Johnny and Shandol. The children were home studying, they said. There was small talk and visiting first and then Shandol learned why they actually came.

Elena was a tall slender woman, a few years older than Johnny. She was neatly dressed in a skirt and sweater, and a light camel colored, fitted coat, which she had taken off. *Her eyes are so like Johnny's,* Shandol thought, *though her hair is as fair as mine.* It fell in becoming waves and curls around her face. Shandol supposed it was naturally curly like Johnny's. Her husband, Hugh, was taller than his wife, and of a heavy build.

"One reason we come," Hugh told them, "is to see if Shandol would like for us to come by on Monday morning to see about a job at the shoe factory."

The shoe factory was located less than a block from where they lived.

"I'm pretty sure you'll get on with no trouble," Hugh explained. "I can put in a good word for you, as you're new here. They lose workers along as you know. Some are drafted, some go to defense plants for more money. What do you say?"

"The work's not hard," Elena added.

"Nope." Hugh interrupted. "If you can handle that tin at that shop out there," he nodded toward where Shandon had been, "then you can handle the work all right.

Shandol looked helplessly at her husband. She wished he would forbid it. But she knew he did not care if she went to work. In fact he had expected it, she was sure. But the idea of facing something new agitated her.

She started to tell them she had planned to do some sewing first, even some embroidery, to make some things she needed or could use. But perhaps she would have time to do such things too when she wasn't working. And she was learning to face and cope with the irritating nervousness which plagued her at every turn.

"Why not," she plastered on a grin for her husband. Johnny grinned back at her and nodded.

"Well, it's settled then," Hugh said. "Just be ready." They told her the time, earlier than they would usually have to go to introduce her before going to work at seven o'clock.

Later Shandol and Johnny discussed it. He reassured her about her nervousness, already knowing she would be frightened. And they planned things they could do with extra money. Perhaps rent a house to themselves, when they could afford to furnish it. There was still the car to pay for, and the rings she wore, as she had learned shortly after marriage. He explained he wasn't sure she would accept them so he could take them back or pay for them every month. And so because she kept them they must be paid for. They weren't able to do it all at once and have money to live.

It was later, after Johnny was asleep and she lay awake that she thought about it more. She was sure she would be more help going to work, despite how she would be dreading it. It would be better, too, if Johnny had to go to war. She realized she would not want to go home. There were enough there already and she liked having her own place. There would be a way. She supposed she could stay there. There was privacy and yet people close by. "If only I don't get pregnant," came a gnawing, fleeting thought. It worried her more that Johnny might have to leave.

But he was here, beside her, and even if she weren't in a defense plant she felt she would be helping, doing her bit. As Hugh had pointed out some were leaving for one reason or the other.

It was a satisfactory thought. She would have reason to get up each morning and be tired enough to sleep at night. Not, as she usually now had been doing, going back to bed to sleep until eight or nine o'clock.

Meantime let the war rage on! We would win! It was only a matter of when.

She snuggled closer to her sleeping husband, warm and cozy, and content.

Had she achieved her goal? Had she "escaped the nest," or had she landed herself smack-dab into another one, only in a different way? The questions she hardly remembered to contemplate. She was too involved in waiting for tomorrow, a new beginning.